THE CASE FILES OF ALDICUS VESCARD

BY

MARK WILLIAM CHASE

PART OF THE WORLD OF MYTHANIA®

This is a work of fiction. Names, characters, places, locations, and events are either the products of the author's imagination or are used fictitiously. Any resemblance to actual persons, living or dead, or to actual events or locations, is purely coincidental.

Published by New Realm Books

ISBN: 978-1-7325456-2-5

Edited by Aaron Sikes
Cover Art by Damonza

Website: mwchase.com
Newsletter: mwchase.com/newsletter
Facebook: facebook.com/markwilliamchase
Twitter: twitter.com/markwchase

This book is dedicated to our sweet Becca.
You will always be loved, and you will never be forgotten.

Table of Contents

MAP OF ARMILLIA

On the continent of Celaphania

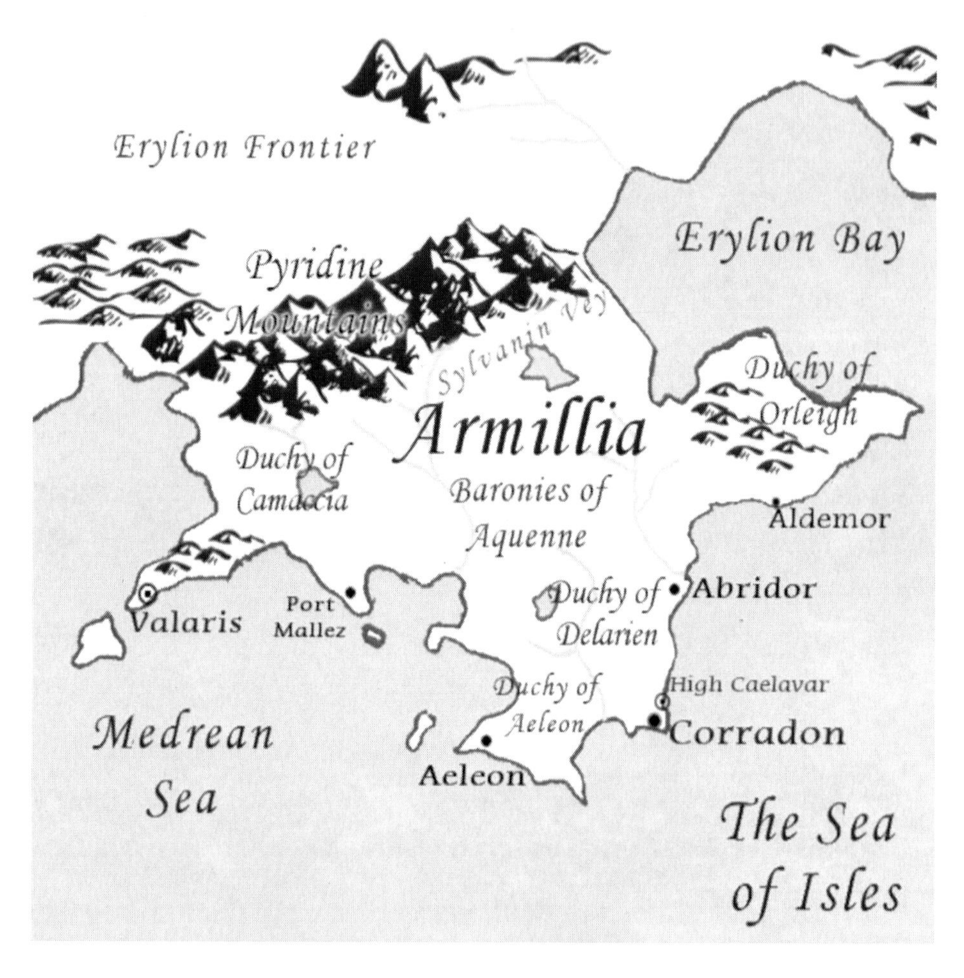

For additional maps and information, please visit:
https://mythania.com/geography/maps

Map of Corradon

1st through 26th Districts

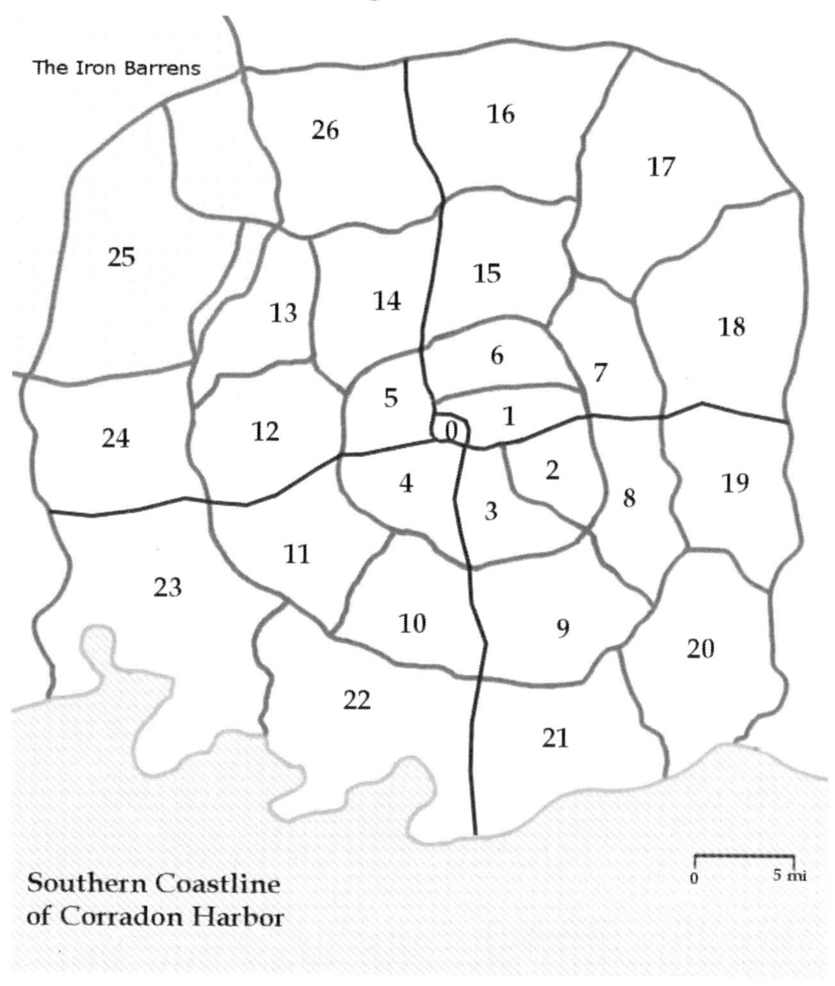

For more on the Clockwork City of Corradon, please visit:
https://mythania.com/corradon

Case File 1:

Deductive Alchemy

Rainwater trickled along the furrows of a face frozen in terror. Had the ossified corpse been placed upright on a pedestal, the deceased could easily have been mistaken for the chiselings of a gifted lunatic, or even a discarded prop from some grotesque cabaret. But here, at the farthermost end of the farthermost alley of Corradon, the Clockwork City, I knew better than to accept the most obvious explanation without first turning an eye to the details.

If the object were a statue, it could only have been carved by an artisan knowledgeable in every subtle variation of anatomy, down to the most minuscule line, vein, follicle, and pore.

"This is no statue," I announced to those behind me. Water spilled from my frock coat as I stood. "This man died in the throes of agony."

Keldon, my apprentice, peered doubtfully at the stone-white body, still garbed in twill coat and trousers. "So, it's not the prank of some mischievous art student?"

"I'm afraid not. Take a closer look at the finer details."

Keldon knelt for a closer inspection. "You're right. I can make out every whisker on his face."

Chief Inspector Tibblemond shook the water from his bowler and plopped the soggy hat back on his head.

"Detective Vescard, am I to understand this here mumper was turned into stone by some dodgy bodgefuddle or another?"

"Bone," I corrected. "No process natural, magical, or alchemical can transmute soft tissue into actual stone. However, there are processes that can ossify flesh into bone, for bone is a natural constituency of animal physiology."

The inspector huffed. "What processes?"

I doffed my top hat and tilted my head back, letting the oily rain beat down across my face. Only a faint sliver of grim sky was visible through the maze of steam pipes, pylons, and clockwork machinery rising to dizzying heights above. "The venom of a spitting basilisk comes to mind."

"There are spells that can mimic a similar effect," Keldon suggested. He drew a large brass skeleton key from his belt and turned it over in his hand. The talisman's vizstone glowed slightly, and the sigils etched along its sides shimmered in the dim gaslight. "May I?"

"By all means," I replied, returning my hat to my head.

Keldon adjusted his newsboy cap, rolled his shoulders, and held his talisman over the rigid form. With eyes closed, he passed the key down the length of the body and back again. "Nothing, boss. Not even a glimmer."

Keldon's findings were not surprising. I touched the severite bonds fastened to my wrists, suppressing a pang of envy. Never again would I feel the ebb and flow of the aetheric energies, nor experience the majesty of the astral realm—living, vibrant, and boundless in measure. I was a man rendered blind, deaf, and numb, stripped of my greatest aptitudes, save for intellect.

"Had sorcery calcified this man, his death would had to have been over a week ago," I said. "That is how long it takes an aetheric imprint to completely dissipate from a body weighing as much as an adult humanoid male. But he did not die a week ago. In fact, he died just last night."

"How could you *possibly* know that?" Tibblemond

demanded, his voice betraying his incredulity.

Tibblemond was not a bad investigator, but he was woefully lacking when it came to unconventional lines of reasoning—as were most in Vandor Tower. Given a straightforward homicide, an organized crime case, or even allegations of criminal sorcery, Tibblemond was more than competent. After all, such matters fell well within the purview of the Vandorian Guard's founding mission. Unfortunately, the Vandorian Guard was largely constrained by those observations and conclusions that could be quickly scribbled down in the narrowly categorized boxes of a standard case report. As a deputized freelance detective, I was not so confined.

I bent down and produced a soggy scrap of paper from the victim's coat pocket. "As you can see, this steamrail ticket is printed with yesterday's date. It follows that the victim was petrified sometime yesterday or last night. Although that could be faked, I should also point out that the body is still fully clothed in coat, trousers, and shoes. The attire is hardly well-to-do, but in this area even a deceased vagrant would have been stripped bare had another night passed. Moreover, judging from the distinct lack of refuse, I would say this alley had been swept clean by the dustmen two days ago, and they would likely have reported this oddity."

A befuddled grimace drooped between Tibblemond's haggard muttonchops. "Fine. But if this isn't the work of sorcery, what else could it be?"

The rain lessened as a construction dirigible drifted high overhead, the scaffolding of some massive framework suspended from its lifting hoist. I squinted my eyes, discerning the emblem of the United Development Concern emblazoned upon its hull.

"It is as I have said," I replied, returning my attention to the body. "Basilisk venom."

Tibblemond shook his head. "There are no basilisks here in Corradon, not even in the Royal Academy's zoological gardens. In fact, there are no basilisks in the entire kingdom of Armillia. Why, you'd have to venture to the darkest corner of the Azanian Jungle just to find such a beastie."

I quirked an eyebrow. "Then you posit that a basilisk must be present to kill a man with its venom?"

Tibblemond was granted reprieve from my question when a steam-carriage clattered into the alley. The carriage drew to a stop and two grimly dressed gentlemen disembarked, bringing a stretcher to carry away the calcareous cadaver.

"Mister Murley, Mister Maves," I greeted with a tip of my top hat.

The two considered me with somber faces frowning in detached indifference, the melancholic rain no more ruffling them than the sight of a man alchemically transmuted into bone.

"If you need to examine this sixer any further," the chief inspector added, "or the other two just like it, be sure to sign—"

I held up a hand. "Did you say there were *two* other bodies just like this one?"

Tibblemond cleared his throat, scratching anxiously at his muttonchops. "We assumed they were just discarded statues at first, and decided to call on your services only after we found the third. I wanted to garner your untainted impression before I mentioned the others."

I folded my arms and sighed. Perhaps that was true, but more likely he had simply forgotten. "In the future, Chief Inspector Tibblemond, I would greatly appreciate being given all pertinent information when I am hired to aid your investigations."

Tibblemond waved his hand dismissively and turned away in a huff. He pretended to busy himself supervising Murley and Maves as they loaded the body into the carriage. "I'll tube the files to you this afternoon," he said, turning to face me again. "The sixers will be in autopsy room four in Vandor Tower should you need to inspect them. Your insight, as always, is very much appreciated. Good day, Vescard."

I touched the brim of my hat. "A pleasure, as always, Chief Inspector."

Tibblemond tipped his bowler and boarded the carriage along with the other two men. He shut the door, gesturing to the driver, and the carriage puttered off down the alleyway.

I turned back to my apprentice and motioned for him to fetch the steam-coach waiting for us on the adjacent street. "Let's go, Keldon. We must hurry if we are to distill what we can from Vandor Tower's latest investigative disaster."

"THESE REPORTS ARE USELESS," Keldon fumed as he shuffled through the papers in the investigation file. "Take this one: 'Broken statue, grotesque, found near conduit junction east corridor 187, sublevel 4, 9th District. No claimants.' It's not even printed on a proper homicide form!"

I flipped a magnifying monocle over my left eye and reduced the aperture with a twist of the adjustment dial. "The district police assumed they were statues, not bodies. It takes a keen eye and a keener mind to distinguish—"

I cut short my discourse, noticing a peculiarity in the arm fragment focused under my lens. All three bodies had been arranged on gurneys in the autopsy room, one next to the other just as I had requested. The coroner had removed their clothes and placed identification tags on their ankles according to standard procedure, but had not yet performed an autopsy. Of course, an autopsy was not even necessary, as one of the bodies had fallen from a great height and shattered on impact with the pavement. This allowed me to inspect the interior of the remains, revealing an oddity I had not expected.

"Keldon, would you turn up the lamps?" I asked.

My apprentice flicked his talismanic key and the room brightened as the gas lamps flared to their full luminance. I clicked a blue filter lens over my magnifying monocle, then switched it out for a red one. Astonishingly, the exposed interior of the arm fragment was not entirely composed of transmuted bone. A quick probing with a surgical pick revealed that much of what appeared to be bone was, in fact, a spongy, fibrous material. If the body had been transformed into such a malleable substance, then it could not have shattered in the manner that it obviously had. I could think of only one logical explanation.

"The ossification appears to be reversing."

"What?" Keldon asked, incredulous. He approached the body that had been found this morning and rapped his knuckles on the chest. "It seems perfectly solid to me—bone through and through."

"True," I said, straightening myself upright. "The most recent body is still solid bone, but this shattered body was the first one discovered. When did the report say it was found?"

"Eight days ago."

"And the second body?"

He looked at another paper. "Four days ago."

I moved to the gurney with the second body, this one of a man who appeared to have been mercifully unconscious during his transmutation. I took a small surgical hammer and struck the abdomen twice, listening to the sound that issued from the torso.

"Dull," I noted. "Dull and muted."

I did the same to the third and most recent body, nodding as I heard the distinct crack I expected.

"The latest one gives a much sharper and solid sound. For whatever reason, the ossification of these bodies is only temporary, lasting perhaps ten to twelve days based on the apparent rate of reversion."

Keldon pushed back his newsboy cap and scratched his head in thought. "Are you saying these people could actually revert back and make a full recovery? Apart from that shattered fellow, I mean."

"Don't be ridiculous, Keldon. No one has ever survived

ossification from basilisk venom. Well, apart from that poor gentleman who suffered partial ossification of his face and arm on a safari a few years back."

Keldon looked over the bodies. "But you said the bodies were reverting."

"Once converted to a simpler form, the law of entropy does not allow for the spontaneous reconstitution of complex organs and tissues back to their original state. In perhaps a week or so, these corpses will be nothing more than human-shaped lumps of spongy, fibrous material."

"That's horrible!"

"On the contrary, it's quite extraordinary. This is not the typical effect basilisk venom has on the human body, which means—" I stopped mid-sentence, realizing I was thinking out loud. "Keldon, bring me my bag."

My apprentice brought over my black leather bag and set it on the table next to the bodies. I popped the latches and tossed back the cover flap, revealing a collection of multicolored vials, powdered reagents, and padded glassware, together with the most compact set of alchemical apparatuses that my ample consulting fees could afford.

I knocked three chips of material off the leg of the most recent victim and dropped each chip into a separate flask. I then added a mixture of chloroform and oil of antimony to the first flask before setting it aside. Into the second flask I poured a measure of fuming vitriolic distillate and then carefully added a single crystal of caloric sublimate. To the third flask I dashed a bit of volatile alkali and a powdering of quicklime, then fastened it above a small gas burner.

"Please recite *The Precepts of the Great Work*, if you would," I asked my apprentice as I set up the equipment.

Keldon sighed, rolling his eyes. "Come on, boss. I'm not a first-year trainee."

"*The Precepts*, Keldon," I repeated.

Keldon folded his arms, breathed out, and cleared his throat. "Initiation, conflagration, separation, circulation, congelation, transmutation, rectification," he recited, speaking flatly and quickly, with a hint of annoyance in his tone. "Through these stages does the sage transform both the subtle and the gross, ascending from earth to heaven and back to earth again, unifying in exalted splendor that which is above with that which is below. In this way were all things created and in this way shall all things be uncreated, through the force of all forces, the power of all power, and the unity of all unity."

"Very good," I said. As an apprentice alchemist and mage-in-training, it was critical for him to know *The Precepts* by heart, even if he did not yet understand their deeper meaning. "Now, a spark, if you would."

Keldon drew his brass key and placed the end near the base of the gas burner. Though I could not sense it, the eddies and currents of the aether converged around his talisman's vizstone as he composed an empowerment to ignite the burner. With a snap and a spark, the oil-soaked filament flashed to life. Keldon twirled the key on his finger and returned it to his belt.

The reagents in the flask began to bubble and steam almost immediately, and I plugged a tube into the top to draw the fumes into a collection beaker. While I waited for the gas to cool and condense, I turned my attention to the other two flasks. The color of the mixture in the first flask gradually gained a pale blue tint, while the reaction in the second dissolved most of the fragment, leaving only a porous lump of material at the bottom.

I smiled. Though I was deprived of my own aetheric abilities, I was not without alternative means.

"See the blue color of the first flask? That would be indicative of a high concentration of calciferic ester, a key constituent of basilisk venom. However, the rapid breakdown of the sample material, as demonstrated in the third flask, suggests a high degree of elemental instability."

I lifted the collection beaker attached to the third flask

and observed the milky white liquid that had condensed at the bottom. A sprinkling of potash resulted in a furious reaction that released a distinctively tart odor. I coughed, waving the vapors from my face.

"Regulus of curcalx. That is not found in basilisk venom, but it can be combined with calciferic ester to mimic its effect."

"Then an alchemist created this?" Keldon ventured correctly. "That doesn't narrow our suspects very much. There must be over a thousand registered alchemists, apothecaries, and spagyrists in Corradon, to say nothing of unlicensed puffers and quacksalvers."

I returned the beaker to its stand and rubbed my chin. "Regulus of curcalx is a restricted compound, as it is violently reactive with most alkalis. Only a handful of alchemists have been granted special dispensation to handle the substance for research purposes. Unfortunately, most alchemical manufactories have rather broad licenses and would have no difficulty importing or even producing regulus of curcalx."

Keldon's shoulders slumped. "Where does that leave us?"

I thought back to the reports. "The bodies were all found in approximately the same area, were they not?"

Keldon looked through the investigation file. "The first two were found eight blocks apart, both in the lower derelict levels of the 9th District, and the most recent body was found some six blocks north of the other two."

"The derelict levels..." I pondered. Then my eyes widened and I snapped my fingers. "Fangle-fop! I should have made the connection the moment I saw that construction dirigible."

"What?" Keldon asked, skimming over the report again. "I don't see anything about—"

"Open bidding for redevelopment of the derelict areas of the 9th District has been hotly contested," I explained. "According to the *Daily Post*, the United Development

Concern has won most of the contracts. They also bought out two other companies that had also won."

Keldon blinked. "Are you saying they're behind this?"

"No, not at all," I replied. "However, just last month they installed a new wastewater reclamation plant to service the district's western quarter. That plant uses a unique purification formula, but I personally know the alchemist who sold them the patents—Doctor Hermeritus Glanch. He has been working for years to devise a cleaner waste reclamation process, banking on the efficacy of caloric sublimate." I paused, but Keldon's bewildered scowl suggested that I needed to say more. "Caloric sublimate can be combined with rarefied antimony and several other compounds to produce regulus of curcalx. Actually, it is the *only* known way to safely produce regulus of curcalx."

"You said you know this Hermeritus Glanch?"

"We were friends, back when I was still a practicing mage." I glanced at my severite wristbands and drew in a sharp breath. I could almost feel the searing elemental energies surging through my body—consuming me, transforming me, *possessing* me, were it not for the severite bands. "In fact, he tried his utmost to cure my curse, though he had no more success than I. But the gentleman I knew was a visionary scientist and an advocate for peace. It is true that people can change for the worst, but Doctor Glanch?" I shook my head. "Unfortunately, I do have reason to suspect him. Do you recall the fellow I mentioned who survived partial ossification?"

Keldon nodded.

"He survived only because Doctor Glanch knew how to treat him. If anyone in this city possesses the knowledge to synthesize basilisk venom..." My voice trailed off and I sighed, unable to voice the unthinkable accusation.

Keldon's eyes widened. "That's it then! I'll get our coats and fetch a coach."

"I must visit him alone," I replied, removing the ocular

apparatus from my head. "There is more to this situation than a once-honest alchemist having turned to madness and murder. I cannot accept the idea that Hermeritus Glanch is our culprit, nor fathom what his motive could possibly be. But, having said that..." I held out my palm. "A tracking pill, if you would?"

Keldon nodded reluctantly. He opened his bag and fished out a small pill box. "I needn't remind you that your severite bonds nullify all aetheric effects. Even if you ingest a tracking pill, I won't be able to sense it or track your movements."

"Then should you suddenly detect the tracking pill, it will mean that my wristbands have come off. As I only remove these bonds under the most dire or life-threatening circumstances, consider it a signal that I require your immediate assistance." I took the pill and swallowed it. "I'll need for you to wait about a block away from my friend's shop. Keep sharp and be ready to come to my aid the moment you detect the tracking pill. Oh, and don't forget to bring the tranquilizer gun, a healing balm, and some spare clothes."

"As always, boss," Keldon assured. "Let's hope the new serum is more effective than the last one."

"Let's hope," I agreed. With that, I took my frock coat and top hat, looped a cravat around my neck, and hastened out the door.

DOCTOR HERMERITUS GLANCH OPERATED a small elixiry just south of Capital Foundry's steamworks in the 9th District. The shop stood adjacent to his extensive private laboratory, although few passersby would suspect that the hundred-year-old crumbling brick façade concealed one of the most spectacular collections of alchemical apparatuses, elemental intermixers, and aethergy generators in all of Corradon. As his lab was closed to the public, I made my entrance through the shop's peeling green door just as any customer would.

"I'm about to close up," came a voice from the back room as the door's bell jingled. "Unless this is a matter of the utmost urgency, you'll have to come back tomorrow."

I drew a deep breath, savoring the familiar tang of vitriol, the sharp aroma of quicklime, the sweet perfume of volatile spirits, and all the delicate smells of countless alchemical concoctions. Shelf upon shelf of multicolored bottles, flasks, and tubes of every shape and size adorned the mirrored wall behind the tarnished brass counter. To my left stood a cabinet displaying all manner of poultices, powders, and elixirs, and to my right was a storeroom filled with glassware, shipping crates, and other supplies.

"Urgent it is," I replied.

Hermeritus Glanch emerged from the back room still polishing a small glass vessel. He froze the moment he saw me, the squinting eyes behind his thick spectacles widening with surprise. "A-ah," he stammered. "Aldicus? Is it you?"

"Detective Aldicus Vescard," I amended. "And I fear it has been far too long, my dear old friend."

The balding alchemist hesitated, then he approached the counter and set the glass vessel on a shelf somewhere below. "It has been some time, hasn't it? I scarcely know where to begin."

I stepped up to the customer's side of the counter and placed my left arm across the railing, brushing my coat open just enough to expose the Vandorian deputy badge clipped to my belt. Although I was a freelance detective, I was fully deputized, as my job often required me to make arrests. Hopefully, I would not be required to do so now.

"Has business treated you well? The last I heard, you had sold a promising new water purification formula to United Development Concern for a rather impressive amount. I'm surprised you've not retired to some idyllic island in the south Medrean."

The prominence in Hermeritus's larynx bobbed as he swallowed. "Yes," he admitted, his voice cracking. He glanced into the room behind him, wringing his hands. Then he cleared his throat and turned back to me. "You might say this shop is really more of a hobby of mine."

As Hermeritus spoke, I noticed a few tiny droplets of sweat forming along the top of his brow. Something was deeply wrong. The man was not just nervous, he was utterly terrified. "Caloric sublimate was one of the formula's main constituents, wasn't it? You must have found a way to stabilize the ancillary reaction chain. Did you use rarefied antimony?"

Hermeritus blinked, seemingly surprised. "Well, yes, as a matter of fact." He removed his spectacles to rub his eyes. "But if you would excuse me, I must tend to a few elixirs in my laboratory. We should have lunch sometime, perhaps at the Morningvale Café over by Dragonberry's?"

I waved my hand dismissively. "Why wait? We can catch up while you introduce me to the latest potions you've been brewing. I'm eager to have a look at your setup, as well. I suspect my own equipment is shamefully antiquated by comparison."

"Somehow I doubt that." The doctor's eyes fell to my severite wristbands. "You always pushed the boundaries of our art, didn't you? You were always ahead of me. You were ahead of everyone... So far ahead."

I pulled my sleeves down to cover the wristbands, then drew in a deep breath as I suppressed the memory of the agonizing fires simmering deep within—waiting, watching, *yearning* to be unleashed again. "I pushed too far, my friend, and I paid the price for my folly. Take it from me. Nature exacts a terrible toll upon all who test the limits of Her immaculate boundaries."

Hermeritus leaned across the counter, his eyes wild and fearful. "Run, Aldicus," he said in a hushed voice. "Get out of here, now!"

The sheer urgency in his voice startled me. His connection to the alchemical murders had merely been a suspicion, and a shaky suspicion at that. I could not imagine how or why my old friend would be involved in such an abominable crime, but involved he was. The only problem with my assessment rested with the fact that I had failed to deduce his role as a mere pawn in a much larger and far more dangerous game.

The bell above the door jingled and I turned to see who had entered. He was a large man, a street tough no doubt, but he was quick for his size and well-practiced in hand-to-hand combat. The impact of this revelation struck me like the butt of a pistol across the occipital bone of my unsuspecting cranium, plunging my consciousness into darkness.

When I came to, I found myself strapped to an examination table in one corner of Doctor Glanch's laboratory. I was pleased to see that my friend had indeed done well for himself over the years, having furnished his workshop with all the latest alchemical apparatuses. Hermeritus himself stood near a table a few paces a way, his head hung and shoulders low as he listened to the upbraiding of a pudgy pomp whose face had been transmuted into bone down the entire right side, along with his right arm, which he kept in a sling. He was dressed in a bespoke suit with a gold pocket watch chain and jeweled lapel pin. Four bruisers stood guard around him, their own stylish suits straining against their bulging muscles—three armed with caplock pistols and the fourth holding an expensive looking clockwork repeater.

"You're that fellow who survived an encounter with a basilisk," I called, trying to ignore the throbbing in my skull. "I'm glad to see Doctor Glanch was able to help you with your misfortune. More or less."

The half-ossified man turned to me and frowned, or rather, half-frowned, as the right side of his face was forever frozen in an awkward expression of astonished terror. "Misfortune?" he demanded, his voice grating like bone. "Hardly! Within this crippled body lies the key to achieving the greatest alchemical transmutation science has yet to unlock. The world will soon know the power I wield, and all will tremble at the name Borphelleus Slurn!"

"Borphelleus Slurn?" I laughed. "You expect the world to tremble at a name like Borphelleus Slurn?" Not waiting for an answer, I gave a nasally snicker, this time making sure to sound as outrageously incredulous as I could. "You, sir, are indeed a madman."

"I don't expect you to understand," Borphelleus snapped.

"Understand what? That you have conspired to develop an alchemical formula utilizing caloric sublimate and rarefied antimony to sell to United Development Concern under the pretense of water reclamation?" I shook my head. "Together with calciferic ester, those particular reactants will combine to form a synthetic allotrope of basilisk venom. But to what end? Madness takes many forms, but rare is the madman who murders without motive."

Borphelleus scratched a bit of bone from his arm, then sprinkled the granules into a flask on the table beside him. "You are quite perceptive, Vescard," he said as the solution in the flask began to bubble. "But no matter. You will not live long enough to expose my plans."

"And those plans would be...?" I prompted.

Borphelleus snorted, a half-sneer forming on the fleshy side of his face.

I thought for a moment, watching the tiny granules of bone react within the solution in the flask. It was a solution of caloric sublimate and rarefied antimony, I realized, considering my own alchemical experiment with the ossified remains of the victims. But what *were* his plans? What was he actually trying to achieve?

I glanced at Hermeritus, then looked to Borphelleus and his well-dressed bruisers, and finally to the bubbling flask. My eyes narrowed. United Development Concern... The water reclamation facility... The 9th District's redevelopment initiative... I sucked in a sharp breath as the pieces at last came together.

"Yes, it is all quite clear," I said with a smile. "Judging from your attire and that of your goons, you are clearly well-to-do, and perhaps even run your own criminal syndicate here in the 9th District. You were hoping to expand your operation through the derelict industrial levels, but when United Development Concern purchased most of the western quarter for redevelopment, your plans were quashed."

Borphelleus's eyes narrowed as I spoke, and I watched him carefully for any twitches or tells as I continued.

"Being the only known survivor of basilisk venom, the ossified parts of your body carry a unique variation of calciferic ester. From Hermeritus's work, you knew that calciferic ester could be combined with caloric sublimate and rarefied antimony to reconstitute a synthetic allotrope of the venom. Conspiring together, you developed a new water purification formula using those reactants and sold the patents to United Development Concern for use in their new water reclamation facility. Once you introduce the calciferic ester into the water supply, thousands within the revitalized district will die in a horrific alchemical transmutation. Blamed for the catastrophe, United Development Concern will be bankrupted, and your syndicate will move in to purchase a great swath of the tainted sectors for pfennies on the ducat. You hope to make millions from the death of thousands."

I shook my head, watching the twitching, tightening muscles of Borphelleus's face contort as he struggled to suppress his rising anger.

"My apologies for calling you a madman," I continued. "You are merely a psychotically deranged swindler plagued by a narcissistic fascination in your own self-propagating delusions of grandeur."

Borphelleus's face turned red with indignation. "Doctor Glanch!" he snapped. "You have your next specimen. Complete the experiment with your newest formulation at once."

Hermeritus nodded in resignation, then approached the table to which I was secured. "Forgive me, Aldicus," he said, his voice low. "I had no choice. He does control a powerful crime syndicate, and his threats were most... persuasive."

"There is always a choice, my friend," I said sadly. "But there is one thing I haven't quite figured out. Why discard the bodies in deserted sublevel alleys?"

"Those were our 'in the wild' tests," Hermeritus answered, leaning in closer to whisper. "We had to know how the reactants would combine with the calciferic ester under everyday conditions. But I introduced a critical flaw into the formula. If I'm correct, its effects should reverse in a few days, restoring the victims to life."

I shook my head. "It is true that the ossification is reversing, but the ravages of entropy cannot be undone. Those men are dead—killed by the noble art you have so horrifically perverted."

Hermeritus's face drew pale. "But your own elemental transformation *proves* it is possible."

"That is the result of hypostatic duality transposition," I whispered, "not the entropic dissolution of reorganized matter."

"I had hoped... But no matter." Hermeritus drew back slightly, his hand touching one of my severite wristbands. "You are correct, as always, Aldicus. You will do what must be done."

My old friend knew me well. I then spoke, loud enough for everyone to hear. "It is necessary to inform you that, by the legal authority of the Vandorian Jurisdiction Proclamation of the High Court of Armillia, you are all under arrest."

Borphelleus bellowed a deep and raucous laugh, his goons joining in a moment later.

"Borphelleus," Hermeritus said, raising his voice above their laughter. He stepped away from me, moving to a table cluttered with alchemical supplies. "This man has severite wristbands to protect him from magic. They could also interfere with the transmutation process."

Borphelleus signaled for his men to stop laughing, then he pointed to one and snapped his fingers. "Remove his wristbands."

Despite the bruiser's clear lack of any discernible measure of intellectual prowess, he experienced no difficulty in removing my severite wristbands. The bonds were easy to remove—a simple twist and pull of the locking pin to release the clamps that held each one in place.

"That's better," I said, wiggling my fingers and flexing my wrists. "Now, if you could just remove these straps holding me to this table, I would be most grateful."

The bruiser only sneered, assuming my cavalier banter was just a feeble attempt to conceal my fear. I was, in fact, steeling myself for the excruciating agony that was about to seize the entirety of my being. Already I felt the heat building within my body—heat upon heat, rising exponentially as the uninhibited alchemical reactions began boiling in my blood. I looked to Hermeritus, watching as he slipped around to the other side of the table, moving farther away. He knew what was about to happen, and he needed to be as far away from me as he could without raising suspicion.

I winced, then convulsed, my internal temperature rising to that of a blast furnace. The heat would have killed me were it not for the hypostatic displacement of my living tissues into pure elemental matter. It did not take long for the bruiser to realize something was amiss. Standing no more than two feet away, the heat radiating from my body would have quickly grown unbearable. But I could no longer see or hear him, nor anyone else in the laboratory. I was deaf to all but my own screams, and blind to everything but the searing fire ripping through every nerve and fiber of my immolating flesh.

Rather than ascending to the pinnacle of alchemical perfection, I plunged body and soul into the corrupt antithesis of all I had once yearned to achieve. My heart rushed like a boiling alembic; my blood pulsed with liquid cinnabar; my innards churned with digestive alkahest; my lungs heaved with burning phlogiston. I held no control over the blazing alchemical being my mortal form had become. I could only watch through eyes of brimstone embers as an unstoppable elemental fiend tore free of the straps and rose upon limbs of flame to stand upon the laboratory floor.

Gunfire issued from the pistols of Borphelleus's men, but the bullets sublimated into harmless gas as they struck the transformative matter of my body. Borphelleus backed away, screaming orders and waving his good arm in frantic gestures. The gunman next to him let loose with his clockwork repeater, confident in the absurd firepower of his weapon. The few rounds that did strike their intended mark disintegrated instantly, while shards of glass and fragments of brass exploded all around.

Reagents spilled from the broken glassware—fuming vitriols, caustic alkalis, and countless other violently reactive compounds that no sane alchemist would dare combine. The toxic solutions pooled around my smoldering feet, and the quintessential energies surging through my body began cooking the ingredients as though within the heart of a coal-fired kiln.

I had no wish to kill my aggressors. Being a devout exponent of law and order, I would have preferred to take the perpetrators into custody to be given a fair trial. Unfortunately, the monster I had become knew nothing of law, justice, or the minimal application of necessary force. Pure in its malice, it knew only rage without reason and wrought destruction without relent.

My diametric antithesis must have perceived the man with the clockwork repeater as the greatest threat. More spilled alchemicals drew up into my elemental form, and a funnel of aqua fortis and ammonia formed above my burning hand, converging to produce a boiling reaction of volatilis ammoniac. The fulminating alchemical compound exploded through the gunman's body like a cannonball, hurling what remained into the far wall. The bruiser who had removed my severite bonds endured no less horrible a fate in the form of a blistering spray of vitriolic chlorinate. As for the other two, I wished only to turn my head and shut my eyes. No one should see what horrors an aqueous solution of caustic alkali and quicklime inflicts upon living tissue, nor hear the screams of those whose boiling flesh sizzled from their bones.

Seeing the last of his men fall, Borphelleus dashed up the stairs leading to the storefront. Hermeritus was now the closest man still standing, and, in my present state, there was no distinguishing friend from foe. My fire-wreathed body moved in his direction, every step drawing in more and more reagents, cooking a frothing amalgamate of alchemical corruption in the fiery crucible of my bowels. *Run, my friend, run!* I screamed in my mind, but no words issued from my flaming mouth.

My attention shot back to the door at the top of the stairs as it burst open just before Borphelleus reached the top. Never had I been more pleased to see my young apprentice than in that moment. He looked down into the room and saw me, or rather, he saw the flaming, alchemical beast my body had become. But his immediate concern was for Borphelleus, who came to a halt scarcely four steps from the now blocked exit. Keldon, of course, was neither aware of the villain's identity nor that he was the culprit. Fortunately, Borphelleus wasted no time making his intentions clear, drawing a small pocket popper from his coat and leveling the barrel at the young man who blocked his way.

As a mage in training, Keldon was well practiced in delvings and simple illusions, but had no experience with offensive empowerments. Yet, he was far from defenseless. His brass key flashed in his hand, bursting with light, color, and sound—a harmless spectacle, but perfectly timed. Borphelleus yelped with a start and staggered back, losing his footing as he missed a step. His pistol fired, but the shot flew wild as he crashed down the stairs to the laboratory floor.

I would surely have snuffed out whatever life remained in Borphelleus's bruised and battered form, but no sooner had I begun to move in his direction than a severite-jacketed dart struck me squarely in the chest. I looked up to see Keldon loading a second dart into the tranquilizer gun, just in case the first one failed to deliver the serum. But deliver it did, and I felt my transmuted body falter and swoon. Although the raging impulse to destroy forced my legs to take one more step, the next step brought me stumbling to my knees.

The room spun, darkness closed over me, and the burning constituents of innumerable alchemical reagents evaporated from my body.

I WOKE TO THE ITCHING STING OF BLISTERS covered in ointment, and a fever that teetered on the cusp of a lethal stroke. Keldon had secured the severite bonds to my wrists while I was unconscious, suppressing the uncontrollable monster whose annihilating fire would otherwise have consumed me. My throat was painfully dry, my eyes and nose stung with the residue of caustic reagents, and my breath stank of ammonia and sulfur. Despite the fever, I could not stop shivering, and I pulled the rough blanket around my sweat-drenched body.

"Water," Keldon said, offering a glass of the utterly common yet undeniable monarch of liquid substances.

I seized the glass and drank what seemed the most delightful elixir my lips had tasted. My fever lessened almost at once, but my burning thirst had yet to be quenched. "More," I managed to rasp.

Keldon took the glass and headed to the faucet in the back of the laboratory. Having regained my composure, I took a moment to survey the devastation. Four bodies lay on the floor, covered by heavy wool sheets that concealed their horrific condition. Chief Inspector Tibblemond stood nearby, taking notes on whatever statement the despondent

Hermeritus Glanch was giving, while two blue-coated jacks held Borphelleus in custody. Regardless of their watch, Borphelleus was in no condition to attempt an escape. His tumble down the stairs had landed him on the hard stone floor, the impact of which had snapped off his ossified arm and completely shattered the right side of his face. Broken, battered, and forever disfigured, the would-be criminal mastermind slouched on the floor in despair.

I drank the next glass of water that Keldon brought me. "Thank you," I said at last.

"How do you feel?" Keldon asked.

"I feel like I've been tossed into the belly of an alchemical furnace, dragged across a crucible of burning sulfur, and stuffed into a vat of concentrated aqua vitriol. But I suppose I'll recover. I always do."

"I brought you some clothes," he added, passing me a matching set of trousers, shirt, and waistcoat.

I managed to put on the clothes in a storeroom adjacent to the laboratory, a rather painful ordeal given the assortment of burns and sores across my body. We then followed Tibblemond and the bluejacks up the stairs and through the storefront as they escorted both Borphelleus and Hermeritus to the plaza outside. Two armored carriages stood by, along with an ornithopter bearing the shield and scales emblem of the Vandorian Guard. A small patrol blimp floated just above the lofty peaks of the great manufactory towers, likely dispatched from Vandor Tower to monitor the situation.

"I have no doubt Borphelleus will be sentenced to spend the last of his days in Angdred Penitentiary under a maximum security spell-ward," I assured Keldon.

"And your friend, Hermeritus?" Keldon asked.

I took a moment to consider as we watched the carriages depart with the prisoners. Hermeritus was responsible for formulating the synthetic basilisk venom and was thus guilty of participating in the crimes of murder and conspiracy to commit mass murder. Even so, Armillian law did provide allowances for cases of extreme duress.

"Given his assistance in apprehending Borphelleus, and assuming he fully cooperates with Tibblemond's investigation, he will likely be exonerated," I said. "It is quite probable, however, that his license to practice alchemy will be permanently revoked."

Keldon sighed. "That's too bad."

"Not nearly as bad as the alternative. All the same, I will put in a good word or two for him with the magistrate. Hermeritus is a good man and a brilliant alchemist. However, even the most admirable of souls can do things they later regret." I looked at my severite wristbands and let out a deep breath. "It is the capacity for remorse that distinguishes those of clear conscious, good heart, and right mind from those wretched fiends who lack even an inkling of compunction. It is what allows us to seek atonement for those past misdeeds that we now remember in shame."

"I wouldn't know, boss," Keldon said, a cajoling smile crooked on his face. "What I do know is that you'd best settle in for a solid week of recuperation. As you often say, crime ever turns in the Clockwork City. Whenever we're next called upon to address those most heinous and inscrutable transgressions of contemptible criminality, the great Aldicus Vescard must be at his best."

"And so he shall," I managed to say, despite the pain of my burned and blistered body. "Just as long as his clever and quick-witted apprentice, Keldon Veldanor, is there by his side."

Case File 2:

A Distillate of Madness

THE GEARS OF THE IMMENSE ORRERY TURNED with undiminished precision, casting doubt on the notion that blood makes a poor lubricant. One might have expected the blood to congeal, gumming up the clockworks deep inside the celestial engine and grinding the entire machine to a halt. But the great Celestarium at the Institute of Thaumaturgical Science generated enough heat to keep its sanguine coating liquescent, maintaining the blood's viscosity to something akin to mineral oil. The mess would require every component to be removed, washed, and fitted back together again, but none of that was my problem. My problem was piecing together a puzzle deeper than the most intricate mechanism of the Institute's crowning centerpiece.

"Well, Vescard?" Chief Inspector Tibblemond asked. "What are your thoughts on the cause of death?"

I looked to the lower half of Doctor Tommas Meldrine's body lying a short distance away, then back to the blood-coated gears of the Celestarium. "Judging from the evidence, I believe Doctor Meldrine was pulverized in the machine's inner workings. Or, at least, his upper half was."

Tibblemond sighed. "I mean, do you think it was an accident, a suicide, or foul play?"

The question was not unexpected or unwarranted. Tibblemond had, after all, brought me into this case due to the conflicting lines of evidence so gruesomely scattered about the room. Nevertheless, I would need more than a cursory survey of the crime scene to draw any substantial conclusions.

"By limiting yourself to only three possibilities, you have introduced a degree of investigative bias that inherently precludes all other solutions."

The chief inspector scratched his scruffy muttonchops. "If not an accident, suicide, or murder, then what?"

I stuffed my hands into my frock coat pockets and looked to the outer room where Keldon searched for additional clues. "If it was an accident or suicide, then why is the lower half of Doctor Meldrine's body on the other side of the room? He could not have fallen, jumped, or walked into the orrery's gearing without his legs. If, on the other hand, it was murder, why would the killer only dispose of half a body? For that matter, why dispose of a body in this manner at all? This is not a murder made to look like an accident—it's far too sloppy for that—and there are countless better ways to make a body disappear. We are, after all, standing in the most prestigious institution of the thaumaturgical arts in all of Armillia."

"Not every murderer must be a criminal mastermind," Tibblemond argued. "In fact, most are bungling fools! This one could have been in a hurry, or perhaps he ran off when he heard—"

"Aldicus, I found..." My apprentice froze the moment he entered the room, his eyes wide and mouth hanging open as he gazed upon the grisly remains.

"Did I not advise you to wait in the outer room?"

"I... I think you should see this," Keldon said, his voice trembling as he worked to maintain his composure. He collected himself, drawing his youthful eyes away from the mechanically masticated victim, and held something out to me. "It was hidden behind one of the smaller armillary models."

I looked at the crystalline stone held between his thumb and forefinger. Although the object resembled an opal, the shimmering glint of rainbow hues sparkling deep within suggested otherwise. "A vizstone is not particularly unusual in an institute of magery."

"Yes, but this one's infused with an encrypted recording," Keldon explained. "The cipher was just a simple logarithmic replacement, which I was able to bypass using a recursive polyglyphic evocation."

I gave an approving nod. "I see you have been practicing." I held out my arms, showing the dull gray severite bonds locked around my wrists. "Unfortunately, there is little I can do with a vizstone since I can no longer sense, shape, or conduct even the smallest chord of aetheric resonance."

"Sorry, boss," Keldon said sheepishly. He turned the vizstone over in his hand, then held it up to his eye. "I believe I can project the message. Just give me a moment to tap into the crystal lattice."

"Make some sense, boy," Tibblemond demanded. "Not all of us here are dilettantes of that blasted bodgefuddle."

"Keldon is hardly a dilettante," I rebuked. "Or perhaps you would prefer that I remove these bonds to delve the vizstone myself?"

Tibblemond fell into an uneasy silence.

My apprentice drew his brass skeleton key and placed the tip against the vizstone, closing his eyes in concentration. After a short moment, a hazy figure materialized in the air, coiling and shifting in formless patterns of inky smoke and bubbling color. The ghostly shape gradually resolved to a more detailed projection of a haggard, middle-aged man with wireframe spectacles and a frumpy tweed coat.

"Is this recording from the victim?" Tibblemond asked.

I shook my head. I recognized the man projected from the vizstone, and he was not Tommas Meldrine. "Not unless Doctor Meldrine lost considerable weight prior to his bodily pulpification."

"Tommas!" the figure said, his voice strained with worry. "Denebus is dead. Those lunkheaded jacks are saying it was suicide, but we both know better. That makes *three* now, plus the other two locked up in Grimhall Asylum." The man looked left, then right, and despite the hazy nature of his ghostly image, I could clearly discern the fear creasing the features of his face. "Listen, Tommas... The only thing I've found that helps the nightmares is a philter of three parts vespersong and one part essence of bloodwort. It may not dispel the curse, but it should give us some time. And... And I think you're right about the O.A.S. If it's true, then Archons help us all. Just be careful and watch yourself tonight. I know how creepy the Celestarium can get in the small hours of the night."

"Whoever sent this message was addressing our victim," Tibblemond said. "He also seemed to know that he would be here late into the night. What do you suppose Doctor Meldrine was doing here last night, anyway?"

I looked to the blood-coated orrery again, watching as the planets turned in their courses about the sun. From what I could tell, the machine appeared to be configured to track an upcoming eclipse, but I could see no connection between that and Tommas Meldrine's death.

"He may have been refining some calculations for the eclipse later this year," I posited. "Doctor Meldrine is, or rather was, the Celestarium's chief researcher."

Tibblemond nodded. "Well, we need to identify whoever sent this message to Doctor Meldrine. He seems to know something about all of this and was clearly distraught."

"That was Doctor Wenthrom Gest," I said, watching as his image dispersed in a cloud of aetheric mist. "He is one of the foremost experts in high resonance metaplasmic condensates. I attended one of his lectures at a symposium last year. His theories were quite brilliant."

"Is he a professor here?" Keldon asked.

"He is a research mage with the Institute, but his office is in an annex on the other side of campus." I turned my full attention back to Tibblemond. "Doctor Gest mentioned three recent suicides. Have you or anyone in the Vandorian Guard recently investigated the apparent suicide of any mages here?"

Tibblemond scratched his muttonchops again, his brow furrowing in thought. "I wasn't part of those investigations, but from my understanding, there was no question that they were suicides. This case is different. The Commissioner General is deeply concerned that we may have a run-amok mage, which is why I brought you into the case. Of course, this could just as easily be a freak accident."

I huffed, stuffing both hands into my pockets. "Did you not think it odd to have three apparent suicides, all recent and all within the same institution, followed by an apparent murder?"

"Then are you suggesting this is also a suicide?" Tibblemond asked, missing my point. "I have a hard time believing anyone would try to kill themselves in this manner." Then he paused, his eyes growing wide as the implication of my question dawned on him. "No... You believe all four were murders, don't you?"

"It is too early to draw conclusions," I admitted. "If they are murders, then we need to compile a list of suspects, beginning with anyone connected to all four victims. Unfortunately, we have only one lead, Doctor Wenthrom Gest, assuming he is not already dead."

Tibblemond thought for a moment, then cleared his throat. "Ah, yes. That would seem a good place to start."

"And what if he *is* dead?" Keldon asked.

"Then his office or apartment may hold additional clues. Grab my bag and meet me in the main hall." I took one last look around the orrery's blood-stained machine room, regretting the rare-cooked roast beef sarnie I had eaten for lunch. I put my hand on Tibblemond's shoulder, feigning sympathy for his job. "Good luck in here. Shall I send for someone with a mop?"

OUR WALK FROM THE CELESTARIUM to the Bruneillé Research Annex was by no means a short jaunt. The Institute of Thaumaturgical Science was merely one college within the Royal Academy of Armillia, and the Academy's many libraries, facilities, and dormitories covered over half of the 4th District of Corradon. Forums, lecture halls, and research buildings lined the Institute's main thoroughfare, bustling with students, faculty, researchers, and academics the world over. The crowd was as diverse as any within the city's core districts—populated not only by Armillians, but by men and woman of every nation of Celaphania, and a few from Tarrona, as well as Dworghs of the Arcrest Mountains, Eldren from Sylvanin Vey and Talyrin Vey, and even the rare Ogrum scholar before whom the churning crowd nervously parted way. Yet, the sprawling campus was little more than a patch of marble and stone surrounded by the Clockwork City's towering ramparts of iron, brass, and fabricrete.

At the colonnaded portico of the Bruneillé Research Annex stood an automaton dressed in a black and red porter's uniform, comically ill-fitted to its boxy shape. Its multi-colored ocular lenses focused on us as we approached, and I showed my badge. The automaton gave a jerky bow, and needless though it was, I tipped my top hat as the front door parted open. On the surface, the facility's security appeared surprisingly relaxed, but quite the opposite was true. Keldon drew a sharp breath as we started down the wood-paneled hall. I could sense nothing myself—the severite bonds clasped to my wrists strangled out every mote of my former talents. But I knew the eyes were there, watching from every corner and lurking in every room.

"What is it like?" I asked.

Keldon shook his head absently, his gaze turning from one seemingly empty corner to another. "Watchdog egregores and intrusion wards are everywhere."

"That's hardly surprising. Some of the Institute's most sensitive research is conducted in the Bruneillé Annex." We continued through a sparsely populated lobby in which the single feature of interest was the bronze statue of Gion Bruneillé, the famed thaumatologist who put forward the theory of transaetheric wave dynamics. "It may not look the part, but this place is a fortress. How any murderer could have entered undetected only deepens the enigma."

"Perhaps the murderer was not seen as an intruder," Keldon suggested.

I quirked an eyebrow, then gave my astute apprentice a smile. "That would certainly narrow our list of suspects, would it not?"

We stopped in front of a rich redwood door, from which issued incoherent murmurings, broken only by the frantic tap and scratch of chalk against slate. The brass plaque read "Wenthrom L. Gest, Doctorate, M. Magus, Sr. Prof." I knocked. After a few more knocks I tried the knob and found the door unlocked.

Keldon shifted his weight nervously, passing my black leather bag from his right hand to his left. "Don't we need a warrant?"

I smiled, pushing open the door. "Not if I'm just a concerned citizen who is merely popping by to catch up with an old acquaintance."

While I fully expected Wenthrom's office to be the same disorganized hodgepodge of stacked books, scattered papers, and unmatched tea sets I had seen years earlier, I was entirely unprepared for the ramshackle mess strewn before me. Heaps of books had been piled upon the floor, papers scrawled in a shaky hand lay scattered over every inch of carpet, and the walls were covered with crudely sketched diagrams and magian notation. A disheveled, wild-haired man hunched over a pair of weathered tomes while his trembling hand dashed glyphic equations upon an ill-treated chalkboard. Although such an appearance was hardly unusual for a professor of theoretical thaumatology, the stretched and hungry features of Wenthrom's terror-drawn face alerted me at once to his plight.

I cleared my throat, brushing my hands down the front of my frock coat. "Doctor Wenthrom Gest—"

"Get out!" Wenthrom screamed, whirling around. He flung his hand in my direction, hurling a meager scrap of chalk past my head. "Get out, get out, get out!"

I held my breath for a moment, then spoke in a calm, deliberate voice. "Doctor Gest, do you recognize me?"

Wenthrom pushed his wireframe spectacles up to the bridge of his nose and jutted out his lower lip. "I know who you are, Vescard. Let me guess—Tommas Meldrine is dead and you were called in to investigate. You found the message I had sent to him and somehow managed to recall it despite your..." He waved in the general direction of my arms. "...inhibited abilities."

"So, you do remember." I pulled up one of my coat sleeves to reveal the dull gray severite bond fastened around my wrist. "I have a few spare ones in my bag, if you think they might help."

Wenthrom frowned. "Why would I want that? I'm not going to bind myself in severite. I'll need every power at my disposal when that *blasted* thing comes for me!"

I gathered up a few of the more interesting diagrams from the floor. Each one detailed a different logarithmic graph charting the entropic limits for various metaforms at specific resonances of aetheric energy. "Your friend, Tommas, is presently being washed out of the gearing machinery of the Celestarium."

Wenthrom took a whiskey flask from his desk and threw back a quick sip. He looked me over, then downed another sip.

I set the diagrams aside and continued. "Your message also mentioned several other mages who have died, as well as a few who have been locked up in Grimhall Asylum. If I did not know better, I would say you're teetering at the precipice of sanity yourself."

"Dead," Wenthrom growled, and took another sip from his flask. "They're all dead, even the ones committed to Grimhall." He turned away and looked over the scribblings on the chalkboard. "We've tried everything—aetheric wards, astral inversion barriers, even metaplasmic refraction fields. But nothing works. We can't escape it."

"You can't escape what?" Keldon asked, slipping past me as he entered the room.

Wenthrom looked up sharply, his face darkening to a glower.

"This is my apprentice, Keldon Veldanor," I introduced. "He is a student of thaumaturgy and was the one who found your message to Tommas."

"Get the boy out of here," Wenthrom said. "If the thing comes for me—"

I held up my hand to interrupt him. "It is not as though we haven't faced all manner of nefarious criminals, unnatural horrors, and ensorcelled abominations before. I just need you to sit down, gather your wits, and tell us everything you know about these murders."

Wenthrom glanced nervously about, as though fearful that someone else was listening, then he stepped closer to us. "It started a month ago," he began, his voice low, but gradually becoming frantic as he spoke. "One by one, killing mages or driving us mad. It comes in our dreams, but then it manifests..." He stopped for a moment, throwing back another swig from his flask. "The thing... It comes from out of the aether!"

I sniffed the air, but I did not catch the odor of alcohol on his breath. I looked at the whiskey flask in his hand. "Precisely what are you drinking?"

"What, this?" He looked at the flask he was holding and shook his head. "I'm not drunk, if that's what you're thinking."

"It's a potion, then?"

"Nothing works to keep it away, but with this..." He shook the flask. "At least I'll have the power to put up a decent fight when it comes."

I raised an eyebrow. "A *vita aurelium* elixir? You should know better than that. How much have you taken?"

He held up his left hand and a ghostly blue wisp of aethergy coiled between his fingers. "I know it could burn me out if I'm not careful, but at least I'll have a chance of destroying the thing before it kills me."

I nodded skeptically. Whatever this thing was, it had pushed Wenthrom to the very brink of delirium. "Could you describe this creature?"

Wenthrom shot a surprised look at me, then he blinked as he realized I had no idea what he was babbling on about. He took another sip of the elixir before indulging my request. "It's different for everyone. Tommas described some kind of dragon-beast. For others it was a chimera or something like a serpent-man. Denebus said he saw an oozing, shapeless blob. In my nightmares, I see this... this... *thing!*" He swept his arm through the air, sloshing blue liquid from his flask. "It was like a spider... *No!* It was a chitinous monstrosity of a man with a spider's head and covered in so many crawling, wiggling spider hairs!"

"Boss," Keldon whispered. He backed away, inching for the door and drawing his talismanic key. At first, I thought he was merely troubled by Wenthrom's incoherent ravings, but his eyes were focused on an otherwise unremarkable corner of the room. Like all mages, Keldon could perceive forms in the aether. If the form resonated at a high enough amplitude, he could see them even without focusing through his talisman.

"...and its fingers!" Wenthrom carried on frantically. "Its fingers were like spider legs! Grasping, wiggling spider-leg fingers!"

My ability to perceive aetheric forms was negated by my

severite wristbands, but even I soon began to see threads of inky black vapor coalescing in the corner. At first the shape was only a shadow, but it grew in thickness and substance as the condensing aetheric metaplasm assumed a humanoid appearance, reminiscent of a carapace covered with nettle-like hairs. The head, if it could be called a head, featured gaping arachnoid mandibles, above which sat six black orbs for eyes. The arms were long and spindly, and from its hands extended spider legs where fingers should have been.

"I see it!" Wenthrom declared. "I can see it in my mind!"

"Actually, it's standing just behind you," I pointed out.

Wenthrom whirled around and loosed a scream of the deepest terror. Perhaps I could have broken the news better, but under the circumstances, expedience of action seemed more in order. Keldon, still in the threshold of the door, could make his escape down the hall should the worst transpire. But if the theory now stirring in my brow turned out to be correct, none of us had anything to fear. In truth, I had more to fear from Wenthrom's reaction than from any monster in the room.

The desk and bookcases exploded in a maelstrom of blue fire and splinters as Wenthrom whipped out his wand and unleashed a barrage of energetic bolts. A siren resounded from somewhere down the hall. No doubt the security egregores had just detected the use of offensive empowerments. I had to act fast—a few ticks more and Wenthrom's potion-bolstered attack would blow through the wall and bring several tons of brick, stone, and fabricrete crashing down on top of us.

"My bag!" I called to Keldon over the deafening clamor of screams, sirens, and exploding energy bursts.

Keldon tossed me my black bag, from which I extracted a pair of severite handcuffs. Unlike my own wristbands, these were more typical of prisoner restraints—complete with lock and chain—and designed to help apprehend mages and sorcerers of a criminal persuasion. Having no desire to be on the receiving end of Wenthrom's relentless barrage, I gripped one cuff in my fist and dashed the metal band against the back of his skull. The professor's legs buckled and I grabbed him as his body fell limp.

The creature flickered as though to fade back into the aether, but it snapped back to my utter dismay, appearing even more corporeal than before. The thing started forward, its horrid, spider hands raised and its glassy black eyes locked on Wenthrom's unconscious form.

"That's not an illusion!" Keldon yelled over the alarm. His talismanic key glowed brightly in his hand. "It's manifest in physical form!"

Of course! Wenthrom was unconscious, but now he was dreaming. Without a moment to lose, I snapped a severite cuff around his left wrist and locked the second cuff to his right. The creature vanished that very instant.

Keldon looked incredulous. "It's... It's gone."

"Of course it's gone," I replied. "You know perfectly well that severite inhibits a mage's abilities."

"But..." Keldon looked at Wenthrom, then to the place where the creature had been, then back to Wenthrom. "He conjured that thing?"

I stood and dusted off my coat. Charred papers settled to the floor, and the stench of burnt wood and the tang of lightning laid heavy in the air. "Ordinarily we would wait for the Vandorian Guardsmen to arrive, but in Wenthrom's present state, he would just end up in Grimhall Asylum, like the others. Since I've not yet completed my investigation, to say nothing of asking the considerable list of questions that need answering, we're going to hold him in protective custody."

"And by that, you mean we need to escape with the suspect before the bluejacks arrive," Keldon surmised, his voice scarcely audible over the wailing alarm.

I nodded. "We need to move quickly. There's a precinct station on campus and they're probably already on their way." I pulled Wenthrom's arm over my shoulder and helped him to his feet. He moaned, then slurred something incoherent. "Oh, and bring that flask. We may get more answers from that than from Wenthrom."

EVERY TERRACED HOUSE ON BRASS LANTERN LANE featured its own spacious cellar, typically used for the storage of wines, cheeses, and sundry possessions, with the exception of #5 Brass Lantern Lane, which I had outfitted as a fully equipped alchemical laboratory. An assembly of glassware, pelican stills, copper condensing coils, and gas burners cluttered every available bench and table, while the wall-to-wall shelves showcased a collection of reagents, elixirs, specimens, and leather-bound tomes. I glanced up from one such folio as Keldon entered lugging the hefty reference catalog I had sent him to retrieve.

"Excellent. Just set it down over here."

Wenthrom had claimed that his flask contained a *vita aurelium* elixir, and while my distillation of the substance had resulted in the expected breakdown of soluletic tonic, amacene extract, and particulated aurium, a mysterious distillate had condensed within the third-stage receptacle. It was odorless and faintly green in hue, but I could not readily identify the liquid, forcing me to consult my collection of alchemical catalogs to determine what the professor had been drinking.

"I stopped by to check on our guest," Keldon said. "He's awake and asking to see you."

"Indeed." I opened the catalog to the middle and flipped through pages of cross-referenced indexes, running my finger down the tiny print as I went. "Odorless, slightly alkaline, green or yellow in hue..." I stopped at one promising entry, then flipped to the back where additional tables detailed more specific properties on the suspected substance. "Oh, fangle-fop!"

Keldon sighed. "I hate it when you say that."

I extracted a few drops of the substance from the sample tube, placed them on a glass slide, and inserted the slide into my magnifying scope. After adjusting the focus and positioning the mirror to collect more light, I could just discern the tiny specks suspended in the liquid. "Spores," I observed. "Of course!"

"Spores?" Keldon looked at the page in the book. "As in some kind of fungus?"

I leaned back in my chair, folding my arms as I thought aloud. "It's an ergot distillate—very dangerous, especially when combined with *vita aurelium* and ingested by a mage versed in the art of aetheric evocation." I shook my head. "Come, Keldon. Let us see if Wenthrom is lucid enough to answer a few questions."

We climbed the steep wooden stairs from the cellar to my foyer. From there, Keldon followed me up the main staircase, winding past the second-floor bedrooms to the townhouse's upper loft. Apart from a small reading room, the loft served as my much-disused guest accommodations, complete with a washroom, a dressing room, and a generously furnished bedroom. Wenthrom was already sitting up in bed, rubbing the back of his skull where I had struck him.

"I should apologize for your abduction," I began, "as well as the welt on the back of your head. I could bring you an anodyne, if you like."

Wenthrom grimaced. "I suppose one small lump is preferable to the alternative, but are these necessary?" He held out his severite-cuffed wrists.

"Consider them a temporary precaution," I replied. "What can you tell me about that creature?"

He sighed. "Not much, I'm afraid. Tommas believed it was a spirit or egregore under the control of some vile sorcerer. But whatever it is, it comes at us first in our dreams. That's how it slips in, I think. It attunes itself to our quintessence, so as not to trigger the aetheric wards."

"If you believed something was getting past your

institution's security, you should have alerted the authorities."

"Some of us did!" he snapped angrily. "They just ended up in Grimhall Asylum." Then he sighed, his shoulders slumping. "I suppose it didn't help that they were gibbering hysterically."

"Tell me, do you have an unusually strong fear of spiders?"

Wenthrom shifted uneasily. "I do, as a matter of fact... Of course, if I hadn't before, I certainly would now."

I nodded. "And you said the creature that came after Tommas was a dragon-beast. Do you know if he had a fear of dragons?"

"Who in their right mind wouldn't fear a dragon?" Wenthrom asked. Then he nodded, as though picking up on my line of questioning. "He wasn't so much afraid of dragons as he was preoccupied with their study."

"And the one who was seeing a serpent-like creature... Did he have a peculiar fear of snakes?"

"That would be Doctor Rensworth. I'm not sure if he was afraid of snakes, but he was quite terrified of the visions he was having."

"Dragons, spiders, serpents—all of these things are archetypes of our deepest and most primal fears. What you were seeing, Doctor Gest, was a manifestation of that which you most feared to see."

"Astral entities?" he asked, using the more technical term for the sundry beings and aetheric detritus native to the higher astral realms.

"No," I replied. "Aetheric constructs, similar to egregores, but materialized into condensed metaplasmic forms. Thaumaturgists such as yourself can materialize such illusionary objects at will, focusing aetheric energy until they gain tangible density and coalesce into physical existence."

"What are you saying?" Wenthrom asked, a hint of agitation in his tone. He looked at the cuffs on his wrists and frowned. “Are you accusing me of conjuring up that creature? I would never—”

“If I knew you were the culprit, you would have awakened behind the severite bars of a high security cell in Vandor Tower. I simply need to know where you have been getting your *vita aurelium.*”

“Why?” he asked after a nervous hesitation. “Is there something wrong with the elixir?”

“If you consider the addition of an ergot alkali to be something wrong, then yes. Now, where were you getting this tainted elixir?”

“An ergot alkali?” Wenthrom asked, stunned by my revelation. “But that’s impossible. We made the elixir ourselves!”

“Who’s this ‘we’ you keep mentioning?” Keldon asked. “You mentioned the O.A.S. in your message to Tommas.” Keldon glanced at me before continuing, but I let him reach his own conclusion. “Would that, by chance, be the *Ordo Argentum Sigilorum*?”

Wenthrom pinched his lips tight, but after a moment he seemed to relax. “I suppose it doesn’t matter. All the others are dead.” He closed his eyes and drew in a deep breath. “I, along with Tommas, Denebus, Doctor Rensworth, Doctor Feldon, and a few others, had formed our own private order, the Darcalion Brotherhood. We were a small group, but we were working to devise a more potent form of *vita aurelium* called *vita excelium.*”

I nodded. “No one has succeeded in creating *vita excelium*, although the O.A.S. claims to be close. Please don’t tell me you were trying to add an ergot alkali into the mix.”

“Certainly not! But we began having nightmares and hallucinations a little over three weeks ago, which was about the time we changed suppliers for some of our reagents. Tommas believed the O.A.S. was attempting to sabotage our efforts by terrorizing us with aetheric sendings, but your evidence points to another possibility…” Wenthrom rubbed the bristles on his cheek. “The O.A.S. could have tainted the reagents from our new supplier, not only poisoning our elixir, but destroying our brotherhood in the process.”

I folded my arms doubtfully and looked at Keldon. The scowl on his face brought a smile to mine. My apprentice already knew our guest was lying or was at least concealing part of the truth.

“Am I to understand that you already suspected the O.A.S., yet you never notified the Vandorian Guard of your suspicions?” I asked.

“Suspicions are one thing, but without evidence...” Wenthrom shrugged. “At least you’re on the case, now. Perhaps we can bring an end to this nightmare.”

“Perhaps,” I agreed. “Does your brotherhood use one of the labs at the Institute to conduct its work?”

“Yes, we have a small lab reserved for our use.”

“Very well. Doctor Gest, you and I will take the rail back to the Institute to conduct a full investigation of the laboratory in question. Keldon, find Tibblemond and inform him of the situation.”

“Is that necessary?” Wenthrom asked.

“It is standard procedure,” I answered simply.

Wenthrom sighed and nodded, then looked to his cuffed wrists. “Must these stay on?”

“I’m afraid so. It may take a few days for the ergot to work its way out of your system, and we can’t have you manifesting every wild hallucination that pops into your head.” I looked at the severite bonds secured around my own wrists. “But perhaps we shall see. As I myself have found, sometimes even the most fiendish curses can have the most surprising uses.”

WENTHROM FIDGETED WITH THE MEDALLION on the lab door, first rotating it one way and then rotating it the other. He looked back at me when it did not open and produced a nervous half-smile. “I’m not the best at remembering these things,”

he explained. Another two rotations and the color of the glyphs changed to a vibrant green. The mechanism clicked in place and the empowerment sealing the door suspended, allowing us entry.

The Darcalion Brotherhood was not a secret order, which I could plainly see by the plaque on the door boldly pronouncing their claim to the laboratory. That, in itself, was not unusual—many small, independent societies operated behind the closed doors of the Institute of Thaumaturgical Science. Some of these groups were associated with larger orders such as the Archidoxy, the Magestrian Order, or the O.A.S., although most were more social clubs than dedicated societies of magery.

But the Darcalion Brotherhood was no mere social club. While their lab was indeed small, it was also very well equipped. The four workbenches were stacked with alchemical apparatuses, custom-made glassware, and assorted crystals and vizstones. Books crowded shelves along the walls, their subjects ranging from alchemy to herbology and from thaumaturgy to advanced aether dynamics, interspersed with aging scrolls, hand-sewn folios, and notebooks stuffed with loose papers and diagrams. Two experiments had been left to boil over and congeal on the floor some days ago, and I could only surmise that other members of the brotherhood had been working right up to the point of their unfortunate demise.

“Over here,” Wenthrom said. He pointed to a case of flasks containing some nondescript green liquid. “This is an aqueous solution of virident amacene, the reagent we recently began ordering from our new supplier.”

I nodded. Aurium powder was the chief component of any *vita aurelium* elixir, but amacene was necessary to extract a sufficient quantity of aethergy from the miniscule flecks of aurium. “And who is this new supplier?” I asked, though my eyes were drawn to a technical text poking out from a pile of papers on the table next to me. “Do they have any affiliation with the O.A.S.?"

"Yes, indeed," Wenthrom replied. "Corbollen-Soliden Alchemicals. Several of their directors are also members of the O.A.S. I'm sure that if we analyze these solutions, we will find the ergot alkali. In fact, this may be the proof we need to show that the O.A.S. sabotaged our research and destroyed our brotherhood."

"That would be exactly the sort of evidence we need," I agreed. I had no doubt an analysis would reveal the ergot alkali, but Wenthrom's pointed observation of that fact seemed just a little too rehearsed. I held up the book I had found, then flipped through the first few pages until finding the contributors' credits. "I see the Darcalion Brotherhood recently published a new research treatise."

Wenthrom waved his hand dismissively. "That was published a few months back by some of the brotherhood. It's not about our experiments to create *vita excelium*, so I don't think it's relevant."

"Oh, but I do think it is relevant. The subject is on metaplasmic condensates, which happens to be your particular area of expertise." I skimmed down the contributors' page, then flipped to the back and nodded. "Not only is your name absent from the list of contributors in the front, but it is also missing from your brotherhood's roster here in the back. That is a most curious omission, is it not?"

The professor stood in silence, but the muscles in his face tensed. I set the book down and picked up an older one, also published by the Darcalion Brotherhood.

"Of course, this book, which your brotherhood printed late last year, does show your name on the roster, alongside that of your now-deceased colleagues."

"It was just an omission, as you surmised," Wenthrom replied. He licked his lips. "We already sent notice to the printer to correct the oversight in the next run. Now, back to the matter at hand. We should take some samples and—"

"While the simplest explanation is not always the correct

one, I have never found the most unlikely sequence of coincidental events and whisperings of conspiracies to be anything but the deceptions of an amateur culprit."

Wenthrom did well to conceal his reaction, but the furrows in his brow did contract ever so slightly. "What are you talking about?"

I threw my shoulders back and drew a deep breath. "Allow me to start from the beginning. My apprentice, Keldon, found the vizstone with your message not on the body of Tommas Meldrine, but tucked away behind one of the planetary models in the Celestarium, which meant either Tommas himself had hidden it for reasons unknown, or someone had planted it for the authorities to find. On that very message, which I doubt Tommas even saw, you played the role of a hapless victim, working diligently to dispel the curse supposedly afflicting you and your former colleagues. You also planted the notion that the O.A.S. might be behind the murders in a clear attempt to throw off the investigation."

Wenthrom opened his mouth to interject, but I was not about to let him interrupt my explication. I paced across the lab, turned, and paced the other way as I continued.

"When we entered your office, I noticed several diagrams that graphed the entropic limits for metaforms at various frequencies of aethergy. At first I thought nothing of it, but it is now clear that you had computed the exact quantity of the tainted elixir that could safely be ingested to make it appear that you were affected, yet still allow you to maintain some control over the manifestation. Although you were never in any real peril, you needed us to believe you were. Furthermore, you did not expect to be handcuffed in severite bonds, even if for your own protection, which is why you have been so anxious to have them removed."

Wenthrom looked at his cuffed wrists and swallowed.

I clasped my hands behind my back. "But your real mistake was in contriving this absurd plot about the O.A.S. being bent on destroying your considerably minor and, I'm sorry to say, rather insignificant brotherhood. Despite the fact that the plausibility of such a conspiracy was diminishingly small, I nevertheless gave you the benefit of the doubt and accompanied you to your brotherhood's lab. Upon arriving, you initially entered the wrong code on the lock, but got it correct the second time. This tells me that your former colleagues wisely changed their code after booting you out of the brotherhood. Even so, you did manage to acquire the new code, and using their new code, you were able to enter the lab at night and inject an ergot distillate into their supply of virident amacene. The fact that you slipped up and entered the old code this time is quite understandable given your obvious distress."

"Aldicus, you can't possibly believe—"

I held up my hand. "The final piece of evidence, which provided your motive as well, was this book published by the Darcalion Brotherhood on the very subject of your specialization. It lacks any mention of your name as a contributor, and for that you were resentful, jealous, and angry. You wanted to punish them for giving you the boot, and for claiming your research as their own. Am I correct?"

The professor backed away, his jaw clenching as he swallowed his own response. While I already knew the answer to my query, I nevertheless demanded his verbal admission.

"Am I correct, Doctor Gest?"

His eyes narrowed and he took another step back, bumping a table and shaking the beakers of experimental *vita excelium*. "*I* founded this brotherhood!" he hissed, stabbing his finger against his chest. "*I* gave us direction and purpose! *I* conducted the research! *I* achieved the critical breakthrough! We could have made a fortune, but they didn't want to sell the formula. They said it was 'too dangerous.' Can you believe the fools? They expelled me from my own brotherhood just so they could steal my research and take all the credit for themselves!"

"I don't care what those men may or may not have done to invoke your ire—such matters are irrelevant to me. What is relevant is the fact that you tormented and murdered those men in a premeditated act of unmitigated malice." I produced my deputy badge from my frock coat, holding it out for him to see. "By the legal authority of the Vandorian Jurisdiction Proclamation of the High Court of Armillia, you are hereby under arrest."

Wenthrom reached back and grabbed a sizable beaker of blue tinged liquid, bringing the glass to his lips. "Tainted or not, this beaker contains sufficient *vita excelium* to overwhelm the effects of these severite cuffs!"

I shook my head. "That much will fry every nerve in your body, to say nothing of what the ergot alkali might do."

Wenthrom's lips turned up in a snarl, his eyes narrowing with resentful indignation. "Tell me, Aldicus, what is the sentence for murder these days?"

He did not wait for my reply, instead downing the contents of the beaker in one gulp. He smashed the empty glass on the floor and drew himself to full height.

"You accuse me of murder, but how are you any better?" the professor demanded, his voice rising with exasperated rage. "I know what you are, Aldicus Vescard. Beneath that veneer of law and order seethes an abomination of alchemical chaos, the living embodiment of creation and annihilation." He bared his fists at me, like a pugilist prompting for a fight, and the severite handcuffs began to glow red-hot. "Remove your bonds, Aldicus. Remove them and let us see who the *real* monster is!"

I touched the pins locking my wristbands and the blazing alchemical being within me screamed for release. I could almost feel my heart pounding like a blacksmith's hammer, burning cinnabar surging through every vein and muscle as the alchemical fire consumed and reformed me into a raging, elemental fiend. But the moment passed, and I drew a deep breath as I let my hands drop to my sides.

"I may be an abomination of science and sorcery, but you, Doctor Gest, are the only monster in this room."

Wenthrom's severite bonds disintegrated in a flare of crackling blue energy, and his wand flipped into his right hand. No doubt incensed by my gelid composure, the fulminating mage enveloped himself in a whirlwind of ghostly aethergy. Rumbling thunder rolled through the floor, the lamps seemed suddenly to dim, and the room sank into shadow as the very elements of light siphoned into the maelstrom of swirling, luminiferous aether, building up within the mage like the boiler of a steam turbine. I could not fathom what desperate evocation his madness-muddled mind had fashioned, but Wenthrom's empowerment resonated with such palpable force that I felt the crashing currents of the aether despite the dampening effects of my own severite bonds.

But the deranged professor never completed his evocation. Formless things emerged from the twisted warpage of space and aether surrounding him. Things I dared not look upon. Things only conceivable to a mind utterly unhinged. Wenthrom's hateful, cajoling expletives melted into shrieks of horrid desperation as the writhing metaforms closed around him. There was nothing I could do to forestall his fate, even if I had wished to help. I turned away, then made my way out of the room, eyes still shut as I stepped into the comforting light of the hall. I closed the door behind me, muffling the horrid screams.

"Aldicus!" Keldon waved at me from the other end of the hall. Behind him followed Tibblemond and two Vandorian Guardsmen. An alarm sounded somewhere, triggered by the professor's offensive empowerments. "What happened? Where's Doctor Gest?"

I stood by the door in silence, trying not to imagine what horrors Wenthrom's demented mind had conjured from the abyssal depths of the aether. The muffled screaming had stopped.

"It is over," I said. "Wenthrom was the culprit. He had poisoned the elixir himself."

"What? He did?" Keldon asked, taken aback. "He admitted it?"

I nodded.

"Is the culprit in that laboratory?" Tibblemond asked as he and the bluejacks came forward. "Well, don't just stand there. Open the door."

I shook my head. "I would advise against that."

The chief inspector sighed. "Just open the door."

The screaming had stopped, and whatever nightmares had beset poor Wenthrom would have vanished the instant he died. Even so, I had little desire to see what remained of his corpse. But this was Tibblemond's case and he did have jurisdiction. So I dialed the same code Wenthrom had used and pushed open the door.

"What is this?" Tibblemond demanded as he stepped inside.

I stood with Keldon at the threshold of the door, staring into an empty laboratory. Save for the shelves along the wall and some clutter on the far side, practically everything in the room had vanished. No sign of Wenthrom remained—not a drop of blood, not a shred of fabric, not even a strand of hair. I realized then that Wenthrom was not dead, and that his nightmare had not ended. His nightmare would never end. He had been taken by the conjured metaforms of his shattered mind into that realm of formless thought and energy beyond the Veil. I could not imagine a more terrible fate, nor wish it upon anyone, no matter how heinous their crime.

"Doctor Gest is dead," I lied, though I wished it were true. "Neither you nor I nor anyone else in this world will ever see him again."

"Blast it," Tibblemond muttered. "Are you sure he didn't just disappear using some kind of trick or illusion?"

"I would be able to detect an illusion or glamour," Keldon

said, scanning the room with his talismanic key. "But I *am* picking up the residual imprint of a massive aetheric disruption. Did he disintegrate himself with an empowerment?"

I considered my answer. "Let's just say he is now and forever more at-one with the aether."

Tibblemond gave a resigned sigh. "The Commissioner General had his eye on this case, so we'll need a detailed report from you, along with an affidavit, signed before a magistrate, declaring that you witnessed his death and that he admitted his guilt for these murders. I'll fill out the requisite forms."

I detested paperwork almost as much as Tibblemond thrived on it, but there was simply no way around the bureaucratic tedium under these circumstances.

"I will see to it first thing tomorrow," I replied, forcing as cordial a smile as I could muster. With that, I tipped my top hat to Tibblemond, brushed some wrinkles from my coat, and started off down the hall. "Come, Keldon. I believe it is half price night at the Broken Spigot and I could do with a few frothy pints."

Case File 3:

Of Orange Peels and Pine

WHAT I FOUND MOST CURIOUS ABOUT THE CORPSE thrashing on the table was the faint, yet distinctly pleasant smell of orange peels and pine. It was not the sort of odor I typically associated with an undead mortifant thrall, yet there it was—a potpourri-scented mortifant, with its bloated black tissues covered in blistering pustules of fetid corruption.

Could its summoner simply have been squeamish, masking the rancid stench of advanced putrefaction with a mild aromatic empowerment? No, that seemed rather unlikely. Perhaps the fragrant odor served a more utilitarian purpose, concealing the mortifant's presence from all but the keenest nose. But that was no less ridiculous. Between its bile-spitting shrieks and wild, convulsive fits, I could not imagine a less stealthy choice for infiltrating an Archidoxy commonage.

I glanced behind me to Shaura Guillerd and Special Inquisitor Thollen, both of whom awaited my comment. Rather than addressing them, I spoke to my apprentice, standing just to my left.

"Your thoughts, Keldon?"

Keldon jumped with a start, nearly dropping his key-shaped talisman. "Sorry, boss," he said, trying not to look at the flailing cadaver even as he analyzed its aetheric spectrum. "I've never had the horror of studying a mortifant before, but if I'm reading this right, it's the work of an amateur. The necrolic aura is like a bramble of writhing worms, barely pinned together by a mesh of metaplasmic sutures."

"And the odor?" I asked.

"Some kind of minor cleansing empowerment," Keldon answered, still looking across whatever spectrum emanated from his talisman. I could not see the spectrum myself, but I trusted my apprentice's analysis. He would be infusing the pattern's signature into the small vizstone pinched between his fingers, to recall later if such evidence was needed in court. "It's well made, unlike the mortifant, but not strong enough to mask this kind of stench. Ugh!"

I nodded. It was as I had suspected. But why?

Shaura Guillerd sniffed with disgust. She was the commonage's resident herbalist and healer, and a devotee of the Order of Mendrus if her red fringed shawl and square white hat gave any indication. She and Eulan Cavaroy had captured the mortifant here in the commonage's cellar, but not before the feral thing had claimed a victim.

"Karcistry is a messy business, young man, and Solenna held no qualms about even the vilest subjects." Shaura drew a handkerchief from her robes and began wiping her hands with some vigor before tucking the cloth away. "She was filthier than a harlot, I say."

I adjusted my cravat, then tilted my head to better direct my voice at the gaunt-faced man inspecting the chewed remains of the mortifant's victim. "This is hardly sufficient evidence to implicate the accused."

Special Inquisitor Sammel Thollen looked up from Borrus Arengam's mangled leftovers and deepened his frown. If the man had any love for his job he did not show it, and if he possessed the faintest talent for sleuthing, he performed admirably at concealing it. A choleric old crank, Thollen had insisted that the investigation was an internal matter for the

Archidoxy. The mages of the Sybastine Commonage were indeed under the Archidoxy's jurisdiction, but murder was a matter of law, and that required a criminal investigation by Vandor Tower.

"Detective Vescard," Thollen pronounced, delivering every syllable with a punctuated inflection. "The fact that Vandor Tower hired an abomination like you to investigate this case, rather than sending one of their own, is an outrage. Were it up to me, you would be chained in severite and thrown into the deepest dungeon of Angdred Penitentiary."

I stuffed my hands into my coat pockets. The severite bands encircling my wrists ensured I would never again wield the splendor of magic. Yet, without their dampening effect I would be consumed, body and soul, by the blazing alchemical chaos boiling in my veins.

"Come now, Your Grace. Who better to catch a monster than one who is a monster himself?"

Inquisitor Thollen rounded the table, his indigo cassock billowing out as though to escape his irascible temper. "Don't be so flippant, Vescard," he snapped, shaking his brass staff at my head. "One mage is dead, and every servant in this commonage is scared witless. I have a mutilated body, the instrument of murder, and fourteen sworn testimonies against the accused. That is more than enough evidence to convict in any court of law."

The instrument of murder lurched against its iron chains, howling over the sound of cracking bones as it strained to break free. "We can neither presume the mortifant was raised by a karcist nor infer the identity of the supposed karcist on account of circumstantial testimony," I explained. "Have you conducted an analysis of the empowerment?"

"What more is there to analyze?" Thollen asked, his voice raised with growing impatience. He looked to Shaura who was now standing at the table where lay the covered remains of Borrus Arengam. She appeared to be in deep thought, her downturned eyes teary with some unspoken pain. "Sister

Guillerd. Put this blasphemous *thing* to final rest."

Shaura jumped at Thollen's abrupt order, but she hurried back to the table where the thrashing corpse strained against its bonds. Keldon glanced at me, as though expecting me to voice some objection, but he had already recorded the empowerment's signature, which was all the evidence we would need. Instead, I simply stood and watched as Shaura brought her pendant-shaped talisman over the thrashing corpse, her eyes closed as she composed a dispellment. She touched the pendant against the mortifant's forehead and the thing gave one final convulsion before collapsing to the table. I caught one last whiff of orange peels and pine, and Shaura wrung her pendant through her handkerchief as she hastily turned away.

Thollen nodded with satisfaction. "Will there be anything else, detective?"

I met the inquisitor's gaze, then gave an affirmative nod. The commonage had only a handful of staff and fifteen—now fourteen—Archidox mages. I intended to take statements from them all. "While I have no doubts as to the... thoroughness... of your investigation, Your Grace, I am obligated to provide my own report to Vandor Tower."

Thollen waved his hand dismissively. "If you wish to take more statements, then go and be done with it. But you will accompany me to the home of this karcist tomorrow and place her under summary arrest."

Still shaken by his first encounter with a reanimated corpse, Keldon followed me in thoughtful silence from the cellar, up the stairs, and down the hall to the oak paneled salon. According to the testimonies Thollen had collected, the mages of the Sybastine Commonage had for the past two weeks been plagued by nightly visitations of shadowy apparitions from beyond the Veil, culminating in yesterday's attack by the mortifant. But how could any apparition or reanimated corpse enter a mage's commonage without detection? Surely they employed some form of spectral warding, if not a host of watchdog egregores primed to repel any such incursion. And why were they so quick to lay blame on Solenna?

"Solenna always was a bit peculiar," Shaura Guillerd mused during the course of her interview. "Just a few months back she was caught rummaging through that old Vernoct Cryptopolis, and she did have those abhorrent books. But a karcist? At the time I had my doubts, but I did vote to expel her. After all, any evidence of blasphemy, spiritism, or spectral summonings is grounds for dismissal."

"But how do you know Solenna Namara sent the mortifant?" I asked. "Or for that matter, the wraiths that have been visiting for the past two weeks?"

Shaura scoffed. "Solenna clearly holds a grudge against us for expelling her. She is wicked and petty, and has always had a macabre fascination with death, spirits, and primitive magic."

I gleaned even less information from Belemus Flannon, an overly anxious illusionist whose fidgeting hands could not keep still. "Sister... That is, former Sister Solenna Namara was hysterical the day she was expelled, screaming threats and curses even as she was led to the door." When I asked him to be more specific about these threats, he paused and wrung his hands. "I do not recall the exact threats, but she was certainly yelling like a madwoman."

"It was a dreadful affair," Larn Amagor informed me, his voice low, almost a mumble. He was an alchemist and elementor, and from what I understood, kept mostly to himself. "I don't know anything about that business with the Vernoct Cryptopolis, but Solenna was twice reprimanded for possession of black market grammaticons. I saw them myself, and she never denied owning them." He looked one way and another before leaning forward to whisper. "Between you and me, I think she was expelled because some blamed her for the loss of our research grants."

I crooked an eyebrow at that. "Research grants?"

Larn nodded. “Oh, yes. One quite prestigious grant, from the Havington Foundation. But during our proposal arguments, Solenna espoused her theories on shamanistic spiritism and higher order spectral intellection. Havington terminated our candidacy the very next day. Word must have gotten around as two other grants we had just received were rescinded not a week later.” Then he sighed. “Solenna was expelled shortly after that on charges of heretical practices contrary to Archidox doctrine. But that certainly doesn’t excuse her attacks.”

Most telling of all was the statement from Eulan Cavaroy, a first-circle master conjurer if his blatantly embellished credentials were to be believed. He had helped Shaura Guillerd capture the mortifant, but neither of them offered any explanation as to how the creature might have entered the commonage.

“Solenna Namara is a karcist, and that is that,” was all Eulan really had to add. “She was reprimanded at least a dozen times for dabbling in black magic and spirit calling, and was finally expelled for breaking into the Vernoct Cryptopolis.”

“I heard she was expelled for her part in the loss of your grants,” I said.

Eulan sighed and nodded. “Well, yes... But that’s just one more example in a long line of offenses. Honestly, I don’t even know why someone like her would join an Archidoxy commonage. She’s a heretic, plain and simple. But who can know what madness twists the minds of the demoniacally depraved?”

Most of the servants and cooks had little to offer, other than attesting to seeing apparitions and being genuinely terrified for the past two weeks. Four servants had left, apparently believing the commonage was cursed, and the head cook had resigned on the grounds that he could find better work elsewhere, which was very likely true. Despite the head cook’s departure, we had a relatively pleasant dinner of roast gillifowl, flat beans, and stewed turnips, and concluded the last interview an hour before the great calendar clock chimed midnight.

Despite the late hour, most of the mages and staff were still up and about, and Eulan and Belemus offered to walk us to the rooms that had been arranged for our stay. A heavy cloud of melancholy lingered in the air. Judging from the downcast eyes and anxious faces of the servants we passed, they expected another attack that night. I could not have been more delighted by the prospect.

"Your bags have already been brought in," Belemus explained as Keldon and I reached the anteroom of our adjoining rooms. "If you require anything, just ring the bell to call a servant."

"There is one more thing," I said before the two could depart. "I am still curious as to how the specters and that mortifant were able to slip past your wards."

Belemus glanced at Eulan who smoothed the front of his coat before answering. "We are a small commonage," he explained, forming a reticent smile. "What defenses we employ are modest at best, and Solenna was quite familiar with them. I am embarrassed to admit that it was she who put up most of the spirit wards in the first place. In retrospect, we were quite foolish to trust her with that."

I nodded, but a doubtful scowl creased Keldon's face.

Eulan attempted a bow. "The demon-moon is full tonight, and I fear its grim visage bears ill-omens. Be wary, gentlemen."

I massaged the bridge of my nose as I watched the two men disappear down the corridor. "I'm afraid we won't find much sleep tonight," I said, gesturing for Keldon to enter the rooms ahead of me. "Now, where did they put my bags?"

SILVER-BLUE LIGHT SHIMMERED FROM THE WALLS of the room, then flickered and vanished with a sonorous *blurp*.

"It's impossible!" Keldon exclaimed, throwing his arms up

in frustration. He waved a sigil-inscribed paper in the air, beating it with his talisman as though to drive his point home. "I'm a mage, not a theurgist, and an apprentice mage at that."

Having carefully uncoiled the mainspring of a disassembled desk clock, I attached one end of the spring to a lead counterweight and the other to the top of a rod taken from the headboard of my bed. "Well, I certainly can't create a spirit ward myself," I said, brandishing one of my dull gray wristbands. "But the ward doesn't have to be perfect. Just try again."

Keldon sighed, then looked to the paper in his hand, crisscrossed with sigils and magian notation. He licked his lips and held his brass key straight out in front of him. "*Salus eremae surum, coriro qam phasmatae vaseram*," he intoned, tracing an intricate pattern in the air. He then turned to face north, repeating the incantation, and again to the west and to the south before facing east again. "*Avelero!*" he exclaimed, thrusting the key straight up in the air.

A voluminous mist of silver-blue light permeated every corner of the room, but this time the lustrous light did not immediately dissolve. I could not feel it, but I knew the surrounding aether hummed with circulating bands of resonant energy impenetrable to all but the most formidable denizens of the Veil. The blue haze gradually faded, sinking like a condensing fog into the floor, walls, and ceiling, but the effect would last well into tomorrow.

Keldon blinked and looked around. "I did it," he breathed, his voice incredulous. "I did it!"

"Of course, you did," I replied, as though his success had been a forgone conclusion.

But his success had not come easily. Ordinarily, mages practiced their empowerments until they knew them by rote and infused the patterns within the vizstones of their talisman, allowing them to compose the empowerments within seconds. To perform an empowerment that was not infused within a talisman was a task fraught with difficulty, requiring words, gestures, and ceremony to help focus the mage's will as he shaped the chords of aetheric resonance into the specific harmonic pattern. Keldon had done an excellent job considering his inexperience and unfamiliarity with theurgical empowerments.

I nodded to another paper sticking out from my black leather bag as I continued working on my own task. "Please familiarize yourself with that banishing rite."

Keldon's shoulders slouched as he resigned himself to the task.

"Just the words, mind you," I quickly assured. "You won't have time to practice the channeling and focusing techniques."

He took the paper in hand, staring doubtfully at the incantation. "But it won't work just saying the words. The words are only needed to help focus the intention, anyway."

"You're right," I agreed. "It won't work. But that in itself should tell us something." At least, I hoped it would.

I finished my work, affixing the rod to a flat piece of board, then stretched the mainspring from the top of the rod to a short dowel bar with the counterweight pulling down. The dowel was balanced precariously between the tension of the spring and the downward pull of the counterweight.

With the contraption complete, I set the device on the dresser and added the finishing touch: a coiled spool of orichalium wire slipped over the spring balanced dowel. It would take only the slightest deviation in the density or elasticity of the aether to trip the jury-rigged device, popping the dowel out of place. Of course, the dowel would also pop out of place if I jostled the dresser, but it should serve well enough as a crude telekinetic echo detector.

"You should get back to your room and tuck in for the night," I said, turning back the covers of my own bed. "Memorize that banishment and be ready to respond at the first sign of trouble."

The brow-pinching, eye-squinting expression on Keldon's face was a study in befuddlement, but my apprentice nodded his head before leaving the room. Already an hour past midnight, I knew it would not be long before some mysterious manifestation appeared. A roaming apparition was unlikely to chance upon one of our two rooms this night, but if it was as I supposed, and its purpose was to implicate rather than intimidate, then the odds were very good indeed.

I tossed my frock coat, waistcoat, cravat, shoes, and belt onto the wingback chair next to the dresser, then dimmed the luminary on the nightstand before settling in under the covers. An hour passed, and I found myself struggling to stave off the heavy lure of sleep. Being a little after three in the morning, the commonage had fallen breathlessly still, with only the creak of heat pipes, the groan of floorboards, and the faint whisper of wind outside. The crimson light of Atracus filtered through the window's gauzy curtain, filling the room with the fearsome glow of the dread volcanic moon.

I was just beginning to drift off when someone cried out from down the hall. A second scream followed just after the first, and then a third cry, which I recognized as Keldon's yelp of surprise. My hand darted for the luminary as I shot up in bed, but I pulled my hand back without tapping it on. In the murky, sanguine moonlight, I could just make out the edges of a twisted shadow floating through the anteroom. The shadow drew near the threshold of my open door, tendrils of inky blackness writhing about its tenebrous form. I was out of bed in an instant. The apparition had passed right through the spirit ward!

"Wraith!" I yelled, if for no other reason than to gauge its reaction.

The apparition poured through the doorway and expanded into the room like the billowing smoke of a brimstone furnace. Shadowy wings spread across the walls, darkening what little red light ebbed from the curtains, and coils of smoke coalesced into the semblance of a shrouded human form. The form rushed toward me, its phantasmal arms extending and gaping mouth widening as though to swallow me whole.

Keldon burst from his room, his slippers skidding across the polished wood floor of the anteroom, and he came to a halt upon seeing the wraith's full form. His eyes widened with terror, but he waited not a moment before leveling his key at the shadowy specter.

"*Do edasos vaelor at phasmata azparamio!*"

He had skipped two of the words, but the apparition shrieked and roiled, then spiraled in on itself until vanishing from sight in a twisting ripple of air.

Keldon looked at his talisman, then blinked. "How... That could not have banished even a wisp, let alone a fully manifest wraith."

I drew a deep breath, then brushed the wrinkles from my shirt and trousers, which I had worn to bed. "No, but it certainly sounded like one. Had it been an actual banishment, the expected result would have been for the apparition to disappear. Thus, to play its part, it did."

Keldon slapped his forehead. "An egregore-guided illusion? I should have seen right through that. You must think I'm an idiot!"

"Illusions can fool even the best illusionist when the mind is caught unaware." I picked up the dowel that had fallen from the contraption on the dresser. A force *had* rippled through the aether, resonating the orichalium spool enough to dislodge the dowel. "If it is any consolation, this illusion was more substantial than most, shored up with some good old-fashioned telekinetic muscle."

Keldon shook his head. "If that's true, then this has nothing to do with karcistry. It's just magery dressed up to *look* like karcistry. Could—"

I held up my hand, hearing footfalls in the corridor outside.

The door to the hall flew open and Thollen, still in his

nightshirt and nightcap, rushed into the anteroom with his brass staff poised for attack. "What's going on? Is it the wraith? Where is it?"

"There's no need for alarm, Your Grace," I calmly advised. "Keldon has already banished our unwelcome visitor."

Belemus Flannon and Eulan Cavaroy followed just behind Inquisitor Thollen, and beyond them I saw a small crowd of anxious mages and frightened servants in the corridor outside our rooms.

"Blast that karcist!" Belemus exclaimed. "Now you see what we've had to put up with night after night. It seems our torment will never end." He gestured to the gathering crowd behind him. "Please, Detective Vescard, you must help us!"

Keldon sniffed the air, his eyes darting around. I smelled it, too—the slightest hint of orange peels and pine. But where was the faintly fruity fragrance coming from? I studied Belemus for a moment, wondering if the illusionist was simply maintaining some kind of perfuming spell. Then I turned my attention to Eulan. He was himself a proficient conjurer, and being a conjurer, was an expert in all forms of energy manipulation, including telekinesis. But conjurers were not known for devising aromatic empowerments. I looked across the faces of all the mages and servants who had gathered, from Shaura the healer, to Larn the elementor, to Thollen himself. One of them was the culprit, of that I was certain. But I would need to place one final piece of the puzzle before knowing precisely who.

"Let me assure you all, this will be settled before dinnertime tomorrow," I said, knowing I would have my answer by then.

"I should hope so," Thollen growled. "I was beginning to question your reputation as Corradon's greatest detective."

I made a short bow and smiled. "Fear not, Your Grace. I will send word to Chief Inspector Tibblemond first thing in the morning, requesting a squad of Vandorian Guardsmen to aid in the arrest."

Thollen furrowed his brow, as though perplexed by my apparent concession. Then he drew up his bony chin and gave a sharp nod. "Excellent."

With that, Thollen turned about and marched out of the anteroom. Eulan and Belemus both gave me an appreciative nod, then followed the inquisitor out. The other mages and servants crowding the hall had not yet dispersed, and I simply smiled at them before shutting the door.

Keldon ran a hand through his pillow-rumpled hair. "So, we're going to arrest Solenna Namara after all?"

I stroked my chin, then gave my apprentice a reassuring smile. "Solenna is the last piece of this puzzle, but she is not the guilty party. Someone is trying to set her up, and in so doing, their little scheme went too far out of hand. Tomorrow we will find our answers, but for tonight we should do our best to catch whatever sleep we can. I have a feeling we will need all the rest that we can get."

SPOKED WHEELS CLATTERED OVER THE RUSTING PLANKS of the ill-kept bridge suspended high above a rushing waterway, itself a minor tributary of the city's expansive waterworks. With a bump we made it to the other side, and I leaned back in my seat as our steam-coach puttered down the mud-washed cobblestone street. The ride from the commonage to the sprawling urban steppes of Corradon's northern outskirts had taken a little under an hour. Being so far from the heart of Corradon, I was not surprised to find the forgotten borough an incongruous mix of aging country stores and traditional Armillian cottages, mashed between ramshackle industrial mills, sheet metal shanties, and corrugated warehouses—a meandering collision, frozen in time, between the old realm and the new.

The coachman pulled back the tiller, easing us to a stop in front of a quaint Royalist-era shop distinguished by its crumbling plaster façade, steeply sloping roof, and tall dormer windows. A hand-painted sign hanging from the door read "Potions and Spellwork," and below that, in smaller words, "By appointment only."

Thollen was out of the coach almost before it had stopped, striding straight up the stone-paved footpath to the shop. I followed just behind him, and Keldon hurried to keep up beside me, pulling his newsboy cap over the hopeless tangles of his hair. A small brass bell hung from the awning, and although its purpose was obvious, Thollen ignored its custom and pounded his brass staff against the door. Scarcely a moment passed before he pounded again, and he deepened his frown to a grimace when no immediate answer came. He raised his staff to pound a third time when the latch clicked and the door inched open.

"Yes?" asked a diffident young woman, her eyes darting between the three of us.

Her attire was quite plain, consisting of an ankle-length dress and simple white blouse, over which she wore a matching blue bodice. Her only jewelry was a vizstone-adorned handflower bracelet, which was likely her talisman. Her straight-brushed copper brown hair was simply cut, and by her anemic complexion, I gathered she was a bit of a recluse—a pity for someone so young.

"I do not recall any appointments..." Her voice trailed off as she recognized Thollen's indigo cassock and his imposing inquisitor's staff. "C-can I help you?"

Thollen's back stiffened. "Disarm and step aside."

Solenna blinked. She glanced at Keldon and myself, then slipped off her talisman and meekly backed away from the door. I could have reminded Thollen that without a properly authorized warrant from a court magistrate he first had to explain the nature of our visit before requesting, not demanding, entry into her home. But Thollen would simply have argued that her storefront was not a private residence or cite some three-hundred-year-old edict that exempted a special inquisitor from such tedious protocol.

Pushing past Solenna without a second glance, Thollen

marched into the shop and whirled around, taking in the crowded bookcases, potion-cluttered shelves, and paper-strewn tables with scornful scrutiny. The man harbored not the slightest inkling of doubt as to her guilt.

"Show us the sanctum of your black art," he demanded.

I stepped casually into the room, hands in my coat pockets. Stunned though Solenna was by Thollen's demand, she seemed even more surprised when I gave her a reassuring smile, her confusion growing when I removed my top hat and hung it on the wall hook as a proper gentleman should.

"Madam," I said, bowing in courtesy. "Allow me to introduce myself. I am Detective Vescard, and this is my apprentice, Keldon Veldanor."

"Madam," Keldon said, removing his newsboy cap.

"And I am Special Inquisitor Sammel Thollen," Thollen announced, "of the Archidoxy Ministry of Inquiry."

Solenna's mouth moved in silence as she mulled over my name. When she finally spoke, her voice was hoarse and breathless. "What is going on, detective? What is this about?"

Thollen scoffed at her apparent disbelief. "It is about your abominable practice of karcistry, your terrorizing of the Sybastine Commonage, and the murder of Borrus Arengam."

"Borrus!" Solenna gasped, hand flying to her mouth. She looked to me again, her eyes wide and her pale face drawing whiter still. "You think that I—"

"We *know*," Thollen answered, cutting her off. The inquisitor crossed the cluttered shop and stood before a plank wood cellar door. "You perform your blasphemous work down there, yes? I sense a strong confluence of negative aetheric resonance."

I glanced at Keldon and he confirmed with a reluctant nod. "He's right about the resonance," Keldon whispered. "It feels... primal... old... But I wouldn't call it negative."

"Perhaps if you showed us the room we could readily dispense with this unpleasantness," I suggested.

Solenna's shoulders drooped in apparent defeat. Defying the inquisitor's request would only have strengthened Thollen's conviction, however circumstantial it might have been. With strained reluctance, she opened the cellar door and led the way down the creaking staircase. We passed through a storeroom crammed floor to ceiling with wooden chests, hooped barrels, and shelves of dried herbs, then entered a candle-lit chamber directly below the main part of her residence.

The room was tiled in rough stone with dark fringed carpets and black wall drapes, in the center of which stood an altar furnished with a bejeweled dagger, a silver chalice, two incense burners, a carved bone fetich, and a painted human skull. A large black mirror dominated the north wall, its frame inscribed with ancient Olarrian petroglyphs, while on the western side of the room stood a bookcase and writing desk. A quick glance at the books revealed that most were handwritten tomes, yellowed with age, each suggestive of spirit summoning, shamanism, and ancestor worship. The printed books dealt with similar topics, one of them being a treatise comparing the shamanic practices of the Kuradan tribes to that of the Eldren and another tracing the ancestral traditions of ancient Olarria to modern practices of spiritism and sorcery. It was all quite damning, at least to the myopic eye of narrow-minded dogma.

Thollen frowned in disgust. "I've seen enough," he growled. "Place this woman under arrest on the charges of karcistry and murder."

"Fangle-fop," I countered. "I have seen no evidence that she raised the mortifant that killed Borrus Arengam. And as for karcistry..." I considered the feather-plumed bone fetich on the altar, admiring the artistry of the small, bird-headed totem. "I fear there has been some confusion over the nature of her research."

"Shamanism... Primal magic," Keldon murmured, his voice almost in a whisper. He considered Solenna, whose downturned eyes seemed to have lost every glimmer of hope. "But you're a mage. Why study these backward customs?"

I wagged my finger. "Now Keldon, what have I told you about keeping an open mind?"

"It's not what you think!" Solenna blurted. She looked at me, then at Keldon, but had the presence of mind not to address the inquisitor. "I've spent the last year teaching myself shamanic magic, and I even managed to reconstruct a few rituals of the lost Kuradan tribes. I've been trying to show is that all magic is one magic. The practices of the shamans, the Eldren, the Ogrum, and even those of spiritors and theurgists are all fundamentally indistinguishable from magery. I've submitted a half-dozen treatises to the *Archidox Fellowship Review*, not that I've ever heard back from them."

I gave a sigh, folding my arms. "You submitted treatises comparing theurgy with shamanic spiritism to the Archidoxy?" It certainly wasn't the wisest decision on her part, but that was not itself a crime.

"Heresy!" Thollen hissed.

"Her theories may not be in line with Archidox doctrine," I said to Thollen, "but that's hardly grounds for accusations of karcistry or murder."

Thollen waved his hand dismissively. "The guise of research does not exempt her from the prohibitions on black magic and spirit summoning, and it certainly does not excuse the raising of the dead to commit murder!"

"I would *never* think to murder anyone, least of all Borrus!" Solenna was shaking now, and she bowed her head, giving a sniff. "He was the only one who supported my work, and the only one who stood by me to protest my expulsion. He was—" She stopped herself suddenly, then swallowed. "We... We were friends."

"Indeed?" I asked, raising an eyebrow. I had assumed Borrus was simply a random victim of a mindless mortifant, but I should not have assumed anything. I thought back to the tears I had seen in Shaura's eyes. Were those tears of sorrow? Anguish? Heartbreak? Or shame? The last piece of the puzzle had finally clicked.

"What about this business with the Vernoct Cryptopolis?" I asked. "You know the deep crypts are dangerous and home to all manner of necrocites, ghouls, ghastuls, and still fouler things that prowl the haunted dark of those long-forgotten passageways."

Solenna looked at me with a start. Then she glanced down, almost as though embarrassed. "Oh, yes... I was just researching ancient customs related to ancestor worship."

I arched an eyebrow. Solenna was a brave one, indeed.

"You cannot seriously believe these lies, Vescard," Thollen protested. He looked around the room, at her substantial collection of shamanic artifacts and spirit fetiches, his face twisting in revulsion. "I already have all the proof I need."

I looked about the room as well, shaking my head. "I see no evidence of murder, Your Grace. As for the prohibition on spirit magic... Well, I suppose that simply depends on your point of view."

"What other point of view is there?" Thollen sputtered. "We would not be here if she was not guilty!"

The inquisitor flinched the moment he had spoken, doubtlessly aware of how easily I could demolish such a fallacious argument. I opened my mouth to reply, but the bell jangled upstairs.

"Hello?" called a muffled voice that I recognized all too well.

"Tibblemond," Keldon and I both said at once.

"Perhaps an *actual* officer of the law will be more accommodating," Thollen grumbled.

He reached out to seize Solenna by the arm, but I held up my hand.

"I believe you will be disappointed. The message I dispatched to Vandor Tower only requested an escort back to the commonage. She will return with us to face her accusers. Then we will carry out the necessary arrest in accordance to due process."

Thollen frowned. "Whether we arrest her here or before her colleagues she has so cruelly terrorized, matters little to me. But we shall have it your way, if you insist. Bring her."

With that, the inquisitor turned and stalked up the stairs.

Once Thollen had disappeared up the stairs, I returned my attention to Solenna. "I would like to take one of these totems or fetiches with us to the commonage. If that is all right with you."

She blinked, perhaps caught off guard by my request, or by the fact that it was merely a request and not a demand. Then she nodded and picked up the ornately carved bird's skull that sat on her altar.

"I did not do those terrible things," she said, handing me the fetich. "You really do believe me?"

"I do," I assured her, tucking the fetich into my inner coat pocket. "Do you trust me?"

She looked into my eyes, and in hers I saw a spark of hope rekindled. After a moment she nodded. "Yes. I trust you, Aldicus Vescard."

So, she had heard of me. It was good to have a reputation. "Excellent!"

But Solenna still looked doubtful. She glanced at Keldon, then turned back to me. "But, if you already know I'm not behind this, who is?"

I clapped my hands together and beamed a chipper grin. "That, my good and curious friend, is for the mages of the Sybastine Commonage to reveal."

"WHAT IS THE MEANING OF THIS, VESCARD?" Belemus demanded as he and the other mages filed into the commonage's great salon. "Why have you brought her back here?"

"This is an outrage!" Eulan yelled, not only his fist but his entire body shaking. "She should be taken to Vandor Tower in chains. Severite chains!"

"This vile woman is a karcist," Shaura added, her arms

clasping about herself as though having taken a sudden chill. “She should not set foot in our sanctified commonage.”

“Quiet, everyone! Quiet!” Thollen yelled over their voices. “Detective Vescard has asked that we bring her here to answer before her victims. Perhaps she will beg for atonement.” He grinned spitefully, his grip on his inquisitor’s staff tightening. “Or perhaps she will stand here, unrepentant and without remorse, denying what is evident to all.”

To say the reaction was what I had expected was not precisely true. I had expected one among them to be notably more outraged than the others, but from Shaura to Belemus to Eulan, the expressions worn by the other mages gathered in the oak paneled salon ran the gamut from surprise to disgust to wide-eyed disbelief. Solenna bit her lip and glanced down meekly. No doubt she had long ago given up defending herself from such spiteful accusations. I placed my hand on her shoulder. She flinched, but she forced herself to lift her head and face her former colleagues.

Tibblemond, standing to my left, cleared his throat. “Ah, you may not have noticed, but she is under guard.” He gestured to the six Vandorian Guardsmen standing with him, each in their full accoutrement of blue body armor with empowered bolt-batons at the ready. The chief inspector smiled, then rubbed his muttonchops absently. “Rest assured, they are quite capable of handling one rogue mage. Or a few.”

“None of us are safe until she is bound in severite!” Eulan repeated.

“There are fourteen of you,” I pointed out. “But even with half that number, a lone sorcerer would not pose any kind of threat, not in this day and age. I suppose a master karcist with a cult of dark disciples, a host of howling wraiths, and a dozen or more mortifant thralls could blast through your defenses in an all-out attack.” I paused, but the range of expressions only grew more worried. I continued. “Therefore,

I must conclude that either you are embarrassingly incompetent, or that you believe Solenna is a Demon Lord straight out of legend."

I received more blank stares, and even heard a few indistinct murmurs. Tibblemond and the Vandorian Guardsmen shifted nervously, their eyes panning from Solenna to Thollen to the gathered mages, almost as though expecting any one of them to suddenly erupt wings and horns and begin vomiting fire in all directions.

"I told you before, she was the one who created our spirit wards," Eulan said, breaking the silence.

Keldon threw his arms in the air, rolling his eyes to embellish the gesture. "And you never reset your spirit wards after the first few wraiths were spotted wandering your halls? The wraiths weren't even real to begin with."

"That's preposterous!" Belemus declared. "You saw the wraith yourself. How could you say—"

"The wraith was a skillful illusion," I broke in. Belemus's mouth hung open mid-sentence, his face going pale. I narrowed my eyes at the master illusionist, then smiled. "Since your own spirit wards seemed ineffective, I had Keldon erect one to surround my room. Being new to such spells, his was admittedly flawed, but it was sufficient to grant at least some degree of protection from wandering apparitions. I also provided him instructions for composing a banishment, but more on that shortly. When the wraith did appear that night, not coincidentally targeting our joint rooms, it slipped through the ward with ease. That would make sense if it was a truly powerful wraith. Fortunately, my excitable young apprentice burst into my room and performed the banishment, and the wraith vanished that very instant."

Belemus breathed a notable sigh of relief. "There, you see? It was clearly a wraith after all and—"

"Except," I continued, holding up a finger, "Keldon only spoke the words of the incantation. He did not actually compose the empowerment itself. Even so, the wraith vanished, just as it would have had it actually been banished. It was as though an egregore was controlling the illusion with instructions to dispel upon hearing a banishing incantation."

Belemus opened his mouth as though to reply, but slowly closed it again. He swallowed, sweat beading on his brow. I continued, this time looking to Eulan.

"Suspecting that some subtle trick of conjury might be involved, I had also rigged up a crude telekinesis detector. When the device was tripped, I knew an empowerment of direct telekinetic manipulation had been used to simulate the illusionary wraith's spectral substance. The wraith, in other words, was a masterful fabrication, and was composed by not one, but *two* mages, each highly accomplished in their respective fields."

Eulan stared at me in wide-eye disbelief, his mouth moving, but no words coming out. Tibblemond began to step forward, but I held up my hand to stop him. I had just one more suspicion to confirm.

"That was no illusion that killed Brother Borrus," Shaura snapped. "We have the body of a mortifant to prove it!"

"You are correct about the mortifant," I agreed. "At first, I thought Borrus had simply been a chance victim, but in this business there is no such thing as a coincidence. He was Solenna's only supporter, and he would have openly refuted any formal charges brought against her. But more than that, he was Solenna's friend." I glanced at Solenna, then added one final qualification. "And I think, perhaps, more than a friend."

A slight blush touched Solenna's cheeks, but she only stood more firm.

Shaura sputtered. "Borrus was a smitten fool!" She stabbed an accusing finger at Solenna, her face pinched with naked hate. "None here have the power to raise such a blasphemous abomination. All the proof you need lies with her and her dark works!"

"She is correct," Thollen said, turning to me, a glowering frown darkening his gaunt face. "Vescard, despite your reputation, I fear your accusations are utterly unfounded. The cellar beneath Solenna's shop was a veritable shrine to karcistry and forbidden sorceries. I would not at all be surprised to find evidence of demonolatry as well. She also has ample motive to seek revenge on her former colleagues. What possible motive would they have to attack their own commonage?"

"Motive, as always, is key," I agreed. "Until I actually met Solenna, the only motivation I could see was petty spite on the part of her former colleagues." Eulan and Belemus stiffened their backs, and the other mages shifted uneasily. "Solenna may not be a karcist, but she is a heretic. She was expelled because her research into shamanism, spiritism, and magical unification theory was an embarrassment to this commonage, to say nothing of calling into question the Archidoxy's deepest tenants. But expelling her should have been the end of the matter. Why go farther? Why seek to implicate her as a karcist and destroy her utterly?"

The room had fallen completely silent, all eyes fixed on me. I reached into my frock coat and produced the fetich Solenna had given me. She looked at the fetich, then looked to me, her face worried but her eyes still trusting.

"The last pieces came together when we visited Solenna's shop," I said. "It was there that I found the final clue that I needed."

I tossed the bird's skull fetich to Shaura. It landed on the healer's robes, then fell to the floor. She yelped and jumped back, brushing frantically at her robes.

"How *dare* you!" She drew her handkerchief and wrung it around her hands, then used the handkerchief to brush at her robes. "Touching me with the vile taint of that filthy offal!"

"Vescard!" Thollen snapped. He glared at me with fury in his eyes. "You removed evidence from the scene of the crime?"

"Not at all, Your Grace," I answered. "The only evidence to be found is within this very commonage."

Keldon sniffed. "Aldicus, that smell..."

I inhaled a deep breath, catching a faint whiff of orange peels and pine. "Indeed," I said, looking to the handkerchief in Shaura's hand. "Chief Inspector Tibblemond, arrest Shaura Guillerd, along with Eulan and Belemus for aiding and abetting. The charges: conspiracy to falsely implicate another and for the unlawful murder of Borrus Arengam."

Tibblemond gave a nod and motioned for the bluejacks to follow him.

Shaura looked up, her face paling and eyes bulging in horror. She looked at her handkerchief, then back to me. Her talisman was in her hand in a flash, and its vizstones shimmered as she pressed the pendant against the handcloth. She was trying to dispel the incriminating empowerment!

"Drop that hankie!" I demanded.

I stepped forward, lifting my left arm to brandish my severite wristband, my right hand gripping the locking pin tight. Shaura froze, her eyes fixed on my severite wristband, but the glow from her talisman remained. In seconds, she could erase every trace of the empowerment infused upon her handkerchief, and that was an outcome I could simply not afford. With no time to delay, I pulled the pin and the severite wristband hit the floor with a thunk.

"Aldicus?" Keldon asked, looking down at the wristband on the floor.

The blood in my veins began to boil, waves of icy fire slicing through every nerve and sinew of my left arm. Welts began forming on my hand—welts that would soon turn into blisters, and those blisters into the transmogrified flesh of the alchemical monster I would become. I would not fully transform, not with the other wristband still on, but the agony was utterly excruciating.

"I am more than capable of subduing you, as you may well know," I rasped between clenched teeth, straining as I fought back the white-hot pain stabbing through my blistering arm.

Shaura swallowed, then with a visible tremble, she let the handkerchief drift down to the floor.

"Keldon, fetch that handkerchief," I managed to say. Then I gave a nod to Tibblemond. "Chief Inspector, if you would?"

Tibblemond's eyes were fixed on my steaming arm. Then he shook his head and drew a pair of severite handcuffs from his belt. "By the legal authority of the Vandorian Jurisdiction Proclamation," he recited, locking each cuff around Shaura's wrists, "you are under arrest."

I retrieved my own severite bond from the floor and quickly snapped it back onto my wrist. The alchemical flames vanished the instant the wristband was secure, but the searing pain my partial transformation left behind was far less fleeting.

Keldon stood, having taken the handkerchief from the floor. "This handkerchief is empowered. It looks like a cleansing spell." He turned the gleaming cloth over and sniffed it. "Orange and pine."

I nodded, then breathed a sigh of relief—not only at the cool reprieve the severite wristband gave to my scalded arm, but also at hearing the handkerchief's empowerment was still intact.

"If we compare the empowerment's signature to the aetheric signature my apprentice recorded from the mortifant's remains, we will find a match." I looked to Shaura, her head now bowed in defeat. "Shaura Guillerd's obsession with cleanliness was her own undoing—a rather problematic compulsion for one trying to raise an undead thrall. Her handkerchief was infused with a cleansing empowerment, and she had used the same empowerment to ward away the filth of the rotting cadaver she called up from the grave to implicate Solenna."

Shaura's shoulders sagged as she conceded the self-incriminating error.

"I wondered at the peculiar scent when I first saw the captured mortifant," I went on to say, "and again when I noticed the smell after the supposed wraith attack—though I could not tell from whom. There were other clues, of course—the patchwork manner in which the mortifant had been bound, the ease with which Shaura dispossessed the mortifant, and her very real display of remorse over Borrus's death. She also claimed, quite emphatically, that no one in the commonage could create a mortifant. But that was a lie. The curious thing about the art of healing is how easily the mastery of life-giving magic can be twisted to dark and terrible ends." I glanced at Solenna standing next to me. "All magic is one magic. The very fact that a theurgist and healer of the Archidoxy Order of Mendrus could raise a mortifant proves Solenna's hypothesis."

Shaura tried to pull away from the bluejacks standing to either side of her, but they tightened their grip on her arms. She let out a despondent sigh, her shoulder sagging as she looked down.

"Yes, I created the mortifant, but I didn't mean for it to kill Borrus!" She looked around frantically, then turned to face me, her tearful eyes pleading. "He was going to write a formal descension against our decision to expel Solenna. We just wanted to frighten him and make him think Solenna sent the thing to kill him. Brother Eulan and I planned to arrive in time to stop it before it could hurt him, but it all happened so fast. I just... I just wanted to save him... To make him see how much I... I..." She began weeping into her severite-cuffed hands.

"Come along," Tibblemond said, pushing his hand against Shaura's back. He motioned for the jacks to take Eulan and Belemus into custody, and the two mages put up no resistance as they were escorted to the door. Though severe, the charges they faced were not nearly as damning as those against Shaura. Even so, murder was murder by whatever means it was executed, and those complicit in the conspiracy were as guilty as the twisted mind behind its orchestration.

Thollan turned back to me and frowned, clearly displeased by the outcome. "None of this changes the fact that Solenna Namara is a heretic and apostate."

"I'm not sure how that is relevant, Your Grace." I tore away what remained of my burned shirt sleeve, then undid my cravat and wrapped the soft fabric over the welts covering my arm. "I, too, am a heretic by my very nature, am I not?" Thollan's sour expression deepened and I gave him as cheery a smile as I could muster. "You have your culprits, and my apprentice and I shall be on our way."

Solenna accompanied us as we left the commonage, leaving behind the pandering apologies of her former colleagues. They may have been willing to reinstate her membership despite her heretical views, but she clearly had no stomach for their hollow words.

"What will you do now?" I asked as we watched the bluejacks usher Shaura and her accomplices into an armored carriage outside.

"I will return to my shop," she replied. "But perhaps it would be for the best if I set my research aside. At least for a little while."

Keldon huffed. "And let that horrible woman win?"

Her head jerked up at Keldon's words. "I—" she began. Then she nodded. "You're right. All magic is one magic. I know it is. I'll prove it is!"

I looked at my bandaged arm and the severite wristband. "Fear and hatred cannot silence the truth. You are not alone in your pursuit of forbidden secrets, but you have proven yourself far more prudent than I ever was." Then, almost absently, I added, "I should probably put in a good word or two for you with the Magestrian Order. I still have a few friends in their upper circle, and I have a good feeling they will be most open to accepting a certain promising mage—

should she choose to tender an application. They are somewhat less dogmatic than the Archidoxy. Somewhat."

Solenna gasped. "But you've done so much for me already. I wouldn't want to trouble you further."

"It is hardly any trouble." I drew my pocket watch from my coat and popped open the cover. "We should still be able to catch the five-thirty to the 6th District, just in time to stop by that new Provanian restaurant on Fairecroft Street. I've been wanting to give their oyster fondue a try." I turned to Solenna. "Would you care to join us?"

She nodded gratefully.

"We're not going anywhere until you get your arm tended," Keldon insisted.

"The burns do not look serious," Solenna said. "I can whip up a poultice that would heal your arm in no time. But I can't imagine what it would be like for you without those severite bands."

Chaos, I wanted to say as we headed to the coach waiting in the commonage yard. Darkness, fire, and chaos, and the monster that burned within.

"Frightfully cross, that's what I'd be—and a bit steamed under the collar." With some effort, I amended my words with a cheery laugh. "But let's do hurry. I don't intend to miss my chance to polish off the best buttery bivalves to bless this city's bustling boulevards!"

Case File 4:

Crucible of the Innocent

THE VICTIM'S ONLY EXTERNAL INJURY was a single stab wound just below the sternum, possibly from a rapier or narrow dagger. But his internal injuries told a different story. Ghostly aetheric light radiated from Keldon's talismanic key as he scanned the body, shining through skin and bones to reveal a mush of burst organs still encased within a cage of splintered ribs, so pulverized that no single organ could be distinguished from another. Few things short of an untimely encounter with a steam locomotive could account for such horrific injuries, but the nearest steamrail line was two sublevels up and a good four blocks west. Unless an oversize stone golem had recently taken to fencing, the most plausible cause of death for poor Andon Galenrad was sorcery.

I stood, dusting the grime from my frock coat. "The internal damage is localized to the torso," I relayed to the men behind me, "and centered around a small stab wound in the chest. Judging from the body's internal condition, I estimate the energy delivered by the attack to be approximately one thousand foot-pounds of concussive force."

"Bodgefuddle!" Tibblemond exclaimed. "How could a dagger inflict that kind of damage?"

I produced a somber smile, grateful for the luminary orb

hovering nearby. It was early afternoon, but only a single band of sunlight crept into this undistinguished chasm of the Clockwork City's decaying depths. Until just an hour ago, my apprentice and I had been on a different case, having come to these ramshackle sublevels following reports of a mysterious blue goblin. But not three hours into our search for the curious beast, we found Chief Inspector Tibblemond interviewing witnesses about a murder. Having no wish to see poor Tibblemond bungle yet another investigation, I offered my assistance as a freelance detective, for the usual fee.

Looking back to the body, I found my apprentice had released the delving empowerment, leaving what appeared to be a perfectly ordinary mugging victim lying in the gutter. "Did you detect any aetheric imprints?"

Keldon examined the patterns shifting along his skeleton key and nodded. "Yes. I think he was killed by some kind of kinetic disruption."

I could probably have made a more precise determination, were it not for my severite wristbands. Regardless, his assessment was clear enough. "So, the murder weapon was empowered."

The dapper-dressed gentleman standing beside Tibblemond breathed on his hands and rubbed them together, shivering against the dank cold of the undercity. "Do you expect me to believe that Andon Galenrad was mugged by a sorcerer in this frothing cesspool of criminal depravity?"

I could not tell if the executive's pale complexion was due to the inclement chill or the fact that he spent nearly every hour of his life behind the cloistered walls of Tavion Spagyricals' industrial enclave. Regardless, Guillard Crambault was the personal secretary to Lord Tavion, and I could only wonder why a man in his position had been sent to confirm the identity of the victim. Even Tibblemond had managed that much on his own, thanks to the punchkey badge the victim had been wearing, which identified Andon Galenrad as a junior-level analytical alchemist with Tavion Spagyricals.

"I did not say the killer was a sorcerer. But consider the puncture wound to his chest." Without Keldon's spell, the only sign of trauma was the puncture wound and bloodstained shirt. "The victim appears to have been stabbed, but he suffered extreme hydrostatic damage. This could only have been inflicted by an empowered weapon—a rapier, perhaps, but more likely a stiletto. And it was no minor empowerment, either."

Crambault frowned, his already formidable glower deepening to a grimace. "What does that matter? This is still just a mugging."

Tibblemond scratched his bristly muttonchops. "I'm inclined to agree. More than one witness claimed that the killer wore a ring of the Unseen Brotherhood."

I immediately dismissed the idea. No member of the Unseen Brotherhood would walk up and stab their mark in the chest. They were thieves, not assassins. I turned to Crambault. "Why did Lord Tavion send his personal secretary to confirm the victim's identity instead of some other paper-pushing flunky?"

Crambault sputtered for a moment, then forced a smile. "This is a *very* sensitive matter. Andon Galenrad was recently dismissed from our employment. When he left, he took with him several vital trade secrets from his department."

A less astute investigator could easily have fallen for such a lie. Over the past year, Tavion Spagyricals had downsized its workforce, citing "improved production efficiency" as their only explanation. Yet, at the same time, they had somehow developed several miraculous elixirs resulting in soaring profits. Stranger still, Lord Tavion had not been seen in public since the company's turnaround, and speculation had been running rampant that the old baron of industry was no longer even in control of his company. Could Andon

Galenrad have uncovered some dubious financial plot or other scheme? That would explain the curious circumstances of his murder, as well as Crambault's overbearing scrutiny.

"Andon Galenrad still had his punchkey badge," I pointed out. "That is how Tibblemond identified him. Am I to understand that you dismissed him without taking his badge?"

Crambault rubbed his hands together and seemed to consider his next words carefully. "Very well. It is clearly an exercise in futility to withhold the truth from the likes of the great Aldicus Vescard."

I cocked an eyebrow at the spurious flattery, but Crambault continued with what I could only assume was a back-up cover story.

"Andon Galenrad was a spy working for one of our competitors—we do not know which one. A few hours before midnight last night, he broke into a secure research laboratory and stole one of our most vital trade secrets. Please understand, this matter could be quite embarrassing for our shareholders."

"One of your competitors?" Keldon asked. He doffed his newsboy cap and ran a hand through his tousled hair. "Doesn't United Thaumaturgicals have a few refineries here in the 12th District?"

"So do Consolidated Omniworks, Corbollen-Soliden Alchemicals, Vylaton Elixiries, and a dozen others," I pointed out. But it hardly mattered. Crambault had just changed his story and I could no longer trust anything he said.

I took a magnifying monocle from my bag and moved a few paces away from the body, motioning for the hovering luminary to follow and give me some light as I studied the ground. Two parallel tracks were just discernable in the muck that lacquered the street, not unlike the imprint left by the wheels of a small pushcart or rickshaw. A set of footprints followed to one side of the tracks, leading to where

Andon's body lay. Not a rickshaw, then. A luggage trunk?

"Inspector, did any of the witnesses describe what was taken from the victim?"

Tibblemond produced his worn notepad and skimmed over whatever illegible gibberish he had scrawled on its pages. "One old mumper said the victim had been pushing a wheeled crate, while another said the knapper carried off a chest or trunk, and others made no mention of anything like that at all." He shook his head. "Ask a dozen witnesses and you'll get two dozen answers."

I knelt and studied the footprints through my magnifying monocle. They were evenly spaced and showed no sign of slipping or smearing, meaning that whomever they belonged to walked at a steady pace. If the footprints were Andon's, he was not fleeing when he was killed. He had come here to meet someone with a trunk in tow, and he either knew his killer or expected to meet someone matching the killer's appearance. According to the witnesses Tibblemond had interviewed, that someone had been wearing a ring of the Unseen Brotherhood.

I adjusted my top hat and stood. "We will take the case."

Crambault licked his lips. "We appreciate your interest in this matter, Detective Vescard, but our security staff is quite capable of tracking down one petty thief."

"This is no simple mugging," Keldon reminded. "The murder weapon was infused with a military-strength empowerment."

Ignoring my apprentice, Crambault returned his attention to Tibblemond. "Chief Inspector, this is a delicate matter for Tavion Spagyricals. We would more than welcome any assistance the district police might provide, but surely a petty mugging is of little concern to Vandor Tower—or the great Aldicus Vescard."

I knew that for the right price, the district police would bow to any request from Tavion Spagyricals, either to assist them or to keep out of the way. But Vandor Tower was not so easily bought, and I could not be bought at all—and Crambault knew it.

"Murder is never a trivial matter, Mister Crambault," I cautioned. I hefted my black bag and tipped my top hat to Tibblemond. "If you will excuse us, my apprentice and I are here investigating another matter. Should we come upon any evidence pertinent to this case, we will certainly let you know."

"Yes, yes, very good," Tibblemond replied, busily scribbling in his battered notepad.

"Come along, Keldon," I said as I started back down the litter-strewn sublevel street. "We have work to do."

"Looking for this blue goblin is not nearly as important as solving the murder," Keldon said. Then he hesitated when he saw my wry expression. "Wait... You think there's a connection, don't you?"

I gave an honest shrug. "A mysterious blue creature is running amok, an alchemist has been stabbed with an empowered stiletto, a major manufactory claims to be a victim of industrial espionage, and someone is trying to pin the blame on the Unseen Brotherhood. I do not yet know how or if these matters are connected, but one way or another, I intend to find out."

THE TICK-TOCK TEMPO OF THE CLOCKWORK CITY had long ago stalled in the derelict Underworks, mired in the dregs of misery, poverty, and crime that seethed beneath the burnished cobblestones of the uppercity's bustling avenues. Abandoned tunnels and empty causeways meandered through the cavernous expanse, the heights above buttressed as much by their support pilings as they were by the crumbling tenements and sunken towers of by-gone centuries. What few underfolk were about hustled along one lost alleyway or another, hunkered in their greatcoats and hooded cloaks—forgotten souls, condemned to haunt these rust-blighted catacombs.

"We're not going deeper, are we?" Keldon asked, holding his nose against the caustic miasma wafting up from the depths beneath our feet.

"Not if my old friend Rognar has done his job," I replied.

I turned down another narrow alley, stepping around a broken-down rickshaw, then crossed a rickety bridge spanning a wide fissure open to the hollows and shanties cluttering the lawless labyrinth below. From there, we followed a causeway lined with black market storefronts and sketchy pubs, all of them oddly closed. I spotted my half-sized contact in the creeping shadows of an alley leading ominously downward and hurried over to meet him. Although I trusted Rognar only as far as I trusted any of my associates who skirted Corradon's rakish underbelly, he was an exemplary acquisitioner, a first-rate informant, and a veritable jack-of-all-trades.

The thickset Dworgh glanced around as Keldon and I approached, shaking the braided locks of his beard. "I poked around, like you asked." He looked behind him, to the tunnel leading to the lower Underworks, and gave us a disapproving once over. "This place isn't as bad as the 9th District, and a far cry from the industrial warzone that's the 13th, but I wouldn't go down there the way you two are dressed." Then he shrugged, his broad shoulders rolling beneath the folds of his buckled duffle coat. "Then again, you're Aldicus Vescard. I should be more worried for whoever you meet."

I pulled down the brim of my top hat. It felt as though someone was watching us, and more likely than not, someone was. "Have you learned anything about this blue goblin?"

"You have to understand, there's a lot of drooka dens down here, so it's probably just the crazed ramblings of some sozzled mumper." Rognar pulled a bully beef and cabbage sarnie from his coat pocket and took a sizeable bite. "Whoever heard of a *blue* goblin, anyway?" he rambled, grease dripping through his beard.

"He does have a point," Keldon put in. "This is probably nothing more than a drunkard's yarn."

I looked back the way we had come. The streets and bridges of the sublevels were never populous, but rarely were they this deserted. The few people I did see hurried along with uncommon urgency, and not a single bludger or bruiser lorded over their gang's territory. "This is no tall tale. The people here are scared. Terrified, even." I turned back to Rognar. "What have you heard?"

Rognar took another bite of his sarnie, then replied through his chewing. "Not many have actually seen the creature. Most I talked to only heard it chattering in the tunnels."

I thought for a moment. According to Crambault, Andon had fled Tavion Spagyricals a few hours before midnight. "Were there any sightings of the creature prior to last night?"

Rognar scratched the hair behind his floppy leather cap. "The earliest report I heard was from one fellow who claimed to have seen it chasing after someone just an hour before midnight. I couldn't get much out of him, though. He just kept babbling about the 'shrieking blue beast.'"

"Did he say if the man was well-dressed?"

"You mean like the sixer you two were looking over?" Rognar took another bite of his sarnie. "Not at all. The man was apparently dressed like a vagrant or thief. The witness even said he wore a thief's ring."

Keldon's eyes widened. "A thief's ring? Could he be the murderer?"

"Faugh!" Rognar laughed, spraying crumbs of food. "If you think the Unseen Brotherhood had anything to do with that murder, then you've got—"

I held up a hand. "On the contrary, I believe the Unseen Brotherhood is a scapegoat. Based on his footprints, Andon was not killed in a mugging, but approached his killer as though he knew him. I believe Andon came here to meet a thief, and the killer was dressed the part, garments, ring, and all. And if the killer had a ring of the Unseen Brotherhood, then he likely murdered a thief to get it." I rubbed my chin in thought. "And then this blue goblin was seen chasing after the killer. Very curious indeed."

Both Keldon and Rognar stared at me in silent bewilderment.

"Are there any members of the Unseen Brotherhood I can speak with?" I asked after a moment.

Rognar shook his head. "I doubt we'll find many thieves willing to chat with a detective. But they have eyes and ears everywhere, and might have some inkling of what's going on." The Dworgh ducked out of the alley and tottered off down the street, tossing the wrapper of his sarnie into a deep chasm off to his right. "If they have a mind to meet, they'll let us know soon enough."

I caught his meaning. "If one of their brothers has been slain, they might be willing to help us find the true villain behind the killings."

We followed Rognar down the subterranean avenue, turning north and continuing on through a well-settled squatters' haunt, evident by the vagrant flophouses and makeshift hovels carved into the foundations of the buildings above. Cook fires crackled in rusting drums, roasting whatever vermin their tenders had trapped, while shifty grifters and rag-clothed urchins pressed in, peddling their stolen wares.

Rognar cut across the dilapidated grotto, motioning for us to follow him into the narrows of a dimly lit tunnel. The rumble of heavy machinery and clattering gears from some distant manufactory echoed down the corridor of dripping sewage pipes and venting steam valves. Something moved in the shadows ahead of us, and from the splash of feet in the fetid water behind us, I realized we were surrounded. Keldon drew his talismanic key to conjure some light, but I held up my hand to stop him.

Three figures emerged from the darkness ahead, the foggy

gloom lifting as one produced a glowstone lantern from beneath his frayed cloak. I glanced behind me and saw two more silhouettes between us and the mouth of the tunnel.

One of the cloaked figures stepped forward. "Rognar," came a stern, female voice. "I see you're still playing both sides of the law. How long can a clever Dworgh survive, being both a fixer and a fink?"

Rognar shifted in his duffle coat. "As long as one can. How've you been, Emileve?"

Emileve. Where did I know that name from? "I am—"

"Detective Aldicus Vescard. We know." The woman drew her hood back, revealing a soot-smudged face with dirty blond bangs draped across red-lensed goggles. She pushed the goggles up and blinked, the pupils of her frost blue eyes dilating in the spectral lantern light. A ring engraved with lockpicks above a coin purse adorned the middle finger of her right hand, and a similar tattoo peeked out from just above the low-cut top of her leather brigandine. But it was not until I saw the distinctive scar hooked from ear to lip that her name clicked: Emileve, the Queen of Thieves.

"I have not come to arrest any of you," I said, speaking over the clang and clamor of the machinery churning above. I glanced to the shadowy figures blocking our only way out. "Not that I find myself in a particularly good position to do so."

Emileve eyed me for a moment, then folded her arms. "You don't think we've been watching you and those bungling bluejacks?" She shook her head. "Why are you here, Vescard?"

"I came to investigate rumors of a mysterious blue goblin, only to discover that an alchemist had been murdered nearby. I believe the culprit killed a thief to don his rags and ring, not only to make the murder look like a mugging, but because the victim was here to meet a thief."

Emileve smiled, pinching the scar on her cheek. "So, you've managed to conclude that the uppercity dandy-fop wasn't mugged by one of our brothers. I'm almost impressed."

"What can you tell me of the real killer?"

"You should've asked what I can tell you of Andon." Emileve brushed past me, heading down the tunnel the way we had come. She motioned for her men to stay back, then gestured for us to follow. "Or have you already deduced his reasons for seeking out the Unseen Brotherhood?"

Keldon and Rognar fell in behind us, their feet splashing through the tunnel's stagnant puddles as they hurried to keep pace. We exited the tunnel and rounded the perimeter of the squatters' settlement, following a causeway flanked by the towering buttresses of the city's ancient infrastructure.

"Are you saying the Unseen Brotherhood already had dealings with the murdered alchemist?" Keldon asked.

I put a hand on Keldon's shoulder. The question was too direct, and Emileve could have taken it as an accusation.

"Had I been told of the plan, I would have put a stop to it," she said with just a hint of acrimony in her voice. "We don't get mixed up in mercantile wars."

"Not told of the plan?" I asked. "You're the Queen of Thieves. Have some of your people been acting alone or against your orders?"

She waved her hand dismissively, but I could see more tension drawing against the features of her face. "It's just an honorific. We're a brotherhood, not a monarchy."

I quirked an eyebrow. "So, although you were not privy to the details, you do know that one of your brothers was killed on his way to meet Andon Galenrad. The killer appropriated his ring and clothes, and then murdered Andon and took whatever he had been carrying. Now I am here, investigating reports of a mysterious blue goblin that first appeared near the time of the two murders, and which was possibly seen chasing after the murderer himself. There is a connection between these things, and when we find that connection, we will have the key to solving both mysteries."

Emileve stopped and looked back at me. "Taimon help us if you do come for us one day."

I gave her a reassuring smile. "Your brotherhood does not condone murder, I know that. There are crimes, and then there are crimes."

She considered me for a moment, then produced a coin purse that looked remarkably similar to my own. "Then I guess you won't mind if I keep this?"

"Hah!" Rognar bellowed, slapping me on the arm.

I didn't bother checking my coat's inner pocket. I just smiled back, remembering the moment she had brushed past me on our way out of the tunnel.

"I'd say she earned the coins if she got one over on you, boss!" Keldon laughed.

Emileve chuckled. "Of course, I shouldn't deprive a young mage of his talisman." She took a brass key out from under her cloak and tossed it to Keldon. My apprentice caught his talisman, his eyes wide and his mouth agape. "Don't feel bad, kid. I've been doing this since I was seven."

She made no move to return my coin purse, instead picking out a few pfennies and ducats to flip to the vagrants of the squatters' settlement. "You're rich," she explained, tossing out coins. "To us, you're a topside prince, and so are the lot of those money-mooching dandy-fops strutting the cobbles in their fancy hats and spotless spats. But upperfolk and underfolk alike, we're either slaves to the barons of industry that run this tick-tock city or we're the refuse spat out the backsides of their infernal manufactories."

She stopped next to a young woman in rags, her face streaked with tears, singing softly as she rocked her wailing infant. Emileve pressed the coin purse into the woman's hand, then nodded when she looked up in disbelief.

"Just tell me one thing, Vescard," Emileve said, turning back to me. "Will you bring the real criminals to justice, no matter where the truth might lead?"

I looked up through the trestles and bridges spanning the

district sublevels, fixing my gaze on the pipe-snarled spires, soot-belching chimneys, and flame-spouting towers reaching high into the hazy sky.

"Always," I said, setting my jaw firm.

She stood in silence for a moment, then continued down the causeway. "All right, Vescard. You want to find a connection? Follow me. There's something you need to see."

WHAT LITTLE LIGHT SEEPED INTO THE STORM TUNNEL came from a single ventilation shaft open to the sublevels above. Harvel and Tobas, the thieves who had come down with Emileve, added the ghostly phosphorescence of their glowstone lanterns, but I needed real light to complete my inspection. I nodded to Keldon, and my apprentice held his key in the air, filling the chamber with the blue-white luminescence of conjured aetheric light.

"A warning might have been nice," Emileve grumbled, pulling off her light-amplifying goggles.

"Ugh! I think I lost my appetite," Rognar said, taking another bite of a greasy meat pie despite his words.

To say the body was completely unidentifiable would have been untrue. Anyone who cared to look could see that the splayed carcass of lacerated flesh, eviscerated organs, and shattered bones was that of an adult human male. Granted, the appalling state of the victim's face would make identification difficult, and would be best facilitated by the recovery of the deceased's jaw—wherever it was. But the most important clue to his identity was on his finger.

"You're certain this is not one of your brothers?" I asked.

"What do you think?" Emileve replied.

The middle finger was adorned with a ring of the Unseen Brotherhood, evinced by the lockpicks and coin purse engraved upon the face. But the ring had been slipped on upside down, with the lockpicks below the coin purse instead of the other way around. No member of the Unseen Brotherhood would disrespect their coveted emblem so.

"The ring is upside down," I observed. "Even so, anyone who saw this man might have noted the ring and assumed he was a thief."

"Those are Jaceil's clothes and ring," Emileve said, referring to her own murdered brother. She knelt beside the mangled corpse and pointed to the score marks on the underside of the ring. "We all mark our rings, and that's his mark. This is the man who murdered Jaceil and then impersonated him to murder Andon."

"So where is Jaceil's body?" Keldon asked. "We should see if he was killed with the same weapon that killed Andon."

Emileve shook her head. "We buried him this morning. He was stabbed in the back, if that's any help."

"A piercing stab wound?" I asked.

She looked at the stiletto lying on the ground a few feet away. "Yes."

Keldon had already scanned the stiletto, confirming that the vizstone on its hilt was indeed infused with a lethal kinetic empowerment.

"Do you know why—" I began to ask, but stopped abruptly. Emileve turned suddenly, looking at a ventilation grate in the tunnel's ceiling. Her men appeared equally concerned. "What is it?"

She remained silently alert for a moment, then shook her head. "I thought someone was watching us." She rubbed her forehead and sighed. "I just get a bit jumpy this deep into the Underworks."

"Curse you, woman," Rognar berated. "You nearly sent me scampering for the exit!"

I looked at the ventilation grate, but saw nothing other than darkness and shadows. "Do you know why Jaceil was meeting with an alchemist from Tavion Spagyricals?"

Emileve looked at her men. "Some of our brothers have been more proactive in their opposition of the syndicates around here. Sabotage, vandalism, theft of mercantile property, that sort of thing. Jaceil was one of the more proactive brothers."

I furrowed my brow. "In what way?"

She sighed, folding her arms over her leather brigandine. "Like I said, I wasn't in on the plan. But I do know that Jaceil and a few others had been working with someone inside Tavion Spagyricals. Word was, that someone had found evidence of a conspiracy big enough to take down the company, and Jaceil was going to help him smuggle it out." She drew a deep breath, then released it in a huff. "Come on. I want to show you something else."

Keldon, Rognar, and I followed Emileve as she headed off down the storm tunnel, Harvel and Tobas trailing behind us. We turned down several connecting tunnels, then entered a smaller service tunnel, its pipes and hatchways rusted over in neglect. Trash littered the floor, but one object stood out clearly from the rest. Emileve gave a nod, and I stepped over to conduct my inspection. It was a grated metal crate, large enough to have held a guard dog, a young scrub drake, or even a goblin. The handle and wheels would have made it easier to pull, but judging from the scuff marks along the floor, the crate had been dragged here in some great haste.

I could only assume the assassin killed Andon to take the crate, then hurried this way through the deeper Underworks to avoid being seen. But wherever the murderer was going, he never made it. Something had torn its way out of the crate, snapping the steel bars as though they were twigs before turning all its vengeful fury upon the assassin. No goblin possessed that kind of strength.

"How far are we from Tavion Spagyricals?" I asked Rognar.

Rognar finished the last of his meat pie. "About four blocks east."

Keldon pointed to one of the outward-bent bars. "Whatever escaped seems to have left some skin behind."

I was already opening my black bag as my apprentice spoke, fishing out a pair of tweezers and a set of beakers. I secured the beakers in a wooden holder and set them on a broken slab of fabricrete. It was far from ideal, but it would have to suffice for a table. I returned to the metal crate with my tweezers. The skin had a distinctive bluish hue and appeared to have the consistency of rubber. No blood was apparent, but a mysterious white liquid coated the skin on one side. I pulled two samples loose, dropping each into one of the beakers.

"Has anyone tampered with either this crate or the body?" I asked, drawing several reagent vials from my bag.

"No," Emileve replied. She peered curiously at what I was doing, or was perhaps appraising the street value of my equipment. "Most underfolk think the deeper Underworks are haunted, and even rustmongers take those kinds of reports to heart."

"And for good reason," Rognar muttered.

I opened a vial of vitriolic chlorinate and calx amalgamate, combining them with the skin sample in the first beaker. Into the second beaker, I poured a measure of cyaniphosphonate and added a pinch of corrosive sublimate, then tightened a cork on the beaker and shook vigorously.

Emileve frowned as the contents of the second beaker began to glow bright green. "Is that dangerous?"

"Not really," I replied. I looked at the tiny bubbles churning inside the glowing beaker, then shook some more. "At least, not unless there is a trace of phlogisticated alkali in the sample, in which case the beaker will explode and fill this area with toxic vapors."

"That's some kind of joke, right?" Emileve asked, taking a cautious step back.

The phosphorescent solution suddenly clouded over, then solidified into a tangle of gummy threads. "That's odd."

Keldon also took a step back. "It's *never* good when he says that."

I drew one of the gummy threads out with my tweezers and laid it across a white strip of paper. "More light, if you would."

My apprentice obliged, and I peered down with my magnifying monocle. The thread was jagged and scaly, and was made up of smaller bundles of fibrous material. "If I didn't know better, I would say this is composed of unmineralized keratin fibers."

I picked up the first beaker, in which the tissue sample had been dissolving, and drew a drop with a pipette. This I applied to the center of a chromagraph plate. The liquid spread out, changing into a pattern of yellow, green, and blue rings. I would have expected some red and far less green from the skin sample of an animal, but instead, the pattern my test had produced suggested the presence of alkaloid atropine, along with antimony and synthetic tallow esters.

"What is it?" Keldon asked, no doubt seeing my puzzled expression.

"Nothing natural," I replied.

I took another skin sample and put it into a third beaker. To reconstruct the makeup of the material, I would need to process the sample through a complete alchemical reaction cycle in accordance to *The Precepts of the Great Work*: conflagration, separation, circulation, congelation, and transmutation. However, I had neither the time to "unify in exalted splendor that which is above with that which is below," nor the equipment necessary to conduct the experiment. But I *did* have my curse.

"Keldon, Rognar," I said, throwing off my frock coat, "stand ready."

Keldon stood in dismay as I pulled the locking pin from my left wristband. A jolt of searing pain blinded my senses and a torrent of liquid fire exploded through every vein and artery of my immolating limb. The beaker shattered in my hand, the sudden alchemical inferno vaporizing the tiny sample as my body absorbed its pure elemental essence. Fearing permanent damage, I slapped the wristband back on, extinguishing the flames.

"Taimon's luck!" Emileve swore. She looked at me, her eyes wide. "The rumors about you... They're all true. You're–"

"A monster, yes," I groaned. I took a moment to recover well enough to breathe, then brushed the embers of my shirt sleeve away from my blistered arm. "An abomination of elemental chaos, born of my own foolish pride."

Rognar had disappeared behind the fabricrete slab along with Harvel and Tobas, only coming out when it was clear I had my curse under control. "Blazes, man, are you insane? I just told you there's an alchemical refinery not four blocks from here!"

"And the material?" Keldon asked.

I smacked my lips, noting the metallic taste of cinnabar and antimony. But my tongue found another flavor, too—bitter and alkaline, with deep, earthy tones. I recognized its acrid bite at once. "It's not just alkaloid atropine, it's *mandragora radixia.*"

"Mandrake root?" Keldon asked.

I ran it all through my head: synthetic tallow esters, unmineralized keratin fibers, and alkaloid atropine from mandrake root. My breath caught. "This creature was not born of nature."

One of Emileve's men screamed, snapping me from my thoughts. His face flushed with fear and he pointed to a grate covering one of the pipes leading into the service tunnel.

"I saw it! A blue face with yellow eyes staring right at us. It was just over there!"

Whatever the thief had seen, it was gone now. I was about to ask him to describe it again when a piercing shriek filled the air, followed by a shrill chattering. Feet scampered along the pipes overhead, and I could just see the blue digits of the creature's hands and feet as it scurried on.

"It's heading east," Emileve said, her eyes wide.

Rognar clenched his fists and growled. "And straight toward Tavion Spagyricals."

"What is it?" Keldon stammered, watching as the creature

jumped and darted up another drainpipe.

I pulled my frock coat on, wincing as the fabric touched my blistered arm. Now I knew why Tavion Spagyricals was so intent on conducting the investigation themselves. They had sent the assassin to stop Andon and take back their stolen property—only their property had not wanted to go back.

"Archons forgive their reckless folly," I whispered. "Tavion Spagyricals has created a homunculus."

EMILEVE AND HER MEN WERE WELL AHEAD OF US, racing down derelict tunnels and ducking through rust-pocked corridors, yelling whenever they caught a glimpse of the fleeing creature by the light of their glowstone lanterns. Our own light faltered briefly when Keldon stumbled on some loose rubble, but he caught himself and kept running, his shining key held high to guide our way.

"Hurry up, Rognar," I called to the Dworgh trailing behind.

"My boots aren't made for this muck!" he yelled, huffing and puffing as he ran.

I lost sight of Emileve after she vanished down another tunnel, but I heard her just ahead. "It ran up another conduit!"

We emerged from the tunnel into a long-abandoned boilerworks, its broken valves and rusting gears petrified in accreted mineral deposits. Emileve and the other two thieves stood at the base of a pipe conduit, and she pointed up the shaft to a narrow opening some forty feet above.

"It went up there," she said, nodding to a ladder that barely seemed attached to the shaft's wall. "I'll go up first to see if it's safe."

I put a hand on her shoulder. She jerked around, her frosty eyes challenging me to stop her. "The creature could have escaped us easily," I explained. "You know that, right?"

She nodded. Without another word she started up the

rickety ladder, flakes of rust falling as she cleared one rung after another.

"We're just beneath Tavion Spagyricals," Rognar wheezed between heaving breaths. He waved his hand in a vaguely upward direction. "But there's no way we're getting through their foundation bulwark. That place is a fortress."

I watched Harvel and Tobas follow their tenacious leader up the ladder. "As fortune has it, we find ourselves in the company of thieves."

More debris fell from the shuddering ladder and I motioned for Keldon to go next. He swallowed back his apprehension, then tucked his key into his belt and took hold of the most secure rung he could find.

"I can't climb that," Rognar said, shaking his head. "I may be short, but I probably weigh as much as you and Keldon combined."

"Not quite so much, I'd wager," I said kindly. Keldon yelped, and I looked up just in time to avoid a rusty ladder rung falling from above. "But your point is well taken. Head back and find Tibblemond. If Crambault is still with him, all the better. Tell him there has been a break-in at Tavion Spagyricals. Make sure he knows to call in a full squad of Vandorian Guardsmen."

The Dworgh nodded, trusting that I had a plan, and he hurried back the way we had come. Of course, I didn't really have a plan. But if Tavion Spagyricals was willing to commit murder to keep their dirty secret a secret, we would need all the backup we could get.

I slung my bag over one shoulder, then started up the perilous ladder. Keldon made it to the top, his legs flailing as the thieves pulled him through the narrow opening. Emileve poked her head out to see where I was.

"Can't you levitate him?" she asked Keldon.

"I'm only an apprentice," he explained.

A rung gave out under my foot and I grabbed the one just above my head. That rung also began to give way, and I clenched my jaw as I stretched for the next rung above. A rope fell across me, and I took hold just as the rung broke loose. With Emileve and the others pulling, I ascended the remaining distance to the upper passage opening. Rognar never would have made it.

Another hundred paces of cramped, rubble-filled corridors led through a maze of viaducts, steam pipes, and pneumatic tubes cluttering our path like some vast jungle skirting the foundation bulwark of Tavion Spagyricals. A cargo train thundered along its tracks thirty feet above, then vanished into the facility's loading dock, which was no doubt heavily guarded. My gaze continued up, surveying the immense assembly of distillation towers, billowing smokestacks, and turning gears.

"We're breaking into that?" Keldon asked. "Don't we need a warrant?"

"Afraid of violating a few laws, kid?" Emileve laughed.

Keldon glanced at me and I gave the only reply that was needed. "There are laws, and then there are laws."

Tobas pointed across the way. "Over there!"

I looked and saw a squat blue form perched on a ledge above a utility conduit. It vanished through a loose ventilation grate too small for any of us to enter. It was showing us the way in.

Emileve and her men started across to the conduit, and I motioned for Keldon to join me as I followed. The utility conduit proved difficult to navigate without tripping over the tangles of pipes or bumping our heads on the low-hanging ductwork. The last fifty paces had us crawling on all fours, and then squeezing through the base of a water main support truss.

"Hold on," Emileve called. She produced a set of tools and rolled onto her back. "This pipe leads straight into the facility."

"That's a water main," I warned. She seemed to be trying to open a maintenance access panel. "I'm not sure flooding this area will help, especially with us directly beneath it."

She tapped on the massive pipe's outer casing with a small wrench, sending a hollow echo reverberating down its length. "Sounds empty to me." After a moment more, she pried the panel off and a gush of water splashed across her and the other two thieves. "Mostly empty," she soddenly amended.

Keldon chuckled, so I volunteered him to assume the lead with me, his talisman lighting our way as we crawled along the interior of the mostly empty water main. Intrusion wards and watchdog egregores were certainly monitoring the facility's perimeter, but with any luck, the wrought iron pipe would help mask our intrusion.

Keldon stopped suddenly, his eyes widening. The sigils on his brass key flickered red, casting an ominous crimson glow along the inner walls of the pipe. "Uh-oh."

"Egregores?" I asked in a whisper.

He nodded.

"What's that?" Emileve asked just behind me.

"We have probably been detected," I replied. "Very shortly, whatever mage is on duty will alert the security guards to our intrusion."

"Wonderful," she grumbled under her breath.

We quickened our crawl until coming to a sealed shutoff valve. Emileve popped the bolts off another access panel, and we dropped out of the pipe onto the fabricrete floor of a dimly lit machine room. The light of Keldon's talisman played across an overgrown forest of pipes, valves, and gauges, but Emileve and her men went straight for the room's locked hatch.

"Got it," Emileve said after a moment at the hatch.

A narrow corridor led away from the machine room, lit by humming induction lamps and flanked by intersecting pipe conduits and ventilation ducts. The polished pipes and brass valves showed no sign of mineral buildup or tarnish, and I estimated that this section of the facility had been overhauled no more than a year ago.

"I saw something in there." Keldon pointed to one of the narrower corridors, then hurried to the intersection, shining his key into the darkness. "It was just a flash of blue, but I'm sure it was the creature."

We squeezed into the corridor single file, following our elusive guide in the dim light, the smells of acrid alkalis and pungent vitriols growing steadily stronger. Emileve caught a glimpse of the scampering creature again, and we followed another narrow corridor to a second machine room. A service door led out of the room, and I pushed both doubt and caution aside as I made my way through the door.

Like the hollowed-out interior of a mountain, the vastness of Tavion Spagyricals' manufacturing complex rose to a dizzying height above. Towering distillation columns and condensing receivers filled the enormous chamber like giant-sized versions of my own alchemistry set. A tangle of glass and copper piping joined the columns and receivers to great brass vessels and dome-covered vats, crisscrossed by platforms, balconies, catwalks, and scaffolding. The earthy smell of roasting mineral clays and boiling tallow esters mixed with the bitter stench of concentrated mandrake extract, wafting from the smoldering crucible that dominated the heart of the clamoring facility.

"Stay down," I warned, pulling Keldon behind a strange brass pod.

We were on a mid-level tier overlooking the main production floor where alchemists, workers, and automatons went about their assigned tasks like bees in a hive. At least two dozen brass pods like the one I had taken cover behind lined the perimeter of our level, as well as the level above. I had no idea what purpose the pods served, but they were not my immediate concern.

A squad of guards brandishing rifles and truncheons marched onto the main level, yelling about a spot security drill. They ushered the alchemists and workers to the other side of the chamber, where the well-drilled employees lined up in file to complete whatever security checks the company required of them. Six guards remained, prowling there and about, no doubt searching for the intruders the watchdog egregores had detected.

"That takes care of the workers," Emileve whispered. She and the other two thieves had ducked behind another one of the brass pods. "But now we have half a dozen guards to contend with."

I nodded to my apprentice. "I know it's a bit far down, but can you muster a little mirage to entertain our friends?"

Keldon nodded. "No problem, boss."

He closed his eyes as he focused, then held out his key. Three shadowy forms took shape on a platform above the guards. Keldon's decoys solidifying into figures strikingly similar to Emileve, Keldon, and myself. The illusions were imperfect, but Keldon set them into motion, running down from the platform and out through another set of doors. One of the guards alerted the others and all six gave chase, leaving the lower level empty.

"Good job, kid," Emileve complimented, sounding a little impressed.

I stood up to inspect the brass pods that filled the tier we were on. They numbered thirty in all, and stood just four feet in height. I looked through the glass view port of the one we had hidden behind and grimaced at the pitiable sight of the diminutive, half-formed creature suspended in its brass-encased womb of bubbling fluids.

"Aldicus, these things are alive!" Keldon called from further down the row of pods.

The creature within the pod he had found was indeed a fully formed two-foot tall humanoid, goblinesque in its basic anatomy, but having smooth blue skin with not a follicle of hair. Its eyes were as large as an owl's—eyes that stared back with an unmistakable glint of conscious perception. It shrieked, throwing itself against its chains, then howled as a jolt of electricity struck down the chains to punish the reluctant captive.

"We have to get them out of these pods," Keldon breathed. "This is... this is..."

"Cruel? Inhumane?" I shook my head. "The creation of homunculi has been forbidden since the age of Marada. To even attempt to do so is beyond arrogance—it is monstrous!" I watched the homunculus inside the pod squirm against its bonds. The creature opened its large eyes again and tilted its head inquisitively. "But no," I added. "These are not monsters. They are innocent of the crime that brought them into being."

I continued down the row of pods, observing the homunculi in all their stages of gestation, when the lanky blue creature we had been chasing dropped on the pod directly in front of me. It chattered and scampered away, heading for a door behind the last row of pods. The creature clawed frantically at the door, jumping aside only as I approached. I tried the handle, but found it locked, and considered calling Emileve over.

"There they are!" a guard yelled as he and the other five rushed back into the level just below us.

Keldon moaned. "The game's up."

"Not quite," Emileve contended. She signaled to Tobas, who ducked back through the service door to the maintenance tunnels we had come through.

Whatever her plan was, we were out of time. I kicked the door as hard as I could, wincing at the sharp pain before kicking again. The door flew open, and the four men inside the room looked up in dismay. The men wore white lab coats, masks, and surgical aprons spotted with blue-white blood, and before each one lay the splayed remains of a dissected homunculus. Jars of formaldehyde lined the shelves along the walls, each containing a shriveled limb, organ, or half-formed embryo, while sealed glass cells displayed still-living specimens, twitching as they lay dying from whatever tests they had suffered. The potions and elixirs shelved on nearby cabinets were numbered, not named, and I realized with sickening horror the true purpose for which these homunculi had been grown: alchemical experimentation on an industrial scale.

"By the legal authority of the Vandorian Jurisdiction Proclamation," I recited, drawing my badge, "I'm placing you—"

All four men broke for the door on the far side of the room. The last man out threw a switch, sounding an earsplitting alarm and lighting up a warning sign above the doorway. The warning sign shone with a single word: "Purge."

"Oh, fangle-fop!" I exclaimed.

I jumped for the nearest containment cell, but I was too late. Murky white smoke fumed into each of the sealed chambers, obscuring the dying homunculus before it flashed to blinding white. *Phlogistonic fulminate!* A blast of exploding gas and shattering glass followed on my heels as I dived out the door and headlong into Keldon.

"We have to free the homunculi!" I exclaimed.

Keldon staggered back. The homunculus on his shoulder shrieked, while a younger one clung tightly to his pant leg. "That's what we're doing!"

"Ah, yes—" I began to say. Seven more thieves had joined Emileve, along with Harvel and Tobas, who had returned. "Where did your friends come from?"

"They followed us here," Emileve explained. "I just had to send Tobas back to ask them to join the party."

I hadn't noticed anyone following us, but they were thieves after all. Twice as many guards joined the six that had found us, and all raced up the ladders and across the catwalks yelling for our surrender. Of greater concern was the murky white gas seeping from the open gestation pods. My eyes followed the lines running from the pods to the larger pipes in the ceiling, and then moved to the junction linking them to the cells in the laboratory. The purge was not meant to just eradicate the test subjects—it was meant to incinerate all evidence of the illegal operation.

"Keldon, Emileve, get away from the pods!" I yelled, dashing to the pipe junction. "That gas is highly flammable."

"And just let these creatures roast?" Emileve asked. She flung open another pod, fanning away the volatile gas as she worked to free the homunculus within. "Jaceil and Andon both died trying to smuggle out the truth, and I'm not about to let Tavion Spagyricals get away with it!"

She was right. If there was any chance that we could rescue the creatures, then we at least had to try.

Four of the newly arrived thieves threw themselves against the charging guards, while the other three helped Harvel, Tobas, and Emileve free more homunculi. Keldon stood his ground, key poised as he conjured up an illusory wall of swirling light and color that, with any luck, would give the guards a moment's pause. I, however, would need more than luck to pull off the ludicrous feat I was about to attempt. I removed the pins from both of my severite wristbands.

"What are you doing?" Keldon yelled, watching in wide-eyed horror. "We're standing in the heart of an alchemical refinery with flammable gas venting all around us!"

I threw off my frock coat and top hat, then tossed both wristbands across the floor to land at my apprentice's feet. My temperature rose exponentially, building as the uninhibited alchemical reactions inside me ignited. Sweat ran from every pore in my body, evaporating into steam as blisters erupted across my skin. I forced back the searing pain and raised a flame-wreathed arm to grab the pipe junction in the ceiling, hoping to delay the flow of the explosive gas. The pipe began to glow red, then turned white-hot as my hand engulfed the couplings and valves of the junction. For an instant nothing happened, then a fountain of fire exploded from the junction, jetting down my immolating arm and into my body.

The blazing alchemical being I had become stood fast

beneath the exploding gas, drawing in the fiery mixture of phlogistonic fulminate pouring from the ruptured pipelines. Fire alarms sounded through every tier and corridor of the refinery, sending scientists and workers scrambling for safety. The guards fled as well, and even Emileve and her thieves backed away in fear. Keldon yelled something to them, though I could no longer hear his words, and Emileve signaled her men to free the last of the captive homunculi.

A commotion two tiers up drew Keldon's attention and my burning brimstone eyes followed his gaze to the facility's main entrance. I spotted Tibblemond first, waving his bowler hat as he fussed with an infuriated Crambault. Rognar accompanied Tibblemond, arms folded and face aglow, his broad grin concealed by his braided red beard. Crambault tried to hold them back, but when Tibblemond saw me he yelped with a start and waved for the Vandorian Guardsmen to follow him inside.

The inferno around me reached its greatest intensity, and then began to diminish as the last wisp of phlogistonic fulminate drained from the ruptured pipe. I had absorbed the full explosive potential of the flammable gas, buying enough time for Emileve and the thieves to pull the remaining homunculi to safety. But now my alchemical form stood poised to unleash a tidal wave of incinerating destruction, and unless I could get my severite wristbands back on, the entire facility would go up like an erupting volcano.

Placing one flaming foot before the other, I strode unwillingly toward my friends, leaving a trail of molten footprints in the grated steel floor. Emileve signaled her men to corral the homunculi and break for the service corridor. Keldon snatched my wristbands off the floor and started toward me, his key raised to project a tenuous aetheric barrier in a futile attempt to buffer the heat radiating from my incandescent body. I wanted to scream for him to get away, to follow Emileve and the others as they fled this doomed facility, but not the slightest sound escaped my flame-spitting mouth.

Keldon staggered back, unable to withstand the sweltering heat, and called out in sudden desperation. I continued toward him, smoldering arms outstretched, the roiling cyclone within me ready to release an all-consuming conflagration.

Just then, a flash of blue scampered down from the scaffolding and sprang for the wristbands clutched in Keldon's hand. I recognized the creature who had led us to this place—I saw the pain and fear that filled its large yellow eyes, and I saw indomitable courage, too. The homunculus jumped straight through the firestorm enveloping me, shrieking as the forge-hot flames disintegrated its synthetic flesh.

Yet, somehow, the creature made it through to deliver the severite bonds to my outstretched limbs. The burning elements of my transmuted body evaporated in an instant, and my mind plunged into the merciful abyss of unconsciousness.

I AWOKE TO CLANGING FIRE BELLS and the noxious stench of burning alchemicals. Despite the pain of my blistered body, I forced open my eyes and sat up. My clothes were gone, burned to ashes in my transformation, and I was grimly thankful for having thrown aside my frock coat as I drew it gingerly around my body. Keldon sat down next to me and held out a battered pewter cup filled with green-tinged liquid. I gladly threw back the restorative elixir, breathing with relief as the warming potion wetted my parched throat.

"Awake at last!" Tibblemond exclaimed as he approached. "Perhaps now you can tell me what in all the names of all the Archons went on in there?"

I opened my eyes again and surveyed my surroundings. We were on a topside street near the outer perimeter of Tavion Spagyricals. Black smoke rose from the alchemical complex, and fire brigades had surrounded the entire area, aided by half a dozen elementors to help douse the flames. Two full squads of Vandorian Guardsmen had also arrived, along with a large transport ornithopter, bringing in an armored HAAMR unit to take Tavion's own garrison force into custody. As much as I disliked the newly commissioned Heavy Armory and Assault Mobile Regiment, they were sometimes a necessary evil.

"Tavion Spagyricals was making homunculi," I replied, my voice hoarse. I drank more of the elixir before continuing. "They were using them for experimentation."

Tibblemond scratched his muttonchops. "Yes, yes, your apprentice has already told us as much. Unfortunately, only a few charred bones remain of those... creatures." He sighed and shook his head. "But we have recovered enough evidence from surviving laboratories to corroborate the story."

Only a few bones? But where were all the other homunculi Emileve and her men had freed? I looked at Keldon, confused, and my apprentice gave me a quick wink and a smile.

"Indeed," I agreed. "The laboratories and gestation pods were piped with phlogistonic fulminate. Dreadfully volatile stuff. I did my best to stop it, but it seems I was not at my best today."

The chief inspector doffed his bowler and shrugged. "It's just as well. We would have had to destroy the creatures, what with them being abominations and all that." I studied his face, noting a slight smile. Did he know? Had he let Emileve and the homunculi go? "Well, at least we have Crambault in custody, as well as their head scientists."

"And what about Lord Tavion?"

Tibblemond shook his head. "It seems Lord Tavion died about a year ago under dubious circumstances. Crambault had been running the company in his name ever since, profiting from his ruthless management while keeping his own hands clean. It's a mighty vile way to run a company, if you ask me."

I nodded. 'Ruthless' and 'vile' were adjectives better applied to the management practices of the Travenni and Seladono crime families. In many ways, the powerful mercantile syndicates that dominated the Clockwork City were just as bad—and in some ways, worse.

One of the Vandorian Guardsmen called Tibblemond away on some matter, and I motioned for Keldon to help me stand. I pulled my coat tighter, despite the pain it caused, and we headed for an alley leading into the chasmal depths below. Rognar soon joined us there.

"Looking for someone in particular?" the Dworgh asked.

"Just a few friends who rallied to the cause," I replied. "Assuming they made it out alive."

"We did," came a voice from the alley. Emileve stepped from the shadows, pulling up her red-lensed goggles and folding her arms across her brigandine. A lanky blue creature, no more than two feet tall, jumped onto a stack of rusting barrels and chattered emphatically. "Along with over two dozen others."

The homunculus sprang away and skittered off down the alley, joining a host of others who disappeared through a storm drain leading to the sublevels below.

"They're just going to run loose?" Keldon asked. He looked at me, then at Emileve. "They're incredibly strong and just as fast. What if they cause trouble?"

"Don't worry, kid," Emileve replied. "Our brotherhood will look after them. They're in good hands now."

I smiled. "The Unseen Brotherhood now has over two dozen new members, each no larger than a child and capable of climbing, crawling, or leaping to places otherwise inaccessible to even the most nimble thief."

Emileve smirked. "An equitable arrangement, wouldn't you agree, Detective Vescard?"

I nodded. "Never forget where they came from, or the brutality they have endured. As timid as they may seem, they are capable of great courage as well."

Emileve closed her eyes, no doubt remembering the one who had thrown himself to the flames to save us all. "This place is crawling with jacks and badgers," she said, glancing past my shoulder. "We'd better get going."

I clutched my coat tighter and began to turn away. "Farewell Emileve, Queen of Thieves. Let us hope you remain true to your principles should we ever meet again."

"Principles?" she called after us. "I've never been so insulted in my life!"

I smiled as we headed out of the alley, trying to contain a laugh that I knew would only bolster her bronzy temperament.

"I can't believe we just brought down a major mercantile syndicate with the help of a gang of thieves," Keldon said.

"Faugh!" Rognar balked. "They're not a gang, they're the Unseen Brotherhood. They're the good guys of the Underworks—or didn't you know?"

Keldon blinked in confusion. "But don't they act against the law?"

I stopped, drawing a deep breath, and pulled my frock coat around me. I looked upward through the rising heights of the city, past the bustling causeways and clattering steamrail lines, to the great airships drifting above the crowning towers and soaring spires reaching into the grim, leaden sky.

"It is not for the law that we fight," I explained, "but for justice and for all that justice stands: fairness, equality, and freedom for all. Law alone does not define what is good or evil, for those of sound conscience will always know right from wrong. But crime ever turns in the Clockwork City, and we who serve the cause of justice must stand vigilant against the monsters and madmen who prowl the fog-veiled streets of Corradon." I balled my hands into fists, looking to the dull gray wristbands locked on my blistered arms. "Even if we must fight the monsters within ourselves."

Case File 5:

Marvelous Mécanique

Arleia regarded my brass-framed display case with suspicion. Her tapered, dagger-like ears twitched, and her teal eyes widened at the meticulously arranged rows of fine artisan pens. She adjusted her glasses and peered closer, then stepped back, shaking her head.

"You collect *pens*?" the young half-Eldren asked incredulously.

Leta Meridian rolled her eyes. "Aldicus has been collecting those pens since before I've known him. Don't bother asking him why." She crossed her legs and sank into the sofa, brushing out the wrinkles from her beige slacks. A matching shrug coat with seven fashionable brass buttons fit snugly around a high-collared pleated blouse, completing her deceptively conservative attire. "Believe me, it's his least annoying eccentricity."

I twirled a gold-etched Swanné Signature pen between my fingers. "There is no greater instrument of truth, no finer apparatus of knowledge, no better tool in the science of investigation than a pen."

Leta's young assistant grew evermore perplexed. Her lips parted in preface to a question, but her breath caught and her face flushed when Keldon returned from the kitchen carrying a tea set.

"Tea is served," my apprentice announced, setting the

tray on the drawing room table.

Leta took a porcelain cup from the tray and gave the steaming brew a sniff. "A hint of ginger and cinnamon... My, Aldicus. You *do* know how to treat a lady."

"But I made the—" Keldon started to say.

I tossed the Swanné pen to Keldon, and he nearly spilled his own tea in his haste to catch the implement. Arleia covered her mouth to suppress a snicker, and Keldon hurriedly returned the pen to the display case, his face reddening.

"We both know your visit is no mere social call," I said to Leta.

Leta sighed, giving her tea a quick stir before returning the spoon to the tray. "As much as I loathe to admit it, we have come to request your assistance."

I managed to keep a smug grin off my face, but masking my feelings from her was an exercise in futility. She was a psychurgist after all, and my emotions might as well have been an open book to her.

"So, the famously infallible Leta Meridian at last comes upon a case requiring advice from her long-time colleague and rival, Aldicus Vescard," I quipped. "Could it be that your renowned powers of clairvoyance have at last failed you?"

Leta's eyes narrowed over the rim of her teacup. "Recent developments have moved from my mystic domain to the shadowy aether of your investigative netherworld. You may have lost your ability to practice magery, but you're still the best forensic alchemist in the city, to say nothing of your considerable breadth of esoteric lore."

I put on my most inscrutable face. She was goading me, and she knew I knew it. "I have not lost my abilities. It is simply that I cannot use them." I pulled back the sleeves of my coat, revealing the gray metal wristbands locked around each wrist. "But that is why I have Keldon as my dutiful assistant."

Leta shifted uneasily. She set her teacup down, paused,

and picked it up again. She was stalling. Something was wrong.

"What could be troubling a veilhunter such as yourself?" I asked. "No simple haunting, spirit possession, or betrayed lover back from the dead this time?"

She shook her head. "Eight cases of *animoptosis catatonia* have been documented over the past three weeks."

I leaned forward in my chair. "Eight cases? Are you certain?"

"*Animoptosis catatonia*?" Keldon asked.

"Catatonic soul displacement," Arleia translated. She beamed at my apprentice, brushing back strands of her lilac hair.

"Pathology?" I asked.

"Every victim was found in a vegetative state and I could find no trace of a soul within their corporeal forms. Someone or something is stealing their vitalic essence, and I've been unable to divine the nature of the culprit. A karcist may be involved, but there's no necrolic residue."

"Did you test for a metaetheric contagion or quintessence alchemy?" I asked.

"That's your area, not mine," she chuckled. "But there is no discernable pattern, commonality, or connection between cases. The victims come from all walks of life, and although most have been human, one of the victims was an Eldren and two were Dworghs. That ratio is striking given the demographics of Corradon, and that leads me to conclude that the occurrences are not random."

"Nothing is truly random," I agreed. "Was there anything in common about where the bodies were found?"

"Only that they were found in lower corridor tunnels or sublevel alleys. Someone might have been trying to hide them, or at least keep them out of sight. None were found in the same immediate vicinity, but all were within the northern quarter of the 10th District, near the border of the 4th."

I nodded. The tangled geography of Corradon was such

that the 4th and 10th Districts neighbored one another, north to south respectively. "Have you interviewed the families of the victims?"

"Those that I could. Most had no families, and those who did provided few useful leads. I do have a good lead on the catatonic Eldren, and that is what brought me to you. Unlike myself, you have full access to the Vandorian case files."

Vandorian case files and a catatonic Eldren... The two pieces click together in my mind. I gave no outward sign, but Leta cocked her head in curiosity, nonetheless.

"What is it?" she asked, her gaze seeming to peer through me. "The spike in your aura is one of astonished realization."

"The Eldren victim—was her name Mirael?"

Leta blinked. "Yes, but how..."

I quite enjoyed catching her off-guard—a particularly challenging feat, given the extent of her mystical percipience. "Keldon, if you would?"

Keldon adjusted his newsboy cap and cleared his throat. "The Vandorian Guard only hires us for a few select cases, but we are tubed the weekly case summaries for review. Most are unremarkable, but yesterday's summary included a report of an Eldren—an *Eldren* mind you—who was arrested for attempting to steal a clockwork ballerina from a street carnival."

Leta looked to Arleia and then to me, but neither spoke. I followed up, filling in the rest. "The case summary stated that the Eldren, Tamethel, insisted that the automaton held the soul of his lifemate, Mirael. The case was closed, concluding that he was mad with grief over his lifemate's affliction—a vegetative coma."

"Tamethel was a successful merchant and was well respected in the Eldren community," Arleia said. As a half-Eldren herself, she would have already pursued this lead as far as she had been able. "According to his friends in the Eldren Preserve, he suffered a complete mental breakdown, raving that his lifemate's spirit had been stolen by a sorcerer.

He went in search of this sorcerer, but that was the last we heard of the matter."

"It's also one of the reasons I suspect a karcist," Leta added.

I drummed my fingers on my armrest. "*Animoptosis catatonia*, an Eldren obsessed with a clockwork ballerina, and a suspicion that a master of dark sorcery lurks behind it all. My job, as always, is to demonstrate that although these disparate lines of evidence are indeed connected, they do not lead to the most obvious conclusion."

Leta smirked. "You mean that a karcist is stealing souls to empower automatons performing at a carnival?"

I scoffed. "No soul-sucking sorcerer would stoop to such menial aspirations. No, the truth is likely far darker: someone, somewhere, is *profiting* from this. To discover who, we must begin by interviewing the despondent husband. Keldon, did the report say if he had been jailed for the attempted theft?"

"He is being held at the 22nd Precinct Station in the 10th District, as I recall," Keldon answered.

"Keldon, fetch my hat and bag, then hail a steam-coach." I pulled my frock coat from the back of the chair and swept it over my shoulders with exactly the kind of supercilious flare that was sure to make Leta roll her eyes. "Crime ever turns in the Clockwork City, and we've neither tick nor tock to spare!"

THE GUARD AT THE 22ND PRECINCT JAIL fumbled the numbers on the cylinder-key again, grumbling to himself about the merits of old-fashioned bit and barrel keys, then tried the lock once more. The key and lock clattered with the sound of the interfacing gears rotating in some complicated sequence. This time it worked and the bolts securing the cell door drew back with three satisfying clicks.

"Mages," he grumbled, returning the cylinder-key to his belt loop. "Nothing's ever good enough for 'em, eh?"

I resisted the urge to point out that the device was purely mechanical and was in no way empowered. Leta strode past me into the cell and Arleia followed. Keldon gave me a sheepish look, and I gestured for him to precede me.

"Thank you, constable," I said. "If I am not mistaken, Tamethel is being held pending his trial on charges of attempted theft. However, the report I was given did not specify who was pressing charges. Would that be any trouble to look up?"

The constable shrugged. "If ye don't mind waiting."

"I'll be right here," I replied, glad to be rid of his prying ears.

The cell was stark and featureless, but clean—the result of new ordinances governing the treatment of prisoners. The same rough white stones that tiled the floor also constituted the walls and ceiling, and the only furnishings were a simple wooden chair, a chamber pot, and a flat cot upon which sat a haggard Eldren. He had not yet been convicted, so he still wore his own attire—earthy-brown trousers, high-laced boots, and an olive doublet with flowing sleeves. A leaf-embroidered sash, of the sort worn by Eldren hailing from Talyrin Vey, was crumpled in the chair.

"...here to help," Leta was saying as I entered. "We have reason to believe your lifemate was the victim of sorcery."

Tamethel nodded, but he was looking at Arleia. "Has the Preserve assigned you to investigate Mirael's ensorcellment? You must tell the elders I was not trying to steal that accursed machine."

Arleia adjusted her glasses nervously. "I have no official connection with the Preserve here in Corradon. I am only half-Eldren."

Tamethel dropped his head, his tapered ears drooping as his face sank into his hands. "I was only trying to save her... To release her captive soul to the Halls of Anuan."

"Tamethel," I said, removing my top hat. "I am Aldicus Vescard."

The Eldren's ears twitched hearing the name, then moved his hands away to reveal an incredulous gaze. "Vescard? *The* Aldicus Vescard?"

Leta sighed. "Just once I'd like to hear someone say, 'Meridian? *The* Leta Meridian?'"

I bent down, meeting Tamethel's citrine eyes with my own. "We will not stop until we have found the criminals who have perpetrated these sorceries against your lifemate and the others who have suffered the same fate."

His face paled. "There are others?"

"Seven others," Leta said. "Of whom we are aware."

Tamethel's shoulders slumped, and he looked to the white stone floor. "She was a dancer, you know. She danced the *Talariáya*, the ancient dance of wind and trees. That thing—that *machine*—it now performs a clumsy mockery of our ancestral dance. But mockery or not, it dances just as she once danced. No one else in Corradon even knows the *Talariáya*."

I took a pen and notepad from my coat pocket and quickly jotted down the details. Elementals and aetheric spirits were often infused into automatons, and I had heard whispers of shades and phantoms being similarly bound. But there were no spells, however dark, that could transfer a living soul into a machine... At least, not since the age of Marada.

"Leta," I said, tapping my pen on the notebook. "Were any of the other victims performers?"

She chewed her lip in thought. "Two of them were fencers, and another played the harpsichord."

"Two others played instruments as well," Arleia added, "and one was a juggler."

I scribbled down the talents. "Jugglers, dancers, fencers, musicians." I thought for a moment. "Automatons can imitate feats of dance and music, but even the best pale before all but the most amateur performer." I drew in a breath. "Where did Mirael perform?"

"Vaugaire," Tamethel answered. And it was all he needed

to say.

Located in the center of the 10th District, Vaugaire Boulevard held the city's largest year-round carnival, covering over ten city blocks in all. The boundless variety of performers, sideshows, menageries, and chicaneries defied all attempts at description, if for no other reason than the fact that it transformed its mood and character almost every other week.

"Had you and Mirael been to Vaugaire before?" Leta asked a breath before I voiced the exact same question. I looked at her and she flashed a wry half-smile.

Tamethel nodded. "She worked there. But I explained all of this to the district police."

"Did she perform near an automaton show?" I asked, quickly cutting off Leta's next question.

"I do not know, but she always came home talking about one show or another. She was fascinated by the exotic and bizarre exhibits she saw there. But she never talked about automatons. We Eldren don't care much for machines, you see."

It always struck me as peculiar when Eldren came to live in the Clockwork City, but was it any stranger than Dworghs taking up farming or humans taking up mining? Now that I considered it, the Eldren Preserve was not far from the 10th District itself. Perhaps the crime was simply one of opportunity.

"Where was she found?" Leta asked, stealing my own question.

Tamethel looked to the floor again. "In the corridors below the street, just six blocks from where we live. They dumped her there, like some discarded husk."

"You have committed no crime," I said to Tamethel, returning the pen and notebook to my bag, "but I cannot ask for your release until the true perpetrator has been apprehended."

He nodded. "And... And what of Mirael?"

I glanced at Leta, but she only raised an eyebrow. We both knew the dangers of severing a soul from its body, a fact that makes astral projection so exceedingly dangerous. From what I recalled of those few fables that spoke of animoptotic soul-bindings, I knew there was no hope for Tamethel's lifemate.

"Her body sleeps, and she does not suffer. Only the animating principles of her being are bound to the machine. The seat of her consciousness, her memories, all that she was in life..." I hesitated before continuing. "Know that she is already free."

Tamethel nodded, tears forming in his eyes. "At least she does not suffer."

I stood and made my way to the door. The constable stood in the hall just outside the cell, waiting for us.

"Got what ye needed from this pointy-eared grifter?" he asked.

I suppressed a scowl. "He is a victim, not a criminal." But the precinct constable only shrugged with jaded disinterest. "Who is pressing the charges?"

"A fellow named Marelle Sandellar," the constable replied, reading from a report. "Says he's the owner of the automaton the suspect tried to steal."

"Did Marelle file the charges himself?"

The constable flipped to another page and frowned. "Well, that's odd. The charges were filed on his behalf. No signature."

"Indeed." I fixed my top hat on my head, checked the time on my pocket watch, and started down the hall. "To Vaugaire Boulevard," I announced to the others.

"To find Marelle?" Keldon asked.

"To find the perpetrator," I answered. "To accomplish that, we must first uncover the single most unique and extraordinary artifact on Vaugaire Boulevard."

Leta gave a huff. "And how do you plan to pull that off? Vaugaire spans nearly two miles of exhibits, sideshows, and curiosities, all purporting to be the most rare and wondrous relics from the darkest ages of antiquity."

"Simple," I replied. "We find the one that's not a phony."

THE BACKSTAGE STOREROOM OF FAUCHERRE'S Magical Cabaret stank of sublimating camphor which, judging from the tattered remains of aging costumes, had done a poor job of staving off moths. Faucherre had been more than happy to lend us the space for a few ducats, and I was glad to have an out-of-the-way corner amidst the hurly-burly tangle of Vaugaire Boulevard. I had just finished setting up my portable aetheric interferometer on a table, attaching the last crystal oscillator and extending the armatures, keeping the antenna-like rods focused on the vial of rarefied quicksilver in the center of the device.

"Have either of you sensed anything?" I asked Keldon and Leta.

Keldon looked at his brass key, its sigils glowing with ghostly blue aethergy. "I am, but that's the problem. This is Vaugaire Boulevard. There's no way I can cut through the discordant turbulence of aetheric activity buzzing all around."

Leta also shook her head. "I don't know how the mediums and fortune-tellers can read anything from their patrons. The psychic noise is overwhelming."

"Most of them are charlatans, anyway," Arleia reminded. She held up her runic totem and panned around. "But there is a clear elemental resonance in the air—fiery, electric, and sylphid all at once."

Keldon nodded. "That would either be the Iceflame Thunder show just across the street, or any number of fire-spinners and lightning-dancers performing up and down the boulevard."

I returned my attention to the aetheric interferometer. Two distinct patterns rippled through the quicksilver. One pattern reflected the usual noise of the lower aether, but the other quivered and stuttered like a kettle drum pounding against the higher astral currents.

"Fangle-fop," I muttered.

"What is it?" Leta asked.

I began breaking down the device to return it to my bag. "Something is creating a disturbance in the higher streams of the astral currents, far in excess of anything the activity here should produce. I believe someone is operating a very powerful mage-engine nearby."

"A *magine*?" Keldon asked, emphasizing the abbreviated term. "Well, this place is bound to have a few magines on display."

"This is no glimmerbox or second-rate hoaxery," I explained, closing my bag. "It is an extremely powerful magine—very likely the product of ancient Maradian over-science."

"Marada?" Arleia gasped, her eyes widening. "Maradian technology is forbidden. Surely, the Archidoxy would have snapped up anything like that."

"Hah!" I laughed, shaking my head as I headed to the door. "We could only wish."

The others followed me out of the room, and we turned down the backstage corridor leading out to the street. We were met halfway down the hall by the dandy-dressed proprietor garbed in brightly striped trousers and a burgundy tailcoat with matching top hat and a puffy cravat.

"Thank you for letting us use the room," I said to Faucherre. "Do you know if anyone here is operating a mage-engine? A real one, I mean."

"A *real* one?" Faucherre gasped with scandalized surprise. He twisted one tip of his well-waxed mustache in thought, then gave a flustered sigh. "Oh, I'm afraid not, my dear. If a *genuine* magine was on exhibit around here, I would have heard about it."

"Do you know anyone named Marelle Sandellar?"

Faucherre clapped his hands together and smiled. "Ah!

You must be looking for Marelle's Marvelous Mechanical Mannequins."

I nodded. "That sounds like the place."

"Just head two blocks north and down one sublevel. When you pass Madame Levieu's House of Eldritch Wonders you'll see Marelle's show. You can't miss it—the sign is all gears and shiny brass. There are no performers, mind you, just those dreary mechanical puppets. The proprietor's a Dworgh by the name of Gulthvar." Faucherre gave me a conspiratorial look, then rolled his eyes. "He's a grouch."

My eyebrow twitched. "If Gulthvar is the proprietor, then who is Marelle?"

Faucherre clicked his tongue. "Marelle's the gearmeister. He's a genius, or so I've heard, but not at all sociable. It's Gulthvar who runs the show, does the promotion, and manages the business." Then he laughed, clapping his hands again. "You know, the *real* work!"

"You have been most helpful," I said, tipping my hat. "Thank you again, good sir."

"Glad to be of service, dear. And do come back for a show, on the house."

Hurrying outside, we collided with the churning mass of confusion winding down the entire length of Vaugaire Boulevard, from the terraced heights rising above to the raucous sublevels below. The night seemed scarcely discernable from day beneath the brilliant glare of gas lamps, empowered luminaries, and marquees lit by every conceivable means—and a few less conceivable, as well.

Meandering throngs of humans, Dworghs, and Eldren stretched for as far as could be seen, all enthralled by a host of entertainers whose appearance and mannerisms ranged from comically outlandish to fascinatingly grotesque. There were masked costumers, beckoning harlequins, knotted contortionists, dazzling fire-spinners, and countless jugglers, pantomimes, stilt-walkers, and street-conjurers. Before every door and outside every tent stood an exuberant promoter, each garbed in flamboyant attire and yelling at the top of his lungs to come and see one oddity or another. More than once I had to pull Keldon from the beguilement of a scantily clad burlesque performer, much to Arleia's apparent amusement.

A flight of stairs brought us down to the sublevel beneath Vaugaire Boulevard, which was no less of a madhouse than topside. We soon passed Madame Levieu's House of Eldritch Wonders, which, according to its brightly colored billboard, had only opened last month. The new attraction was particularly popular, judging from the line of patrons waiting to be duped a few pfennies just to see some rusty artifacts made up to look exotic. Following Faucherre's directions, we approached an assemblage of pavilions, stages, and wagons that could easily have constituted a carnival in their own right. Spectators milled about, entering and leaving one tent or another, while others made their way to the stages further on.

I had no need to consult the clockwork sign arched above the street, its gears ticking and clicking as the letters revolved about one another. The fact that we had found Marelle's show was clear enough. A pair of automatons stood on either side of the entrance to the main pavilion, one taking money and the other bowing to spectators as they entered. Near another pavilion I saw what looked to be a kind of mechanical elephant and possibly a mechanical tiger. Both were in cages and surrounded by wonder-struck onlookers. I could not see the open-air stage, but the rhythmic sound of ballet music, together with the 'oohs' and 'aahs' of the crowd, suggested the musician and dancer automatons were in full swing.

I stopped some twenty paces from the main pavilion. "Keldon, Arleia, have a look around. Try to learn how many automatons are here and how many of them are ensorcelled. If you see any automatons peering eerily in your direction, head the other way."

Keldon grimaced. “Thanks for the creepy imagery, boss.”

I flipped him a ducat. “Now, be a gentleman and buy your date some sweet confections, and maybe a pack of shimmer sticks.”

“My...” he blinked and looked at Arleia. “Hey!”

Arleia hooped her arm around his. “Just try acting like a normal boy for once,” she said with a grin.

“You can be so cruel, Aldicus,” Leta mused, watching her apprentice drag mine to the pavilion. “And just where are you planning to take *your* date this inauspicious evening?”

I shifted my black bag from my right hand to my left, then started for the wagons clustered near the back wall of Levieu’s, just north of the show tents. “To find and question the proprietor.”

We walked the short distance to the wagons, which seemed oddly deserted. At any typical show they would have been bustling with stagehands, gaffers, and assorted performers preparing for their next act. But apart from a few dust-covered footprints, an unhinged door or two, and the smells of rotting wood and stagnant gutter water, I found nothing of note but the utter lack of activity itself.

Leta glanced from one vacant wagon to another. “If there’s no one here, who’s running the show?”

I looked back to the main pavilion spilling over with light, laughter, and the sounds of clockwork gears. A figure garbed in tailcoat and pinstripes stepped from the shadows of the tent and walked with sudden jerking motions to the open-air stage. At the same time, two child-sized silhouettes emerged from a holding pen escorting a mechanical horse to a cluster of show tents. They were automatons—every single one of them.

“The show seems to be running itself quite efficiently,” I answered.

Leta swallowed, her worried eyes glancing across the halting, jerking forms moving in and around the pavilions. “You’re not suggesting everyone—”

“Can I help you?” a recriminating voice rose from behind.

I turned to see a stout figure no more than four feet high and as broad-chested as a four-banded cask of Norithian ale. His curling black beard draped over a garish green vest that no more matched his scarlet coat than it did his blue striped trousers. Behind him stood a much taller and altogether less lively figure whose ocular lenses stared vacantly from a steel skull fixed upon a neck of pneumatic actuators.

“Gulthvar!” I exclaimed, presuming he could be none other. I tipped my hat and smiled. “Just the Dworgh we were looking for.”

He jutted a lip, eying both Leta and myself suspiciously. “The show is that way,” he grumbled, pointing with an intricately etched brass cane. *Very* intricately etched. “You’d best be off if you hope to catch the main act of the evening.”

I gave a polite chuckle. “Allow me to introduce myself, sir. I am Davon Sulkar, and this is my secretary, Berthandra Whipplethorp.” Leta clenched her jaw, but managed to smile and curtsy all the same. “We represent the interests of Barrington and Company, an automatronic manufactory here in Corradon.”

The Dworgh turned his head slightly, his eyes darting to the machine standing patiently behind him. “Never heard of ‘em.”

“Be that as it may, my company is impressed with the sophistication of your automatons.” I gestured to the machine behind Gulthvar. “Take this one, for instance. See how it stands there behind you, holding itself in a pose of utmost confidence and surety? Why, one might even say it looks *intimidating* the way it simply looms over you, gazing at us with those black, unblinking lenses. Most impressive, if I do say so. To that end, my company wishes to secure any patents or trade secrets that you might be willing to sign over. For a sizeable sum, of course.”

Gulthvar snorted at the prospect. “Our automatons come from rustmongers and second-hand junk dealers. We fix ‘em up, but any so-called sophistication you see is just a carnival trick. Ordinarily, I'd swindle you, but I never get mixed up in the bloodthirsty, backstabbing business of the profiteering syndicates that grease the gears of this tick-tock city. That's a sure way to wind up dead."

I smiled pleasantly. "I have been authorized to offer no less than 50,000 ducats, which I must say is a considerably handsome price for what we're asking."

"Look here, now," Gulthvar began, his voice raised. He shook his cane at me as he spoke, then thought better of the threatening motion and hid the implement behind his back. "I just told you there's nothing to it but a few crafty tricks and gimmicks."

I looked at Leta, who made a slight motion with her eyes. She sensed Gulthvar was lying, perhaps with every word. But I did not need a psychic to tell me the Dworgh was pushing to be rid of us. "May we extend the offer to Marelle Sandellar?"

The folds on Gulthvar's brow deepened for an instant, but his reaction was fleeting. "Be my guest," he laughed. But it was a hollow laugh. "His answer will be the same as mine."

I held my back straight and put my hand on Leta's arm. "Come, Berthandra. Let us find Mister Sandellar and make him a well-to-do gentleman of leisure." We turned and walked away without so much as a glance back.

"Berthandra?" Leta snapped once we were amidst the crowds.

"It's a charming name," I blithely replied. "Why, my great aunt had that very name. Or was it her horse?"

She balled her fist to punch me on the arm when, as fortune had it, Keldon and Arleia emerged from the pavilion. They hurried over as soon as they spotted us, and I was pleased to see Arleia carrying a set of shimmer sticks. The phosphoriferous compounds glowing within could come in handy.

"Anything to report?" I asked.

Both nodded emphatically and began speaking at once. Keldon described the dozens of automatons on stage while Arleia explained that there were no people, save for those in the audience. Keldon detailed the performance of a mechanical band and the two clockwork dancers who executed the most extraordinary sequence of movements. Arleia jumped in to say that none of the automatons were bound with elemental spirits or empowered in any way that she could detect. Keldon added that he felt something like icy shards cutting through the local eddies of the aether, but had no idea what it was.

"I fear we won't find a soul working here," I said when they were done. "Not even a soul chained captive to a machine."

"What do you mean?" Keldon asked. "The automatons could only be operating in this fashion if—"

"If," I interjected, holding my finger in the air, "their analytic mill was transfused with the animating principles of a once living, conscious being."

Keldon threw his hands up. "What's the difference?"

"You mean a *shade*," Leta whispered, realizing the truth. The blood drained from the veilhunter's face. "Not the soul, but the aetheric echo of a departed soul."

"Precisely," I confirmed. "The soul, and by that I mean the seat of emotion and intellect within all sentient beings, cannot be infused upon the gears and springs of a simple machine—a machine of equal intricacy and complexity to the human mind, perhaps, but not the sort we have today. From what little is known, the Maradians did dabble in just such experiments of human-machine soul transference. But to attempt such sorceries today..." I drew in a breath and looked around. "Well, you have seen the ghastly results for yourselves."

"You mean the automatons are possessed by ghosts?" Keldon asked.

Arleia gasped in horror. "Like the rustwraiths and

geargeists of the Iron Barrens?"

"Worse," Leta said. "These are the mangled remnants of once living souls, stripped of consciousness and burned into the movements of cold iron gears. But this still doesn't explain how Marelle and Gulthvar are doing it. We need to find this magine."

I nodded. "For that, we must break into Madame Levieu's House of Eldritch Wonders."

Keldon and Arleia both stared at me, bewildered. I looked north across the crowded street to the cluster of derelict wagons where we had met Gulthvar and his menacing mechanical manservant. Just beyond the wagons rose the brick wall of Madame Levieu's.

"Leta," I said, "where did Gulthvar and his automaton come from, and where did they go when we walked away?"

She looked past the wagons and her mouth dropped open. "That's Levieu's," she replied, glancing at the building across the lot. "You mean—"

"The wagons are abandoned. No one works here, not even Gulthvar. The entire show is automated. It certainly did not start out that way, and I'm sure Gulthvar was once the proprietor and manager, just as I'm sure Marelle Sandellar built the automatons for the show. Did you notice Gulthvar's cane? Did you see the intricate etchings down its length? Those etchings were inscribed in red metal, orichalium no doubt, and they were distinctly Maradian in design. Although I had detected a powerful mage-engine nearby, I could not determine precisely where it was. And Keldon, you say you felt something icy cutting through the local aether?"

My apprentice nodded.

"And it is stronger here than elsewhere?"

He looked to Levieu's House of Eldritch Wonders and nodded again.

"While that could have a dozen different causes, from astrological alignments to an abundance of aurium or other aetherically reactant ores, one noteworthy source would be the aetheric resonance given off by a poorly tuned, or perhaps clumsily rebuilt, Maradian magine."

Leta raised an eyebrow. "So Gulthvar is in league with Madame Levieu, who has a magine from the age of Marada that they use to ensorcell the automatons for his show?"

"No, not at all," I said. "Gulthvar is a puppet, metaphorically speaking, and I doubt Madame Levieu is even a real person. The billboard outside Levieu's said it had opened last month, and the first case of *animoptosis catatonia* was about three weeks ago. Tamethel said that his lifemate recently explored some of the more exotic exhibits, although she never visited the automaton show. Eldren have little interest in such things. However, she probably visited the newly opened House of Eldritch Wonders. I would wager all the victims had."

Leta considered this, then shook her head. "If the victims had their psychic essence stripped away at Levieu's, they would have fallen into their catatonic state there, not elsewhere."

I shrugged. "They could simply have been dropped off in any sublevel tunnel or deep alley."

"I assume we aren't going to just wait in line with the other dupes," Keldon said.

Arleia nodded. "If you say Gulthvar appeared from nowhere, there must be a back door."

"Precisely," I replied. I started toward the abandoned wagons and gestured for the others to follow. "The door is, of course, concealed. But we will need something to draw any watching eyes away from our surreptitious undertaking. Perhaps a distraction, a counter-clairvoyance veil, and our own little illusion might be in order."

We quickened our pace as we headed for the back of the building, and my three companions jumped into action. Leta furrowed her brow in concentration, her eyes open just enough to mind where we were going. Keldon caught his breath, no doubt sensing a ripple through the aether as

Leta's mystical barrier took form. Bringing out his talismanic key, my apprentice went through a few quick motions, drawing in currents of ambient aethergy and spinning the harmonic chords into a subtle smoke-and-mirror illusion. Striding by Keldon's side, Arleia produced her runic totem and whispered inaudibly. With a flash and a pop, every gas lamp for nearly half a block erupted in jets of flame. Yells and panicked cries rose from the crowded street, but the flames vanished as regulator valves clicked on. Blanketed in darkness, the people muttered in confusion as they search for the way back up to the topside boulevard.

Under the cover of darkness, illusion, and Leta's mystical veil, we wove through the dim shadows of dilapidated wagons to the weather-worn back wall of Madame Levieu's. Arleia shook one of her shimmer sticks and the phosphorescent rod's sallow alchemical glow panned against the crumbling masonry in front of us. Keldon swept his brass key across the wall, then jerked to a sudden stop.

"Right here," he said, pointing to an area of the wall. "It's a refractive inversion glamour, and a weak one at that."

I moved to the spot he pointed to and brushed my hand along the shoddy brickwork. The wall seemed to ripple, then pinched in on itself and bulged back out again, following the movement of my hand. I smiled. The severite of the wristband wreaked havoc with the empowerment. Following another pass of my arm, the illusion dissolved like an effervescent foam revealing a rusty metal door. The door had no apparent lock, knob, or handle, but that scarcely constituted an obstacle.

Keldon placed his key an inch from where a knob should have been, then flexed the finger of his other hand as though turning a dial. His eyes moved one way, then another, and his face tightened with a moment's concentration. Then a latch clicked as the locking mechanism gave way.

"Got it," he announced in a hushed but gleeful voice.

"Keep quiet," Arleia protested, although her rebuke

seemed even louder.

I pushed the door open, revealing a short hallway of crumbling plaster and peeling paper. The passageway's deplorable state left little doubt that it served no other purpose than to access this back door, but recent footprints in the dust attested to a redoublement in its use. Anxious voices murmured from other rooms within the darkened museum, confirming that the gas had shut off here as well. The door at the far end likely led to Levieu's exhibit hall, and the only other door—just to our left—was a kind of oval-shaped hatch.

I stepped up to the hatch and turned the handle, cringing at the squeak of unoiled hinges as I pulled the heavy door open. A set of rusty metal stairs led down into the murky darkness below.

"This way," I whispered to the others.

Arleia looked past my right shoulder, her eyes wide behind her glasses and her ears perking up in attention. Keldon looked past my left, his breath held as he considered the pitch-black darkness below.

"Down there?" Keldon asked.

"If there's a mage-engine here, it won't be in the exhibit hall," I explained. I adjusted my top hat and nodded down the stairs. "Now come on. This blackout won't keep them distracted for long."

EVERY STEP CREAKED AND SHUDDERED under foot, threatening to give way with a groaning complaint. I continued down, daring one step after another, and the others followed with well-warranted caution. The only light came from the glow of Arleia's shimmer stick, and although I could have asked either she or Keldon to conjure more light, we risked being detected should our adversary indeed prove sorcerous.

The rickety metal stairs zigzagged through three full flights, each with a rust eaten landing, before terminating at the pockmarked fabricrete floor of an old storm tunnel.

Looking down either direction of the tunnel, I realized that we were in the city's long-forsaken derelict levels, just above the uppermost levels of the dreaded Underworks.

Leta moved to whisper in my ear. "I sense—"

I held up my hand. A faint flicker of light danced from the tunnel to the left, and I could just make out the sound of heavy footsteps on the hard stone floor. "Someone's coming."

Leta sighed. "Yes. I was just about to—"

"Hurry," I whispered. I pulled my frock coat tighter, then ducked down the tunnel heading the opposite way.

The tunnel ran for some twenty paces and ended at a large metal door. With the footfalls drawing closer, we hadn't a moment to lose. I worked the door's latch hoping for the best. With a click, the door creaked open, and I motioned my companions inside. The greenish-yellow glow of the shimmer stick spilled into the unlit chamber, but we had no time to survey our surroundings. I began to close the door once everyone was inside, but paused to listen when words echoed from farther down the tunnel.

"An explosion?" growled a voice that sounded like gravel in a can. "And you're certain it was only an accident?"

"Yes," echoed a voice I recognized as Gulthvar's. "Just a ruptured gas line, I suspect. That would explain why all the lamps shut off."

"No... This can't be an accident," growled the other. "Not now. Not at this crucial juncture. Someone is on to us, and that explosion was a distraction. We must complete the experiment."

"But sir, with the gas off, there's no light for the exhibits. Everyone is trying to leave."

"Engage the reserve gas supply," the gravelly voice ordered. "Then go topside and tell everyone in the exhibit hall to remain calm. Offer them refunds. I don't care. Just keep them in there and return as soon as you are done. I will prepare the machine."

"A-as you say," Gulthvar stammered.

I held my breath and eased the sizable door closed, wincing at the squeak of hinges and the clang of its latch. It was only then that I chanced to take in the room. "Out of the foundry and into the furnace," I whispered.

"Where are we?" Leta asked.

I took the shimmer stick from Arleia and held it high above my head. Dim light spilled across the cavernous chamber, casting eerie shadows of mannequin-like forms along the water-stained walls. Among the boxes, crates, and workbenches stood over two dozen automatronic figures in various states of repair. Some had not yet had their limbs attached, while others slouched with breastplates open, their gears and cogs exposed as though awaiting the final fitting of their punch-tape reels. But these machines would not require reels to supply their locomotive routines. Indeed, the very engine of their morbid animation sat in the center of the room.

"There," I said, nodding my head to the bulky apparatus. "That must be the magine."

All eyes turned to the box of metal, crystal, and glass. Built in three distinct sections, the central cylinder stood roughly five feet high with three coppery-red bands encircling it. The bands, composed of orichalium, were etched with intricate lines and interlocking patterns, similar to those I had seen on Gulthvar's cane. Four crystal orbs were fixed upon the top, each circumscribed by coils of orichalium wire. To either side of the main section were trapezoidal boxes, one having a panel of buttons, wheels, and opalescent vizstones, while the other glowed with the faint blue light of aetheric energy.

Heavy footsteps came to a stop at the metal door. I discerned a series of ratcheting clicks, then the sound of the door's latch turning.

"Aldicus," Keldon whispered urgently. "There's no other way out."

"You two, behind the magine," I said to Keldon and Arleia.

Keldon began to protest, but I shoved my bag into his arms. "Take this and go!"

Leta glanced at me and arched an eyebrow, silently inquiring where we were to hide.

"We stand here," I said to her, motioning with the shimmer stick. "And try on that wonderfully audacious smirk that so becomes you."

With a snap and a hiss, the gas lamps flared to life. At the same time, the large metal door swung open, and I was struck with a pang of both pity and reproach for the thing that lumbered into the room. It was like an automaton, but it was more than the gears that drove its legs; more than the actuators of its clockwork arms; more than the ocular lenses and vibrating vocalizer within its helmeted head. For harnessed within a compartment riveted to its metal-plated chest hung the gaunt and shriveled figure of what once had been a man.

The gaunt man's eyes widened upon seeing us. The barest whisper parted from his withered lips, and the automaton boomed his query: "What are you doing here?"

He was probably a young man, perhaps in his late twenties, but his body was utterly wasted away. The atrophied vestiges of his arms and legs dangled uselessly in the air, and the features of his emaciated face bore little resemblance to the handsome lad he must once have been.

"*Necrodystrophia cachexia*," I immediately diagnosed. "The wasting death. I'm so sorry, Marelle. There is no cure."

The floor trembled as Marelle's automatronic frame ducked through the large door and lumbered into the now fully lit room. Behind him followed another automaton, either the same or identical to the one we had seen with Gulthvar.

"Oh, but there *is* a cure," Marelle mouthed. Above him the machine amplified his whispered words. The automaton's arm moved, pointing to the over-science magine behind us. "Once I complete my experiment, I will bind my soul to this immortal frame of steam and steel!"

"It all fits," I said to Leta while keeping my gaze fixed on Marelle and his machine. "Perhaps profit motivates Gulthvar, but Marelle himself is driven by a far more primal urge—the urge to *survive*. His affliction is in its final stages, which means the first symptoms must have struck sometime last year. Since then, he has likely sought cures from one end of Celaphania to the other, only to be sent away with the same grim prospects."

"Be quiet!" rumbled the mechanical voice of Marelle's machine. He stepped forward, the floor shaking. "How did you get in here?"

Ignoring him, I continued. "At some point during his search, he came upon this Maradian artifact—perhaps in some remote corner of Vanamar or darkest Azania, or even buried deep in the Underworks of Corradon. Being a gearmeister, he engineered a scheme to use the magine to transfer his consciousness into an automatronic machine. But first he had to experiment, transferring the minds of hapless patrons into the bodies of automatons. Although only the merest fragments of his victims' minds imprinted on the machines, the great success of their automatronic show brought wealth enough for him to continue his insidious research."

"Who *are* you?" bellowed Marelle's machine.

"I am Detective Aldicus Vescard, and this is my colleague, Leta Meridian." I threw back the right side of my coat and produced my badge. "By the legal authority of the Vandorian Jurisdiction Proclamation of the High Court of Armillia, you are hereby under arrest."

The vocalizer of Marelle's automaton burst with the most grating buzz of a laugh I had ever heard. "Under arrest?" he mocked. The laughter resumed, then abruptly cut off. He gestured to the automaton behind him. "Kill them!"

Leta shook her head. "They never go quietly, do they?"

The mindless automaton lunged for us, its crushing

hands raised as though to throttle our necks. But at that exact moment, another automaton clamored to life, gears clattering and pneumatics sputtering as orange flames ignited within its chassis. The blazing machine plowed headlong into the attacking automaton, slamming it against the wall. The two clockwork mannequins grappled one another like wrestlers in a brawl, crashing into boxes and stumbling over spare parts as smoke and oil streamed from their straining limbs.

Marelle appeared to be as startled as I was, but I regained my composure when Arleia and Keldon emerged from hiding. Arleia held her runic totem in one hand, her lips moving and fingers weaving as she manipulated the elemental spirit empowering the appropriated automaton. She strained to maintain her tenuous control, her brow furrowed and beading with sweat. Keldon, too, strained to sustain an empowerment of his own, but I saw no evidence of what that empowerment might be.

Tumbling past us, the two clamoring machines crashed against a workbench, then stumbled through a packing crate, scattering straw, splinters, and broken bits of wood. The opposing automaton drove a fist into Arleia's machine, bursting fire and broken gears through its ruptured chassis. Arleia's then grappled her opponent in a crushing bear hug and slammed it into the wall. Burning oil engulfed both machines, and with one last tumble, their ruined forms crashed to the floor.

Marelle's emaciated face filled with rage. He spun around to attack the audacious half-Eldren, a garble of shrieking noises issuing from his mechanical vocalizer.

"Arleia, get back!" Leta screamed.

I put my hand on her arm. "You give our apprentices too little credit."

With three great strides, Marelle's frame bounded to the magine where Arleia and Keldon hunkered. He swept an arm through the air to smash both of them to the floor, but the mechanized limb passed through their images as though nothing was there. They flickered and vanished, reappearing on the exact opposite side of the magine from where they seemed to have been before. Keldon grinned, twirling his brass key on one finger.

"A mirror mirage," I explained.

"No matter," growled Marelle's augmented voice. His automaton's metal fingers clicked across the magine's control panel, and in moments, the engine hummed to life. "When Gulthvar returns, we will add four new automatons to our show."

I watched as the mage-engine's aethergy generator flared with iridescent blue light. The rings encircling its central cylinder began to rotate and the four orbs on its top spun up to speed.

Based on what Marelle had just said, the cane Gulthvar carried must have served some critical purpose—perhaps allowing him to select the victim for their grim experiment. I had no idea how long it would be until the Dworgh returned, but no sooner had I wondered than my question was answered.

"What's going on?" Gulthvar demanded as he appeared in the doorway.

I showed my badge to the Dworgh. "By the legal authority of the Vandorian—"

"Quickly!" Marelle boomed. He jabbed a metal finger in my direction. "Designate this one!"

Gulthvar looked at me, or more precisely at my badge, then he turned back to Marelle with ice-cold fear glazing over his eyes. I knew an opportunity when I saw it.

"Fifteen hundred years ago," I said, speaking over the growing whine and rumble of the powered-up magine, "amidst the horrors of the War of Golla and Marada, the scientists of Marada sought to imbue the minds of soldiers directly into their empowered war machines. But only a fragment of the human mind could be imprinted—the rest was lost to the aether."

"Designate them!" Marelle's machine thundered.

"You see, Gulthvar," I continued, "this device does not transfer souls. It rips the soul away, consumes it, and burns a pale echo of sense and mannerism into the automaton. Either way, Marelle, your fate is death, and yours, Gulthvar, is a life sentence in Angdred Penitentiary."

Gulthvar held up his cane, but rather than aiming it at me, he pointed it at Marelle. "What is he saying?" Then his voice raised in panic. "Is that true? You said this machine would just copy their minds. You said they would wake up in a few days. Well? Answer me!"

Marelle stepped forward, his mechanical hands balling into fists. "Just designate them, you fool!"

"You've... You've made me a monster," Gulthvar sputtered through his beard. He lifted the cane higher, stabbing it toward Marelle. "A monster... As horrible as you!"

"Gulthvar, don't do it!" I yelled, but it was too late.

The cane shown with brilliant white light, and the light focused into a beam that spilled across Marelle and his machine. Marelle howled in agony, his emaciated body thrashing against the buckles that held him within his automaton. His jaw clenched, his body stiffened, and his eyes rolled up into his skull. Every thread of his vitalic essence vacated his crippled body and he slumped limp in his harness.

Leta clasped her hands to her mouth, her eyes widening in horror. No doubt she had sensed the abrupt excision of Marelle's twisted soul. "The fragments of his essence have been transposed into his automaton," she whispered. "Transposed, at the climax of his hatred and rage!"

I drew in a sharp breath. "Oh, fangle-fop—"

The automaton rose taller, stretching its arms to either side and flexing its bulging pneumatic actuators like a strongman on stage. It threw its head back and loosed a roar like a thousand iron shards ripping through steel. Marelle's limp body still dangled in the harness drooping from its chest, but no consciousness resided there. Marelle was gone, his mind obliterated, leaving only his hatred and malice impressed upon the grinding gears and whirring motors of his automatronic mobility frame.

I looked to Gulthvar, but the Dworgh dropped the cane and sank to the floor, hands covering his face in despair.

"Hold this," I said, passing Leta the severite bond that I had just removed from my left wrist. "I will need it back momentarily."

Her face blanched white, looking at the severite wristband. She now seemed more terrified of me than she was of the raging automaton. "Are you *insane*?"

I simply nodded. Already I could feel my blood pumping, burning, and boiling as vital humours converted to their purest elemental forms. With my right wristband still on, my alchemical transmutation would not be complete. I could only hope it would be enough to stop this mad machine before I was forced to become a more terrible monster still.

I tossed the shimmer stick from my right hand to my left, closing burning fingers around its fragile glass tube. "Keldon, formaldehyde!"

The crazed automaton lumbered forward, but my assistant snapped his gaze away and hurriedly opened my bag.

"Got it!" he exclaimed, then tossed the bottle my way.

I caught the bottle just as the automaton lunged for me. Scalding blisters opened down my left arm and across the back of my hand, while waves of heat washed along the burning fibers of my coat sleeve. The shimmer stick's glass tube had already begun to glow red, and the phosphoriferous liquid flared bright as it boiled. In three strides the automaton was upon me, its clawed hands extended for my throat. I slammed the formaldehyde bottle against the alchemical furnace of my arm, shattering both it and the shimmer stick's tube. Sparked by the quintessential energies unleased by the transformative reaction, the improvised reagents sublimated and recombined in a violent gaseous diffusion of instantaneous exothermic combustion.

With a blinding flash and searing heat, the incinerating jet of flame blasted straight through the charging automaton and continued on, ripping into the heart of the whirring Maradian engine. I threw myself to the side as the monstrous machine careened past and crashed into the wall before toppling backward to the floor, smoke bellowing from the molten cavity punched through its chest.

My fire-wreathed arm trembled more from my struggle to control it than from the blinding pain rippling across my body. "Leta—" I gasped through clenched teeth.

Her eyes stayed fixed on my blazing limb, but she spared not a moment's hesitation before braving the flames to slap the band around my wrist. She snapped her hands away just as quickly, shaking them in the air and swearing under her breath. I staggered back and dropped to the floor, clutching my blistered arm through the charred remnants of a coat sleeve.

Keldon knelt by my side, throwing open my bag and fishing out a healing salve and a roll of gauze. "What about him?" he asked, nodding to Gulthvar as he began applying the balm to my burns and blisters.

I was not particularly concerned with Gulthvar, guilty though he was as an accomplice in Marelle's twisted plot. The Dworgh sat despondent on the floor, his head bowed and his face grim as he accepted his lot with silent resignation.

"How did you..." Gulthvar began to ask. Then he shook his head. "What—what are you?"

My eyes turned from Gulthvar to the smoldering remains of Marelle's automatonic frame. Beneath that heap of half-melted metal lay the charred bones of Marelle himself. Across the room, the Maradian magine appeared equally demolished, with smoke and sparks still spewing from the gaping hole where the explosive blast had terminated.

"Within me seethes a monster," I admitted to Gulthvar, feeling a chill as the last embers of alchemical chaos faded to an icy smolder. "A monster of my own making, by my own foolish whims and arrogant fancies. For all his rage and malice, for all the pain and suffering he wrought, Marelle was just a man crippled by a cruel disease. Yet, he was more a monster than I could ever be."

Gulthvar looked at the cane and shook his head. That control rod was useless now—as useless as the ruined magine it once operated. "I didn't know it would take their souls away," he lamented. "I thought..." he stopped and looked down again. "But no. I should have known better. I just... I just didn't *want* to know."

I rose to my feet with Leta's help. Every inch of my arm burned as though a colony of jungle ants had made their nest beneath my skin, but I donned a stolid face and fixed my eyes sternly upon the surviving culprit.

"You did what you did not out of fear or under coercion, but in collusion with a madman. You saw an opportunity for profit and willingly took part in these vile experiments. Perhaps you do feel remorse for your actions, but it is not my place to judge the extent of your culpability. That is a matter for the courts of Armillia."

Keldon and Arleia had by then surrounded Gulthvar, blocking any flight he might attempt, but the Dworgh made no move to suggest he would even try. "I understand," he muttered shamefully.

"Can anything be done for the victims?" Arleia asked. "For Tamethel's lifemate and the others?"

"I will make certain Tamethel is released from jail now that the mystery is solved. But as for the victims..." I shook my head. "The essence of their being has been wholly destroyed, and their bodies are condemned to an unwaking slumber until the ravages of atrophy end their torpid existence. I will order the automatons dismantled, but I fear nothing more can be done."

❖

A CROWD HAD GATHERED in the wagon yard behind Madame Levieu's, no doubt drawn by the commotion. A district constable edged his way through the throng, and he grimaced when he saw us emerge from the building.

"What's going on here?" the constable demanded, shouldering past two stubborn onlookers. "First half a block of gas lamps erupt like a war zone, then there's reports of another explosion down below this building."

"Aldicus Vescard," I said, showing my deputy badge. I looked to Gulthvar, his right arm held firmly in Leta's grip. "Take this suspect into custody and notify Chief Inspector Tibblemond at Vandor Tower."

The constable blinked. "What's the charge?"

I frowned. A crime such as this had no precedent. "Multiple accounts of theft. Soul theft. Add to that malicious destruction of said articles."

"Soul theft?" the constable asked. Then his face grew suddenly pale. "Destruction? Ah... If you say so, sir."

"I will fill Tibblemond in on the details," I added before turning back to my associates. "For now, I intend to slip down to the Broken Spigot for a relaxing evening with my friends and a few nips of their finest brandywine."

Leta smirked at the suggestion. "I know a few places markedly more lively than that somber salon of social sobriety."

"I'm quite certain you do," I bantered back, "but Keldon and I have already been called on for another big case. It may prove to be even more baffling than this befuddling business."

"And what might that be?" Arleia asked as we pushed our way through the crowd.

"A case of gelatinous *goo*," Keldon replied, childishly emphasizing the word 'goo.'

Arleia scrunched up her face in disgust. "Yuck!"

"It's always something with you two," Leta reproved. "I'd

take an ordinary haunting, a vengeful wraith from across the Veil, or even a run-amok vampire any old day."

"A veilhunter through and through," I laughed. "I'll be sure to call on you if I get word of a murderous wraith haunting the abandoned steam tunnels of the Underworks."

Leta folded her arms and shook her head. "Now that you mention it, there *have* been some rather mysterious reports from the derelict zones of late."

I drew in a deep breath of crisp night air as we made our way down Vaugaire Boulevard. "By all means, fill me in, and do not leave out the slightest detail."

Case File 6:

A Case of Gelatinous Goo

FOUR WITNESSES ADMITTED TO SEEING THE MAN DISSOLVE, while the other seventeen patrons of the inebriating establishment fervently insisted they had no recollection of the freakishly bizarre event. Perhaps a few of the more intoxicated individuals had overlooked the victim's abrupt liquefaction, but how anyone could have failed to notice his screams of excruciating agony as he crashed flailing and wailing against two tables, a half dozen chairs, and a cabinet of bottles, before finally deteriorating into a substance roughly analogous to jelly, was quite beyond my ability to fathom.

"No, sir," said the barkeep in response to my query, the follicles of his ample mustache puffing with every word. "Hadn't said a thing 'cept to order his drink."

"But you have seen him here before," I stated with the inflection of a question.

"Oh, no, sir," the barkeep replied emphatically, disputing two other testimonies. "Hadn't seen that poor fellow in me life. Ya don't suppose he was 'flicted by some contagious blight or curse, do ya?"

I straightened my frock coat, then stepped back from the grimy bar counter and turned to survey the room. To say the tavern was in shambles would have understated the obvious, though how much of the wreck was due to the unfortunate patron's misadventure and how much to its usual state of disarray I could not decide. While the toppled chairs and broken bottles were certainly a result of the incident, the water-stained walls, cracked ceiling, trash-strewn floor, knife-scoured fixtures, and the peculiar scorch marks throughout only attested to the Wet Weasel's colorful history as one of the more disreputable alehouses hindmost of the law. On the far side of the room Keldon studied the gelatinous heap of what once had been a man.

"Curses are not contagious. Not usually." I rubbed the bandages beneath my left coat sleeve where my blistered skin continued to heal from yesterday's excitement on Vaugaire Boulevard. "Would you mind telling me what he ordered?"

The barkeep shrugged. "Just a pint of house ale and two bowls of salted pretzels." His eyes suddenly widened. "Not that there's any funny business in it, mind you!"

"Then were I to produce a warrant, you would be more than happy to allow a detailed inspection of your drafts, ales, potions, and elixirs? Those up here as well as those—" I nodded my head to the cellar door, "of more surreptitious notoriety?"

The barkeep quickly wiped his hands on the grease-stained towel looped through his belt. "This is no drooka den, sir! I run a legitimate business here." He sniffed and glanced around, his eyes narrowing. "Ya don't actually have a warrant, do ya?"

Rather than relieving the man's concerns, I merely raised an eyebrow. A healthy dose of ill-ease often made such characters surprisingly cooperative. "Keldon, what have you determined?" I asked, stepping over a splintered chair as I returned to the scene of the incident.

My young apprentice stood and the shimmering glow surrounding his brass skeleton key faded. "There is a faint trace of aetheric residue, but it could be anything. I do know one thing for certain—I'm never eating strawberry jam again." He coughed, then pinched his eyes shut as he forced himself to suppress a gag. "And that smell!"

"He does look rather like strawberry jam," I said, slapping Keldon on the back. "Shall I fetch some toast?"

Keldon grimaced. He was about to reply when the tavern door opened and Chief Inspector Tibblemond strolled in, still scrawling notes on his pad.

"Useless," he muttered, slipping the pad into his coat pocket. "Another useless testimony from a silver-tongued swindler. I have half a mind to arrest the lot of those free-booting scoundrels!"

"Eh, now, those are me customers," the barkeep protested. "Decent working-class folk, they are."

Tibblemond crossed his arms, ignoring the barkeep. "Tell me we have probable cause, Vescard. My men and I could take down half the criminal element this side of Coalbrick Street this very night."

I knelt beside the mass of jellied flesh, morbidly sheathed in a rumpled bag of clothing. A pistol and magical charm were partially submerged in the gooey, putrid mass. "Do you honestly believe any patrons of this establishment could have rendered a two-hundred-pound man armed with a holdout pepperbox and a contrahex charm into a lump of gelatinous goo in a mere ten seconds?"

"Perhaps the killer was a sorcerer," Tibblemond mulled doubtfully.

I took a pair of tongs from my black bag and plucked the charm from the remains. Keldon passed his key over the engraved disk, then shook his head.

"Never mind," I said. "The charm's a dud."

"That's a mighty awful way to die," the barkeep suddenly offered. "Blackest sorcery if there ever was! But no sorcerer or mage has ever set foot in this tavern, I can tell you that." He nodded to a fetich of bones and beads fixed above the tavern's door. "The fellow that sold me that said it will make quite the racket should any conjurer pass beneath."

Keldon rolled his eyes.

"I fear that charm's a dud, too," I replied. "Otherwise, it would have sounded the moment we entered." Or at least it would have when Keldon entered.

The barkeep looked suddenly abashed, rubbing his hands together and looking at the floor before resuming his work polishing his glasses.

"You should have brought this case to us sooner," I said, turning to Tibblemond. I rubbed my sore arm again, then straightened out my coat. "According to the files you sent me, four others have died like this over the past two weeks, and all here within the southeast quarter of the 15th District."

Tibblemond scratched his scraggly muttonchops. "And all of them duffers, dupers, grifters, knappers, and mumpers. That's why we didn't call on you from the start. Still, we need to get to the bottom of this before it spreads from the wretched rabble to the right and proper folk of the city."

I looked to the chief inspector and sighed. "No, Chief Inspector, we must stop the villains responsible for this because their true motives are far more sinister than simply rubbing out a few small-time miscreants."

Tibblemond blinked, genuinely shocked by the suggestion. "And those motives would be?"

"That would be what you have hired me to determine." I fished a slip of paper from the goo-covered pocket of the victim's coat and showed it to my apprentice. "Look, Keldon, a sourdrop wrapper. This may prove vital."

Tibblemond shook his head. Then he started suddenly, seeming to remember something. He snatched his pocket watch from inside his coat and clicked it open. "Blast! I still need to finish my report for the Commissioner General."

"On the gelatinous goo case?" I asked, putting the wrapper in another bag as I stood.

"No, no," he said shortly. "On that rash of museum heists. Haven't you been reading the papers? Or the weekly case summaries we tube you?"

Of course, I knew of the robberies. The papers had been

making quite a fuss over them, and several of the museums and depositories were high profile establishments. But as far as I was aware, no culprits had yet been identified.

"Still no luck cracking that case?" I asked. "Will you be needing our assistance on that one as well?"

Tibblemond shook his head. "We're doing just fine, thank you. But that case will need my undivided attention. This—" He waved his hand about the tavern. "This blasted bodgefuddle is more your thing, so I leave it in your capable hands."

"Right you are, inspector," I agreed, tipping my top hat. "The strange and bizarre are our specialty—the stranger and more bizarre, the better."

Tibblemond touched the brim of his bowler, bidding farewell. "The carters should be here shortly to haul off whatever remains of this sixer." With that, he turned and hurried out the door.

"Now we can finally get around to solving this puzzle," I said to Keldon. "But I do wish he had called us in sooner."

Keldon scratched behind his newsboy cap. "Should we take a sample before the carters arrive?"

"Thank you for volunteering." I produced tweezers and a sample jar from my bag and passed them to my apprentice. "Try to get a nice juicy gob of it right from the middle."

Keldon took the jar and tweezers, and his face changed from a pasty pale to a kind of sickly green.

I returned to the bar where the proprietor kept an apprehensive watch. "Mister Perney, isn't it?" The man nodded hesitantly. "Before my assistant and I take our leave, I suspect you could spare me the trouble of procuring a warrant if you could merely recall this poor fellow's name."

"Ah, yes." Mister Perney's eyes darted from one side to the other. "After considering it, I think I did overhear someone mention that his name was Gnasher."

"An alias," I said flatly.

"Same as half me customers. Why, just the other night we

had a Bruiser, a Boxer, a Lucky, and a Lefty."

Mister Perney was not in a state of mind to lie without sweating, stammering, or stuttering. The essence of unease I had distilled in his mind had successfully fermented into a potent brew of acrid apprehension. I glanced back to check on Keldon's progress and saw the young lad standing restlessly above the remains.

"Now, Keldon, you will need to overcome this squeamishness if you hope to become a forensic alchemist or detective magus one day."

"There is one more thing," Mister Perney interjected with a wavering hesitation. "He had a..." The barkeep looked down, as though uncertain how to proceed.

"Yes, go on," I encouraged.

"I'm just telling you what I saw, mind you." He drew in a deep breath and blew it out through his nostrils, rustling his mustache. "He had a strip of cloth sticking out of his arm. I don't mean like the bandages you've got there on your arm. It was just a piece of cloth, hanging right out from his left forearm. Strangest thing I ever saw." He blinked having said this and looked to the heap of jellified flesh in the middle of his tavern. "Well, the second strangest thing I ever saw."

I nodded. "Thank you. That could be very useful."

I returned to the amorphous blob of mucilaginous tissues, then stood for a moment, rubbing my chin as I pondered the gelatinous mass.

"Where would the left arm have been." I bent down, then stopped. "No, that's the liquefied residue of a lung. Or possibly the liver. Keldon!"

Keldon looked up suddenly, his face wracked with horror at the prospect that I might ask him to dig through more of the remains.

I held out my hand. "Tweezers and jar."

He scrambled to hand over the collection tools, nearly dropping them in his haste to escape the dreaded task.

Using the tweezers, I managed to pull free a strip of cloth

from deep inside the viscous blob. The strip was three inches long, ragged on one end and cleanly cut on the other. It appeared to be of a coarse burlap material, better suited for sacks and draperies than clothing. I dropped it in the sample jar and twisted the lid shut.

A pair of morose-looking gentlemen garbed in sullen accoutrements of black and gray dragged themselves into the tavern carrying a stretcher between them. The taller of the two set his end of the stretcher down and stiffly stood up.

"Get the shovel, Mister Maves," he said, his voice flat and solemn.

The other nodded grimly, languidly blinking his sunken eyes. "Straight away, Mister Murley—and perhaps a bucket, too."

Keldon shuddered. "Always a joy, those two."

I gave the gentlemen a cordial smile and an appreciative nod. Mister Murley and Mister Maves were, without a doubt, the best corpse-carters in all of Corradon—singularly focused and admirably unflappable. "They could teach you a thing or two about stalwart self-possession," I replied with a chuckle. "Should I arrange for a supplementary apprenticeship?"

Keldon held his breath, nervously glancing back and forth between the pair as they began their cheerless work.

Leaving the grisly remains in the capable hands of the two uncanny carters, we made our way out of the Wet Weasel and into the cold and foggy night. A light rain had begun, pattering down on a grimy, litter-strewn street that still wasn't half the mess as the tavern. Several district constables milled about, but Tibblemond was already gone. We hailed a steam-coach and climbed inside, and I watched the weight of anxiety lift from Keldon's shoulders the moment the driver eased the vehicle forward.

"Number Five Brass Lantern Lane, 8th District," I said to the driver before turning to Keldon. "Have you ever tried jellied eels? Perhaps a savory slice of well-salted jellied pork or a pungent plate of jellied lutefisk delight?"

Though the sallow light of the passing streetlamps made it difficult to tell, my assistant seemed to grow even more green in the face. "No," he gulped. "And I likely never will."

"The process of gelatinization is nothing more than the dissolution of skin, bone, cartilage, and connective tissues by boiling in a kettle of brine with lye or vinegar. Normally, that takes several hours, or even several days, but in these cases, the victims were rapidly converted into a gelatinous goo without the benefit of extended boiling. That would require a highly potent transmutative reaction, be it magical or alchemical in nature."

Keldon nodded. "I did detect a trace of aetheric residue, but it was relatively weak."

I sat back in my seat and considered the possibilities. "That only adds to the mystery."

The driver heaved the tiller left, sharply cutting the corner of Copper and Bulwark Street, and narrowly missing a collision with an ichor-burning motor-wagon puttering past. Ahead, I caught sight of Mainspring Causeway—the great thoroughfare of Corradon—flanked on either side by cliffs of towering buildings and manufactories.

Even at this deep hour, the pedestrious masses ebbed and flowed like teeming shoals through the rolling mists rising from the abyssal Underworks far beneath their feet. A steamrail thundered down its elevated track, blaring its horn as it clattered down a tunnel to descend into the endless labyrinth of the sublevels below. Great airships drifted lazily in the midnight sky, the red light of Atracus blazing across their gleaming silver hulls. And there, rising above it all, soared the needle-like profile of the Aetherspire—the great wonder of our age—its enormous scaffolding abuzz with workers and automatons laboring tirelessly into the night. Once complete, the Aetherspire would resonate with near-limitless aethergy for the city of Corradon, paving the way for a new Golden Age.

I leaned back in my seat and sighed, closing my eyes. True to its name, the cogs of the Clockwork City never ceased in their turning.

❖

THE NIGHT WAS AS LATE as the morning was young when we reached my townhouse on Brass Lantern Lane. Sparing not a moment, we hastened to the cellar and into my generously furnished alchemical laboratory. With a wave of his key, Keldon ignited the lamps, bathing amber gaslight across an eccentric collection of glassware, brasswork, and clockwork contrivances of every conceivable kind. I set my bag on a table and went for the canister in the pneumatic delivery tube holding today's copy of the *Corradon Daily Post*.

Keldon had already begun to attach a condensing coil to one of the alembics when he noticed my interest in the paper. "I don't believe Vandor Tower has released any information about this case to the press."

"Actually, they have," I explained, spreading the pages across a table. "Only they do not realize it is part of this case."

Keldon shook his head. "What are you talking about?"

"Poor Tibblemond," I sighed. "He's a good man, and perhaps one of the best investigators in the Vandorian Guard. But he is too singularly focused on the facts of each individual case to apprehend the interrelations of the whole."

Keldon blinked, obviously confused.

Instead of explaining, I grabbed yesterday's newspaper and the one from the day before, spreading the pages out across the table beside today's paper. I threw the front pages aside, shuffling past salacious political scandals, sensational reports of piracy in the Sea of Isles, and articles covering the many recent worker strikes and walkouts. Finding the articles I was looking for, I drew Keldon's attention and pointed to the pages.

"Take a look at these," I said.

As Keldon began to study the articles, I retrieved from my bag the evidence we had collected at the Wet Weasel—

namely, the sourdrop wrapper and the goo-coated strip of cloth—setting each on the table where Keldon had arranged my alchemistry set.

"The upcoming eclipse?" he asked, looking at an article in the 'Amazing Events' column.

I sighed. "No, no. On the other side of that page."

Keldon continued reading, and I busied myself setting up the experiment. Using a glass rod, I scraped away a small quantity of Gnasher's viscous remains and placed the rod, covered in goo, into the alembic. I then dashed the merest pinch of regulus of azoth into the alembic, followed by a quart and a half of highly distilled water. The water erupted in a spume, bubbles fizzing as the azoth sundered the elements into the primordial modicum of which all matter is formed. I then uncorked a flask of aqua vitriol and added the entire measure to the swirling brume. As Gnasher's transmogrified flesh had already begun to dissolve, the addition of the aqua vitriol should catalyze and produce what I hoped would be a clue.

"Oh, the recent artifact thefts," Keldon said, picking up the page. "But what does that have to do with our case?"

"Everything," I answered.

In truth, the connection could have been purely circumstantial—a coincidence of geography and timing. In a city as large and populous as Corradon, multiple thefts and homicides have been known to occur in the very same building at approximately the same time, yet be entirely unrelated. But when *five* bizarre deaths occurred near a similar number of inexplicable thefts, I preferred to tender a more open mind.

I spread a map of the 15th District on the floor beside the table and, with a handful of valve caps, marked the locations of the recent deaths along the district's southeast quarter.

"According to the Vandorian case summaries, the jellified bodies were found here, here, here, here, and most recently here at the Wet Weasel. Now, let us consider the burglaries."

I took a moment to consult the newspaper articles, then placed a cap at each of the corresponding locations throughout the 15th District. Assuming my theory was correct, then the proximity of the burglaries from the location of the bodies was entirely dependent on where the thieves happened to venture in their last few hours following each heist. "One robbery was at the Pradovon Gallery, the second at Pfarphenber's Museum of Lost Oddities, the third at the Medrean Bank Depository, the fourth at the Armillian Private Antiquities Exchange, and the one last night at Servelle's Jewelry of Hewning Street."

Keldon doffed his newsboy cap to dishevel his hair while examining the map. "Wait," he said, furrowing his brow. "Those aren't all museums. In fact, only two of them are museums. But how is Pfarphenber's Museum of Lost Oddities in any way related to the Medrean Bank Depository or a jewelry store?"

"An excellent question!" I lauded. "It's the broadsheets that have styled these as 'museum heists,' but there is a good reason. What all these places hold in common is that they contain ancient relics and empowered artifacts, some dating back to the time of Marada, Elinica, and even the lost ages of Keshim and Eram-Ur. The Medrean Bank Depository and the Private Antiquities Exchange have extensive private collections of ancient artifacts, but they boast fanatically tight security. Not only are their vaults sealed by empowered clockwork magelocks, but they are further protected by watchdog egregores, heavily armed guards, and numerous sentry automatons. On the other hand, Pfarphenber's Museum of Lost Oddities showcases little more than knickknacks, replicas, and hoaxy fakes. Servelle's Jewelry, as I recall, is a high-end purveyor of fashionable amulets and empowered vizstones. However, they are allegedly associated with the Travenni crime family, and only a lunatic would rob from them."

"Do we know what was taken?" Keldon asked.

I shook my head. "The paper does not detail what was stolen, other than saying they were empowered artifacts. And since we're not on the case, Vandor Tower has only sent us the summaries which have even less details than the papers." I looked up at my apprentice and smiled. "Now, do you see any connections between the locations of the burglaries and the locations of the bodies?"

Keldon studied the map for a moment, scratching his head. Then he sighed, his shoulders slumping. "As far as I can tell, there's no connection at all. Most of the bodies are over ten blocks from the burglaries, although the deaths seem to cluster around the lower west quarter of the district."

I glanced at the alchemical process still boiling in the alembic, then turned back to Keldon. "Here is what we know. Over the past two weeks there have been five unsolved burglaries and five unsolved deaths, all within the 15th District. All five deaths are essentially the same, and all five burglaries seem to involve empowered artifacts. Although the burglaries have occurred throughout the district, all the deaths have been in or near the same area. Furthermore, each of the deaths have occurred some four to six hours after each of the burglaries."

Keldon blinked, apparently expecting me to explain more. "I don't follow, boss. Are you saying these thieves break into high security vaults and then, a few hours later, turn into goo? If the vaults were booby-trapped in some way, why wouldn't the spell just kill them on the spot? And for that matter, why would five different places employ the same booby-trap? That seems rather unlikely." Then his eyes widened and he snapped his fingers. "They're being offed by whoever hired them!"

I smiled. "That is a very good deduction. But I'm afraid there is just one problem with that theory. If the thieves were being killed to silence them, then whoever is behind this would do so quietly and subtly, not in a manner so shockingly bizarre as spontaneous tissue liquefaction. That would draw far too much attention, just as it has."

"Well, what then?" Keldon asked.

"I fear the thieves are suffering some horrific side-effect related to the thefts themselves." I looked at the alembic again and watched the last of the jellied flesh dissolve in the bubbling vessel. "As to what that is, we shall have our answer momentarily."

I fixed an ocular amplification monocle over my left eye and tightened the straps around the back of my head, then screwed on the highest magnifying lens. Peering down at the alembic, I saw exactly what I feared I would see. It was not in the glass vessel itself, but floated like tiny, glittering motes of dust just outside the alchemical apparatus. I moved my hand through the air and watched the particles pass through, unperturbed by either motion or matter.

"Fangle-fop," I said, removing the monocle. "This poor soul was subjected to a diaphamorphic matter state. Such a state of matter is highly unstable and extremely detrimental to one's life expectancy following any significant exposure."

"Diaphamorphic matter?" Keldon asked. "Didn't the Magestrian Order carry out some experiments a few years ago, proving that such substances not only violate the entropic principle, but would require a complete rework of both the general and special theories of aetheromagnetic numinosity?"

"The entropic principle was in no way violated. The victim's bodies were irreparably destabilized by the transformation and eventually broke down to a lower state of particulate organization—or, as we say, goo." I shrugged. "The fact remains that the dissolution of this tissue sample has released residual particles exhibiting a diaphamorphic state of matter. These particles are nearly invisible and do not interact with normal matter. Not only did they float out of a completely sealed alembic, but they also passed through my hand as though it was not even there."

Keldon's eyes widened. "That's how the thieves got in and

out of the vaults. They were transformed into diaphamorphic matter! But if that is so, how could they have picked up the artifacts and carried them out?"

"Another excellent question," I praised. "But remember, it is getting *into* a high security vault that is the hard part. I suspect the effect only lasted a few minutes, enabling the thieves to walk through the walls of the building and right into the vault. Two of the burglary reports suggest that the vaults were opened from the inside, rather than being forced or broken, which corroborates my theory that they entered in an immaterial state, returned to a state of normal matter, grabbed the goods, and walked out by simply opening the doors from the inside. Also, the proprietor of the Wet Weasel said that he saw a strip of burlap hanging out of Gnasher's arm. He was probably transitioning from an immaterial state to a material state when he grabbed a bag. Part of the bag passed through his arm before he fully materialized and it got stuck there. Nevertheless, neither the thieves nor the burglaries concern me at the moment. Finding the criminals who are hiring these knappers, and who have either acquired or invented this extremely dangerous technology, is my sole concern."

Kelden scratched his head again. "Where do we begin?"

"Anyone who suffered such a sudden metabolic transmogrification would likely lose a substantial quantity of water, salts, and sugars, leading to a sudden craving for sweet candies and salty foods." I picked up the sourdrop wrapper that I had found on Gnasher's remains and turned it over in my hand. "Doctor Inglebart's Confectionery," I read. "If memory serves, a delightful little parlor on the corner of Brassbell and Bulwark Street."

I marked the spot on the map with another cap.

"Let us suppose," I continued, "that our most recent victim hurried from a successful burglary last night to an unknown location somewhere in the southwest quarter of the 15th District where he turned over the goods and received payment for his services. Sometime thereafter, he purchased a few sourdrops from Inglebart's Confectionery to satisfy his gnawing craving for salt and sweets. Later in the evening, he made his way to his regular nocturnal haunt, the Wet Weasel, where he had a quick drink and some salted pretzels before settling down into a heap of gelatinous goo."

Keldon blinked, looking at the latest cap I had placed on the map. "That confectionery is square in the middle of the deaths. That *can't* be a coincidence."

"No, but it could simply be a product of the city's geography," I said. I took one of my finer artisan pens and plotted lines from the confectionery to the five caps that marked the locations of the deaths. Each was within six blocks of the store. "All we know is that Gnasher visited Inglebart's Confectionery, either on his way to deliver the stolen goods or on his way to the Wet Weasel, which is four blocks farther east. In fact, all the deaths appear to be within eight blocks of Inglebart's Confectionery. If I were a betting man, which as a jonko player, I am, I would say the criminals have their base of operations within a few blocks of this confectionery."

Keldon nodded. "Well, the confectionary is probably closed this late at night."

"Indeed," I agreed. "I will inform Tibblemond of our findings and see if he can accompany us. I'm sure the proprietor will be more than happy to talk about any unsavory sorts who might have recently stopped by for a few dainty sweets or salty treats."

Keldon pinched his eyes shut and placed a fist over his mouth as a gaping yawn seized his weary expression.

I flipped open my pocket watch and frowned. "We should both turn in for what remains of the morning and get a good day's rest before heading out to close this grisly affair. If the pattern holds, I estimate that we have between ten to twelve hours before the masterminds dispatch their next ill-fated patsy. Let us hope we can stop them before then."

FOLLOWING A FITFUL SLEEP that took me almost past noon, I tubed Tibblemond a quick missive informing him of our findings and requesting that he accompany us to the confectionary. Following a frustrating back and forth, I finally rendezvoused with him at Vandor Tower and spent far too long explaining the connection between the unsolved burglaries and the mysterious deaths. The concept behind diaphamorphic matter, and how it could allow the thieves to simply walk through walls as though they were nothing, had him particularly befuddled. Eventually, I simply resigned myself to saying "it's magic," though I could as well have said "it's science," or "it's alchemy," or "it's physics."

"Bodgefuddle!" Tibblemond huffed as we neared the confectionary in our coach. He padded his coat pockets, then drew out his battered notepad. "Where you come up with these ludicrous ideas is truly beyond me."

"Undoubtedly," I heartily agreed.

Keldon just smiled, shaking his head.

"The fact that the victim in the Wet Weasel had purchased a sourdrop from this place may be worth a follow-up," Tibblemond went on to say, "but it has nothing to do with the artifact heists."

I raised an eyebrow, folding my arms over my frock coat. "We shall see."

By the time the coachman stopped in front of the whitewashed storefront of Inglebart's Confectionery, the sun had sunk beneath the great spired towers to the west, and the crimson light of Atracus shown through the foggy veil of the deepening sky.

I had feared the shop would be closed by this late hour, but the warm glow of gas lamps illuminated shelves of candies in the windows. Beyond the colorful glass display was the storekeeper—Doctor Inglebart, I presumed—pacing worriedly behind a counter cluttered with bulging jars of licorice knots, bubble gobs, and sourdrops. He was a gangling man, well past his middle years, and dressed in striped trousers with a bright blue coat, puffed sleeves, and a whimsical blue top hat tailored to evoke the laughter of children. Yet, his pensive frown and worried brow exuded an air that was anything but amusing.

"Good evening, sir," I said, pushing through the door, the little bell chiming as I entered. "I feared no confectioneries would be open at this hour, but I am truly delighted to find your store still welcoming."

Doctor Inglebart's attention jerked our way. "I'm sorry, I was about to close up." He wrung his hands, his eyes darting from me to Tibblemond and finally to Keldon. "Oh, yes. Would the young sir enjoy a few cinnamon drakes or a fizzle pop?"

Keldon rolled his eyes. "I'm nearly eighteen."

"Ah, but the years have been far too kind," I blithely gibed. "In truth, we are here on a matter of urgent—"

"Yes, yes," Tibblemond interrupted, elbowing past. He produced his Vandorian badge and cut straight to the questioning. "I am Chief Inspector Tibblemond of the Vandorian Guard. It has come to our attention that your establishment may have been visited by one or more sinister fellows involved in a series of recent crimes."

I could only clench my fist as I listened to the inspector's rambling pronouncements, lacking even the slightest hint of subtlety or finesse.

"I... I..." Inglebart stammered. He wrung his hands again and swallowed. "All sorts come here, mostly youngsters or parents with their children. All manner of gentlemen and ladies also have a sweet tooth, especially the ladies, but I would remember seeing any thieves!"

I raised my eyebrows. To his credit, Tibblemond had not specifically indicated that the men were thieves. For a moment, I considered the possibility that my recrimination of the inspector's tactics were unjustly harsh. But only for a moment.

"You see, Vescard?" he asked, crooking a mocking smile in my direction. "If such sordid men had come by this shop, don't you think he'd tell us? Now stop wasting my time with these preposterous theories of yours!"

"How silly of me." I approached the counter, gesturing for Keldon to follow. "If these men have threatened you into silence, understand that we are on the verge of cracking this case and will bring to justice all who are in any way involved. Of course, those who are involved but who choose to cooperate will benefit from the clemency of the courts." I looked down at one of the jars and smiled. "I say, are those sizzle sticks?"

Inglebart stared blankly at the jar. "Yes," he said after a slight hesitation. He drew in a breath and touched a trembling hand to his brow. "Yes... They were thieves... I'm sure of it. They had that look, you know? A different one came by every couple of days, and usually at night." He glanced at the clock on the wall, then cast the slightest glance at the door. "I have no idea why they wanted all that candy, but they did. And they even paid for it! Most wanted salty tarts and sourdrops. Do you think they might be part of a gang?"

I nodded doubtfully. He was telling me everything he thought I wanted to hear. He was even trying to cover for his earlier slip, explaining that the men simply looked like thieves.

"Doctor Inglebart, I do not care about the thieves and I already know why they needed to metabolize so much salt and sugar. I also do not care about the patsies and middlemen involved in this demented crime. I only care to find the real villains who are behind—"

The door chimed open.

"I can't believe that belt worked! You'd never believe—" the man froze mid-sentence, mouth open and burlap sack in hand. His eyes flitted between Tibblemond, Keldon, and me. "Oh..."

I gave Keldon a nod.

Of course, Keldon was only an apprentice mage. He could not restrain a man in a field of compressive force, knock him down with a concussive blast, or even deliver a jolt of incapacitating electricity, but he *was* a clever illusionist in his own right. His talismanic key flipped into his hand, and with a sudden flash, a shimmering barrier filled the threshold of the door. A gasp rose from both Doctor Inglebart and the newcomer, their eyes bulging and mouths agape. They could easily have passed through the illusory barrier to make their escape had they known it was just a trick of distorted light and air conjured from the lower eddies of the aether. As it was, both men assumed the barrier was real, and resigned themselves to the inevitability of their arrest.

"By all the blazing stars above!" Tibblemond exclaimed. Then he composed himself enough to take a good look at the man who had just arrived. He looked him up and down, now noting his black attire, his strange metal belt, the black mask he held in one hand, and the hefty sack he carried with the other. "You look as though you've just returned from a burglary! I am hereby placing you under arrest." Then he looked at Inglebart and frowned. "Both of you!"

"There is no need to be hasty, Inspector Tibblemond." I studied the newcomer, paying close attention to his metal-banded belt of silver and brass with a snap-lock buckle and two large disks on either side of the hip. "This poor fellow is a pawn, as is Doctor Inglebart. But unlike Inglebart, our newest acquaintance should be granted a reprieve. He is, after all, going to suffer a rather horrific death in a few hours."

The man looked at me aghast. His mouth opened as though to speak, but he choked his own words back. I truly did pity him. If he had been subjected to a diaphamorphic matter state, nothing I nor anyone else could do would save him.

"I am sorry," I said to him with my deepest sincerity. "I

truly am. You and at least five other thieves were hired to commit burglaries using a device that allowed you to walk through solid matter. But there is a terrible side effect to its use that results in a rather grisly death within five hours or so."

The man dropped the bag with a clatter, then scrambled to unbuckle the belt as if removing it would somehow do any good. He stopped, perhaps realizing the pointlessness of his action, and he looked me in the eyes. "Is... Is there anything you can do?"

I shook my head. "If I knew of a way to reverse the damage, I would do whatever I could to save your life. Consuming a large quantity of sugar and salt will temporarily stabilize your metabolism, but it will only prolong the inevitable. There is nothing to be done."

The thief looked to Inglebart, then to Tibblemond, Keldon, and finally back to me. His shoulders slumped, and his eyes turned down in defeat. Neither he nor Inglebart were the masterminds behind these crimes, but one of them could provide the key to learning who was. After all, someone needed to collect the stolen goods.

Curious, I took the thief's burlap bag and pulled the drawstring open. Inside was a coppery-red disk etched with a complex pattern of lines and bejeweled with opalescent vizstones arranged in an intricately lined grid. "This artifact is from the War of Golla and Marada.

I turned the disk over and nearly dropped the device upon seeing the inscriptions etched on the back. Although my knowledge of ancient Maradian was spotty, I was familiar enough to read part of the inscription naming the purpose of the device.

"This is a *neuroflayer*—an instrument of horrific torture, designed to burn away nerves. It delivers unimaginable pain as it slowly renders its victim blind, numb, and paralyzed. What kind of madman would want such an abominable device?"

Inglebart scoffed. "And what self-righteous old miser would lock away such wonders in the darkest depths of obscurity, never again to be seen, studied, or used?"

I looked back to the confectionary owner, his question catching me off guard. He was clearly referring to the Fathomless Vault, where for centuries the Archidoxy had gathered and contained countless artifacts from the War of Golla and Marada.

"That is a rather interesting and unorthodox view. Is your master plotting to pilfer the Fathomless Vault?" I paused, watching the expression on Inglebart's face. But I did not detect so much as a flinch or twitch. "No... He knows that is impossible, even with a device such as the belt. And so, he seeks any and all over-science technology that remains in private hands."

Inglebart frowned, no doubt realizing he had said too much. This man was no patsy as I had originally surmised. He was probably a middleman serving as the agent who received the stolen artifacts and disbursed payment to the petty thieves whose bodies would soon succumb to the belt's side effects. It was a grotesque arrangement—the candy store had been aptly chosen not only as an unlikely front, but also to stuff the dying men with sufficient sugar and salt to stabilize their metabolisms long enough for them to get far away from the base of operations.

"The belt," I demanded from the thief.

His face was still drawn with shock and disbelief, but he finished unbuckling the apparatus and handed it to me without a word. A quick inspection told me nothing. While it was clearly an advanced over-science contraption, there were no markings of any kind. I did not recognize the design to be either ancient Maradian or modern construction, but what else could it be? I put the mysterious belt in the bag with the Maradian torture device and pulled the drawstrings tight.

"These will be delivered to the Archidoxy's Fathomless Vault," I announced, "where they will be sealed away for all time."

"Nothing remains sealed forever," Inglebart hissed.

I quirked an eyebrow. So, there was a larger plot in motion...

"You will tell me where I can find the mastermind behind this operation," I said to both Inglebart and the thief. "Cooperation may find you some small leniency in court."

Inglebart clinched his jaw and looked down. "I will not help you bring down everything we have worked to achieve."

"I'll take you there," the thief said. "I'm not exactly sure where, but I figure it must be one of those abandoned tenements near the old steamworks on Bronzewell."

But for the quickest twinge of the eye, Inglebart managed to maintain his dour-faced veil. Slight though his reaction was, it was enough to make clear that the thief's guess was close to the mark.

"Very good," I said. I turned to Tibblemond. "Inspector, if you would arrest Doctor Inglebart for his involvement in this affair, Keldon and I will proceed to bring the case to a close."

Tibblemond shook his head. "Vescard, I must accomp—"

I raised a hand to cut him off. "Time is of the essence, and procedure dictates that you must call in the full support of a Heavy Armory and Assault Mobile Regiment before storming what is sure to be a criminal stronghold."

"Criminal stronghold?" Tibblemond asked, clearly befuddled. "A HAAMR unit?"

"Just as a precaution," I assured. I abhorred the need for HAAMR, but if we faced adversaries in possession of powerful, over-science artifacts, their presence would likely be needed. "And those procedures do not apply to a freelance detective such as myself, so we are free to go on ahead of them."

The chief inspector grumbled something under his breath, then he cuffed the grimly impassive Doctor Inglebart whose flamboyant attire now stood in sharp contrast to his somber countenance. I could not help but wonder what his few enigmatic admissions meant. He seemed as equally concerned that the artifacts had been in museums or private hands as he was with the prospect of them being confiscated by the authorities.

"Do you have a list of the other artifacts that were stolen?" I asked Tibblemond.

He sighed, then reluctantly flipped through the pages of his battered notepad. "We're not at liberty to release specific details," he said, settling on a page filled with haphazard scribbles. "But I did jot down—"

"Obliged," I said, tearing the page from the notepad.

"Now just a moment!" Tibblemond yelled, but I was already ushering the thief to the door.

Keldon released the illusionary wall of energy and the three of us were in the street before the chief inspector could raise any further objection. The thief, who gave his name as Geb, motioned to a cross street a few blocks down and suggested it as the quickest way to Bronzewell Boulevard. For a man who was only hours from death he was uncannily calm. Then again, the glazed look in his eyes was that of a man bewildered by a reality he could not accept. I, too, wished it were not so. Other than his ill-chosen profession, Geb did not seem to be a particularly reprehensible character. Indeed, under these circumstances, he was the victim, not the culprit.

I studied the scrap of paper from Tibblemond's notepad as we crossed the street and rounded the corner of a steam utilities substation, straining my eyes in the sallow gaslight as I tried to make sense of the meandering scrawls that passed for the chief inspector's clumsy shorthand. "Amaldiere's Masque of Illusions, said to grant its wearer any desired form," I read aloud, slowly teasing out the shorthand strokes that at least bore some resemblance to common Kellian stenography. "Multi-ringed obsidian sphere with strong aetheric resonance, effects unknown. Void Scepter of the Embersoul, of possible Gollan origin. A nine-pointed amulet of unknown origin and unknown purpose. Reliquary of the Infernal Desolator, said to contain the remains of a demonsworn servitor." I considered these for a moment. Adding to the mysterious belt and the Maradian torture device, it was evident that whoever was behind this sought to amass a collection of the most dangerous artifacts they could find.

"Those were all in private hands?" Keldon asked.

"Unfortunately," I replied. "Every single one of them should have been consigned to the Fathomless Vault centuries ago. Now they are in the hands of criminals."

We turned another corner, finally coming to Bronzewell Boulevard—a cracked and pitted cobblestone street flanked by condemned tenements that were long due for demolition. As the demarcation line for the industrial quarter of the 15th District, Bronzewell saw few visitors outside the skives and scabs of the smoldering ironworks and churning manufactories rising above the rundown tenements. But I soon realized that the bellowing chimney towers were not the only source of smoke. A black column plumed above the roofs of the dilapidated buildings no more than two blocks away, while a fiery red glow shown upward through the sooty air to meet the crimson haze of Atracus, shining through the overcast sky.

"Keldon, find a fire beacon!" I yelled before grabbing Geb's arm and turning to make a dash for the blaze.

The acrid stench of smoke grew steadily sharper as I hurried past vacant tenements and gutted stores, and the air became thick and turbid as though a heavy fog had rolled in from the bay. After passing the second block, the source of the smoke became clear: a five-story tenement engulfed by a raging inferno. Ash and burning cinders floated upward from the conflagration, and an explosion of sparks and flame erupted from every window as part of the roof's fire-stripped framework caved in.

"That must be the place," Geb said, breathing hard from

his run to keep up with me. "They set it afire. I think they—"

I startled at a crack and a flash, and Geb fell backwards as snapping blue arcs lashed across his thrashing body. I reached for him reflexively, then recoiled when his skin began to bubble and melt, dissolving into a liquescent goo. Turning from the horrid sight, I fixed my gaze on the burning building. There I saw the black silhouette of a man standing before the towering bonfire.

"A small mercy," the shadowy man called over the crackling din. He twirled a golden staff in his hands, the light of the fire glittering down its length as he aimed the end in my direction. "Be grateful he was spared a slow and agonizing death."

A beam of light struck up into the sky, flashing on and off as a bell began to sound. Keldon had found a fire beacon. "Drop the staff and surrender peacefully," I said. I still could not make out the shadowy man's face, even though he glanced up to study the beacon. He was not merely silhouetted by the flames—he was concealed by an empowerment. "The fire brigade and district police will be here any moment, and soon after, the Vandorian Guard with a full HAAMR unit."

The Shadow Man remained impassive, tightening his grip on the golden staff. "It is of no consequence, Aldicus Vescard. We knew you would unravel this case as soon as you were brought in, but we had to contain as many of those artifacts as we could find—for the good of this city, of course."

Contain? What did he mean? I stepped forward. "Who are you?"

The Shadow Man stood silent for a moment, his staff still pointed in my direction. "I am but a servant of a greater cause."

"You must stop what you are doing. Men are dying, and you have no right to use them as your pawns."

"I have every right," the Shadow Man said coldly. "Those artifacts could not be left in private hands. Or do you disagree, Vescard?"

"They belong in the Fathomless Vault!" I yelled.

A laugh echoed over the cracking and crashing of the roiling inferno. "And you believe the Archidoxy's motives are pure? Such arrogance! Such presumption!"

"At least their motives are purer than yours." I pointed to Geb's oozing remains still bubbling behind me. "How can you justify such brutal acts of murder?"

"Some must die to serve a greater good." His voice was as cold as it was self-righteous. "All the better if they are thugs and thieves."

"You are a monster," I hissed. My left hand touched the severite wristband fastened to my right wrist, fingers brushing the pin that held the aethergy-dampening band tight. I had only to pull that pin and the other one, too. And then...

"You call *me* a monster?" The Shadow Man laughed again. "You are a weapon more dangerous than all these artifacts combined. Work with us, Vescard, not against us. Like you, we seek to bring justice to this world. We seek a glorious, new order!" His shadow-masked face turned to the sky, looking to Atracus as the volcanic moon peeked out from behind a sooty cloud. "As above, so below... The dark above, the dark below. A greater power is stirring, Vescard. Have you not felt it? Have you not *tasted* it? Have you not seen the shape of things to come?"

The man was mad. *He had to be.*

The frantic peal of three fire engines joined the ringing toll of the beacon as they skidded onto Bronzewell Boulevard, their steam boilers sputtering and iron wheels clattering. In the sky to the east, a deepening rumble became a deafening thunder, and I looked up to see the airship *Justiciar* closing overhead. Two ornithopters descended from the airship, siren lights flashing as their battering wings carried them over the scene of the fire and around the great column of smoke.

"Goodbye, Aldicus Vescard," the Shadow Man said. "You have been of greater assistance than you can possibly know." He performed a quick bow—perhaps in earnest, perhaps in jest—then faded into the sooty veil gathering between buildings.

The flames had spread to two more abandoned tenements by the time the fire engines came to a stop in the yard. Men jumped from their seats, wasting no time connecting hoses to the engines' water pumps. One of the ornithopters landed a short distance away and two cloaked passengers exited the rear compartment. They were mages, I knew—elementors trained to combat the ever-present threat of fire in this great urban tinderbox we called a city.

"What's going on? Who was that?" Keldon asked as he jogged up to my side.

"A problem," I admitted. I looked out across the crackling pyre and watched as one wall of the tenement collapsed like the logs of a bonfire.

Keldon glanced at Geb's remains and quickly looked away. "Don't tell me they eluded you. We've never failed to close a case before."

"We haven't failed," I said, holding up the bag. "We have the belt they used to commit the thefts and the most recent artifact they sought to acquire. And the case *is* closed. In fact, we have closed two cases tonight. Not only have we put an end to the rash of gruesome deaths by jellification, but we have also solved the case of the artifact burglaries. We even have a middleman in custody, though I doubt he can provide any useful information."

"But?" Keldon asked. He had picked up on the hesitation in my voice.

The two elementors had already extinguished half the fire with a tandem assault of strategically manipulated vacuum bubbles and jets of water condensed from moisture in the air. The fire brigade added their own streams of water, dousing the flames that had just spread to another building.

"But," I continued, "all evidence pointing to the mastermind of this operation has probably just gone up in smoke. Whoever that man was, he has knowledge, power, resources, and a fanatical devotion to a sadly misguided ideology." I drew a deep breath, tasting the burnt ash in the air. "What scares me the most is that I can almost agree with his intentions. *Almost.* These artifacts should not be in private hands, but their methods and motives for securing them are entirely reprehensible."

My apprentice nodded, seeming to understand. "A vigilante," he said. "And a ruthless one at that."

No, not a vigilante... A *fanatic.* But I let the colorful appellation stand. Another vehicle rolled into the yard and came to a stop, this one more like an armored steam tractor when compared to the fire brigade's clumsy wagons. Brandishing a distinctive sword and shield emblem on its side, it proclaimed the arrival of a Vandorian HAAMR unit. Another ornithopter buzzed overhead, and the airship *Justiciar* turned sharply southward, keeping well away from the ballooning column of smoke and steam.

I looked away from the scene and gave Keldon a reassuring pat on the shoulder. "Save for a monstrous share of the paperwork, our part in this is finished. No doubt we will again encounter whoever orchestrated this plot, and on that day, I will gladly convey the bounty of justice he is due."

Case File 7:

A Pfenny For Your Thoughts

DOLDEN GRESSON WAS INNOCENT. His face flushed with fear and sweat glistening on his brow, the well-dressed talent manager had the very countenance of a man trapped like an animal in a cage. Looking into his glazed and searching eyes, I saw a man wishing he could wake from the nightmare that had brought his entire world crashing down. His was not the face of a calculating criminal or a villainous sorcerer caught at his own game, but that of a broken man resigned to the fate that cruel injustice now condemned him.

Two Vandorian patrol automatons led Gresson down the short walk from his office to the armored wagon where a gathering crowd awaited. Chief Inspector Tibblemond and Detective Eucas Pfennigus followed just behind the slouching figure. Passing by where I stood, I heard poor Gresson mutter, "I didn't kill her… I didn't. I did everything I could to help her. She just lost her will to live." His mutterings cut off as Pfennigus pushed him into the armored wagon and slammed the door shut.

"Detective Pfennigus," cried reporters from every tabloid and circular that littered the gas-lit streets of Corradon. The crowd pressed forward, swarming the wagon in a sea of hats, pens, pads, and the bumping horns of newfangled phonographic recorders.

"How did you discover her manager was behind it?" asked one reporter pushing through. "Have you confirmed her death was not a suicide?" yelled another. "Is it true she was cursed, as she claimed before she died?" a third reporter inquired.

"We don't have time for questions," Tibblemond replied, his voice muffled under the chattering deluge. "Briefings will be tubed to all papers and presses by this evening."

But Pfennigus stepped around the patrol automatons and held up a hand, broadening his self-sure smile to a boastful grin. "This case is all but closed, inspector, and surely the people have a right to know." The young freelance detective brushed a hand across his side-swept hair, then dusted some imagined smudge from his smart tailcoat before adjusting his bright blue cravat. "It is without dispute that the beloved Marion Melodor, perhaps the single most famed singer our fair city has ever known, took her own life after tragically losing her singing voice. But it is the how and the why that any good detective must ask when facing such a mysterious affair."

Tibblemond sighed, but made no move to stop the brash upstart. The crowd silenced, and Eucas Pfennigus turned to address the reporters, the only sound the scribbling of pens and the tick-tock turning of wax cylinders recording. Spotting me he smiled again—a mocking smirk filled as much with arrogance as bile.

I folded my arms over my frock coat, drawing a breath as I listened to his dramatic account of the crime.

"Yes, Marion Melodor committed suicide, but she was driven into despair by the swindling villain who managed her illustrious career—Dolden Gresson! It was Mister Gresson who arranged her kidnapping, and it was Mister Gresson who employed a sell-spell sorcerer to bind her singing voice and implant a psychic block to suppress her talents."

Keldon shook his head in disbelief. My apprentice was experienced enough in both the aetheric arts and the investigative sciences to see how ridiculous Pfennigus's statement was. The facts of the case were already known to us, and the facts refuted every word he had spoken. Dolden Gresson had nothing to do with the loss of Marion Melodor's voice, for Gresson's agency had been financially ruined by the sudden fall of her career.

Moreover, Mister Gresson himself had no alibi to account for his whereabouts on the night of Miss Melodor's kidnapping. While that certainly lent credence to the allegations, if Mister Gresson was indeed the criminal mastermind Pfennigus made him out to be, he would have done everything in his power to ensure an ironclad alibi. But most telling of all was Pfennigus's utter disregard for the many similar cases that had plagued the Clockwork City over the past few months. Marion Melodor was not the first individual of extraordinary ability to lose her talents, nor, I feared, would she be the last.

A flurry of questions followed, but Pfennigus silenced the reporters with another upraised hand. It was then that I caught sight of the coin held between his fingers—a coin that he rolled from one finger to another with a strangely familiar ease.

"I am no mage," Pfennigus said, his eyes fixed on mine, "and I claim no special power of supernatural apprehension. It is only by the pure means of the science of deduction that I have unraveled this most heinous crime. Although Gresson's agency has declared itself insolvent, Mister Gresson himself received a handsome sum from the underwriters who had insured Marion Melodor's voice on a 10,000-guild policy. Yet, Gresson's agency provided Miss Melodor with only a marginal stipend in the weeks following her disability. With her career ruined, and her every pfenny spent seeking aid from shamans and charlatans alike, Miss Melodor fell into a deep depression and ultimately partook of the poison that ended her life. Having committed the perfect crime, Mister Gresson would have no doubt retired to some tropical shore of the south Medrean, had I not offered my humble services as a freelance detective to Vandor Tower."

Applause erupted from the gathered crowd of reporters and curious onlookers, and Pfennigus even had the gall to bow. A jumble of fresh questions babbled from the reporters in an incoherent din, but Pfennigus and Tibblemond strode for a steam-carriage parked just in front of the armored wagon.

"Inspector Tibblemond," I called, slipping past a young lady from the *Corradon Daily Post.* I offered her a quick apology and tipped my felt top hat, then proceeded to ignore her narrow-eyed glare. "May I have a word with you concerning this case?"

The chief inspector turned from the carriage, scratching his scruffy muttonchops as he considered what to say. "Ah, Vescard... It's good to see you again, but this is hardly the place to discuss such matters."

He was right, but my questions couldn't wait. The suicide of Marion Melodor had captured the public eye, and with Pfennigus flatly proclaiming her manager's guilt to the scandal-hungry press, the outcome was more disastrous than a bulgore in a porcelain shop. "The evidence in this case is far from conclusive," I began to say, lowering my voice to just below the babbling din. "Where is the evidence for the underwriter's policy? Who was the sorcerer hired to kidnap Miss Melodor? How is this connected to the other similar cases springing up around the city?"

Tibblemond removed his bowler and drummed his fingers on the rim. "I'm sorry Vescard, but I believe Detective Pfennigus has this case well in hand." He cleared his throat, then lowered his voice as he cast a nervous glance at the severite bands clasped to my wrists. "I know you're the best detective we have on retainer, but the Commissioner General wants a less notorious figure to head such a high-profile case. There are some who still regard your curse as evidence of your dubious past endeavors."

I was about to reply to my longtime associate when Pfennigus forced his way by, his voice a whisper as his eyes locked with mine. "Perhaps you were once the greatest detective this city has known, Aldicus Vescard, but what is that to a true virtuoso of all sciences?"

My breath caught as a surge of boiling sulfur stabbed through my veins. The sensation passed as quickly as it had come, thanks to the dampening effect of my severite wristbands, and I schooled my face to maintain an impassive composure.

"You, sir," I whispered back, my voice hushed and straining, "are a charlatan and a fraud."

"There's no need to be jealous, Vescard," Tibblemond said as he and Pfennigus stepped up to the steam-carriage. He plopped his bowler back on and pushed his ample form aboard, motioning for the driver to get underway. "I will contact you as soon as another case comes up requiring your uniquely qualified perspective. Until then, good day."

The steam-carriage door shut and the driver released the brake, taking the tiller as the vehicle chugged into motion. The armored wagon lurched after Tibblemond's carriage, its heavy iron wheels clattering on the cobblestone boulevard. Both were followed by a third wagon carrying the Guardsmen and patrol automatons. The crowd of reporters chased after the convoy for nearly a block, their chattering flood of frivolous questions fading to a merciful murmur. Overhead, the Vandorian airship *Justiciar* turned southward, rising high above the district's forest of lofty spires and clock-topped towers, trailed by two patrol thopters buzzing overhead. So much effort and manpower for such a poorly justified raid.

I stuffed my hands into the pockets of my frock coat and drew a breath of the city's oil-spritzed air. "Fetch a coach, Keldon, as fast a one as you can find."

"Right away, boss." Keldon started off, then turned back with a worried look. "Where are we going?"

“To Vandor Tower,” I replied. “I’m afraid we’re about to conduct a most unauthorized autopsy.”

THE BRAIN OF MARION MELODOR held none of the elegant beauty for which her enchanting voice was famed. The forensic preservation empowerment had kept the body and its organs relatively fresh since the time of her death, which meant the localized hemorrhaging I observed along the prefrontal cortex and lower cerebellum had been present at the time of her death. The hemorrhaging did not appear to be recent, being evident only in the tiny dark specks distributed across the affected regions, and had most likely occurred two months ago when she lost her ability to sing. But was the hemorrhaging the cause of her affliction or was it a symptom of something more sinister?

“I’m only picking up the preservation spell,” Keldon said, passing his large brass key above the body of the victim. Sigils shimmered down the length of the talisman, then blinked out when he released his concentration. “There is no aetheric imprint from any other empowerments. But if she was cursed two months ago, any traces of it would have dissipated by now.”

I nodded, jotting down the observations in my notebook. “I do not believe any sort of empowerment could have done this. The hemorrhaging may be evidence of a telepathic mind-burn, which would mean our culprit is a psychurgist, not a sorcerer.” I gently capped the cobalt nib of my Swanné Signature pen and tucked the implement back into my coat’s inner pocket. Although not the most valuable pen in my collection, it was the most comfortable in my hand. Unfortunately, Mister Swanné had recently been committed to Grimhall Asylum, so it was unlikely I would ever enjoy another of its like again. “It could also mean she simply experienced a stroke. Either way, we need to know. An innocent man is sitting in jail right now.”

“Well, I sure hope you’re right,” Keldon said, shaking his

head. "We could get fired for this, you know?"

"I know," I admitted.

Performing an illegal autopsy could easily end my career as a freelance detective, and it put Keldon's future prospects at risk as well. But it was a risk I had to take. Pfennigus had come to his conclusion without ordering an autopsy, which was a gross oversight by my estimation. He had no physical proof to back up his assertion. No proof, whatsoever.

A relative newcomer, Eucas Pfennigus had joined Vandor Tower as a freelance detective just three months ago. In that time he had solved three perplexing murder cases, unraveled two cold cases, and brought a happy ending to a kidnapping and ransom case that might otherwise have turned tragic. He was a pretentious dandy so full of himself that calling him an arrogant egomaniac only understated the obvious. Yet, his criminal insight and talent for deduction were genuine. The investigative methods he employed were not unlike those of the late Pergus Controise, of whom I had once been a pupil, and I wondered if perhaps he, too, had studied under the old master before he died. Nevertheless, his findings in this most recent case were negligent in almost every respect.

But something else about Pfennigus bothered me. Although he had shown himself to be a master detective, he also performed piano concerts, had authored a book on natural philosophy, was a knowledgeable art critic, and had recently patented an innovative alchemical osmosis precipitator. In short, he was a man too extraordinary to be believed.

"Aldicus, your experiment," my apprentice reminded.

I returned to the laboratory's workbench and glanced over the cluttered collection of retorts, belly flasks, alembic stills, and condenser coils, all bubbling and hissing as they digested a sample of Marion Melodor's cerebral fluid. The four receiving flasks at the end of the process held only thimblefuls of murky white liquid, but it would be enough. Using a pipette, I extracted a single drop from each flask and placed them on separate chromagraph plates. If her cerebral fluid were normal, there would only be a slight yellow tinge to each of the plates. But what I saw caused my breath to draw short.

Bleeding into view on each of the plates were colorful patterns of overlapping circles, interwoven lines, and a dense speckling of tiny colored dots. The patterns on each of the plates were different, for each showed only a small portion of a more complex pattern. Although it was impossible to reconstruct precisely what composed the contaminant, I understood its staggering implication.

"There is no doubt," I said. "Her brain has been tainted by a psychoactive alchemical elixir of stupendous complexity. Whatever kind of elixir this was, its formulation is an order of magnitude beyond even the most advanced dream potions yet conceived." I shook my head, pondering the possibilities. "Why would anyone go to such lengths to suppress a famous singer's talents? It's completely absurd. We must be missing something."

"Vescard!" boomed a voice from the hallway door.

I turned and saw Tibblemond standing in the doorway, his muttonchops sagging as his frown deepened to a glower.

"Fangle-fop," I muttered.

"The coroner said you were slinking around the morgue, but I couldn't believe it." The chief inspector opened his mouth to continue, but his eyes widened with horror at the sight of Marion Melodor's corpse, her brain resting in a tray on the autopsy table just above her hollowed out skull. "By the Archons! What have you done?"

I rubbed my hands together and drew a deep breath. "Good timing, inspector. I was about to send for you. I have taken the liberty of performing my own analysis on Miss Melodor's brain and cerebral fluids, and have discovered a most—"

"The case is closed," Tibblemond remanded. "We already have the culprit in hand!"

I held up a finger, then pointed to the chromagraph plates on the table. "The results of my analysis contradict Pfennigus's own conclusions. It is my belief that an alchemist, not a sorcerer, performed—"

The chief inspector huffed, folding his arms and shaking his head. "Bodgefuddle! You have no authority to perform an autopsy, so whatever you have discovered will be completely inadmissible in court. It astonishes me that your impetuous rivalry with Detective Pfennigus would descend this low. You ought to be ashamed of yourself. Now, get out of Vandor Tower before I call the jacks to throw you out!"

I sighed, motioning for Keldon to bring my coat and hat. It seemed I was the old wolf and Pfennigus was the new. Yet, it was not professional jealousy that I felt, but rather, a deep-seated concern, gnawing in the pit of my stomach. Pfennigus's charming personality and celebrity status had seduced most of Vandor Tower, Tibblemond included. Tibblemond and I were long-time colleagues, and whatever jealousy I felt came from the pained realization that I was, day-by-day, losing a friend.

"I had hoped that you might be more open to considering the evidence I have uncovered." I pulled my frock coat on and donned my top hat with a flourish. "If you could spare a moment to hear me out, I'm sure—"

But Tibblemond cut me off, gesturing at Miss Melodor's exenterated brain. "I don't know how I'm going to explain this to the Commissioner General, but I'll think of something. I have half a mind to bring you up on charges, but fortunately for you, I'm in a bit of a hurry. I was just on my way to meet Detective Pfennigus for our interview with Selus Oberus, who, as I'm sure you know, was burned out of his magical abilities by some demented enemy of his."

I raised an eyebrow. "There have been at least a dozen cases of inexplicable ability loss over the past three months. Do you not think there could be a connection?"

"Detective Pfennigus is following up for that very reason."

With that, the chief inspector gestured to the door. "Now, collect your things and make a peaceable departure. If you're lucky, I might be able to back-date an autopsy authorization form. If not, then perhaps you'll only be suspended for a few months."

I tipped my top hat to Tibblemond and hurried out of the morgue, my apprentice in tow.

"What now?" Keldon asked once we got to the street and hailed a coach. "I know you're not giving up. You have that look on your face."

I thought for a moment, trying to recall Selus Oberus's address. I didn't know it, but I did know he lived in the 3rd District, somewhere on Habercroft Boulevard. I told the coachman to take us there, then joined Keldon on the seat.

"What look on my face?" I asked as the coach puttered forward.

Keldon shrugged. "You know, the one that says, 'I'm not giving up.'"

I smiled. "Whether he knows it or not, Tibblemond just handed us a critical clue. Right now, Eucas Pfennigus is on his way to visit Selus Oberus, likely to see if his loss of ability is in some way related to the case of Marion Melodor."

Keldon narrowed his eyes in confusion. "But Pfennigus has accused Marion Melodor's manager of hiring a sorcerer to lay a curse on her. What would that have to do with a mage being burned out of his quintessence?"

"On the face of it, they appear to be completely unrelated," I admitted. "Yet, it is no coincidence that Pfennigus has investigated several other, similar cases of ability loss that have popped up around the city. Selus Oberus is another such case. The fact that Pfennigus has already made an arrest and filed his conclusions for the Melodor case is quite disturbing. He is either a fool or a fraud, or more likely, both."

I sighed, sinking back on the seat as I thought. There had been at least a dozen reported cases of mysterious ability loss over the past three months. Many more had likely never even been reported to the police or Vandor Tower, or if they were, no one ever followed up on them since no obvious crime was involved. The only common thread that I could see was that most of the victims were either exceptionally talented or prominent in their field.

But that only made the case with Selus Oberus all the more mysterious. Selus Oberus was neither a powerful nor noteworthy mage, serving as a clerical administrator in the bureaucratic bowels of the Magestrian Order. I had worked with him some years ago during my apprenticeship at the Armillian Institute of Judicial Magery, but last I heard he had gone abroad seeking better fortunes. Now he had returned, stripped of his abilities like so many others.

The steam-coach soon reached the ivy-crept terraces of the affluent 3rd District, and I kept my eye out for Oberus's house when we turned onto Habercroft Boulevard. Spotting his well-manicured terrace villa, I instructed the coachman to stop. Warm light flickered from between the brightly painted shutter slats, and the jingling tunes of a harpsichord issued from somewhere inside.

We made our way to the house and I tapped the knocker twice. "Oberus, it's your old acquaintance, Aldicus."

The harpsichord stopped. "Aldicus?" came a muffled reply. "Aldicus Vescard?" The latch drew and the door creaked open, revealing a balding man with a neatly trimmed goatee. He pressed his spectacles to the crest of his nose and gave an appreciative nod. "Ah, have you come to commiserate with a fellow debilitated mage?"

Sweeping off my top hat, I gestured for Keldon to precede me into the house. "My disability is entirely self-imposed," I said, following my old friend from the lamp-lit foyer to his cluttered drawing room. "Without these severite wristbands, I would undergo a most uncomfortable alchemical metamorph—"

I froze. Eucas Pfennigus stood up from an armchair near a darkened fireplace, a silver coin rolling between the fingers of his hand. He crooked a smile, then pocketed the coin and casually brushed out the wrinkles in his tailcoat. "Aldicus Vescard. You are not privy to this investigation."

"Oberus is an old friend," I said, "and I recently received word of his unfortunate affliction. If I had known you were here..." I shrugged, letting my words trail off.

"Aldicus is always welcome in my home," Oberus stated. He hurried to the fireplace and began prodding the coals with a rusty poker. "Blasted flames! Why won't they keep up? Once I could have lit this with a snap and a flick."

Keldon's shoulders slumped and he gave me a disheartened glance. It was not Pfennigus that troubled my apprentice, but his right concern for my ill-fortuned friend. Selus Oberus had been a mage, and to see him in such a helpless dither chilled me more than the bitter breath of the deepest winter night.

"Renew the fire," I bade him. Keldon nodded, then moved to help Oberus at the fireplace. With the most amiable face I could muster, I then turned my gaze upon my rival. "Fear not, Detective Pfennigus, I am not here to assume the case you are investigating. I merely wish to comfort my friend and reminisce of the days before his powers were so cruelly stolen."

I saw a twitch on Pfennigus's face, and his back stiffened with resolve. "He was cursed," the detective corrected, "quite possibly by the very same sorcerer that Miss Melador's manager hired. That is, of course, why I am here."

Keldon drew his talisman and, after a few sputtering sparks, struck a modest aetheric dart into the fireplace. The logs erupted in a blaze of crackling blue flames and shortly defused to the warm red tongues of enkindled firewood.

"Keep practicing, my boy, and you'll get the hang of it," Oberus said, slapping Keldon on the shoulder. "A fine apprentice you have, Aldicus. Although he is a bit young for blasting aethergy bolts."

Keldon smiled weakly. "I sense you still have some latent

aetheric quintessence, sir. Are you saying you can no longer compose empowerments?"

Oberus nodded. "That is what I was told by the healer who first tried to treat my condition. I retain every bit of my aetheric quintessence, for that is as much a part of me as my nose. By all rights, I should still be able to compose empowerments, but whenever I try, I find I have completely forgotten how!"

I crossed my arms and glanced at Pfennigus. The detective had begun flipping the coin between his fingers again—a nervous tell, to be sure. Then it struck me as to why his coin trick seemed so familiar: it was the habit of Pergus Controise, the same great detective whom Pfennigus's own methods seemed to parody.

"Just magery?" I asked, turning back to Oberus. I drew a pen and notepad from my coat pocket and jotted down the details. "Are you sure that's all? You have experienced no other inexplicable mental or physical disabilities?"

Pfennigus frowned at me, but said nothing.

"Well, I am getting up in my years, so there's the usual forgetfulness and physical decline," Oberus admitted. "But I still know a great deal about other subjects, from history to literature to how best to bluff you at jonko." He nodded to the harpsichord filling one corner of the sitting room. "And as you can see, I've even taken up a new hobby to while away the time in my forced retirement."

I looked to the harpsichord and nodded. From the case summaries I had read, the sudden loss of oddly specific abilities that had struck Oberus and Marion Melodor were but two examples in a four-month rash of inexplicable debilitations. Surgeons who could no longer operate, accountants who could no longer count, swordsmen who could no longer fence, and gearmeisters who could no longer build. Oberus was not the first victim who was a mage, either. A conjurer and a disruptor mage had both turned up with similar afflictions, but Oberus's humble proficiency was minor compared to theirs.

"Do you recall anything about *how* you lost your abilities?" I asked Oberus. "Or did you just wake up one morning, unable to perform magery?"

Oberus opened his mouth to answer, but it was Pfennigus who replied. "Detective Vescard, this is not your investigation, and I have already troubled Mister Oberus with enough of these questions. But if you must know, he does have about half a day's amnesia preceding his ability loss. It is the same for the other subjects, but you would already know that if you were privy to the reports." Pfennigus continued flipping the coin between his fingers as he spoke, and his face turned up in a knowing grin. "This sorcerer, whoever he is, is a crafty villain indeed."

I nodded and smiled back, suppressing the urge to glower. Was Pfennigus truly this incompetent, or was he actively working to conceal the most critical details of these crimes? More worrisome still, why were his methods and mannerisms so similar to those of the great Pergus Controise? If he had studied under Controise, then incompetence was not a factor.

I was about to ask Pfennigus if he knew Controise, hoping to unsettle him with the question, when he abruptly shoved the coin into his pocket. He had noticed that I had noticed, and I was glad I had not asked. If Pfennigus possessed even a fraction of Controise's deductive abilities, then even the most oblique question would alert him to my suspicions.

"Detective Pfennigus," I said, forcing a courteous smile. "I know you will do everything you can to track down this vile sorcerer, but if you find you need a fresh set of eyes, my services are at your disposal."

Pfennigus stiffened, then he tilted his head and flashed a smile as clearly fake as my own.

Turning to Oberus, I took my old friend's hand in a cordial shake. "Be well, my friend. I'll leave you in the capable hands of my esteemed colleague. We should get together soon for a few drinks and a round of jonko, just like old times at the Broken Spigot."

He nodded in somber agreement, then showed us to the door and bid a melancholy farewell.

From around the corner down the street, I watched Tibblemond's carriage arrive just minutes after our departure. Would Pfennigus tell the chief inspector of our visit? Would Oberus? I added these last questions to my notes, then put the notepad away and capped my pen. I studied the pen for a moment—my Swanné Signature pen—and drew a sharp breath.

Swanné... *Of course!*

I nodded to Keldon and we hastened back to our own coach waiting half a block farther down.

THE DISPLAY CASE ABOVE MY MANTLE held forty-seven pens of exquisite elegance, design, and artistry, and twelve of them were Swanné Signature pens. In the whole of his thirty-eight years as an artisan penmaker, Elmeire Swanné had produced only twelve distinct designs, issuing a new design every four years with anywhere from fifty to one hundred individually inscribed and numbered pens. Having been committed to Grimhall Asylum just last month due to an intractable case of severe cortical dementia, according to *Branweir's Medical Journal*, there seemed little chance of there ever being a thirteenth Swanné design. It thus came as a considerable surprise that I now held in my hand not one, but *two*, brand new Swanné Signature pens.

"Counterfeits?" I asked Rognar, letting more than a hint of incredulity slip through.

The stocky Dworgh shook his head, swaying the straps of his floppy leather cap. "Oh, it's genuine, all right." He stroked his braided beard, then chuckled. "Swanné's old apprentice took over after he went mad. And I do mean Aban Olengier. You know, the one he gave the boot to for being a bungling fool? He's not only crafting these new pens now, but making reissues of the older ones. Fifty ducats each, if you can believe it! But there's no rush paying me back. I know you're good for it. Plus my usual fee, of course."

Rognar was one of my more trusted informants, which was not really saying much since all the others were so grossly untrustworthy. But Rognar was different. More than merely an informant, he was also a professional acquisitioner and a skilled artificer in his own right. After all, Rognar had furnished many of my more unique laboratory contrivances and newfangled devices, and he had even designed the pneumatic tranquilizer gun Keldon kept for when the monster inside me came out to play.

"Reissues?" I demanded. "Fangle-fop! These pens are collectable only because of their rarity."

"Wait," Keldon said, closing his copy of Jan Arlengel's *Elements of Conjury*. "Didn't you tell me those pens were worth a small fortune? Why would he be selling them for just fifty ducats, not that I could even buy the end cap at that price?"

"Quantity," I replied. I took a magnifying monocle from the table and inspected the intricate gilded etchings of one of the pen's cobalt nibs. The etchings were an authentic Swanné style, with their elegant lattice work of interlocking knots matching to the most minute detail. "Aban Olengier is not an artisan, he's an opportunist. But he does have an artisan's skill, otherwise he would not have the talent to handcraft authentic Swannés. The paradox is that Aban Olengier was not a good apprentice. Swanné dismissed him for good reason." I placed the pens on the mantle and folded my hands behind my back. "Thank you, Rognar. I had hoped I was wrong, but this only confirms my most troubling suspicions."

Keldon tightened his lips in thought. "You mean that someone is stealing other people's talents?"

"No," I replied. "That desperate fools are buying them."

Keldon and Rognar both blinked.

"Consider the evidence," I continued. "For the past few months, mysterious cases of skill and memory loss have been on the rise—Marion Melodor's lost talent, Selus Oberus's mysterious debilitation, and the abrupt onset of dementia that resigned Elmeire Swanné to Grimhall Asylum. There are surgeons, swordsmen, mages, and gearmeisters who have all been similarly afflicted. Yet, none have been able to recall what happened, other than waking in some strange alley or sublevel tunnel. It is even possible that the great detective Pergus Controise fell victim just before he died. At the same time, other individuals with no connection to the victims, or even to each other, have displayed a remarkable development of new talents: Swanné's formerly inept apprentice and our own self-proclaimed virtuoso, Eucas Pfennigus. There are certainly others as well, but it would be both foolish and erroneous to assume every neophyte savant is complicit in these crimes."

Rognar snapped his fingers. "There's a new street doc in the 14th District Underworks who's said to be a miracle man, and the dancers in a few of the joints I frequent have suddenly got real talent. There's even a singer who makes a fair imitation of Miss Melodor!"

Keldon's eyebrows lifted. "Don't tell me we're on the trail of another Maradian artifact like the one mad Marelle used to empower his automatons."

I shook my head. "If I'm correct, our culprit is using an alchemically powered device, unlike that old soul-sucking machine. But it could be of Maradian origin."

From my sitting room's bookcase, I selected a leather-bound copy of *The Last Cataclysm* and flipped to one of the many bookmarked pages. What little was known of the War of Golla and Marada was veiled in legend, obscured all the more so by the ravages of that brutish dark age that followed its cataclysmic culmination. But fables always held some glimmer of truth.

I began reading, quoting from the page for Keldon's

benefit. "'Regardless of whether the sorcerers of Marada or the demons of Golla devised the abominable practice, mind-leaching was widely employed by agents of both this world and Atracus in the final decade of the War. While the technique is thankfully lost, accounts attest that mind-leaching was used not only to extract knowledge, but also to transfer valuable talents and abilities.'" I nodded, skimming over the rest of the text. "It goes on to explain that mind-leaching was an alchemical process, distilling mnemonic patterns in the brain into soluble extracts. There is also a description of a side effect called bleed-over, in which the individual who consumed the extract exhibits various tendencies, habits, or mannerisms of the victim."

Keldon shook his head in disbelief. "Mind-leaching..."

I closed the book, then rubbed my chin as I considered our next step. "There is the small matter of tangible evidence. Although we may suspect Detective Pfennigus, Aban Olengier, and others, they are not the criminals we are after. If we are to have any hope of locating the actual culprits behind this nefarious scheme, we must backtrack any suspicious money exchanges made by these individuals. As my mentor, Pergus Controise, often said, 'Follow the funds and you'll find the felons.'"

Rognar folded his arms and smiled through his beard. "Already ahead of you, boss. Word is, Aban Olengier's in a barrel of pickles over what he owes some rather bronzy duffers. I'd say he's selling those pens at bargain prices just to meet his extorter's demands. They come by his shop every other night around nine, and last time they left none too pleased."

I glanced at the brass clock above my cluttered writing bureau. "Nine o'clock. Keldon, grab your things. We have a shop to reconnoiter."

"Mind if I join you?" Rognar asked. The Dworgh patted a bulge on the left side of his buckled duffle coat, and his smile broadened to a grin. "Varla here tells me you might be needing her special brand of diplomacy this fine evening."

I grabbed my coat and hat from the coat rack and started for the door. "I wouldn't have it any other way, my streetwise friend. Just try not to demolish the neighborhood if things get out of hand."

THE THREE BRUISERS WERE ANYTHING BUT SUBTLE. They pulled into the alley behind Swanné's shop in a clattering steam-coach, then bulled their way through the back door with cudgels and saps. One of the men was either a half-ogre or was a grotesquely muscled man with severe dental abnormalities. His two fellow ruffians were almost as ugly. A fourth man, the driver, was the only one who seemed even marginally presentable, and he wore a drab sack suit and grimy bowler. His coat hung open and he slipped his right hand beneath his opposite lapel, where he no doubt concealed a pistol or blasting rod.

Rognar leaned around the corner of the building where we had parked, adjusting the knobs and lenses of his elaborate clockwork goggles. "Are you seeing this?"

"Of course, we are," I replied from where we sat, still inside the locomobile's passenger cab, "and in much greater detail I'd wager."

Rognar pushed his goggles over the brim of his leather cap and frowned at the shimmering sphere floating just above Keldon's talismanic key. The conjured image showed the scene in the unlit alley, distorted as though looking through water, but much nearer and with the light greatly amplified. It was a simple optical trick, channeling light through a compressed aetheric tunnel from one point to another, and considerably less elaborate than an all-seeing-eye or reconnaissance egregore. It was easy to detect, of course, but not by these goons.

"Faugh!" the Dworgh grunted. He put his goggles back over his eyes and resumed his own surveillance effort.

The three goons returned a moment later, shoving a

stumbling man ahead of them out the door and into the darkened alleyway. The man was frantic, his mouth working as he pleaded with the driver atop the coach. Based on the fact that he wore a smock and eye loupe, it was a good guess that he was Swanné's former apprentice, Aban Olengier.

"Keldon, some sound if you would," I said.

Keldon drew a breath and closed his eyes, focusing on the tenuous threads of his espial conjuration.

"...little more time and you'll have the money," came Aban's voice, cavernous and distorted though it was. "I swear!"

"Ye had yer time," the goon's driver growled. He drew a caplock pistol and motioned Aban to the back of the coach. Aban hesitated, and the burly half-ogre took him by the scruff of the neck and shoved him through the door. "But don't worry—we ain't gonna kill ye, see? Boss just wants to take back the goods, with interest. If ye're lucky, ye might even learn how to read and write again. Eventually." He chuckled and the other men laughed. Then they were off in their rumbling coach, the suit at the driver's tiller and the others in the back with their captive.

"Benson," I said to the man sitting at the front of our own vehicle. "Can you follow that steam-coach, keeping well behind?"

"I could follow one a'them 'fernal machines with just me nose, detective," Benson replied with a tip of his hat.

Rognar returned to the passenger cab, joining Keldon on the seat across from me. We settled back as the locomobile started forward, its alchemical battery humming quietly as rubber-padded wheels eased along the cobblestones. The fare for a newfangled alchemically powered cabriolet such as this was nearly twice that of a comparable steam-coach, but the ride was far more comfortable and the engine unquestionably quieter. I would have gladly paid the toll twice over, for tonight stealth was our greatest ally.

I sat back, watching the lamp-lit streets of the Clockwork

City roll by. The polished brass and gleaming glass of the 5th District's upscale storefronts soon gave way to the grease and grime of the industrial 14th. We eased down several narrow sublevel tunnels, then followed a corridor beneath the pipe-tangled underpass of some foul-smelling manufactory. I grew increasingly concerned that our quarry might vanish through some darkened passageway into the Underworks—for we would surely lose them in that haunted labyrinth of desolate tunnels and deserted habitations. Thankfully, our locomobile drew to a stop before descending further into the darkened underpass.

"We've arrived, detective, sir," Benson called from the front. "The clanker pulled into that old foundry over there."

I climbed out, impressed that Benson had stopped at such an inconspicuous location. The red light of Atracus spilled across the fog-veiled scrapyard of the abandoned ironworks across the street. Despite its derelict condition, warm light shown from the lower windows of the rusting facility, and a thread of smoke snaked from one of its towering chimneys.

"Good work," I said, handing Benson three ducats.

Benson touched the brim of his hat. "And thank you, sir. I'll be right sure to frequent your street more often."

Keldon grabbed the tranquilizer gun from beneath the seat, Rognar buckled up his duffle coat, and I pulled my frock coat tight as we hustled across the lonesome square to an alley on the other side. There were two entrances from what I could see: one was the loading dock where the steam-coach had parked, and the other was a lobby outside of which another carriage and its driver waited for his passenger's return.

After a few minutes, a gentleman strolled from the lobby, stopping to adjust his scarf and top hat before climbing into the carriage. Despite appearances, no legitimate business would set up shop in this less-than-licit precinct. And yet, through the still open door I could see a reception desk and small waiting area, complete with ornamented fixtures and plush sofas. It was a troubling juxtaposition, but not nearly so troubling as the well-to-do quality of their apparent clientele.

Keldon hung the tranq gun over his shoulder by its strap, then tapped his key to the side of his head. "Shall I take a peek?"

I shook my head. "We cannot chance it. A place like that could easily have scrying wards or watchdog egregores. But Rognar," I added, turning to the Dworgh, "it would be most helpful if you could introduce yourself to the receptionist, rambling on about your need for one obscure talent or another."

Rognar harrumphed and patted the sides of his well-traveled duffle coat. "They'd throw me right out, judging from the look of that dandy-fop who just left."

"Excellent. Do whatever you can to stir up trouble."

A wide grin spread beneath the Dworgh's braided beard. "Of that, I'll be happy to oblige!"

I motioned for Keldon to follow me as Rognar made for the lobby entrance. We rounded the east corner of the building, crouching low against the crumbling brick wall as we approached the loading dock.

"I must ask you to leave, sir," came the muted voice of the lobby receptionist from a window near the building's front entrance.

"Leave?" Rognar bellowed. "This is the place selling talents, isn't it? Surely, you've got something for an old Dworgh who just wants to live out his fancy as a fire-juggling, cross-dressing burlesque dancer. You may laugh, but I've always—"

"Whoever told you this, they are mistaken. If you do not have an appointment, then I will call for the guards."

"You have no appreciation for the arts! Why, my great-grandfather..." Rognar continued on, but his voice faded as we moved out of earshot.

I stopped just short of the loading dock entrance and motioned for Keldon to come up beside me. A single bruiser stood inside, pacing a fabricrete platform between the steam-coach and a rusting rear door. He carried a longarm, but in the dim crimson light I could not discern if it was a caplock, a pneumatic, or a clockwork automatic.

"Tranq gun," I whispered to my anxious apprentice.

Keldon caught his breath, but I gave him a reassuring nod. He readied the weapon, then switched the dart out for the least potent one. We didn't want to kill the man, after all—just incapacitate him. "Here goes," he sighed, and flipped the switch to prime the compression valve.

Keldon fired, and the pacing goon jumped with a start. His left hand flew to the dart jutting from his side, then he groaned, staggered, and stumbled to the ground.

Hoping Rognar's antics had drawn the attention of any other bruisers inside, I dashed up the steps to the loading dock platform. The back door proved to be unlocked, but I cringed as its corroded hinges squealed in piercing protest. Glancing inside, I saw a dingy hall of half-rotted floorboards and peeling paint, which ended in a rich oak door, starkly out of place in the dilapidated interior. Situated near the front of the building, the elegant door likely led to the upscale lobby and whatever consultation rooms these criminals provided for their wealthy clientele.

"Unhand me, you brutes!" came Rognar's muffled protest from behind the oak door. "A Dworgh's got a right to follow his dreams no matter how short he is!"

Knowing my quick-witted friend had the diversion well in hand, I motioned for Keldon to follow and started down the opposite way. The corridor led past several other rooms, these haphazardly stocked with bottles, beakers, and vials of innumerable sizes and colors. The pungent stench of potent alchemical compounds wafted from what was likely a laboratory further on.

We headed straight for the lab, making our way down a

worn set of stairs to a crumbling brick archway, but Keldon stopped to pick up a small card from the floor. "Have a look at this."

I took the card and frowned at its glossy header and neatly printed type. "'Any knowledge, any talent, any profession that you can dream,'" I read from the top. Then I scanned the list below, reading it like some vulgar tavern menu. "'Mnemonic extracts available now. Artistry, musical talent, jonko mastery, politics, law, physician, fencing, boxing, analytical engineering, gearmeistery, alchemistry, thaumatology...'" And the list went on. Beside each extract was a price, each appallingly high. Five hundred guilds was the lowest on the list—a year's wage for a craftsman of excellent repute. My stomach turned with sickening disgust and the beast in my blood burned with sulfurous fury.

I tossed the card aside. "Behold the luxury of conceit, for those of privilege and wealth shall build their empires upon the blood and toil of all who labor true."

Keldon's eyes widened and he looked to a place beyond the reach of my severite dampened senses. "Egregores," he hissed. "We've been detected!"

A warbling alarm sounded through the air, echoing from the unseen watchers warding the heart of this iniquitous enterprise. "Fangle-fop," I muttered under my breath. Our time was up and our ploy was made. With reckless haste, I dashed into a grim chamber that seemed more dungeon than laboratory.

The nocturnal fires of Atracus spilled through the clerestory windows above, commingling with the sallow glow of gas lamps to reveal a stark fabricrete room stacked with shipping materials and shelving. One other door led out of the room, but I gave it only a passing glance. In the center of the room sat Aban Olengier in a metal restraining chair, convulsing and shivering with eyes wide in terror. A tangle of tubes and needles protruded from his head, each one leading to a whirring, churning clockwork apparatus of gurgling pipes, bubbling bottles, and oscillating coils, crowned by three spinning orbs pulsing with currents of galvanic aethergy.

Of course, our most immediate concern was the dapper young man standing in the back of the room, sneering as he flipped a silver coin between his fingers. Eucas Pfennigus was guarded on either side by two well-armed bruisers and a knobby-faced half-ogre, and he did not look at all surprised by our arrival.

“Pfennigus!” Keldon exclaimed.

I raised a hand to calm my excitable apprentice. Eucas Pfennigus was not our man. I looked at the extraction chair, studying the intricate mechanisms draining poor Aban of his ill-gotten aptitudes. The machine was not an artifact from the age of Marada, and it looked too new to be anything other than modern. Yet, it was of a design far beyond any science of our present era. To build such an over-science machine, Pfennigus would have to be a genius surpassing any other. But no, someone else had built this machine, and Pfennigus was merely a pawn whose sole purpose was to subvert any investigations that might uncover this horrific operation.

“I thought you might track one of our clients here,” Pfennigus said with a sigh. He unlocked the restraining chair and yanked the extraction tubes from Aban’s head. Aban collapsed on the floor, quivering. Pfennigus only sneered. “Throw this trash into the rubbish bin, then bring that squat diversion back here,” he said to the half-ogre. “And tell the boss that Aldicus Vescard has arrived.”

The half-ogre hoisted Aban over his shoulder and plodded out of the room through the second door.

“Your boss?” Keldon asked. He looked at me confused. “Pfennigus has been throwing off the investigation all along. He must—”

“He’s just a pawn,” I stated. Pfennigus frowned, but said nothing more. I listened for a moment, then nodded. “The egregore alarm has stopped. Keldon, some dazzling lights if you would."

Keldon snapped his key from his belt and flicked it forward. But rather than a burst of dazzling lights to stun Pfennigus, my apprentice staggered back gripping his head in pain. "Gah!"

It was just as I thought. An aetheric feedback field now encompassed the room, undoubtedly the handiwork of a master disruptor mage. One of the mages who had succumbed to this mind-leaching operation was a disruptor, but that mage was *not* Selus Oberus. Oberus had never been a mage of noteworthy talent. He would never have been targeted by this operation. So if Oberus was not actually a victim, why had Pfennigus visited him under the pretense that he was?

"Sorry, Keldon," I apologized. "I had to know if a feedback field was in place." I then returned my attention to Pfennigus. "Where is Selus Oberus?"

Pfennigus drew a sharp breath. He was about to speak when a familiar voice came from behind. "Eucas warned me that kidnapping Aban might lead you here," my old acquaintance said. "It seems the deductive capabilities of Pergus Controise truly do rival your own. I'm sorry to say we had to kill him. Even with the amnesia, Pergus would have pieced it all together months ago. That's more than I can say for you, Aldicus."

Keldon shook his head, still dazed, but otherwise all right. "A feedback field? But how could..." his voice trailed off when he saw Oberus.

"Ah, but I did piece it together," I explained. "Eucas Pfennigus was a dead giveaway, with uncanny habits and mannerisms too similar to those of Controise to be mere coincidence. I admit, I did not suspect you at first, and your performance playing the victim would have been convincing were it not for one small detail."

"Oh?" Oberus chuckled. "And what was that?"

I shrugged. "One does not master the harpsichord with

just a few weeks practice."

"Ah, well," he sighed. "Even the best jonko players have their tell."

"But the real tip off was the fact that you were just a minor clerical mage of no real talent or noteworthy potential. Why then would the culprit behind this mind-leaching operation target you? Knowledge of magery is useless to anyone lacking aetheric quintessence. The only person who could benefit from the talents stolen from the two master mages would be another mage—and presumably by one who has an abundance of quintessence, but who is hopelessly inept. You feigned the role of a victim merely to have a convenient excuse for your meetings with Pfennigus. And, perhaps, to throw off suspicion."

Oberus frowned, his eyes narrowing and brow creasing as his face reddened with indignation. "It is a pity that your curse prevents us from extracting *your* talents. I would enjoy seeing the great Aldicus Vescard reduced to a drooling imbecile. I suppose I shall have to settle for your death."

I drew my badge from my coat pocket. "By the legal authority of the Vandorian Jurisdiction Proclamation of the High Court of Armillia, I—"

The shock wave hit with such force and speed that I found myself buried in a pile of broken shipping crates before realizing I had even been hit. My head spun, my ears rang, and I could scarcely breathe with the wind knocked out of me. Knowing I had but seconds before my adversary struck again, I pushed aside the boxes and staggered to my feet. I saw a flash and ducked to the side just as a searing blast of blue-white aethergy exploded through the crates where I had been. Keldon was still struggling to his feet, and seeing that he was otherwise unharmed, I fixed my attention on Oberus. But where was Rognar?

The door to the second hall erupted in a shower of splinters and flaming embers, and the still burning carcass of a fully cooked half-ogre careened into the room. Rognar stood within the shattered doorframe, the forge-hot barrel of his empowered clocklock blunderbuss still steaming from the blast. Wheels spun and gears clattered, and Varla belched another thundering fireball straight for Oberus. The air around the mage became a solid silver shield, and the fireball exploded across the mirror-like surface.

"Keldon, Rognar, get back!" I yelled. "He's a disruptor mage!"

Incited by Rognar's attack, Pfennigus and the two bruisers drew their own weapons and opened fire in a succession of deafening cracks. Oberus must have dropped the feedback field when he conjured his shield, for in that same instant, both Keldon and Rognar shifted in a blur of motion. It was one of Keldon's illusions, a simple twisting of light and perspective, and the bullets struck well away from their intended targets. The shield surrounding Oberus vanished, and with his face contorted in rage, the mage lashed out with his ivory wand held high. The illusionary distortion vanished, and Keldon yelped in a mix of pain and start. Rognar whipped around and another blast from Varla thundered through the room, missing Oberus but exploding through one of the bruisers. An imprint of the man's skeleton sizzled on the flame-scorched wall.

My severite wristbands hit the floor and I tossed the locking pins to my dazed apprentice. "Ready the tranq gun," I said to him. "Take me down before there's too much collateral damage."

I threw my frock coat aside, and the once tempered fire within me erupted like the backdraft from a blast furnace. My vision went white from the searing pain, and my ears filled with the wrenching agony of my own horrific scream. My blood boiled with liquid cinnabar, my flesh burned to sulfurous ash, and my bones baked to blackened coal. Around my immolating form blazed the all-consuming flames of the unchained elemental fury.

"You fool!" Oberus screamed. "This room is filled with

volatile alchemicals. You'll kill us all!"

He was right, of course, but I could no more stop the conflagrating monster than a leaf could stop a hurricane. The remaining bruiser rounded the extraction chair, unloading the last four shots from his caplock pistol. Bottles of reagents and reactants exploded on their shelves, and with flaming arms outstretched, my alchemical form absorbed a bubbling brew of corrosive sublimates and scorching alkahests. A sudden blast of catalyst-ignited vitriol tore through the guts of my foolhardy attacker, dropping him as he dissolved from the inside out—screaming.

Horrified, Pfennigus threw down his gun and bolted for the door, and I watched through burning ember eyes as a blistering amalgamation sprayed across his path. More's the pity, I considered as he dropped to his knees clutching his liquefying face with bone-raw fingers. I had hoped to see him stand trial for his part in these abominable crimes.

Oberus stumbled back, then turned and grabbed a handful of vials from a nearby table. "Deft reflexes," he muttered, and drank the extract down. "Boxing. Acrobatics. Metaplasmic conjury. Combat magery." He downed them all, one mnemonic extract after another, heedless of any danger or side effect.

The frantic mage spun around to face me, laughing as he hurled wave after wave of disruptive aethergy. Unfazed by the assault, the blazing alchemical reactor I had become drew in a noxious mix of caustic alkalis and fulminating sulfates, igniting the volatile concoction in a swirling furnace of white-hot fire. The blast exploded across Oberus's shield, followed by another and another, but nothing penetrated his defensive wards. Oberus leveled his wand and struck back with a molten beam of metaplasmic aethergy. Although my alchemical form absorbed the attack, the enveloping flames radiated such heat that my companions were forced back to the furthest corner of the room. Back and forth our futile exchange continued: fiery waves of combusting acids against pulsing bursts of blue-white light; searing streams of alchemical reactants against crackling claws of mage-conjured lightning. Glass shattered, shelving crashed, tables splintered, and walls cracked.

Oberus's assault suddenly wavered, his eyes growing wide as he gazed upon the smoldering heap that had been his mind-leaching machine. "No!" he gasped with horror. His face flushed red, brow pinched and cheeks swelling with the unquenchable rage boiling within him. "You've ruined everything!"

Bolts and beams of blistering energy surged from the mage's ivory wand, his piercing scream rising above the thunderous report of his redoubled barrage. And then, for the first time in all my years of struggle against the fiery foe within me, my diametric antithesis took pause. Here it had found a kindred spirit—a man driven to madness and rage, his lifetime of petty toil and unfulfilled dreams corrupted to those most virulent poisons of avarice and greed. The beast made no move to attack poor Oberus, but stood with ember eyes gazing and infernal mouth grinning as the mage's attacks thundered on.

It admired him!

Oberus's attacks abruptly stopped. The wand dropped from his hand and he stood with eyes glazed over, as though staring to some distant and imperceptible point. His limbs went slack, blood dripped from his nose, and he dropped leadenly to his knees. An orb of blinding white fire erupted in my hand, and I turned unwittingly to face Keldon and Rognar. But before the monster could unleash its rage upon my friends, a severite-jacketed tranquilizer dart shot straight into my chest.

An agony of scalding burns and scorching heat hit me like a barreling locomotive, and I crashed to the floor beside my shallow breathing foe. I felt the cool metal of my severite bands clasp around my wrists, and in the blink of an eye, the flames of the alchemical fury fizzled away and were gone.

I smiled, hearing the voices of Keldon and Rognar both asking if I was all right. They were alive, and that was all that really mattered.

"The dark above... the dark below," Oberus rasped, almost too faintly to be heard. He looked to the shattered windows in the fire-charred ceiling above, where the swollen volcanic orb of Atracus blazed like an anti-sun in the black void of night. The dying mage drew his final breath, sputtering on the blood filling his mouth. "He was... like a shadow... like a shadow man."

With that his head sagged to one side, his eyes frozen and lifeless. Unable to resist the effects of the sedative, my own eyes fluttered closed and I welcomed the oblivion of sleep's merciful embrace.

I PULLED MY COAT AROUND ME TIGHTER, wincing at the sting from the countless burns pot-marking my skin. It would take at least a day for the healing balm to mend my wounds, but its analgesic effect at least mitigated what would otherwise be an excruciating few hours. A HAAMR unit had arrived to secure the scene of the crime, and a half-dozen Vandorian bluejacks scoured the burned-out room for whatever bits of evidence remained. Mister Murley and Mister Maves had just entered as well, the grim-faced corpse-carters hefting their stretcher between them.

Chief Inspector Tibblemond watched as the carters began to collect the half-dissolved body of Eucas Pfennigus. "Pfennigus had us all duped, even the Commissioner General." He shook his head and rubbed his muttonchops in apparent befuddlement. Then he sighed, turning back to study me. "Well, at least he didn't have you fooled. I'm sorry I ever doubted you, Aldicus. You have my word that Dolden Gresson will be released with all charges in the murder of Marion Melodor dropped." He scratched his head as he wandered on his way. "And perhaps we should take another look at those other cases he closed."

"Indeed," I agreed. I took a drink from the cup in my hand, soothing my parched throat. "That would probably be wise."

"So, it was Oberus all along," Keldon said, sitting down beside me, "with Pfennigus as his partner in crime."

I glanced at the sheet covering poor Oberus. Although it would take an autopsy to be sure, he had most likely died of a massive brain aneurism caused by the inundation of so much memory extract all at once. But Oberus was not my reason for concern. I studied the slag heap of what once had been the mind-leaching machine. "No, Keldon, I'm afraid Oberus was as much a pawn as Pfennigus. Do you honestly believe a second-rate mage like him could have constructed such a machine?"

Rognar eyed the wreckage skeptically, then folded his arms over his duffle coat. "Isn't this some kind of Maradian artifact?"

That was a fair question, but I already knew the answer. With my coat buttoned tight, I stood and made my way over to what was left of the machine. Reaching down, I picked out a bit of metal frame from the pile, noting a string of curious, circular-shaped glyphs etched along one side. The glyphs bore no resemblance to ancient Maradian, nor that of any other language on our world.

But if not our world...

I narrowed my eyes. "This machine is not Maradian, nor is its construction ancient. It is, in fact, remarkably new."

"Faugh!" Rognar barked. "If it's not an artifact, and Oberus didn't build it, then who did?"

Drawing a sharp breath, I looked up through the broken windows above to the fire-wreathed face of Atracus.

As above, so below; the dark above, the dark below.

Those were the words the Shadow Man had spoken to me. So too had Oberus quoted the last part of that cryptic rhyme in his dying words. He had looked to the demon-moon as he spoke, just as the Shadow Man had. But what did it mean? What was he trying to tell me?

I tossed the bar back into the pile of half-melted metal and sighed. “We may never know, with the state the machine is in,” I said, perhaps even trying to convince myself. “Regardless, the machine is destroyed, the culprits have met their end, and an innocent man is now free. Best of all, we made it out alive. Who could ask for a better resolution?”

My friends nodded in agreement, and we made our way from the black charred building to Benson’s waiting locomobile. Keldon excitedly recalled the highlights of our battle, while Rognar related the more amusing points of his comical lobby interlude. But I paid little mind to their banter, pausing to pull my coat tighter before following them to the vehicle.

Looking up, I gazed past the dilapidated warehouses and ramshackle tenements around us to the fog-veiled morose of billowing manufactories and machine-cluttered cliffs of the 5th District. Beyond rose the vast urban plateau of gleaming glass and brass that was the city’s Central Core, and surmounting even those reaching towers and lofty heights soared the great needle-shaped marvel that was the Aetherspire, still sheathed in scaffolding and tended by construction dirigibles.

And there, rising above it all, loomed the black volcanic face of Atracus—the demon-moon—its fiery visage now high in the smog-choke sky.

I closed my eyes and drew a breath. Crime ever turns in the Clockwork City, yet now I knew an even greater mystery awaited. The real battle was about to begin, perhaps a battle for our very world. And yet, for all my instinct and intuition, I could not begin to guess how the battle would end.

CASE FILE 8:

MURDER ON THE *GAMBLER'S BOON*

BREAKING CLOUDS SWEPT PAST THE SKY-STEAMER'S wide mezzanine deck, their rich scarlet hues muted somewhat by the spell-tempered tektite glass surrounding the ship's vast gambling hall. Twin paddlewheels of magnetized novarite turned in the rushing winds, keeping our ship aloft, each driven by the elemental furnace rumbling deep within the tick-tock symphony of her clockwork heart. Polished brass fixtures and crystal chandeliers sparkled like rubies as the sun sank beneath the turquoise waters of the majestic Sea of Isles, and to the east rose Atracus, burning with the infernal pyres of that demon-haunted moon.

I leaned back in my chair, looking to the other four passengers with whom I enjoyed the present jonko match. The well-dressed vampire sitting directly across from me smiled, his topaz irises brightening with the coming of twilight's dawn. He sipped his drink, a sanguine vintage notably thicker than wine, and he considered his cards with a haughty air. The Scaithi sorcerer beside him carefully arranged his own cards, his dagger-like ears twitching and his gray skin blanching with notable unease. At the end of the table sat Tylon Meldanel, a mage whose gaunt-face stiffen as he studied his hand, while to my right sat Dupraine Rothorp III, a slim Armillian attorney whose grandiloquent courtroom maneuvering had won the freedom of more than a few criminal masterminds.

"It is your turn, Vescard," said the vampire, Armez, "and although I may have eternity, I don't have all night."

I needed one more seven for the pair I held to qualify for a match, but my spread of crowns looked more promising. With a nine, ten, and knight, all of the suit of crowns, I could at least make the minimum play. But if I got either an eight of crowns or a duke of crowns on the next round, I could play a spread of four. "I'm afraid I must pass," I gambled.

Tylon Meldanel muttered something under his breath, then folded his cards on the table. "I drop," he sighed. He stood, brushing out his old-fashioned green and gold justaucorps coat before removing the severite lapel pin that had inhibited his powers during the game. "But the night may yet be mine, gentlemen." With that, the gaudy-dressed mage gave a short bow and headed down the mezzanine stairs to the gambling hall's lower deck.

The Scaithi sorcerer, Ralathoz, sneered after the defeated mage, then laid down four dukes leaving him with two cards in hand. I caught my breath. So much for getting the duke of crowns. Armez played a match of three queens, leaving him with four cards in hand. Dupraine dealt everyone their next card, and mine was a seven of coins. I may not have had the spread I needed, but it did give me a match. Dupraine passed, leaving six cards in his hand, and I played my three sevens.

Armez glanced at me over his cards, quirking an eyebrow. "And here I thought you were strategizing. Please do not disappoint me, Vescard."

"Who says I'm not?" I asked. On the next round I would get one more card, and although it could not be the duke of crowns, I could still play my triple match and call the game. Even if my remaining card was a low value card, I would still win by default—assuming everyone kept three or more cards in hand and no one got a jonko.

Ralathoz considered his three cards, and his dark complexion flushed to ashen grey. He shook his head, indicating he would pass, and everyone looked to Armez.

The vampire grinned, flashing his pronounced canines. "Jonko," he claimed, laying down all five of his cards. And so it was: a ten of swords, a knight of swords, a duke of swords, a queen of swords, and the court wild card, the mage.

Armez reached for the pile of tokens in the center of the table, but Dupraine cut in, laying his cards next to Armez's hand. "Double jonko," the lawyer cheerfully proclaimed.

The vampire's eyes widened at the sight of Dupraine's rider play—a five of swords, a six of swords, an eight of swords, a nine of swords, and the jester wild card in place of the seven. Higher or lower, a double jonko rider always wins.

"Impossible!" Armez fell back in his chair, hand raking through his glossy black hair. "I was sure I had this one!"

Someone clapped from behind. I glanced over my shoulder to the stairs as the ship's first officer approached our table. "I see we have a winner at table four." He smiled, turning up the corners of his thin mustache, and he brushed his hands down the sides of his white uniform coat. Marcel Barquez was Captain Darmoro's first mate, and the second in command of the *S.S. Gambler's Boon*, crown jewel of the Venture Ship Company. "Might I accompany you to our showroom gallery? We have a most exquisite mesmer wand which a man of your profession must not be without."

"A mesmer wand you say?" Dupraine asked as he gathered his winnings before following the commander. "What a splendid idea!"

I pushed back my chair and stood, then adjusted the sleeves of my frock coat to cover my severite wristbands before taking my leave of Armez and Ralathoz. The spiral stairs led down from the mezzanine to the lower level of the gambling hall where a panoply of empowered luminaries bathed the vibrant space in golden light. Automatons in black tailcoats and white shirts served patrons clustered around dicing tables and roulette wheels, fire-throwers and illusionists performed their flashy spectacles on nearby stages, and the dark beauty of scantily clad Scaithi danced on levitating platforms to the skull-pounding rhythms of a full percussion ensemble.

I pressed my way through the raucous throng to the back of the hall where, not far from the barroom lounge, stood a row of automatronic jackpot machines. My apprentice was there, and although he did not chance a go at their decidedly unlikely probabilities, he sat in ogle-eyed fascination of a girl who clearly was. She took a few coins from him, and he followed her signal to distract a floor spook with some urgent question or another. It was then that I spotted the clockwork device rigged to the side of the machine: a highly illegal autorotor employed by gearmeisters for any number of unscrupulous endeavors, from clockwork safe cracking to automaton sabotage to analytical engine espionage. But the girl gave off an air of something even more peculiar—something about her raven black hair, her bright amber eyes, and the teeth that showed behind her mischievous smile.

"Your assistant?" came a velvety voice just to my left.

I had not heard him approach from behind, and I forced myself not to flinch or turn. "My apprentice, Keldon." I nodded in the direction of the girl. "Your apprentice?"

"My sireling, Quiniece," Armez confirmed. He stepped up beside me, his topaz eyes looking me over and his lips curling with the hint of a smile. "She is quite fond of new toys. Please tell your young apprentice to take care."

The bell on the jackpot machine sounded, and Quiniece swiped the autorotor before an attendant approached with her ill-gotten tokens. Keldon returned as soon as the attendant left, pulling his newsboy cap over his unkempt hair and chuckling lightly at something she said. Perhaps his overt willingness to help her cheat should have concerned me, but it was hardly a crime to rig an already rigged game. Keldon waved, spotting me in the crowd, and Quiniece folded her arms across her tight-laced bodice as she narrowed her eyes at Armez.

Armez donned a teal top hat that not only matched his cravat, but complemented his bright scarlet tailcoat. He then placed his hands on his dragon-headed gentleman's cane and produced a loud, deliberate sigh. "Why is the most renowned detective in all of Armillia, and perhaps even the world, here aboard the single most exclusive sky-steamer to operate outside the law? Somehow, I doubt you are on vacation. Half the patrons aboard are as criminal as they come, and the other half are twice as bad." He turned to me, crooking a wry smile on his ghastly white face. "Your present company included."

I took a wine glass from the tray of an automaton making its rounds and surveyed the discordant den of thieves. There and about were dapper-dressed Travenni mobsters eyeing their blood rivals, the ruthless Seladono family. There were gray-skinned Scaithi from darkest Kendes, Ogrum chieftains from the frozen north of Tarrona, wealthy Dworghs from the isle of Nuram, sorcerers garbed in flamboyant robes and dazzling accoutrements, and more than a few of the most notorious pirates to plague the Sea of Isles. All were aboard this underground ship cruising high above the clouds—gambling, plotting, dealing, and cheating in the hopes of winning some of the most dangerous artifacts known to myth and legend.

I took a sip of wine. "I am waiting for something to go horribly wrong."

Armez nodded, but said nothing further.

I waved to my apprentice. Trusting, however unwisely, that he had sense enough to keep out of trouble, I headed down a hall to the showroom gallery. The vampire followed, a silent shadow keeping up just behind.

"I'm not hunting you, if that's what worries you," I said.

"Oh, I wasn't worried," Armez replied. "You're no veilhunter. But I do wonder at the real reason for your presence aboard this ship. Vandorian jurisdiction does not apply out here, nor does Armillia's or that of any other country. And surely you have not turned in your badge to become some questing knight determined to confiscate these priceless relics for the Archidoxy."

"I'm a freelance detective," I said as we stepped past the ogres guarding the showroom door. "Yes, I have been deputized, but I'm not here on behalf of Vandor Tower."

From one end of the empowerment-lit showroom to the other stood rows of ornate pedestals, each displaying a unique artifact of unparalleled darkness and infamy: the Eldritch Staff of Sundering, the Bone Crown of Dagoroth, the Chalice of the Blood King, and countless swords, helms, and orbs of arcane sorcery. And there, bathed in prismatic light upon a black obsidian pillar raised above them all, reigned a mysterious crystalline relic said to have originated from Atracus itself—the Chaos Hexillion.

In truth, every one of them should be sealed away in the Fathomless Vault for all time. Yet, as impressive as they were, none of them were real. I passed my hand through the artifact nearest me and the wicked black helm wavered as the illusion met the dampening effect of my severite wristband. The real artifacts were secured in a well-guarded, severite-shielded vault just below the showroom. Yet, even the best security was no match for the ingenuity of the thieves I pursued. Their crime spree through Corradon had gained them a treasure trove of ensorcelled artifacts. With Keldon's help I had foiled at least part of their operation, but the true mastermind remained at large. More than merely tempting, the contents of this sky-steamer's vault would be the crowning heist for that shadowy cabal.

"Mister Vescard," came the sultry voice of a buxom Scaithi, her bosom barely contained by a corset designed to reveal far more of her grey-toned skin than it concealed. She lifted the lid of the silver platter in her hand, revealing an exquisite brooch imbued with vizstones and finely etched orichalium. "Your prize from this morning's match."

"Yes, of course," I said, collecting the brooch. I had won a match of jonko earlier in the day, but this was my first time since then to visit the showroom. It was one of the lesser prizes, of course, but it could nevertheless prove useful.

Armez pulled his gaze away from an artifact he had been studying, his eyebrow raised. "I can't say I'm familiar with that brooch."

I glanced to where Armez had been looking and saw the Chalice of the Blood King. Turning back to the vampire, I smiled. "Let's just say, should I find myself in harm's way, my attacker will be most disheartened."

Armez's jaw tightened, but he gave an approving nod. "A wise precaution, considering the complement of this ship."

I stepped aside as Dupraine hurried out of the gallery, the long black box tucked under his arm no doubt containing his newly won mesmer wand. Other patrons moved through the showroom as well, some admiring the illusory images of those coveted artifacts, while others hastened to collect their priceless winnings.

"Oh, do relax, my dear Vescard," Armez laughed, perhaps sensing my unease. "We still have a high enough rank to buy into the final round eliminations. I very much hope to see you there."

"You can count on it," I replied.

"Then I shall consider it a date," Armez bid, winking as he turned to leave. "I could not have chosen a more worthy adversary to test the measure of my cunning and duplicity."

With that, he donned a pair of red-tinted spectacles, then tapped his cane to the brim of his top hat and strolled out the showroom door.

I WAS STILL HALF ASLEEP in the predawn hours when the *S.S. Gambler's Boon* turned lazily to the west, her novarite paddlewheels chugging to the rhythmic pulse of her spell-fired engine. A gust of cold night air blew into my cabin through the open window, a window I distinctly remembered shutting before going to bed. I cracked an eyelid just in time to see a fleeting shadow dart across the crimson moonlight. The intruder was as silent as a midnight specter, and I steeled myself to jump from bed at the first glimmer of the assassin's blade. Instead, I heard the desk drawer slide open, followed by the quiet rustling of the papers in my files. A floorboard creaked, the air pressed thick around me, and I felt a presence edge its way to the bedside table.

The intruder was going for the brooch!

Throwing the covers off, I sprang to my feet. No sooner had I seized the brooch than a sudden force rammed into my chest, knocking me breathless and crashing me into the desk. I cringed, realizing my severite wristbands had negated the brooch's protective empowerment, and I braced myself for a second attack. My assailant lunged again, but instead of attacking, flew straight out the open window in a dizzying blur.

I stood in the darkness, still gripping the brooch as I heaved one labored breath after another. A knock pounded on the door and I heard my apprentice call anxiously from the hall. "Aldicus, are you all right?"

Not waiting for an answer, he threw the door open and charged in. The shimmering blue light of his talismanic key spilled shadows through the cabin. My hand found the wall sconce. With a turn of the knob, the room brightened with the warming radiance of the luminary.

"Were you attacked?" Keldon asked. He moved to put away his key, then paused, noticing he wore only his nightshirt and longs. "Who was it?"

I tossed the brooch onto the bed and drew my night robe around me. Through the window, I glimpsed the fading light of Atracus giving way to the fledgling rays of the pre-dawn sun, painting the clouds drifting alongside us in brilliant orange hues. I shut the window and pulled the curtains, then released a breath I had not known I was holding.

"My list of suspects is considerably short," I replied. "No human can move that fast, nor even the most agile Scaithi assassin."

"Do you think he was after that?" Keldon asked, nodding to the brooch on the bed.

I almost answered yes, but the jumble of loose papers scattered across the desk seemed to suggest a different motivation. The portfolio contained numerous newspaper clippings, crime reports, case summaries, and notes scrawled in my own hand. All pertained to two months' worth of investigations into crimes involving ancient artifacts from the War of Golla and Marada and what little I knew of the Shadow Man who seemed to be the mastermind of the nefarious operation.

Among the papers was my report on the mind-leaching apparatus Selus Oberus had employed in his talent-stealing scheme, the Maradian soul-binding machine used by Marelle Sandellar to animate his ghoulish automatons, and the diaphamorphic transmutation belt which, though fatal to use, allowed the mysterious cabal to procure countless artifacts of wonder and terror. Those items included the Reliquary of the Infernal Desolator, the Void Scepter of the Embersoul, a multi-ringed obsidian sphere of unknown purpose, and Amaldiere's Masque of Illusions. If Armez or his sireling had been in my cabin, what were they looking for in these files? Was the vampire connected with this sorcerous crime ring? Could Armez be the Shadow Man? But no. The Shadow Man, whoever he was, had only ever use pawns to do his bidding.

"Aldicus?" Keldon asked, drawing me from my musings.

Hurried footfalls pounded on the deck above, and I could just make out the muffled call of frantic voices down the hall. "Get dressed," I said, going for the dresser. "Our culprit may have just played his hand."

Minutes later, we were up the stairs and moving quickly down the hall, following the commotion to a stateroom crowded with guards, officers, and crewmen. Four grim-faced men stood to one side of the room—Travenni goons, judging from their striped waistcoats and pork pie hats. A man lay face down in the middle of the room. He was garbed in a red-stained nightshirt with blood pooled around his neck. I frowned. Had the throat been slit or was it a bite?

"Them Seladono moochers did this, I tell ya!" yelled one of the Travenni goons. His tight face was flushed with anger and he paced back and forth beside the body. "They's got every reason to off the boss!"

"Just let us at 'em," said another, popping his knuckles. "We'll make sure they won't cause no more trouble."

Commander Barquez shook his head as he considered the brutally murdered man. He looked up, surprised to see me, then forced a smile. "Ah, Aldicus Vescard, yes? I wish we could have met under better circumstances, but I'm glad you're here. It seems Bardel Alanonni has met a rather unpleasant end."

I motioned Keldon over to join me, pulling on my inspection gloves as I knelt beside the body. The victim, Bardel Alanonni, was an older gentleman with a wide, drooping mustache after the fashion set by Vacciano Travenni himself. The immediate cause of death was profuse blood loss resulting from severe trauma to the neck. A quick inspection of the wound revealed a deep but clean cut, likely inflicted by a large knife. The blood showed only moderate coagulation, placing the time of death inside half an hour and maybe as little as fifteen minutes.

"No bite marks," I whispered with relief.

Keldon flinched. "You were looking for bite marks?"

I nodded. "Yes. And that reminds me. I should probably tell you something about your new friend—"

"Well, well, well! If it ain't the famous Detective Vescard," the first Travenni goon mocked with an exaggerated Glaven accent. He brushed out his sharp suit coat, then rolled his shoulders as he glanced around. "So, I guess this investigation is well in hand, ain't that right, detective?"

"And you are?" I asked.

"Giono," he said proudly. "Giono Gallinaro. My great uncle is Vacciano Travenni, so don't you forget it!"

"I won't," I replied. I rose to my feet and made my way to the windows. Testing the first one proved it was locked and the second one seemed equally secure. The goons were probably his guards, so how anyone could have gotten past them was the crux of the mystery. "You were guarding this man?"

Giono scratched behind his hat, then he brushed out his coat again before clearing his throat. "I'm Mister Alanonni's second. Luigo was the one on watch." He gave his best attempt at a nonchalant shrug. "Now he's gone missing. If he sold out to those Seladonos, why I'll pop a..." Giono blinked, apparently remembering who I was. "I'll pop his ears. Yeah. That's what I'll do."

I picked up a broken box from the floor and turned it over. With its gold leaf latches and padded satin lining, the exquisitely crafted leather-bound case must have held an artifact of considerable value. "What did Bardel Alanonni win yesterday?"

The goons grew more nervous at the question. "Didn't he say it was a blade or something? The forgotten blade of combustion, or maybe it was corruption..." Giono looked to the others, but they just shrugged.

I drew a sharp breath, recognizing the name. "The Forsaken Blade of Soulless Corruption," I corrected, "thought to have been lost over twelve hundred years ago during the savage dark age that followed the fall of Marada."

"Yeah, that was it," Giono confirmed.

"He was killed by his own prize?" Commander Barquez wildly conjectured.

I shook my head. "Had that been the murder weapon, it would have annihilated his soul and transformed his body into a rampaging, living-dead abomination. I believe we would have noticed that by now. No, it seems someone has slit his throat with a perfectly mundane blade and taken the artifact. For now, this Luigo fellow is our prime suspect."

"Commander," said one of the ship's crewman as he ducked into the stateroom. "We've found another body."

"Where? Who?" the commander asked.

"A storeroom two decks below." The crewman nodded to the Travennis. "He's dressed like them, sir."

"Tall and skinny, with a poor excuse for a mustache?" Giono asked.

The crewman nodded.

"And so much for Luigo," I sighed.

Commander Barquez pushed through the crowd and hurried after the crewman, no doubt troubled by the events aboard ship. Keldon and I followed the commander down the stairs to the second-class deck, with Giono and two other Travennis keeping pace just behind. It felt odd working to unmask the murder of a Travenni crime boss, though I suspected it was even less comfortable for them. For all of their bluster and bravado, the Travenni goons kept eying me with more than a little apprehension coloring their faces.

Keldon glanced back at the Travennis and worried his lip, but when he turned back to me he had a different question on his mind. "You started to say something about Quiniece?"

I nodded. "You do know she's a vampire, right?"

Keldon blinked. "That would explain why she kept looking at my neck. And why she's just so *pale*... But you don't think she's involved with this, do you? Not just because she's a vampire."

"Not *just* because," I answered. "I had a pleasant chat with her sire, Armez. He's a charming gentleman, but he made no effort to hide the fact that he's up to something. He may even have been taunting me. But more than that, I believe he was the one who broke into my cabin."

Keldon's eyes widened. "That's why you were checking for bite marks. But that only means a vampire didn't bite him.

It doesn't mean a vampire couldn't have slit his throat."

I nodded. "Which any killer could have done, leaving us no closer to an answer. The fact is, if Armez was trying to enter my room when this murder took place then he, at least, has an impeccable alibi."

Keldon grimaced, recognizing the implication at once. If Armez had broken into my room at the time of the murder, he could have sent his sireling to steal the artifact from the Travennis at the same time. But as plausible a theory as that might have been, something about it did not sit right. Armez, if he was my intruder, had not simply broken into my room as a diversion—he had come to find something in my files. But what was he looking for?

The crewman led us into the storeroom and stepped aside for the commander and myself to have a look.

"By the Light of the Archons," Commander Barquez whispered. "This man has killed himself!"

I knelt beside the body, shaking my head at the commander's tendency to jump to the most presumptive conclusions. He was even worse than Inspector Tibblemond. The fact that the man's throat had been slit and a bloody dagger rested in his hand did not necessarily imply the wound was self-inflicted. Suicide victims rarely slit their own throat, preferring instead to cut their wrists or plunge the dagger into their gut. Furthermore, the cut stretched from one ear to another, and the likelihood of him completing the full cut was diminishingly small. Yet, equally perplexing, the expression on the dead man's face was disturbingly serene. He was not killed in a struggle, nor did he die in a moment of terror as though taken by surprise.

Giono spat. "See what that got ya, Luigo? Do the Seladono's dirty work and they'll pay ya good for sure!"

Commander Barquez sighed. "So, they killed their patsy to keep him quiet, making it look like a suicide. I'll put some guards to watch the Seladonos, but I doubt we'll be able to pin this on them. It's not as though these things don't happen from time to time."

Something was not right. I dabbed my handkerchief against the blood on the dead man's neck and found it to be a sticky, solid mass. He had been dead for at least an hour, maybe two, but Bardel Alanonni could not have died more than twenty minutes ago. "Do you know for certain Luigo was guarding Alanonni's room?"

"Yeah, and I checked on him about half an hour ago," Giono replied. "I didn't see nothing fishy."

Half an hour ago. If that was true, then Luigo could not have killed Alanonni. "Keldon—" I began to ask, but my apprentice was already on it.

"There's a residual aetheric imprint," he reported, squinting as he focused on his key. The sigils glowed bright, but after a moment he shook his head. "Best I can tell, there was some kind of enthrallment along with something else—maybe a glamour or illusion, but I'm pretty sure he was enthralled."

"A spell?" Commander Barquez asked. "Don't you Travennis have wards against this sort of thing?"

The Travenni goons shifted nervously, one of them fingering a small lapel pin which was probably empowered with just such a warding.

"For every ward against one sort of enthrallment, a new ensorcellment comes along to defeat it," I said. "And I fear there is no shield or ward that can defend against the sort of artifacts that are aboard this ship."

"The mesmer wand," Keldon whispered.

I could not discount the possibility that Armez, a master vampire, had enthralled poor Luigo, but a mesmer wand seemed the more likely implement. Even so, it was not the only artifact that could be used to dominate the mind of another. I had seen both the Soulstone of Kesh and several Triclopes psyorbs on display in the showroom. Still, as far as I knew, only the mesmer wand had thus far been won.

"Has anyone else won a mesmer wand?" I asked the

commander.

"Anyone else?" the commander asked, his brow furrowing. "Besides whom?"

"Besides Dupraine," I replied. "You accompanied him to the showroom after he won the jonko game last night, and even suggested he pick the mesmer wand as his prize."

Commander Barquez rubbed his thin mustache. "I'm afraid I was on the bridge for most of the evening. But now that you mention it, I do believe one of the mesmer wands was claimed."

I frowned. Not only had Commander Barquez been standing at the table when Dupraine won, but he had accompanied him to the showroom to collect his prize. Then it struck me—Dupraine had been alone when I saw him leaving the showroom, but Barquez was not with him.

"Claimed, indeed," I said. "By Dupraine Rothorp III. Could you send someone to check up on him?"

"Right away," the commander replied. He snapped his fingers, bringing the crewman to attention. "Check on Mister Rothorp and bring a few guards with you. Shall we presume he is your prime suspect?"

"No," I replied grimly. "Dupraine Rothorp III is dead, his mesmer wand has been stolen, and you, Commander Barquez, should consider yourself very fortunate to be alive."

"AMALDIERE'S MASQUE OF ILLUSIONS?" Captain Darmoro scratched the bristles of his grizzled beard, pondering my assertion. With his weathered face, crinkled brow, and knobby nose, he looked the very part of a hardened arctic whaler, and as captain of this lawless ship of thieves, I had no doubt he was twice as tough. "I've never heard of it, and it certainly isn't in this ship's manifest. Are you sure this killer is planning to crack the vault?"

I nodded. The officer's wardroom was cramped and unadorned by the extravagant standards of the guest facilities. Between its bare wood walls were two tables with some chairs, a cabinet of books, a few nautical knickknacks, and two large portholes beyond which hung the rosy clouds of a late afternoon sky. Compared to the events of this morning, the rest of the day had passed uneventfully.

Unfortunately, a thorough search of the ship had turned up no trace of Dupraine Rothorp III, and all that was found of his mesmer wand was an empty case discarded in a waste bin. No other significant clues had turned up in his cabin. The first of the evening's jonko matches were already underway, and if Dupraine was going to turn up at all, he would have turned up there.

"I am certain," I said in answer to the captain's question. "But I suspect that whoever is behind this is backed by a powerful organization bent on amassing an arsenal of artifacts from the War of Golla and Marada. They already have Amaldiere's Masque of Illusions and could use it to impersonate anyone aboard this ship."

The captain gave a gruff laugh, and his chair creaked as he leaned back. "I'm afraid you're chasing shadows, detective." I just nodded. He had no idea how right he was. "There's always a few thefts and killings on a voyage like this. You've seen our passengers. They're not the sort you'd find lolling about some leisurely South Medrean cruise."

The captain's dismissive attitude had much to be desired, but this was a private vessel, not a military ship. The officers and crew of the *S.S. Gambler's Boon* were as mercenary as her profiteering passengers, kept in line by the simple fact that the Venture Ship Company was about as forgiving of disloyalty as the Travenni crime family. But could I truly discount Commander Barquez as a suspect, or even Captain Darmoro? If Amaldiere's Masque was involved, then nearly everyone was a suspect—crew and passenger alike. The only catch was, the wearer of the Masque needed to be roughly the same size and build as the one being impersonated. Commander Barquez was a rather lanky fellow, and both Dupraine and Luigo had tall, lean builds as well. I glanced the captain over and quirked an eyebrow. Though he was certainly more stout than Commander Barquez, he was almost as tall. He, too, could be a target for the culprit.

"Have any other passengers been found dead or gone missing?" I asked. "Any crew?"

The captain drew a deep breath, then nodded. "After Mister Rothorp's disappearance, we did a deck-by-deck cabin check, bow to stern. That turned up only two other passengers unaccounted for, but no other bodies have been found."

I leaned forward, folding my hands on the table. "Who are the other two missing."

"Gustace Gabron, an antiquities dealer, and Tylon Meldanel, a mage I believe. It's odd for a mage to go missing. I could call for a full complement muster, but I'd rather not. On a voyage like this, dragging everyone out of the gambling hall, lounges, and private suites to stand on deck for a head count won't go over very well. You've seen our clientele."

I nodded. Tylon Meldanel had been at the jonko game with myself, Dupraine, Armez, and the Scaithi sorcerer, Ralathoz. Now both Dupraine and Tylon were missing, and were most probably dead.

"Had Tylon Meldanel or Gustace Gabron won any of the ship's major prizes?" I asked.

Captain Darmoro shook his head. "I'm actually not sure, but I can have my first officer look into it."

"How well do you know your first officer? Do you trust him?"

"Marcel?" Captain Darmoro asked, using the commander's first name. He drummed his fingers on the table, then drew a deep breath and slowly let it out again. "He came aboard three months ago when the Company gave my old first mate his own boat. He's a competent enough officer, though a bit too by-the-book to fit in. He was formally with the Armillian navy, if that tells you anything. But trust him?" The captain shrugged. "I wouldn't trust a soul aboard this ship."

I nodded, leaning back in my chair.

Captain Darmoro gave another sigh, then he pushed his chair back and stood. "If you'll excuse me, detective, we have a resupply dirigible docking with us in less than an hour and I need to get topside to supervise the mooring deployment. My first officer still hasn't quite gotten the knack of it."

I thanked the captain for his time and made my way back to my quarters still pondering the mystery. The real Commander Barquez had been on the bridge at the same time that his double had appeared at the jonko tables, meaning the culprit had impersonated him to get the jump on whoever won the match. That, at least, eliminated Commander Barquez as a suspect, as well as the captain and the other bridge crew who had been on duty at the time. It also meant that neither Armez nor Ralathoz could be suspects since both were still at our table when the false Barquez had so generously escorted Dupraine to his demise. If my hunch was correct, then the false commander had killed Dupraine, then used Amaldiere's Masque of Illusions to impersonate him and collect his prize.

But there were still more questions to be answered. Dupraine, Gustace Gabron, and Tylon Meldanel had all gone missing—their bodies' presumably thrown overboard to forestall discovery. But just because they were missing did not mean they were dead. In fact, the likelihood that one of them was himself the killer was actually quite high. I knew nothing of this Gustace Gabron, but Tylon Meldanel had been at the table with Dupraine, Armez, and myself, and had excused himself shortly before the false commander arrived. In truth, the man who had been at the table might not have been Tylon Meldanel at all, but the masked killer himself. But why impersonate Commander Barquez? Perhaps the killer knew Dupraine, with his ego, would be far more likely to accompany the commander to the showroom than a rival jonko player.

Then came the question of Alanonni and Luigo, and why their bodies had been left in such a way as to be found. Luigo had obviously been killed so the murderer could impersonate him without worrying about the real Luigo turning up. But why had the culprit stashed Luigo's body in a storeroom rather than tossing him overboard? And the same could be asked about Alanonni's body, although the disappearance of Bardel Alanonni would probably have caused as much of a stir as his murder. In fact, the whole scenario seemed to be set up to direct attention to the Travenni and Seladono rivalry. The culprit, whoever he was, knew I was onboard and was likely counting on me to investigate. If so, then was Alanonni's murder a ploy to throw my investigation off track, or had the killer truly been after the Forsaken Blade of Soulless Corruption? Perhaps the killer was just buying time while he prepared for the next stage in his murderous scheme.

And what of Armez and his sireling? I was sure it had been Armez who had broken into my room, but he had been after information, not the empowered brooch. Armez might not be connected with the murders, but he was still my only real lead.

"I think I have it," Keldon said as I entered my room. The apprentice mage sat cross-legged on the floor, pages scrawled with magian notation strewn all around him. He held a pair of spectacles up to the luminary light, watching as bands of color glittered off the oddly angled crystals attached to either side of the lenses. He tapped his talismanic key against the empowered spectacles and smiled. "Now I just have to see if it works. You don't mind, do you, boss?"

I opened my mouth to answer, but before I could, Keldon aimed his key at me and gave the talisman a flick and flourish. Glancing down, I found myself garbed in a ridiculous floral dressing gown. The illusion was imperfect, shifting unnaturally against my movements and fading out near my severite wristbands, but it was passable for an off-hand mirage.

"Ugh," Keldon said after putting on the glasses. He adjusted the crystals and squinted his eyes, then blinked a few times and shook his head. "It sort of works. I should be able to spot anyone shrouded by an illusion, and if I adjust the crystals just right, I might even catch a glimpse of their real face."

My illusionary dressing gown vanished and I absently brushed the lapel of my frock coat. "Anyone wearing Amaldiere's Masque will be far more difficult to spot than a simple glamour veil." I glanced out the room's window and drew a breath. Dusk was half an hour away, and the vampires would be stirring soon—assuming they were not already awake. "Have you made plans with your new friend this evening?"

Keldon rolled his eyes. "She's probably still sleeping, or whatever it is they call it."

"Torpor," I replied. I took the empowered brooch from the dresser and tossed it to my apprentice. He was proficient enough with illusions, but his knowledge of wards and barriers was still incomplete. If, in the course of this investigation, we were forced to confront an aggressive opponent, he would likely need the brooch's defensive capability. "Put the brooch on. If you plan to be in her company tonight, you should bring some protection."

"Right, that's probably—" He stopped mid-sentence, squinting as he eyed me with suspicion. "Did you just make a joke?"

I crooked an eyebrow. "Oh? Did I? Or did you just infer your own suggestive meaning? What would Arleia think?"

Keldon's cheeks reddened and he formed a sheepish grin. Then he stood and pinned the brooch to his vest. "At least tell me you have some idea of who's behind the murders. You don't think it's Quiniece and Armez, do you?"

"My instincts tell me no. But Armez *is* up to something. What, I do not know." I adjusted my top hat, straightened my coat, and turned to open the door. "Whoever the culprit is, I intent to catch them this very night—perhaps with the aid of our new acquaintances. Now, get those spectacles and come on. We have vampires to track."

ARMEZ AND HIS SIRELING HAD ALREADY left their rooms by the time we got there, but we had only missed them by a few minutes. After a quick stroll around the ship's mezzanine, Keldon spotted Quiniece scoping out the gambling hall and I caught sight of Armez taking refreshment in the main lounge. Armez soon rejoined Quiniece in the gambling hall, and both vampires casually disappeared through a door leading into a maintenance corridor. Tailing quarry as cunning as these two would be a bigger gamble than any I had taken since boarding. Being the masters of stealth and concealment that they were, the pair proved formidable to shadow. My one advantage came in anticipating their destination: the vault directly below the showroom gallery.

The ship's interior accessways were rarely visited by the well-pampered passengers and looked more the part of a commercial freighter than a luxurious sky-steamer. More than once I bumped my head on a low-hanging pipe or protruding steam valve, and Keldon tripped on practically every hatch frame. Were we to chance upon an officer or guard, we would surely be escorted back to the gambling hall, and we took care to avoid the crewmen going about their daily routines. Twice I glimpsed the flash of a scarlet tailcoat rounding a corner just ahead of us, and I grew increasingly concerned that Armez knew of our presence and was leading us on a wild squonk chase.

Hoping to head the vampires off before they reached the vault, I motioned to Keldon and ducked down a narrow side corridor.

"You shouldn't be here," rumbled a deep voice as we stepped into the corridor. Two scowling Ogrum stood to either side of a tool closet, both armed with breech-loading blunderbusses and both bearing chipped tusks through their widening snarls.

"Well?" growled the second ogre, his yellow eyes narrowing as he glared down at me.

"I was told I might find the commander down here," I said, taking what I hoped was an unthreatening step back.

"Hah!" the first ogre balked. "You missed him by half an hour." He slung his blunderbuss to his armor-padded shoulder, then shook his shaggy head in puzzlement. "He and the cap came down here to check on something. I can't remember what."

I had been meeting with Captain Darmoro just over half an hour ago, and he had clearly stated that he was going topside to supervise the supply ship docking. Whoever had come down here with Commander Barquez was now impersonating the captain, and that meant the commander was probably in danger.

I looked again to the nondescript door of the unassuming tool closet. "May I ask what it is you're guarding?"

The ogres glanced at one another. "The vault," the first one replied. He stabbed a massive thumb at the closet door. "What do you think this is?"

Keldon opened his mouth, but I held up my hand.

"Yes, of course. I believe we'll just be going now."

"What was that about?" Keldon asked as we retreated around the corner. "It looked like they were just guarding a closet."

"They believe they are guarding the vault," I replied. "Which means the vault is presently unguarded."

Keldon adjusted his empowered spectacles and glanced back. "Do you think Armez enthralled them?"

I shook my head. If this ship's security protocols were anything like those of other ships transporting high-value cargo, then no officer could open the vault alone—not even the captain. Three officers were likely required to open the vault, or two if they were the captain and commander.

Assuming that was the case, the imposter must have used Amaldiere's Masque to impersonate the captain and either ordered Commander Barquez, or compelled him with the stolen mesmer wand, to accompany him to the vault. Upon gaining access, the culprit could have enthralled the guards with the mesmer wand and then made a clean getaway with the vault's contents.

I stopped at the corridor junction and peered cautiously around the corner. Armez stood at the vault door keeping watch, while Quiniece knelt at an open panel tinkering with the maze of clockwork mechanisms inside the supposedly uncrackable lock. Armez glowered with concern, no doubt wondering why the vault was unguarded. He checked his pocket watch, then glanced both ways down the hall. I pulled my head back just before he looked in my direction.

"Hurry," Armez said. "I don't know why it's been left unguarded, but that can't be a good sign. If he's taken it..."

"Don't worry," I heard Quiniece say. "I've almost got it."

Not wanting to risk even a whisper, I signaled for Keldon to get ready. He nodded, and I braced myself. I had caught the vampires in the act of breaking into the vault. Of that, if nothing else, they were guilty. But Armez seemed genuinely worried that someone had beaten him to the vault's contents. I had to know what he was up to, and for that, I needed to let them finish.

"Amateurs," Quiniece scoffed. A loud clatter of gears prefaced the heavy *clunk* of locking bolts disengaging. "You'd think they would at least have the decency to employ double-recursion anti-tamper gears. I'm almost insulted."

I waited a few seconds more, then peeked into the hall. The vault's massive severite steel door was partway open, and both vampires had disappeared inside. Taking my badge in hand, I started down the hall, moving slowly at first before picking up speed as I drew near.

"Stars be cursed!" Armez swore from inside. "What happened here?"

I rounded the vault door, brandishing my badge. "By the legal authority of the Vandorian Juris—"

"Oh, give it a rest, Vescard," Armez cut back with a dismissive wave of his hand. "You're outside your jurisdiction. And besides, we have a much bigger problem now."

Keldon entered the vault behind me and gasped. Whoever had beaten Armez to the take had been quite selective in their plunder, judging from the fact that only a few strongboxes had been opened. But that was not my most immediate concerned.

"Commander Barquez," I sighed, looking at the body sprawled across the vault room's floor. His throat had been slit, just like Alanonni and Luigo, and the dark red pool of blood still had a sheen of wetness. He could not have been killed more than fifteen minutes ago.

"Gone!" Quiniece exclaimed. She slammed her fist into the wall, leaving a respectable dent next to one of the pried-open alcoves. The text on the brass plaque beneath that empty alcove did not surprise me in the least.

"The Chalice of the Blood King," I read. "That's why you're here, isn't it? That was your plan all along. If you could not win the Chalice, you would simply steal it."

Armez frowned, folding his arms over his coat. "And what of it? By all rights the Chalice belongs to our kind, and it may well prove to be our salvation."

I looked around the room to see what else had been stolen, and immediately saw that only a handful of artifacts were missing. The Eldritch Staff of Sundering was still in its case, as were numerous empowered orbs, helms, and swords. But the real question was not what the thief had left behind, but what he had taken. And why.

"Look at this, boss," Keldon said, pointing to the largest of the strongboxes. The spellworked lid had been rent apart by some tremendous force and looking inside I saw nothing but a padded satin lining. Whatever had been inside was gone. I looked to the plaque and a cold shudder ran through me.

"The Chaos Hexillion," I whispered, my breath drawing short.

"They took the Bone Crown of Dagoroth as well," Armez added, pointing to another empty alcove. "The Crown, the Blade of Corruption, and the Chaos Hexillion were all said to have come from Atracus. But why would they take the Chalice? It can only be used by a master vampire."

"Collateral," Quiniece said. "They know we're after it, and they probably hope to use it as a bargaining chip." She then cocked her head, considering Keldon with a bemused smirk. "What is that ridiculous thing on your face?"

Keldon touched his empowered spectacles and smiled. "They're for seeing through illusions. Whoever the culprit is—"

Quiniece rolled her eyes. "—has Amaldiere's Masque of Illusions. We know. Do you really think your hocery-pocery glasses can see through *that* kind of sorcery?"

I drew myself up and straightened my coat, then turned to face Armez. "You seem to know a lot about what's going on here. What do you know of the criminals behind this heist?"

Armez cocked his head to one side, arching an eyebrow. "We know more than you, apparently. At least, that's what I gathered from the sorry state of your files."

"So, it was you who broke into my room last night."

Armez twirled his dragon-headed cane and smiled. "Would it surprise you to know we're on the same side? The only difference is, not only do I know who we're dealing with, but I also know their designs for this world. You only know of them through chance encounters with their operations in Corradon. But we have pursued them—and been pursued by them—from the dark cities of Kendes to the highest peaks of Carsovia to the savage plains of the Bloodland Wilds. They go by many guises and are known by many names, for they are the servants of the lords of darkness. They are the

Servants of Vosh."

Vosh? My blood froze. For an instant, I hoped I had simply misheard. Surely, he did not mean Voshthok-ung'Ulkoth, more commonly known as Vosh, the Demon Lord of Wrath. But judging from the grave expression darkening his alabaster face, the vampire's meaning was all too clear.

"Impossible," I breathed, harboring some faint hope he was mistaken. But the facts agreed. Apart from the mesmer wand and the chalice, every artifact that had been taken was of Gollan origin. The Maradian artifacts were untouched, as were those of Elinican, Eldren, and Dworghen origin. "Do you know what this means?"

Armez curled his lips with disdain. "Our world was all but destroyed when the Demon Lords were last unleashed. Only with the full might of the empire of Marada did we vanquish the Gollan hordes back to the fiery pits of their scorched, volcanic prison. Now the Servants of Vosh seek to release their masters once more—only this time, no power on this world can possibly oppose them."

"The thief must still be aboard this ship since there's no way off," Quiniece reminded. She took a clockwork gauntlet from her satchel and slipped it over her left hand, then began adjusting the dials and gauges adorning the wrist. "If I can pinpoint the highest concentration of aetheric resonance—"

"Fangle-fop!" I exclaimed. Everyone looked at me, their faces puzzled. "I just learned from Captain Darmoro that we're about to dock with a resupply dirigible. It's no coincidence that our culprit made his move now. He plans to get off this ship tonight."

"Kalith's spit," Armez growled. He gave the dragon head of his cane a sharp twist, then drew a gleaming rapier from the disguising scabbard. "I'll down a pint of quicksilver before I let them take that chalice!"

Quiniece balled her gauntleted hand, galvanic arcs leaping and snapping like angry serpents between its copper-coiled rivets. "Just let them try!" she hissed through gnashing teeth.

Keldon looked from me to the vampires and back to me again. He touched the brooch pinned to his vest and flipped the key from his belt to his waiting hand. "Let's do this, boss."

I nodded, and wasting not a moment more, held onto my top hat as I dashed for the stairs at the end of the corridor. I had no idea what power the Bone Crown of Dagoroth or the Chaos Hexillion held, but coupled with the artifact heists in Corradon, it seemed more than plausible that the Servants of Vosh, whoever they were, would soon have everything they needed to set their harrowing plans into motion.

The two Ogrum called out as we charged past their fallacious post, and several crewmen took chase behind us, having noticed the open vault door. Ignoring them all, we took the stairs two at a time and burst through the doors at the back of the gambling hall. No one looked up from the card tables or roulette wheels as we dodged through the crowd of reveling patrons, and the angry calls of the pursuing crewmen fell mute in the deafening din.

Glancing up to the windows arched high above the mezzanine, I caught sight of a massive ship breaking from the deepening twilight clouds. The air trembled as the flying ironclad descended, thundering with the roar of a dozen whirling impeller engines.

"That's no cargo dirigible," I whispered, drawing to a stop just below the mezzanine.

"That's a military aircruiser!" Armez confirmed, his eyes widening in panic. "Where did they get a blasted *aircruiser*?"

I dashed up the steps to the mezzanine, making straight for one of the more crowded tables. The throng of stripe-suited men in pork pie hats turned as I approached, with more than a few hands slipping into their coats.

"Do you want to know who killed your boss?" I asked the grim-faced gathering. "It so happens we're just on our way to meet him."

The Travenni goons glanced between one another, and I

hurried on with a chorus of cocking guns and locking breeches following behind me. Armez and Quiniece raced past in a preternaturally accelerated dash, beating me to the doors at the far end of the mezzanine. They burst through the doors to a flight of metal stairs, and I picked up my pace with Keldon running by my side. We followed the vampires to the top of the stairs, a cavalcade of footfalls and angry calls trailing just behind us. The hatch at the top led straight into the cold night air, and we charged onto the sky-steamer's upper loading deck.

A whirlwind of turbulence whipped across my face, sweeping away my top hat and filling my lungs with sooty black smoke washed back from the ship's twin stacks. I threw my arm up, shielding my eyes from the blinding searchlights spilling from the enormous aircruiser hovering directly above. Forcing myself to look through the glare, I saw Commander Barquez, or the illusion of the commander at least, his arms raised as though to welcome the descending ship. The captain's crumpled form lay at the base of a nearby cargo crane—dead or unconscious I did not know.

"That's not the commander," Keldon yelled over the rushing wind. He tweaked the crystals on his spectacles, then nodded. "I can't make out his face—he's wearing an ornate mask. But he's dressed in a... Is that an old justacorps coat?"

The mask Keldon saw was Amaldiere's Masque of Illusions, and if the culprit was wearing a justacorps coat beneath the illusion...

"Tylon Meldanel," Armez called. He bared his teeth, his fists clenched by his sides. "If that's even who you really are!"

I nodded, feeling some small relief that my faint suspicion had proved correct, however tenuous it might have been. The gaudy dressed mage had abandoned our jonko game shortly before it ended and just minutes before the imposter commander first appeared. Tall and lanky, Tylon's build was similar to both Dupraine and Commander Barquez, and he was only slightly taller than Luigo. He didn't have Captain Darmoro's stout frame, but he could pass well enough for the captain, especially with that justacorps coat bulking out his figure.

"Where'd that ship come from?" Giono demanded as he and the other Travenni goons rushed out onto the deck. "Hey, isn't that Commander Barquez?"

The massive aircruiser descended—a veritable battleship of the sky—and its boarding ramp touched down on the deck just paces from where the imposter commander stood. A squad of mercenaries appeared at the mouth of the boarding ramp, armed and armored with the best battle gear money could buy. Tylon glanced back at us, his sneer turning up in a grin.

"Commander Barquez is dead," I called over my shoulder. "That's Tylon Meldanel, using an illusion to disguise himself as the commander. He's the one who killed Bardel Alanonni."

Giono cocked his pepperbox pistol and leveled it at the impersonator. "Take 'em down, boys!"

Tylon signaled to his mercenaries. "Kill them all!"

Gunfire cracked over the roar of wind and engines, and the mercenaries stormed down the boarding ramp as the Travennis split for cover and opened fire. I seized Keldon by the arm, hotfooting it across the deck as bullets burst through landing lights and ricocheted from mooring trusses all around us. We dropped behind the marginally less exposed cover of the loading crane near the body of Captain Darmoro. A nasty gash decorated the left side of his neck, clearly meant to sever his carotid artery, but the cut had missed its mark by a hair.

"He's still breathing," Keldon said, kneeling by the captain's side.

I whipped off my cravat and placed the cloth against the wound, applying pressure to stifle the bleeding. "I'm just glad Tylon didn't cut him with the Forsaken Blade."

Keldon looked up at me and blinked. "Oh, yeah? Why?"

A red blur struck across the starboard walkway, and three of Tylon's men went down—each skewered by a flashing rapier blade. The blur wheeled about, tailcoat billowing in the wash of the aircruiser's engines, and Armez dashed to the mercenaries forming up to protect Tylon. Quiniece pounced to the middle of the deck, losing a deluge of snapping electric arcs from her clockwork gauntlet and dropping three more men in the crackling storm. She tumbled aside as a hail of bullets cut through the deck where she had been. Taking aim as she rose, Quiniece fired a whirling bola from her gauntlet's pneumatic launcher, catching a fourth man in the legs and sending him toppling over the side of the ship, screaming.

"Don't just loll around, you wag!" she yelled at Keldon as she charged past. "Blast them!"

Keldon jumped up and flicked his wrist, thrusting out with his key as though to hurl an aetheric bolt at the mercenaries. Nothing happened.

"Hey!" he yelled, trying to yank his arm from my grasp. "Watch the severite, boss!"

"Don't draw their attention," I warned, still holding his arm. "They might—"

A battery of bullets hammered into my apprentice, three straight into his chest and a fourth striking him square in the head. With each impact the empowered brooch flashed to brilliant white, and, with a crackling pop, transposed the projectiles at their exact opposite trajectory. Two mercenaries dropped dead, both struck through the chest, and two others fell back gripping their gun arms in agony.

Keldon blinked, then touched the protective brooch pinned to his shirt. "Thanks for the brooch," he breathed.

I was about to ask my apprentice to get Captain Darmoro out of harm's way, but two crewmen were already at my side, fussing over their wounded skipper.

"His throat's been cut," I said to the pair. "Keep the pressure on with that cloth and get him below deck. Quickly now! Try to find one of the shamans onboard, and hurry."

Not even batting an eye at the battle raging around them, the crewmen lifted their captain and made straight for the hatch leading back into the ship.

With four of their number already down, the Travennis found themselves heavily outgunned. But Armez and his sireling more than made up the difference, cutting through the opposing mercenaries as they made straight for Tylon. Quiniece dropped another one, ducking the whirling teeth of his buzz-sword and finishing him with a crackling jolt from her gauntlet. Unconcerned by the bullets ripping apart his coat, Armez shoved his sword through the heart of his next victim, then punched another with such force that he flew clear over the ship's railing.

"Stop!" Tylon yelled. He drew a gleaming gold chalice from the bulging sack at his feet and held it in the air. "You want your precious chalice, bloodsucker?" he demanded, a cruel sneer twisting his face. "Then fetch it!"

With that, he hurled the chalice over the side of the ship. Tylon probably expected the vampires to launch themselves in mad pursuit of their precious relic, but he stood dumbfounded when a grappling line struck out, snagged the cup mid-air, and retracted.

"Never finagle with a newfangled gearmeister girl," Quiniece chided, the Chalice of the Blood King clutched in the grip of her clockwork gauntlet.

Tylon snatched up the oversized sack and dashed for the boarding ramp. But he stopped short of the ramp, his panicked eyes fixed on a shadow-shrouded figure standing at the threshold of the aircruiser's entrance. The sack lurched from his grasp and flew straight into the shadowy figure's arms.

Tylon looked at his empty hands, then turned his gaze to the Shadow Man. "M-my lord?"

"That's no illusion," Keldon whispered to me, adjusting his empowered spectacles. "All I can see of him are shadows... Shadows veiling shadows."

Tylon fell to his knees, his hands clasped together, pleading. "I have done all you have asked, my lord!" he called over the rushing wind and thundering engines. "The Bone Crown, the Forsaken Blade, and the Chaos Hexillion... They are all yours!"

The Shadow Man held out his inky black hand and the Forsaken Blade of Soulless Corruption floated up from the burlap sack. "You have done well," the Shadow Man commended in his sonorous voice. "But there is one final task you must complete."

"Yes, my lord?" Tylon asked, his voice trembling with fear. "What is your command?"

"Ravage!" the Shadow Man hissed.

The Forsaken Blade struck through the air, stabbing into Tylon's heart with a bone-crunching thump. He staggered back, the illusion around him flickering and vanishing as Amaldiere's Masque dropped from his face. With a scream of abject agony, Tylon reeled backwards, throwing his hands to his head and digging his nails through the skin of his forehead. Black veins coiled across his body like writhing worms, his justacorps coat splitting at the seams as bony protuberances erupted from his shoulders, spine, and skull. Chitinous scales burst from beneath his sloughing skin while clawed hands tore away what little human flesh remained. Tylon's mortified scream twisted into a chilling howl of mindless rage, and the hulking beast stepped forward, the deck trembling with the force of its terrible might.

"Choose your battle wisely, Vescard," boomed the Shadow Man's parting taunt. "Thwart our escape or save your friends and this ship from the rampaging abomination your dogged meddling has unleashed."

I clenched my jaw. It was no choice at all.

The remaining mercenaries watched in disbelief as the boarding ramp retracted, the Shadow Man laughing in certain victory as his thundering aircruiser pulled up and away. Gunfire erupted from both the mercenaries and the Travenni mobsters pelting the transmogrified fiend with bullets, but I knew nothing short of total annihilation would stop the demonic abomination.

With one swipe of its massive hand, the bellowing creature hurled three mercenaries over the side of the ship, then seized one of the Travennis in its crushing grip. Armez flourished his rapier and leaped to attack, only to be clubbed to the deck with what remained of the crumpled Travenni's corpse. Quiniece dashed forward to aid her master, depleting her gauntlet's galvanic vial in a crackling discharge that merely agitated the beast. When she ejected the spent glass tube and drew another glowing blue vial from her satchel, I knew what I had to do.

"Quiniece, throw me that vial!" I yelled, tossing my frock coat to Keldon.

She glanced at me, then looked to Armez who gave a quick nod. I caught the vial when she threw it to me, then pulled the locking pins from my severite wristbands. Knowing Keldon could not subdue me without the tranquilizer gun, I tossed the wristbands to Armez hoping the vampire, at least, might have some chance of restraining me. A heartbeat later, a flash of heat erupted through every nerve and fiber of my body. The vial shattered in my hand, and the volatile alchemicals surged through my veins as I convulsed in white-hot agony. My blood turned to molten cinnabar, my lungs burned with ignited phlogiston, and my flesh charred to scorched black coal.

The blazing alchemical fiend I had become threw back its flame-wreathed head and roared, unleashing a blazing deluge of combusting, vapor-point gas. Unfazed by the attack, the monstrous foe charged through the torrent of alchemical flames, delivering a bone-crushing punch that sent me crashing through one of the ship's bellowing smokestacks. But I was not alone in my struggle. The remaining Travennis and mercenaries had regrouped, bringing the full force of their firearms to bear, and even Armez took up two blow-back repeaters, one in either hand, gnashing his teeth as he pumped volley after volley from the pneumatic-powered guns. Dazzling lights and blinding bolts flashed from Keldon's talismanic key, and beside him stood Quiniece, her clockwork gauntlet spitting jolts of lightning.

Drawn by the clamor of the ongoing battle, a dozen of the ship's guards poured on to the deck followed by two private enforcer mages in glittering spellworked mail. Unfortunately, no one told the new arrivals who was friend and who was foe, and I soon found myself pelted by rounds of shock-charged bullets and concussive blasts of kinetic force.

The abomination landed another pulverizing punch, nearly sending me over the side of the ship, but my transmuted self held its ground, digging red-hot feet into the molten deck plates. I burned through the last of the concoction from Quiniece's vial, blasting an explosion of reactant fulminate from my outstretched arms. Waves of fire washed over the bone-knotted monster, but the alchemical blast did more harm to the loading deck than it did to our rancorous foe. Even as waves of searing heat coursed through my immolating body, a cold shudder struck down my spine. Without more reagents to fuel the alchemical reactor raging inside me, the demonic abomination would soon overwhelm me through sheer brute strength.

As though hearing my fears, my alchemical antithesis drove its fist like a hammer through the melting deck plates, focusing the last of its roiling energy straight down into the ship's engine room. Fire and smoke belched up from the decks below as tendrils of living flame sought the greatest source of power they could fine. And there, in the ship's beating clockwork heart, my quintessence touched a roaring maelstrom of pure elemental aethergy driving the empowered paddlewheels that kept our ship aloft.

A cascading fountain of fire, air, and light surged back up from the elemental furnace, siphoning into my arm and surging like a wellspring of energy through the blazing core of my being. The full force of that onrushing power seethed within me, coursing into my outstretched hand where it exploded in a devastating, molten white beam. The twisted abomination stood against the thundering river of elemental light and dazzling metaplasmic particles, screaming as its upheld arms blackened and crumbled into ash. Guards and mobsters alike fled as the air burned in the scorching conflagration—deck plates melting and glass panels exploding one after another down the length of the ship.

The abomination staggered backwards, buffeted not only by the torrent of elemental aethergy, but by volleys of bullets, cracking arcs of lightning, and sizzling fire bolts as the mages, guards, and mobsters joined my friends in the desperate assault. At last, the monster's bony carapace gave way, and the wash of sundering fire blasted it through the portside paddlewheel—its burning skeletal remains plunging to the night black sea a thousand fathoms below.

But one monster still lived. I turned from the smoldering ruin of the portside paddlewheel, the pulsing light of pure elemental energy surging through my veins, and gazed with burning ember eyes upon my friends' horrified faces. I screamed, a prisoner within my own transmogrified body, watching helplessly as the monster I had become stepped forward to slaughter them all.

Armez tossed my severite bonds to Quiniece, then darted straight at me with his twin repeaters rattling off salvos of lead. The bullets vanished to vapor before my upraised hand, but Armez's attack was just a distraction. From the corner of my fire-filled vision, I watched Quiniece prep her pneumatic launcher with a bola, my severite wristbands tied to either end. She leveled her gauntlet and fired, sending the bola whirling through the air toward me.

I reared back to release a deluge of fire and burning light upon both vampires, but the bola struck home, whipping around my legs and snaring me in the severite bonds. The severite's dampening effect swept over me, and I dropped to my knees in a cloud of scalding hot steam. Waves of excruciating agony ripped through every inch of my blistered skin, and I doubled over convulsing uncontrollably.

Keldon rushed to my side, throwing my coat over me as he knelt down to help. "Someone get a healer!" he yelled as I slipped into the merciful arms of unconsciousness.

We had not won the day, but we had survived. And for that, I could not have been more grateful.

ARMEZ PLAYED A MATCH OF THREE with the six of crowns, the six of coins, and the six of swords. His eyebrow perked as he considered the four cards still in his hand, but the slight expression was just a deception. The vampire had no tells. Keldon, unfortunately, was a different story. His shoulders slumped, his larynx bobbed, and he worried his lip as he pondered his cards. I had a lot left to teach the boy.

He began to lay down three cards, then stopped as he reconsidered. "I guess I'll pass."

Quiniece rolled her eyes. "Amateurs." She glanced at her own cards, her alabaster face an inscrutable mask. "Pass," she said, leaving no question that she was holding back.

"I was never very good at jonko myself," Captain Darmoro said, pairing two of his cards together. He rubbed the scar on his neck, then gazed across the toppled chairs and tables of the half-vacant gambling hall before looking up to the walls of broken glass. Outside, the first light of the morning sun peeked over the eastern horizon, casting a dim orange haze across the sandy beach where the *Gambler's Boon* had made an emergency landing. "But what else have I to do until the rescue ships arrive?" He laid down a spread of four crowns—a seven, an eight, a nine, and the knight of crowns. "No thanks to all of you."

Without the duke of crowns, I couldn't ride Darmoro's play with my own queen and king of crowns. But I did have a match with my newly dealt four of coins. I laid down the two, three, four, and five of coins, then leaned back in my chair with only the queen and king of crowns in hand.

"Would you have preferred that the man who murdered Commander Barquez got away?" I rubbed the newly healed scabs on my face and sighed. "At least we recovered Amaldiere's Masque and the Chalice of the Blood King."

Captain Darmoro shook his head. "I would have preferred that you not demolish half my ship trying to stop them. And the fact that you recovered those artifacts hardly counts when I'm obligated to surrender them."

I gave the captain a sympathetic smile. "You do realize that all of the remaining 'prizes' will also be confiscated, to be sealed forever in the Archidoxy's Fathomless Vault?"

Captain Darmoro sighed. "They aren't mine, detective. I just captain the boat."

"Well, they won't get their hands on *this* artifact," Armez said, pouring the sanguine contents of the golden chalice into his wine glass. "It would be such a waste for anyone other than myself to possess this fine heirloom of my ancestors' proud heritage." He added more water to the chalice, smiling as it instantly turned into blood. "Care for some?" he asked Quiniece. "I can't help but notice the way you keep licking your lips whenever you eye the nice young lad sitting beside you. Or is there perhaps another reason for your present state of distraction?"

Quiniece sank into her chair, hiding her face behind her cards. "No thanks, boss," she mumbled. "I'm good."

Keldon shifted in his chair uneasily. Armez quirked a smile, then dealt everyone their next card. I peeled mine off the table and forced myself not to grin. It was the duke of crowns. Together with my queen and king of crowns, I could call the game on my turn. Although five cards were needed for a jonko, a win was still a win, even if it was a weak win.

"We can at least be thankful that the Forsaken Blade has been lost to the sea," I said.

Armez narrowed his eyes. "Yes, but they have the Chaos

Hexillion." He laid down the three, four, and five of stars. "As well as the Bone Crown of Dagoroth."

"Hah!" Keldon exclaimed. He dropped the six and seven of stars, riding Armez's spread, and followed up with a matching nine of coins, nine of swords, and nine of stars. "Beat *that*."

"Jonko," Quiniece chimed, producing an astounding seven-card spread: a two, three, four, five, seven, and an eight of swords, with the jester for the six of swords.

Keldon's grin drooped in dismay.

I laid my cards on the table. "I certainly can't beat that."

"Neither can I," Darmoro lamented. "And it seems rather unlikely that anyone can double jonko a seven-card spread."

Quiniece grinned as she piled the cards together, then split the stack and began to shuffle. "Care for another round, boys?"

Armez looked to the dome of shattered glass above. "The sun is coming up," he said, his eyes fixed on the volcanic visage of Atracus, fading to a dim specter before the dawn. "Though I fear it only heralds portents of the coming midnight storm. The dark above, the dark below—as it has ever been. Yet still we busy about our petty affairs, complacent in our ignorance of the ancient powers that stir once more." The vampire took the chalice and stood, donning his red-tinted spectacles and tapping his cane to the brim of his top hat in a kind of mock salute. "Farewell, my dear Vescard. Until we meet again."

I worried my chin as I watched him turn and leave, Quiniece following with a grudging huff. Armez knew far more than he let on, for not only had he named the Servants of Vosh and hinted at their monstrous plans, but in his parting words he spoke their enigmatic epigram that twisted the very words of *The Precepts*: 'As above, so below; the dark above, the dark below.'

Yes, we would be seeing Armez and his sireling again. But would they be friends or would they be foes?

CASE FILE 9:

THE MADNESS OF DOCTOR MALDAN ZAVEROI

HAD I NOT BEEN TOLD OTHERWISE, I would have guessed that the victims had been sucked into a pneumatic compressor, passed through a steam press roller, and spat out the nasty end of an industrial-sized ore grinder. The fact that there were two victims, and not simply one overly corpulent individual, would not have been apparent, save for the fact that I had identified more than two humerus bones. Shattered glass, splintered tables, and broken tiles littered the area around the mangled remains, and a six-foot crater scarred the manor's fabricrete foundation, heaped with the twisted wreckage of what once had been Doctor Zaveroi's aetheric amplification modulator.

I knelt beside the imploded ruins of the machine to examine the pieces that were more-or-less intact. "And you are quite certain this was not an accident?"

Doctor Maldan Zaveroi threw a linen sheet over the remains, then brushed out the wrinkles in the ruffled shirt beneath his tailored morning coat. "For it to have been an accident, three independent safety regulators would have to fail simultaneously while the machine experienced a catastrophic overload. I cannot say that is impossible, but it is supremely unlikely."

Doctor Zaveroi was a renowned aetherological theorist, a preeminent teratologist, and a pioneer in the field of thaumaturgical engineering. He even held a chair on the advisory board of the Royal Academy of Armillia. For him to have made a careless mistake was unlikely. Unfortunately, too little of the machine remained to perform a proper analysis.

"Do you have reason to suspect either of your assistants?" I asked. "Or former assistants, I should say."

"No," Zaveroi admitted. "But neither would I rule out their involvement." He watched me examine the crumpled husk of the aetheric modulator, stroking his neatly trimmed beard as though in thought. "The only motivation I can imagine is money. I did not pay them what I should have, and it is possible that a rival of mine bribed them into sabotaging my life's work. You must understand that the contention for research and development grants is quite competitive these days."

It was a reasonable hypothesis. Tampering with a high-energy aetheric modulator was dangerous business, and the machine could well have overloaded and imploded once the safety regulators had been disengaged.

I looked across the laboratory to Keldon, who seemed uncomfortably anxious as he paced in front of a row of bookshelves. In any other investigation I would have enlisted his assistance to scan for residual aetheric imprints, remnant spell fragments, or other evidence of culpable ensorcellment. However, the machine's catastrophic overload had another startling effect beyond turning two laboratory helpers inside out. In fact, it was the sole reason I had put my investigation of the Shadow Man on hiatus to take the case.

I stood, dusting off my hands. "Explain to me how an imploding aetheric modulator could leave a void in the aether?"

Zaveroi's shoulders dropped slightly. "I am still trying to figure that out myself. From what I have determined, the overloading modulator funneled all ambient aethergy into a self-sustaining cascade vortex, dragging the fabric of the aetheric substrata along with it. Whether Jorven or Dechon sabotaged the machine or were simply unfortunate enough to be in the room at the time, you can see the resulting effect. But the effect on the local aether was just as bad." He paused for a moment, as though unsure how to phrase his next words. "It may sound callous, but the real damage lies in the fact that magic no longer works within this laboratory, and throughout most of my manor as well. I will have to relocate if I am to continue my career."

"I still don't see how this is possible," Keldon said from across the laboratory. "We call it magic, but aetheric energy is still subject to the laws of nature. Just as heat moves from areas of higher heat to lower heat, so does aethergy. Saying there's a null-aethergy void is like saying there's a null-heat void. More aethergy should just flow into the area to fill the void."

Zaveroi frowned, but only for a moment. "Your apprentice is well versed in the laws of aetherodynamics, Vescard. But it is not that simple. You see, the damage was done to the aetheric substrata itself."

I looked to my severite wristbands, my brow furrowing as I contemplated the implications of the null-aethergy void. "I am not so much concerned with the effects of this phenomenon as I am in its cause. If this was sabotage, then we need to uncover the villain who is responsible."

Despite my words, I was *very* curious about the effect. Severite dampens aetheric energy, suppressing my uncontrollable alchemical transmutation. Would not a null-aethergy void have the same effect? Could I safely remove my severite wristbands here, within this null-aethergy void? Dare I risk it?

"Quite right, detective. Would you like to see the rooms where Jorven and Dechon stayed?"

Still lost in my own thoughts, I had only caught part of what Doctor Zaveroi had said. "Yes, of course." I dropped my arms to my side and straightened my frock coat. "We should inspect their rooms."

"I am aware of your condition, Vescard." Zaveroi clasped his hands behind his back and smiled, his eyes brightening. "I can see you are wondering what effect this aetheric void might have on you." He looked to Keldon and nodded. "Here, your apprentice is as incapable of wielding magic as any mage bound in severite bonds, for the effect of this void is much the same. Remove your wristbands and I think you will be pleasantly surprised."

Was it possible? Was it too much to hope for? Had Doctor Maldan Zaveroi discovered, quite by accident, a cure to my infernal curse?

Drawing a deep breath, I pulled the pin from my left wristband and let it fall to the floor. I felt no searing pain, no boiling fire within my blood, and no scalding blisters on my skin. With growing hope, I removed the second wristband and waited.

Nothing happened.

"Aldicus?" Keldon asked. His eyes widened as he realized what was happening—or rather, what was not happening. "Aldicus, do you know what this means?"

I handed my apprentice my wristbands, along with the black bag containing my collection of alchemical supplies and investigation tools. "It means that we are indeed within a null-aethergy void." I looked to Zaveroi. "Does the void extend all the way to Jorven's and Dechon's rooms?"

"It extends through most of the manor," he confirmed. He started for the door leading to the hall and motioned for us to follow. "Allow me to show you the way."

I massaged my wrists as we followed Doctor Zaveroi through his manor, which doubled as his private research facility. Leaving the laboratory wing behind, we found ourselves in the south wing, which he dedicated to his other chief interest: teratology.

The yawning hall he led us through was as tall as it was

wide, nearly fifteen feet, and containment cells of various sizes ran along either side. Each cell featured its own observation window and reinforced metal door, many of them battered as though from inside. I had already verified that Zaveroi was licensed to keep the creatures in his extraordinary menagerie, but that fact lent me little comfort as we strode down the aisle flanked by the shrieking, roaring, clawing horrors of nature's most aberrant monstrosities.

Keldon's jaw hung open, his finger pointing as he singled out the most dangerous of the lot. "There's a forest troll, and over there a frilled drake. I think there's a couple of barghests in that cell, right next to that pair of chimeras. And is that a bulgore?"

I looked to where he was pointing and drew a sharp breath when I saw the hulking brute. It was akin to a massive bear, but with cloven hooves, ape-like arms, and the head and horns of a monstrous bull. "That's definitely a bulgore."

"I wouldn't worry," Zaveroi said. "The walls are composed of polymetalloid quartzstone and the glass is spell-tempered tektite. Not even dragon's fire can burn through."

Keldon stopped in front of one of the cells. The frilled drake inside hissed and launched itself straight at him, slamming against the tektite glass. He jumped in start, but the fear quickly vanished. "Arleia would be fascinated by this collection. She and Leta aren't far from here, you know?"

"Oh?" I asked, raising an eyebrow.

Keldon grinned. "I gave Arleia one of my empowered tracker beacons. You know, just in case. I think they're in the lower wards, across the East Axis investigating a rash of wraith activity in the sublevels there."

I nodded, rubbing my wrists again, scarcely able to believe I could go without my wristbands. "Perhaps Doctor Zaveroi would give a private tour for all of us once this business has been resolved."

Zaveroi bowed his head and smiled. "I would be delighted."

He led us further down the menagerie wing, and we passed a number of empty cells, some piled with dust and rubble. The doors to those cells were open, and Zaveroi probably intended to clean them out.

"My elemental constructs and mortifant undead did not survive the null-aethergy void," Zaveroi explained, looking to the empty cells. "Their existence is bound to the aetheric quintessence, much as your own elemental form, Vescard."

"Mortifants?" I asked with a frown. "You're not licensed to keep or study undead. In fact, there are no such licenses. You risk charges of karcistry, even if you did not raise them yourself."

"True, but I would be remiss as a teratologist to ignore the splendid diversity found among the undead—mortifants, ghouls, ghastuls, necrocites, bone-walkers..." He stopped and looked at me with a troubling grin. "There are few monsters more terrifying than the risen dead. In fact, there is only one that I can think of. One that would be the crowning jewel of my treasured collection."

I stopped and took a hesitant step back. A sudden wildness gleamed in Doctor Zaveroi's eyes as he considered me. Considered me, as a predator might consider its prey.

"Keldon," I whispered, holding out my hand. "Keldon, my wristbands..."

Zaveroi's grin widened to a sneer and he drew a small control disk from his coat pocket. "Welcome, Vescard, to my singular collection." With a laugh, he gave a dial on the disk a sharp twist.

The null-aethergy void vanished and the aether came crashing back in. Burning pain struck through my body, searing nerves and boiling blood as the elemental chaos within me took hold. Keldon yelled, and I whirled about only to watch as a lumbering brute of a man, with arms like boulders and a face pockmarked with pebbles, seized my young apprentice. Keldon kicked and struggled, trying in vain to escape the stone man's unyielding grip.

"Hold him!" Zaveroi ordered. "Hold him and watch the alchemorph incinerate his helpless apprentice!"

Flames erupted along my arms, then spread across my entire body. My heart blazed like a blast furnace; my blood surged with liquid cinnabar; my lungs heaved like a blacksmith's bellows. "Fangle-fop!" I managed to breathe as I staggered back.

Zaveroi's deception was complete. The entire case had been a ruse to lure me to his research manor and draw me into his trap. Without my severite wristbands, the raging, alchemical being within me would surely kill Keldon, along with everyone else that stood in my way. With only seconds to react, I threw myself into the nearest empty cell hoping Zaveroi was right about its indestructibility.

Laughing, Zaveroi slammed the cell door shut and locked it tight with a spin of the hatch wheel. Having lost all control over the monster I had become, I slammed against the cell window, exploding liquid fire and molten light in all directions. I struck the window again and again, shrieking in mindless rage. But the diamond-hard glass did not falter or give way.

"At last!" Zaveroi declared, clapping his hands in delight. His eyes quivered with euphoric rapture. "The living calamity of Aldicus Vescard at last belongs to me!"

I AWOKE ON THE ICE-COLD FLOOR of a polymetalloid quartzstone cell, a sackcloth gown draped over my naked body like a blanket. I looked at my wrists, but my severite wristbands were nowhere to be found. Doctor Zaveroi must have reactivated his null-aethergy field, but whether or not the field encompassed his entire manor, or was focused on my cell alone, I did not know. Despite my exhaustion, I managed to sit up and pull on the sackcloth garment. The coarse material chafed my skin, but I felt no pain from the burns and blisters that would normally have covered me. In fact, I was completely free of any sign that I had been a blazing alchemical monster only hours before.

The stone-covered man who had seize Keldon stood just beyond the wall-sized window of my cell. Tall and broad shouldered, he wore burlap trousers and a tunic like a blacksmith's apron, but was covered in tough skin embedded with rocks and pebbles, like aggregate stone. He was not an elemental construct, but a man sure enough, for the eyes staring out from his gravel-knotted face were all too human. In his rough hands he held a pewter tray heaped with tuber mash and sliced beef.

My stomach rumbled.

I staggered to my feet and approached the window. "Where is Keldon?"

The stone man said nothing at first. Then he nodded slowly. "The other one? Your friend?" he asked, his deep voice muted through the tektite glass. "He in other cell."

"Is he all right? Did you harm him?"

The stone man's sunken eyes widened. "No. I not hurt him. I hold him, like master say. Put him in other cell." He looked down at the tray in his hands, apparently remembering the reason for his visit. "I bring food."

I waited for the stone man to slide the trade through the slot at the base of the cell door, then yelled through the glass before he lumbered away. "What is your name?"

The stone man turned to face me, wincing as he put too much weight on the leg he favored when he walked. "Borthon," he replied, and winced again as he drew himself up.

"Are you in pain, Borthon? What has Zaveroi done to you?"

"Master make me strong," Borthon replied. He then seemed to remember something else. "Master say I no talk to you."

Undoubtedly. Borthon was simple of mind, but had he always been that way, or was it an effect of his transmutation?

"He fused your body with a stone elemental, didn't he?" I asked. Borthon stared back blankly. He probably had no idea what I was talking about, but the agony he endured from such an unnatural fusion of flesh and stone had to be unbearable. "I can stop your pain. I can cure you. I just need you to get—"

"No!" Borthon exclaimed, waving his rock-covered arm. "Master say he make me better. Say he must learn from you, then he finish work on me."

"Borthon, wait," I said as he turned to leave. But he just shook his head, limping out of sight.

I dropped back onto the floor and hung my head in shame. I had lied to Borthon, hoping to trick him into setting me free. In truth, I could do nothing to ease his pain, and I doubted anything could be done to reverse his transformation—just as there was no cure for mine.

I ate the cold mash and dried beef from the pewter plate, only then realizing why it was pewter. If I refused to return it through the slot, hoping to somehow use it as a tool or weapon, it would simply melt and evaporate the next time I transmuted into... What had Zaveroi called it? An *alchemorph.* It was as good a name as any.

"How is my prize specimen this morning?" came a voice seemingly out of thin air. But not out of thin air, of course. If Zaveroi had found a way to dampen the currents of the luminiferous aether, he certainly possessed the means to control vibrations in the air. "Are we ready to begin the first experiment?"

"Would it matter if I said no?" I asked the doctor's disembodied voice.

"Not particularly."

I stood, holding myself as dignified as I could, being garbed in nothing more than a sackcloth bag. "Release my apprentice and I will fully cooperate in your experiments."

Doctor Zaveroi's laugh echoed between the cell's quartzstone walls. "Your cooperation is neither required nor desired. Resist, Vescard. Resist with every dram of strength you can muster!"

I balled my hands into fists. He was right, of course. I could not resist the transmutation. "Then I beg you, do not harm him."

"Why would I harm the boy? I only wish to improve him. You have already met my servant, Borthon. But do not fear. I take meticulous care when learning from my previous mistakes. The knowledge that I will gain from you will advance my experiments to their supreme perfection. Your apprentice will be made... Better."

"You are a *monster*," I growled through clenched teeth.

"So says the worm to the inquiring knife of science."

The jolt of searing hot pain nearly knocked me unconscious. Zaveroi had switched off the null-aethergy field, and within seconds of its release my entire body erupted in flames. My nerves burned as though torn by white-hot needles, blood boiling into liquid cinnabar as my flesh and bones ignited like coal. Scarcely had my transformation finished when the alchemorph blasted the tektite window with a stream of molten fire. The glass remained wholly unscathed, and my diametric antithesis howled with insatiable rage.

With a thump and a rumble, the back wall of my cell slid open to reveal a second room beyond. My alchemorph surged into the room like a rolling firestorm, shrieking as it entered yet another inescapable chamber of quartzstone walls. Four glass receptacles lowered from tubes in the high ceiling, each one filled with a different alchemical liquid or powdered metal. But before my alchemorph reached them, an opening on the far side of the chamber slid away. From the cell beyond charged a nine-foot-tall forest troll, bellowing in torment as it raised its crude iron club to attack.

The poor creature never stood a chance. The glass receptacles shattered as I drew in and absorbed the alchemical reagents, mixing and reacting them within the volatile bowels of my immolating body. I watched through eyes of brimstone embers as a spray of fulminic acid and burning phlogiston exploded across the room to engulf the troll. Rushing through the infernal deluge, the savage troll fell upon me even as its leathery skin peeled away like flakes of burning paper. The iron club swung, melting to slag as it passed through the churning alchemical furnace of my transmuted form. Seconds later, the troll's disintegrating skeleton spilled across the floor like the logs of a collapsing bonfire.

No sooner had the troll perished than the fiery maelstrom of my body grew suddenly cold. Elemental matter snapped back to corporeal flesh, and bone, sinew, and muscles reconstituted to their original form. I dropped to my knees, my aching lungs straining for breath in the smoke-choked air, the noxious stench of burnt troll flesh causing me to double over and retch.

"Observe how your body is free from burns or other injury," Zaveroi's voice announced. "This evinces my theory of spontaneous alchemical transubstantiation—provided that your transition occurs as near to instantaneous as possible."

"Why?" I managed to ask between gasps of air.

"It is simple, Vescard. The faster the phase change between the alchemorph and your mortal body, the less damage will—"

"No," I interrupted, still coughing. "Why... Why are you doing this?"

Zaveroi gave no reply at first. "To learn, of course," he answered after a long silence. "For what other reason do men such as us probe the darkest secrets of Nature's outermost boundaries?"

Had I once been as deranged as this madman? No, not even during my most ambitious experiments had I dared to commit such unspeakable atrocities against another living creature. My experiments had been upon myself, and I alone had paid the price for my reckless folly. But Zaveroi was a man of ruthless determination, indifferent to whatever suffering he wrought.

"Boundaries exist for a reason!" I yelled.

"Boundaries exist to be *broken*!" barked the reply. "Shall we continue the experiment, Vescard?"

Four more glass receptacles descended from the ceiling, and another door opened on the wall releasing a pair of savage barghests—howling as their black, bristle-haired forms lunged toward me. I screamed as flames engulfed my body, and the scream melted into the roar of a blast furnace as my alchemorph rushed to obliterate the hopelessly outmatched opponents. The bloody trials continued, victim after victim and hour after hour, until that ceaseless conflagration of pain, fire, and death blurred into a single moment of consummate awareness.

It was then that my conscious mind touched the chaos raging in the fiery depths of my tortured being. And, in that instant, I felt the chaos within me shudder in fear.

BORTHON FINISHED SECURING MY ARMS to the severite chains on the wall of my cell, muttering quietly to himself as his stony hands locked the bonds tight. I could not discern precisely what he was muttering, his voice was too gravelly and deep, but I did catch something about patching crossbeams. I could only assume that my long days of fighting had begun to damage the structure of the building.

"Why am I being chained?" I asked Borthon for the third time. I looked to the high ceiling. "Zaveroi, can you hear me?"

"He busy." Borthon stopped and shook his head. "No. Master say I no talk to you. Master busy. Must work."

I gave the chains a futile yank. "Were you not supposed to let me eat before chaining me up?" I asked, glancing to the tray of food on the floor.

Borthon looked around confused, then he shook his stony head. "Food for other. For your friend."

I sighed. At least Zaveroi was doing something to care for Keldon. I could only hope he had not yet begun whatever abominable experiments he had planned for him.

"The two men who were killed in the laboratory—were they actually Zaveroi's assistants?"

Borthon shook his head. "They..." He paused, perhaps trying to recall the word. "They vagrants." He took the tray of food and started out the cell door.

"Borthon," I called, causing him to stop. "Your master is a bad man. You do know that, don't you?"

Borthon glanced down, but said nothing.

I had to try. "He hurts you, doesn't he? You try to do what he asks, but he is never pleased and he punishes you, even when you do not know why. I know what kind of a man he is, and he is a monster."

After a moment Borthon replied. "No. He study monsters. He master of monsters."

"No, Borthon. There is only one monster in this place. His name is Zaveroi."

Borthon shook his head and began muttering again. He closed my cell door and I watched through the tektite window as he limped across the wide hall to the cells on the other side. If I recalled correctly, there were two empty cells on my side of the hall and three on the side opposite. I could see into the window of the empty cell directly across from me, and a good quarter of the one next to it. If Borthon was bringing the food to Keldon, then he had to be in the third empty cell on the other side of the hall, just out of sight. Although that information did me little good, I felt somewhat better having deduced where Keldon was being held.

Most of the day passed before Borthon returned. My arms had grown sore in their constrained position, and my sackcloth garment did little to warm the chill of the quartzstone wall at my back. The only explanation I could surmise for being shackled in severite was that Zaveroi needed to work on his null-aethergy device, either to improve it or, more likely, to fix some component that had worn out. That meant the device required periodic maintenance and could break down if left running for too long.

Borthon tried his best to ignore me as he unlocked my bonds, but he continued muttering, this time about bracing the support pilings. He left after letting me down, leaving me with another pewter plate of tuber mash and dried beef.

"I hope you are well rested, Vescard," resonated Doctor Zaveroi's voice through my cell.

I had only just finished off the unsavory dinner, and I gulped down the last of the water in the battered pewter cup before answering. "Why? Is the alchemorph weakened by my fatigue?"

"A valid question, but I have already discounted it," Zaveroi replied. "You, however, are debilitated in direct proportion to the energy expended by the alchemorph. In our next set of experiments, I will be correlating this pattern with the alchemorph's consumption of alchemical reagents. Precise regulation of the flow of alchemicals, together with pinpoint adjustments to the attenuation of the aetheric field, should enable me to stabilize the reactant conversion. After all, the alchemorph is a living alchemical reactor, and like any reactor, it can be controlled."

"How long do you think you can keep these experiments up?" I demanded, looking to the ceiling. "Days? Weeks?"

"As long as necessary," Zaveroi answered. "Your original experiment came very close to the pinnacle of alchemical perfection, but where you failed, I shall succeed." He paused, then continued, quoting from *The Precepts of the Great Work*. "'Through these stages does the sage transform both the subtle and the gross, ascending from earth to heaven and back to earth again, unifying in exalted splendor that which is above with that which is below. In this way were all things created and in this way shall all things be uncreated, through the force of all forces, the power of all power, and the unity of all unity.'"

"Do not quote *The Precepts* to me," I growled. It was those very words that had led me to my failed experiment, resulting in the creation of the alchemorph. Zaveroi was clearly pursuing the same line of forbidden research. "You defile its sacred truth with these abominable experiments."

Zaveroi chuckled. "As did you, Vescard. Your quest to transmute your own living quintessence to pure elemental essence was flawed, for you did not consider the subtle influence of the higher aetheric currents. I would like to see if the astral confluence of the upcoming ecliptic conjunction stabilizes the alchemorph's negative energy resonance. Sadly, that will have to wait another few months. I can only hope you will survive until then."

The back wall of my cell slid open, revealing the testing room beyond. I cringed, bracing myself for the coming pain, then screamed as my body ignited in a furor of all-consuming flames. I was helpless to resist the overpowering impulse to destroy, and my alchemorph roared into the adjacent room hungry to slaughter the coterie of goblins waiting there. The diminutive creatures scattered at the first sight of the fire-wreathed abomination racing toward them, dropping their primitive spears and shrieking in pitiful terror. Doctor Zaveroi knew that such woeful opponents would do nothing to hinder the alchemorph—they were merely targets for its power, as were all the doomed captives of Zaveroi's menagerie.

After the goblins came a pair of giant arachnidons, followed by four barghests. The two chimeras, both of the lion-boar-scorpion variety, proved markedly more challenging, but only because they possessed innate aetheric defenses. With each attack, I pressed my will upon the raging chaos that was the mind of the alchemorph—if a mind that roiling fury could be called. Perhaps I was nothing more than an itch to the frenzied fiend, but when I narrowed my focus in one direction or another, I found that the alchemorph glanced the same way.

In the fight with the arachnidons, I was able to distract the alchemorph from its attack for a few seconds at a time. Again, I drew the alchemorph's attention away when the four barghests rushed into the room, though only for three seconds before it dissolved the beasts in a deluge of caustic alkali and corrosive sublimate. The alchemorph's eagerness to attack the chimeras was overwhelming, but I used its own fervor to my advantage. Fixing my focus on the chimeras caused the alchemorph to lash out against the creatures before it had finished absorbing the alchemicals from their receptacles. The fight was all the more difficult for it, but when the battle was done, two of the receptacles remained full—one with phlogistonic fulminate and the other containing vitriolic chlorinate.

I had not expected Zaveroi to release the frilled drake for the next battery of tests, but the fifteen-foot-long fire-breathing beast provided an opportunity I could not ignore. Four empty receptacles filled from the tubes leading into the room, one with volatilis ammoniac, one with an aqueous solution of aurium, and the other two with corrosive sublimate and caustic alkali. Dragons were all but immune to both acid and fire, and Zeveroi no doubt wished to see if the alchemorph preferred one set of alchemicals over the other. What he had failed to consider were the alchemicals that remained in the receptacles from the previous battle. Neither had he considered the potent brew of flammable acids in the belly of the beast before me.

The drake thrashed forward on its arching legs, its rainbow-colored frills flaring outward as fire vomited from its maw. Unfazed by the flames, my alchemorph went straight for the receptacles of corrosive sublimate and caustic alkali. Although I could not direct the alchemorph to take any one specific action, I *could* direct its attention. Narrowing my focus on the frilled drake's belly, I flashed thoughts of the volatile alchemical mixture boiling in its gullet.

Dragon physiology is a field unto itself, but for an

alchemist, it is the unique blend of acids and compounds found in the special pouches of their first stomach that is of greatest interest. Ammonia, aqua fortis, palmitic acid, and pyrophoric phosphate, along with partially digested peat, are vomited up and ignited by the gnashing of a pair of specialized teeth, resulting in the dragon's blast furnace breath. Although normally quite stable within a dragon's belly, a well-placed cannon shot can rupture the stomach and detonate the compounds, killing the dragon and anything else unfortunate enough to be nearby.

With almost sadistic glee, the alchemorph launched itself straight for the dragon's mouth. It came as little surprise that the one-ton frilled drake erupted in a bone-charring fireball the instant my alchemorph projected its incendiary arms down its throat. Most of the explosion was absorbed when the alchemorph consumed the reacting compounds into its own fiery bulk, leaving the burned-out husk of the beast gutted from jaw to bowels.

I had only moments to put the rest of my plan into action. If Zaveroi even suspected that I held the slightest influence over the alchemorph, he would terminate the test in an instant—and with it, my only chance of escape. I focused my thoughts on the receptacles containing volatilis ammoniac and aqueous aurium, as well as the two receptacles that remained from the earlier test. Then I pictured a pencil-thin jet of scorching hot flame striking my cell's tektite window. Thirsting for freedom as much as I, the alchemorph responded immediately.

The glass receptacles shattered as the alchemorph siphoned their contents with unquenchable ferocity, reacting aqueous aurium, volatilis ammoniac, vitriolic chlorinate, and phlogistonic fulminate together with the roiling hot contents of the dragon's stomach. The explosive stew of volatile reagents combined and combusted, creating new and unique compounds the likes of which I had scarcely imagined, each one forming and dissolving in the blink of an eye.

Yet, rather than exploding outward, the alchemical inferno crushed in on itself, burning hotter and faster as the alchemorph drew in the very air of the room, creating an ever-shrinking bubble of impossibly dense pressure. Blistering red fire flared to blinding white as the aurium burned, releasing vast quantities of aethergy, and the accelerating reaction rebounded with such tremendous force that I thought it would blast the alchemorph into oblivion. Instead, the alchemorph wheeled around to face the tektite window and opened one tiny aperture in the collapsing pressure bubble, allowing the full force of the explosion to escape in a tightly focused beam of coherent energy.

The window exploded in a shower of molten crystal shards, as did the window of the cell on the other side of the hall, leaving a sizable hole punched clean through the quartzstone wall beyond that. My hopes rose, and I felt a rush of unbounded exhilaration from the alchemorph as it roared free from our imprisonment. Zaveroi would activate his null-aethergy device any second now, but I had one last thing to do before my ploy was ended.

Keldon's cell was just across the hall and three cells down, exactly where I had surmised. I held his image in my mind, focusing on my hopes for his safety and well-being, and recalled Borthon's mutterings about the building's damaged structure. Like a boilerman stoking the coals of a furnace, a flash of hate flared within the alchemorph's blazing heart as the monster reveled in the thought of burning my apprentice to cinders.

Keldon stood in the window of his cell, his wrists bound in severite handcuffs, staring in wide-eyed disbelief as my alchemorph surged forward with murderous intent. He must have guessed what was about to happen, for he ducked down and tumbled to the back of the cell just before a torrent of boiling, burning alchemical fire erupted from the alchemorph's outstretched hands. Although the cells themselves were enclosed in polymetalloid quartzstone, the floor of the hall was ordinary granite tile over floorboards, crossbeams, and pilings. Following a second fulminating fireball, the floor exploded in a shower of burning splinters and shattered boards, and the already weakened crossbeams and pilings finally gave way.

Mere seconds had passed, but I heard Zaveroi scream over the crashing thunder of collapsing wood and stone. Keldon's cell, and the ones to either side, broke from their foundations and the quartzstone cracked under its own immense weight, opening a great fissure in the floor. I could do nothing as the alchemorph lashed out with a volley of scorching fire, continuing its relentless march for Keldon's broken cell across the burning, smoke-filled hall. Through the rising dust and falling embers I saw a flash of movement heading for the fissure, and the alchemorph blasted the darting shape without hesitation.

An ice-cold chill gripped my entire body and I dropped to the floor, limp and exhausted, as the fire of the alchemorph dissipated. I could barely breathe in the smoke-filled hall, my skin blistering as I lay on the still burning embers of charred floorboards where the alchemorph had stood only seconds before. The last thing I saw before slipping into unconsciousness was Borthon bounding into the hall with a keg of water in tow and a wet blanket to throw over me.

"THAT WAS A MOST IMPRESSIVE DISPLAY."

I opened my eyes and looked up. Doctor Maldan Zaveroi stood in the window of my new cell, his eyes narrowed in consideration. He stroked his neatly trimmed beard, then turned his smile to an impish grin.

"I had no idea the alchemorph could generate an elemental annihilation reaction, not unlike that of a solaonic reactor of Maradian over-science," he went on to say. "If only I had some radiant aurium we could test your ultimate potential." He then sighed and shook his head. "It's too bad about your apprentice, though. I will have to find a new specimen for the next stage of my experiment."

"Keldon!" I sprang from the floor and slammed my fists into the tektite glass. "What has happened? What have you done with him?"

Zaveroi blinked in surprise. "I have done nothing, Vescard. You are the one who killed him in that wonderful rampage of yours. Don't pretend you have forgotten. I know you are conscious of everything that transpires while you are in that form."

I remained silent for a moment, looking beyond Zaveroi to the still-smoking ruins of the cells behind him. The last I had seen of Keldon, he had been running for the fissure in the floor just before my alchemorph blasted the entire area into rubble. I swallowed down the fear clenching my stomach. Had he gotten to the fissure in time?

"Where..." my voice shook as I spoke. "Where is his body? I... I need to see the body."

"Somewhere in that mess," Zaveroi replied, nodding his head to the rubble. "Borthon is digging around for whatever might be left, though I doubt he'll find more than a few charred bones."

Keldon wasn't dead... If Zaveroi could not produce the body, then there was no body to produce. I nearly cried out with joy, but Zaveroi had to see me broken by the pain and anguish of Keldon's death. I quickly covered my face with my hands, then slid down the glass to crumple into a ball on the floor. I began to rock where I sat with my coarse sackcloth garment pulled tightly around me, delivering my best imitation of weeping.

"There is no need to despair, Vescard," Zaveroi said, his voice full of smug derision. "My experiment is far from ruined. I still have you, and I still have my laboratory and my aetheric negator."

Zaveroi chuckled and walked away, and I waited a few moments before moving to a corner in the back of my cell. The cramped room stank of troll, and it had only been given a cursory wash down after its last tenant had been vacated—no doubt the same troll I had fought in my first trial.

I could only wonder at what new experiments Zaveroi had in mind. Most of his menagerie had already been wiped out, either during my earlier trials or as a result of my alchemorph's recent rampage. Many of the cells I could see were destroyed or empty, but some were still host to one captive beast or another—two more chimeras, a few barghests, and, of course, the bulgore. Of those, only the bulgore might give my alchemorph pause. While bulgores were not immune to fire, the one-ton half-bull, half-bear brute was tougher than a mastodon and more aggressive than a rabid barghest.

Regardless of Zaveroi's plans, at least I knew Keldon had escaped. Zaveroi believed him dead, and so much the better, for if the mad doctor even suspected my apprentice had gotten away, he would likely resort to drastic measures to cover up his crimes. Knowing Keldon, he would seek help from the nearest ally, but Vandor Tower was halfway across the city and he knew better than to call for the dismally inept district police. Who then would he seek?

"Leta," I whispered under my breath. Keldon simply needed to follow the tracker beacon he had given Arleia, and they were just one district over, investigating a sublevel haunting.

Hours passed, and I paced anxiously in my cell, wondering if Zaveroi would resume his experiments today or wait until tomorrow. I was uncertain as to the time of day, but my stomach told me that mealtime was near. Another hour passed, by my estimation, and I was beginning to wonder where Borthon was. Perhaps my perception of time was more distorted than I suspected, and it was actually sometime late at night, or early morning.

I sat down, hoping to catch a short nap, and felt a tremor run through the floor. Another tremor followed the first, and then a third, preceded by the reverberating bang of a rolling thunderclap. Alarm bells clanged through the hall, and Borthon lurched past my window, his eyes wild with panic. Several more blasts rattled the manor, raining dust and debris from the hall's already battered ceiling, and the bellows, howls, and shrieks of Zaveroi's menagerie grew louder as they riled into a frenzy.

Borthon hobbled past my window again, then, to my amazement, he came back to unlock the door before limping off.

I pushed open my cell door and stepped out, ready to thank Borthon for having come around to help me. But as I entered the debris-strewn hall, I realized the terrible truth. Borthon was opening *all* the cell doors as he limped along, muttering incessantly about 'intruders' and 'protecting master.' No, I was not free. I, like all the beasts of the menagerie, were Zaveroi's last line of defense.

Zaveroi's voice resounded through the air. "It seems your apprentice *did* survive, and he has returned with a few friends." Then, with a near-delirious laugh, he continued. "I can conceive of no better way to conclude our experiment!"

A host of horrors burst from their cells and stormed into the hall—howling barghests, hissing chimeras, skittering scarapods, chittering arachnidons, and following behind them charged the roaring bulgore, bellowing with pure unfettered rage. Blinding pain stabbed through every fiber of my body and I dropped to my knees, straining to hold back the white-hot torrent of volatile reagents surging through my veins. But I could only scream, helpless to impede the accelerating reaction, and I felt my own flesh give way to liquid flame, transmuting me, body and soul, into the most monstrous abomination of them all.

The doors at the far end of the hall exploded inward, blasted from their hinges by a conjuration of tightly focused air. I saw three figures through the cloud of fluttering debris and wafting dust, and at the head stood a woman of fearsome temper and indomitable resolve, her copper-brown hair swept forward in the rush of summoned wind. She was Leta Meridian, veilhunter, and behind her followed Keldon with his brass key at the ready and Arleia with her runic totem held high. Now that Zaveroi had disengaged his null-aethergy device, they were free to use their empowerments unhindered.

Leta signaled for the others to find cover, then pressed the rings of her right hand together as she evoked a ward of mystical energy. A pair of arachnidons sprang for her, mandibular fangs extruding, only to bounce aside when they struck the defensive barrier.

"Aldicus!" Keldon yelled. Terror filled his eyes when he saw me, but his jaw clenched in staunch determination. "We have to get to Zaveroi's laboratory and find that machine."

"Then don't just loll around—get moving, you two!" Leta yelled back, her hands thrusting out to bolster the barrier.

A stampede of monsters thundered past me as I stood, my horror growing as my alchemorph turned with fiendish delight to join the onslaught charging for my friends. Keldon clambered over the rubble piles, firing a few sparkling darts at a barghest, while Arleia struck down the scarapod with a blast of elemental fire.

The half-Eldren wheeled around as two chimeras darted in, teeth snapping and fangs flashing. Before either could strike, both reeled away, thrashing as though snared by some unseen leash. Arleia whispered inaudibly, pressing forward with her totem, her teal eyes narrowing behind her glasses. The chimeras quivered, hissing and growling as they backed away from her, shaking each of their three heads. Then they turned and took their place to either side of her, entranced by the potent weave of Eldren magic.

"Defend!" Arleia commanded.

The chimeras launched forward, snarling and hissing at the barghests. My alchemorph blazed right past them all, eager to incinerate my friends. A ray of mystical light struck from Leta's outstretched hand, bathing my alchemorph in a ghostly blue glow. Even in my transmuted form, I knew Leta could read me. She felt my fear, my helplessness, my cry for them to run and save themselves. And she could feel the full fury of the alchemorph, too—its unbridled hate, its insatiable hunger, and the malevolent chaos that roiled within.

I could not hear Leta's thoughts, but I felt her presence in that ghostly light—a presence serene, certain, and strong. And in her strength, I found my own strength.

Our captor, I thought, pressing Zaveroi's image into the burning chaos of the alchemorph's mind. *Find Zaveroi. Find our captor. Find our tormentor.*

The alchemorph wavered, howling in rage and holding up its flaming arms to shield itself from the tranquilizing light of Leta's mystical intercession. With another fire-spitting roar it charged forward again, hurling a blast of fulminating alchemicals and molten stone toward Leta, but the veilhunter was no longer there. She had utterly vanished.

My alchemorph spun around, and I spotted Keldon and Arleia dashing down the hall. I smiled to myself. Keldon had fooled the alchemorph with an illusionary image of Leta, distracting it long enough for them to make a break for Zaveroi's laboratory. But where was the real Leta Meridian? The question would have to wait, as my alchemorph charged after the two young apprentices—a roiling fury of combusting alchemicals racing past the frenzy of monsters in pursuit.

Keldon and Arleia had nearly made it to the doors at the opposite end of the hall when the one-ton bulgore smashed through a wall of fallen rubble, charging straight at them with horns down. Both slid to a stop and looked back, only to see me closing in on them from the other direction.

Arleia gnashed her teeth and raised her runic totem before her. She glanced at Keldon, clearly irked by his dumbfounded expression. "If you ever wanted to impress a girl, now would be a great time!"

Keldon jumped, shaking himself from his bewilderment. He whipped his key around and flooded the hall with a shower of flashing orbs and blinding strobes. The bulgore veered away howling, but was back on them in an instant, sweeping down to skewer them with its massive horns. Both Keldon and Arleia flickered away as my apprentice's illusion dissolved, and I saw them again a second later, standing not far from the doors to the laboratory wing. Arleia grimaced in concentration, straining with all her will to compel the charging beast.

"I can't control it!" she exclaimed. "It's mad with rage!"

The bulgore, I thought to the alchemorph, hoping to goad it into attacking the indomitable beast. My alchemorph hesitated, and I felt its power begin to weaken as it burned through what little remained of its alchemical reagents. Drawing upon all the strength I could muster, I focused on the bulgore's imposing image. *Is it not a most formidable opponent?*

Despite its waning strength, my alchemorph surged forward with savage zeal, enveloping the bulgore in its immolating arms. Wicked bullhorns speared my chest, tearing through the blackened coal and burning elemental matter, while the bulgore's stone-crushing fist drove into my abdomen with the force of a pneumatic hammer.

We tumbled over in our struggle, crashing through the doors to the laboratory wing and taking a good part of the surrounding wall with us. Burning wood and smoldering debris rained all around, and both floor and ceiling began to crumble as we wrestled down the adjacent hall. I feared for Keldon and Arleia, then I spotted the pair ducking into Zaveroi's main lab. The mad doctor was there, watching the battle unfold, and neither apprentice would be any match for his sorcery and ruthless guile.

I felt the fires within me dwindle as the last of the alchemorph's reagents fizzled into vapor. The bulgore, its fur scorched and hide smoking, barreled into me with the force of a speeding locomotive. The wall caved in behind me, and we exploded into Zaveroi's main laboratory in a shower of shattered bricks and splintered support beams. I caught a glimpse of Keldon and Arleia as the bulgore rammed me once more, just in time to see Zaveroi unleash a storm of arcing lightning from a copper-coiled staff. Both apprentices dived behind a table before the lightning struck, but the table was entirely pulverized in the crackling blast.

"Kill those two!" Zaveroi yelled to Borthon. The stone-covered man seemed stunned by the command, so Zaveroi smacked him on his head with his staff. "Kill them, you hopeless dullwit! Crush the life from them with your hands! I'll deal with Vescard."

My alchemorph tried to strike back at the bulgore, but the enraged beast slammed into me again, hurling me into the shelves along one wall. The shelves exploded in a shower of broken bottles and glassware, spilling copious alchemicals across the laboratory floor. In an instant, the alchemorph siphoned up the sizzling concoction of volatile reagents, and its inner fires erupted in a blinding white blaze, reigniting the furnace of its heart. With a booming laugh, the alchemorph bound together a fireball of boiling acid and burning phlogiston.

"I can't allow you to destroy my life's work!" Zaveroi screamed. He turned to the cabinet-sized machine just behind him and threw the handle of a knife switch, activating its whirling collector coils and aetheric lenses. "Let's see how you fare against the bulgore now!"

The fire flashed out of me in a second, and I collapsed to my knees on the steaming, half-melted tile floor, my body quivering in the sudden cold. The bulgore dropped to all fours and snorted, its black eyes narrowing as it prepared to charge.

"Do something!" Arleia yelled.

Keldon shook his sigil-etched key, but nothing happened. "I can't. He's activated the negation field."

"Kill them," Zaveroi yelled to Borthon again. "Why are you standing there, you mindless oaf? Are you deaf?"

"Borthon," I managed to gasp. "Your master... is the real monster..." The bulgore lowered its head, its horns tearing through the floor as it charged. "Borthon... Smash that machine!"

Borthon looked up, the sunken eyes beneath his stony brow widening in sudden realization. "Monster!" he roared. With that, he spun around and drove his rock-hardened fists straight through the center panel of the whirling machine.

The rattling clatter of breaking gears, bursting pneumatics, and shattering spark tubes eclipsed Zaveroi's horrified scream, and was eclipsed again by the spontaneous combustion of the igniting inferno that revived my alchemorph. The bulgore was already on top of me, and in that instant the alchemorph resumed the fulminating alchemical reaction, slamming the exploding fireball straight into the charging beast's chest. The bulgore tumbled past, its own momentum carrying it another twenty feet through workbenches and tables to crash in a burning heap scarcely a pace from Zaveroi and his ruined machine.

The alchemorph turned to face the mad doctor, its rage boiling like a blast furnace as it brought its hands together, forming a blistering fireball as it siphoned up the remaining alchemical reagents. Zaveroi tried to flee, but Borthon grabbed him by his arms and hoisted him off the floor. I screamed in my own mind, helpless to stop the alchemorph as it poured forth an incinerating deluge, bathing Borthon, Zaveroi, and his machine in all-consuming flames. Zaveroi's horrified screams turned to a wail of agony, then fell silent as his disintegrating skeleton crumbled to cinders. A pile of charred stones collapsed on top of Zaveroi's remains, Borthon at last having found both peace and justice in his final act of valor.

Keldon and Arleia fled into the rubble filled hall and my alchemorph took chase behind them. With Zaveroi's machine destroyed, my only hope remained with my friends. Yet, with my alchemorph inundated with a reservoir of boiling alchemicals, anyone who came close enough to attach my severite wristbands would be incinerated in seconds. To my horror, I found myself wondering which of my friends would give their life to stop me.

I roared into the menagerie hall, pursuing the two apprentices across the scattered rubble and mangled corpses of Zaveroi's ill-fated collection. My alchemorph reeled back almost immediately, shrieking with rage as a black chain whipped out from the left and wrapped around my burning arm. Just as I turned, a second chain joined the first, this one entangling my right arm. Leta stood just a few paces away, her teeth bared and face grimacing against the sweltering heat, gripping in either hand the severite chains that Zaveroi had once used to confine me.

The aethergy-dampening metal felt as cold as ice, and the inferno around me snuffed out with a smothering fizzle. I winced, shutting my eyes as the boiling alchemicals evaporated and the super-heated air clapped back around me, scorching my resubstantiated skin. But after a heartbeat, all thoughts of pain vanished and my eyes shot open when I realized my rather unbecoming predicament.

"Fangle-fop," I muttered.

Arleia yelped and turned the other way, and Keldon buried his face in his hands, shaking his head. But Leta just dropped the chains and folded her arms, forming a wry smirk without so much as a hint of a blush.

"Now there's a side of you I don't see every day," she mused, eyebrows quirking.

"This is terribly embarrassing," I said, pulling the severite chains over my naked body. I looked across the rubble, hoping to find something to throw on.

Leta snickered. "Believe me, Aldicus, you don't have a thing to be embarrassed about." Then she stepped away to rummage through some of the rubble. Finding a few torn sheets and part of a sackcloth garment, she came back over and tossed them my way. "I'd look for something better, but this whole place is about to burn down around us."

Acrid smoke had already filled the hall, and the crash of falling rafters and buckling support pilings shook the charred floor beneath my feet. I dropped one of the severite chains and wrapped the other around my body like a bandolier to hold my ragged garments on. Taking one final look around the thoroughly demolished interior of Doctor Zaveroi's manor, I let out a long, exhausted sigh.

"Let's get out of this place," I said to the others.

No one objected in the least.

BURNING EMBERS SWELLED into the cloud-laden sky, and we watched from a safe distance as the fire brigade worked feverishly to control the flames, aided by a few highly trained elementors. They had arrived posthaste, and thanks to their efforts, had prevented the fire from spreading to the neighboring buildings that crowded this jumbled district quarter. A squad of Vandorian bluejacks had also arrived on the scene, along with a HAAMR unit in their fancy empowered armor. The bluejacks helped the district police with crowd control, but the HAAMR troopers had apparently been called to contain and eliminate any of Zaveroi's menagerie that had escaped. I was quite confident that none of those creatures remained, but HAAMR stood on guard, ready to charge in the moment the fires were stifled.

"Was it bad?" Leta asked. She leaned against the retaining wall where I sat, the concern on her face now replacing any trace of her teasing smirk. "What he did to you, I mean."

I drew a deep breath and closed my eyes. The past few days were a blur, and I had been shocked to discover that only three days had gone by. It had seemed like a week. A week of torment, fear, and *humiliation*. All at the hands of a madman.

"Yes," I replied simply. I tried not to dwell on the heavy severite chain looped about me, and I pulled my ragged coat tighter, grateful for the passing beggar who had exchanged it for a silver ducat. “It was bad.”

Leta nodded, worrying her lower lip. “You can always talk to me, Aldicus, if you need someone to talk to.”

“I know,” I whispered, looking down. She was a psychurgist, and I knew she could read me. Was she reading me now? Did she sense the pain within me? Could she feel the horror I felt, recalling the gruesome trials Zaveroi had put me through? “Perhaps... Perhaps I shall. But not today, Leta. Not today.”

She nodded again, saying nothing more.

The remaining fires went out in a cloud of smoke and steam, and the HAAMR troopers stormed into the charred remains of Zaveroi’s manor. I wondered at what they expected to find. Nothing could have survived that inferno.

“Zaveroi’s research might have led to a cure, you know?” I said after a moment, trying to steady my voice. “Or, at the very least, a way for me to control it.”

Keldon and Arleia returned as I spoke—Keldon with a cup of water and Arleia with a full set of clothes she had found somewhere.

“A cure?” Keldon asked, passing me the cup of water. “Zaveroi was insane. He...” His voice quivered and he looked down at his own hands, tightening them into fists. “We were nothing but test subjects to him. If you hadn’t managed to free me when you did, he would have...” He looked away suddenly, closing his eyes. “He would have done to me what he did to poor Borthon.”

Borthon... I thirstily downed the cup of water Keldon had given me, hoping the cool liquid would quench my parched throat. “Borthon gave his life to save us all.”

“I know. It’s just...” Keldon’s voice trailed off and he sighed.

“It’s over now,” Arleia said, putting a comforting hand on Keldon’s shoulder. “That madman has met a fitting end.”

I shook my head. “Zaveroi was no madman. He was a genius, singularly driven and supremely confident in his self-declared right to push every boundary in his search for ultimate knowledge." I clenched my jaw, my thoughts burning with the memory of the alchemorph and the wanton destruction it had wrought. "I should know. I, too, was once so driven."

My friends were silent for a moment, then Leta gave a lighthearted laugh. "You were never *that* crazy, Aldicus. You were just brash. You never tortured animals or experimented on people—besides yourself, I mean." She shrugged. "Zaveroi tormented you enough, so don't keep tormenting yourself. Every crime you stop, every killer you catch, every plot you thwart, and every life you save repays whatever debt you imagine you owe a hundred times over. Isn't it about time that you moved on?"

What she said was true, but that truth could never vanquish the monster I carried inside. Zaveroi had shown me the alchemorph *could* be tamed, and yet, however hard I had fought, however much I pushed my will to gain even the smallest measure of control, in the end I had lost. I could not control the beast within me—not on my own.

My friends stood looking back at me, and in that moment, I realized that I was not alone.

"You're right," I replied, nodding as I forced a smile. I drew a deep breath and started for the steam-coach across the street with Keldon, Arleia, and Leta following beside me. "Crime ever turns in the Clockwork City, and though my debt has long been paid, I shall never cease in my quest to bring justice to the streets of Corradon."

"That's good," Leta said back. Then she smiled as she slipped into the coach, taking the seat across from Keldon and Arleia, and sliding over to make room for me. "For the day you stop being Aldicus Vescard will be the day that justice dies in the Clockwork City."

Case File 10:

On a Wheel and a Prayer

Neb Dorlen's chest had exploded from the inside—not directly outward, but upward, tearing open his neck just above the sternum and nearly taking his head off. The pressure from the explosion had escaped through his esophagus, a much easier path than blasting through the ribcage, but extensive damage had also been inflicted to his abdominal region. I knelt closer, examining the internal damage through the ghostly blue haze surrounding the victim's torso. The stomach had been obliterated, confirming my suspicions that Neb had ingested a highly volatile compound.

I stood up, pulling my frock coat around me. "This man was poisoned."

The glowing sigils of Keldon's brass key darkened and the eerie haze melted away. The body on the floor of the pavilion was no longer transparent, but the gruesome hole blasted through Neb Dorlen's neck was evidence enough that the inventor's death had been a tragically violent affair.

"Poisoned?" my apprentice asked, incredulous. "It looks like he ate a bomb!"

I returned to the cluttered table where I had laid out my alchemistry set and inspected the bubbling, smoking vials. Like all the pavilions of the rally's mobile encampment, this pavilion was large enough to house a single locomobile, along with tools, equipment, spare parts, and a pair of workbenches, one of which I had appropriated for my on-site investigation.

"A poison is any substance that impairs health, damages the body, or results in the death of the victim," I replied, taking one of the vials from the table. "Neb Dorlen's health is quite impaired, and the other two points are equally incontestable."

"But how could poison cause his chest to explode?" Joard Estuvon asked, stepping up to the workbench.

The mechanic, who was somewhere in his late twenties, had been Neb's partner and co-driver for their entry into the 23rd Annual Golden Gear Locomobile Rally. Crossing half of Armillia, the race began in the Baronies of Aquenne, then cut across the haunted borrows of Ravenvale to the perilous Gloombog Swamp, and would continue on to the narrow hallows of Drake Valley in the Duchy of Delarien, only to finish in Corradon after surviving the treacherous industrial wasteland of the Iron Barrens. The winner would receive the coveted Golden Gear trophy, along with a lucrative contract with their sponsor. The rally was the most challenging competition of its kind, and inevitably sparked a firestorm of cutthroat rivalry.

I touched a drop of the solution from one of the vials to the center of a chromograph plate and watched a rainbow of rings spread across its surface. The pattern indicated the presence of aqua fortis and ammonia, which together with the catalyzed reaction I observed in the other vial, led to one incontrovertible conclusion. I picked up the empty brandy glass on the table and peered through its wide bottom.

"This glass was laced with volatilis ammoniac. Together with certain other catalysts, volatilis ammoniac will react quite energetically with stomach acid."

"Energetically?" Joard asked, peering at the brandy glass.

I nodded. "It will explode." I looked to the bullet-shaped vehicle nestled between stacks of boxes and tool racks inside

Neb's workshop pavilion. "I understand your racer uses something other than alchemically refined ichor. Tell me about it."

Joard hesitated. "The fuel mixture is our trade secret."

"I can assure you, I will be discreet."

Joard glanced nervously about, as though looking to make sure no one else but myself and Keldon were present inside the small pavilion. "Our engine is actually a cycloaetheric compressor using two fuels," he said, speaking quietly. "An azeotrope of phlogisticated oleum, which is injected to react with a mix of vitriolic ethynate and..." He paused, then gave a reluctant sigh before continuing. "Volatilis ammoniac."

He knew the implication was incriminating, but other than his understandable hesitation, he had done nothing to conceal the fact. "Did you know the taste and odor of volatilis ammoniac can be masked when mixed with distilled alcohol and salicylic ester?" My query was a lie, of course. The bitter taste of volatilis ammoniac could only be disguised when combined with equal parts of formetic distillate, which is readily available from any apothecary. I waited for Joard to contest my assertion, which a knowledgeable alchemist might do to avoid implication.

But Joard just shifted his weight to his other leg and bit his lip. "I know how this looks, but you must believe me! Neb was my friend. We've worked together for over two years on this project, and—"

I held up my hand. He was either clever enough to second guess my trap or he truly lacked the background necessary to have committed the deed. "I'm sure several other drivers have access to volatilis ammoniac. The question is, which one of them wants to see Neb Dorlen dead?"

"All of them, probably," Keldon put in. "As of today, Neb had gained the lead."

I nodded. "And now that Neb and Joard are out of the picture..."

“No!” Joard looked at the racer and balled his fists. “Neb would have wanted me to continue, and I’ll be damned before I let whoever murdered him win!”

I narrowed my eyes. Was I wrong about Joard? With Neb out of the way, Joard stood to win the trophy for himself alone—and all the gold and glory that came with it. “I understand. With any luck, I will have the killer in custody before this race is finished.”

Joard simply nodded.

I put on my top hat and stepped out of the tent, Keldon following me.

The roar of engines and clattering of gears rose above the chattering drivers and team crews milling about the field of tents, pavilions, and make-shift garages. Evening had settled, and the warm glow of gas lamps mixed incongruously with the crimson light of Atracus rising to the east. I looked north, to the distant outskirts of Ravenvale, wondering at the perils the drivers had endured racing through those ancient, haunted borrows. Turning south, I saw the foggy tree line of Gloombog Swamp, and pondered what greater perils yet awaited.

“First someone steals Neb’s engine plans, then they kill him the very next day,” Keldon muttered. “But why kill him if the thieves got away with the plans? And why steal the plans if the goal was to remove Neb from the race?”

Both were excellent questions. I had met Neb Dorlen at an aether mechanics conference three years ago, and we had corresponded intermittently since. He was a brilliant inventor and an accomplished alchemist, and while many of his ideas were too theoretical to ever prove viable, he was determined to realize his designs. He had dispatched a missive to me just yesterday, stating only that someone had stolen the plans for his cycloaetheric compressor.

As it turned out, the theft had been the least of the inventor’s concerns.

Nevertheless, Neb could have called on any freelance

detective, or even the local authorities, but he had sought my aid specifically, perhaps because of our occasional correspondence. With my investigation into the Shadow Man and the mysterious Servants of Vosh having hit a wall, and with no meaningful cases coming my way from Tibblemond or Vandor Tower, I certainly had time to spare.

"Aldicus Vescard," came a brassy female voice. I turned and thought I was seeing double, then realized the women were twins. Both wore identical racing suits with leather bodices and chaps, gauge-cluttered bracers, and racing goggles pushed up over their dreadlocks. Their low-slung gun belts each held a clockwork pistol holstered to either side. Nera and Vera, I recognized at once—the notorious Nyasha Twins.

"You be here to catch the killer?" asked the second twin, her inflected Arkanan accent rolling each word together.

"Or maybe you be here to admire us?" continued the first, quirking a grin.

Keldon blinked in stunned silence, then gulped. He was always so awkward around ladies.

"I see I need no introduction," I replied, tipping my hat. "Nor do either of you—Nera, Vera."

The dark-skinned twins glanced at each other and smiled. "I be Vera," said the first. "She be Nera."

I crossed my arms over my frock coat and nodded. "Judging from the leader board, you two moved up to second place today."

"That we did," Nera answered, her lips curling to a smile.

The twins turned and started back to their own pavilion, clearly assuming I would follow. I did so. "You're going to tell me how you couldn't have committed the murder and how you both have impeccable alibis, yes?"

"Why bother?" Nera asked. She pulled open the flap to their pavilion, then glanced back to me. "You be the great Aldicus Vescard. You'll not be discounting no one, whatever they be saying."

"Truth be, we liked the old man," Vera continued. "He be..." She stopped and drew a sharp breath. "He was a good man."

She nodded to one of the other pavilions where a young man stood, garbed in a white racing suit with scarf and goggles, and brandishing a cocky grin. Reporters and spectators surrounded a spit and polish speedster just outside his pavilion. Atop the vehicle's bulging engine compartment sat a bored looking woman minding her hair in a hand mirror.

"That be Cylus Deuvel," Vera said. "He took third place, but be nearly tied with us. He be sponsored by Dragar Industries."

Dragar was best known for manufacturing weapons, mobile artillery, and armored carriages, but they also produced motors and engines as well. "And the woman?" I asked, looking to the lady sitting on Cylus's racer.

"She be his new squeeze, Meretta," Nera answered, a notable touch of disdain in her tone. "But he no be bringing the dollymolly for his co-driver, that be certain."

Vera looked to a massive vehicle parked some distance away, tended by two men—one large, the other skinny. Their racer had the appearance of a locomotive engine, but with six massive tires instead of train wheels and two smokestacks rising above its boiler and firebox. "The bruiser there be Gunther Viggs, a former convict, and skinny boy be his boilerman, Toben Gall." Gunther, who looked like a carnival strongman, was working on the locomotive's pipeworks, cursing and swearing at the scrawny poll of a man trying to help him. "They came in at fourth place, but that beast be fast once it gets going. They be sponsored by United Coal and Rail."

I nodded. Gunther's locomotive monstrosity was exactly the sort of racer United Coal and Rail would sponsor, hoping to extol the virtues of coal and steam over newfangled ichor engines.

"Kargeth took fifth place, tying with Svotgar," Nera continued. She looked across the rally field to a tent just large enough to cover a racer. A grey-skinned Scaithi sat outside the tent, eating his dinner alone. "Kargeth be exiled from darkest Kendes, but make no mistake, he be a banging gearmeister and a brutty driver. He be sponsored by Lord Cumbervain and Sons."

"And Svotgar?" I asked.

Vera looked to another tent, not far from Kargeth's. Through the tent's open flaps I saw a grease-covered Dworgh adjusting the large rear wheel of his three-wheeled racer. "Don't know much about the Dworgh, but he be mighty funny when he's drunk. He be lucky, too. His sponsor be Consolidated Omniworks."

Consolidated Omniworks was indeed an impressive sponsorship, being the world's largest manufacturer of vehicles, engines, machinery, and ships of both sea and sky. "And who might your sponsor be?"

Vera grinned, pulling the tent flap open just enough for me to see their twin-wheeled vehicle inside. The racer looked like a single motowheel, but was in fact two large wheels fixed side-by-side, with twin rotary engines mounted below and behind the seats inside each wheel.

"Sturmont Motors," she replied, nodding to their striking duowheeler. "We have the winning racer for sure, so we no be needing to off the competition this year."

I narrowed my eyes. What did she mean, *this* year?

"And what about Neb's sponsor?" Keldon asked.

I glanced at my apprentice and smiled. I had hoped he would pick up on the omission, as Joard had made no mentioned of their sponsorship at all.

Both twins shrugged. "Neb says we all be sellouts," Nera explained. "He turned down every sponsor. But Joard always be saying they needed one."

That grabbed my attention. "What do you mean?"

Nera and Vera glanced at Neb and Joard's pavilion before

stepping inside their own. “You best not discount no one,” Nera replied. “No one who be ranking to win.”

The twins disappeared into their pavilion.

“I guess this means everyone’s a suspect,” Keldon said. “What do we do now?”

“Why, we enter the race, of course,” I replied. Keldon’s eyes grew wide. “Kargeth and Svotgar are both driving solo, but I’d wager Svotgar will be far more accommodating to letting you ride with him. I’ll be riding with Joard, as it would be mighty suspicious if he refused. Just remember, any use of magic is forbidden in this race, except in self-defense.”

Keldon nodded. He drew a deep breath and surveyed the clamoring, revving rally yard. “I can’t believe I’ll be riding in the Golden Gear Rally…” his voice trailed off. “Do you have any idea how high the casualty rate is?”

“Higher than usual this year.” I stuffed my hands into my coat pockets and started for Svotgar’s tent. “And I fear it shall grow even higher before we cross the finish line.”

MUDDY WATER SPLASHED from the wheels of Kargeth’s racer and Joard veered right, barely avoiding the foul spray. I ducked low into the cockpit seat, pulling down my leather racing cap as vines and branches whipped past. Our racer hit a bump and lurched upward, fortuitously clearing a pile of rotting logs before speeding on—wheels ripping furrows through the shallow mire of the swamp’s murky silt.

“Is it always like this?” I yelled over the roar of the alchemical engine.

“It’s usually worse,” Joard yelled back. He threw a lever at his side and the engine’s flywheel kicked in, giving a jolt of speed to break through a curtain of vines. “You should have seen the mortifants and gaunt-wights back at the Ravenvale barrows. They are *not* fans of this race, I can tell you that!”

I picked a piece of vine off my coat, then hurled it away when I saw it was a bloodfang viper. “I would venture that

Gloombog Swamp is no less perilous."

"You've never been chased by a necrocite, have you?" Joard asked.

A crash of trees drew me to look behind us and I saw Gunther's locomotive racer barreling through a coppice of mangroves. The ten-ton iron beast should have sunk in the sodden mud, but its hefty tires had inflated to provide enough buoyancy for the colossal vehicle to ride across the mire. Gunther waved at us from his cabin window, laughing as his vehicle demolished a swamp troll's nest mound, exploding dirt, rocks, and mud in every direction. The troll lumbered out, bellowing in anger and waving a ladle as Gunther's massive vehicle thundered away.

I wiped the mud from my goggles and sank back in my seat. "Something tells me we're the real monsters here."

Joard cursed and threw the tiller hard to right, sending us careening over an embankment as a writhing mass of hooked tentacles erupted from the water next to us. One tentacle snagged the rear of our racer, but the appendage tore free from whatever beast it had belonged too.

"You were saying, Vescard?" Joard asked, his words nearly lost to the roar of engines and crashing foliage.

I glanced back just in time to see Gunther steer his locomotive straight for the tangle of writhing tentacles. Viscous goo exploded across the boiler and front wheels, and the vehicle's thundering steam engine eclipsed the creature's dying shriek.

"I stand by my position," I moaned.

Something fluttered at my feet and I looked down. A piece of paper stuck up from a loose floorboard and I leaned down to pull it out. It was a pneumatic mail missive.

"What have you found?" Joard asked. He glanced at the missive and frowned, then returned his attention to the race as Svotgar and Keldon sped past in their agile three-wheeler.

The missive was to Neb Dorlen from Dragar Industries and was dated the tenth of Stormspell—three months ago.

Short and to the point, it was an offer for sponsorship granting an advance of 500 guilds, plus 3000 more if they won and a lucrative license for their patents. At ten ducats to a guild, that was nothing short of a fortune.

"Neb turned down this offer?" I asked.

"Over my objection," Joard grumbled. A pair of will-o-the-wisps came at us from the right and Joard steered left, avoiding the infuriated elementals. "He wanted to give this engine design to the world, not some profiteering manufactory."

"And you?"

Joard shook his head. "The winnings would have pulled us both out of debt, and the patent license would have made us rich for life. Now that dandy-fop, Cylus, has Dragar's sponsorship. Well, good for him, I say!"

"When did Cylus get the sponsorship?"

"A week after Neb tubed back a missive to reject their offer. Just over two months ago."

I nodded. That would have been around the first of Summertide. Neb and Joard had been at odds over whether or not to accept sponsorship, and next to jealousy and revenge, money was the next most common motivation for murder. But if Dragar Industries had already picked Cylus as their driver, it would be too late for Joard to accept sponsorship even with Neb dead. Then again, why had the missive been stashed under the floorboards if Neb had no interest in Dragar's offer? Could he still be hoping to negotiate a deal for the engine patents?

Gunther cut directly in front of us, sending up a wave of bog water and splintered trees, forcing Joard to jog left to avoid the worst of it. Svotgar and Keldon were not so lucky, and their racer slammed into a mound of mud as Gunther's locomotive thundered past.

"We have to stop!" I yelled.

"I'm barely holding third place as it is!" Joard objected.

But he knew arguing with me was pointless. Shaking his

head, he pulled the stick to the right and came back around, slowing to a stop just a few paces from Svotgar's mud-drenched three-wheeler. Svotgar was already out of the vehicle, pulling with all his strength to free the oversized rear wheel from the sinking bog.

"Get out here and help me, boy!" the Dworgh yelled to Keldon. "You're not going to let Gunther get away with this, are you?"

Keldon staggered from his seat, still dazed from the crash. He pushed up his goggles and waved when he saw me climbing out of Joard's racer. "Aldicus!"

My boots sloshed through the muck as I made my way over to help, but I had scarcely taken two steps before another racer went by, spraying rank silt over Keldon and Svotgar.

"Lose your way to the finish line?" Cylus yelled. He laughed, and his speedster's ichor-pumped engine slammed into high gear, flames jetting from the brass tubes hemming its sides. Meretta blew a taunting kiss as they tore away.

Keldon stood rigid, clumps of muck dripping from his helmet, goggles, and jacket. "I hate swamps..."

"Did you see that?" Svotgar wiped his goggles with the back of his glove, then rung a pint's worth of bog water from his beard. "Dandy's got himself a top-of-the-line, dual-intake dragon fire injector. I hope he blows a gasket!"

I raised an eyebrow. Dragon fire was the more common name for volatilis ammoniac. "Are you certain? Is anyone else using volatilis ammoniac in their engine?"

"I doubt it," the Dworgh replied, his voice straining as he hefted his racer again. "Only an idiot like him would—"

The twins' duowheeler bounded over a nearby embankment, then turned sharply and skidded to a stop. "Anybody be hurt?" yelled one of the twins—Nera, I guessed, judging from her somewhat longer dreadlocks.

"Gunther will be hurting if I ever catch up with him!" Svotgar barked back.

Joard joined Svotgar and Keldon at the back of his racer, and all three gave a heave as they tried to pull the vehicle free. Nera and Vera jumped out of their duowheeler and slid down the embankment, adding more mud to the layers already covering their leather boots and chaps.

Two more racers sped past, both sputtering steamers, followed by a third belching oily black fumes. "You seem to be ranking at the top of the rear today," I said to the twins.

Nera narrowed her eyes. "We tangled with a hydra, if you must be knowing." She drew the two clockwork pistols holstered at her side and gave the guns a twirl. "And these be no good slaying such a brutty beastie."

I nodded. "At least you got away."

Vera pushed her goggles up and stabbed a thumb back in the direction they had come. "Oh, it still be chasing us. We just be stopping so you don't be dying on our account."

A massive, undulating form crashed through the mangrove trees, the mouth-like grippers of its thrashing tentacles snapping as they struck toward us. Vera whipped her pistols from their holsters, joining her sister who was already firing her clockwork repeaters.

"Anybody bring a flamethrower?" Nera yelled over her own gunshots' report.

"Or a mage?" Vera added, throwing a look my way.

I brushed my hand against my left wristband and glanced at Svotgar's racer. The vehicle used a steam turbine engine and was likely fueled by flashwood or compressed coal pellets—combustible, but not explosively so. I had no idea what fuel the twins' duowheeler used, and that left Joard's racer with its potent mixture of phlogisticated oleum, vitriolic ethynate, and volatilis ammoniac.

"What are you doing?" Joard yelled, sloshing through the soupy muck after me.

I leaned into the cockpit and tried to pry up one of the loose floorboards, hoping to find a fuel hose underneath. "I need your fuel."

"Move aside," Joard insisted. He forced his way in and opened the storage compartment behind the cockpit seats. "There's no need to go tearing my racer apart."

"Aldicus," Keldon yelled to me. "I know the rules say we can't use empowerments, but—"

"You can in self-defense," I reminded.

Nera and Vera emptied their clockwork pistols, the bullets having proven as dolefully inadequate as they had warned. The snapping tentacles struck out from the hydra's central mass and the twins cartwheeled away. Keldon rushed forward as soon as they were clear, a beam of dazzling white light flashing from his brass key.

"You be trying to blind us?" Nera yelled, throwing an arm over her face.

Vera tackled Keldon, knocking him into the muddy water as the hydra's jaw-like tentacles lashed out to snare him. "Hydras hunt by feel," she berated. "Not sight!"

"This is my emergency supply," Joard explained to me, pulling a red canister and a blue canister from the racer's storage compartment. "The blue one is phlogisticated oleum and the red one is vitriolic ethynate and volatilis ammoniac. But please use them sparingly."

I watched as the hydra surged forward again, the dagger-like teeth of its radial feeding maw yawning hungrily. "I would certainly classify this is an emergency. Now go help Svotgar pull his racer free."

Joard nodded and dashed away. I rolled up my sleeve, poured a pint of fuel from the red canister across my left arm, and yanked the locking pin from the wristband. My arm erupted in a blaze of elemental matter and whirling flames, the agony like red-hot irons tearing into flesh. I ground my teeth against the searing pain, then grabbed the blue canister with my other hand and tossed a splash of the second mixture into the air.

Conflagrating fingers touched the splash of phlogisticated oleum, and the burning mixture of volatilis ammoniac and vitriolic ethynate catalyzed instantly, exploding outward in a fiery blast of combusting vapors. The scorching flames poured across the hydra's body, and the shrieking beast recoiled in a fury of thrashing tentacles and splashing water, retreating into the impenetrable shadows of Gloombog Swamp.

"We got her free!" Svotgar yelled.

I slapped my wristband on, extinguishing the flames, but leaving my skin red and blistered. Looking back, I saw Joard and Svotgar had pulled the racer out of the mud and were now heaving Keldon from the sodden layers of silt.

"Good job drawing the hydra's attention," I called.

"Thanks, boss," my apprentice groaned.

"Pleasantries be over, boys," Nera quipped as she and her sister hurried to their racer. "Try not to die."

Vera lowered her muddied goggles over her eyes as the duowheeler's rotary engine spun to life, and she gave a parting salute. "We'll be waiting at the finish line."

Joard was already in his racer's cockpit, opening the choke valve and giving the starter crank a spin. "Get in, Vescard, or you'll find yourself waiting for the rescue teams."

The howl of Svotgar's steam turbine eclipsed our own engine, white smoke blooming from the brass pipes to either side of his rear wheel as his racer sped off in pursuit of the twins' duowheeler. Joard frowned as he took the control tiller and shoved the throttle stick all the way forward. We were off with a sudden lurch, wheels spraying muddy water behind us. Within minutes we caught up with Svotgar and Keldon, bumping and bucking down the crude path cut through the tangled swampland by the racers ahead of us. Judging from the wide wheel tracks to either side, Gunther had taken the lead, leaving everyone else to follow the trail of splintered trees and uprooted ferns made by his barreling locomotive.

We passed a half dozen pneumatic wagons and puttering steamers as we raced side-by-side with Svotgar and Keldon, then pulled ahead when Svotgar swerved to avoid a tree stump, plowing through a thicket of bog reeds and bulrushes. I looked back to make sure they were all right, and was pleased to see Svotgar steer his racer back on course.

Minutes later, we were out of the swamp and skirting the peat marshes to the grassy hills and vineyards beyond which lay the village of Dommel on the northern border of Delarien. The inhabitants of the rustic hamlet knew what to expect from the annual rally, and while they may not have appreciated the inevitable assault of clattering engines, oily fumes, and rowdy drivers, they no doubt enjoyed the coin brought in by troves of reporters and spectators booking rooms in every hospice, inn, tavern, and cottage for miles around. Those same reporters and spectators lined the main road leading into Dommel, jumping, hooting, and clapping as the thundering menagerie of eccentric vehicles roared past.

Joard engaged the reduction gear as we sped down the village's main road, following the trail of mud and scattered vegetation. We passed the finish line in fourth place, just behind the twins. Cylus took second place and Gunther claimed first, although Gunther's ten-ton trackless locomotive continued for another quarter mile before grinding to a complete stop. Svotgar's battered racer limped across the finish line a few minutes behind us. The remaining stragglers puttered in as dusk settled, Kargeth being one of them, his drive axle having broken loose on the final mile.

Gunther Viggs slammed his mug on the tavern table, sloshing foam across the savaged remains of his meal. "E'eryone laughed at my Bruntilga," he growled, wiping froth from his horseshoe mustache with the back of his meaty hand. "Said Gloombog 'oud swallow 'er whole. Well, who's laugh'n now, eh?" He roared a boisterous guffaw.

"You apparently are," Kargeth grumbled. The gray-skinned Scaithi leaned back in his chair across from

Gunther, kicking one boot up on the table. "Had my axle not mysteriously come loose, I would have beaten you soundly." He looked thoughtfully into his drink, his turquoise eyes narrowing and tapered ears drooping flat. "It should not have come loose the way it did," he muttered softly. "Those bolts were secure last night. I'm *certain* they were."

Gunther laughed again and slapped his scrawny co-driver on the back, nearly plunging the poor man's face into his stew. "The race is ours this year! Ain't that right, Toben?"

Toben just choked in reply, trying to clear whatever soup had gone down his windpipe.

I looked across the dimly lit tavern room of the Ox and Badger where we had been boarded for the night. I felt somewhat sorry for the innkeeper and his two daughters, who by now were at wit's end keeping up with the demands of their ill-mannered guests. Raucous laughter and drunken tavern songs filled the smoky air, drowning out the clang of forks on pewter plates and spoons on empty tankards. Svotgar stood on his stool, bringing himself to eyelevel with another driver to yell rude implications about his ancestors' heritage, while Vera egged him on with another brimming mug of ale. Nera sprang from her table whooping, having just won an arm-wrestling match with a driver twice her size. She threw back a mug of spiced rum, then shouted an open challenge to anyone man enough to beat her. Meretta was notably more reserved, sipping a gin and fluffing her freshly washed hair as she waited for Cylus to return from outside. Through it all, Keldon tried to recluse himself in one corner of the tavern, his hands against his ears and face buried in one of his thaumaturgical study books.

The back door of the tavern opened and Joard strode in with Cylus fast on his heels, yelling over the clamor in the room.

"You grease-grubbing cheat!" Cylus went on. "I saw you slinking around my racer!"

"Your racer is parked right next to mine," Joard

contended. He threw his tool bag on a table and crossed his arms. “I was working on my engine.”

Cylus scoffed and brushed back his hair. “So you say. But it’s too dark out there to fix anything.”

Joard poked a finger back at Cylus. “If that’s so, then what were *you* doing out there?”

I excused myself from the table, stepping over one drunken patron while avoiding another who nearly staggered into me. But before I could cross the hopelessly crowded room of toppled chairs and broken tableware, Meretta had already joined her suave companion in his verbal assault.

“I don’t care if you killed your partner or not,” Meretta snapped, “but you’d better keep your hands off our racer!” She looked Joard up and down, then shook her head. “And didn’t I see you poking around Gunther’s junk heap just after the race?”

Gunther bolted from his chair, knocking it over. “He done what?”

“No!” Joard protested. “I didn’t... I wasn’t...”

The room did not fall completely silent, but most conversations quieted as heads turned to the roiling commotion. I could see where the altercation was going, and I raised my hands hoping to disarm what was surely a thoroughly inebriated time bomb.

“Why don’t we all just—” I began to say.

“Kick this skulker out of here,” Meretta cut in. She shoved Joard against a table, then jabbed his chest with her finger. “He’s sabotaging this race! He’s probably the one who sabotaged Kargeth’s racer, and everyone knows he killed Neb!”

“That be enough from you,” Nera called, rushing up to Meretta with her sister not far behind. “You don’t even be a driver. You just be dandy-boy’s bed warmer, you floozy tart!”

“You will apologize for that!” Cylus yelled, his face turning beet red. He reached for something behind his back and the twins’ hands flew to the pistols at their hips.

"Stop!" I yelled. My badge was in my hand, held high in the air. "As a deputized freelance detective for Vandor Tower, I have the full authority to arrest the lot of you. Just try finishing the race from behind bars." I looked around, happy to see I had everyone's attention. "As all of you know, I am here investigating Neb Dorlen's death. It would be in everyone's best interest if you refrain from shooting each other and allow me to do my job."

"Faugh!" Cylus threw his hands up and stalked away. "I'm giving my racer a thorough check first light tomorrow, and if even one bolt is out of place, I'll ki—" He stopped himself from finishing the threat, his eyes glancing to me. "Then I'll know who's responsible."

Meretta patted the golden curls behind her head. "I believe I shall retire for the evening." She turned her nose up as she brushed past the twins. "There's a foul stench in the air and I don't think it's the swamp."

Vera's face pinched into a snarl and she shook a fist after Meretta. "Try sniffing between your—"

"Ahem!" I interrupted, clearing my throat.

Both twins glared at me, then rolled their eyes.

Keldon pushed through the crowded tavern, his brass key drawn and book open to one of the more lethal conjurations. "What's going on? Has something happened?"

"You're not ready to practice those kinds of empowerments," I said, nodding to the book.

Keldon shut the book and stuffed his talisman back into his belt. "The hydra..." He glanced at the twins, then looked away. "I should have been able to do more. What good are tricks of light and illusions when we're in danger?"

I sighed. He had a good point, but he wasn't ready for combat magery. He was more likely to injure himself than his opponent. "You've done brilliantly," I assured him, giving him an encouraging smile.

Joard grabbed his tool bag from the table and shoved an empty chair out of his way, heading for the staircase leading to the rooms upstairs.

"What happened out there?" I asked, catching him by the arm. "Cylus was right about one thing. It *is* dark, and you didn't take a lantern with you."

Joard glanced at my hand holding his shirt sleeve. "I was just tightening a few bolts and checking the fuel hoses." He pulled his arm away and straightened out his mud-stained shirt. "There's enough light to do that much with Atracus up and the sky clear."

I glanced over his shirt and nodded. "You might want to get that button fixed."

Joard looked down at his rumpled shirt and poked the hole where one of his mother-of-pearl buttons should have been. "It must have torn off while I was working." He looked nervously about the room, then shook his head. "I'm going to call it a night as well. I've had enough of one day to fill a week."

With that, he hefted his tool bag and trudged up the wooden stairs to the guest rooms.

"He's in a rather sour humor tonight," Keldon observed. "I guess coming in at fourth place will do that to you."

The jocular din of the tavern had resumed, and I looked to Svotgar who was now dancing on a nearby table, sloshing ale as he sang some horrifically off-key mining shanty, his onlookers laughing and slapping their knees at the spectacle. Svotgar had come in at fifth place, and having ranked poorly the previous days, his chances of winning were remote at best. In contrast, Joard had little reason to worry as he could still win if he placed well tomorrow.

No, Joard wasn't upset about the race or his ranking. Something else had rattled his nerves—something serious. But whether he was shaken by his partner's recent death, or by Cylus's and Meretta's accusations, or because those accusations rang all too true, remained to be seen.

PEBBLES AND GRAINY BITS of sand battered Joard's racer as we bounced across the tortured terrain, with more rock chips pelting my goggles than seemed to strike the dismally short windshield. The blackened desolation stretched from the northern end of the valley to the weathered roots of Daggercrest Mountain, scarred by rocky gorges and riven clefts smoldering with the ancient fires of the subterranean tar pits burning far below. Wormwood, thornscrubs, and needle brambles were the only living plants I could see, and the charred stumps and shattered trunks of what few trees had dared to grow here were a grim reminder of the land's eponymous apex predators.

"Watch out for that—!" I began to scream, my voice scarcely audible over the racer's alchemical engine.

But Joard had already seen the scaly beast charging at us from between two rock pillars. He veered right and accelerated, then swerved left, and the horned drake stumbled past, its bone-crushing jaws snapping shut on empty air. The reptile shrieked as it lumbered after us, growing distant in the wake of the dust kicked up by our wheels.

I sighed, leaning back in my seat as I looked across the blasted hills and blackened gullies of Drake Valley. Fire elementals leaped and looped around the smoldering fissures hewn deep into the lowland basin, their flighty antics overshadowed by the appearance of vermatherion crawling from their cavernous holes, nostrils flaring as the spiny reptiles sniffed the desiccated air. A pack of mountain wyverns alighted upon the craggy heights of a barren ridge, while pennapterexes and dracavians circled in the sky, their majestic plumage glittering with metallic hues in the late afternoon sun.

The high-pitched whine of rotary engines split the air as the twins' duowheeler vaulted off a butte and skidded across the ground in front of us, kicking up a spray of rocks and dirt. Nera and Vera gave us a thumbs-up, then revved their engines and sped ahead, pursued by a pair of screeching wyverns, their head crests flushed red with the thrill of the chase. Joard cursed and swerved again as a third wyvern swooped in, its talons extending to snatch us from our seats. I ducked low as the beast passed overhead, missing me by a hand span.

"Blasted dragons!" Joard yelled. He sat back up and righted our course, shaking his fist at the wyvern now following the other two in their pursuit of the twins. "The way they're acting, you'd think we were their prey."

I was about to remind him of the fact that we *were* their prey when I noticed the floorboards were no longer loose. I tapped a foot on the plank where I had found the missive the day before, only to find the board had been firmly battened down. Joard must have secured the boards while he was working on the engine last night, and doing so certainly made for a sturdier place to put my feet. On the other hand, he had seemed rather surprised when I found the missive sticking up between the planks, and was nearly frantic when he saw me trying to pry up one of those boards in search of a fuel hose. Had he simply been concerned I would damage the racer, or was he afraid of what I might find beneath those floorboards?

Gunther's Bruntilga thundered past us, black smoke belching from the stacks to either side of its boiler. The exhaust should have been light gray, not black, meaning far too much smoke was being exhausted in proportion to the venting steam. Something was wrong. The speeding machine surged ahead of us with a blast of smoke and sparks from its stacks, and a bang like a gunshot cracked through the air. The six-wheeled locomotive swerved to the left, nearly tipping over, and then swerved right again as Gunther regained control. We tore past the convulsing iron beast, leaving her behind in a cloud of settling dust and choking black smoke.

"We have to stop," I said.

"Are you serious?" Joard demanded. "If I stop now, I'll lose for sure. And let's not forget about those dragons!"

I glanced over my shoulder. Bruntilga chugged to a stop behind us, a final ring of smoke puffing from the smokestacks. "Gunther and Cylus were in the lead, followed by you. Cylus caught you skulking about his racer last night, and Meretta claimed to have seen you near Gunther's. What do you imagine the other racers are going to say?"

Joard shook his head, his hands tightening on the tiller. "I told you, I was working on my engine!"

"I probably shouldn't tell you this, but right now, you are my primary suspect." It was not exactly a lie. Cylus, Kargeth, Gunther, Svotgar, and even the twins were suspects as well, but I needed Joard to feel the pressure. Apply just the right pressure at just the right moment and a man's true nature will shine through—for good or for ill. "If you want to demonstrate otherwise, then turn around and go back."

Joard bit his lip. He shook his head again and swore under his breath, then he pressed the break and turn the tiller hard to the left. We spun about on the parched ground, skidding wheels kicking up a cloud of dust and dirt around us, then sped back the opposite way we had come. Bruntilga was still rolling to a stop when we pulled up beside her and I hopped out of my seat before our racer had stopped moving.

Gunther yelled something from inside the cabin and I rushed up the steps to the side door. The big fellow knelt beside Toben who was splayed out on the floor with his face smashed in as though struck by the rude end of a war hammer. Blood and water soaked the boilerman's overalls, and the skin of his arms and face were bright red, as though scalded by a jet of hot steam.

"Toben!" Gunther yelled, shaking the limp form.

I placed a hand on Gunther's muscled shoulder. He shot a glance at me, his teeth bared in a mix of anger and anguish, then he slowly lowered his head, closing his eyes as he realized nothing could be done.

"What happened?" I asked.

Gunther nodded to the snarl of pipes, valves, and gauges

cluttering the front of the cab. “Steam injector done seized up. Toben tried to clear the block, but the o’erflow valve blew up in his face.” He scratched his horseshoe mustache, then stood and looked over the clutter of valves. “Boiler water don’t e’en flow that way, not unless the compressor coupling done cracked.”

I knelt beside the body as Gunther lumbered to the front of the cab. The profusion of blood covering Toben’s face gave him the appearance of having been mauled, but it was in fact only the superciliary ridge just above his right eye that had been crushed in. A few feet away I spotted the small valve wheel that had done him in, spattered with blood.

“There’s a dracavian circling just above,” Joard warned as he climbed up the steps to the cab. “We’d better...” His voice trailed off when he saw Toben’s body. “Is... Is he dead?”

I nodded. “It seems he took an overflow valve to the face.”

“Star’s blast it!” Gunther cursed. He slammed his fist into the wall next to the firebox backhead, his brow furrowed in rage. “The compressor coupling ain’t cracked. The locking bolt’s been loosened!”

Accidents do happen, especially in the Golden Gear Locomobile Rally, but if what Gunther said was true, then this might indeed be sabotage. I began to ask if the locking bolt could come loose on its own, but a glint of light from beneath the co-driver’s seat caught my eye. I picked up the tiny round object, tensing when I recognized the distinctively patterned mother-of-pearl button. The button matched those on Joard’s shirt, one of which was still missing from last night.

“You done this, didn’t you?” Gunther barked, wheeling around and stabbing a finger at Joard. “Cylus said you was slink’n ‘round last night. What’da you have to say to that?”

I slipped the button into my pocket hoping Gunther had not seen it. If he realized the button matched those on Joard’s shirt, he would probably bash the man’s skull in even as I watched.

"We have no definitive evidence," I said, standing up. I rolled the button in my pocket, knowing it was about as definitive a piece of evidence as we would likely find. "This may be sabotage, but Joard is no more likely a suspect than Cylus or Kargeth."

Gunther balled his fists, looking me up and down. "You're suppos'd to be some famous detective, huh? Well, I ain't see'n it. If you so great, you'd already be cuff'n this here killer!"

The twins had explained that Gunther was a former convict, but I could not guess what crime the man might have committed. He looked tough enough to be a killer himself, but whatever his crime, he had likely seen more than his share of judicial discrimination. "Everyone deserves equitable consideration under the law. Equal justice and equal protection for all."

Gunther stared me straight in the eyes. He then turned away and sniffed, folding his arms over his broad chest. "Yeah, you're right," he admitted. "Stars help me, but you're right."

"Aldicus, what's—" came Keldon's voice from just outside the cab. I turned and saw him staring at Toben's body. He pushed up his dirty goggles and took a step back. "An accident?"

"Doubtful," I replied. I would have elaborated, but Svotgar rushed up, his eyes wild with panic.

"What are you lolling about for!" the Dworgh yelled. "Don't tell me you've gotten yourself stranded." He then saw Toben's body and drew a sharp breath. "By Kromal's bones!"

A piercing shriek tore through the air, followed by a violent gust of wind. I rushed to the cab door and looked up, fear gripping me when I spotted the pennapterex swooping down, its wings spread and talons extended for the attack. Another roar came, this time from a different direction, and a second dragon—a vulture-like dracavian—slammed into the first. The brightly plumaged males tumbled through the air as they fought, a whirlwind of teeth, talons, and shooting flames.

"They're fighting over food rights," I surmised.

"Food? What food?" Keldon asked, looking over the few brambles and scrubs growing in the parched soil of Drake Valley. His shoulders slumped when he took my meaning. "Oh."

"Can you get this iron beast moving?" Svotgar yelled to Gunther.

"No yellow-bellied grifter's gonna stop my Bruntilga," Gunther called back, already attending to the broken valve with a pipe wrench and torque driver. "But I'm gonna need a boilerman to keep her blaz'n belly full."

Svotgar sighed, his beaded beard rattling as he shook his head. "I might as well help you out, as I've already lost this blasted race. Just give me two ticks and a tock to hitch my racer to the back."

Keldon turned to follow Svotgar, but I placed a hand on his shoulder and pointed to the airborne battle of beating wings and thrashing tails. The larger dracavian tore into the pennapterex's left wing and blasted the smaller foe with a deluge of searing blue fire. Wounded, though not mortally so, the pennapterex shrieked in defeat and retreated into the sky trailing blood and smoke behind it.

"We appear to have a victor," I said to my apprentice. "And to the victor go the small, crunchy morsels scampering about their obnoxious mechanical rides." Keldon tensed, perhaps anticipating what I was about to suggest. "We shall need a good distraction. A fine job for an illusionist, wouldn't you say?"

Judging from his blanched complexion, Keldon might have held a different opinion on the subject. But he nodded anyway and drew his talisman from his belt. The large brass key glinted in the late afternoon sun, its vizstone glowing faintly blue as he focused his concentration. I did not wait to see what wily mirage he might conjure to distract the dragon, and instead climbed back into the cab to help Gunther get Bruntilga's iron heart pumping.

Joard dragged Toben to an out-of-the-way corner in the back of the cab, and I found a small survival blanket in a storage compartment to lay over the body. Gunther finished his work on the overflow valve, then began turning wheels, winding cranks, and checking gauges. Another screech reverberated through the air, and I poked my head out the door to have another look around.

Svotgar was busy securing his racer to Bruntilga's rear hitch, and Keldon stood a few feet away, his shimmering key held out before him. The dracavian circled back around, having chased away its lesser rival, and with one swoosh of its great feathered wings, the beast came swooping down toward us. No, not toward us, but for what appeared to be a herd of bison charging eastward. Never mind the fact that bison hadn't roamed the plains of Armillia in over two centuries, nor that a single mote of dust rose in the wake of their stampeding hooves, carrying them in eerie silence across the valley floor. The spectral herd shimmered and began to fade as they grew evermore distant, testing the limits of Keldon's ability. The dragon would not be fooled for long.

"Svotgar!" I called to the Dworgh.

"I got it!" he yelled back. He locked the chains secure, then hoisted his racer off its two front wheels leaving only the single large rear wheel on the ground. "Come on, lad. That old wyrm will be mighty bitter when he learns he was fooled."

The dragon had already turned from the phantasmal bison, so Keldon simply released the illusion and hurried after Svotgar. Bruntilga rumbled to life and Gunther began throwing shovelfuls of lustrous ebonite into the sweltering furnace. The rare coal burned twice as hot and twice as long as common coal, but the real innovation had to be the vehicle's firebox and boiler. The extreme temperature and pressure of the supercritical steam would blast any ordinary locomotive to smithereens.

"All aboard who's com'n aboard, and e'erybody out who ain't," Gunther announced. He tossed the shovel to Svotgar and motioned for him to continue scooping ebonite coal, then began opening valves, pulling levers, and tapping gauges as they crossed their redline limits. "I'll be push'n her someth'n fierce, and she might blow more than just one or two valves. Fair warn'n and all that."

Keldon's eyes widened at the warning, but I gave him a reassuring pat on the shoulder and smiled.

Bruntilga was already moving at a fair clip when Joard and I jumped off, and we ran, half stumbling, back to his racer. The cycloaetheric compressor roared to life. Joard cranked the gearbox and hit the accelerator, tearing after Bruntilga as the massive vehicle slowly but surely gained speed. I opened the small compartment behind my seat and fumbled around for my black bag, glancing skyward only to see the dracavian gaining fast.

"What are you doing?" Joard asked.

There was no time to explain. "I can't conjure an illusion, but I *can* devise a distraction."

Searching through the alchemistry set in my bag, I quickly located my paltry supply of powdered phosphor, zinc filings, and muriatic acid. It would be enough, if barely. I then retrieved the spare canister of vitriolic ethynate from the rear compartment and breathed a sigh of relief when I found that at least some of the fuel additive remained. Dumping each reagent into the quarter-filled container, I topped it off with a pinch of alkahest to serve as a catalyst. The contents of the canister began to fizz and bubble, growing steadily hotter, and I hefted it up to rest on the back of the racer, pointing directly behind us.

"Was something supposed to happen?" Joard asked, glancing back. His eyes widened when he saw how close the dragon was, and the vehicle lurched forward as his foot slammed the accelerator pedal. "Archons help us!

I nearly dropped the canister when the racer bounced over a shallow knoll, just managing to catch it as a single puff of smoke burped from the top. I frowned, fearing I had misjudged the proportions, then nearly dropped the canister again when a billowing column of white smoke erupted from the end.

"Bring us in front of Bruntilga and circle around," I called over the engine's whine and rushing wind. Bruntilga was fast once she got up to speed, but until she did, the dragon could easily catch up to them. "We need to draw that monster away."

Joard shook his head in obvious frustration, but he followed my directions nonetheless. The billowing plume of smoke pouring from the canister expanded behind us, widening as it blanketed everything in a rolling cloud of opaque white. I could barely see the dragon through the alchemical brume, and with luck, the beast would have just as much difficulty seeing us. We swept across Bruntilga's path, blanketing the locomotive racer in the enveloping cloud, then broke left and accelerated, heading away from the slower vehicle.

I watched with a smile as the dragon followed the smoke screen trailing behind us, and smiled again when I saw the orange glow of dragon fire through the murky haze. The volatile cloud ignited in a flash, exploding around the dragon in a cascading fireball of vaporescent phosphor, zinc, muriatic acid, and vitriolic ethynate. I threw the smoking canister aside, a tongue of fire streaming after it as we sped away. The shrieking dragon tumbled from the conflagration and crashed to the ground, feathers burning. Joard steered us back on course and we soon joined up with Bruntilga, leaving a burning cloud of ash and cinder—and one very angry dragon—smoldering behind us.

After crossing another ten miles, we sped through the rocky pass leading from Drake Valley to the southern hills of the Duchy of Delarien. A fusillade of cannon blasts saluted our approach as the naval dirigibles patrolling the outskirts sent up a wall of drakesbane shrapnel, repelling any winged reptiles attempting to breach the borders of the reservation. We passed four more racers on the final stretch to the day's finish line, but trailed far behind those in the lead position.

Cheering spectators crowded the bumpy dirt road ushering us into the bustling trade town of Doriville, cluttered up against the towering iron walls of Fort Calithion. We crossed the finish line just a head of Gunther, but only managed to claim fourth place. Cylus took first place, with the twins and Kargeth placing second and third. Of the forty some-odd teams that had begun the race four days ago, only ten remained, the rest having met with accidents or break downs, or simply dropped out knowing they would be lucky just to survive, let alone win.

Tomorrow would bring the rally's most perilous and challenging leg yet: the haunted wasteland of rust and ruin known simply as the Iron Barrens.

NERA THREW BACK HER ALE and slammed the mug on the table before returning her attention to her cards. I wondered if she had a bad hand, but then she cast a disparaging glance at Cylus and Meretta as the pair strolled through the inn's common room, looking for a table. Both wore immaculately washed racing outfits, Cylus with his puffed-up scarf to complement his equally pompous grin and Meretta with a lavish cartwheel hat over her curled blond hair.

"He be fixing to win," Nera grumbled. She played a triple match of fives, then frowned when I played a two card rider of fives over hers. "He and that dollymolly of his."

"Are you certain they'll win?" I asked.

Nera shrugged. "We might take second place, Taimon's luck be with us."

Cylus had placed high enough that he would most likely win the Golden Gear tomorrow. Second place could easily fall to the twins, and they still had a fair chance at winning first. If anyone was going to be sabotaged tonight, it would either be Cylus or the twins. I glanced around the common room, hoping to account for everyone. Cylus and Meretta had just sat down at an empty table, Keldon, Svotgar, and the twins were at my table playing jonko, Gunther brooded quietly over several tankards of ale, and the remaining, lower ranked drivers laughed and carried on at a table near the back. I frowned. Both Kargeth and Joard were missing.

"I'm out," I said, laying my cards down. I stood, adjusted my frock coat, and headed for the door. Keldon began to follow, but I waved him back to the table. What I had to do, I had to do alone.

The sun had already set, but enough light came from the streetlamps to see the scattered tents and pavilions filling the inn's front yard. I spotted Kargeth stepping out of the tent housing his racer, wiping his hands with a rag and muttering to himself. I looked to Joard's pavilion where a small light was glowing, but I did not see Joard in the tent.

"Have you seen Joard?" I asked Kargeth as he passed me in the yard on his way back to the inn.

Kargeth pinched his mouth shut and narrowed his eyes. "No," he answered curtly. "But someone tampered with my axle again. If you really are here to catch the saboteur, then might I suggest you keep a better eye on the obvious culprit?"

The Scaithi pushed pass me and headed inside. I continued to the small pavilion housing Joard's racer and finally spotted him working on something underneath his engine.

"Joard?" I asked.

"Just a minute," he replied from underneath.

I folded my arms and waited, but found my eyes drawn to the racer's floorboards. Why had they been loose before, only to be securely nailed down now? Why had a missive from Dragar Industries been stuck between the boards? Why had Joard seemed so anxious when I was poking around there?

Taking a pry bar from Joard's toolbox, I quickly jimmied one of the floorboards up. What the gap revealed caused my breath to catch.

Joard banged his head on the undercarriage, then he scrambled up from the floor. "What are you doing?"

I turned to meet Joard's horror-filled eyes. "That is the question I should ask you." I pointed to the rolled-up blueprints stuffed between the floorboard and the undercarriage chassis plate. "Are these not the plans Neb claimed had been stolen?"

"I..." Joard's face grew pale in the sallow lamp light, his hands visibly shaking. "Whatever you think... Whatever else I might have done... I swear, I didn't kill Neb!"

I would like to have believed him, but the mounting evidence could not simply be ignored. "And the sabotage to Gunther's and Kargeth's racers?"

Joard shook his head. "No! I had nothing—"

I took the button from my pocket and held it against a button on his shirt. The buttons matched. "I found this in Gunther's cab."

Joard's eyes widened. "But I..." His voice trailed off. After a moment, he drew a deep breath and seemed to recover some measure of his wits. "We stopped to help him. How could you believe I sabotaged his vehicle if we—"

"We stopped only *after* I insisted on it," I reminded him. "Now, I ask you again: why were the supposedly stolen designs for Neb's engine stuffed under the floorboards of his racer?"

Joard pinched his eyes shut, his shoulders slumping. "Yes, I stole the plans," he admitted. "I hid them hoping I could sell them to Dragar Industries, or to anyone else who might pay."

I folded my arms, eyeing him suspiciously. "Have you already contacted them?"

"Dragar?" Joard asked. "No. If we placed, I knew I could demand more..." He sighed again and shook his head. "Arrest me for stealing the blueprints if you must. But not for Neb's murder, and not for the sabotage. I don't even care if I win. I just wanted to rank well enough so I can sell these designs to pay off my debts."

I set my jaw and studied Joard's face. "You will answer for your crime, but I must see this race to the finish if I am to uncover the identity of our murderous saboteur." I paused, then made a point of looking him up and down, my face as stern as I could make it. "Whoever that turns out to be."

Joard hesitated, then gave a somber nod. I took him roughly by the arm and led him back to the inn.

In truth, the button could easily have been planted by the saboteur. All someone needed was a button from Joard's shirt. With Joard already a suspect, the culprit probably hoped to throw me off, allowing them free reign to complete their scheme. But what *was* the scheme? Cylus had held the lead for most of the race, so there was no reason for him to sabotage the opposition, at least, not at the risk of being caught. Kargeth or Gunther had both been sabotaged, and Svotgar seemed content to simply finish the race as Gunther's boilerman.

That left Nera and Vera. Their duowheeler had not suffered any mysterious breakdowns, and they were second only to Cylus in ranking. Then again, Cylus had not suffered any mishaps either and his vehicle did use volatilis ammoniac as a fuel additive. If Cylus and Meretta...

"Meretta..." I heard myself whisper.

"What?" Joard asked.

Meretta could easily have torn the button from Joard's shirt when she shoved him the other night. I pushed through the door to the inn's common room and looked to the table where she and Cylus had been sitting. Cylus was still there, but not Meretta.

"Have you seen Meretta?" I asked Nera, returning to the table where she, Vera, Keldon, and Svotgar continued their jonko game.

"Pfff!" Nera sputtered into her drink. "Why would I care where she be?"

I looked between Nera and her sister. "You mentioned she was Cylus's new girlfriend. How new?"

Both shrugged, but Vera answered. "Two or three months. Like we be saying, she only be with him for fame."

Neb had rejected the offer from Dragar Industries two months ago, but according to Joard, Cylus had gotten the sponsorship one week later. "Was it two months or three? This is critical."

"Two," Vera said. "She be with him at the practice track about the second week of Summertide."

My eyes grew wide. We didn't have a saboteur lurking in our midst, we had an industrial spy. "Fangle-fop!"

Keldon looked up from his cards. "What's that noise?"

An engine roared to life outside—not the smooth revving of a driver testing his latest tweaks, but the shrill howl of a racer taking off at full speed. Everyone was out of their seats in an instant, throwing cards, drinks, and smoking pipes into the air as they scrambled for the door. I hurried back outside with Joard and the other drivers, but judging from Joard's ghost-white face, I knew he recognized the fading drone of his own engine.

"My racer!" he yelled, stumbling for the shredded remains of his pavilion before dropping to his knees in the middle of the yard. "Someone's stealing my racer!"

Cylus also stood in wide-eyed disbelief, staring in utter shock at the dusty trail rising in the night. "What...?" he asked, his voice trailing off. "What is she doing?"

I crossed my arms and raised an eyebrow. "I'm afraid your girlfriend just stole Joard's racer."

Cylus stood in stunned silence for a moment more, then shook his head. "But no... But why... She can't..." His eyes widened. "I'll be disqualified!" With that, he bolted for his own speedster.

"Meretta?" Keldon asked, stepping up beside me.

I nodded, the pieces clicking together all too late. "Meretta must have seen me confronting Joard. She probably assumed I had taken him into custody and believed that I or the local constabulary would confiscate his racer. More importantly, this is our last stop before the race's final day, and the best opportunity for her to make her break. We are close enough to Corradon that she can make it to the city in about two hours, assuming she drives through the heart of the Iron Barrens, rather than keeping to the race's safer course. She knows there's little chance I can even pursue her, since any driver absconding from this rally point will be immediately disqualified. No driver would take that kind of risk just to help us."

"What about Cylus?" Keldon asked. Then he looked to the fluttering remains of Cylus's tent, watching as his speedster raced after the dusty trail, the howl of its engine fading in the cold night air. "Oh, I guess he's already off. Is he helping her?"

I shook my head. "Cylus was duped. It seems Meretta is an agent of Dragar Industries, sent to eliminate Neb and steal the plans for his revolutionary engine design. She killed Neb, but failed to find the plans, and my arrival threw another wrench into her schemes. Stealing the racer itself is an act of desperation, but since Joard had hidden those plans beneath the floorboards, she just made off with both. The irony is, Joard was going to sell them those very same plans. But he hadn't contacted Dragar yet, so as far as they knew, Neb was going to release the designs to the public like he said he would—something Dragar desperately wanted to avoid."

"What?" Keldon asked, clearly stunned by the revelation. "We have to go after her!"

I sighed, looking around. "Name one driver who would voluntarily forfeit the race to help us."

"Svotgar," Keldon said simply.

My eyes widened. Of course! Svotgar had already dropped out of the race, but unlike the others who had dropped out, he had chosen to remain in our company, helping Gunther. "Svotgar!" I yelled, glancing around for the Dworgh.

"What?" he yelled back.

I turned to see Svotgar strolling out of the inn, a tankard of ale in one hand and a roasted mutton rib in the other. Just before I could ask for his aid, the Dworgh's racer tore past, its massive rear wheel kicking up rocks and dust as it sped away. Svotgar dropped his ale and mutton rib, his bearded jaw falling slack. I had never seen a Dworgh run as fast as he ran then, his ambling stride becoming a loping gait with arms waving as he screamed for the thief to come back. I squinted as I watched the three-wheeled racer thunder after the other two, then shook my head when I saw the driver.

"Joard has just stolen Svotgar's racer to chase after his own." I was going to need to take notes just to keep track of which infraction was committed by whom. I slapped Keldon on the arm and pointed to Gunther. "It's time to get the pursuit underway."

Gunther backed away as we drew near, his hands waving in a frantic gesture of protest. "Oh, no!" he objected before I had even said a word. "I ain't throw'n away my chances, not with Cylus and Joard hav'n forfeited the race."

"Then I should just let Toben's killer get away?" I asked.

Gunther's shoulders slumped in defeat. "I'll get Bruntilga started," he mumbled before climbing into his cab.

Kargeth's racer tore away from its tent with Svotgar at the tiller, the clatter of its clockwork engine rising to a whirring buzz as it smashed through a wooden fence and skidded onto the main road. Kargeth chased after him, shaking a socket wrench and yelling Scaithi obscenities.

I sighed. "Well, there goes the race..."

One of the referees finally made an appearance, his face flush with panic and eyes bulging in disbelief. "Where is everyone going? The final leg of the race isn't until tomorrow morning!"

"That so?" Nera asked, strapping on her goggles.

Vera slammed her foot on their duowheeler's starter and a flash of blue-white aethergy flared within its whirling rotors. "I think the real race be starting now!"

"You can't enter the Iron Barrens in the middle of the night!" the referee yelled after them. "It's suicide!"

"Check for sabotage," I called to the twins. If anyone's vehicle had been tampered with, it would be theirs.

Vera threw me a burned-out spark valve as their duowheeler skidded past. "Already be fixed, old man," she countered with a grin. "Keep up."

"Old man?" I shot back, but the duowheeler was speeding fast away. Keldon just laughed.

An eruption of smoke and steam belched from Bruntilga's smokestacks as the mighty locomotive engine came alive. I hopped up into the cab and lent a hand to help Keldon clamber inside. Kargeth jogged up beside us, his trot becoming a run as Bruntilga built speed.

"I'm coming with you," he indignantly announced. "My racer was stolen too, you know."

"You can come, but only if you tend the firebox," I bargained.

He snarled, his tapered ears flattening back, but he thrust out his hand for me to pull him inside. Soon, Bruntilga was barreling down the road after the other five vehicles, the heat of her blazing furnace boiling away the bite of the cold autumn night. I leaned out the window and held on to my top hat, the wind whipping across my face as I looked down the tangle of pipes and pneumatic vents adorning the locomotive's boiler. A vast black expanse stretched before us, the skeletal forms of long abandoned refineries and derelict manufactories rising from the industrial desolation like the petrified bones of ancient titans. *The Iron Barrens*—ten miles of festering alchemical mires, wraith-haunted scrapyards, and cursed machines blighting the northwestern outskirts of Corradon.

Bruntilga sailed from the Barren's outer barricade and crashed back to the ground, wheels ripping through the rust-speckled soil. Gunther swore, opening a series of pressure valves and motioning for Kargeth to shovel faster. The sweat-drenched Scaithi muttered under his breath as he wiped his brow, smearing black soot across his lead gray skin. He heaved an even bigger scoop of ebonite into the engine's roaring white fire. The locomotive surged forward, its blast pipes erupting with sparks and every gauge crossing its redline limit.

"The Iron Barrens," Keldon groaned, looking out the window as we thundered past shadow-veiled scrapyards and crumbling quarry pits. "No one comes here... No one."

"Of course people come here," I replied, trying to instill some measure of assurance. "Deranged clockwork cultists, gearbinder sorcerers, half-crazed mechanomancers, the odd karcist... A few actually manage to come back alive, although most do end up committed to Grimhall Asylum."

Keldon wrapped his arms around himself and shivered despite the sweltering heat of the furnace, and his worried frown dropped to a grimace. I looked out the window again, glad to see we were gaining on Svotgar. The twins had already pulled ahead, cutting through the gutted husk of a warehouse before speeding down a caved-in tunnel trench, heedless of the cog spiders and scraplings crawling out from the haunted ruins around them. Gunther proved equally reckless, plowing Bruntilga straight through the corroded gates of a dilapidated manufactory before jogging left to avoid a horde of clattering clockwork elementals.

I looked behind us and regretted it immediately. The wakened denizens of the decaying industrial necropolis poured after us, a tidal wave of howling geargeists, spectral engines, reanimated detritus, and scrap-fashioned rustwraiths. Bruntilga crashed through a wall of corroded sheet metal and turned sharply to avoid a churning river of noxious alchemical sludge. We sped under a gantry of fallen smokestacks and support pilings, catching up with Svotgar only to find him pursued by a formation of ghostly apparitions riding mechanical steeds. The twins' duowheeler cut directly in front of the phantasmal host, drawing half of them away. Gunther chuckled as he pulled the control tiller left and cranked the pressurizer, sending Bruntilga barreling through what remained of the spectral cavalry.

I gathered myself off the floor and kicked a few twitching gears and writhing chain belts out of the cab. "Are you out of your mind?"

"I did let you talk me into follow'n these lunatics, didn't I?" Gunther replied.

"You're *all* lunatics—every blasted one of you!" Kargeth spat. He shoveled more ebonite into the furnace, shaking his head as he heaved another scoop. "And I'm as much of one for coming with you!"

The volcanic orb of Atracus loomed high above, spilling crimson hues across the jagged peaks of forsaken refinery towers and mountainous junk heaps. In the distance, I saw the warm amber light of the city's skyline. The gleaming brass towers and bustling cobblestone avenues looked so near, and yet, were so terribly far. I was about to tell Keldon that Corradon was in sight, but my words caught in my throat when an undulating shadow eclipsed my view of the Clockwork City. It took a moment for me to realize what I was seeing, for the sheer size of the mechanized agglomeration was beyond anything I had feared we might encounter.

"By the Archons..." Gunther breathed. His hand reached to pull back the throttle, but I prodded him on the shoulder.

"Faster," I said. The ensorcelled construct was massive, but we had only one chance to get past it. "As fast as Bruntilga can go."

Gunther looked back at me in shock, then swallowed and nodded. He disengaged the governor, opened two more pressure valves, and edged up the throttle. "E'erybody, hang on!"

The monstrous form rose from the scrap-strewn landscape, a patchwork mountain of rusting sheet metal, conjoined machinery, and whirring, interlocking gears. Fires blazed deep within its churning core, shining hot and red from the gaps in its junk accreted body, while snapping electric bolts arced between rows of twisted poles protruding from its spine. Looking ahead, I caught sight of Joard's racer, and following not far behind was Joard in Svotgar's vehicle and Cylus in his own speedster. I watched as Svotgar, in Kargeth's racer, suddenly broke left, and the twins' duowheeler jumped directly across our path. Nera pulled a lever at her side, and the duowheeler suddenly split into two separate motowheel racers, each veering off in a different direction with one of the twins inside.

Confused by the scattering prey, the ensorcelled construct reared back and howled, a fountain of living fire erupting from the spinning grinder rings of its metal-shredding maw. It crashed back to the ground, sending a bone-jarring tremor through the layers of rubbish and refuse compressed beneath our wheels. To my surprise, Meretta kept straight on course with Cylus quickly gaining on her, but she hit the brakes just before coming into range of the colossal foe and skidded away. Cylus raced headlong into the monster's waiting grasp, swerving too late. The beast's shovel-like claw hoisted Cylus and his racer high into the air, then dropped him, speedster and all, into the iron-melting furnace of its pulverizing gullet.

"She led us straight to its lair!" Keldon yelled, his voice quivering with the horror of what he saw.

My apprentice was right. Meretta had known exactly how to lose us in the Iron Barrens, and could easily have avoided the feral agglomeration altogether. I watched as she sideswiped Joard, knocking him off course before speeding away. A barrage of buzz-saws and grasping pincers lashed out from the monstrous construct, smashing into the ground behind Joard as he deftly maneuvered Svotgar's three-wheeler through the gauntlet, narrowly avoiding Cylus's sorry fate.

"We'll need some cover if we hope to make it through ourselves," I said to Keldon. "An illusory mirror mirage might be enough to distract it."

"On it, boss," Keldon replied, drawing his key. We continued on course, barreling straight for the construct as Keldon whispered to himself, the sigils inscribed along the sides of his talisman glowing brighter with every passing second. "Break right, now!"

Bruntilga listed so sharply as we turned that I feared we might topple over. As we turned, a diaphanous replica of our locomotive racer split away from us, continuing on our original heading. The colossal construct crouched down to attack, steam-actuated arms striking forward as its fiery maw widened to consume its prey. By the time the illusion dispelled we were already well out of the monster's range, thundering down a long-abandoned road leading south, out of the Iron Barrens and into Corradon's largely derelict northwestern quarter.

The 13th District marked the border zone between the Iron Barrens and Corradon proper—a perilous no-man's land of roving scavenger gangs, sorcerous shadow cults, and desperate criminal outlaws. Only a handful of these desperate denizens took chase, following in rickety steam-buggies and firing the occasional potshot as we raced through their contested territories. This was not the main road the rally called for us to follow, which would have taken us through the 26th District and onto Mainspring Causeway, the great thoroughfare of Corradon. No, this was a less populated avenue, heading south from the 13th District and straight into the vast industrial complex of the 14th.

I stroked my chin and nodded. Dragar Industries was headquartered in the 14th District, but then again, both Consolidated Omniworks and United Coal and Rail had extensive facilities there as well. Even so, Dragar Industries remained my prime suspect.

Block by block, the sights and sounds of Corradon grew from its decaying outskirts to the burnished brass, crystalline glass, and iron-cast fabricrete of the sprawling metropolis. The crimson shadow of Atracus faded under the warming glow of countless gas lamps and hovering luminary orbs, and the dark of midnight gave way to the eternal half-light of the sleepless Clockwork City. Gunther pushed and pulled the control tiller, frantically avoiding oncoming street trollies and puttering steam-coaches, reluctantly backing off the throttle as we raced deeper into the crowded district center.

"I can't keep up," Gunther warned. "Bruntilga's too big for the streets. It's too dangerous."

"Get us alongside Svotgar," I said, pointing to Kargeth's clockwork racer zigzagging around the panicked pedestrians scattering through the street ahead of us.

"You mean my stolen racer," Kargeth reminded. He threw another load of ebonite into Bruntilga's blazing firebox.

Gunther nodded, accelerating just enough to close the distance with the other vehicle.

"I'm coming with you," Keldon said as I edged out of the cab to the narrow catwalk running the length of Bruntilga's boiler.

"Not this time," I replied. "Stay here with Gunther and Kargeth."

Keldon sighed, but nodded. "Right, boss."

I turned to Gunther. "Get to Dragar Industries as quickly as you safely can."

Gunther gave a mock salute and grinned. "Will do, boss."

I held on to my top hat as I followed the catwalk, half crouched, to the front of the speeding locomotive. Dead ahead I saw a double-trussed causeway leading into the heavy industrial jungle of the 14th District. I had just seconds before Gunther would have to pull away. I doubted

Svotgar could hear me over Bruntilga's engine, but I yelled for him to get his racer closer, anyway. The Dworgh must have seen how close the locomotive had come and glanced up at me with a start. I signaled to him, then braced myself for the jump as our distance to the causeway shrank with astonishing speed. Feeling a change in momentum as Gunther began to pull away, I sprang for Svotgar's speeding racer.

I crashed onto the back of the vehicle, my fingers grasping the brass roll bar just behind the cockpit. Glancing behind us, I saw Bruntilga turn sharply away from the causeway, thundering down a ramp to the less crowded sublevel avenues.

"Are you insane?" Svotgar barked at me.

I pulled myself into the seat next to him and straightened out my ruffled frock coat. "Just determined." I began to adjust my top hat, then frowned when I found it had blown away. "I trust you can catch up with Meretta."

Svotgar shook his head, his beaded beard jingling. "I might catch up with Joard, but Meretta's got too much of a lead."

I nodded. "Good enough."

Svotgar navigated the cluttered obstacle course of the causeway, weaving between horse-drawn coaches, puttering steam-carriages, and pneumatic rickshaws, even while the racer's chattering clockwork engine accelerated us to greater speeds. A pair of shadows descended as we reached the end of the causeway, and I looked up to see the Nyasha Twins sailing off the top of a bridge just above, each one in their now separated racers. Their motowheels ripped across the street in front of us, and both twins glanced back with impish grins before surging ahead to catch up with Meretta and Joard.

Svotgar clearly took their smirks as a challenge, his brow furrowing as he tightened his grip on the tiller and accelerated Kargeth's racer to ever more dangerous speeds.

Startled crowds scattered and slower traffic made way as we careened down one busy avenue after another, skidding beneath steamrail tracks and skirting the walls of narrow access corridors. I looked up as we exited a sublevel utility corridor, and saw a massive shape filling the black night sky above. The Vandorian dirigible *Justiciar* cruised just above the district's reaching spires, search lights panning as a flight of ornithopters descended from its launch bays, pursuit lights flashing.

"We seem to have drawn the attention of Vandor Tower," I commented.

"These velocities are not exactly legal inside the city," Svotgar grumbled back.

I smiled. "Don't worry. I'll make sure they know I recruited you and the others to help apprehend the suspect."

Svotgar accelerated again, closing the distance with Joard. The twins were already flanking him, but Meretta was still a good six blocks ahead. I climbed out of the cockpit and slid down the front of the racer, the hood buzzing with the pulsing harmony of the clockwork engine inside.

"I want my racer back intact!" Svotgar yelled, as much to me as to Joard who was driving his vehicle.

I waved to Joard, and Joard's eyes went wide behind his goggles when he saw what I planned to do. Before he could object, I jumped for the racer, narrowly missing the massive rear wheel and catching myself on the dorsal support strut. Pulling myself forward, I clambered ungracefully into the cockpit, half-falling into the co-driver's seat.

"Faster," I said simply.

Joard shook his head, then pushed the throttle. The steam turbine's pitch rose to a whine, flames kicking from the exhaust pipes as we sped across another chasm-spanning causeway. The twins followed on their motowheels, Svotgar receded behind us, and in the air above, a flight of patrol thopters closed in fast. Just ahead loomed the imposing iron walls of the Dragar Industries manufactory enclave. The massive doors of the facility's expansive loading bay stood open, and Meretta was taking Joard's stolen racer straight for it. Those doors would close as soon as Meretta was in, locking us out of the fortified enclave. I grimaced at the thought. Unless I caught her in the handover, a syndicate as powerful as Dragar Industries, with teams of lawyers and well-placed political bribes, would have no difficulty worming out of any legal repercussions.

"Disable those doors!" I yelled to the twins, hands cupped around my mouth.

Nera and Vera both nodded, their motowheels striking off for each door's machinery encasements. Aetheric spark bolts and pneumatic thumper blasts erupted from the enclave's battlements the instant we crossed the intrusion ward perimeter. Explosions flanked the doors as the twins did their dirty work, knocking them out of commission, and we launched into the air when one thumper blast struck too close. I gripped the side of the cockpit, but the vehicle's massive rear wheel stabilized us like a gyroscope, and we crashed back to the road, speeding past rows of freight railcars and into the loading bay tunnel.

We were moving too fast for the sentry automatons to get a bead on us, but a host of egregores was likely converging on our position. I could not sense them, thanks to my severite wristbands, but no industrial enclave would be without their own army of aetheric watchdogs. If Keldon were here, we might have had some small chance of slipping past them, but it hardly mattered as our entrance had been somewhat less than subtle. Every mage on guard duty would know we were here, and that fact sat well enough with me. The game was already up.

Meretta spun Joard's racer to a stop at the far end of the loading bay, stumbling out of the cockpit and yelling to the guards as they emerged from the doors. Joard slammed the brakes, locking the rear wheel with such force that the front end of our vehicle dug into the fabricrete floor with a shower of sparks. We were both out of the cockpit and over the side in seconds, keeping the racer's body between us and the cracking shots of the guards' longarm repeaters.

"Svotgar is going to be rather put out about this," I said to Joard.

Joard winced as the racer shook from the impact of a concussive blast. "I think we were safer in the Iron Barrens than we are in Corradon."

Nera and Vera screeched to a stop and tumbled from their motowheels, drawing their clockwork pistols and firing back at the guards as they ran to join us behind Svotgar's racer.

Nera grinned at me, guns in hand. "We be outnumbered, outgunned, and facing one brutty bad syndicate!"

"Just the way we like it," Vera cheerfully added.

Svotgar skidded into the tunnel in Kargeth's racer, stopping just short of our position. "My racer!" he exclaimed, seeing the vehicle's sorry state. Volleys of gunfire and pneumatic blasts sent him jumping from the cockpit and scrambling for the cover of his own battered, bullet-riddled vehicle. "I told you I wanted it back intact!"

I gave Svotgar a conciliatory smile, then glanced up just long enough to get a quick look around. A red-cloaked mage had joined the guards, the air distorting around the coils of his staff as he began conjuring another kinetic blast. Just behind the mage stood a heavy-set fellow dressed in coat, waistcoat, and cravat, his scowling gaze fixed firmly on Meretta.

I dropped back behind the vehicle, my eyebrows rising in surprise. So, Meretta had unwittingly implicated Lord Dragar himself.

"Eliminate those fools," Dragar said to his mage. "And dispose of this incompetent moll."

"It's not my fault!" Meretta protested. "I had to make my move before Vescard uncovered the plan. I thought I could lose him in the Iron Barr—ahh!"

Her words became a scream, then silenced with the

sickening crunch of breaking bones and ripping flesh.

"Detective Vescard," Dragar said in a low voice. The gunfire had stopped, Dragar having likely signaled for his men to stand down. "We seem to have a rather unpleasant misunderstanding. I assure you, this thieving rogue operated on her own volition without my prior knowledge. Perhaps she hoped to sell this stolen property to my company, but we have no interest in dealing with criminals."

I shook my head. Such a pathetic attempt to cover his own culpability would be laughable, were it not for the fact that the High Court would likely accept such testimony, given the number of lawyers he would hire.

Against my better judgement I stood, my eyes glancing to the blood-soaked heap of twisted flesh and bones that had been Meretta. "Unfortunately, Lord Dragar, I just witnessed you ordering your mage to murder her."

Dragar's frown deepened, but I saw a nervous twitch in his eye. "She was a criminal and an intruder, and you will find she was armed as well. It is within the provisions of the law to exercise lethal force against any interlopers having hostile or criminal intention." He fixed his eyes on me and grinned. "*Any* interlopers."

I looked to the numerous guards and sentry automatons, and though their weapons were lowered, their eyes and ocular lenses were trained squarely on me. "The measure of your guilt will be determined by the courts. If not the courts of law, perhaps the court of public opinion... And the opinion of your shareholders as well." I drew the badge from my belt and held it out for him to see. "By the legal authority of the Vandorian Jurisdiction Proclamation of the High Court of Armillia, I am placing you under arrest."

A cruel sneer curled on Dragar's face. "Dragar Industries is one of the most powerful manufactory syndicates in all of Corradon." He waved for his guards to pull back, then started for the numerous transport containers lining the far side of the loading dock. "Who do you think supplies Vandor Tower with its arsenal of aether-powered weaponry? Who do you think produces the advanced articulated armor and battle-ready automatons used by your new HAAMR units? I have allies in high places, Vescard. *Very* high places."

Whatever Dragar was up to, it was clear that he was not going to come quietly. I threw off my frock coat and took hold of the locking pins in my severite wristbands. "Everyone, get back," I whispered to my friends huddled behind the crumpled frame of Svotgar's racer.

"We be going nowhere," Vera protested. She checked the ammo in her clockwork pistols and nodded to her sister. "We be with you, bossman, whatever that grifter be doing."

"Just take cover," I insisted, my tone firm.

Vera pinched her lips. She glanced at my wristbands, then tossed her dreadlocks as she threw a quick gesture with her head. "We best be doing what he say."

She hustled the others away, taking cover behind Kargeth's racer. I stepped out from around Svotgar's bullet-riddled racer and started forward, making sure Dragar saw I was prepared to drop my severite wristbands. Already I could hear the ornithopters descending, along with the deepening rumble of something else approaching.

"You will order your men to stand down and surrender into the custody of the Vandorian Guard," I ordered.

Dragar grinned as he stepped up to one of the larger transport containers. "Perhaps I should have mentioned, we also produce for the Armillian military."

He placed his back to the container's hydraulic doors, then pulled a locking lever to his right. Alarm bells sounded as the hydraulic doors opened, the platform beneath Dragar lifting him into the pilot's harness of the hulking armored suit berthed inside. Chest plates closed around him, and a plume of smoke bellowed from the rumbling engine. Dragar gripped the control handles to either side. Taking one floor-shaking step and then another, the military moto-armor lumbered forward, raising its pneumatic clockwork arms bristling with an array of horrifically lethal weaponry.

I took a hesitant step back. The automatronic armor looked like some kind of walking juggernaut war machine, with its pilot held securely behind layers of spellworked armor and advanced alchemical steels. Flamethrowers and mechanized rotor guns spun up to pour forth a veritable firestorm of destruction. With Neb's revolutionary engine in his possession, what greater terrors could a man such as Dragar unleash?

I shook my head, realizing I had no choice. My fingers tightened on the wristbands' pins and I closed my eyes, preparing to release the monster within.

"Go ahead, Vescard! Show me your worst!" Dragar challenged over the rumbling engine behind him, now laughing like some deranged lunatic. "Let's see how you fare against the might of Dragar Industries' most powerful moto-armor!"

A steam whistle sounded from behind, the floor shaking as though seized by an earthquake, and I glanced back just in time to see Bruntilga thundering down the loading bay corridor. The others scattered and I took a diving leap to get out of the way. The locomotive raced by with heedless speed as it crashed through barricades and ranks of sentry automatons. Dragar screamed, the clattering whirr of his moto-armor's rotor gun eclipsing the drumming chug of Bruntilga's supercritical steam engine—but only for a heartbeat.

With a deafening crash, the speeding locomotive slammed headlong into Dragar's moto-armor with the force of a fifty-ton steam-hammer, driving him into the crystal-tempered fabricrete wall. I threw my arms over my head as fire, smoke, and shrapnel showered the loading bay, the boom of the exploding boiler eclipsing all other sounds. A moment passed, and the cloud of dust and burning debris began to settle in the stark silenced that followed.

I looked up, breathing with relief when I saw that

Bruntilga's cabin was still intact. But Dragar and his moto-armor had been utterly pulverized by the crushing impact.

Gunther staggered out of Bruntilga's cab, shaking his head as he looked over the damage to his locomotive. "Did... Did I hit something?" he asked, clearly dazed and disoriented from the crash.

"Only some worthless rubbish," Nera answered, popping out from behind cover.

Keldon tumbled out of the cab next, Kargeth catching him as he started to fall over. "Remind me to never ride with this maniac again."

I stood, dusting myself off, and approached the squad of guards still standing in the back of the loading bay. The men threw down their weapons and raised their hands in surrender. Even the mage lowered his staff, his shoulders slumping as he realized the trouble he was in. The rumble of armored carriages and landing ornithopters filled the air just outside the loading bay where a force of Vandorian Guardsmen and HAAMR troopers prepared to storm the premises, bolt-batons primed and ready.

"Come along," I said to Keldon. "I probably have a great deal of explaining to do."

JUSTICIAR FLOATED IN THE NIGHT SKY ABOVE, a leviathan of gleaming steel and shining brass whose mere presence was a scathing pronouncement of the panic our reckless race through the bustling streets of Corradon had provoked. The grounds around Dragar Industries swarmed with Vandorian Guardsmen, district police, and HAAMR troopers. The mage and guards that had accompanied Lord Dragar were already in custody, but Dragar's body had yet to be cut from the twisted wreckage of Gunther's locomotive racer. Keldon waited by my side, while Nera and Vera milled around the enclave's crippled loading bay doors where Gunther, Kargeth, and Svotgar stood reminiscing about the chase. Joard sat alone off to one side, resting his head on his arms folded across his knees.

A HAAMR colonel named Ordin Dolgrim was apparently in charge, and the battle-scarred officer seemed less than pleased with the situation.

"I've half a mind to arrest you myself," Colonel Dolgrim said in his gravelly voice. Between his flat-cropped hair, his square jawline, and the optographic receptor filling his left eye socket, I could scarcely tell that he had removed his helmet at all. He frowned, twisting the jagged scar that ran from his artificial eye to the edge of his jaw. "You'll be lucky if the Commissioner General doesn't boot you off the force for good."

I suddenly found myself wishing for the levity of Tibblemond's affable badinage. Something about the colonel made my stomach knot. "Come now, colonel," I said, dusting out my frock coat before throwing it back on. "I just unraveled an underhanded plot to assassinate an inventor, steal his revolutionary engine, and ruin the world-famous Golden Gear Rally."

Colonel Dolgrim folded his arms over the articulated plates of his empowered armor. Armor, I grudgingly noted, that had been manufactured by Dragar Industries. "And with both Dragar and his alleged agent dead, how will you prove any of this, apart from a few disreputable testimonies and whatever circumstantial evidence you've scrounged up?"

I shrugged, stuffing my hands into my coat pockets. "If I am not mistaken, justice has already been served."

The colonel looked me up and down, his expression darkening, but he turned away to direct his men as they rounded up more Dragar employees for questioning.

"What happens now?" Keldon asked as we made our way back to the others. He looked at Joard. "What about him?"

I honestly did not know. Joard had stolen the engine plans, but it was the fact that he had hidden the plans that kept Meretta from finding them and stealing them right off. In a way, his single act of criminality had ensured the failure of Dragar's murderous plot.

"Everyone makes mistakes," I explained.

Joard looked up to find me standing over him. "Aldicus?" he asked. He glanced around, then nodded and held out his hands to be cuffed. "I am prepared to turn myself in."

I shook my head. "I should arrest you, but your actions this day have shown me that you are a good man. You will regret your mistake for as long as you live, and that is a punishment far greater than any that the rule of law can offer."

He hesitated, then nodded. "I will do what Neb wanted. I will freely give his designs to the world."

I considered telling him to destroy the cycloaetheric compressor along with its designs. But in time another would surely develop the very same engine, again granting the advantage to a single ambitious individual or ruthless mercantile syndicate. At least this way there would be no monopoly over such a revolutionary machine.

"You be a brutty bossman," Vera said, joining me as I walked with Keldon to the road leading out of the enclave. Her sister swaggered after her, thumbs hooked in her gun belt. "The Nyasha Twins got your back if you ever be in trouble."

"They ain't the only ones," Gunther broke in. "'Course, I gotta fix my Bruntilga first." He boomed a boisterous laugh.

I could not help but smile at their joviality, savoring the refreshing break from our long night's contest. We came to the edge of the causeway, and I looked out across the vast cityscape stretching for as far as I could see. Enormous foundries, alchemical refineries, and clockwork manufactories rose like mountains of brass and steel, while beneath them snarls of pipes spread like creeping vines across the iron valleys of districts farther on. Great airships docked with mooring gantries reaching high into the black night sky, while steamrails thundered across tracks overhead or through tunnels in the sublevels below. The terraced plateau of the 1st District loomed above the city's tangled morass, the countless towers of the Central Core surmounted by the Governor's Tower, Vandor Tower, and the soaring needle-like profile of the Aetherspire, half-encased in scaffolding, rising above them all.

I turned to Keldon and saw the others had gathered just behind him—Nera, Vera, Gunther, Svotgar, and even Kargeth. "Crime ever turns in the Clockwork City, my friends, and there may come a day when I will need to call upon each and every one of you."

They all nodded, arms folded or hands braced on hips, their expressions attentive and resolved. I looked back to the city once more and drew in a breath. Somewhere out there was an evil I had yet to unmask—the Shadow Man, and his mysterious cabal, the Servants of Vosh—their schemes and designs as yet unknown to me, yet working steadily and fiendishly toward their hidden goal, even as I wondered.

"And I fear that time may come far sooner than I had ever dared to imagine."

Case File 11:

A Curious Case of Karcistry

THE CONTAGION ISOLATION FIELD INHIBITED the corpse's rank stench, but did nothing to mitigate the thick fetor of rain-sodden refuse hanging over the 20th District's squalid slums. I covered my face with a handkerchief as I studied the bloated body, lying half submerged in the polluted gutter water of this star-forsaken sublevel alley. Livid blue splotches and ruptured pustules covered every inch of exposed skin, and the moldering flesh looked ready to slough off the bone like melted tallow. Judging from the advanced putrefaction, I would have estimated the body had been decaying for at least two weeks. However, witnesses claimed to have seen the victim stumble into this sublevel alley just eight hours ago, the welling boils and lesions already spreading.

"No disease works this fast," I whispered.

But if not a disease, what *was* it? Sorcery? Alchemy? Karcistry? A rogue artifact of power? Or perhaps something even more sinister.

I looked to the blue and white wagon at the other end of the alley where Keldon and Tibblemond stood listening to whatever hastily concocted drivel the APHID official prattled on about. The Administration for Public Health, Illness, and Disease had been called in the instant an outbreak was suspected, but the department was woefully inadequate when it came to handling ensorcelled maladies. Worse still, APHID was a chronically underfunded adjunct of Corradon's phlegmatic, bureaucratic machinery, scarcely more competent than the notoriously inept district police.

"Doc says it's probably a blood contagion," Tibblemond said, making his way back to where I stood. He held a handkerchief over his mouth and nose, and made a point of keeping his distance from the body. "It's a good thing we called them when we did," he added, glancing back to the APHID official following him.

"Doctor Edwell Seltoc," the official introduced without the slightest hint of inflection.

He was a lanky man with a lean face, dressed in a straight-cut coat with APHID's blue and white winged emblem pinned to his lapel. Although he wore a low brim top hat, he was clearly bald, and I could just discern some scarring along the exposed edges of his scalp, likely due to a bungled attempt at hair transplantation.

"Detective Vescard," I said simply, giving a nod.

"Yes, I know," Seltoc droned, his dull tone matching his dismal attire. He glanced down to consult the report he was holding. "The symptoms match five other cases this week. We must act quickly if we are to contain the outbreak."

"Let me see that," I said, snatching the paper away.

I held the paper to catch the light of the hovering luminary orb, a difficult task considering how it kept bobbing about. The report detailed the autopsies conducted on the other five victims. Three were human and two were Dworghs, but all had been found in an alleyway or sublevel corridor along the border of the 20th and 21st Districts, and each had been subjected to accelerated decomposition. Alchemical tests revealed high concentrations of drooka, enraptuphine, and other addictive euphorics, but missing was any definitive diagnosis of their illness. The symptoms mirrored a ghastly concoction of lethal diseases: blood-rot, grimpox, tropical hemorrhagic fever, and some kind of virulent systemic necrosis.

I arched an eyebrow. Such highly contagious diseases should have resulted in a wide-spread epidemic here in this crowded, poverty-stricken district, yet no such outbreak had occurred. The victims had numerous scars on their arms and faces, and two had suffered repeated fractures to their fingers, wrists, and elbows, possibly inflicted from fights or beatings.

Odd.

Keldon tried not to look at the bloated, pox-covered corpse as he came up beside me. He wore a breather mask, its vizstone empowered with a purification spell, and his voice came out muffled, as though speaking through pillow stuffing. "Are you sure this man was murdered? Isn't it just some disease?"

"The mask is quite unnecessary," I told my apprentice. "The body has already been sealed by an isolation ward. But even if it wasn't, I doubt whatever killed this man is contagious."

"That's what APHID is here to determine," Tibblemond said, still speaking through his handkerchief. A steamrail thundered down its tracks overhead, showering us with grimy water. The chief inspector cursed, then took a moment to shake out his bowler before continuing. "You might be Corradon's greatest detective, but they're the experts when it comes to plagues."

"Six deaths do not constitute a plague," I stated.

Doctor Seltoc frowned. "Do you have an alternative theory?"

I considered the body. Whoever the man was, he had not been wealthy. His clothes consisted of a tattered raincoat, muck-stained overalls, and muddied wader boots like those used by fishermen, sewer workers, and slaughterhouse hands. Both of his arms were wrapped in blood-stained bandages, no doubt covering an assortment of cuts similar to those of the other victims.

"Scan the body for residual aetheric imprints," I said to Keldon.

Keldon's shoulders slumped. Sickened though he was by the sight of the half-decayed corpse, he drew his key to begin the delving. "Sure thing, boss."

Tibblemond scratched his muttonchops and sighed. "I'm sorry for calling you in and wasting your time, Aldicus, but this seems to be a matter best left for APHID." He patted his coat and drew out a battered notepad. "But since you're here, Vandor Tower does need your help in another urgent matter."

Doctor Seltoc motioned for two of his medics, and the men hurried over with a stretcher. The men were covered from head to toe in sealed oilcloth suits, complete with respirator facemasks and protective goggles. The stretcher they carried was equipped with its own set of isolation vizstones. The precautions seemed almost farcical, especially since Doctor Seltoc was not even wearing a breather mask himself. Of course, APHID regulations were often more procedural than practical.

"If this was an infectious disease, half of this district would already be dead or dying by now," I pointed out, "and we ourselves would be dead in a few hours more. Is that not correct, Doctor Seltoc."

Seltoc waved his hand dismissively. "The contagion is obviously not airborne. I suspect it is blood borne, and only during a narrow infection window. Even so, every precaution is warranted until we know more."

"Your findings?" I asked my apprentice.

Keldon stepped aside as the medics began the unhappy task of hauling the corpse onto the isolation stretcher. "I detected a faint aetheric imprint, but it could have been anything." He studied the sigils on the side of his key before putting it away. "With the isolation field in place, there's no way I can get a precise reading."

I turned back to Tibblemond. "Have the body transported

to Vandor Tower. I would like to perform my own alchemical analysis."

"This body will be quarantined in APHID Central Research Laboratory, along with the others," Seltoc put in.

Tibblemond huffed. "As I was trying to explain, this matter has already been transferred to Doctor Seltoc's department."

My hands tightened into fists, crumpling the APHID report. Realizing I still held the only set of clues I was likely to gather, I slipped the crumpled paper into my coat pocket. "This is not a disease. What can APHID possibly do about it?"

Seltoc studied me impassively, then he sighed and shook his head. "If you will excuse me, gentlemen, I have a great deal of paperwork to fill out." He moved off to supervise the medics.

Tibblemond put away his handkerchief, then motioned for me to follow as he started back to the steam-coach parked just past the APHID wagon. "I'm sorry, Aldicus, but this is clearly a matter of public health." He looked at his battered notepad again and gave a weary sigh. "As for the other matter, there has been a violent upsurge in vandalism and rioting in the 13th District—more than usual, that is. I'm sure you've read about it in the *Daily Post*. The Commissioner General believes an anarchist movement is responsible, and he's directed the full focus of Vandor Tower to apprehend the ringleaders before these radicals do something even more rash."

I stopped in my tracts and Keldon nearly crashed into me from behind. "When did the Vandorian Guard get into the business of quelling political dissenters?" I looked up through the tangled web of pipes, crosswalks, and steamrail lines to what little of the distant gray sky could be seen. "Regardless, I'm a freelance detective, so you can tell the Commissioner General I have no interest in chasing down a few ideological miscreants."

Tibblemond's shoulders slumped, his brow drooping with

some unspoken weariness. The poor man was probably more frustrated by this new directive than I was. "I don't like it any more than you do," he admitted. "It feels... Well, I don't know how it feels. It just feels..."

"I believe 'wrong' is the feeling you are looking for," I suggested.

Tibblemond doffed his bowler and scratched his head, then put his hat back on. I had known Tibblemond for many years, and I knew his habits and nervous ticks. Tibblemond was not simply nervous, he was utterly unnerved.

"It is what it is, Aldicus. There are riots and anarchist overrunning the 13th District as we speak, and it could easily spread to the 12th and 14th. The Commissioner General has ordered all HAAMR units to full alert, and has ask every Guardsman and inspector to be on the lookout for seditious activities."

"Seditious activities?" I asked, incredulous. "What is that even supposed to mean?"

"I can't blame you if you don't want to accept the job, but there are no other cases that aren't already assigned or turned over to the district police." Tibblemond sighed. "The growing anarchist movement is Vandor Tower's top priority."

I forced a smile. If the majority of Vandor Tower's cases had been handed over to the district police, then they were already as good as botched. Just as this case was already botched.

"Perhaps," I replied. "But it is not *my* priority."

Tibblemond nodded. "There are days I wish I had the luxury of being a freelance detective." He touched the brim of his bowler and bowed. "Well, until next time."

"Until next time, chief inspector," I bid, bowing my head in return.

With that, I stuffed my hands in my coat pockets, wheeled around on my heels, and started off down a small side alley. Keldon jumped to catch up with me as I picked my way around heaps of garbage.

"Are we giving up on this case?" Keldon asked, his voice still muffled by the breather mask. He quickly took it off, then started to head back to the APHID wagon. "Hold on, I forgot to give this back."

I caught his arm and nodded for him to keep moving. We could not afford to go back on the off chance that Doctor Seltoc remembered the report I still had. "APHID is not going to see this as a criminal case. They just want to isolate any potential outbreak. But whoever is behind this is either a deranged sorcerer or a master karcist, and we cannot allow them to continue."

Keldon nodded. "What was Tibblemond saying about an anarchist movement? Is this about those riots I read about in the *Post*? I thought those where just over some labor disputes."

We headed back to the main thoroughfare following a different alleyway, but I was certain it was the right direction. "I make it a point to give all matters of politics a wide berth. If what Tibblemond says is true, then Vandor Tower is on a fool's errand. As for the putrefied victim—no, I'm not giving up. Fortunately for us, that doctor forgot I had kept his report." I pulled the crumpled paper from my coat pocket and smiled. "This may not be much, but it's the only evidence we—"

Something moved in one of the alley's dark corners. I squinted, trying to discern shapes in the perpetual gloom, but saw only piles of crumbled brick and twisted metal bars. Realizing we had ventured too far into this labyrinth, I hastened our pace and turned down a larger corridor hoping it would connect with the main thoroughfare. But the sublevel alley ended in a kind of sunken grotto, its hollow filled out by the rusting husk of a derelict garbage scow.

"Aldicus!" Keldon gasped.

I spun around and saw two figures in a gaudy mishmash of ragged clothes, one gripping a hefty knife and the other wielding a sledgehammer. I took a step back, then saw three others emerge from the wrecked scow brandishing chains and cudgels. Keldon reached for his talisman, but I caught his arm. He wasn't skilled enough to fend off five armed men, and the last thing I wanted was for them to see an empowered talisman. Even if they couldn't use it, the crystals and metals would be worth a small fortune down here.

"Looks like we caught us a pair'a topside dandies," the man with the knife growled. He grinned, showing what few yellow teeth he had, and shook his knife at us. "Give us all ya got, and ya might leave 'ere with yer hides."

"I am Aldicus Vescard." I pulled up my coat sleeves, revealing my severite wristbands. "And I believe you will be directing us to the main thoroughfare instead."

The man eyed my wristbands, his face twisting in confusion. "'Dat name suppos'd ta mean someth'n?"

Of all the times to find someone who hadn't yet heard of me... None of the man's cohorts seemed to recognize me, either.

Not wanting to unleash my alchemorph, I reached for my Vandorian deputy badge, hoping to dissuade them. But a scream from behind drew my attention. I turned, catching a glimpse of a fast-moving shadow darting into a recess between the crashed scow and an abandoned building. The two men standing near the base of the scow glanced at one another, then frantically looked around. Hadn't there been three men near the scow? Another scream came, and I spun around just in time to see the man with the sledgehammer vanish in a blur of darkness.

"Botch this!" the gang leader exclaimed. "I'm outta 'ere!"

Two more screams echoed through the under-street grotto, and I turned back to the wrecked scow as the remaining men disappeared in a whirlwind of fluttering shadows. The gang leader was already running back down the dilapidated alley, babbling prayers to every Archon his panicked mind could recall. With a final scream he, too, vanished like the others, borne away in the fearsome flurry of those whirling shadows.

"What the—" Keldon breathed, his words hushed with fear.

"Truly, my dear Vescard," a dapper voice intoned, "you must take care when venturing into these forsaken, sublevel hollows."

I looked to the wrecked garbage scow where the gentleman stood, garbed in a brocaded scarlet tailcoat with a teal top hat, red-tinted spectacles, and a dragon-headed cane. On the wreckage above him perched a young lady with raven black hair and a tight-laced bodice, her clockwork gauntlet complementing the eccentric collection of gauges and gizmos adorning her brass belt.

"Armez," I said, recognizing him at once. The last time I had seen the vampire and his sireling had been aboard the *Gambler's Boon* where the two proved to be invaluable allies—but only because it had suited their goal. "Did you kill those men? Doesn't the Chalice of the Blood King quench your need to feed?"

"The Chalice sustains us," Armez replied evasively. He smiled, showing his pronounced canines. "But if you must know, we did not kill those men. We simply deposited them in one of the less pleasant accommodations of this steaming subterranean cesspit."

"And by that he means an open sewer," Quiniece laughed. She licked her canines and grinned, swinging her legs in the air as she looked down from her perch. "Hi, Keldon," she said, a teasing lilt to her voice. "Miss me?"

Keldon pulled off his newsboy cap and balled it up nervously in his hands. "Ah... Well... That is..." He glanced at me, then back to her, his face drooping sheepishly.

I clasped my hands behind my frock coat and met Armez's gaze. "You know I could have handled those men."

Armez arched an eyebrow. "And who would have handled you? I fear that unfortunate task would have fallen to me, as your apprentice does not appear to be carrying his tranquilizer gun." Then he beamed a wide grin. "I simply averted the crisis before it came to such drastic measures."

He was right, of course. If worst had come to worst, that could easily have been the outcome. "Why are you here?"

The vampire brushed out his lacy cravat and shrugged. "You fascinate me, Vescard. It is touching how much concern you show for the plebian rabble of this decaying city, while far more momentous events stir in the shadows around us. But you do have an uncanny knack for connecting the most insignificant minutia to the whirling currents of the greater whole." Then he smiled, his exaggerated canines gleaming. "You might say I find you... deliciously refreshing."

The vampire's ramblings were as cryptic as they were evasive, and I had no time for whatever game he was playing. "If you have a point to make, then make it. Otherwise, you are hindering my investigation."

"I doubt we could hinder your investigation any more than Vandor Tower already has."

Armez grinned, perhaps waiting for me to demand how he knew as much as he did. Instead, I motioned for Keldon to follow as I started back the way we had come. We only managed to make one turn down the alley corridor before a flutter of shadows cut us off. I looked up and frowned, seeing Armez and his young sireling perched on a scaffolding above us.

"You already have all the clues you need, my dear and lovely Vescard, save for what that report cannot tell you. So, I shall tell you this. The man who died today is no different from the others—a broken soul, lost in the misery of his own hopeless melancholy, condemned by cruel fate to the darkest dens of horror and despair." The vampire tapped his cane to the brim of his top hat and winked. "See you around."

Armez and Quiniece disappeared like shadows folding into the perpetual twilight of the Clockwork City's fathomless roots.

"That made about as much sense as an ogre at a tea

party," Keldon stated.

I nodded my agreement. "How does lunch down at the wharf sound? I don't know about you, but I'm famished."

Keldon's face blanched, possibly recalling the ghastly state of the day's unfortunate victim. "Only you, Aldicus. Only you."

❖

I LEANED BACK AGAINST THE BENCH, considering the APHID report as I took another bite of my pickled herring sarnie, the newspaper wrapper catching whatever greasy drippings the soggy bread could no longer sop up. According to the report, the other five victims had been low-wage scabs with various off-and-on jobs near the East Wharf, here in the 21st District. Three lived in the 20th District, where rents were even cheaper, and the latest victim probably hailed from there as well. I saw no pattern to the locations where the bodies had been found, but judging from the times of death and proximity to various nearby tenements, it seemed reasonable to conclude they had died heading home in the early morning hours.

"Are you sure the food is safe around here?" Keldon asked, joining me at the bench with a steaming meat pie in hand.

I looked to the street vendor's rusty cart, now mobbed by drudgers, dustmen, and dock workers as hungry as they were grubby. "Pickled herring, yes. But as to whatever might be in that pie..." I took another bite of my sarnie and shrugged.

Keldon leaned over and sniffed, nearly gagging when he caught a whiff of my pungent meal. "I'd hardly call what you're eating any more appetizing. How can you stomach that?" He then sniffed his own dinner doubtfully. "Why not return to Brass Lantern Lane? At least in the 8th District we can be reasonably sure the meat's not cat, dog, rat, or worse."

"Because," I replied, stuffing the APHID report back into

my coat pocket, "the trail we are following leads here."

Keldon surveyed the crowded market rows along the fog-smothered avenues of the 21st District's lower east side, his gaze lifting to the cranes of the colossal dry docks and loading piers. Flocks of crying gulls filled the hazy gray sky. "The body was found in the 20th District. Why do you think the crime happened here?"

I finished my sarnie, then crumpled the grease-soaked wrapper and looked for a waste bin. There were none, but judging from the heaps of rubbish clogging the district's already cluttered arteries, no one particularly cared. I sighed, grudgingly tossing the wrapper to the litter-strewn street. "The other victims worked various odd jobs here in the wharf district, and if what Armez said is true, so did our latest victim."

Keldon bit into his meat pie and grimaced, pulling out a strip of tendon. "The East Wharf spans the entire 21st District. That's nearly four miles of shipyards, piers, and canals. And that's not even including the city's main port, which takes up most of the 22nd." He nibbled a bit of the crust, then gave a sigh. "How are we going to find anything in this jumble?"

I drew my frock coat around me as I stood. "The most recent victim wore overalls, waders, and a raincoat. Judging from the muck staining his outfit, he was most likely a grubber or mudman employed in the unenviable job of cleaning pier pilings. Because he was found dead in a sublevel street on the border between the 20th and 21st District, he likely walked from his place of work to his home in a low-rent tenement in the 20th District, narrowing our search to the 21st District's lower east quarter."

Keldon's expression turned suddenly apprehensive. "Wait... Doesn't the Travenni crime family control a good chunk of the lower east quarter? Do you think..." He drew a deep breath, then continued. "Do you think they're behind this?"

I shook my head. "No. The Travenni always make it clear when they've made a hit. These deaths are not their doing."

Keldon threw the rest of his meat pie to some scrawny dogs who took one sniff before leaving the suspect scraps where they landed. "Well, that's a relief."

The low-town denizens gave us more than a few spiteful glances as we pressed through the throng, their envious eyes lingering on our moneyed attires. We passed through a curtain of miasmic steam rising from the dank tunnels beneath the muddy street, our feet splashing through pools of rusty runoff water.

"This is something far more sinister," I went on to say. "Armez suggested all the victims hailed from similar circumstances, and considering the APHID report, I would agree. All appear to have died returning home in the early morning hours, which means they either worked a late shift or had spent the night drowning their sorrows in drink and debauchery. Not even the most desperate mudman would dare work under the piers in the dark of night, so the latter explanation is most probable."

Keldon looked around the grungy narrows we had entered. "Uh, Aldicus, where are we going?"

The narrows led underneath an aging trestle of corroded viaducts, then opened into another sublevel avenue, sparsely populated by rag-clothed vagrants and shuffling gutter-dwellers. "The APHID report mentioned that all the victims had imbibed drooka and various other euphorics. There were also indications they had suffered numerous cuts and broken joints over an extended period of time. But most importantly, Armez hinted that the men had condemned themselves to, and I quote, 'the darkest dens of horror and despair.'"

Keldon nodded. "So, a drooka den?"

"Not just any drooka den," I replied, giving a sigh. "A tormentorium."

Keldon stopped, his eyes widening at the very mention of

the word. "Archons, help us!"

I had wanted to send him off the moment I realized where this trail was leading. But if Keldon was ever going to become a detective magus one day, then a tormentorium was exactly the sort of place he needed to cut his teeth. Better that his first encounter with one be on my watch than when he was out investigating on his own.

"Whatever rumors you've heard are just the fabricated ramblings of hackneyed reporters," I replied. "A real tormentorium is far worse."

I had only heard vague whisperings of a drooka den in this area that served up more than just a few gurgling drooka pipes. Such reports were impossible to corroborate, but I grew evermore confident that those whispers had been right as we drew near a shambled stretch of abandoned store fronts. The street had grown steadily more deserted, with not a coach or rickshaw in sight. Those few figures we did see all hurried by, hunkered in their baggy coats as they made for the only door not boarded up.

Keldon stopped and reached for his talisman. "I'm sensing something."

"Intrusion wards," I guessed. "They'll detect we have money and will probably let us pass."

"And what if they detect my talisman?" my apprentice asked nervously.

I frowned. Between my severite wristbands and Keldon's talisman, we would probably trip every intrusion ward they had, assuming we hadn't already. "Come on."

A man just ahead of us was let through by a bouncer on the other side of the door, and I began to ponder how I might bluff our way in. The peep door slid open as we drew near and a pair of shadow-framed eyes looked us up and down.

"I ain't never seen you before," came a hoarse voice from the other side. The eyes glanced at Keldon. "This ain't no place for a kid. Get lost."

I paused. No questions? No passwords? Not even a

derisive quip about our dandy-dressed topside attire? "My boy has to learn to be a man sometime," I whispered through the peep door. I held up a single guild coin. "Something for your troubles."

The man snorted and shut the peep door. I was about to double my bribe when the latch clicked and the door swung open. The bouncer was more fat than muscle, and judging from the frayed, unbuttoned waistcoat draped over his sweat-stained shirt, he cared as little for his appearance as he did for his job. He held out his hand and flexed his fingers, and I deposited the coin onto his grubby palm.

The stench of cheap pipe smoke, wet garbage, and urine wafted through the murky air of the barely lit room, mixed incongruously with the floral undertones of percolating drooka. Like most drooka dens, this one bore the frail façade of a third-rate tavern or dive. But I knew at a glance that nothing about the seemingly seedy establishment was remotely genuine—not the cracked walls and crumbling plaster, not the vermin scurrying along rotting base boards, not the frowning barkeep spit washing glassware with his filthy rag, nor even the inebriated patrons slumped on their tables. It was all part of the highly orchestrated illusion we now found ourselves inside.

Keldon covered his mouth against the smell, then glanced at the sigils on his key. "This place is awash with aetheric resonance," he whispered. "I'm picking up intrusion wards, scry veils, a whole host of illusions, and half a dozen other patterns pulsing from somewhere farther in."

"Put that away," I whispered back. Then I thought better of it. "On second thought, keep scanning. And make it obvious."

Keldon gave me a curious look, but I knew our best chance for discovering the truth behind the sorcerous killings was to draw out the den's proprietor—whoever that was. The barkeep watched us with a skeptical eye, but his overt glare was meant to draw our focus away from the slouching 'patrons' who were, in fact, the establishment's actual bouncers, ready to spring from their feigned stupor at the first sign of trouble.

We passed one such sentry as we crossed the room, and though his face lay buried under his tattered raincoat, I glimpsed a watchful eye peering out from the folds of the sleeve. Yet, no one made any move to stop us as we opened the battered door at the back of the barroom. Oily rags and water-soaked boxes cluttered the tiny room, which had the appearance of a carelessly arranged supply closet. The smell of drooka was strongest here, and I could just discern the slightest hint of some hollow murmurings. I stretched one arm into the closet, watching as ripples of light skittered from the nullifying effect of my severite wristband.

"A mirage," Keldon whispered. He drew a deep breath, then held out his brass key to begin an aetheric dispellment.

I shook my finger. "Now Keldon, you know better than to spoil such exquisitely crafted ambiance. They put great effort into cultivating the appearance of a ramshackle, rat-infested, sublevel dive. Some might even consider this a work of art."

Keldon gave me a sidelong glance, but I just straightened my top hat and stepped into the grungy supply closet. With two more strides I passed through the illusion and found myself in a narrow hall lit by dimly glowing luminaries. The wood relief panels, scrollwork accents, and beaded wall hangings harkened to the original drooka dens and pleasure houses of Kendes, and the hypnotic drone of tanpuras and glass armonicas seemed strangely in tune with the groans and moans emanating from curtained alcoves down the length of the velvet-draped corridor.

Keldon coughed, covering his nose against the sickly-sweet vapors and intoxicating smoke that hung like a haze in the air. "I'm going to get sozzled just on the fumes." He rubbed his watering eyes, then remembered the breather mask strapped to his belt. "That's better," he mumbled, fitting the mask to his face.

I glanced into one of the curtained alcoves, knowing whoever was inside would hardly notice the intrusion. The poor wretch was sprawled on the floor of his cramped cubby, convulsing as though suffering a seizure, but moaning in the throes of ensorcelled ecstasy. Those in the next two alcoves suffered much the same, either lost in the intoxicating vapors of spell-infused drooka or entranced by the mindless delirium of a dream potion. These ill-fated addicts who could scarcely afford to feed themselves were now slaves to soul-consuming vice, unable to find the slightest joy or solace outside the ever-heightening extremes they experienced here in this damnable sty.

Keldon's eyes widened when a scream issued from another room—a scream that shifted into a bout of laughter followed by a euphoric gasp. "Uh, Aldicus?"

"This is a tormentorium," I reminded. "Here, the sorcerous vapors and enrapturing spells blur and magnify the mind's sense of both pleasure and pain. The greater the one, the greater the other. In the height of their fevered delirium, these victims tear their own flesh and disjoint their own limbs seeking to further intensify the... experience."

Keldon's face paled with horror.

"Quite correct," came a sultry voice from just ahead of us.

She stepped out from the room, her azure eyes narrowing as her blue glossed lips curled into a smile. From her black silk gloves to her pushed up leather corset, her ash gray skin displayed an exotic collection of tribal tattoos. She brushed back her lavender hair, revealing her dagger-like ears, then put hands to hips above her lace skirt in a seductive pose.

"Half-Scaithi," I said, quickly assessing every detail of her person. "Not among the most common denizens of Corradon. Judging from your use of charcoal-based makeup to darken your complexion, you wish to emphasize your Scaithi heritage while masking your human side. Since Scaithi are almost universally distrusted outside of Kendes and Tir Scaith, this would be quite unusual for a Scaithi who has been exiled. You have therefore come here for a very specific purpose, but it is not to make a fortune as some exotic courtesan. After all, an establishment such as this could never afford a paramour of your caliber. Moreover, several of your tattoos are distinctive of the Dungh'gar cults of northern Kendes whose ranks you would never have been permitted to leave alive—or dead for that matter." I paused, noting the interlaced orichalium wire and vizstones woven into her right arm glove. "You are also a sorceress, as attested to by the talisman on your right hand."

She dropped her hands to her sides and rolled her eyes. "*Kshoth*," she swore. "You're Aldicus Vescard, aren't you?"

I simply answered with a smile, glancing to look into the room she had stepped out from. Although I could not see much of the room, I did spot a shelf crammed full of potions and elixirs. Was there a laboratory back there?

"I would say you have me at a disadvantage," I said, "but that would merely be my way of opening a lengthy line of questioning that will ultimately lead to your admission of the crime I am investigating."

"Then skip the spurious persiflage and get to the point," she replied, her vowels inflecting a thick Kendes accent. "You may call me Mistress Agona. Now tell me—why are you here, Vescard? Drooka dens are not strictly illegal."

That was unlikely to be her real name. Judging from her accent, she had not been in Corradon for long, and had probably not even entered through official channels. There would be no record of her true identity. "This is no drooka den," I asserted. Another scream came, shifting to laughter before growing to a scream once more. "This is a tormentorium."

Agona's watchful gaze darkened, and she glanced back as the scream diminished to a whimper. "That is merely a passing bout of delirium from one of our more temperamental patrons." A different scream came from a room further down the hall. Her jaw flexed with growing tension. "Perhaps more than one."

I took a step forward, gesturing for Keldon to move behind me. "I thought you preferred to dispense with the spurious persiflage." I brushed back the side of my coat, showing my badge. "Allow me to cut to the point, Mistress Agona. What you are doing here is illegal, and I am not referring to the drooka or your ensorcelled ecstasy potions."

"You have no authority here," Agona hissed. Her hands balled into fists, the vizstones of her talisman flashing bright. "Produce a warrant or depart these premises at once."

"She just brought up a defensive ward," Keldon warned from behind me.

Considering the screams I had heard, I already had grounds for probable cause. "With or without a warrant, I'm shutting you down. If you don't like it, you can file a complaint with Vandor Tower." Agona began to protest, but I cut her off. "Six men have died over the past week, each from a lethal concoction of the most horrific diseases known to man. The diseases were ensorcelled, evinced by the fact that we do not have a district-wide epidemic on our hands. The victims were transient workers, taking whatever odd jobs they could find here in the East Wharf. I doubt they even knew each other's names, but they had one thing in common: they were all patrons of this perverse establishment."

Mistress Agona met my eyes with her own, fear flashing behind her bright azure irises. "Conjecture," she breathed, her voice a low whisper.

"Deduction," I refuted.

"Aldicus," Keldon said, his voice quivering.

I glanced back, only now noticing how heavy and oppressive the air had grown. Four men from the tavern room entered the hall behind us, each wearing filthy tattered raincoats and muck-covered waders. One of the men stepped forward, pushing back a hood to expose a bloated, pustule-covered face and vacant eyes. It readied a crude iron mace, and its desiccated lips drew back to reveal a jagged set of broken teeth.

"Has it already come to this?" I asked.

"I fear it has." Agona sneered, raising the hand bearing her talisman. "A pity, though. My master would have enjoyed dissecting you."

I cocked my head. "Your master?"

A blast of seething metaplasm surged from her outstretched hand and I flung my arms up reflexively. The impact slammed me into the wall, pain exploding across my back as waves of heat washed over me. The white of my dazzled vision resolved to a swimming haze of stars, and I looked down fearing I would see nothing of my hands but charred stumps. The fear was irrational, of course—my severite wristbands had absorbed most of the empowerment's energy, leaving only its concussive impact to have any real effect.

"Aldicus!" Keldon screamed. He brought up his brass key and a bolt of aetheric light struck from the talisman as he attempted his first real offensive empowerment.

The bolt flashed and vanished as it dissipated across Agona's ward, and the sorceress spun away, sweeping around to face Keldon as lightning arced and coiled about her talismanic glove. I had to act fast—my apprentice was no match for this foe. With no time to think, I charged forward, ramming my shoulder into Agona's side and grappling her in the hopes that my severite wristbands would impede her aetheric empowerments. But she twisted from my grasp like a contortionist and cartwheeled away, landing next to the door leading back into what I guessed was a laboratory.

I scrambled to my feet, glancing back to make sure my apprentice was all right. The first of the rot-blighted thralls advanced with its iron mace raised, the others following just behind it.

"Keldon, watch out!" I yelled, my fear spiking to panic.

Keldon wheeled around and gasped, staggering

backwards as he fumbled his talisman in his haste to compose a defensive empowerment. I lurched forward to pull him away, but I was too slow. The ghastly foe swung its mace for Keldon's head, cracked lips curling in a sadistic grin. The blow would surely have killed my apprentice had it managed to connect. Instead, the weapon struck the floor with a thud, and the thrall looked down at its chest from which protruded its own heart, grasped in an articulated metal claw. The claw retracted, wrenching the eviscerated organ out of its back as the steel cable reeled in its catch.

"Not quite the heart I hoped to steal," Quiniece quipped, plucking the bloody lump from her grappling claw. She pulled a lever on her clockwork gauntlet, resetting the pneumatic launcher. "But it'll do for now."

Armez tipped his top hat, then gave his dragon-headed cane a twist and drew the hidden blade. "I see you've found yourself in another fine mess, Vescard. It's a good thing we followed you."

Armez and Quiniece sprang into a flurry of flashing steel and clattering brass gears, the thralls proving to be no match for their speed and power. Facing two enraged vampires, Agona cursed and dashed into the laboratory, no doubt to make her escape. I bolted after her, ignoring the other five thralls rushing into the hall from an adjacent corridor. Armez and his sireling would handle them, and keep Keldon from harm. But as soon as I entered the room, I realized it was more apothecary than laboratory. Shelves lined every wall, full of potions, elixirs, and bottles of spell-infused euphorics. Mistress Agona spun around before reaching the door on the other side of the room, blasting a metaplasmic bolt from her jeweled glove. I ducked aside and the white-hot bolt exploded through the shelf beside me, showering me with bits of glass and splashing elixirs on my coat.

I grabbed one of the remaining vials, an aqueous solution of caustic alkali, and hooked a finger around one of my wristband's locking pins. "You know who I am, so you know what I'm capable of. Drop your talisman and surrender, immediately."

Agona sneered. "Do that and everyone here dies, screaming in the flames of the beast within you."

I looked down at my coat soaked through with star's knew what kind of alchemicals. She was right, and she knew it. She tightened her fist, her talisman's vizstones flashing bright as she prepared another blast. I threw my arms in front of me, hoping my wristbands would absorb the attack. But the empowerment was purely kinetic this time, blasting me out of the room and into Keldon as he ran up to the door.

"We don't have time for this," Armez yelled, his voice barely audible over the ringing in my ears. "She's escaping!"

The floor shook beneath me, then heaved and shook again. For a moment, I thought my head was still spinning from the impact, but when a third blast came, I realized something had exploded several floors below.

"Was that a boiler room explosion?" Quiniece asked.

"Not unless they have three boilers." I struggled back to my feet as another explosion rattled the building. "Make that four."

"It's a failsafe," Armez growled, his teeth bared and his eyes narrowing. Black smoke began seeping from the seams in the floorboards. "They would destroy everything before letting one shred of evidence fall into our hands!"

Evidence? What Evidence was Armez talking about? Or, perhaps more importantly, what evidence had he been hoping I would find?

I quickly helped Keldon off the floor, then looked down the hall at the line of violently disemboweled bodies. Armez and Quiniece had been disturbingly expedient in dispatching the thralls, and judging from the apparent ferocity of their attack, they had made no attempt to restrain their primal bloodlust. Both vampires stood wiping their hands and weapons clean, but displayed no interest in the profusion of blood coating the walls and floor. Had they drunk their fill from the Chalice of the Blood King, or was the blood so tainted they found it utterly unpalatable?

A few inebriated patrons wandered out of their alcoves, staggering through the smoke-filled hall and slipping on the oozing pools of blood, too dazed and confused to realize what was going on.

"We have to get these people out of here," I said, covering my mouth against the thickening smoke. Heat wafted up from below as the fire in the basement spread. "This entire building is going up in flames."

Armez returned his blade to its cane sheath and frowned. "There's no time to bother with these..." His voice trailed off and he forced an amicable smile. "You're right, of course. Come, Quiniece. Let us herd these drooling dregs of humanity to some semblance of safety."

The illusion disguising the door to the tavern room had dispelled, revealing the threshold as it really was: a plain wooden doorframe, beyond which roiled a wall of smoke, lit red from beneath by the fires burning below. The crack of breaking timbers and a mighty crash signaled the collapse of some support joists.

I grabbed the nearest inebriated patron and shoved the sozzled fellow into what remained of the apothecary room. The door Mistress Agona had escaped through was still open, and judging from the rusty stairwell just visible in the gloom, it probably led to some long abandoned storm tunnel or steamworks corridor. I grabbed another man staggering into the room and shoved him after the first.

"Keldon, escort these people down those stairs and to whatever tunnel leads back to the more populous streets." I saw the fear in his eyes and gave him a pat on the shoulder. "That sorceress will be long gone by now, but keep your talisman out and stay sharp for any surprises she might have left behind. You are ready for this. I am counting on you."

He gave a nod and started down the rusty stairs as two

more semiconscious men followed behind him. Armez and Quiniece ushered in four more, and judging from their darkening expressions, they were growing increasingly concerned by the inferno raging beneath us. I could hardly blame them—fire was one of the few things certain to kill a vampire.

The floor shook again, timbers cracking and walls groaning as sweltering smoke thickened the air with unbreathable fumes. I threw open every drawer and cabinet I could see, shuffling through the contents with one hand while my other held a handkerchief to my face. There had to be something here—some clue Mistress Agona feared we might find. Why else would she burn down this building?

"That's all of them," I heard Armez say.

I squinted against the burning smoke, barely able to see the two gray silhouettes against the darker gray of the billowing soot. Red firelight blazed somewhere behind them. "Are you sure?" I asked, punctuating my question with a coughing fit.

"You have my word," Armez assured, his silky voice utterly unaffected by the smoke. He knelt and took something from the floor. "We must go. Now."

I coughed again, but forced myself to make one final pass through the drawers and shelves, blindly grabbing whatever I guessed was most valuable—some loose papers, a mechanical implement of some kind, and a case of glass vials. The floor buckled, the falling timbers exploding in a spray of burning sparks as a wave of heat washed up from below. My feet pounded on the crumbling floor, flames licking at my heals as I dashed for the stairwell. But something was wrong—it should only have been a few paces to the exit. Too late, I realized that in the confusion of the smoke and flames, I had run the wrong way!

The floor collapsed beneath me even as I turned to head back. A metal claw grasped my shoulder and my coat drew tight around me, the sudden retracting force jerking me through the air. It was all I could do to hold on to the items I had gathered as the clockwork grapple reeled me in like a sailfish on an angler's line. Hands grabbed me, pulling me into the stairwell.

"Oh, my dear and foolish Vescard," I heard Armez lament. "Are you simply insane, or are you trying to restart my heart on purpose?"

The black of unconsciousness enveloped me before I could manage a reply.

I RUBBED MY TEMPLES, trying to press back the relentless throbbing in my skull, then heaved over in another painful coughing fit. The blistering smoke and red-hot cinders of a burning building should not have fazed me in the least, considering the pain of spontaneous immolation I experience during my self-inflicted transmutation. But, as Armez was apt to say, my physical body could not escape the ails of its mortal frailty. My eyes watered, my lungs burned with every breath, and my scalded skin felt as though someone had scrubbed me down with a handful of stinging nettles. Worst of all, the stench of smoke and ash had taken up permanent residence in the fibers of my frock coat.

The vampire and his young sireling stood in the shadows farther down the street, the foundation bulwarks of the city's upper stratum rising behind them like the stepped cliffs of some block-cut rock quarry. Night had fallen, and the vibrant light of streetlamps and towering industrial enclaves mixed incongruously with the crimson shadow of Atracus, peeking out from a break in the cloud-strangled sky. Black smoke rose from where the drooka den had been, and bells clanged all around us, calling more fire brigades to the scene. It had taken half an hour for the first brigade to answer, sadly swift for these derelict haunts, and the flames had spread to consume four more sublevel blocks—all thankfully empty. Most of the den's patrons had fled after their escape, and those few who remained were passed out in their delirious stupor.

Keldon handed me a battered tin cup. “Any luck?”

I took the cup and gulped down its contents, the cool water giving some relief to my painfully dry throat. He had probably tapped one of the test spigots in a utility corridor, but I wasn’t going to ask.

“Not as yet,” I replied, only to be seized by another coughing fit.

Drawing in a slow breath of air, I sat back up and looked over the meager evidence we had plundered from the burning tormentorium. Most of the vials in the case were broken, save for two—one of vitriolic chlorinate and the other a potent alkahest reagent. The vials bore APHID’s blue and white emblem, and I grimaced, wondering what else the perpetrators might have stolen from APHID’s labs. I had no clue as to the purpose of the mechanical apparatus I had pulled from the drawer, but it was cylindrical in shape, and had several ratcheting gears and a set of oddly shaped bits at one end. Perhaps Quiniece would know what the device was for.

The papers proved more promising, and I sifted through the remaining pages hoping to distill some meaningful clue. Most were instructions for handling various elixirs and alchemical reagents, but a few were written in Kendes, while others appeared to be in some kind of cipher. The elixirs called for various ratios of enraptuphine and drooka, as well as newer euphorics apparently imported from Kendes, including red ice, liquid velv, and sweet malice, none of which were known to me.

“What have we here,” I mulled, coming to one of the last pages. The drawing was annotated in Kendes and depicted a circular band of vertebra, finger bones, and jawbones, surmounted by a crown of ribs behind which rose the twin ilium of the hip bones. “Could it be...” I whispered.

“What is it?” Keldon asked, leaning over to look.

I shook my head, but could not deny the horrid artifact

drawn upon that page. “The Bone Crown of Dagoroth.”

Armez cocked his head, then motioned for Quiniece to follow as he started back to rejoin us. “What is this about the Bone Crown?”

I looked up at Armez, pursing my lips doubtfully. During our earlier encounter, aboard the *Gambler’s Boon*, we had thwarted a heist orchestrated by the Shadow Man and the Servants of Vosh. But the Shadow Man had escaped with several artifacts, including both the Bone Crown of Dagoroth and the Chaos Hexillion. Was it mere coincidence we found ourselves working with Armez again, only to pick up the trail of those stolen artifacts?

“I seriously doubt you are surprised by this development.” I passed the drawing to my meddling colleague. “Can you at least read Kendes?”

Armez pushed up his red-tinted spectacles and smiled. “I’m afraid I never took the time to learn.” He handed the sketch back to me. “That lady was a Dungh’gar sorceress, judging from those tattoos. Is it not possible she simply had a sketch of this lying about, perhaps as a matter of her own occult studies?”

I pulled out two more pages. Although also written in Kendes, the word “Dagoroth” stood out several times in the text. “She was conducting research, yes, but that drawing is so detailed it could only have been made while studying the genuine article.” I coughed again, then downed more water before continuing. “The priests of Dagoroth, the Demon Lord of Pestilence, were said to have cursed their enemies with horrific plagues and diseases. Together with Abothog and Voshthok, the Demon Lords of Carnage and Wrath, they form an unholy triumvirate worshipped by the ancient Dungh’gar cults.”

“The Dungh’gar?” Keldon asked. “But wasn’t the Bone Crown of Dagoroth stolen by the Servants of Vosh?”

I nodded. “If Mistress Agona is herself a member of the Dungh’gar, then perhaps that brutish cult is in some way connected with the Servants of Vosh and the Shadow Man."

I looked across the street, watching as one of the drooka den's patrons staggered into the shadows, his arms hugging his shaking body.

"Fangle-fop!" I exclaimed, slapping the paper with my hand. "Why didn't I see it before? That drooka den wasn't just a tormentorium—it was a Dungh'gar recruiting facility. First they addict these wretched souls to ever greater extremes of pain and depravity, then they twist the broken shell that remains to serve their murderous ends."

"And the diseased bodies?" Keldon asked.

I closed my eyes, remembering the fetid things that had attacked us in the hall. "Failures."

Armez folded his hands on his cane's brass dragon head. "Then I suggest we follow the sorceress and hope she leads us to this unholy cult's base of operations."

"Unfortunately, Mistress Agona has given us the slip," I admitted.

"There's no need to fret, Vescard. I have a blood trace on her." Armez held out a shard of glass with one edge stained in red. "I found this on the floor of that storeroom. She must have been cut when the glassware exploded, and this was just enough blood for me to bind a trace."

I breathed out slowly and nodded. "Which way does your trace say she's heading?"

"North and somewhat east—most likely to the rusting depths of the Derelict Zone."

"Then she is very likely heading the complete opposite direction," I stated. "She recognized you were vampires and knew you would bind a blood trace the instant you had a chance. That trail is a decoy, planted to throw us off her scent."

Armez stood silent for a moment, then he tossed the shard of glass over his shoulder and casually adjusted his teal cravat. "Ah... Yes." He looked off in one direction, then another. "Where do you say we should search?"

I handed Quiniece the clunky apparatus I had found. “What do you make of this?”

She turned the device over in her hand. “It’s a jury-rigged interlock spanner. Rather crude, but the build’s solid enough.” She flipped the spanner around and studied the bits attached to the clamp on one end. “The splines on the coupling joint are outdated and the camslide follows a rather obsolete design. I would say this was made to override hydraulic switching arrays from at least two centuries ago.”

“Hydraulic switching arrays?” I asked.

“They were commonly used in the waterworks for pumping timers and levee gates about half a century ago,” Quiniece explained. “Most have now been replaced with oscillator relays, but I’m sure some of the older switches are still in operation.”

I considered her explanation. “What else could someone use it for?”

Quiniece looked over the interlock spanner again. “Besides the day-to-day operation of an outdated levee gate or pumping timer?” She thought for a moment, then shrugged. “Well, they could use it to control the over-spill gates for one of the old backflow reservoirs. That would let them flood and clear the storm tunnels whenever they like.”

I nodded. “The main reservoir for this district is actively manned and operated by the Authority for Sewage and Sanitation, and probably uses those newer switches. But if I remember correctly, there’s an abandoned backflow reservoir half a mile south and eight sublevels down from here, once used to manage the over-spill from seawall levees of the harbor. The Dungh’gar cults preferred dank and decaying cloisters, deep underground, and the lower waterworks are about the dankest and darkest places you will find in Corradon.”

Armez studied me for a moment, then nodded. “Very well, Vescard. We will follow your hunch. That is, of course, the reason we’ve been shadowing you all this time.”

"Why are you so interested in this case?" I asked. "Am I to believe it is pure coincidence that I find myself pursuing the Servants of Vosh with you and your sireling once again in tow? Are you looking to recover the Bone Crown of Dagoroth?"

Armez cocked an eyebrow. "To the latter, no. As for the rest..." He hesitated, looking to the towering heights of the city. "Perhaps I simply wish to bring these nefarious criminals to justice."

I cocked an eyebrow, making sure Armez knew that I knew better than to believe his spurious pretext. He crooked a wry smile, confirming he knew I wouldn't buy it.

I slipped the pilfered papers into one of my coat pockets and the two unbroken vials into another, then started for the lower access corridor paralleling the bustling streets above. Keldon, Armez, and Quiniece followed, and soon the flurry of commotion stirred up by the fire brigades and district police faded far behind us.

Descending through the cavernous corridor, itself lined with shanty tenements and ramshackle storefronts, we soon entered a vast, sunken plaza, heaped with refuse and piles of construction debris—the abandoned leavings of some topside development project. A few people milled about or hurried on their way, though most were homeless vagrants or pfenniless underfolk who had found some measure of refuge in these forgotten haunts. What faint light there was filtered through ventilation grates above or flickered from the simmering barrel fires lit by the sublevel denizens.

"You have a history with the Servants of Vosh," I said to Armez as we continued deeper in. The vampire did not reply, but his silence was admission enough. "What did they do to you?"

"Is it not sufficient that I see them for the threat they pose to this city, and, indeed, to the world?" Armez asked in return. "But if you must know, I have the extreme displeasure of counting myself among the ill-fated victims of their sadistic experimentations. What they did to me..." He stopped for a moment, then breathed in deeply. "They changed me, Vescard. Change me and tortured me in ways I cannot begin to describe." He resumed walking again, his cane tapping the ground with every other step. "That was many years ago, and if you do not mind, I would rather not dredge up those memories again."

I nodded, understanding all too well the helplessness he must have felt under the ministrations of a madman's scalpel.

Descending another access corridor, the sprawling undercity block had grown dark enough that I could barely see more than ten paces in the gloom. The vampires suffered no such impediment, and Keldon drew his talisman to conjure an orb of mage's light.

But Quiniece put a hand on his arm and produced a small, crystal-capped device from a pouch on her belt. She whispered something in his ear and Keldon nodded, placing one end of his key against the crystal. Quiniece adjusted two tiny pin knobs on the base of the device and the crystal began to glow as Keldon applied a stream of aetheric current from his talisman. The darkness evaporated, shadows brightening as the dim light receded, and the cavernous sublevel revealed itself in striking hues of inverted contrast and reversed color.

"Shadow light?" I asked.

"It is not so different from mage's light," Armez contended. He removed his red-tinted spectacles and slipped them into his coat pocket. "Merely a subtle shift in the ambient aetheric vibrations."

I looked around, and despite the unsettling nature of the inverted colors, I found I could see surprisingly well. We had made our way into what might have been a thriving market square a hundred years ago, now buried and forgotten under the city's ever-accreting layers of sprawling urban developments and industrial manufactories. Makeshift lean-tos and cold fire pits attested to the vagrant dwellers who called this forsaken hollow home, but the cluster of dilapidated hovels had been vacated for some time. The south end of the subterranean plaza had caved-in, and the barest trace of a footpath wound between lichen-covered support pilings and crumbling buttresses, leading into the deeper ruins beneath. We followed the path, skidding down the embankment on a landslide of plaster and broken masonry, and splashed feet first into the dank muck of a flood tunnel.

"Could you be any more noisy?" Quiniece hissed, alighting silently beside Armez on a ledge just above the mud-caked floor.

"Probably," Keldon replied. He wrenched one foot free of the muck, the sucking slurp of thick, oozing silt threatening to pull his shoe away. "But I doubt I'd be heard over that waterfall."

I tried to look farther down the tunnel, hoping to discern the source of the thundering water, but Quiniece's shadow light device only illuminated the tunnel for a hundred paces or so. "Some part of the old waterworks is still operational here. Where there is mud, there is a regularity of water. And regularity means timing."

Quiniece tapped the interlock spanner hooked to her belt. "As in clockwork timing?"

I nodded. "Precisely."

The muddy quagmire would have swallowed any footprints left behind, but whoever had last passed through had likely used the same ledge Armez and Quiniece had found. I helped Keldon up, and we started down the tunnel following the sound of crashing water. We passed several seized-up machine rooms and hatchways rusted shut, as well as the door to a deep silo which, judging from the half-corroded placard, held a store of caustic soda used in the reclamation cycle.

We ventured on, the sound of crashing water growing to a deafening roar, and the tunnel soon emptied into the upper level of a vast overflow reservoir. A maelstrom of water boiled up from below, quickly rising as seawater spilled in from two other tunnels on either side. In the inverted color spectrum, the water shown bright white, while the reservoir walls and piping fixtures were a strange mix of violet, teal, and black.

"This entire chamber is going to be flooded in a matter of minutes!" I screamed over the deafening deluge.

"One minute seventeen seconds, judging from the velocity and volume of the inflowing water," Quiniece added, clicking through a series of cogs and number dials on her clockwork gauntlet.

Keldon stared at her slack jawed. "You have an enumerator built into that thing?"

She rolled her eyes. "Of course, I do. I'm a gearmeister."

I looked to the level above ours where a rusty catwalk led to a small control room, hued in splotches of blue and gray in the shadow light. We had no way to access the catwalk from our side of the reservoir, and the gushing water was rising too fast for us to find another way around. "Can you get up there?" I asked Armez, nodding to the control room.

He sighed, rapping his cane on the floor. "We can jump far, climb fast, and move as quick as a shadow. But despite what many have been led to believe, vampires cannot technically fly."

"But I can," Quiniece answered with a mischievous smirk. "Once I'm up there, I'll used the interlock spanner to reverse the water flow."

She cocked the priming lever of her clockwork gauntlet's grapple, then jogged back a dozen paces to get a running start. With a blur of speed, she hurled herself out above the surging maelstrom, her grapple firing for the mess of pipes just above the catwalk. The grapple struck home, cable drawing taunt, and she swung to the far wall as the gauntlet's motorized windlass reeled her upward. In seconds, she ascended two full stories, then kicked herself from the wall and landed with uncanny grace on the catwalk. Bolts popped and metal groaned, but somehow the rusting structure held. Her grapple released, retracting into her clockwork gauntlet, and she dashed into the control room.

The churning waters had risen another ten feet, nearly reaching our level. I looked back to the control room where the young vampire studied a bank of grime-covered gauges. She glanced at a set of levers and tapped the spanner on her hand, then looked to a panel on the wall.

"Not to rush you," I yelled over the deafening deluge, "but we are in pursuit of my prime suspect."

"To say nothing of the rising water," Keldon added, backing away from the edge of the reservoir.

Quiniece connected the interlock spanner to the wall panel and tried to rotate the spanner both clockwise and counterclockwise. She then removed the spanner, made a few adjustments to the coupling joint, and tried again. I looked down as she continued her efforts, watching as the water swelled with astonishing speed. The frothing spume had already soaked my trouser legs and had likely ruined my calfskin shoes. I was about to order Keldon to retreat the way we had come when a shuddering thud resonated through the reservoir. The torrential waterfalls from the inlet tunnels petered to trickles, and the clamor of massive pumping machinery filled the momentary silence before the deafening roar of siphoning water thundered anew.

"If they didn't already know we were here, they certainly do now," Armez yelled, his voice barely audible over the rush of draining water.

The whirlpool receded into the depths, revealing a set of rusting stairs circling the reservoir's inner wall and descending into the darkness beneath. The drop to the landing nearest us was only ten feet, and I lent Keldon a hand climbing down before Armez helped me down in turn. The vampire dropped beside me with almost casual ease, and his sireling quickly rejoined us, rappelling on her grappling cable. Although the rusting stairs appeared to be on the verge of collapse, they actually felt quite sturdy. A quick inspection of the support braces fastening them to the reservoir's wall revealed the structure had been recently reinforced.

We followed the stairs down, winding around the dank interior of the now empty reservoir. In one respect I had to admire the Servants of Vosh. Using the backflow reservoirs of the city's flood tunnels to conceal their lair was a stroke of genius, as the water filled reservoir provided a cunning barrier against all manner of snoops and trespassers. But Mistress Agona had left behind a painfully obvious trail. The makeshift interlock spanner had been our best clue, as it served no other purpose than to regulate old-style pumping machinery. Furthermore, the rot-blighted thralls had worn tattered raincoats and muddy waders, not unlike those of the victim we had found—an attire indicative of grubbers scavenging in the waterworks. But Agona herself had provided the final bit of evidence for her destination. If she was a sorceress of the Dungh'gar cults, as her tattoos suggested, then the abandoned waterworks would be almost homely to her and her foul ilk. In fact, the clues were so obvious that I grew increasingly concerned we were heading into a trap. But trap or not, at least we were on the trail.

"This door is out of place," Keldon said.

The door we had come to was a sealed hatchway, similar to those found on naval ironclads, but fitted with a complex clockwork lock. Quiniece pried the cover off the lock, then took an autorotor from her belt and attached the illicit device to the arrangement of gears and tumblers inside.

"Hardly a worthy challenge," she scoffed. After a few moments of winding and adjusting the autorotor, her sneer turned to a grimace.

"Maybe you need to turn it the other way around," Keldon chuckled.

Quiniece glared at Keldon with narrowed eyes, then turned back to her work. After a few more adjustments, the mechanism clicked into place and the hatch's locking bolts ratcheted back. Armez pushed the hatch open and strode into the corridor beyond.

"It seems clear," he reported, moving further in.

"The aether is humming with energy in there," Keldon whispered, drawing his key from his belt. "I think they are intrusion wards, or something like them."

Quiniece held up her crystal-capped device and twisted the knobs on its base. The inverted colors of shadow light vanished, plunging us into darkness. "Just in case that sorceress is watching," she explained.

Or her master, I reminded myself.

"Thanks... Now I can't see anything," Keldon complained. "Wait, what's that glow?"

I saw it, too. Instead of being entirely dark, a sickly green glow emanated from the cavernous chamber at the far end of the grime-plastered corridor. The stench of rot and decay grew increasingly repugnant as we ventured farther in, putrid vapors rising around us as our shoes sloshed through the oozing black water pooled in the ruts and furrows of the corroded tunnel.

"You'd better put the mask back on," I said to Keldon. The two vampires would be fine, but if we faced a karcist endowed with the power of the Bone Crown of Dagoroth, Keldon could be infected as easily as any of those hapless victims.

"What about you?" he asked, fitting the breather mask on his face.

"I'll be fine," I lied, showing him my severite wristbands. In truth, severite would do nothing to protect me from a direct infection, even an ensorcelled one.

As my eyes adjusted to the dim viridian light, I began to discern unnerving etchings carved along the tunnel's moss-coated walls: a chilling collection of thorn-crossed Dungh'gar runes intermixed with crudely transcribed glyphs of Gollan design. Dark intonements murmured from the unseen chamber at the end of the corridor, carried upon the noxious currents of the dank and clammy air. Shadows crept across the moss-slick walls as fetid things moved about the haunting green light, and the droning chant abruptly ended in a bout of chilling laughter.

Armez staggered into the wall, dropping his cane and throwing his hands to his head. At first, I assumed he had slipped on some blot of slime mold before remembering such a casual misstep did not befit a master vampire. Keldon brought his talisman up as he stepped back, his eyes widening in the sickly green light. I braced myself, hoping we had not tripped a deadly empowered trap.

"Sire!" Quiniece yelled, grabbing him by his coat sleeve.

Armez bared his teeth, his face contorting in pain. "No..." he moaned. He clutched his chest and dropped to his knees in the stinking muck. "Not here... Not now!"

Quiniece gasped, backing away from him. She snatched his cane from the floor and unsheathed the sword. "Armez, resist!" she yelled, her voice trembling in horror.

"Resist what?" I demanded. I took a step toward him, then stopped. "What is happening?"

"No! It can't be," Armez choked. His coat bulged out and tore open, the fabric splitting as his body ruptured with fleshy protrusions. "I'm too late... They still have me!" he screamed, his voice cracking as he writhed and twisted in agony. "Archons, no! Don't let them take me!"

With a tormented roar, Armez threw his head back and reared upright, bones cracking and muscles rippling beneath his blackening skin. The stricken vampire flung his arms wide, clawed fingers lengthening as membranous wings stretched between them. Red eyes peered out from a face now marred by armored scales and boney horns, its mouth agape as rows of needle-like teeth extended from blood-red roots.

I staggered back, an ice-cold shudder cutting through me. *This* was why Armez had pursued the Servants of Vosh with such fervent determination. He had no interest in the Bone Crown, nor did he care about the victims or seek to bring their murderers to justice. He was himself a victim of their sinister designs, and he hunted them either for vengeance or to find a cure for whatever they had done to him. But the monstrous fiend rising before me was not the Armez I knew, and by the fear draining from her alabaster face, he was not the sire Quiniece had grown to trust.

Whatever curse afflicted Armez, Quiniece herself seemed unaffected. I grabbed her arm and pulled her around, then snapped my fingers to draw Keldon's attention. The transfigured vampire stalked forward, blocking our escape route, so I pointed to the only path remaining: to the chamber at the end of the corridor.

"Run," I breathed, my voice low and hoarse.

The two looked at me, utter terror painted across their too-young faces. But they knew, as I knew, that we had no other choice. Either we ended this now or we would die without the faintest hope of escape.

"Run!" I yelled.

And we ran.

ROCKS AND WATER EXPLODED BEHIND US, a piercing shriek gaining with every bound. I jumped, following just behind Keldon and Quiniece, stumbling as I hit the scraps of rusting metal and broken gears scattered across the cavernous room. Man-like shapes cloaked in tattered raincoats and wader boots closed around us, each one baring heavy iron maces or cruel serrated blades. The winged beast Armez had become flew into the chamber behind us and circled the derelict machinery high above, then dived with claws extended.

I threw myself down as Armez swooped overhead, and a shower of flashing lights and dazzling colors erupted from Keldon's key, causing the ranks of encroaching thralls to shriek and fall back. Quiniece lashed out with Armez's sword, beheading one thrall and then another, and I jumped up to catch the arm of the foe nearest me as it swung its wicked sword. I pivoted to pry the weapon from its hand, a swath of putrid skin peeling away with the hilt, and I shoved the blade into the chest of its former owner. Keldon and Quiniece got behind me as the host of rotting thralls closed in, with the beast Armez had become landing in their midst. We were outnumbered and outmatched, and not only lacked the support of our strongest ally, but faced the worst of his immortal wrath.

I slipped a hand into my pocket where I had stashed the two alchemical vials from the tormentorium—one of vitriolic chlorinate and the other an alkahest reagent. *At least I still had those...*

"Welcome, Aldicus Vescard," boomed a voice from a balcony overlooking the chamber. The speaker was not Mistress Agona.

A man draped in robes of green and black made his way down a short catwalk to the balcony's edge. He held a gnarled black staff in one hand and a rotting leather tome in the other, and upon his head he wore the Bone Crown of Dagoroth—its skeletal spines digging into the scars encircling his scalp. When I saw the man's lean and sunken face, my grip tightened on the vials in my pocket. The vials baring the blue and white emblem of APHID. *What a fool I had been!*

"Doctor Seltoc," Keldon whispered for me.

"That is *Lord* Seltoc, to you," Mistress Agona spoke, emerging from a shadowed corner of the room. "High Priest of Dagoroth, Grand Adjutor of Abothog, and Holy Seneschal to his Eternal Majesty, Prince Voshthok-ung'Ulkoth, Implacable Lord of Justice."

"The Demon Lord of Wrath," I corrected. "Not Justice!"

Agona crooked a hateful sneer. "Have some perspective, Vescard."

"Our master had great plans for you," Lord Seltoc growled. He leveled his black staff toward us and frowned. "But your dogged meddling has made you more trouble than you're worth."

Jagged green lightning erupted from Seltoc's staff, and I raised my arms hoping my wristbands might absorb at least some of the attack. Quiniece ripped a canister from her belt and sprang forward, slamming one end into the muck as it telescoped into a four-foot pole, a mesh of orichalium wire blossoming from its top. She tumbled away as the lightning diverted and surged into the aetheric countermeasure, turning the device into a white-hot rod under the crackling barrage. At the same time, Keldon conjured a prismatic wall of twisting light, causing the infected hordes to shrink back. Quiniece tossed Armez's sword to me, and I ducked low and struck out, dispatching one of the thralls as the young vampire fired her grapple to entangle her former master.

Armez launched into the air, catching Quiniece's grapple and hurling her across the chamber by its cable. A deluge of aetheric fire blazed from Mistress Agona's bejeweled hand, shattering Keldon's mirage in a shower of disjointed reflections. I kicked one tatter-clothed thrall away, then rammed my shoulder into another before skewering a third, my eyes growing wide when I saw what I had impaled. The thrall was not garbed in a raincoat, but wore the oilcloth suit and facemask of the APHID medics we had seen earlier. Three other medics moved among the grisly throng, each shambling with the same mindless determination as the others.

If the Servants of Vosh now infested APHID, how deep did the infection go?

I had no time to ponder such questions. A squall of howling black wind and spectral currents swept through the chamber as the vile karcist pressed his terrible will upon his blight-spawned army.

"Arise, plague golem!" Seltoc bellowed. Ghostly vapors of coal-black corruption poured from the Bone Crown of Dagoroth, washing over the rot-blighted horde. "Arise!"

The diseased thralls burst open one after another, their

putrescent flesh spiraling into a festering mass of bloated viscera, leaving piles of blood-soaked raincoats and waders scattered throughout the chamber. Tangles of writhing sinew bound their flesh-stripped bones together, forming a crude skeleton of asymmetric limbs and vertebral tentacles, while skin, muscles, and entrails coalesced, fleshing out the monster's twisted anatomy. The abomination drew in its first breath of unliving life, then blasted a sonorous howl, shaking the chamber and raining rust and debris from the machinery in the ceiling high above.

Keldon and Quiniece stood staring in dumbfounded horror, eyes wide as the enormous plague golem rose to fill the chamber with all its loathsome bulk. I tossed the sword back to Quiniece, then dashed for the pestilent monstrosity as she whipped around to fend off the transfigured Armez. Agona darted across my path, and with a blast of kinetic force, hurled a tangled ball of wire and rusty metal straight at me. I brought up my arms in a vain attempt to block the attack, but the crushing impact slammed me against the wall. Realizing all other options were out, I crossed my arms to pull the locking pins from my severite wristbands. But something was wrong. I couldn't move my arms.

Looking down, I saw the tangle of twisted wire and metal had knotted around my wristbands, holding them fast.

"Did you think we would not be ready for you?" Agona spat. She levitated a scrap of iron pipe from the floor, the jagged end aimed at me like a spear. "Did the great Aldicus Vescard not suspect a trap?"

I threw myself into a running dive, the iron pipe missing me by mere inches as I hit the ground—slick with muck and moldering ooze. I slid right past Agona on a path straight for the still white-hot rod of Quiniece's countermeasure, my wire-tangled arms stretched out before me.

Pain and heat washed over me, and my hands and wrists began to blister as I pressed my tangled bonds against the rod's molten metal. Agona spat some vulgar Scaithi curse, but I could scarcely hear her over my own scream. At last, the severite bonds broke free, and I flung the wristbands to Keldon.

"Get those on Armez!" I forced out, just before the raging inferno exploded through me.

Keldon caught one of the wristbands as he tumbled away from the sweeping reach of Armez's transmuted talons, and Quiniece snagged the other with her grapple. Mistress Agona threw everything she had at me, but the blast of aetheric fire had no effect on my already immolating flesh. The remains of my coat went up like oil-soaked torch wrappings, instantly consuming the alchemicals within the vials in my pocket.

My heart became a blast furnace; my blood boiled to liquid cinnabar; my innards churned with digestive alkahest; and the very flesh and bones of my body converted to the purest elemental matter.

A fireball of combusting phlogiston tore from my outstretched hands, exploding just short of the sorceress as she levitated a sheet of metal between herself and the attack. The impact slammed the shield into her, throwing her against the far wall and burying her in an avalanche of crumbling masonry and rusting machine parts.

Compelled by its own chaotic impulse to destroy, my alchemorph turned from the downed foe and surged for the plague golem. A spray of burning alchemicals erupted from my incendiary hands, searing through the abomination's tumorous flesh. But no sooner had the monster's outer skin dissolved than it shifted and reformed, healing itself faster than the wounds could appear. The alchemorph pressed on, redoubling its attack, yet with every passing moment I felt the energy drain from me. The two vials were not nearly enough to sustain the blazing alchemical reactor within me, and these dank, abandoned depths held nothing but rust, rocks, and filthy water.

From the corner of my burning brimstone eyes, I watched Keldon and Quiniece split to either side to flank and attack

Armez. Quiniece darted in first, sword swinging, but Armez hurled her aside with ease. Keldon aim his key to loose some diverting empowerment, and Armez swept around to swat my apprentice with his gruesome six-inch talons. But the talons tore through empty air, and as Keldon's illusion flickered away, he reappeared behind a pile of rubble where Quiniece had landed. Armez flew at them shrieking, and the pair shifted in the twisting blur of a second illusion, reappearing a dozen paces away.

In their place stood a jury-rigged tripwire affixed to two bowing rods with my severite bonds attached to either end. Armez landed right on top of the trap and Quiniece yanked her grapple's cable, snapping a snare hidden just beneath him. The snare pulled taunt around Armez's legs, drawing my severite bonds against his monstrous form. Armez fell thrashing and screaming into the muck, his scaley skin crumbling away as his leathery wings retracted.

"Agona, exterminate these vermin!" the karcist yelled.

Mistress Agona erupted from the rubble, launching herself across the chamber on a wave of kinetic force, rays of aethergy streaming from her talisman. Keldon and Quiniece dashed away as rocks and debris exploded around them, but in my present state I could do nothing to help them. The plague golem barreled into me, limbs enveloping me even as my furnace-hot fires scorched its flesh to cinders. We crashed to the floor, and the monster's fetid bulk pushed me deeper into the muck and mud, smothering the alchemical reactions sustaining my elemental form.

Pressed deeper into the muck-sodden floor, my alchemorph looked upward past the festering plague golem to the ceiling where I saw a pair of sealed hopper doors. Thinking back to the path we had taken through the tunnels, I realized the silo of caustic soda was directly above this very chamber—a chamber filled with water, rusting metal, and dissolved limestone. It was a perfect catalyst for a volatile exothermic reaction. My alchemorph understood the instant

I realized the truth, and a jet of fire launched from its outstretched hand, reaching in desperation for the hopper doors high above. But the distance was too great, and my alchemorph roared with unsated rage as the fiery plume fizzled to a trickle.

Lord Seltoc bellowed laughter, black light streaming like noxious mist from the ghastly crown atop his head. "My victory is complete!"

Mistress Agona pressed her attack, ignoring Keldon's diverting illusions and blasting a bolt of aethergy straight at him. Quiniece knocked him aside in a sudden blur of motion, and the two tumbled across the ground, shattered rocks falling around them. Having seen the desperate spout of flame from my alchemorph, Quiniece looked up and spotted the hopper doors with her keen eyes. She aimed her clockwork gauntlet and fired her grapple for the gears that held the doors closed. The claw clamped onto a locking lever, and Quiniece threw her cable spool into reverse, pulling back hard. The hopper doors burst open, releasing a cascade of caustic soda grains into the chamber like a hailstorm.

The plague golem howled, Agona cursed, and Seltoc screamed. But I scarcely heard them over the popping, hissing symphony of molten sparks and white-hot flames erupting as the alkaline pellets splashed into the metal-tainted water. Keldon and Quiniece dashed from the roiling waters, but Mistress Agona found herself facing Armez. Muck and viscous black ooze covered the restored vampire from head to toe, and he held his sword before him with the severite bonds now locked firmly to his wrists. A burst of light exploded from Agona's talisman, and the sorceress jumped away as Armez shrank from the blinding white flare. Quiniece began to take chase, but Armez pointed with his blade and charged for Lord Seltoc.

"Ignore her," Armez yelled above the din. He locked eyes with the sinister priest, lips curling with a hatred I had not seen in him before. "Destroy that crown at all cost!"

My alchemorph sprayed corrosive vitriol and alkahest across the churning brew of caustic soda, water, and metal pooling on the chamber floor. Flammable gas steamed from the bubbling reaction, then ignited in a scorching flash as fulminating metal sparked and sizzled all around. The plague golem howled in agony as it died, its rotting, ulcerous flesh disintegrating in the blazing conflagration. Lord Seltoc clutched his head at the same instant, screaming as black vapors recoiled into his blasphemous crown.

Seeing their chance, Keldon fired an aetheric dart from his key and Quiniece launched a pneumatic bola from her gauntlet. Energy surged across the invisible ward surrounding the karcist, absorbing Keldon's dart and deflecting Quiniece's bola. But their attack opened the way for Armez, and the vampire sprang for the balcony, screaming as he crashed into Seltoc's empowered shield, pressing his blade against the barrier with all his might.

The room shook as another burst of explosive gas erupted from the burning, bubbling muck, and Keldon and Quiniece scrambled up a mound of debris to escape the roiling inferno generated by the volatile reaction. A column of cinder blocks crashed from the ceiling above, smashing through the catwalk leading to the balcony, but the catwalk reappeared an instant later—a tenuous illusion conjured by Keldon's cunning skill. Seltoc cursed as Armez pressed on, lunging again as he tried to penetrate the defensive barrier. The karcist took another step back, his feet scraping over rubble as he edged his way for the now illusionary catwalk.

"You were once *ours* to command!" Seltoc snarled, coils of crackling green energy forming around his black staff. "You cannot escape our grip so easily."

"Once, perhaps," Armez growled in reply. He threw all his strength into the next strike, smashing one severite wristband into the aetheric shield as he plunged his sword for the karcist's crown. "But never again!"

Seltoc stumbled back to evade the attack, his feet slipping

to the catwalk that was not there. The illusionary catwalk flickered, and the karcist screamed, arms flailing as he fell backwards from the ledge. The still burning husk of the plague golem sloshed and undulated in its final death throes, and Lord Seltoc dropped into that simmering mass of boiling pus and liquified entrails.

"Mistress Agona!" Seltoc shrieked as the burning broth of gore washed over him. His arm reached out even as the flesh melted from his bones. "Help me!"

Agona watched from the tunnel leading out of the chamber, her dark gray face twisted with fury. "This is a mercy, considering how our master rewards failure!" With that, she turned and fled down the tunnel.

My alchemorph surged forward, a torrent of elemental fire and molten metals washing over what remained of Seltoc and the withering plague golem he had created. The karcist screamed again, his body crumbling like burning paper in the blast furnace winds. The Bone Crown of Dagoroth imploded around the dark priest's head, then shattered outward in a deafening shock wave, scattering shards of broken bone—some, undoubtedly, from Seltoc's own obliterated skull.

Water crashed into the chamber from an enormous pipe, and my alchemorph looked up just in time for me to spot Keldon and Quiniece standing on a platform beside the wheel of an inflow release valve. Armez jumped from the balcony, pulling my severite bonds from his wrists as he fell toward me. The deluge of seawater engulfed me and all went black—the merciful embrace of unconsciousness at last taking hold.

I PULLED THE TATTERED RAINCOAT around my blistered body, trying not to think of the diseased thing that had worn it only hours before. At least the coat had been flash baked by the alchemical fire and washed clean in the deluge, the stench of stagnant mud and seawater overwhelming whatever fetid odors might have remained. I was topside now, resting on the curb of a litter-strewn concourse near the main steamrail station for East Wharf's market row. The area had been evacuated by the Vandorian Guard under Tibblemond's supervision, with a thirty-block dragnet thrown by the imposing presence of two HAAMR units, their officers fully outfitted in articulated, empowered armor. Despite their efforts, there had been no sign of anyone matching Mistress Agona's description. She had either died or escaped, but the latter seemed more likely.

Justiciar and one other dirigible hung in the night sky above, distinguished by the shield and scales emblem of the Vandorian Guard, both accompanied by an armored dirigible bearing HAAMR's sword and shield. Atracus sank to the west, wreathing shipyard cranes and ironwork foundries in its fiery, crimson glow.

"I doubt some ancient, diabolical cult has actually infiltrated APHID," Tibblemond said. He flipped through his notepad and scratched his muttonchops. "I just received word that Doctor Seltoc's credentials never checked out, and APHID has no record of him or any member of his team. Whoever they were, they were posing as APHID, not APHID themselves."

Tibblemond had only now received word? That seemed a little too convenient. "But they had APHID equipment, uniforms, and vehicles. Moreover, those vials I found in the tormentorium were taken from an APHID laboratory."

"Perhaps they do have someone on the inside helping them," Tibblemond said. "I'll open an inquest, but with everything else going on, it might be some time before I dig anything up."

I spotted Keldon returning from across the street with a bundle of clothes in his arms. He glanced at Tibblemond, but the chief inspector had moved off to talk to one of the HAAMR officers.

"Quiniece gave me these," my apprentice said, dropping the clothes beside me. "I didn't ask where she got them."

"I fear we are well beyond worrying about petty theft," I replied.

I looked at my severite wristbands, closing my eyes as I pictured the monstrous beast Armez had become. It had been a guess that the severite would work on him as it did on me, but if the karcist had triggered the transformation, then the severite's dampening power would have blocked the spell. Even so, Armez clearly had some connection with the Servants of Vosh, and they still held some degree of power over him.

"Did you see Armez?" I asked.

Keldon shook his head. "Quiniece said he was changing." He paused for a moment before continuing. "I assume she meant he was changing into new clothes, not back into that creature. How do you think that happened to him?"

"I do not know," I admitted. "He did say he had been their captive, and was subjected to horrific experiments that he has tried his best to forget. The Bone Crown must have allowed Seltoc to awaken whatever dark form they had buried within him. With its destruction, he was freed. I am not so fortunate."

A HAAMR officer approached, his armored boots clopping on the cobblestone street. He carried his helmet under one arm, and I saw his square-jawed face, flat-cropped hair, and optographic receptor where his left eye should have been. Colonel Ordin Dolgrim.

"My men have found no sign of this supposed sorceress," Colonel Dolgrim said, his gravelly voice edged with doubt. He shook his head, looking to the storm drains leading down to the waterworks. "And thanks to you, whatever evidence we might have dredged up was either incinerated or washed out to sea."

An ornithopter landed nearby, its wings still beating even as a passenger hurried from the craft. "Colonel!" the young officer yelled. He saluted and handed Dolgrim a piece of paper. "We have more reports coming in and all units have been mobilized."

"Reports?" I asked.

The colonel glanced over the missive, then crumpled the paper in his gauntleted hand. "If you will excuse me, more urgent matters demand my attention." He started away, calling for his men to form up.

"The bombings, I'd wager," Tibblemond explained.

I staggered to my feet, pulling the raincoat tighter. "Bombings? What bombings?"

Tibblemond sighed. "If you hadn't been so obsessed with chasing this one case, perhaps you might have paid better attention when I tried to tell you about—"

"Yes, yes, the so-called radical anarchists," I interrupted. "Now, tell me what has happened."

"There were two bombings in the 13th District." The chief inspector put his battered notepad away and strained to button his coat over his ample belly. "Yes, there have been bombings there before, but these were in the new housing development, near the border with the 14th District. Several dozen manufactory workers were killed, with twice as many wounded."

Colonel Dolgrim boarded a transport thopter, then turned to look out across the city as its thundering pneumatic engines lifted the craft into the air. The remaining HAAMR troopers boarded their armored wagons, each one more like a military juggernaut than any common patrol carriage, their massive wheels turning and furnace pipes flaring as they headed out of the steamrail concourse to the northbound causeway.

I shook my head. When had the police become a military force?

"So much for the dragnet," Keldon grumbled as he watched the armored vehicles pull away.

Tibblemond touched the brim of his bowler. "I'm sorry, Aldicus, but I must get back to Vandor Tower. Knowing the Commissioner General, he'll be calling for all hands on deck.

We could be on the verge of a state of emergency."

The chief inspector hurried off to join the remaining bluejacks as they made ready to depart in their considerably less impressive steam-carriages. I grabbed the bundle of clothes Keldon had brought me and changed behind an empty vendor's stall. The rugged work shirt, tweed vest, and loose trousers were a poor fit, but I was thankful to be rid of that cursed raincoat.

Keldon fell in beside me as I started down the empty concourse. I saw real fear in his eyes—fear that was not at all unwarranted. "What's going on, Aldicus? How could this be happening? Why are the protesters bombing housing developments?"

"I doubt they are," I said.

Keldon looked at me and blinked.

I pushed my hands into the pockets of my illicitly borrowed trousers, then drew a breath of the crisp night air. "A darkness is closing fast upon this city—a darkness we have faced and fought, yet failed utterly in divining the depths of their designs. My own hubris was my blindness, for I now see the enemy is far more dangerous and infinitely more insidious than any common crime ring or cult of sorcery. They have not merely been a step ahead of me, nor have they simply outmaneuvered me. They have played me every step of the way. Played me, like a rigged game of jonko."

The HAAMR dirigible turned away with *Justiciar* and the smaller airship trailing in formation. I watched the ships recede into the fog-veiled skyline—a seemingly endless expanse of refineries, manufactories, and tenement sprawls, bathed in the blood-red light of the waxing demon-moon.

The haunting words of the Shadow Man whispered at the corners of my thoughts: *As above, so below; the dark above, the dark below.*

I drew a deep breath, closing my eyes. "I fear our most perilous trials still lie ahead, and our darkest days have yet to dawn."

CASE FILE 12:

FALL OF THE HAMMER OF JUSTICE

RUBBLE FILLED THE STREET AROUND ME, and the acrid stench of burning oil and smoldering cinders choked the dusty air. Black smoke billowed from fires deep within the demolished gasification refinery, the impenetrable cloud blotting out all signs of the rescue dirigibles only a few hundred feet above. Despite the danger to themselves, search and rescue teams clambered about the rubble scanning with empowered rods for any remaining survivors—a dim hope, given the totality of the disaster. It was a scene repeated half a dozen times over the past few days, seizing all of Corradon in the chilling grip of terror.

"I heard the refinery explode," said the man in front of me. He coughed into his hand, then wiped the soot from his haggard face. "The next blast came from below. The gas main, maybe? I don't know. The building was on fire. I heard others screaming, but I..." He shook his head. "I..."

"Take your time, Mister Melard," I said, pulling my new frock coat around me. "Could you see the refinery from your office?"

"I didn't see anything unusual before the blast, if that's what you're asking," Melard replied.

Despite the soot and grime covering him, Guillem Melard had fared better than most. Nearly all of the refinery workers were dead or critically injured, but Melard had been working in his office at the Dalewerth Archeological Institute two blocks east of the explosion. The Dalewerth Institute was a poorly funded research center, but had recently made headlines with Luthus Dalewerth's most recent foray into the deeper reaches of the Underworks. Rumors persisted that the famed archeologist had brought back artifacts of dramatic historical importance, but no public announcement had been made. I could only wonder what Dalewerth had found in those sunken depths of forgotten antiquity. If they dated back to the War of Golla and Marada, then the Shadow Man would top my list of potential suspects.

"What can you tell me of the artifacts Luthus Dalewerth recently brought back?"

"Artifacts?" Melard asked, furrowing his brow. He shook his head and blinked. "Mainly some treasures and palace frescos from the reign of King Lothair, we believe. We haven't catalogued any of them yet."

I considered him doubtfully, then turned my attention back to the collapsed ruins of the Dalewerth Institute. Although the gasification refinery was the apparent target of the bombing, the neighboring buildings sustained extensive damage. But among them, only the institute had been totally demolished. Judging from what remained, the building had been an overbuilt mongrel of mismatched veneers, overhanging jetties, and haphazard additions—a common sight in the older reaches of the 5th District. It was easy to see how the building might suffer a catastrophic collapse, but only a secondary explosion of sufficient concussive force could have so utterly shattered its foundations. But if the explosion traveled the gas main from the refinery, the safety cutoffs should have engaged within seconds of the detonation.

A half-burned sheet of paper flitted through the ash-laden wind. The manifesto was identical to countless others scattered both here and at every bombing site across Corradon, and its fiery rhetoric only deepened the enigma of these attacks.

> "We are the Scales of Liberty. We are the Sword of Righteousness. We are the Brethren of Justice. We will not stop until the Merchant Princes and Barons of Industry hear our voices. No longer shall the common man be trod upon by the relentless march of untempered progress. No longer shall the toiling laborer be crushed beneath the iron wheels of unceasing manufactories. The Lord Governor and his Chamber of Industry have usurped the rights of the people, but no more! We demand these villains step down from their haughty towers and admit their crimes of gluttony and cronyism, lest we purge their foul corruption from the rotting heart of Armillia. To arms, fellow citizens! To arms! Together we will rise up and usher in a new age of justice, equality, and prosperity for all."
>
> - The Disciple

Keldon's shoes crunched on loose debris as he walked up. "I found him," he said. He glanced over his shoulder, then dropped his gaze to the ground. "The triage station, critical ward." His jaw tightened and he drew a sharp breath. "It's bad, Aldicus. Doctor Dalewerth might not pull through."

"Luthus is alive?" Melard gasped.

I narrowed my eyes. Melard's slack-jawed expression seemed more shocked than relieved. "No doubt you are anxious to wish your injured friend well."

Melard rung his hands, his eyes darting to one side. "I... I should inform his wife. She will want to be with him."

"An excellent idea. Do you know where to find her?" I asked. Melard stammered and stepped back, and I seized him by his sleeve. I knew a guilty man when I saw one. "Come along. Perhaps you could relate to me how you escaped this carnage with only a few scratches to show for it."

Melard blathered on as I dragged him along behind me. His excuses were meaningless, and his stuttered words and trembling voice told me all I needed to know. He was a liar, but more than that, he was an exceedingly bad liar. Perhaps he was nothing more than a patsy, having simply been paid for whatever his role was in this terrible attack, or perhaps the degree of his involvement was something more substantial. He seemed genuinely troubled that Doctor Dalewerth was still alive, and that was not the reaction one might expect from a friend and colleague.

The triage station was a picture of blood and butchery, more akin to the savage battlefields of war-torn Tarrona than anything familiar to a civilized metropolis. Cots and bedrolls crowded the pavilions, each one occupied by a moaning, bloodied form. The astringent bite of antiseptic salves and alchemical coagulants mixed with the nauseating fetor of burned flesh, overwhelming the sooty reek lingering in the air. Physicians, Eldren healers, and priests of Mendrus scrambled to save those who could be saved, while surgeons tended the grisly task of heaping ruined limbs upon an ever-growing pile.

A fretful Eldren tended the figure Keldon brought us to, his green and silver tunic stained brown with crusted blood. He glanced up from his charge, his ageless eyes distant and haunted, and he shook his head in answer to my unspoken question. Not even Eldren magic could sooth the suffering of this dark day. I looked to the man on the cot, his broken body wrapped in salve-soaked bandages surrounded by glowing vizstones and healing runes. A clockwork apparatus ticked and sputtered beside him, its tangle of tubes filtering blood through alchemical treatment ampules while pneumatic bellows pumped air to the mask covering his mouth.

"Doctor Dalewerth?" I asked, uncertain if this mangled remnant of a man was indeed the institute's founder. If he was, then I had to cut straight to the matter at hand. "I am Aldicus Vescard. The artifacts you found, were they Maradian—"

"This isn't Luthus," Melard interrupted. He strained to pull away from me, but I only tightened my grip on his coat sleeve. "He couldn't possibly have survived. Now, let's be off."

"Why?" Dalewerth rasped through his breathing mask, his one unbandaged eye fluttering open. "Why, Guillem... Why let them take it?"

Guillem Melard jerked from my grasp, but I seized his other arm and twisted it behind his back, causing him to yelp.

"Who?" I demanded, looking at Dalewerth. "What did they take?"

"Don't know who..." Dalewerth wheezed, his words muffled to a whisper. I had to lean closer just to hear. "He... He let them in... Just before the blast..." The archeologist convulsed in a coughing fit, then drew in a ragged breath through the respirator mask. "They took it..."

"Took what?" I asked, fearing he was about to slip away. "What did they take?"

"They... They took..." Dalewerth rasped. "They took... The doomseed."

My hold on Melard nearly slipped at Dalewerth's fading words. "A doomseed?" I hissed under my breath, scarcely able to believe I had heard correctly.

Keldon looked at me, his eyes bulging. "What did he just say?"

"Doctor Dalewerth," I said, forcing my voice steady. His chest had stopped moving. "Luthus!"

A bell sounded from the clockwork apparatus and the Eldren rushed to the dying man. After checking vitals and placing hands to Dalewerth's head and chest, the Eldren switched off the machine and bowed his head in solemn respect.

"Speak!" I demanded, pulling Melard around. I seized his

shoulders and held tight, looking deep into his fearful eyes. "What is this—" I stopped and glanced about the triage tent. No one was paying us any particular attention, and the Eldren had moved away to tend to other victims. Even so, I dropped my voice to a whisper. "What is this about a *doomseed*?"

Melard's lower lip quivered. His face had drained of color and I felt his shoulder slump in my grasp. "They just paid me to turn it over," he blubbered, shaking his head. "But it can't possibly work. It's fifteen hundred years old, and there's not a speck of radiant aurium inside. I... I didn't know they would blow-up the refinery. You must believe me!"

My grip on Melard's shoulder tightened. "You botch-brained fool! You've just consigned *millions* to unimaginable destruction. Not since the War of Golla and Marada have such sorcerous weapons—"

"Aldicus, there you are!" a gruff voice called. Chief Inspector Tibblemond stumbled down a bank of crumbling debris, a team of Vandorian Guardsmen and armored HAAMR troopers following just behind him. "Why are you over here? Shouldn't you be hunting for clues at the bombing site?"

I pulled the sobbing Melard up by his coat collar, then shoved him to the ground at Tibblemond's feet. "My investigation of the secondary explosion at the Dalewerth Institute has turned up a considerable clue. Luthus Dalewerth has succumbed to his injuries, but his research fellow, Guillem Melard, aided the bombers."

"He did?" Tibblemond asked incredulous. Then he scratched his scraggly muttonchops and looked down at Melard. "Well, speak up. Who is this Disciple? And why is he blowing up the city bit by bit?"

Melard clasped his hands together, pleading tearfully as he answered Tibblemond. "I don't know who they are. They just wanted the artifact. I had no idea they would do this. Please believe me!"

"This man is just a patsy," I explained. "Place him under arrest and have him escorted to Vandor Tower. Perhaps we can get sketches of the men he was dealing with."

"All right," Tibblemond agreed. We watched the jacks handcuff Melard and lead him away, the HAAMR troopers following close behind. "What is your theory on all of this, Aldicus? I assume you have a theory. You always do."

"A premise only," I admitted. "Not yet distilled to theory."

I slipped my hands into my coat pockets and headed back to the collapsed ruins of the Dalewerth Institute with Keldon and Tibblemond following behind me. Beyond the institute, the remains of the still-burning refinery smoldered like a dying bonfire. Had the bombing just been a distraction? Was it a tactic to cover their tracks and eliminate any evidence that the doomseed had been stolen, or that it even existed? If so, then what of the other bombings across the city? Was chaos their goal, or was a more sinister plan at work? The riots and bombings already had the public in a panic, and the manifesto's dire pronouncement only escalated the fear. News of a stolen doomseed would throw the city into outright hysteria.

Tibblemond fell in beside me, shaking one of the manifestos in his hand. "This Disciple and his Brethren of Justice are a menace. Not only have they killed hundreds in their bombing spree, they now threaten the Lord Governor and the Chamber of Industry!"

"The manifesto is nonsense," Keldon put in. "It aims to sway the common working folk, but the bombings have killed and injured the very people they seek to rally."

I smiled at my apprentice. He already saw through the manifesto's absurdity.

Tibblemond waved his hand dismissively. "Who can know the mind of a madman. The point is, we have a credible threat against the government of our city and we must act accordingly."

"No, inspector, my apprentice is correct," I put in. Keldon

smiled. “The manifesto is a work of pure misdirection. I doubt the Brethren of Justice are even real, and whatever this Disciple’s goal might be, it has nothing to do with a people’s revolution.”

“Are you suggesting this is all part of an elaborate ruse?” Tibblemond blew a frustrated huff from his nostrils, rustling the scraggly follicles of his unkempt mustache. “To what end?”

We had made our way back to the collapsed ruins of the Dalewerth Institute. A few rescue workers sifted through the rubble searching for bodies, but all were outside of earshot. “The reason I needed Melard taken to Vandor Tower was because of what he knows of the theft this bombing was meant to cover.”

“Theft?” Tibblemond asked. “What theft?”

I stopped and turned to the inspector. “Luthus Dalewerth recently returned from an expedition to the ancient ruins deep below the Underworks of Corradon. But he kept secret his most sensational and dangerous discovery, and for good reason. You see, the late doctor brought back—”

A series of gunshots rang out, followed by the sharp crack and clap of a concussive blast. Yells of panic turned to barking orders, and Vandorian Guardsmen and HAAMR troopers alike rushed to the source of the commotion.

“Archons above!” Tibblemond exclaimed. Hand to bowler, he dashed off in the same direction as the others, his stout legs carrying his ample form with surprising haste.

Keldon and I passed the chief inspector with no great effort, and quickly came upon a scene roiling with activity. Uniformed bluejacks and plain-clothed inspectors squabbled with the armored HAAMR troopers blocking their way. Reporters from the *Corradon Daily Post*, the *Sunrise Herald*, and half a dozen other circulars demanded an official statement, and civilian onlookers babbled in excitement from behind yellow safety lines.

The jacks made way as I approached, but the HAAMR

troopers stood unyielding. I glanced around the excessive bulk of their empowered armor, catching a glimpse of a body and what might have been one of Melard's shoes.

"Is that the suspect?" I demanded, my stomach clenching. *Melard was my only lead.* "Let me through!"

I tried to push passed the HAAMR trooper blocking my way, and I was soon joined by several Guardsmen adding their own arms and shoulders to my effort.

"Let Vescard through," a gravelly voice ordered.

The HAAMR troopers stepped aside and I dashed forward, only to reel back when I saw the grisly corpse sprawled on the rubble-strewn ground. The body was indeed Melard's, the back of his coat shot through with smoking holes. His limbs were twisted and broken, and the debris around him appeared to be crushed, as though impacted by a shock wave.

"What have you done?" I gasped.

Colonel Dolgrim stepped up, his frown twisting the scar that ran from his optographic receptor to the base of his jaw. "I only just arrived myself." He nodded to three HAAMR officers—two troopers and one mage judging from his talismanic staff and the eight-pointed star emblazoned on his armor. "According to my men, the prisoner broke and ran."

"So blasting him to smithereens was the answer?" I clenched my fists, resisting the urge to jab an accusing finger against Dolgrim's breastplate. "Your men have bolt-batons, the same as any Guardsman, which they could easily have used to stun him. What happened to the appropriate application of measured force?"

"The circumstances are unfortunate," the HAAMR mage calmly explained. "Lieutenant Garvon discovered his bolt-baton's vizstone was defective and Lieutenant Dagreth had not readied his. With little time to spare, Lieutenant Dagreth attempted to shoot the perpetrator's legs with his repeater, and I discharged a concussion strike intending to stun. Alas, my strike proved somewhat more lethal than I had expected, and, in his haste, the lieutenant's aim was higher than intended."

I shook my head. Equip the police like an army and they will treat every crime scene like a warzone.

"You're a mage!" Keldon bared his teeth, making no effort to conceal his outrage. "Did you even attempt to project a confinement field or slow him with a dazzlement?"

The HAAMR mage frowned, regarding my apprentice with a shocking measure of disdain. "What would you know of it, little conjurer boy?"

Colonel Dolgrim held up his gauntleted hand. "Enough, Major Caldrus. It is true that what happened here is unfortunate. Although I was too far away to assist, I saw the entire incident. The suspect did flee, and I believe my men acted appropriately under the circumstances. Nevertheless, we will open an internal investigation. If their actions cannot be justified, then Lieutenant Dagreth and Major Caldrus will be disciplined accordingly."

I turned away in disgust, waving aside the colonel's hollow assurances that such a lapse would not occur again. Whatever clues Melard might have provided had died with him.

"Our HAAMR units should be better trained than that," Tibblemond said, ambling up beside me. He doffed his bowler to scratch his head. "But their numbers have greatly expanded over the past few months. I suppose new recruits are apt to make such mistakes, however well trained."

We had come to another building partially demolished in the bombing, its broken fabricrete walls towering above us. I glanced back to make sure we were well away from anyone who might overhear, then took Tibblemond by the shoulders. "The sole reason for this bombing was to cover a theft. Guillem Melard admitted he was paid to take the artifact from the Dalewerth Institute, and he harbored no doubt that the men he turned it over to were the same men behind the bombing."

"Are you certain?" Tibblemond asked, his brow furrowing. "What is this artifact?"

I closed my eyes, dreading the very word. "A doomseed."

Tibblemond's face froze, his jaw open and eyes wide. "That's impossible! The Archidoxy destroyed every remaining one centuries ago. But stars above, you're serious, aren't you? What was Luthus Dalewerth doing with..." He stopped, perhaps realizing why I had led him to this secluded spot. "...with a *doomseed*?"

I dropped my hands from Tibblemond's shoulders and looked to the ruins of the Dalewerth Institute. "Dalewerth discovered it on his last expedition, and like any good scientist, he was probably trying to verify its authenticity before announcing the discovery. According to Melard, there was no radiant aurium inside. That means the thieves, or whoever they work for, will not be able to use the artifact. Radiant aurium is so rare now as to be practically non-existent."

"Thank the Archons for that," Tibblemond breathed, shaking his head. "Even so, we'd best make contingency plans to evacuate the Lord Governor and the Chamber of Industry before these lunatics make good on their threat."

I looked beyond the smoldering ruins around me, through the slowly clearing veil of smoke and ash. Dirigibles filled the midday sky above the rising towers of the Clockwork City. If the ancient legends were to be believed, the devastation wrought by even a single doomseed was utterly unimaginable. Yet, such wanton destruction was incongruous to the Disciple's stated goal. His manifesto sought to fuel the flames of an uprising, but the bombings instilled only fear. If he wished to stoke the fires of terror, why would he conceal the theft of the doomseed? The most terrifying possibility was that he wanted none of these things, and his true goal remained buried far beneath the chaos trailing in his wake.

"I doubt evacuating a few politicians will help matters." I

turned from Tibblemond to Keldon, clasping my hands behind me. "But there is one place I can go to find help. Come along Keldon. It is time we dropped by the Broken Spigot for a few frothy pints."

THE LAMP IN THE CORNER of our cramped nook had gone out, which suited me just as well. The enveloping shadows gave an added sense of privacy and kept the more curious patrons from gazing too long in our direction. Thankfully, no one in the Broken Spigot particularly cared about our conversation. Those who weren't engrossed by the dodgy jonko game on the far side of the common room were equally absorbed in their drink. But the boisterous merriment and jolly laughter that had always graced this old tavern was vexingly absent, a symptom which could only be attributed to the lingering specter of the recent bombings.

Rognar tore off a bite of ox tongue sausage, then washed it down with a gulp of thick stout. "Davlen help us all," he grumbled, plunking the tankard on the age-worn table. "An actual doomseed... Are you certain?"

"Quite certain," I answered. "I doubt they would have gone to the trouble of demolishing the Dalewerth Institute in an apparent gas main explosion unless they were trying to cover something up. Moreover, Luthus Dalewerth died believing he had found a doomseed, and Guillem Melard admitted to handing the artifact over to his mysterious associates just before the bombing."

Keldon sipped his ginger ale and leaned back in his chair. "A single doomseed can't possibly be as powerful as the legends say. Wiping entire armies from existence? Entire *cities*?" He shook his head. "Nothing can do that."

I studied the bottom of my empty mug and sighed. From what little was known, in the final days of that war, Marada threw its doomseeds against Atracus even as Gollan pyroclysms and thanathage plagues devastated our world. Blossoming above the demon-moon's black cities, they brought the war to its cataclysmic end. So fell Golla, and so fell Marada—each destroyed by the other. At least, that was what the legends told. Fifteen centuries had passed, and the shadow of that demonic war lingers still.

"There is no way to be sure," I admitted. "All we have left are legends."

"But without radiant aurium, the doomseed is useless, right?" Keldon asked. "They can't use ordinary aurium... Can they?"

My jaw tightened. The science of converting cold aurium to radiant aurium had thankfully been lost in the long dark age following the fall of Marada. But if the Servants of Vosh were indeed agents of the demonic forces of Atracus, then perhaps they did possess such knowledge.

"I certainly hope they can't," I answered simply. "Rognar, have you heard any murmurings of radiant aurium for sale in the black markets of Corradon?"

Rognar stroked his braided beard. "Aurium's hard enough to find on the black market, but radiant aurium's about as common as an Eldren lass in a Scaithi brothel. Bah! Is there even any still around?"

I nodded. "The largest remaining quantities are sealed in the Archidoxy's Fathomless Vault, in Valaris. But that's the most heavily fortified installation in the world. It would take nothing short of a fully mobilized army with juggernaut divisions and an aerial armada to even scratch their defenses."

"What about the Grand Lodge?" Keldon asked, referring to the largest and most prestigious lodge of the Magestrian Order.

I worried my chin. He was right. "The Magestrian Order has experimented with radiant aurium before, mostly in failed attempts to replicate the aetheric enrichment process used to create it. If there is any to be found in Corradon, the Grand Lodge would be the best place to look."

"Faugh!" Rognar balked. "They're no Fathomless Vault,

but only a clodnog with a death wish would try to pilfer the Grand Lodge's spell-warded vaults."

"Shorty's right," came a stern female voice. A cloaked figure swept into our corner nook, dropping to the bench beside Rognar and kicking battered boots up onto the table. She threw her hood back, revealing locks of dirty blond hair and a hooked scar on her cheek. "I wouldn't try breaking into the Grand Lodge even if I brought my best brothers with me. Lethal doesn't begin to describe the traps they've rigged around those vaults."

"Emileve," I said, surprised to see her. "Several bombings have hit the 12th District. I would have thought you'd be seeing to your people."

She nodded. "Already taken care of. We've corralled most of the underfolk through the sublevel tunnels into the 4th and 5th Districts, hoping to find refuge closer to the Central Core." She snagged a sausage from Rognar's plate and took a bite, then spat it out just as quick. "Taimon's luck! What's in this?"

"Ox tongue and onions," Rognar replied, snatching the remaining half back from her. "Maybe that'll teach you to ask before taking something that's not yours."

Emileve rolled her eyes. "Anyway, if you think it's bad topside, you should take a peek below the surface. Marauding gangs and armed thugs are pouring out from the 13th District into the sublevels of the 12th, and even here into the 5th District. Every industrial enclave from United Thaumaturgicals to the Omniworks have deployed their own mercs to guard their turf, leaving the masses to fend for themselves. This city is fast falling into chaos, but all you jacks and badgers seem interested in are these bodging mooks calling themselves the Brethren of Justice."

Rognar nodded. "It's even worse in the 14th District. Consolidated Omniworks barricaded the boarders of the 24th before the riots even started, leaving refugees from the 13th with nowhere else to go. There's already rioting along the Oppidan Causeway, and looters set fire to the Primavio Bazaar."

"What about the Armillian army?" Keldon asked. "If it's even half as bad as you say, shouldn't King Darius step in?"

"Most of Armillia's army is busy guarding the Erylion Frontier or aiding Glaven against the Karghen Warhold," I replied. "Besides, Corradon is a semi-autonomous city-state. The Lord Governor would have to place a formal petition through the Armillian Parliament to request a military intercession."

Emileve snorted. "There's not a whit of a chance of that. King Darius might rule Armillia from High Caelavar, but it's the counts of commerce and barons of industry that run Corradon. The Lord Governor is just a fat coin in the purse of the city's profiteering syndicates, and I doubt you'll find the Commissioner General of Vandor Tower of any better quality."

I leaned in toward Emileve, folding my arms on the table. "If your people are coordinating evacuations, then you should direct your efforts to getting as many as you can into the sublevels of the 26th District."

Emileve shook her head. "No one wants to tread that close to the Iron Barrens. We'd rather face roving gangs and mad bombers than the rusting horrors of those thrice-cursed boneyards. But if you're referring to the danger posed by the stolen doomseed, I'll just trust you to thwart whatever dastardly plot is afoot."

I straightened up and blinked, utterly taken aback. "How did you—"

"I've been eavesdropping ever since you sat down with Rognar." Emileve smirked when she saw my eyes widen, then she nodded to the Broken Spigot's inebriated patrons. "Don't worry. No one else here has enough wits about them to listen in."

I drummed my fingers on the table, then breathed out a resigned sigh. "Unfortunately, with the death of my only suspect, the trail has gone cold. Our best chance now is to ensure they never acquire a sufficient quantity of radiant aurium. Even so, I am not convinced they even intend to use the doomseed. They may simply want to hold it over us as a threat."

"But can you be certain?" Emileve argued. "These Brethren of Justice are not the crusaders of the common man they make themselves out to be. Their indiscriminate bombing spree is evidence enough of that."

I nodded, glad that she saw through their thin veneer. "The Brethren of Justice are a façade for a criminal organization that has orchestrated events over the past year to bring us to this bloody culmination."

Emileve's brassy smirk dropped to a frown, and she glanced at Rognar who just shrugged beneath his bulky duffle coat.

"They call themselves the Servants of Vosh," I explained, "and they have been gathering artifacts from the War of Golla and Marada to serve their own insidious ends. The doomseed is only the most recent addition to their collection."

Emileve pulled her boots off the table and leaned in closer, her frosty eyes narrowing as her expression grew more grave. "If they're as dangerous as you say, then there's good reason to think they'll carry out the deed." She glanced up for a moment, then return her attention to me. "In fact, this might explain what my scouts have been seeing."

"Your scouts?" I asked.

She gestured in sign and a lanky shape dropped onto the back of Keldon's chair. My apprentice yelped in alarm, and he might have sprang to the ceiling had his legs not collided with the table, knocking him back into his chair. The goblinesque creature jumped to the table and scampered up to Rognar, sniffing the remaining bits of sausage before turning away in disgust. Although it wore short knee breeches and an embroidered vest, I immediately recognized the creature's distinctive blue skin and large, owl-like eyes.

This one even had a small tool belt and a set of custom-fitted goggles over its flat wool cap.

"The homunculi we rescued," I said, raising an eyebrow. The homunculus inched up to me, then chittered excitedly as it remembered me, tiny hands forming quick gestures. "Is that some form of sign?"

"Mutespeak," Emileve replied. "It's used by our brotherhood to communicate silently when pulling a job. I had to expand the vocabulary, but they picked it up pretty fast. They're quite intelligent."

Scarcely two feet tall and as gangly as a goblin, these homunculi could sneak through ducts and drains that not even the most limber thieves could attempt. With over two dozen rescued from the brutish laboratories of Tavion Spagyricals, they had no doubt proved themselves indispensable to the Unseen Brotherhood.

"And the report?" I asked.

"As we move more refugees into the sublevels of the core districts, I've had to send my scouts further afield. When they returned with reports of unusual construction below the 1st District, I just assumed it was support pilings for that blasted Aetherspire. But they kept repeating the signs for 'dangerous men,' 'far deep,' 'lost place,' and 'round cave.' None of it made sense, until I realized the construction was deep within the Underworks."

"The Aetherspire?" I asked. The great Aetherspire—crown jewel of Corradon—was promised to provide the city with a near-limitless supply of aetheric energy, powering everything from levitating rails to engineless airships to telaetheric missives. Although construction had begun over three years ago, the Aetherspire was now all but complete. "There shouldn't be any more foundation work going on. Where is this construction, precisely?"

Emileve shrugged. "Directly beneath the Central Core, somewhere around the deep ruins of the city's old boilerworks complex."

"The Central Core?" Keldon asked. "If they activate the doomseed there..." his voice trailed off and he shook his head.

I leaned back in my chair, finding myself no closer to an answer. "If they want to maximize the doomseed's destructive effect, they might hide it somewhere below the core districts. But, in truth, they could put it anywhere in Corradon and be relatively certain of the city's complete annihilation. They could just hide it under a rubbish heap in any abandoned warehouse or derelict foundry and no one will ever find it."

"It could be scavengers," Rognar suggested. "The old boilerworks were picked clean by rustmongers centuries ago. But maybe someone found an older, untouched area deeper down."

Emileve tapped her finger on the table. "These weren't scavengers. I had trouble understanding what our little brothers were trying to tell me, but I got the impression the workers were professionals and were guarded by a crack mercenary outfit."

"Someone may be up to something down there," I agreed. "But Rognar's right. It could be anyone—archeologists, treasure hunters, salvage crews, or, indeed, the Servants of Vosh."

"I'll try to get some of my men into the area, but it won't be easy." Emileve nodded to the homunculus, who chittered excitedly and scurried back up to the rafters. "Our little brothers can sneak into and out of almost any place in this city completely unseen. Even so, it may be several days before I know more."

I stood up from the table and began buttoning my frock coat. "Unfortunately, we cannot afford several days. We will find out what we can from the Grand Lodge. If they do have some small supply of radiant aurium in their vaults, we can only hope it is still secure. And if it has been stolen, then we will at least find ourselves on the trail again."

Rognar chortled gruffly. "That's a mighty peculiar way of

looking at it."

"That's as may be, Rognar, but I still need you to root around your street contacts to see if anyone has been in the market for radiant aurium."

He nodded. "Will do, boss."

I tipped my hat to Emileve, and the Queen of Thieves mock-saluted in return. Keldon gulped down the last of his ginger ale and fell in behind me as I crossed the common room heading for the door. I now had three avenues to explore: the Grand Lodge, Emileve's report of mysterious construction beneath the city's core, and any leads Rognar might dredge up. None held any greater promise than the other, and all could be dead ends.

I could only hope that at least one might uncover some clue to unravel our enemy's elaborate web of crime and terror.

KELDON WATCHED THE CLOCKWORK CITY roll by, his fretful face reflected in the sooty window framing that great tapestry of industry and invention. Our steamrail leaned to one side as it entered the curve skirting the 1st District's outer perimeter, wheels clattering on rungs as it thundered across a bustling urban canyon. The city's Central Core rose like a vast plateau of gleaming glass and brass high above the sprawling landscape of alchemical refineries and automatronic manufactories. And in the center, the needle-like profile of the Aetherspire—now all but free of its scaffolding—rose hundreds of feet above Vandor Tower and even the Governor's Tower.

In the streets below, rioting crowds pressed against newly erected barriers setup by HAAMR units. We were too distant to hear their voices or read the signs they carried, but the fuel that enflamed the protesters was clear. The *Corradon Daily Post* had just released the Disciple's latest rambling tirade, purporting evidence of the grave corruption running through every level of the city's government. Three more bombings had followed the proclamation, each site scattered with pamphlets threatening that Corradon would soon 'tremble to its foundation' if the Lord Governor did not immediately stepdown.

Our train crossed beneath Mainspring Causeway, the great thoroughfare of Corradon, leaving the 5th District and emerging into the terraced city blocks of the opulent 6th. The view soon changed to brass-trimmed guildhalls, marble-columned libraries, and spire-crowned temples. We pulled into the terminal a few minutes later and disembarked with the train's other passengers. Not wishing to wait for a steam-coach, I flipped a ducat to a loitering rickshaw boy and gave him our destination. The ride through the crowded 6th District was bumpier than I would have preferred, and Keldon seemed genuinely terrified by the driver's reckless maneuvering across footbridges and down steep alley stairs. But the puttering cart made the trip in half the time of a more ponderous coach.

The Grand Lodge of the Magestrian Order dominated six square blocks of the district's eastern quarter. Walled by spellworked quartzstone, the Grand Lodge was an enclave in itself, made all the more impressive by its soaring statues, ancillary research facilities, private airship moorings, and the six levitating castle turrets orbiting the central tower. A fountain of light blazed like a golden crown upon the tower's pinnacle, radiating beams of prismatic aethergy which, though visually spectacular, served the more practical purpose of empowering the enclave's legendary defensive wards.

Keldon followed me through the main gate and up the marble steps to the visitor's entrance, his eyes wide and mouth agape. "This place is humming with chords of aetheric resonance," he whispered. "It's a veritable symphony!"

I looked to my severite wristbands and smiled, remembering the days before the accident that infused the alchemorph within me. All magic was music—a whirling fugue of resonating chords, shifting harmonies, elemental waveforms, and the resounding silver chorus of the higher astral light.

"You are old enough to apply," I said to him, pushing my hands into my coat pockets. "Your references and qualifications will more than guarantee your acceptance into the Magestrian Order."

Keldon looked away, his brow furrowed and eyes downcast. His apprenticeship with me was fast coming to an end and he would soon move on, as all apprentices must.

"Aetheric pattern verification," buzzed a voice nearby. The monitoring orb descended from its nook above the visitor's entrance, its crystal lenses focused squarely on my face. The orichalium coils of its twin antennae flickered with sparks as the spell-empowered automaton circled us in the air. "Expulsion in effect. Entry denied, Aldicus Vescard."

I sighed. "That is odd. I am still on relatively good terms with the present Grand Magister."

Keldon crossed his arms, looking up at the orb. "Or so you thought."

The guards standing to either side of the entrance glanced at each other, then looked back to me. Their expressions tensed and their hands tightened on their shock-staffs as they considered what to do should I not peaceably depart. But the hovering orb quickly resolved their quandary.

"Priority override authorized," the orb chirped as it bobbed in the air. "Entry permitted."

"There, you see," I said to Keldon, stepping passed the relieved guards and into the lobby. "I am already back in their good graces."

"That remains to be seen, Aldicus."

A richly garbed gentleman descended the lobby's wide marble staircase, his voluminous blue robes dragging behind him and his ornate staff tapping with every step. His silver beard was trimmed short and angular, in the Glaven style, and on his head he wore an orichalium skullcap, the coppery-red metal etched with sigils connecting its arrangement of empowered vizstones.

"Grand Magister Barthemius," I said, tipping my top hat and performing a quick bow in difference to the elder archmage. "Thank you for granting my entry. I know my past transgression prohibits me from—"

Barthemius waved his hand dismissively. "Others here will disagree, but as far as I'm concerned, you have more than paid for your infraction." He nodded to my severite wristbands. "And you will forever live with the consequences of your errant quest for immortality."

The muscles of my face tensed. My thoughts rarely dwelt upon those days, or upon that foolhardy endeavor that had nearly extinguished me—body, mind, and soul. The elemental transmutation of living quintessence was forbidden for good reason, but I, in my arrogance, had believed I had found the key hidden within *The Precepts of the Great Work*. My misinterpretation of 'the sage transforming both the subtle and the gross... through the unity of all unity' led me to the belief that I could convert my own body to a perfect entity of pure, elemental essence. I had been wrong—*horribly wrong*—and Barthemius had tried, in vain, to dissuade me from my mad pursuit. Ultimately, Barthemius had been the one who saved me, chaining me in severite when the alchemorph took hold. For that, I was forever in his debt.

I must have looked the fool standing there in silence, but a warm smile grew beneath the Grand Magister's beard and he slapped me on the arm. "So how does my old apprentice fair?"

Keldon blinked in surprise. "You apprenticed under the Grand Magister?"

"He wasn't the Grand Magister back then," I replied before turning back to Barthemius. "But I have come here on a matter of dire concern."

"Yes, and I do thank you for coming." Barthemius started off down the hall, flanked on either side by ornate tapestries and luminaries of shifting color set into the wood paneled walls. "To be honest, I am surprised Vandor Tower sent you, considering your past history with us. But what am I saying? You are the best detective this city has. Truth be told, with all the bombings, I had not dared to hope anyone would come around. What is a mere burglary compared to the threat of this Disciple and his ilk?"

I stopped, Keldon nearly crashing into me. "There has been a break-in?" I ask, my voice a whisper. "Just recently?"

"Isn't that why..." Barthemius turned and considered me, his brow furrowed in confusion. Then he stood a bit straighter and nodded. "Ah, I see. So Vandor Tower did not send you. Curious."

I drew a sharp breath, my fists clenching. "The radiant aurium... How much of it did they take?"

Barthemius blinked. "The radiant..." Then he sighed and shook his head. "Aldicus, what little radiant aurium we had was on loan from the Archidoxy, and it was under constant watch by a contingent of Temple Knights. But it was all returned to them several years ago when they reasserted the moratorium. The only aurium we have now is cold aurium, and most of that is burned to power the aethergy generators."

My body relaxed and I breathed out in relief. Had I truly been that terrified? I drew a deep breath and put on a diffident smile. "I had not been informed."

"Why would you have been informed?" Barthemius asked as we continued down the corridor. "The research was classified. Oh, it still is, so please don't go talking about it. One day, we might rediscover how to enrich cold aurium to create radiant aurium, but I'm afraid it will not be for centuries, if ever."

"I, for one, hope we never do," Keldon whispered.

Barthemius nodded. "Why did you come, if not about the theft?" He took a side corridor, then started up a set of stairs leading to one of the ancillary research wings. "I doubt you would be here for a social call with the city fast falling into anarchy."

"I have reason to believe this Disciple, as he calls himself, is trying to acquire a quantity of radiant aurium."

Barthemius shook his head. "I doubt the Disciple is anything more than a madman, or at worse, a fanatical cult leader. Should he manage to get his hands on radiant aurium, he is more likely to disintegrate himself than harm anyone else. Even with all our precautions, our own research efforts cost the lives of four mages and crippled six others, and that was with just a thimbleful of the stuff. Radiant aurium is not a substance to be trifled with."

"What, exactly, was stolen from here?" Keldon asked. He quickly looked down and gulped. "Grand Magister, sir."

"Keldon Veldanor, isn't it?" Barthemius gave my apprentice a once over and smiled. "Are your studies progressing well?"

"Yes, sir," he replied. "But that's not important right now. If something was stolen, there could still be a connection with the Disciple and his schemes."

Barthemius shook with a jovial laugh. "Here you stand, prompted to proclaim your accomplishments before the Grand Magister of the Magestrian Order, and instead you insist upon pursuing matters of more pressing concern." He smiled through his beard, then stepped into the room we had come to. "Good lad."

Following the Grand Magister, we found ourselves in one of the Grand Lodge's many research libraries. Custodians and researchers alike hastened between densely packed rows of technical journals, astrological almanacs, and reference volumes, while studious mages hunched over softly glowing tomes in their reading alcoves. The library's two delving mirrors were both in use by security mages, distinguished by their black and silver robes, and the codicon transcriptor was also under scrutiny by a wild-haired gearmage mumbling to himself as he poked at the empowered mechanism's brasswork innards.

Two helper orbs descended from their nests in the room's chandelier, chirping happily about how they could assist in any matter of research. Both looked practically new. I shooed the automatons away, then noticed the remains of their thoroughly smashed predecessors heaped on a table nearby.

"Someone broke into this repository?" I asked.

"This is an ancillary repository, and it's not as heavily guarded as Magestrian Tower," Barthemius explained. He brought us to the table where they had collected the remains of the two smashed helper orbs, along with several other pieces of evidence. In addition to a sizable lump of melted tektite glass, the table held a pile of shattered aetheronic emission tubes and a silver amulet set with three burned-out vizstones.

I took a moment to study the items. "Whoever is behind this was fully prepared to get in and out as quickly as possible, and they knew what they were after." I glanced up, spotting a window near the ceiling that had recently been sealed over. "The perpetrator entered through that window, having come with some means to quickly melt tektite." I nodded to the lump of tektite on the table. "But the intruder first needed to disrupt the watchdog egregores and counteract any perimeter intrusion wards. I suspect those broken emission tubes were part of an aetheric device designed for that task. Once inside, the helper orbs approached to greet the intruder, as they are apt to do, and were summarily dispatched when the intruder mistook them for security automatons."

"Or perhaps he was just annoyed by their incessant nagging," Keldon offered, waving his arms as he shooed away the two hovering orbs once more.

"He or she," I amended, "then invoked an incredibly sophisticated empowerment, possibly even an egregore, burning out three vizstones on that amulet—an expensive sacrifice to say the least."

Keldon, with his key in hand, began scanning the

vizstones. The security mages had certainly already done so, but I allowed him to continue.

"There's not much left of the empowerment's residual imprint," Keldon said after a moment. "But there was definitely an egregore inside. Probably a verimorphic simulacrum or a specialized circumvention egregore."

Barthemius nodded approvingly. "Very good. Now, what might you surmise from this assessment?"

Keldon glanced at me, but I only raised an eyebrow. He swallowed nervously, then cleared his throat. "Your libraries have curator egregores, right?" When Barthemius nodded, Keldon continued. "I would surmise that the intruder was attempting to seize control over the curator egregore. That would grant access to the archive's index, as well as all codicons. Has the curator been analyzed?"

"You have certainly instructed your apprentice well," Barthemius said to me. Then his beaming smile drew serious. "Your assessment is correct, Keldon Veldanor. Unfortunately, the curator was completely destroyed—either in the attempt to take control or after the fact to remove evidence."

I looked to the delving mirrors. They were typically used to recall visual recordings stored on specialized vizstones, but they could also show anything seen by the curator or watchdog egregores during the night or previous day. The mirrors presently displayed nothing more than shifting patterns of mist, and both security mages were now bickering with one another.

"It appears your security mages have grown quite frustrated in their attempt to recall any impressions of the break-in," I pointed out. "The intruder must have been scry-guarded."

Keldon sighed. "This was a master heist. But why leave so much evidence behind? Given enough time, those empowerments could be reconstructed, perhaps enough to learn something about whoever composed them."

Barthemius nodded to the codicon transcriptor. “The intruder attempted to use the transcriptor to copy several codicons. I suspect the intention was to copy the codicons, destroy the curator, then take the remains of the broken emission tubes and the burned-out amulet before escaping back through the window. That would leave us without any clue as to what was taken since the original codicons would still be here. However, our perimeter egregores detected the disruption in the intrusion wards and alerted security. A team was here within minutes, and the intruder chose to flee with the codicons before copies could be transcribed.”

I nodded. “Which codicons were stolen?”

“We still have other copies, of course.” Barthemius took a neatly bound book from a nearby desk, its boarders trimmed in brass with a lattice of orichalium woven between the vizstones imbedded on its front and back covers. He opened the book to the middle and a waterfall of softly glowing text and diagrams spilled down the pages. “The codicons held centuries worth of research on Maradian over-science, along with their accompanying commentaries, rebuttals, and appendices. None of it was particularly secret, but the archivists are combing through the texts to be sure.” He nodded to the other researchers in the room.

I took the codicon and the book immediately went dark, the text vanishing from its pages. “Blast,” I said, glancing at my severite wristbands. I handed the book to Keldon. “Have a look for me, would you.”

“Sure, boss,” Keldon replied, taking the empowered book. The vizstones lit up once more, and text scrolled across the pages as my apprentice thumbed through. “Am I looking for anything in particular?”

“We are looking for any reason why the thief would be interested in these treatises.” I considered this for a moment, wondering how much I should reveal to the Grand Magister regarding the Shadow Man and the Servants of Vosh. Barthemius was a good fellow, but he had an unfortunate tendency to babble, and I was not particularly keen on having anyone else overhear a sensitive tidbit or two. "The cult this so-called Disciple leads has a rather perverse interest in artifacts from the War of Golla and Marada."

"You mentioned radiant aurium, fearing someone had broken in to steal the substance," Barthemius said. "Are they in possession of a device fueled by radiant aurium?"

"Radiant aurium is extremely dangerous, even by itself," I replied, evading the answer. "This is one occasion I am thankful to have been mistaken about the perpetrator's intentions."

I looked over Keldon's shoulder as he continued through the pages, sometimes giving one of the vizstones a twist to switch the codicon to the next treatise. Diagrams, sigils, and text flowed like endless streams across each new page, revealing research and commentaries on Maradian over-science. But from what I saw, the treatises contained little more than theories, suppositions, and outright flights of fancy. So much had been lost after the War of Golla and Marada that we seemed as children before the unfathomable height of their marvelous wonders.

"Is there anything in these texts you would consider to be of interest?" I asked.

Barthemius folded his arms, pressing his staff against his shoulder. "To scholars such as myself, it is all of great interest. But nothing that could be of any practical use to these anarchists. You must understand, these are not designs or schematics for Maradian technology. We have only deciphered a fraction of their over-science, and know even less of Golla's." He scratched his short beard in thought. "Having said that, Varcconi's treatise on teleaetheric communications is probably the most important of the works, although Mannius's theories on the astral bridge comprises the most compelling research."

I nodded. According to the Archidoxy, the War of Golla and Marada began when Marada opened an 'astral bridge' to

Atracus, pressed by their hunger for new resources. But the Demon Lords of Atracus held appetites infinitely greater than even Marada's mythical greed. Legions of fellspawn warriors, monstrous abominations, and sorcerous war machines crossed through, decimating our world a dozen times over. Out of sheer desperation, the mages of Marada devised the most destructive weapon ever conceived: doomseeds. But by then, all was already lost. The Archidoxy held this as an object lesson on greed and hubris, but I was only concerned with the historical facts.

"Do any of the works touch on radiant aurium?" I asked.

"Indeed. May I?" Barthemius held out his hand for the codicon and Keldon promptly returned the book. The Grand Magister shifted the text through several different works, skimming through the pages as he did. "Many of the treatises mention both cold aurium and radiant aurium, but only in reference to powering Marada's most advanced technology. Varcconi detailed his theories on the conversion of aurium to radiant aurium, but we have since disproved his ideas in our own failed attempts to create the substance. Mannius's work cataloged the various uses of radiant aurium, from powering solaonic reactors, aether vortex engines, doomseeds, and the astral bridge itself." He stopped paging through and smiled. "Ah, here we are."

The page was from Mannius's *Fifth Treatise on the Inquiry into Maradian Aetheronics*, and showed a sketch of lines, boxes, and coils, the accompanying text describing it as a mirage projector, or miragram. Barthemius turned through several more pages detailing numerous other sketches crudely illustrating wonders the author knew of only from legend.

"Marada's technology advanced beyond the limitations of physical mechanisms, developing into the aetheric machinery of their supernal over-science," Barthemius explained. "As such, we are quite limited in our ability to study what few artifacts remain, let alone reconstruct even their most rudimentary devices. But they still needed to generate aethergy to power their machines. Although most of their generators burned cold aurium, their solaonic reactors harnessed the awesome potential of radiant aurium."

He stopped on a page detailing a solaonic reactor, drawn here as a circular cavern with a convex column at the center. The text described, in only the vaguest terms, that such machines harnessed radiant aurium in their elemental annihilation reactions, releasing prodigious quantities of aetheric energy.

"Nothing here could allow anyone to build such devices." Barthemius turned several more pages and shook his head. "However, this text would be an excellent guide to their use for anyone possessing a well-preserved artifact."

The next page showed the narrow, ovaloid-shape of a doomseed, followed by passages taken from the colorful prose of mythology describing the blinding rainbow blossoms of their all-consuming light. At the bottom of the page was black-shaded sphere, circumscribed by metal rings. The text identified it as a radiant aurium containment sphere.

"Thankfully, nothing capable of harnessing radiant aurium survived the War of Golla and Marada," Barthemius went on to say. "We have only the vaguest hints as to—"

"Wait," I said, stopping him from turning the page. The image of the sphere was familiar, but I could not place where I had seen it before. "What is this?"

"Ah, yes." Barthemius said. "Radiant aurium was contained several ways, but this was how it was stored for use in doomseeds. Only a few of these have ever been discovered, and those are safely contained in the Fathomless Vault. Most radiant aurium was kept in spell-seal diamanium cylinders, and occasionally stasis boxes. Woe be the soul who opens a Maradian stasis box containing radiant aurium."

A black sphere circumscribed by rings. No, not black, but obsidian. *A multi-ringed obsidian sphere...* My breath caught and my skin prickled with a sudden chill as I remembered where I had seen that description before.

"It was on the list," I whispered, recalling the list of items the Servants of Vosh had stolen using their diaphamorphic transmutation belt. "Archons, no... They already have it!"

Keldon looked at me befuddled, then his eyes widened in shock.

"Who has what?" Barthemius ask. "Aldicus, you look as though you're about to faint, and your apprentice looks little better."

My panicked eyes met Barthemius's questioning gaze. "They already have the radiant aurium!"

I spun on my heels and hastened for the arched door leading out of the library. Barthemius called after me, but I had not a moment to spare.

"Where are we going?" Keldon asked, hurrying to keep up with me.

"To Vandor Tower," I replied, my frock coat billowing as I swept down the corridor. "If that doomseed blossoms beneath the core districts, *millions* will perish. Only the Lord Governor can authorize the evacuation of Corradon, assuming a city such as this can even be evacuated. I cannot fathom how the Servants of Vosh might profit from such senseless destruction, but I will not risk the lives of millions on a hunch that this is all some mad ruse. Those are stakes that even *I* would not dare gamble."

JACKS, CLERKS, AND INSPECTORS HUSTLED through the halls of Vandor Tower, a roiling turmoil of pounding feet, slamming doors, shouting orders, and urgent replies. Reporters jammed the stairwell, bombarding every passing officer with a rush of questions. Their efforts to storm the Tower were only kept at bay by a valiant clutch of panic-faced recruits. Somewhere, the all-hands alarm bell clamored its three-two-three knell, and voices rang through brass call tubes alerting personnel to changes in the duty schedule. Two HAAMR troopers clomped into the hall, fully armored but for the helms carried at their sides, and the crowd broke like parting waters to let the pair lumber by.

I ducked into a maintenance stairwell, motioning for Keldon to follow, then dashed up six narrow flights pausing only to make way for the clerks hurrying about their errands. The pneumatic lifts on the administration level connected to the Tower's summit, and would be far less busy than those in the hectic lower levels. Even so, nearly two dozen personnel milled about waiting for one of the two lifts. The Tower was three times busier than normal, with every shift called upon to pull double duty.

"Do you think he'll have time to see us?" Keldon asked as we squeezed into the crowded lift. We were met by more than a few disparaging frowns, but no one voiced an objection.

"He will *make* time," I replied, pulling Keldon further inside as the gate rattled closed.

Gears groaned and pneumatics hissed, and the lift began its sluggish ascent, laden by twice its certified load. The lift stopped several floors up, letting two people off. We stopped again two more floors up, and another inspector impatiently shoved his way aboard. I sighed. At this rate, we could have climbed the remaining forty stories in half the time this would take. When we finally reached the upper floors, only two Vandorian officers remained with us on the lift. Both wore the winged shield badges on their uniform coats distinctive to the Vandorian Air Corp. I had seen *Justiciar* docked at one of the Tower's airship moorings, along with a cargo dirigible docked at the other.

"Do you serve aboard *Justiciar*?" I asked.

"Yes, sir," both men crisply replied.

Captain Cheyron ran a tight ship, but something was wrong. "Wasn't *Justiciar* undergoing maintenance?"

"We were recalled early, sir," one of the men replied. "The city is in a state of emergency."

The pneumatic lift hissed to a stopped and the gate rattled

open. Both officers hurried into the hall and joined a line of other men heading up the stairs to the mooring deck. Turning the other way, I looked down a decorated hall of plaques and memorials that ended at the burnished bronze doors of Vandor Tower's highest office.

I straightened my hat, buttoned up my frock coat, and fluffed out my cravat. "Time to see if the boss is in."

"Aldicus!" Tibblemond exclaimed. The chief inspector barreled in from an intersecting hall, huffing to catch his breath. "I'm so glad you're here. I wouldn't trust anyone else to the Lord Governor's safety."

Keldon looked from Tibblemond to me and back to Tibblemond again. "The Lord Governor is here?"

The chief inspector nodded. "He is. All members of the Chamber of Industry as well. They're being evacuated."

"Evacuated?" I asked. I had come to advise the Commissioner General to evacuate all of Corradon, not just the Lord Governor and his Chamber of Industry.

A second man followed Tibblemond into the hall, first glancing to the stairs leading up to the mooring deck, then turning back to consider us. He, too, wore a wing and shield badge on his shoulder, but his golden epaulettes and double-breasted service coat distinguished his rank, as did his traditional captain's cap.

"Detective Vescard," the man said with a nod.

"Captain Cheyron," I greeted back. He was a deputy commissioner by rank, effectively equivalent to a brigadier, but the old navy title held honorific meaning for any shipmaster. "I was just on my way to see the Commissioner General. Have you seen him?"

"The Commissioner General is personally overseeing the deployment of all HAAMR units to secure the core districts, leaving me in charge of evacuating the Lord Governor and the Chamber."

I drew a sharp breath. "*All* HAAMR units have been deployed?" I looked to Tibblemond. "Is this true?"

Tibblemond nodded. "Along with scores of patrol automatons, armored wagons, and full airship support." He sighed, seeing the concern on my face. "There have been four more bombings, two of them in the 3rd District. But that's not all. Have a look at the latest manifesto."

I took the paper from Tibblemond's hand. The manifesto read much the same as the others, but ended on a more ominous note.

> As a forest blaze must burn away the old growth to make way for the new, so must we burn away the rotting heart of Armillia by the righteous light of our Holy Conflagration.
>
> - The Disciple

"The doomseed," Keldon gasped.

The manifesto crumpled in my hand. The meaning of the threat could not have been more clear. "The Lord Governor must order the immediate evacuation of the city."

Tibblemond sputtered. "Aldicus! You know Corradon couldn't be evacuated even if we had a week. And didn't you say they still need to acquire some radiant aurium?"

"They had it all along," I admitted, my voice grim. But he was right. Corradon could not be evacuated without starting a mass panic, and then no one would escape in time.

"Archons help us," Tibblemond gasped.

"So, they really mean to use it?" Captain Cheyron asked, clearly aware of the doomseed. Tibblemond must have filled him in, probably as part of his briefing to the Commissioner General. "I take it you were unsuccessful in tracking down the doomseed's location."

I grimaced, the sudden realization of my failure striking like a sledgehammer. "I have enlisted additional help, but if the doomseed has been planted in the sublevels of this district, or in the Underworks below, I doubt we can find it in time."

Cheyron set his jaw, then started up the stairs to the mooring deck, the crewmen pressing to the side as their captain hurried passed. "*Justiciar* will depart with the Lord Governor and the Chamber of Industry as soon as we're aboard."

I followed Captain Cheyron onto the mooring deck, Keldon and Tibblemond just behind me.

"Arleia," Keldon choked. I could see the fear and anguish painted across his face, tears forming in his eyes. "We have to find Arleia and Leta. And Rognar, too. We can't just leave them here to..." His face grew pale. "Aldicus, what do we do?"

I didn't answer. Nothing about this case made any sense. Why would the Servants of Vosh destroy Corradon? What did they have to gain? Chaos for chaos's sake? Destruction for destruction's sake? No, the designs they had set into motion were neither the schemes of petty criminals nor the whims of deranged lunatics. Every plan had an objective, every theft had a purpose, and every act of subterfuge brought them that much closer to the end game of their sinister conspiracy. The destruction of Corradon could not have been their goal. They sought something greater and far more terrible. But what, I did not know.

I picked up my pace, falling in beside Cheyron as we neared the gangway to *Justiciar.* "Captain, where are you taking the Lord Governor?"

"To High Caelavar," Cheyron replied. "There is no safer place in all of Armillia. King Darius, the First Minister, and all members of Parliament are already there, defended by the First Fleet and two divisions of the Armillian army."

I stopped at the gangway door. *High Caelavar...*

Corradon was the largest city in Armillia, and indeed, the world. But High Caelavar was the ancient palace-city of House Anthocles and the seat of the Parliament of Armillia.

I took the crumpled manifesto from my pocket and unraveled the paper. "They shall burn away the rotting heart of Armillia," I read, my voice a whisper. Not Corradon.

Armillia. "Oh, fangle-fop!"

"Aldicus?" Tibblemond asked.

With King Darius, the First Minister, and Parliament all gathered in High Caelavar, the arrival of the Lord Governor and the entire Chamber of Industry would place every member of Armillia's highest offices in a single, concentrated location. Releasing a doomseed above High Caelavar would throw Armillia into utter chaos, opening a power vacuum which, in the absence of the King, Parliament, and Corradon's government, would result in a succession war as the old aristocracy clamored to exert their claims to rule. The bait was placed, the trap was set, and the prey stood but a breath away from slaughter.

The doomseed wasn't hidden anywhere in Corradon... But then, where was it? And how were they going to secret it in to High Caelavar?

"*Justiciar* was undergoing maintenance, yes?" I asked the captain, recalling what the crewmen had said in the lift. "Where?"

"Omniworks dry dock 7, in the 24th District," Captain Cheyron replied. "We had to cut it short to come here, but the work was only part of our routine engine upkeep."

"Consolidated Omniworks?" Keldon asked. "Didn't Rognar say something about them deploying their own mercenary security force and blockading the 24th District before the riots even started?"

I nodded. "How many Omniworks personnel had access to your ship?"

"Around sixty, perhaps more," Cheyron answered. "But they were all cleared by..." He hesitated, then glanced to the gangway bridge. "By Omniworks security."

I stepped closer to the captain. "Get the Lord Governor and the Chamber members off your ship immediately." Cheyron furrowed his brow, and I continued. "The doomseed is not hidden beneath the streets of Corradon. It has been smuggled aboard *Justiciar*."

The captain's eyes widened in sudden realization. "I'll order the ship evacuated. We will search her stem to stern, and if—"

"No," I said, cutting him off. "They could still activate the doomseed if they realize we're onto them. Your ship must depart precisely as planned." I looked across the mooring deck to the gangway bridge leading to the cargo dirigible. "Get the Lord Governor and the others aboard that cargo dirigible and have the ship set course due west. If we fail to find and disarm the doomseed in time, they'll at least be able to establish an interim government in Aeleon."

Captain Cheyron nodded, then rushed down the gangway shouting orders even as he ducked through the boarding hatch. We followed just behind the captain, moving aside as the Lord Governor and the sixteen members of the Chamber of Industry filed back out of the ship, arguing profusely with the poor crewmen who had the misfortune of escorting the pompous city lords. The Lord Governor—a duke by title—was a rotund peacock of a man, and the clutch of merchant princes and barons of industry following him looked equally garish in their brightly colored tailcoats, double-high top hats, and ruffles all around.

"You! You're that Vescard fellow, aren't you?" the Lord Governor barked as he passed me in the gangway. He stepped up to me, fat finger waving in my face. "What's the meaning of this? The Commissioner General tells me there's a doomseed somewhere in this city and I have no wish to remain a moment longer than I must!"

I considered, if only for a moment, that we should simply let them stay aboard *Justiciar*. "This is for your safety, Your Grace. I have reason to believe your evacuation aboard *Justiciar* has been anticipated, and so you will be secreted away aboard a less conspicuous vessel."

The Lord Governor turned away in a huff, but followed the crewmen to the cargo dirigible's gangway, the Chamber lords trailing just behind like a grumbling gaggle of goslings.

"See that they get safely aboard the ship," I said to Tibblemond. "Then do some digging into Consolidated Omniworks. If they have been infiltrated, or worse yet, if they are fully cognizant accomplices, we will need to act before that trail is swept as clean as the others."

Tibblemond gave a quick nod and hurried off. I gave Keldon a reassuring pat on the shoulder and wondered if I should send him along with Tibblemond. But the grim truth was, if the doomseed did blossom, he would probably be better off aboard *Justiciar* than in Vandor Tower. At least then he would be disintegrated instantaneously, rather than suffering his last agonizing moments in the screaming maelstrom of the doomseed's horrible light, the city and all within slowly crumbling to inert cinders and desiccated ash around him.

For a ship as large as *Justiciar*, her corridors proved to be surprisingly narrow, cluttered by pipes and conduits, and divided by bulkheads passable only through low clearance hatchways. Captain Cheyron stopped at an intersecting corridor just ahead of us, waving down several of his officers on their way to the bridge.

"Lieutenant Dallin, Sergeant Greston," Cheyron said to them. He turned back to me and nodded. "Aldicus Vescard has come aboard to locate an extremely dangerous device that may have been smuggled aboard. Lend whatever assistance you can and make sure he has everything he needs."

"A device, sir?" one of the men asked.

Cheyron nodded. "Yes, sergeant. A doomseed."

The two men stood frozen in dumbfounded disbelief, but Captain Cheyron just continued down the corridor calling out orders to passing crewmen as he went. "Retract the gangway. Release all moorings. Make ready the impellers. And will someone please tell me where I left my pipe?"

The two men continued to stand in shock, neither one having recovered from the captain's revelation.

“Perhaps we should begin at the stern and make our way forward,” I said to them. “But I am open to suggestions.”

“Sir,” Sergeant Greston said, snapping to attention. He was decidedly younger than Lieutenant Dallin, perhaps a year or two older than Keldon, but he spoke with a crisp voice, absent even a hint of hesitation. “This ship is 800 feet from stem to stern. It could take hours to root through every trunk, crate, and locker.”

Keldon took out his key, then turned from one side to another holding the glowing talisman before him. “Radiant aurium should have a strong aetheric resonance. I may not be able to pinpoint its exact location, but...” He hesitated, then shook his head. “Blast. What kind of engine does this ship have?”

The two men glanced at one another. “Two turbines drive the ship’s impeller engines,” Lieutenant Dallin replied. He glanced at Keldon’s key, then elaborated. “Elemental steam turbines, supplemented by auxiliary ebonite vapor boilers.”

I thought for a moment. The swirling storm of raw aethergy generated by the elemental turbines would washout all but the most intense aetheric impressions. “The radiant aurium will be well-shielded within its containment sphere,” I explained. “Even so, it should give off a distinctive aetheric resonance, detectable once we are close enough. Unfortunately, the noise from these elemental turbines will likely washout such aetheric impressions.”

Keldon looked at me and smiled, no doubt deducing the answer I had also arrived at. “They’ve hidden it in the engine room. Or at least near the engine room.”

I smiled back at him, then looked to Dallin and Greston. “We will begin our search in the engine room. Please lead the way.”

Dallin and Greston nodded and we followed them as they started off down the corridor. The droning hum of the impellers grew louder, and I felt the deck beneath me gently sway. Officers and crewmen dashed through the corridor as the ship got underway, hatches opening and closing, boots clattering up and down ladders and across the grated metal floors of the decks above and below us.

A whistle sounded and Captain Cheyron's voice piped over the ship's call tubes. "All hands, assume action stations. Make ready for clipping speed as we head out to sea."

"We're heading out to sea?" Keldon asked.

"A wise precaution," I replied. "If we fail, Corradon might actually stand a chance, assuming this ship is fast enough."

"Fast?" Lieutenant Dallin asked, a proud smile growing on his face. "You've never been aboard *Justiciar*, have you, sir?"

The ship listed suddenly to starboard, impeller engines howling as we accelerated, gaining altitude. I stumbled into the corridor wall, catching Keldon as I did, but Dallin and Greston just leaned into the turn. After a moment of grumbling, Keldon recovered his footing and we continued astern, following Dallin and Greston down another corridor skirting the ship's outer hull. The occasional porthole provided an unprecedented nighttime view of the city, and my breath caught as I gazed upon that vast expanse of towers, refineries, manufactories, and bustling avenues far below.

The ship continued its turn, rounding an immense, needle-like tower rising higher than *Justiciar*'s present altitude. *The Aetherspire.* Now all but complete and crowned by a coil-wrapped finial, the tower already seemed to hum with its promise of limitless aethergy for all. I narrowed my eyes, considering what Emileve had said. Something was going on in the derelict depths of the Underworks directly beneath the Central Core. No, not simply beneath the Central Core, but beneath the Aetherspire itself. The Aetherspire, whose chief construction contractor was none other than Consolidated Omniworks...

"Aldicus," Keldon called, pulling me from my thoughts. We had come to a hatchway open to a flight of ladder stairs leading up. "I think I'm picking something up." He looked at his talismanic key and nodded. "It's faint, but it could be the shadow of some extremely powerful aethergy source seeping through the interference from the turbines."

"That's the engineering deck," Sergeant Greston said, nodding to the deck above the ladder. "We have a lot of ground to cover if it's hidden in that tangled nest of gears and pipes."

Once up the ladder, we passed through several more hatchways and entered the steaming bowels of *Justiciar*'s clattering engine room. Men in grease-stained overalls and striped caps hurried about their work, checking gauges and adjusting valves, then rushing to where the next piercing whistle demanded their attention.

We pressed on, moving along the catwalk paralleling the twin axle shafts, spinning like whirlwinds wreathed in crackling arcs of aetheric energy. A set of hypoid gears connected the axles to the ship's spell-empowered engines, and the howling maelstrom of their captive elementals drove the twin turbines with all the fury of a thunderstorm. They were not sentient elementals, of course, but the wild flotsam common to the lower aether.

Keldon said something, pointing to an access panel in the grated floor off to one side of the turbines. His words were lost in the deafening engine room noise, but he clearly intended to open the panel and venture into the oil-greased snarls below. Several mechanics approached as he struggled to lift the access panel, their expressions both bemused and befuddled.

"We have the captain's permission to be here!" I yelled, my voice scarcely audible. "We believe a dangerous device has been smuggled aboard."

One of the men stepped closer. Although he wore the same overalls as everyone else, the patch on his shirt sleeve identified him as a major. He was only just shorter than myself, but with his stocky frame and the bulbous nose jutting out above his scraggly beard, I could not help but wonder if there wasn't a bit of Dworghen blood in his veins.

"I be Beldwick, the chief engineer," he barked back. "Nothing gets into me engine room without me knowing 'bout it."

"Then you know about the doomseed?" I asked. "Excellent. Please direct us to its present location."

Chief Beldwick looked aghast, and though it took a moment for the other men to realize what I said, all were soon glancing about in fearful expectation.

"What did you say?" the chief engineer demanded. "That's impossible!"

"Is it?" I asked. "Did you personally supervise every worker from Consolidated Omniworks? Did you search through every crate and box they hauled in here? Did you double check every pipe, bolt, and gauge they might have modified?"

Beldwick shook his head slowly. "I do me final inspection when they be done," he yelled over the din, "but the ship be called to duty before the refit be finished. I haven't had time..." his voice trailed off, and his eyes fell upon the access panel Keldon had been trying to open. "Is it down there?"

I nodded, and the chief engineer motioned for two of his men to lift the access panel. Below, a hodgepodge of pipes, conduits, and gears crowded the cramped and dirty crawlspace. I grimaced, realizing it would be a tight fit for any of us to climb down there, let alone find and disarm the doomseed. Then Chief Beldwick gave a few more orders, and the men jumped to work with spanners in hand, loosening bolts and pulling away entire sections of the grated metal floor above the crawlspace.

"That should make finding it easier," Keldon yelled.

I stepped up to the edge of the exposed crawlspace, brushing back my frock coat as I began to step down. I stopped and pulled my foot back, my brow furrowing as I caught sight of something scurrying along the shadowed edges of the pipe-cluttered trench.

"Keldon, do you detect—"

A scream eclipsed the engine's howling turbines and clattering gears. I wheeled around and saw one of the crewmen's staggering away, hands grasping some mechanical apparatus clinging to his face. *No, not an apparatus...* With its four crystal eyes, eight articulated legs, and spark tubes rising from its abdomen, it could only have been one thing. The man fell to the deck dead, blood spraying as buzz-saw mandibles ripped into his skull with horrifying efficiency.

"Clickspring spiders!" I yelled. Someone had left a nasty surprise for anyone unfortunate enough to stumble upon the doomseed.

"By Dodecon's Hammer!" Beldwick swore. Another hand-sized spider sprang from the crawlspace and he battered it away with a hefty pipe wrench. "We be under attack!"

More spiders scuttled up from the crawlspace, their razor-edged legs clattering on the deck, serrated mandibles buzzing as optographic registers scanned for the nearest prey. The boilermen scrambled to arm themselves, yelling as they seized sledgehammers, pneumatic rivet guns, and pipe wrenches. Someone sounded the alarm, and the engine room became a battlefield—crewmen screaming, dying, and mechanical spider parts flying. Dallin and Greston drew their bolt-batons and threw themselves into the fray, spark-bolts striking the swift moving targets.

"These things are empowered!" Keldon exclaimed. He flipped his key in his hand and snapped a dart of aetheric energy, blasting one spider into scrap. I was in no position to complain about his use of offensive empowerments. "I think they're siphoning aethergy from the turbines. We have to shut them down."

"We can't shut down those turbines," I yelled over the now deafening clamor of roaring engines and frantic battle. "If we fail, Corradon's only hope lies with Captain Cheyron's efforts to get *Justiciar* out to sea."

I considered pulling a pin to drop one of my severite wristbands, but with so many men in the close confines of the engine room, the result would be disastrous. Thankfully, the alarm had brought a squad of Vandorian Guardsmen, and the bluejacks charged through the hatch with bolt-batons sparking. I forced my attention back to Keldon and the crawlspace.

"We have our job to do," I said, pointing to the open crawlspace. "Let the Guardsmen do theirs."

Keldon's face grew pale, his eyes widening as he considered that brutal killing trench now overrun with clickspring spiders. But we had no choice. We had to find the doomseed before all was lost.

I jumped into the crawlspace trench, kicking aside one of the spiders and raising my arm as another sprang for my face. The small automaton bounced aside and hit the floor curling into a ball, my severite wristband having disrupted whatever spell empowered its control gears. Keldon blasted two more, and I knocked aside another one, pressing on as the jacks and crewmen battled the swarm. Bodies fell around us, and Keldon gritted his teeth, his eyes half-closed as he tried not to look at the mangled remains.

A dozen or more spiders scurried about, but I spotted four standing guard before a recessed alcove at the end of the crawlspace, hunched low and ready to pounce. Two attacked immediately, leaping with forelegs raised and mandibles buzzing. I brought my left arm up to block with my severite wristband, but the thing landed on my upper arm—its legs jabbing like tiny spears as buzzing blades tore into my coat sleeve. I screamed, hot pain ripping through my arm, and I slammed myself against the side of the crawlspace, crushing the mechanical menace between my shoulder and the pipe-laden wall.

Keldon dispatched the second spider in a blast of sparkling blue light, but the two remaining spiders pounced for him even as he fired. Throwing myself in front of my apprentice, I grabbed one of the spiders and slammed it against another iron pipe, but the last one latched onto my back. Buzz-saw mandibles tore into the fabric of my frock coat, and I flung the coat from my shoulders, yanking my arms free as I spun around. The machine thrashed beneath my coat, and I brought my shoe down against the bulging form, shattering its glass-encased spark tubes with a satisfying crunch.

"Aldicus, you're bleeding!" Keldon yelled. "I'll get help."

"No time," I gasped. My white cambric shirt was soaked through with blood, sticking wetly to my left arm and back. "Find some tools... Hurry!"

I threw my hat aside, then whipped off my cravat to serve as a tourniquet for my arm. Keldon returned with a hefty toolbox, and he helped tie off the tourniquet while I hurried to find the right sized socket wrench. Loosening the bolts around the alcove proved even more time consuming, and when I had finally removed the panel, my heart sank seeing the intricate mess of twisted wires, copper coils, ticking gears, and glowing spark tubes cobbled together atop a casket-like box which must have been the doomseed. I had no idea where to begin, and the baffling tangle of clunky modern components jury-rigged to the advanced over-science weapon only made my prospects grimmer.

"I wish Quiniece were here," I mumbled. I ran my hands down the sides of the weapon, feeling for the seams of the compartment where the radiant aurium was stored. "We could use a gearmeister right about now."

Keldon looked around. "Should I get one of the mechanics?"

Although I still heard the cries of the injured above the thundering turbines, the buzzing clatter of those savage clickspring spiders had thankfully fallen silent.

"There is too much at stake," I replied. "This burden is mine alone."

My fingers brushed the edges of a compartment near the base of the doomseed, and I took one of the multi-spanners to extract the machine-tightened bolts. The pneumatic tool made short work of the bolts, and I lifted the panel cover off. Underneath I saw another tangle of wires and actuators interlaced with flickering arrays of crystal parts. Many of the original components were still covered in mineralized stone, and the modern additions must have been intended to compensate, however crudely, for the damage. I reached in slowly, feeling around for a switch or latch, then froze when I heard a soft click and a whir. A pair of emission tubes suddenly lit up, digits ticking down from a count of twenty.

"Fangle-fop!"

Keldon took a step back, not that a few feet would make any difference. "What happened?"

There was no time to answer. The slightest mistake now would trigger whatever safeguards were in place. But why wasn't it simply booby-trapped with an empowerment? I pushed the question aside and scooted around to find a better view of the interior, searching desperately for a way to get at the radiant aurium containment sphere. If I could just find a way to remove the fuel sphere, or break it open, the weapon would be disabled. We would all die horrifically from the enriched ore's blistering aetheric light, but at least Corradon would be saved.

Blood trickled down my left arm as the tourniquet came loose, and I ground my teeth, forcing back the stabbing pain. The counter hit ten and continued down. I reached in again and pushed aside a bundle of wires, sliding my other hand along the base of the doomseed. The counter reached five. My fingers brushed another row of bolt heads and I peered in. There was the fuel compartment, sealed by eight bolts. I grabbed the multi-spanner, my hands shaking as I started on the first bolt. The counter hit three. The first bolt clattered off and I moved to the second bolt. The counter hit two. My hand worked frantically, ratcheting the spanner as I worked the second bolt out. The counter flashed to one. Time was up.

I closed my eyes.

"Forgive me, Corradon," I whispered, bowing my head. "I have failed."

A moment passed, but nothing happened. I opened my eyes. The counter showed zero, then blinked out. The glowing crystals faded, the spark tubes went dark, and the whirring within the ancient device fell suddenly silent. *A dud?* Impossible! I continued working at the bolts, removing the remaining six, then threw aside the compartment cover. The cavity, large enough to hold a sphere about the size of a grapefruit, was empty save for a single piece of paper. I took the note and turned it over, reading the fine calligraphy.

> As above, so below.
> The dark above, the dark below.
> And in-between the Gate of Ages.
> Behold, it opens, as the Black Sun closes!
> - The Disciple of the Servants of Vosh

"A diversion," I choked, crushing the note. *How could I have been such a fool?* "This was all a diversion!"

"What's going on?" Keldon asked, his voice shaking in panic.

I pulled myself out from the crawlspace, then staggered passed the crewmen and Guardsmen crowding the engine room on my way to the bank of call tubes on the wall.

"Captain Cheyron," I yelled into the call tube labeled 'Bridge.'

"Vescard," the captain's voice echoed back. "Did you disarm the weapon?"

"It was a diversion," I answered, still breathing hard. I pressed a hand against my upper arm, wincing at the pain. "Bring this ship about and make top speed for the cargo dirigible."

There was a pause. "We sent that ship in the opposite direction. It must be twenty miles away by now."

"I know," I breathed out grimly.

I looked to the mechanics and boilermen, to those who had survived the onslaught of the clickspring spiders. Four had died, and three more were seriously injured. And for what? Then I saw the mangled body of Sergeant Greston, and a mournful Lieutenant Dallin kneeling beside his fallen comrade. He had been so young—scarcely older than Keldon. I glanced away, then set my jaw and turned to the chief engineer.

"How hard can you push those turbines?"

Beldwick gave a sharp nod. "We'll push 'em past the redline 'til every boiler whistle blows."

I was off in an instant, racing down the ladder to the main corridor even as the ship listed hard to port in a turned. I crashed into the wall, nearly banging my head on a set of low hanging pipes, then staggered on, a trail of blood following me, dripping from my soaked-through sleeve. Keldon stumbled down the ladder behind me, yelling for me to stop and tend my wounds. But there was no time. Ignoring both his protests and the pain throbbing through my arm, I hurried on, hoping to reach the bridge before it was too late. But as swift a ship as *Justiciar* might be, and as determined as her captain and crew were, I knew we would never reach the cargo dirigible in time. The trap was already sprung.

Officers and crewmen made way as I dashed from one corridor to the next, then up another ladder to the front of the ship. *Justiciar* leveled out as I charged onto the bridge, and I staggered to the right before catching myself on the railing. Officers and crewmen flitted about their duty stations monitoring gauges, adjusting flight controls, and calling out distances and bearings, while Captain Cheyron watched from the center of the bridge. The wide panorama of windows looked out and down upon an unobstructed view of Corradon, its forest of towers and spires blazing like a thousand wakeful eyes. A dozen other dirigibles floated there and about above the Clockwork City, but dead ahead I spotted the distant shape of what must have been the cargo dirigible.

"Detective Vescard," Captain Cheyron greeted, taking his emberless pipe from his mouth. He turned in his chair, his eyebrows lifting his captain's cap when he saw my battered state. "Stars, man, what happened?"

Keldon dashed through the hatchway and onto the bridge, nearly colliding with an officer striding by. "Aldicus! We need to get you to a medic." He glanced frantically about. "Is anyone here a medic?"

"I'm fine," I breathed. The cuts to my arm and back were by no means trivial, but at least the bleeding had slowed. I stepped up to the captain's chair, looking out through the forward windows. Considering how distant the cargo dirigible was, I could see the ship surprisingly well. "How long until we catch up with them?"

"Five minutes," the captain replied. "The engines are already past the redline, and I dare not risk pushing—"

A flash of red and yellow flared on the distant dirigible's hull, then swelled to engulf the entire ship. The force of the blast threw burning debris in all directions, and the smoldering shape of what must have been the dirigible's gutted frame plunged from the expanding fireball to the city below.

"What happened?" Captain Cheyron demanded, his pipe clattering to the floor as he sprang from his chair.

My own voice failed me, and I stood in stunned silence as the thundering blast wave rattled the hull of our ship. It was a conventional explosion, and judging from the color and intensity of the fireball, it had probably been triggered by some alchemical reactant devised to ignite the ship's volatile lifting gases. Phlogistonic fulminate most likely, or perhaps...

Keldon grabbed me from behind. I shook my head and steadied myself on the railing, then looked out the window to the dissipating cloud of black smoke and the burning debris raining down on the city streets below.

"All hands to ready stations!" Cheyron ordered, yelling over the ship's now blaring battle alarms. "Alert all medical teams and emergency crews..." He stopped himself and swallowed, then shook his head. "There is no one to rescue, is there? No one could survive that."

"The Lord Governor," Keldon whispered. "The Chamber of Industry. They're all... dead."

Perhaps it was the blood loss, or perhaps it was the shock, but I felt a rush of ice-cold needles prickling through every nerve and fiber of my body. "He killed them," I managed to whisper. "He killed them all."

"Who? The Disciple?" Captain Cheyron asked. "But what about the doomseed? Why plant it aboard this ship? How could he even know we would evacuate them on the other ship?"

How indeed. The Shadow Man, or the Disciple as he called himself, had been a dozen steps ahead of me. He knew I was on the trail of the stolen artifacts, and he knew I would investigate the theft of the doomseed. He knew I would check up on the Grand Lodge, and he knew I would find the clues confirming that the Servants of Vosh possessed a radiant aurium fuel sphere. But it had all been a ruse. The doomseed had been concocted as a preemptive crisis to send me scurrying from one planted clue to another down a false trail, diverting me from the Shadow Man's true aim.

But even that false trail had served the enemy's sinister ends, for the Shadow Man knew the threat of a doomseed would prompt Vandor Tower to evacuate the Lord Governor and the Chamber of Industry. He knew I would surmise the doomseed was aboard *Justiciar* once I saw his latest manifesto and learned of Consolidated Omniwork's suspicious activities, and he knew I would demand the city's leaders be secreted away aboard the cargo ship so conveniently docked at Vandor Tower. Yes, the Disciple knew exactly how I would act to each and every clue that had been so carefully planted, and he had made absolutely certain that events would unfold according to his designs.

But who had that kind of power? Who had that kind of information? Who could manipulate me and, indeed, all of Vandor Tower, with such consummate duplicity?

Another chill ran down my spine and I caught my breath as the only possible answer came to me.

"Bring us back to Vandor Tower, captain," I said, my voice trembling even as I spoke. "It is time I had a word with the Commissioner General."

THREE HAAMR DIRIGIBLES AND AN AIRCRUISER had each claimed one of Vandor Tower's four mooring docks, and *Justiciar* had to divert to the 2nd District precinct tower. It was another hour after that before the steam-coach I hailed managed to inch its way through the crowd-strangled arteries of Corradon. Though the clock was well past midnight, thousands had taken to the streets as news spread of the airship bombing that had claimed the life of the Lord Governor and all members of the Chamber of Industry. The frightened multitudes flocked almost instinctively for the city's Central Core, to Municipal Plaza where stood the Governor's Tower, Vandor Tower, and the Aetherspire rising high above them all.

"I can go no further, sir," our coachmen said as he brought the vehicle to an abrupt halt, the way blocked by a milling mass of people.

I flipped him a ducat and stepped into the pressing crowd, nearly losing Keldon despite the fact that he followed right behind me. A pedestrian bumped me, and then another, each jostle sending a sharp lance of pain through the wounds on my arm and back. I pulled the sack coat I now wore closer to my body, ambling along with the churning throng meandering between the towering brass statues and streamlined monuments girding Municipal Plaza. The constant drone of the crowd was deafening, but above it blared emergency sirens and a voice on a bull horn calling for everyone to remain calm.

We entered the plaza, rounding a globe-shaped monument, and I saw a contingent of HAAMR troopers donned in full empowered armor. With them stood battle-dressed mages, moto-armor commandos, and hulking patrol automatons armed with their own substantial arsenals. The floodlights of the HAAMR dirigibles panned across Municipal Plaza and the buildings rising on all sides, while flights of ornithopters and monitoring orbs circled like vultures above the pressing crowds, wings droning over the deafening din. I could only shake my head. Military garrison and crowd control were not among HAAMR's duties. The Heavy Armory and Assault Mobile Regiment had been established for the sole purpose of defusing standoffs deemed too dangerous for Vandorian Guardsmen. *Everything here was wrong.*

"What is HAAMR doing here?" Keldon asked. Judging from his fearful tone, he already knew the answer. "What does it mean?"

A familiar figure emerged from the pressing crowd, gripping his bowler as he hurried toward me. "Aldicus, I thought that was you!" Tibblemond yelled above the clamor. "How did the Disciple know you would discover the doomseed was aboard *Justiciar*? And how did he know we would move the Lord Governor and the others to that cargo dirigible?"

I shook my head. "The question you must ask, chief inspector, is who has the power to call HAAMR out in force?" Tibblemond threw a glance at the imposing HAAMR units and frowned, clearly perturbed. "And who has such intimate knowledge of our procedures and operations to anticipate our every action? Where is the Commissioner General?"

Tibblemond turned back to me, his brow furrowing. "He headed straight for the Governor's Tower after the airship exploded. Something about emergency protocols. HAAMR has Vandor Tower on complete lock down, and I'm only out here because I was sent to help control this blasted crowd." He nodded to several bluejacks and inspectors moving through the throng. Wearing Vandorian uniforms and plain clothes like Tibblemond, they were far less conspicuous than the heavily armored HAAMR troopers blocking the entrances to Vandor Tower and the Governor's Tower. "So were most of the inspectors and Guardsmen, now that I think about it."

I breathed out a long sigh. "So, the Vandorian Guard has just been evicted from Vandor Tower."

Several floodlights converged on a mid-level balcony of the Governor's Tower. The riotous throng quieted of its own accord as all eyes turned expectantly to that high terrace. A man appeared at the balcony railing, flanked on either side by armored HAAMR troopers. One of the troopers raised a staff and the air shimmered just in front of the center figure, then expanded in an illusory projection of light and sound. The magnifying empowerment grew to a quarter of the height of the Governor's Tower, making the Commissioner General in his fitted suit coat and tall top hat clear for all to see. I recognized the HAAMR officer to his right as Colonel Dolgrim, with his distinctive optographic receptor. To his left stood Major Caldrus, the HAAMR mage who had killed Melard as he fled, and very likely cleared of all wrongdoing.

The Commissioner General held up his arms, bidding the still murmuring crowd to fall silent. "Fellow citizens!" he called, his voice amplified by Caldrus's spell. "Dire tragedy has befallen our great city, shaking the very pillars of Corradon to its deepest foundations. The Lord Governor, along with all members of the Chamber of Industry, perished when their airship was deliberately and maliciously destroyed in a cowardly bombing orchestrated by the so-called Brethren of Justice. These radical anarchists, and all subversive dissenters like them, seek to stifle the ideals that have made our city great, killing without remorse or regard for the hundreds of innocents who stand in the way of their treasonous plot. Yes, the crime and corruption that has long plagued Corradon must be addressed. But neither the tyranny of terror nor the sword of sedition can bring about the peace and freedom cherished by enlightened society."

An incongruous mix of fearful voices, anxious demands, and hopeful cheers erupted from the crowd, but the Commissioner General raised his hand, bringing silence before he continued.

"So it is that I, the Commissioner General of Vandor Tower, by the full authority provided by the Vandorian Jurisdiction Proclamation of Armillia, do hereby invoke the Emergency Crisis Protocol. Under this lawful directive, I humbly assume the weighty burden of Lord Protector of the Independent City-State of Corradon until such time as stability and rule of law is restored. The radicals and fanatics that now besiege our beloved metropolis shall not prevail, and through the courageous efforts of HAAMR and the Vandorian Guard, justice and order will reign triumphant over this terrible adversity we now endure."

The self-declared Lord Protector stretched his arms wide, his broad smile resplendent in all of his deceitful pretense.

"Rejoice, good citizens of Corradon! We shall soon have peace for our time."

Cheers and applause thundered from one end of Municipal Plaza to the other, reverberating from the reaching towers and echoing down the weaving causeways and avenues of the Clockwork City. I looked to the HAAMR dirigibles circling the needle-like pinnacle of the Aetherspire, stabbing like some victorious rapier into the cloud blackened sky above, and an icy chill shivered down my spine.

The Shadow Man had prevailed...

"So fades the light of liberty as the shadow of tyranny descends," I said, the barest whisper slipping through my lips. "Archons help us all."

Case File 13:

The Harrowing Beneath

A SICKLY RAIN DRIZZLED FROM THE COAL BLACK SKY, spilling through the maze of viaducts and causeways laced between the rusting edifices of soot-stained manufactories and noxious refineries of the 14th District. The thrumming drone of a HAAMR ornithopter faded in the distance, sirens howled somewhere in the night, and to the south, the loudspeakers of the core districts called for all citizens to observe curfew under martial law. Hours remained until Atracus rose, a waning crescent heralding the dawn, and only the faint lamplight from streets above allowed me to make out the body lying face down in the gurgling gutter wash.

"We were on our way back from the 1st District Underworks when one of my scouts found the body," Emileve said softly. She crossed her arms over her leather brigandine, her red-lensed goggles reflecting the dim half-light.

I knelt, my hand shaking as fingers brushed a scorched hole seared through his rain-soaked coat. A crushed bowler bobbed in a puddle of runoff water, and the remains of a battered notepad was mired in the muck beside him. I hung my head, eyes pinched closed as I fought back the tears threatening to overwhelm me.

"I'm sorry, Aldicus," Emileve continued. "I know he was a colleague of yours."

"He was more than a colleague," I whispered, not caring to hide the quaver in my voice. "He was..." I choked. "He was my friend."

My jaw clenched, my hands tightening into fists. Half a minute passed before I could breathe out again. I bit my lip, forcing myself to put aside the heart-twisting anguish so I could press on with my forensic analysis.

His skin was cold, as cold as the ambient air, and judging from the stiffness of his limbs, rigor mortis had already set in. I rolled the body over as gently as I could, noting how dry his waistcoat was. The rain had started some eight hours ago, and the fact that the front of his body was still mostly dry further narrowed the time of death. The body had been here for between eight to ten hours, and the cause of death was likely some kind of projected energy bolt that struck him from behind.

A quick search of his coat turned up nothing more than a cheap pocket watch, some loose coins, and the keys to his apartment. But the coat was torn along one side, as though forcibly pulled open, and the knees of his trousers had tears in them as well. I furrowed my brow, studying Tibblemond's hands. Both bore long, shallow cuts across the palms, not even deep enough to cause significant bleeding. It was a strange injury, but one that could have been caused if he had been struggling to hold on to a folder or some papers.

Drawing another breath to still my rattled nerves, I tasked myself with reconstructing what had happened. Tibblemond had been trying to make his way back to us with some vital evidence on his person when his killers caught up with him. One of the villains attacked, struggling for the papers he held, when another one came up from behind and blasted him in the back. Then they fled, leaving his corpse here in the dark cold of this long-deserted sublevel alley. But in their haste, might they have left some scrap of evidence behind?

I fished Tibblemond's notepad from the muck and pealed the covers apart, my hopes dwindling when I saw the tattered remnants of several torn-out pages along the notepad's spine. But why would the killers have torn out just these pages? Why not simply take the notepad when they made off with the other evidence he had been carrying? I was about to tuck the pad into my pocket when I noticed what appeared to be a recent bite mark on the back cover. Odd.

Keldon stepped up beside me, his too-young eyes glinting with tears even as he clutched his talisman in hand. He started forward, no doubt to scan the body, but I caught his arm.

"It's all right," I whispered softly. As much as I could have used a bit of aetheric insight, I would not subject Keldon to delving our late friend's remains. "You don't have to do this. Not this time."

He stood in silence for a moment, then pulled his arm from my grasp. "Whatever it takes," he choked, kneeling beside the body. The oily rain pattered around him, soaking his cap and clothes. "I'll do whatever it takes to find whoever did this."

"We will," I said, my stomach clenching. I stepped back to let him conduct his scan. "I promise you, we will."

"Do you think Consolidated Omniworks had him killed?" Emileve asked, brushing back the locks of her dirty blond hair.

"It is too early to say," I admitted.

Tibblemond had been helping me unofficially, following up on a few leads linking Consolidated Omniworks to the decoy doomseed smuggled aboard *Justiciar*, and with the mysterious construction work going on deep beneath the Aetherspire. I could only assume he had discovered something vitally important—something important enough to kill for. But whatever evidence he had found, it was gone now. Consolidated Omniworks was the largest and most powerful industrial syndicate in the world, and if they were somehow involved in the Commissioner General's coupe, the implications would be astounding.

Keldon stood, consulting the sigils glowing on the side of his key. "I'm detecting traces of aetheric energy and a degraded pattern suggestive of a highly focused aetheric empowerment."

"He was killed by a sorcerer or mage," I concluded. I pulled off my inspection gloves and returned them to my black bag along with Tibblemond's notepad. "That doesn't narrow our suspects much, but—"

An excited chittering drew my attention and I looked up through the rain to see one of Emileve's homunculi perched on a cluster of corroded pipes. The goblinesque creature was difficult to see in the drizzly night, but its owl-like eyes, made all the larger by its custom-fitted goggles, glittered in what little light there was. Two more joined the first a moment later, and their tiny hands flashed through a series of urgent signs. Emileve swore under her breath and the two cloaked thieves who stood guard just behind her bolted for either end of the alley.

"What is it?" I asked, sensing the sudden concern.

"Trouble," she confirmed. "There's a HAAMR patrol headed this way."

Even as she spoke, I heard the distinctive thrum of a patrol ornithopter growing near. My eyes narrowed. Had the body been left here as bait? I looked down at Tibblemond's corpse, silently cursing the fact that we still had no real clues to go on. We were out of time, but I had to give the body one last search before we made a break for it. Perhaps I had missed something.

"Give me a moment," I said, kneeling again.

"We don't have a moment," Emileve protested. "We have to go."

I patted through Tibblemond clothes, but again found nothing. Whatever evidence he had carried was gone. The rising thrum of the thoptor's beating wings grew steadily louder, joined now by the sound of metal footfalls pounding on pavement. One of Emileve's men came running back down the alley, calling for us to head out. Then I remembered the bite mark on Tibblemond's notepad. I blinked. *Of course!* Drawing a sharp breath, I placed my thumb against Tibblemond's jaw and forced it open with the sickening crack of breaking cartilage.

"What are you doing?" Keldon demanded, his face twisted in a mix of horror and disgust.

I didn't have time to concern myself with the nuances of social decorum. If Tibblemond knew he was being pursued, then maybe—just maybe—he had left the bite mark on the notepad as a subtle clue. I pushed my fingers into the corpse's open mouth, swallowing back the bile rising in my throat as I tried not to think about what I was doing. After feeling around for a moment, my fingers brushed against something pressed against his inside cheek. Pulling it out, I caught my breath, seeing the folded-up square of several pages matching those torn from his battered notepad.

"Good man," I whispered to my departed friend, another tear forming in my eye. "A hero to the last."

"We have to go, now," Emileve repeated, her tone insistent as she seized me by the scruff of my coat. "And by now, I mean *now*!"

As much as I loathed the thought of leaving Tibblemond's body behind, I staggered to my feet, grabbed my bag, and followed Emileve with Keldon hurrying along beside me. The thopter buzzed overhead, still out of sight thanks to the tangled canopy of catwalks, scaffolding, and conduits, but the sound of clomping armor echoed from the walls as HAAMR troopers entered the far end of the alley.

We turned down another alley and came to a rusted-over utility junction. A new set of footfalls drummed from just ahead as a second HAAMR patrol swept in to cut off our escape route, but one of Emileve's men threw open a ventilation grate and jumped down. Emileve climbed down next, with the three homunculi scurrying ahead. Keldon and I both ducked low to follow while the thief behind us locked the grate back in place.

The pitch-blackness of the sublevel access corridor would have been absolute were it not for the occasional glint of the thieves' empowered goggles. Although Keldon could have illuminated our way, he wisely refrained. We meandered through several twists and turns of the tunnel before coming to an abrupt stop when our shoes clamored onto some kind of metal flooring.

"Hold on tight," came Emileve's voice from the darkness.

I was about to ask what she meant when the floor lurched downward. Keldon yelped, his cry muffled by the clattering of chains, pulleys, and wheels, and I grasped for something to hold on to—which, as it so happened, turned out to be Emileve's arm. She gave a derisive snort and pushed me back, but before I could apologize, the rickety lift squealed to a stop.

My eyes had adjusted well enough that I could just make out the pipe-cluttered walls of the service corridor we had entered. Judging from the century-old accretion of mineralized soot and sediment along the walls and floor, we were below the lowest of the city's aging sublevels, having entered the upper reaches of the long-forsaken Underworks. Not that the Underworks were in any way forgotten or deserted, I reminded myself, and I brushed my fingers against my severite cuffs, pondering what to do should we cross paths with any of the deepening realm's more ravenous inhabitants.

"Just so you know, my men have finished scouting the outer periphery of the construction work beneath the Central Core," Emileve said, leading us through the dark, undercity corridor. "But apart from our little brothers, we haven't gotten in for a look. We've haven't managed to backtrack their supply chain, either, as they seem to change their routes daily, but the workers appear to be scabs. On the other hand, the mercs watching the place aren't your typical pfenny-a-dozen bruisers. If I didn't know better, I'd venture to say they're either ex-military or the private security of a major industrial syndicate."

I was still so unsettled by Tibblemond's death that I only caught part of what she had said. Of course, I was not about to ask her to repeat herself, for a detective of my renown should naturally endeavor to remain astute at all times.

"And what is the biggest industrial syndicate you can think of?" I asked, shaking some water off my top hat.

The Queen of Thieves gave a half-amused snort. "Consolidated Omniworks, of course. But you do know they're not the only company working on the Aetherspire, right? There's at least a dozen others contracted for one part of the construction or another, and every one of them has more than enough power and capital to field an army of engineers, workers, and mercenaries—even secretly."

"Yes, but Tibblemond was following the leads on Consolidated Omniworks." I pushed my hands into my frock coat pockets, my fingers brushing against the paper I had found in Tibblemond's mouth. "And someone wanted him very dead for his troubles."

"It just doesn't make sense," Keldon mulled. He doffed his newsboy cap to ruffle his wet and tousled hair. "With so many people working on the project, how could Consolidated Omniworks keep whatever plot they're behind a secret?"

"Because their workers are not behind this plot," I posited. I pulled the paper out of my pocket and began to gently unfold it. "If Consolidated Omniworks is involved, they're probably just another pawn in an even bigger game."

The old service corridor eventually led through another debris-littered room and then into the remains of what might once have been a storm tunnel, now mired in rotting refuse and sludge-filled water. Emileve quickly ushered us through an ancillary corridor leading to the more populated sublevels of the 14th District. We soon emerged onto a covered street deep within Corradon's labyrinthine undercity. Assuming I had not gotten completely turned around, we were now ten blocks west of where Tibblemond had been murdered, and several sublevels below. Given the round-about way we had come, it seemed unlikely the HAAMR patrols would be able to track us here. That was one advantage of running with the Unseen Brotherhood—evading the law was their cream and cake.

I finished unfolding the pages and squinted, trying to tease out whatever clues they might contain. The light level was now sufficient for me to discern the hasty scribbles, though I would need several hours to interpret the muddled collection of lopsided scratches and undulating squiggles that densely filled all four pages, front and back. Tibblemond had a habit of falling into his own distinct shorthand whenever he was in a rush, and although it was similar to common Kellian stenography, he regrettably employed his own unique derivation of its single-stroke shortform words. Shortform words only existed for the most common words, while proper names still had to be spelled out—even if in shorthand. A quick once-through revealed several lists of proper names, so I would likely be able to decipher most of his notes with a good stenographic reference at hand.

"Preferred Logistics," I said, as I began to read a few of the more legible names. "Industrial something Partnership." I paused, considering the mysterious shorthand squiggle. It was similar to the Kellian shortform for 'fish,' which was also similar to the shortform for 'resource.' Although he could have been referring to a fishery or fishing partnership, the latter interpretation made more sense. "I think he means Industrial Resource Partnership."

"What?" Keldon asked.

"The notes Tibblemond hid before he was murdered," I replied. "They are scrawled in his own peculiar shorthand."

Keldon nodded, then looked down, his shoulders slouching and arms hugging himself. "I still can't believe he's gone..."

"Anything about Consolidated Omniworks?" Emileve

asked.

I squinted at the notes in what little light eked down into these abandoned depths. The word 'Omwrk' occurred several times, spelled out in the looping lines of shorthand script. Unfortunately, most of the surrounding text was illegible, apart from some mention of a 'spcl drctrt' and a tantalizing bit about a 'scrt cmplx.'

"There is something," I replied after a moment. "But I will need time to distill enough of the text before I can even guess at what these notes might actually contain. They are quite extensive."

Emileve grunted doubtfully. She brought us through a dimly lit tunnel, haphazardly bored beneath the rusting roots of an old but still operating alchemical refinery. We covered our faces against the acrid fumes of vitriolic chlorinate seeping from a tangle of corroded pipes dripping above our heads. Moments later we were clear of the toxic tunnel, emerging into the dusty half-light of the wide utility chasm cutting through the center of the district. I nodded to myself, now recognizing where we were. The towering edifice of Corbollen-Soliden Alchemicals rose above like some scabrous iron mountain, while the dilapidated boneyards and aging scrap pits of the rustmongers' quarter blighted the city's outer reaches to the west.

Many of the district's unlicensed ale and dicing joints pockmarked the area, and we soon found ourselves ducking into one particular dive called the Chancy Step, so named for the wobbly brick midway down the stairs to its otherwise nondescript entrance. The Chancy Step had none of the Broken Spigot's quaint charm, with crumbling plaster where rich wood paneling would have been and grungy crates instead of resin-lacquered oak tables. But the seedy undercity establishment did have two key advantages over my usual haunt: it was entirely unknown to HAAMR or Vandor Tower, and served as a safe house for the Unseen Brotherhood.

The portly proprietor nodded as we entered, as did the half-dozen thieves guised as thoroughly sozzled patrons, and we made our way down the stairs to the cellar. Glad though I was to leave behind the reek of cheap pipe smoke and even cheaper rotgut, the cramped basement room hardly smelled any better with its lingering fetor of stagnate water and well-ripened rubbish.

"Where the stars have you been?" Rognar demanded from his chair at the cellar's card-cluttered table. He glanced at a scuffed-up fob watch pulled from the depths of his baggy duffle coat and sighed. "We have to hurry before Leta does something rash. You know she doesn't have half the patience I've got, and that's not—"

"Tibblemond is dead," I found myself saying.

Two more of Emileve's men sat at the table with Rognar, both engaged in a round of jonko, but they dropped their cards and looked up when they heard my words. The Unseen Brotherhood had no love for anyone in law enforcement, but Tibblemond, along with what remained of the true Vandorian Guard, had become their unlikely confederates in the struggle to reclaim the city from the Shadow Man and his cronies.

"Blast!" Rognar swore. He swept off his floppy leather cap and bowed his head in respect. After releasing a deep breath, he shook his head and looked up at me again. "What happened?"

"I suspect he got too close to the truth." I held up Tibblemond's notes. "This is all that remains of his investigation into Consolidated Omniworks, but I need time to study it."

Rognar shook his head. "There's no time, Aldicus. I came here to let you know that Leta and Arleia tracked Mistress Agona to the Vernoct Cryptopolis. They're still there, keeping an eye on that skulking Scaithi sorceress to see what scheme she's about. But knowing Leta, she might not wait for back up."

I frowned, shoving the notes back into my pocket. The Vernoct Cryptopolis was buried deep beneath the border of the 15th District in a precinct largely dominated by residential terraces, mercantile plazas, and guildhalls spilling over from the 5th District. Like most of the city's older catacomb complexes, the Vernoct Cryptopolis had been sealed centuries ago and left to sink into the forgotten pages of history as the city grew, layer by rising layer. Yet, as was often the case for such ancient ruins, looters, treasure-hunters, and the morbidly curious inevitably found their way in through one hidden entrance or another, and the Vernoct Cryptopolis had more than its share of secret entrances.

"Mistress Agona?" Keldon asked, his eyes growing wide. "Aldicus, we can't let them face that sorceress alone. She's probably the Shadow Man's right hand!"

I grimaced at the name. Until recently, the Shadow Man was the only name we had for him. Operating as the Disciple of the Brethren of Justice, he had brought Corradon to its knees with a string of bombings to incite fear and turmoil, culminating with the murder of the city's Lord Governor and the entire Chamber of Industry. But my discovery of his true identity as the Commissioner General of Vandor Tower had come too late, and now he ruled the city with absolute autonomy as Corradon's so-called 'Lord Protector.' Now he commanded the vast military resources of HAAMR and operated with complete political impunity as he conducted the final movement of his grand symphony of mayhem. We still had no inkling of what his end game might entail, and that, more than anything else, terrified me. But whatever Mistress Agona was up to, it was certainly at the heart of the Shadow Man's master plan.

"Did they at least promise not to move against her until help arrived?" I asked.

Rognar scratched his head in thought before plopping his floppy leather cap back on. "Well, not as such," he admitted with a quaver of hesitation. "But, ah... You know Leta."

Emileve hissed. "I'll get my men."

"No," I said, holding up a hand. "I need you to keep on the trail Tibblemond was on."

"Then give me those notes," Emileve said, opening her hand to take them. "I can't read shorthand, but one of my men might be able to."

I shook my head. "As hard a time as I have making any sense of Tibblemond's shorthand, I'm probably the only person who even has a chance at it." I glanced at the notes again, skimming over what few legible names stood out. "See if you can find any dirt on Preferred Logistics or Industrial Resource Partnership. Tibblemond must have uncovered a connection. Perhaps Consolidated Omniworks was a false lead, or perhaps these are subsidiaries or fronts. They might even be the companies managing whatever work is going on deep beneath the Aetherspire. Either way, the more we can find out the better."

Emileve sighed, then nodded. "We'll start digging."

I grabbed my black bag and headed for the stairs, then glanced over my shoulder. "Oh, and if you happen to run into Armez, let him know where we're heading. Be sure to tell him that Mistress Agona might be there as well."

Emileve rolled her eyes and grumbled something under her breath.

"Rognar," I added, "grab whatever you need and lead the way. We've no time to waste."

The streetwise Dworgh patted the bulge on the left side of his duffle coat and smiled through his braided red beard. "I've got everything I need right here. Isn't that right, Varla?"

Rognar gave a quiet chuckle and nodded to himself as though hearing some kind of answer, then he hurried up the rickety stairs, his heavy boots pounding the half-rotted wood.

"Does it ever worry you that he named his gun and talks to it?" Keldon asked, keeping his voice low.

"There are plenty of named swords and relics of power

about, most of them empowered," I replied simply. "How is this any different?"

Keldon arched a doubtful eyebrow, but nodded anyway.

We followed Rognar out of the Chancy Step, carefully avoiding its loose, namesake brick, and we picked up our pace as we made our way through the sublevel streets of Corradon's 14th District.

IT TOOK THE BETTER PART OF AN HOUR to make our way from the Chancy Step to the 15th District's mercantile precinct. With the late-night curfew in effect, all passenger steamrails and street-level coaches had stopped running, although a few beaten-up rickshaws and carriages still operated in the deeper sublevels. Yet, not even those illicit conveyances could bring us to the forgotten depths of a Corradon six centuries past.

The shimmering blue light of Keldon's talismanic key played across a diverse panoply of calcified stonework and crumbling archways as we pressed deeper into the city's ancient roots. No gears, steam pipes, or pneumatic tubes cluttered these buried cobblestone streets, and the only hint of the ever-growing city above were the enormous iron and fabricrete pilings driven like spikes through the decaying corpse of the old city.

Rognar led us down another passageway, apparently opened by intrepid explorer some years earlier. The tunnel soon emptied into the time-entombed halls of the Vernoct Cryptopolis. Like all cryptopolises of its era, it was a labyrinth in its own right, housing the dusty remains of countless thousands of Corradon's former citizens who had passed from life during the golden age of the Three Realms. The light of Keldon's key illuminated only the merest fraction of the cavernous gallery before us, and the moss-slick floor sloped treacherously downward, stretching into still greater depths below.

This deep beneath Corradon, the effects of the city's

slowly sinking bedrock were far more pronounced, and I was not at all surprised to see the catacombs had settled at this precarious angle. The path lay scattered with loose bones, collapsed support columns, and the broken fragments of sarcophagi long ago looted or toppled by subterranean quakes. Lichen covered the walls, and the sound of rushing water echoed from somewhere deep within. The musty smell of stagnant decay hung heavy in the still air.

"We should have brought a rope," Keldon lamented, his foot slipping on one of the floor's moldy stones.

I nodded, though I was beginning to wish we had brought more light. Keldon's key provided ample illumination for our immediate area, but the sheer immensity of the great galleries made his talisman little better than a candle flickering in some vast abyss. Rognar had already donned his ocular amplification goggles, pausing only to adjust the position or aperture of his lenses. Despite his visual advantage, Rognar missed more than a few obvious clues, walking past the fresh scrapes and scuff marks that broke the mossy carpet of the ancient stone floor. Although some of these were no doubt Leta's and Arleia's footprints, there were other tracks that could not be so easily explained.

I scuttled sideways across the sloping floor and knelt to inspect a snake-like track winding down the sepulchers' lopsided descent. Keldon joined me there, his aetheric light revealing the undulating curve and centipede-like scrapes cutting through the oozing mycoflora that fouled these long-abandoned halls.

"What is it?" my apprentice asked, his whispering voice quavering in the too-still air.

The tracks were those of a necrocite, but Keldon was better off not knowing that such a flesh-scavenging horror was about. "It's difficult to say," I answered evasively.

In truth, I was surprised we had not already encountered a few of the cryptopolis's more distinctive denizens. Necrocites, mortifants, and ghastuls were as common in ancient catacombs as rustwraiths and geargeists were in the Iron Barrens. And yet, we had stumbled across none. Leta and Arleia could have already eliminated such threats—they were veilhunters after all—but the lack of any visible remains suggested a more disturbing possibility: something had frightened even the deathless hordes away.

"Are you sensing anything?" I asked my apprentice.

Keldon nodded, eyes glancing back and forth with understandable trepidation. "This place..." he whispered. "This place is suffused with necrolic energy. It's like..."

"Like we're in a six-hundred-year-old, light-forsaken tomb, interred beneath the deepest chasms of the Underworks?" Shadows fell away from the speaker as she emerged from a recessed passageway—one hand propped on her hip and the other holding a luminary lamp. "It's about time you got here, Aldicus. You know better than to keep a lady waiting."

Leta Meridian stood with all the bronzy confidence deserved by a psychic veilhunter versed in the mystic arts, as fearless of the dark as the very nightmare creatures she pursued. Her apprentice, Arleia, stood quietly beside her, anxiously adjusting her glasses as she glanced discreetly at Keldon. The soft glow of her totem's light was warmer and more natural than the harsh-blue radiance of Keldon's talisman, though it was dimmer by compare.

"We were delayed," I admitted. "I have some..." I hesitated, my words catching in my throat, and I looked away from Leta. "I have some bad news."

Leta glanced at Keldon and blinked, then looked to Rognar before returning her gaze to me. Her face drew pale, her psychic senses no doubt alerting her to the bitter melancholy brooding within me. "What is it? What has happened?"

"Tibblemond..." I managed to say. "We found him, murdered, in a sublevel alley. Whatever evidence he was trying to bring to us was gone, save for some scribblings on his notepad."

Arleia gasped, her tapered ears flattening back as she clapped a hand over her mouth, stifling a cry.

Leta closed her eyes and turned away, her fists tightening. "We've all lost friends since the Disciple—the Shadow Man—seized power. The only thing we can do to honor them is to see this nightmare through to the bitter end."

I nodded my agreement. "Rognar tells me you've tracked Mistress Agona here. What is she up to?"

"Nothing good." Leta's eyes glanced to the impenetrable darkness farther down the tilted hall and she let out a weary sigh. "Despite what you're thinking, I *do* have enough sense not to face her without back up. But if you hadn't gotten here when you did, I might not have had a choice. I think she's nearing the end of her ritual."

"Ritual?" I asked. "What ritual?"

"I'm not sure. But I'm fairly certain the incantation is in Gollan."

"Gollan?" Keldon choked. "The demon-tongue of Atracus?"

"Then why are we standing here gabbing about it like a gaggle of tea-touting dandy-fops?" Rognar balked. "Let's get down there and give her what for!"

Keldon and Arleia followed behind me as Leta led us through a low ceiling passageway, and Rognar brought up the rear. We soon entered another wide hall cluttered with a macabre collection of hollow-eyed skulls, discarded death shrouds, and disturbingly empty sarcophagi. A crumbling set of stairs brought us to the lower levels, and we passed through a stretch of chambers half-flooded with stagnate water and murky silt. Leta darkened her luminary lamp and returned it to her satchel, and Arleia dimmed the light of her runic totem, nudging Keldon to do likewise.

The murky gloom closed around us, but a hazy red light issued from a chamber just ahead. Agona's fervent voice resounded from that secluded grotto, her alien words sharp and strident, with every phrase echoed by a chanting refrain from the others gathered with her.

"You didn't mention there were others," I whispered to Leta.

"Don't worry," she said. "They're probably just a few dark acolytes. Maybe a karcist or two."

"Karcists? Dark acolytes?" Keldon whispered, aghast.

I gave Keldon a reassuring pat on the shoulder. "You've faced this sorceress with me once before. You did well then, and you'll do well again." In truth, I would have felt a lot more confident if Armez and his sireling had joined us, and perhaps Emileve and her men as well. But between a battle-proven veilhunter and a half-Eldren elementor, we could probably put a serious crimp in whatever sinister ritual Mistress Agona had devised. "Besides, you have Arleia here to pull you out if things get really rough."

Arleia flipped her runic totem in her hand, then grinned and gave Keldon a teasing wink.

"Thanks, boss," Keldon grumbled, his face growing red.

Leta and Rognar moved on ahead, and both crouched low behind a toppled pillar just around the corner from the ritual chamber. Leta motioned us over, then spoke in a low whisper. "The room is one of the larger catacomb galleries, about sixty paces long and twenty paces wide, with support columns on either side. Those should provide some degree of cover."

"Is there any other way in or out?" I whispered back.

Leta nodded. "Unfortunately, yes. Are you worried that they'll escape?"

I drew in a deep breath and sighed. "Actually, I was working out a plan for *our* escape if things turn sour."

"I'm more worried that they could call in reinforcements," Rognar grumbled.

I grimaced. "There's that, too."

"Arleia, you and Keldon stay back until it's clear what

we're up against," Leta said. Arleia looked affronted, but both apprentices nodded. "Aldicus and I will go in first, and Rognar, you take the right flank and give them your worst." She looked to me and smiled. "Sound good?"

I adjusted my top hat and smiled back. "Far be it for me to dismiss a well-reasoned plan. Our best chance is to catch them unawares. If we can surprise..."

My voice trailed off, leaving only a hollow silence hanging in the stagnant air. A second passed as my mind reconciled what was wrong, and I watched Leta's eyes widen as she came to the same realization: the chanting had stopped.

"Botch it all!" she cursed, scrambling to her feet.

Without another word, she charged straight into the chamber, gnashing the talismanic rings of her right hand as she drew in the mystic essence of the astral light. I bolted after her, frock coat billowing behind me.

The hall was larger than I had imagined, with a barrel vault ceiling precariously supported by what few unbroken pillars hemmed the burial alcoves lining the walls. Torchieres illuminated much of the vast chamber, each crowned by a blazing elemental flame. Seven black-robed acolytes waited impassively with cowls lowered, each holding an iron pole supporting a banner of some demonic design. Two other figures, garbed in robes of black and gold, bore the distinctive facial tattoos and thorn-like nails of Dungh'gar priests. Agona stood just in front of an angular black obelisk, garbed in hardened leather armor and adorned in an impressive collection of Dungh'gar tattoos. And there, lurking in the darkness just beyond the chamber's fiery red light, moved emaciated shapes of jutting bone and rotting flesh.

My jaw clenched. *At least now we knew where the catacombs' usual haunts had gone...*

Mistress Agona turned to face us, her azure eyes burning with all her ardent hate. "Seize Vescard," she hissed, a cruel smile curling on her lips. "Extinguish the others!"

Three of the acolytes dropped their banners, drawing

curved knives as they rushed forward to attack. The four remaining acolytes held their position, and I could only conclude that they served some vital role in the ritual. Agona returned her attention to the strange obelisk, raising her bejeweled right hand to resume her sinister ceremony. But while she completed the ritual, the two Dungh'gar priests turned to face us, their hands outstretched as they whispered their own gibbering incantations.

"Oh, no you don't!" Leta exclaimed.

A shimmering sphere of mystical energy expanded from Leta's outstretched hands, colliding a split second later with a roiling beam of phantasmal energy striking out from the Dungh'gar priests. Leta staggered back, her face contorting in a grimace, but she held her ground with hands outstretched, repelling the dark priests' sorcerous malediction.

The three acolytes were upon us a heartbeat later—the first one slashing at me with his ritual dagger, while the others surrounded Leta even as she defended against the priests. A sudden *whoomph* sounded through the chamber, and a scorching fireball from Rognar's gun incinerated one of the acolytes attacking Leta. My own assailant lunged with dagger slashing, and I ducked and spun aside, the rip of fabric vouching for the near miss that clipped my coat sleeve.

Seeing our peril, our two apprentices dashed into the room, Keldon with his key glimmering bright and Arleia with her totem brandished before her. One of the Dungh'gar priests shifted his attention from Leta to the youths, bringing his hands together and opening his palms to unleash a screaming blast of metaplasmic energy. The pair blinked out as the searing beam surged through their insubstantial images, and they reappeared moments later not six paces away, Arleia striking back with a razor-sharp blade of coalesced air. Rognar fired Varla again at the very same priest, but the karcist grinned with contempt as his warding barrier repelled both attacks. Leta's own mystical ward began to crack against the barrage of the first priest's attack, but rather than bolstering her defenses, she released her ward and dived aside, lashing out with a near-invisible lance of psychokinetic energy. The karcist was too stunned by the move to react in time, and the lance sliced a nasty gash across his left shoulder.

I tossed my frock coat aside as I backed away from my own fanatical assailant, and took four glass vials from my black bag. Three of the vials went into my belt, and the fourth I gripped in my left hand. The dark acolyte snarled and lunged at me again, and I pulled the locking pin from my left wristband. The severite cuff fell away, and a spike of searing pain cut through my arm as flesh and bone ignited like aether-fired ebonite. The vial cracked, then shattered, splashing fulminic acid across my burning fist and flaring to a torch of alchemical flames. Scorching pain tore through my outstretched arm, but the Dungh'gar acolyte didn't even stand a chance, his scream melting into silence as a torrent of molten fire washed over him.

With jaw clenched and arm ablaze, I whipped around to face Mistress Agona. But what I saw instead could have turned my boiling blood to frigid ice.

A shrieking tide of gaunt husks and skeletal forms charged from the darkness beyond the torchieres' flickering red light, clambering over empty sarcophagi and broken pillars in their mindless onslaught. The ghastly host swarmed past the ceremonial circle, but Mistress Agona remained focused on the obelisk, her devout acolytes standing with banners held high as her blasphemous incantations echoed through the chamber. A glowing blue seam split down the center of the obelisk, while strange glyphs shimmered in phosphorescent hues down either side of its glass-smooth surface.

Our time was up!

The rest of my shirt sleeve burned away as I swept an alchemical firestorm across the charging mob. Leta reenergized her defensive ward to deflect the enemy priest's phantasmal strike, and Rognar's empowered blunderbuss belched a fiery blast, exploding through another attacking acolyte. Keldon and Arleia took cover behind a pile of rubble—the illusion of their running forms distracting the second priest, while Arleia hurled a ball of elemental fire at the mortifant horde, conjured from the enemy's own torchieres. Rognar leveled Varla and fired again, the fireball finishing off the priest attacking Leta and freeing the veilhunter to invoke the full force of her mystical intercession. Coruscating silver light spilled from her upraised hands, reducing the desiccated flesh and brittle bones of the ghastly horde's forward ranks to smoldering ash.

Yet, even as I dared to hope that we might stand a chance, Mistress Agona's invocation reached its harrowing crescendo. Leta staggered back, her eyes wide with horror as tendrils of inky black smoke struck from the obelisk's widening seam, each impaling the chest of the four remaining acolytes. Screams of agony and terror tore from the men as their mouth's stretched open, their body's thrashing and quivering against the necrolic tendrils stabbing into them. Pulsing streams of spectral light drained from each of the acolytes, their sacrificial souls surging into the obelisk, fueling whatever deathless fiend stirred within its ancient hollow.

But no... That was no obelisk. It was a stasis box.

A Gollan stasis box!

Leta dropped to one knee, hands clutching her head against the shrieking psychic backlash, and both Keldon and Arleia grimaced, their faces growing frightfully pale. Despite the dampening effect of my remaining severite wristband, I, too, felt a chilling shudder ripple through the aether. An oppressive force crushed down upon the air, and the flickering light of the torchieres dimmed as the cold of the catacombs became a deep and penetrating chill that not even the heat of my flaming arm could dispel.

The last of the acolytes' living souls drained into the open stasis box as a hulking form emerged from its ancient prison. What little illumination remained slipped away from the creature, but its hunched posture straightened to an imposing eight feet. Two pairs of forward swept horns curved from the back of its elongated skull to the front of its reptilian maw, and a guttural growl rumbled from deep within its carapace-covered chest. It raised its terrible hands, revealing grossly elongated fingers with four-inch talons and a second thumb where its fourth finger should have been. I took a step back, my mind racing with both wonder and dread, and the flames of my arm diminish before the creature's light-stifling presence.

"And now, Aldicus Vescard," Agona mewed, her azure eyes narrowing and lips twisting with cruel hate, "you will be ours."

I glanced to my friends—to Keldon, Leta, Arleia, and Rognar, standing just as dumbfounded as I must have appeared. The horde of emaciated mortifants, centipedean necrocites, and white-eyed ghastuls closed in around us. Together with Mistress Agona, the remaining Dungh'gar priest, and the newly awakened fiend, I saw only one course of action.

"Run!" I screamed. Then I bit down on the locking pin of my right wristband and yanked the pin free.

Blinding pain exploded through every vein, muscle, and bone in my body as the alchemorph roared to life with the heat of a blast furnace, unfettered by the dampening effects of severite. My clothes incinerated in an instant and my three remaining vials exploded, the volatile reagents fueling the raging elemental chaos I had become. Crackling fire washed across the moss-slick floor as my flaming form stepped forward, sending the undead horde scampering for the shadows. The nightmarish creature we faced swept straight past Mistress Agona, condensing threads of necrolic energy as it stalked toward me. A blistering conflagration erupted from my alchemorph's hands, but the firestorm fizzled like a snuffed-out candle, leaving nothing more than a cloud of steam that sank in a cold, sinking mist.

The abominable creature met my burning ember eyes, a guttural laugh rumbling from its chest as it stretched out its terrible hands, taloned fingers weaving together the inky smoke seething around its shadow-darkened form. The pain of a thousand freezing needles replaced the inferno within me, wrenching away every whit of reactant alchemical energy coursing through my immolating body. I screamed, my own voice joining the primal howl of my enraged alchemorph, then the alchemorph fell abruptly silent. My knees hit the steaming floor, the blinding white pain ebbing to a frigid chill numbing every inch of my shivering skin. Horror and panic swept over me, and I looked from my trembling hands to the otherworldly creature looming above me, a swirling vortex of flame gathering between its massive hands.

The alchemorph... The alchemorph was gone!

"Aldicus!" I heard Keldon yell.

Heat washed over me as the flaming vortex reformed into a blazing figure of elemental fire standing beside the fiendish creature. A moment passed before I realized that I was seeing my own alchemorph, now separated entirely from myself. The alchemorph stared back, the incandescent eyes of its flame-wreathed face burning with all its seething hatred. Keldon called again, and I glanced back only to see my friends gathered in a defensive circle, braced to fight what they each knew would be their final battle. I pinched my eyes shut. *They should have run...* Now they would share my fate—a doom of fire and agony, here in the abyssal depths a thousand feet below the night-conquered streets of Corradon.

"Behold, the triumph of the Dark," Mistress Agona sneered. She, together with the primordial fiend and my stolen alchemorph, started forward to unleash their final, killing attack.

I braced myself for the end, but a rising rumble resounded through the air, growing steadily louder until I could discern the clamor of iron hooves and carriage wheels. A pale green light spilled from far down the catacombs, growing brighter as the bray of phantasmal horses echoed through the ancient halls. From out of the lingering gloom a midnight coach appeared, flying as though born upon an unseen aetheric wind and drawn by four clockwork steeds glowing with spectral light. Atop the unearthly carriage rode the vampire Armez, festooned in his scarlet tailcoat and teal top hat, with raven-haired Quiniece sitting by his side, a panoply weaponry poised to attack.

"I see Emileve found us just in time," Armez chimed with a goading grin. "Now, quit your gawking and climb aboard!"

Leta flung out a defensive ward, deflecting Agona's barrage of crackling aetheric energy, while Rognar blasted potshots from Varla. Keldon threw my frock coat over my shoulders and I staggered to my feet, pulling the coat tighter as I followed the others to the vampire's timely ride.

Armez glanced down from his perch atop the coach, making sure everyone was inside. "Hang on," he called as Leta shut the carriage door. "The takeoff might be a little rough."

The dapper vampire whipped the heavy brass chains he held as reins, and with a sudden upward lurch, I felt the catacomb floor fall away—iron hooves thundering and clockwork gears clattering. Glancing out the coach's rearward window, I watched the ghostly streams of light trailing in our wake, leaving far behind the bolts of crackling energy and blazing alchemical fire streaming after us.

"What in Davlen's name *was* that thing?" Rognar yelled, turning to look back as the chamber receded into darkness.

Keldon shifted nervously in his seat, and both Leta and Arleia were as speechless as my apprentice. No one had an answer for Rognar, and the horror reeling in my own mind precluded any chance that I might conjure up even the slightest semblance of a guess. I shivered, the emptiness inside me aching like a hollowed-out cavity, and I pulled my coat tighter as I sank back into the coach's plush interior couch.

The enemy's plans had come to a head, and we had failed to put even a dent in their nefarious scheme. Our only chance now was to unravel the mystery of the Aetherspire and uncover whatever treachery undermined its design. I could only hope that the faint trail Tibblemond left for us would be enough to find our way before all was lost.

THE 5TH DISTRICT'S LOWER PRECINCT rolled beneath Armez's flying coach as the spectral clockwork steeds carried us through the smoggy night with untiring dedication. Industrial cranes and heavy-lift dirigibles gave way to gaudy jumbles of luminary signboards and the advertising arc-lights of businesses, alehouses, and tenements—all eerily empty thanks to the imposed nighttime curfew. Yet, despite the declaration of martial law, the populous remained oblivious to the scheming machinations of those imperious powers operating beyond the realm of their day-to-day affairs. So long as order was restored and a semblance of normality resumed, the general citizenry would go about their lives in blissful ignorance.

I drew the window drape closed and leaned back in my plush seat. "From the doldrums of apathy rise the kingdom of tyranny."

"Hmm?" Keldon asked, turning away from the left side window.

"Hold on tight," Armez called from the driver's box at the front of the coach.

No sooner had he spoken than the pit of my stomach lurched to the top of my throat, and the coach plummeted for what must have been three hundred feet before leveling out again. Keldon grabbed the interior chair rail, and Leta and Arleia held onto their seat with teeth clenched in sudden surprise. Rognar just sat back and kicked his boots up on the center footrest, pulling a grease-soaked liver and onion sarnie from one of his countless duffle coat pockets.

Keldon groaned, watching Rognar eat. “How are you able to stomach that when we’re spending as much time falling as flying in this thing?”

Rognar shrugged. “If anyone knows how to fly an ensorcelled clockwork passenger coach, it would be vampires.” He took a bite of his greasy sarnie and smiled through his beard.

“Please, don’t remind me,” Leta growled, her narrowed eyes fixed on our dapper-dressed driver and his young sireling sitting at the head of the coach. “Were it any other day, we’d be hunting those two.”

The lamplit night turned pitch-black, and I glanced out the window to watch the hazy glow of the coach’s eerie green light glint across the conduits and steam pipes of a sublevel utility corridor. A short time passed, and we exited the corridor into the silent vastness of a colonnaded storm cistern before descending into the confines of an even deeper tunnel. I did not know where Armez was taking us, but I would not have been surprised if the ancient vampire had more than a few well-secluded haunts in the depths of the Clockwork City.

The coach lurched again, and with the rolling clatter of wood wheels and iron hooves battering against cobblestone, we finally set down on solid ground. We continued for what might have been a few blocks more, bouncing along the rough remnants of some long-buried avenue. We were deep beneath the top-side streets of Corradon—perhaps even in the Underworks. Although darkness shrouded much of the sunken building we approached, I glimpsed enough of the intricate stonework to deduce it might once have been a spectacular guildhall from centuries long past.

My suspicions were confirmed when we rolled into a well-lit coach house tucked away at the foot of the building. Most of the parking stalls were empty, save for a small collection of pristine coaches and carriages—all of them black and outfitted with velvet drapes and elegant interiors, much like our own. The clopping hooves fell silent as we came to a stop, and the ratcheting crank of wheel brakes signaled that we could safely disembark. Leta opened the door and jumped out, with Arleia following just behind her. Rognar stuffed the last bite of his sarnie into his mouth before exiting the coach, and Keldon nearly stumbled on top of him as he staggered out on motion-sick legs.

I followed a moment later, still clutching my frock coat around my otherwise naked body. I spared a worried glance at my wrists, which were as distressingly bare as the rest of me. Without my severite wristbands, I should be a flaming monstrosity of pure elemental chaos—and yet, not the slightest hint of the alchemorph's presence remained. In its place there was only an empty hole carved out from the very core of my being.

What had that fiendish creature done to me?

Quiniece twisted a small vizstone on her side of the driver's box and the spectral light radiating from the mechanical steeds winked out with a snap of discharging aethergy. My skin prickled at the sensation, and I drew a sharp breath as I felt the metallic tingle of diaphanous aethergy pulsing through the luminiferous aether. It was a welcome sensation, and one I had not felt in many years. I could not help but smile, slowly breathing out as I listened to the distant, crystal chimes of the higher astral light.

"Hi, Keldon," Quiniece greeted. She hopped down from the top of the coach, then stepped past Keldon, brushing a finger along his neck before giving him a wink. "Miss me?"

Keldon blinked, lost for words, and his gaze dropped involuntarily to the low-cut top of her tight-laced bodice. Arleia shouldered herself around him, her fists clenched and lips pursed as she locked eyes with the vampire sireling.

"We *hunt* creatures like you," she snapped, her tapered ears drawn back. "We *slay* creatures like you!"

A wicked smile crept across Quiniece's alabaster face. "I wouldn't be so sure about that. We aren't your deadlurk-variety thralls or blood-ghouls, you know." Then she licked her pronounced canines and winked, this time at Arleia. "We're the real deal, sweets."

Arleia's face pinched with indignation and she looked to Leta, but Leta replied with the slightest shake of her head. Face flushed and temper fuming, the half-Eldren spun away in a huff, pausing just long enough to give my apprentice a scornful glare before stalking off with arms crossed.

"What?" Keldon asked, apparently bewildered. "What did I do?"

"I see we're all well acquainted," Armez said glibly, striding into our midst. He smiled, brushing out a few wrinkles from his brocaded scarlet tailcoat before fluffing the ruffles of his satin cravat. "Ah, my dear and lovely Vescard," he continued, looking me up and down, eyebrows arched in mock surprise. "You appear to be suffering a most scandalous wardrobe deficiency. But as much as I might prefer your company in your present state, there are young ones about, and we must find you something more suitable to wear." He clasped his hands together, looking from me to the others and back again. "But first, allow me to show you around my humble haven, Harrowdeep."

Armez led us past the coach stalls and up a flight of polished stone stairs to the main floor of his 'humble' guildhall-turned-mansion. An oak panel door opened to a wide hallway embellished with luxurious velvet drapes and carpeted by an ornate runner rug, the warm glow of gas wall sconces illuminating our way in soft, twilight hues. We passed several side corridors and closed off rooms, continuing through an archway into a handsomely furnished foyer leading to Harrowdeep's Great Hall.

Armez removed his top hat and gestured with a flourish,

ushering us through the tall double doors into a chamber of richly veined marble and polished quartzstone. Between each fluted column supporting the vaulted ceiling above stood ornate stained-glass windows, lit from behind by hidden luminaries, and depicting mythic scenes from long lost ages. Three crystal chandeliers hung above a thirty-foot long dining table, providing ample illumination for the expansive space. The far side of the hall featured a cozy sitting area arranged about the hearth of an enormous fireplace flickering with the bright red flames of cinnabar coal. Yet, despite the roaring fire, a perpetual chill lingered in the air, made worse by the cold marble floor against my bare feet. I pulled my frock coat even tighter, but the garment did little to help my numbing toes.

"Quaint," Rognar muttered, crossing his arms as he took in the full immensity of the hall. "The stained glass is a bit dated for modern sensibilities, but the stonework is worthy of some small note—for human craftsmanship, I mean."

Armez cracked the barest hint of a smile, though he was clearly holding back some sassy repartee to counter the Dworgh's genial raillery. Leta and Arleia spread out as we made our way across the room, the former taking careful note of the chamber's entrances and exits, while the latter kept a watchful eye on Quiniece. Keldon stumbled after me, his wide-eyed gaze jumping from one ornate fixture to another, too overwhelmed to apprehend the scattering of clues our host had deliberately left out in the open.

The most obvious clue was the golden cup placed prominently on the hall's banquet table—the Chalice of the Blood King—and next to it sat a carafe of water, which, when poured into the chalice, would transmute into blood. Two dinner sets also graced the table, along with wine glasses and several bottles of excellent Armillian vintage. Although vampires required only blood to sustain them, Armez certainly enjoyed the occasional self-indulgent meal, if for no other reason than the sheer vanity of it. The far end of the table was buried beneath a sizable map of the city, spilling over with markings, scribblings, and tacked on notes. Armez had been far more involved in the planning of our little insurrection than his nonchalant attitude let on, and that, at least, boded well.

But perhaps the most telling clue of all was the dust—not a copious amount of dust, but rather, the fine gray layer coating the banisters, fixtures, and furnishings, with cobwebs garnishing every corner of the Great Hall. A mansion this large could only be kept clean with the help of a considerable staff of housemaids and butlers. Any other master vampire would have had an army of thralls at his beck and call, tasked with everything from guard duty to maid service, but not Armez. Perhaps Armez had such thralls in the past, but today there was no sign that anyone other than himself and his sireling occupied his half acre, subterranean abode.

Leta and Arleia were not wrong to mistrust the pair—vampires were, after all, notoriously cruel, and considered humans prey. But Armez and Quiniece were different. They had gone out of their way to acquire the Chalice of the Blood King, and not simply as a relic of their ancient heritage, but to satiate their need to feed on other sentient beings. They had helped us thwart the sinister plans of the Servants of Vosh, and now they had joined our struggle against the Shadow Man's tyranny.

But why? What had happened to Armez that changed him so dramatically? Although he had spoken little of his ordeal at the hands of the Servants of Vosh, I knew they had tortured him, experimented on him, and exposed him to untold horrors. In them, he had seen a darkness—a *true* darkness, darker even than the darkest dreams of his own bloodthirsty nature. And in the madness and agony of their sadistic ministrations, perhaps they had sparked a long cold ember of humanity buried deep within the desiccated husk of his black, unbeating heart.

Perhaps.

Or perhaps he was just Armez.

"Make yourselves at home," the vampire invited. He gestured to the plush settees and leather armchairs of the sitting area, then indicated the porcelain tea set arranged on the table. "The finest yellow tea, imported from far Arkana."

Rognar plopped down on an oversize armchair, his heavy boots kicking up but not quite reaching the table, which was probably for the best since he would have knocked over the tea set. Arleia took a smaller armchair, Leta settled into one of the settees, and Keldon slid into another settee across from them. Quiniece brazenly squeezed into the settee next to Keldon, her amber eyes narrowing as they fixed on Arleia. Arleia glared back, ears flattening and face tensing.

"Oh, yes, I should get you some clothes," Armez said, as though only now remembering that I had nothing but the battle-frayed frock coat pulled around my body. "We can't very well have you running around my mansion naked—at least not with these young ones here." He cracked a knowing smile and sighed. "Such a shame."

The awkward silence grew even more awkward and silent, with everyone, save for Leta, shifting uneasily in their seats. Leta just arched an eyebrow at Armez, her eyes narrowing.

"This way, Vescard," Armez indicated as he started for a side door near the southeast corner of the hall. "I believe you will find my wardrobe as stylish and diverse as that of the most fashionable clothiers of Bridgecroft Avenue."

I sighed and followed Armez, glancing back just as we reached the door to catch the rising banter between our amiably contentious apprentices.

"I have a fully equipped workshop," Quiniece was saying to Keldon, her eyes glancing fleetingly to his neck, "complete with cobalt-ilmenium lathes, pneumatic tooling, and even a switchable gearmill I built myself. Come on. I'll show you around."

"You're not going anywhere with him," Arleia cut in before

my cornered apprentice could voice his reply. "I saw you eyeing his neck!"

"You can come, too, sweets," Quiniece said with an unconcerned shrug. "But I think you'll find our three thousand volume library more to your liking."

Arleia sucked in a breath, her hand reaching up to adjust her glasses. "You... You have a library?" she asked, her inflection raised a notch.

"What an excellent idea," Armez called back before ducking through the doorway. "I'm sure Leta and her protégé would quite enjoy perusing our rare book collection."

"I'd like to see this workshop of yours," Rognar put in. Then he patted the pockets of his duffle coat as though searching for something. "Or better yet, your larder."

"Well, we do have some fresh black pudding," Quiniece offered.

"Black pudding? I love..." The Dworgh's voice trailed off, as though just now remembering that our hosts were vampires. "Wait... What's it made from?"

But we were already out the door and making our way down the corridor, the quarrelsome exchange receding behind us as Armez led me deeper into the depths of his hidden lair.

I FOLLOWED ARMEZ DOWN THE RICHLY PANEL HALL, admiring the hanging tapestries and old oil paintings warmly lit by the softly glowing luminaries fixed in brass wall sconces. We passed the arched doorway for what I suspected was the library and continued down the corridor until arriving at an elegantly furnished parlor.

"Right this way," Armez said, gesturing to another door across the parlor.

The door opened into a small anteroom, and from there into the dressing room attached to Armez's chambers. The dressing room was a picture of aristocratic indulgence, complete with porcelain vanity and gilded mirrors, sumptuous lounging chairs, four chests of drawers, and an expansive wardrobe spilling over with coats, hats, scarfs, and every imaginable garment to complete a gentleman's attire. Although I was certainly no authority on fashion, a quick survey of the enviable collection revealed styles and accessories that must have dated back at least four centuries—brocaded justacorps coats, knee-breeches, frill-laced shirts, and even a few heeled shoes, all in the most diverse assortment of colors imaginable.

Even today, Armez's preferred attire seemed to reflect aspects of these older fashions, combined and refined with a measured balance of modern overtones. I had never inquired as to how old Armez might be, but as a master vampire, he may well have witnessed the collapse of the Three Realms, the Patrician Wars, the War of Tyranny, and the full-steam-ahead rise of our modern Age of Progress. I shuddered, wondering at the vast expanse of history my formidable colleague had seen.

"Oh, you must be freezing," Armez said, noticing my shudder. "You will have to forgive me. I do forget what it was like to be mortal."

He curled an impish smile, then spun about to look through a wardrobe containing a collection of more-or-less modern attire. After a moment of careful consideration, he picked out a bright purple tailcoat, a gaudy floral waistcoat, and tight-legged trousers, along with a selection of silk cravats in various shades of rose and pink. He turned back to me, presenting the ludicrous selection with a deadpan expression.

I furrowed my brow, but Armez held a straight face for a moment longer, then burst with laughter.

"I'm only fooling, Vescard! But a little color would make you look absolutely fetching."

I sighed. "Why can't you just dress in black like all the other vampires?"

"To be different is not a crime." He returned the garments

to the wardrobe and continued his search, pausing only to glance back at me, his eyes narrowing and lips curling in an unmistakably seductive grin. "And I do enjoy showing off in your company."

I did my best to return his grin with a courteous smile. He was clearly enjoying the chase, though he certainly knew my inclinations did not match his own. Yet, I found I appreciated his efforts for what they were. As bleak and dispiriting a time as this was, his playful disposition was oddly refreshing. How strange that the flirtatious badinage of a vampire could so lighten the sullen mood these darkest days.

"This should be more your style," Armez said, bringing out a blue frock coat, matching trousers, and a white pleated shirt. To these he added a brocaded waistcoat, a gold cravat, and a pair of wingtip shoes surprisingly close to my size. "Respectable, conventional, and dreadfully boring. But you'll be pleased to know I have a set of undergarments that have never once been used."

Armez arranged the clothes on one of the dressing room's lounging chairs, then indicated where I could find the undergarments. He remained for a moment longer, arms folded as he casually leaned back against a chest of drawers.

"Oh, that's right," he sighed, as though only now remembering the finer points of propriety. "I suppose you shall want me to leave." He gave a seemingly indifferent shrug, then donned his red-tinted spectacles and left through the door leading out to the parlor.

With Armez gone, I assembled my new attire with as much haste as I could manage. I transferred Tibblemond's notes from my battle-frayed frock coat to the pocket of my new coat, glad that I had not put it in my trouser pocket, which had been incinerated. After making sure the cravat was properly tied and tucked, I made my way back into the parlor.

"Oh, be quickened, my black, unbeating heart!" Armez

exclaimed, hand pressed to his chest as he looked me up and down. "You are as dapper as ever, my dear Vescard. Perhaps even more so, thanks to the remarkable breadth of my fashionable sensibilities."

I followed Armez down the wood-paneled corridor, but instead of returning to the Great Hall, we entered Harrowdeep's lavishly embellished library. Half as large as the Great Hall itself, the library boasted a white marble floor and quartzstone columns supporting not one, but two balcony tiers, accessible by four spiral staircases. What few sections of wall were not covered in bookshelves were either paneled in rich walnut boiserie or featured a receded alcove holding a statue of pre-Maradian antiquity. Two chandeliers of empowered luminaries hung from the barrel-vaulted ceiling, between which turned the blades of a fan driven by a complication of brass clockworks doubtlessly assembled by Quiniece. Considering the tightly packed bookshelves of the first level, and the rows of shelves lining the balcony tiers, the collection had to number in the thousands—perhaps even three thousand, if Quiniece's statement had not been a boast.

Leta and Arleia were already present, their eyes wide in bewilderment as they walked, half-dazed, through the library. Keldon had found a sizable tome on thaumaturgical arts and was eagerly thumbing through, while Rognar lounged in the enveloping folds of a plush leather armchair. Quiniece stood quietly by, hands on hips with a smile wide enough to rival even Armez's most grandiose grin.

"Welcome to the new headquarters of the Corradon resistance," Armez proudly announced. He swiped a sheet away from a large easel, revealing a map of Corradon along with another, close-in map of the city's core districts.

"We already have a headquarters," Rognar objected. "Or is the Chancy Step's seedy ambience beneath your genteel refinement?"

"You may return there if you prefer," Armez said. "Please

give my best to the HAAMR troopers who've now secured that rusty old dive, along with all surrounding establishments for a six-block radius."

"Fangle-fop!" I exclaimed. My fingers brushed against my wrists and I flinched at the absence of my severite wristbands. *That was going to take some getting used to.* "They must have tracked us from the scene of the murder, despite Emileve's precautions." Then I froze. "Emileve... The Unseen Brotherhood... Were they captured?"

"No, of course they escaped," Armez replied. Then he sighed as though explaining the obvious was too much of a tedious chore. "And before you ask, the Broken Spigot is also out of the question, since I'm sure the Shadow Man knows all your usual haunts. I wouldn't count on returning to Number Five Brass Lantern Lane, either. HAAMR agents are watching your house like a pack of starving barghests." He then nodded to Leta. "The same holds for your fashionable uptown flat as well, I'm afraid."

"Wonderful," Leta mumbled, her eyes rolling.

"So, what you're saying is, since no one knows about your modest little apartment in the 5th District Underworks, we should just convene the resistance here?" Keldon asked.

"I wouldn't say *no one* knows," Armez corrected. "But apart from us—no. No one who's still alive, at any rate."

"I do not find the prospect of hiding out in a vampire's lair particularly comforting." Leta ran her hand along a row of leather-bound books, then stopped to pull one out. "Still, the resources here are considerably better than those of the Chancy Step."

"Bah!" Rognar barked. "I'd like to see our swanky host match the Chancy Step's unrivaled supply of rust-bottom rotgut!"

Quiniece glanced at Armez and he smiled in return.

"That reminds me," Armez mused. "We've not given you a tour of the undercroft, have we?"

Rognar looked up and blinked. He scratched his beard,

then cleared his throat, shifting uneasily in his chair. "This would be an undercroft stocked with ale, rum, and spirits, right? Not a dungeon full of bones, rotting guts, and... well... actual spirits."

"Aromatic gins, spiced rums, vintage wines, brandy wines, malt beers, and amber ales," Armez rattled off. "Only the best, of course—not the watered-down swill of your middling sublevel alehouses." He stood a bit straighter, brushing out the creases of his tailcoat. "I may be a vampire, my staunch little friend, but I do have taste."

I joined Keldon at the table where he sat studying *Orvan's Grammaticon* by Dergus Orvan, and a first print from the looks of it. Leta and Arleia had already picked out a sizable pile of books for their own perusal, flipping through the pages of ancient lore, too engrossed to mind the ongoing raillery between Rognar and Armez. I skimmed the titles along the shelf where Keldon had found his book, then smiled as I pulled out a copy of Izaron Ty's *Manual of Talismanic Empowerments*.

For the first time since my encounter with the fiend in the depths of the Vernoct Cryptopolis, the fact that I was well and truly cured of my affliction finally sank in. Without the dampening effect of my severite wristbands, I could once again hear the distant harmonies of the ever-shifting aetheric currents—could touch it, channel it, and mold it to my will. And yet, without the resonant empowerments of my old talisman, stashed away in #5 Brass Lantern Lane, I could scarcely harness even a fraction of that power. But artificing a proper talisman to replace my old one could take over a week—or a month for a proper job—and that was time we did not have. I sighed, returning the book to the shelf, and drew Tibblemond's notes from my pocket.

"Do you have any books on stenography?" I asked Armez. "Specifically, Kellian stenography and its lesser-known variations?"

"Stenography?" Armez laughed. "My dear Vescard, I have

books on every subject from the rise and fall of Marada, to the whimsical anecdotes of backcountry folklore, to the latest research treatises on aetheronic engineering, theoretical thaumatology, and metazotic bioalchemy. And yes, I do have a few books on stenography."

Armez nodded to Quiniece, who rolled her eyes before heading off to fetch the books. Then he took a few tomes from a still dustier shelf and dropped them on the table before me.

"Making sense of whatever clues Tibblemond left us is important, but let's get some perspective," he went on to say, removing his red-tinted spectacles as he cracked the cover of the first book. "Mistress Agona and her cronies just unleashed a demon-spawned abomination from its ancient slumber—a creature of immense and terrifying power. And that, my friend, is more than a little worrying. I've seen a lot in my days, but I've never seen something quite like what I saw today." He pushed one of the books over to me and smiled. "Now, let's see what we can find out, shall we?"

"Don't bother," Leta whispered. She had grown increasingly pale as Armez spoke, the blood draining from her face as she stared at the faded pages of an old illuminated manuscript, handwritten in ancient Relican. "I was hoping I was wrong, but now..." She hesitated, drawing a deep breath and slowly letting it out again. "I... I think I know what that creature was."

I blinked, first looking to Armez, who arched an intrigued eyebrow, then to Keldon, Arleia, and Rognar, who all appeared nearly as befuddled. "You do?"

"I don't know how it's possible, and I could be wrong," she went on to say, her voice trembling. "I certainly hope I'm wrong. But the similarities are too—"

"Out with it, already!" Rognar insisted, bolting up in his chair.

Leta rotated the book, revealing a crude illustration of a dark, hunched form with four distinctive horns thrusting out from beneath the drooping cowl of its cloak and reaching arms with monstrous, taloned hands, each having an extra thumb where the little finger should have been. The rendering was in the early monastic style, at least a thousand years old, and the distortions were so exaggerated that it could only have been drawn from a rough description passed down over the centuries. But there was no question in my mind: the creature depicted was identical to the fiend we had encountered.

"What..." I found myself rasping, shivering as the memory of its chilling, alien presence threatened to overwhelm me. "What is it?"

"A Darkweaver," Leta said, her voice trembling as she pointed to the Relican text. "A demonic servitor of pure malevolence and corruption—a supreme master of the blackest magics, exalted commander of the forces of ancient Golla, and emissary to the Demon Lords of Atracus."

The room fell silent and remained silent as the tick-tock timing of the gearwork fan marked out what must have been a minute. I stared at the page, unable to think, unable to move, and scarcely able to breathe.

Atracus. The demon-moon. The eternal prison of the Demon Lords and the fell legions of the empire of Golla. It was impossible. It was *unthinkable.* But there it was. After fifteen hundred years, the ancient enemy had returned.

I slumped back in my chair, the cold emptiness within me becoming a tempest of chilling terror. "Archons help us all."

Case File 14:

As Above, So Below

I WOKE THE NEXT DAY TO THE ENVELOPING WARMTH of a plush mattress, luxurious silk sheets, and a down-stuffed quilt. I could almost forget last night's disturbing revelation, wrapped snugly in the blissful oblivion between languid dreams and wakeful awareness. Why Armez had such comfortable beds, or even guest rooms, was a mystery. Vampires had no need for either, as for them sleep was a death-like torpor, typically inside a cassone bed often mistaken for a coffin by the uninformed. Regardless, I had slept through what little remained of the morning and most of the afternoon, only now rousing as footsteps and voices echoed from the gallery hall outside.

"Wake up, Keldon," I called to my apprentice, throwing on the dressing robe Armez had loaned me. "We have a lot of work to do today. Or rather, this evening, as the case happens to be."

Keldon groaned and rolled over on the spare mattress tucked into the corner of the room, pulling his pillow over his face as he mumbled incoherent objections. I splashed my face in the vanity wash basin, then dressed in the clothes Armez had provided, throwing on the blue frock coat and reminding Keldon to get up before leaving our quarters.

The hall on this wing of the mansion was a colonnaded gallery that had likely served as a reception area when the building was still a guildhall. Armez had made the gallery the main residence wing, decorated in the neoclassical style with the surrounding rooms converted into two master suites, two guest rooms, a parlor, and a small drawing room. Leta and Arleia shared one of the rooms, with myself and Keldon sharing the other. Rognar had to make do with a sofa in the Great Hall, but the resourceful Dworgh didn't seem to mind. It was, after all, right next door to the larder and kitchen.

Muffled voices and clinking teacups issued from the parlor, so I picked up my pace, eager for a strong cup of tea.

"Look what the crypt-rat dragged in," Leta said, cracking a smile. She took another sip from her teacup and nodded to the porcelain pot on the table. "Care for a little morning refreshment?"

"It is five fifteen in the evening," I corrected, after a quick glance at the room's case clock. Quiniece no doubt kept every timekeeping fixture in Harrowdeep as tick-tock accurate as the city's Grand Complication—anything less would be an insult to even the most maladroit gearmeister. I pulled up a chair and sat down, breathing out a despondent sigh as I took one of the remaining teacups. "This should be dinner time."

"It's morning," Quiniece clarified. She leaned back in her chair, swirling the crimson contents of the golden chalice she held. "Morning for vampires, anyway—and an early morning at that." She glanced at Arleia sitting opposite from her and a mischievous smile crept across her face. "Does Keldon always sleep in?"

Arleia jumped, nearly spilling her tea. "How should I know?" she squeaked, her face turning red.

"I'b abbake," Keldon muttered as he stumbled into the parlor. His clothes were as disheveled as his tousled hair, and he staggered to the table, greedily ogling the remaining teacup with bleary, sleep-leaden eyes.

Quiniece pushed up the bosom of her tight-laced bodice, then patted the chair to her left. Oblivious, Keldon plopped down beside the young vampire and tried to pour himself a cup from the teapot before noticing the cup in front of him was already full.

Quiniece looked to Arleia, grinning triumphantly.

Arleia scowled, her tapered ears flattened back, and she almost seemed ready to throw herself across the table at Quiniece. Leta glanced at me from over the rim of her steaming teacup, as though to ask if we should intervene to stop their flirtatious spat. But before anyone could say anything more, Rognar lurched into the parlor hefting a tray piled high with pan-seared sausages, bread rolls stuffed with bacon and cheese, and assorted sweet pastries.

"Breakfast!" he cheerily announced. "Or dinner if you prefer."

He dropped the tray onto the table and plopped into the remaining chair before grabbing a handful of sausages. Except for Quiniece, who sat sipping from the Chalice of the Blood King, everyone reached in for the food, though wisely leaving the majority of sausages for Rognar who devoured them without shame.

"Where is Armez?" I asked Quiniece before taking a bite of a stuffed roll.

"Out," Quiniece replied. She took another sip from the chalice, but offered no further clarification.

It was indeed early for a vampire to be out and about, but only a dim memory of sunlight ever made it into the lower sublevels, and none at all into the Underworks. Assuming Armez had spent sufficient time revivifying in torpor, Armez would have no difficulty pursuing his errands. As to what those errands were, I could only speculate.

Vampires were predators, and ordinarily I would be as keen to stop him as Leta or any other veilhunter. But Armez and his sireling had given up their nocturnal hunts long before acquiring the Chalice of the Blood King, instead subsisting on undercity vermin and the occasional criminal whom they likely regarded as much the same. Perhaps Armez had gone out to get food, clothing, and other supplies for us lowly mortals. On the other hand, being the self-indulgent gourmet that he was, Armez already had a well-stocked larder, as Rognar had uncovered.

I sighed. "Did Armez go out to find Emileve and the Unseen Brotherhood?"

"No," Quiniece answered, still failing to elaborate.

"Well, someone needs to," I suggested, giving Rognar a quick nod.

Rognar grinned beneath his braided beard. "On it, boss!" He grabbed the last four sausages and stuffed them into his pockets, then hustled out the door.

Quiniece frowned as the Dworgh disappeared down the corridor. "I'm not sure Armez would approve of more people knowing about our hidden refuge."

"If he wants this to be our new headquarters, he will need to accept the responsibility that entails," I explained. "Besides, the Unseen Brotherhood is rather good at keeping secrets."

Quiniece glowered, but said nothing more.

With a meal in our bellies and tea in our veins, we returned to the library to continue our research. The next few hours passed with the kind of frenetic silence I had only seen in the Grand Lodge's research libraries—the soft rasp of turning pages, the shuffle of feet from shelves to tables, and the occasional whisper of colleagues consulting one another. Even Quiniece behaved, quietly studying a few choice books while Keldon and Arleia poured over ancient monastic manuscripts, undisturbed by her typical provocations. She glanced at them only when Arleia snickered at some wisecrack Keldon had made, smiling ever so slightly before settling back into her own quiet studies.

"This is so frustrating," Keldon blurted from behind his pile of books. He slammed shut the tome he had been reading, then ran a hand through his unruly hair. "Most of these accounts were written by Archidox monks, six hundred *years* after the War of Golla and Marada, and in poetic religious verse. If I see one more elegiac couplet or lyric quatrain, I think I'll scream!"

"You're screaming now," Quiniece pointed out.

Leta looked up from her own books and sighed. "We're supposed to be searching for references to Darkweavers, demonic emissaries, or anything suggestive of that."

"There are references aplenty," Keldon admitted. "Darkweavers commanding the demonsworn legions and emissaries carrying out the will of one Demon Lord or another. But none of it tells us anything useful. What *was* that blasted thing? What are its powers and what can it do?"

"More importantly," Quiniece added, "how do we kill it?"

I pushed Tibblemond's notes aside, then folded my hands on the table. Although I had made good progress translating my late friend's haphazard scribblings, I needed a break. "The real question is, where did that creature come from and what does the Shadow Man hope to gain through its allegiance?"

The room fell silent, save for the rhythmic ticking of the clockwork complications driving the fans above.

"Do we have anything substantial, beyond the vague whisperings of myth and legends?" I asked Leta.

Leta sat back and adjusted her shrug coat, taking a moment to think before answering. "Most of what we've found just mentions these creatures in passing, usually referring to them as commanding the forces of Atracus during the War of Golla and Marada. I was already familiar with some of these accounts, but Keldon's right. Most were written centuries after the war, in the cloistered sanctuaries of mountaintop monasteries by monks who had never laid eyes on the creatures. Almost no direct accounts of the war survived the dark age that followed, leaving us with little more than the passed-down fables, allegorical parables, and pseudo-histories written in the early days of the Archidoxy's reconstruction."

I perked up, reading into her words. "You said *almost* no direct accounts survived the war."

Leta nodded. "The Archidoxy's histories, which cast the war in the poetic language that typically obfuscates all mythical narratives, do quote a few passages from just after the war's end. Most of these excerpts are given to validate the legendary deeds of Emperor Kullan or other sanctified heroes of Marada, but we have come across two that are of particular note."

I arched an eyebrow, waiting for Leta to continue. Instead, she looked to her young assistant and waited. Arleia bit her lip, her teal eyes darting to Leta before returning to her books.

"Well, you're the one who found the passage," Leta prompted.

Arleia sighed, her tapered ears drooping. "It's not much to go on," she said, adjusting her glasses as she shuffled through her notes. "The text, which is from around 290 CA and was written by a monk in the Monastery of Sabarrial, chronicles the invasions of the region of Glaven by Gollan forces near the end of the war. In it, he summarizes a visual record from a supposedly surviving crystex recording."

She cleared her throat in preparation to quote the text.

"'There, upon the shores of the last stronghold of Glaven, fell the thundering wings of the enemy. From their wings marched the demonsworn legions and their sorcerous machines, and at their head walked those vile weavers of darkness and corruption, with twelve unholy priests of Voshthok and Abothog bearing the blasphemous standards of their demonic lords.'" Having finished, she looked up and sighed. "That is, of course, translated from Maradian to Relican, which I have translated to modern Celanic."

"Weavers of darkness and corruption," Leta repeated. "Darkweavers."

"And then there's this one," Keldon said, pointing to another open book. "In it they refer to something called

Drazaki the Desolator."

"That's not exactly what it says," Leta stated. "I found another manuscript that also refers to Darkweavers as Drazaki. I think that's what their race is called, or it's the closest approximation from Gollan."

"Desolator," I said, considering the word for a moment. A spark of recognition tingled in the back of my mind. "What does the manuscript say?"

Keldon studied the Relican text for a moment, his mouth moving as he silently sounded out the words. All mages were versed in Relican, including apprentice mages, but Keldon had never been particularly fluent in the long dead language.

"'At great loss of life, Kullan's mages... Um... the mage's of Kullan's expedition... closed devices of starry bridge to Atracus,'" Keldon read, slowly. Arleia leaned over and whispered something to him, pointing to a few of the words. "Oh, right. They 'stopped the machines of the astral bridge to Atracus... But some had come through already... Led by Drazaki Desolator. By his knowledge great and terrible he awoke those machines... calling forth... the...'" Keldon stopped and Arleia whispered to him again. "Thanks. 'The blazing vortex of darkness-light... opening the bridge again. Thus entered...' I mean, 'thus came the Third Wave, and the world shook... or trembled... as the demon-moon swallowed the light of the sun.'"

I furrowed my brow. "Swallowed the light of the sun," I whispered, mulling the poetic phrasing. An eclipse?

"Among them was *a* Drazaki, *the* Desolator," Leta corrected. "Relican lacks both definite and indefinite articles, but take another look at the declension of 'desolator'."

Keldon nodded his head. "This Drazaki, or Darkweaver, has a title naming him the Desolator."

"Fangle-fop!" I exclaimed, slamming my hand on the table.

Everyone turned to look at me, but I was already out of my chair and skimming the length of the library's titles. The pieces were coming together, forming the first hints of a picture I now dreaded to complete.

"The Reliquary of the Infernal Desolator was stolen by the Servants of Vosh several months ago," I said over my shoulder, before resuming my search for the book. "The Reliquary was said to contain the essence of a demonic servitor."

Keldon sucked in a breath, coming to the same horrifying conclusion. "It didn't contain its essence. It contained the creature itself. The Reliquary was a Maradian stasis box!"

"A *Gollan* stasis box," I corrected. I found the book I was looking for—a thick astrological ephemeris for the current year, full of astrological tables and charts. "That's probably why no one has been able to open it. Maradian stasis boxes are exceedingly rare, but at least the procedure for opening them is known. On the other hand, that Gollan stasis box must have been keyed to a very particular ritual, and it must have required a considerable quantity of necrolic energy, which explains why Mistress Agona needed to open it in the Vernoct Cryptopolis."

Leta tapped her fingers on the table. "Then this Darkweaver is from the War of Golla and Marada." She looked at the text Keldon had read from. "It was even mentioned by name in the Archidoxy's chronicles. But why raise such a fiend? What could they hope to gain?"

"Read the text again," I said, returning to the table with the ephemeris. "Consider *exactly* what the words are saying. What does the text say the Desolator was able to do?"

Silence was my answer. Then, after a short moment, Quiniece spoke up. She, of all who were present, was most likely to make the connection. "It's a scientist... An engineer," she whispered. Then her amber eyes widened with terrible realization. "It repaired the machinery powering the astral bridge all those years ago. That creature knows how to open a portal to Atracus!"

"A portal to Atracus, indeed," I confirmed. "But there's

another clue." Having found the pages I was looking for, I set the book down for everyone to see. "The astral bridge was only reopened when the demon-moon 'swallowed the light of the sun.'"

Leta studied the astrological chart for a moment, then her jaw dropped. "That's right! There's an eclipse coming up, crossing over much of northern Celaphania... Including Armillia. With everything going on, I had completely forgotten about it."

"I did see something about that a few months back," Keldon said. "But why hasn't there been any recent articles about it in the papers?"

I shook my head. "With all the riots and chaos, and the city-wide declaration of martial law, it's back page news. I also suspect the Shadow Man has had his hand in suppressing the fact as well."

"It looks like the eclipse will be in three days," Arleia said, peeking over Leta's shoulder to look at the book.

"That's our deadline for the Shadow Man's end game," I said. "It cannot be a coincidence that everything is coming to a head."

"Technically, it *could* be a coincidence," Leta refuted. "Although, I must admit, the timing is more than a little ominous."

"It's more than that," I explained. "Ever since my first encounter with the Shadow Man and the Servants of Vosh they have left a cryptic epigram behind: 'As above, so below; the dark above, the dark below.' That phrase was recently appended to a message left for me to find in the empty shell of the doomseed we were tricked into chasing down." I paused to clear my throat before completing the sinister rhyme. "'And in-between the Gate of Ages; Behold, it opens, as the Black Sun closes.' Although it has all the qualities of a riddle, I fear we have just unearthed the remaining piece that makes its meaning all too clear."

"So, it's the end of the world, is it?" came a velvety voice from behind. "It looks like I've returned just in time."

I RECOGNIZED THE VOICE, OF COURSE, but if that had not been enough, Quiniece's expression confirmed that our absent host had returned. Catching the whiff of burned fabric, I turned to see Armez stepping up to the table. His normally pristine tailcoat was singed along every seam with deeper scorch marks along the left side and back. His top hat was missing, and deep, black burns pockmarked his alabaster face. Master vampire though he was, he was still vulnerable to silver, sunlight, and fire. Wherever he had gone, he had gone at great peril.

"And precisely where have you been?" I asked.

"My dear Vescard, I was merely collecting some of your personal effects," he answered, dropping a fire-scorched duffle bag on the table in front of me. He put a similar bag in front of Leta, though it appeared to be entirely unblemished. "Your effects were notably easier to come by. You'll also find clothes and such for your apprentices as well."

"My personal effects?" Leta asked, her brow furrowing. "You broke into my apartment and rifled through my..." She cut off as she drew out several articles of clothing, then quickly shoved them back into the bag, her face reddening. "My *unmentionables*!"

Armez tisked and rolled his eyes. "Oh, don't be so scandalized, Leta. You're not my type."

I opened the duffle bag and dumped out the contents, finding several sets of clothes, both for myself and for Keldon, along with toiletries, a set of severite handcuffs, and my spare black bag containing an assortment of alchemical reagents. Another bag fell out, and I gasped when I opened it, finding my entire pen collection.

"Why?" I asked. "Why risk your life for this?"

Quiniece handed Armez the Chalice of the Blood King, and he drank deeply before answering. "Ah, yes," he mused, his topaz irises growing brighter, overwhelming his inhumanly black sclera. "I should probably inform you that your house exploded... Rather catastrophically, thanks to the numerous volatile compounds in your cellar." He shrugged. "Well, that, and the bomb the Servants of Vosh set off when they spotted me inside. I think they mistook me for you." He paused again, lost to his own thoughts. "Those poor fools. Oh, how they screamed when I caught up with them..."

I sat in stunned silence, struggling to come to terms with the news Armez had just relayed. "My townhouse?" I asked, incredulous. My prized book collection, my Royalist-era drawing room set, my fully stocked alchemical forensics laboratory... *All gone...* "They blew up my townhouse?"

"To their credit, it was a well-executed plan," Armez reassured, the burns on his face mending even as he spoke. He took another sip from the chalice and smiled. "On the bright side, I rescued your pen collection."

I steadied my hand as I sorted the pens, still half-dazed. Of all the things in my house, why save my pen collection? Why even risk going back to my house in the first place when he knew it was a trap? I was grateful for the gesture, but strictly speaking, nothing in my house was worth the risk, and by going there Armez had not only put his own eternal life in jeopardy, but had triggered the bomb that resulted in the destruction of #5 Brass Lantern Lane.

Then I remembered the one thing that might have warranted such reckless action.

I emptied the rest of the pens onto the table and began sorting the Swannés from the others. Elmeire Swanné had only made twelve distinctive, limited edition designs, discounting the counterfeits created by his apprentice, and I possessed all twelve—plus one more. A tingle raced from my hand and up through my arm as my fingers brushed the smooth contour of the pen's artisan-worked metal, and I gently lifted the exquisite implement I had not dared to touch since the fateful accident all those years ago.

Although cosmetically similar to the seventh Swanné

design, with its intricate cobalt nib, platinum-etched barrel, and corundum-tipped finial, the pen I held was of singular distinction. Instead of platinum, its etchings were of precisely interconnected orichalium. Its emeralds and rubies had been replaced with opalescent vizstones and shimmering crystal conductors. Along its inner feed cylinder was a spiraled helix of orichalium coils, crowned by a spellworked focal lens concealed within the cap covering its still functional writing nib.

"My talisman..." I whispered, too overwhelmed to say anything more.

Armez grinned, his ivory-white skin now free from all signs of injury. "I thought you might be needing it."

I had resigned myself to knowing I could neither retrieve my talisman nor construct a new one in the time we had. But here it was, cradled in the palm of my hand. I closed my eyes, sensing the cool, aetheric energy pulsing through my body, the gently flowing eddies of the aether coursing all around me, and beyond those, the distant, silver harmonies of the astral light. I turned the talisman over in my hand and closed my fingers around its streamlined contour, tears forming in my eyes as chords of aetheric resonance condensed and bound together at the slightest prodding of my will.

This was more than I could have hoped for; more than I could have asked for. A world I had thought closed to me had now reopened in all its glorious wonder!

"Should we leave the two of you alone?" Leta asked. "Perhaps I should fetch some candles, silk pillows, and scented oils?"

I opened my eyes and blinked, then caught the meaning of her jest. "I..." I began to say, still struggling to find words. "I'm just overwhelmed. I never thought I would touch the aether again. I—"

"You don't have to explain, Aldicus," she chuckled. "We might not know what that creature did to you or why, but we can at least be thankful that your curse has been lifted."

I nodded, but my stomach knotted as I recalled how the Darkweaver so effortlessly ripped the alchemorph away from me. The cold hollowness was still there, like a gaping cavity carved out from my soul.

"Oh, and before I forget." Armez drew a small object from the pocket of his tattered coat and tossed it to Keldon. "I retrieved a little something for you as well."

Keldon caught the object, his eyes widening when he saw its glittering vizstones and finely etched orichalium. "It's the brooch!" he exclaimed, looking from the empowered artifact to me and back again. "The Brooch of Reversion you won on the *Gambler's Boon.*"

"So it is," I agreed, glad that my apprentice would have the item's defensive power to aid him in the struggles to come.

Armez looked himself up and down, patting at the singe marks on his coat. "Now, if you will excuse me, I really must change. I fear I look more bedraggled than Keldon."

Arleia snickered, and Keldon turned several shades of red.

Despite the welcome break, we soon found ourselves back on various lines of research, with Keldon scouring for more references to Darkweavers while Leta and Arleia hunted through ancient myths, hoping to uncover some weakness. As for myself, my ability to concentrate on deciphering Tibblemond's notes had waned, and my eyes kept straying to my talisman. Even so, I made fair progress, having discovered that Tibblemond had actually used a variation of Salgner, which was a modern derivative of Kellian stenography.

Armez reappeared after another hour, dressed in a scarlet tailcoat, black brocaded waistcoat, satin cravat, and teal top hat—identical in nearly every respect to his previous attire. He carried a hefty steel tray heaped with breads, cheeses, fritters, and dainty cucumber sarnies. I glanced at the library's great clockwork ceiling fan, which also featured hour and minute hands to show the time, and saw that it was one o'clock in the morning—well-past lunchtime on our new nocturnal schedule.

We were just finishing off the last crumbs of the midnight meal when Rognar returned.

"I missed lunch?" were the first words out of his mouth. He then produced a grease-soaked sarnie from his coat pocket and chomped down. "Good thing I brought my own."

Emileve strolled into the library behind him, her eyes darting back and forth as she instinctively appraised the opulent statues, priceless paintings, and one-of-a-kind books. She was, after all, a thief through and through.

"Nice haunt," she said, nodding approvingly.

Armez sighed. "Why do I have the nagging suspicion that I'm going to have to relocate?"

"Probably because you're not an idiot," Emileve quipped. If she realized she was talking to a centuries old master vampire, she did a superb job concealing any sign of fear. "But don't worry. Your secret's safe with us."

"Yes," Armez said slowly. "But will my property?"

Emileve crooked a wry grin. "It'll be safe with us, too."

"Have you learned anything more about the construction going on beneath the Aetherspire?" I asked the Queen of Thieves.

"Your clues on those front companies helped," she replied. "We didn't find out anything on Industrial Resource Partnership, but Preferred Logistics operates a private cargo rail from the northern edge of the 12th District all the way to the core districts. Their cargo train makes five bogus transfer stops before disappearing into a service complex, but several of our little brothers scouted the last leg of the route. They have confirmed the train is delivering equipment and materials to the secret construction site below the Aetherspire." She then nodded to the clutter of papers and stenography books scattered around my side of the table. "Have you deciphered the rest of Tibblemond's notes?"

"I have," I replied. "Tibblemond spent most of this past week combing through the city's business registrars and tax offices for any suspicious activity by companies having some relationship to Consolidated Omniworks. I believe he was carrying several files of evidence when he was murdered, but the results of his findings are summarized in these shorthand notes."

I cleared my throat and skimmed over my own notes, gathering my thoughts before summarizing the meandering narrative of Tibblemond's ill-fated investigation.

"Preferred Logistics, Capstone Construction, and Industrial Resource Partnership were three such companies, created only eight or nine months ago, but having fake paper trails showing several years of operation. Those companies received considerable funding from Consolidated Omniworks for general contract work related to the Aetherspire, but they apparently have no employees. However, all three companies are held by a parent company called Abalone Capital Holdings, which had also been given several years of fabricated business history."

"Abalone?" Keldon asked. Abalones were plentiful in Corradon Bay and were harvested by the ton for use in stews, chowders, fritters, and clam bakes. "As in the mollusks?"

"As in their shells!" Armez laughed. "Rather audacious of them to use so obvious a reference for their surreptitious *shell* company. I'm betting that's what tipped Tibblemond off."

"Indeed," I agreed. Tibblemond may have been a bureaucratic stickler most of the time, but when he put his mind to something, he could really be a top-notch forensic analyst. I winced and closed my eyes. *Had been*, I grimly corrected myself. "Tibblemond notes that Abalone contracted Capstone Construction to build a secure research facility within the 13th District, called the Special Directorate. Public records indicate that the project was abandoned, but the bank transfers Tibblemond found suggest that the facility was completed."

"Let me get this straight," Armez said. "Through a series of fake companies, Consolidated Omniworks contracted *another* fake company to build a research facility in the 13th District, which was canceled, but was in fact fully funded and completed in total secrecy?" He sighed. "Well, that's not the least bit suspicious."

"It's not just suspicious, it's crazy!" Rognar barked. "The 13th District's a blasted warzone. Why would they build anything there?"

It was a fair question. The 13th District was a seething cesspit of criminal factions, half-crazed cultists, violent mobsters, black marketeers, and rogue vigilantes, all vying for control over their ever-shifting territories within the city's most notorious district. The 13th District had no government departments, no police, no fire brigades, and no city services. Even the Vandorian Guard considered it effectively off-limits. Making matters worse, the Iron Barrens, which had long ago consumed the 25th District, had steadily encroached upon the 13th like an ever-spreading infection of rusting blight. Even so, countless companies kept heavily guarded manufactories running there, chiefly to leverage the barrel-bottom wages and utter absence of law.

"No police, no oversight, and no questions asked," I answered simply. "Tibblemond's notes also suggest that Abalone contracted a company called Blackhelm to provide security for the facility, but all he could find on Blackhelm was a rubber-stamped private security permit from Vandor Tower."

"Tibblemond had all that in his notes?" Leta asked.

I held up the pages from his notepad and nodded. "It's just a summary of what he found, in dense shorthand. And I did infer some of it. Unfortunately, whatever documents, files, or other proof he was carrying was taken when he was killed. That means we need to collect the evidence ourselves."

Keldon leaned forward in his chair. "Evidence for what,

exactly?"

I took a moment to consider before answering. "All lines of evidence point to one terrible, inescapable truth. The Shadow Man and the Servants of Vosh are building an astral bridge to Atracus."

The room stilled. Everyone held their breath, looking at me in silent anticipation.

"Consider the evidence," I continued. "The Shadow Man—the Disciple—has been collecting artifacts from the War of Golla and Marada, and chiefly Gollan artifacts, as we have learned. As the Commissioner General, he has manipulated events to seize control of Vandor Tower, not only to throw off investigations into his scheme, but to establish martial law across the city. He has worked through a shadowy cabal to create a secret over-science research facility—a facility that is directly connected with the mysterious construction going on beneath the Aetherspire. Moreover, his apparent righthand, Mistress Agona, has just awakened an ancient demonic servitor who likely possesses formidable knowledge of the original astral bridge. We have also learned that the astral bridge can only be opened during an eclipse, and there will be an eclipse in three days. It is no coincidence that construction of the Aetherspire itself is now all but complete. When the Aetherspire activates, it will not be to provide Corradon with a limitless supply of aetheric energy, but to open a gateway to the demon realm of Atracus."

The library remained silent, the ticking of the clockwork complication the only sound to be heard. Everyone looked stunned, and even Armez and Quiniece seemed paler than usual.

"So, it really is the end of the world," Armez said after a moment.

"Archons help us all," Leta muttered.

Keldon shook his head. "I... I can't believe it..."

Arleia slumped in her chair, her ears drooping. "Tibblemond must have been close to the truth. Close enough that someone murdered him for it."

"He did some crack work, that one," Emileve agreed. She folded her arms over her leather brigandine and sat down, kicking her boots up onto the table. "I guess he was pretty sharp... For a badger."

Leta frowned, leaning back in her chair. "So, what are we supposed to do? We can't just go to Vandor Tower about this, and I doubt we can convince the Armillian Parliament of anything. Certainly not in three days."

"We start by finding this secret research facility in the 13th District," I replied. I nodded to Emileve. "Can your people help us locate it?"

"We'll focus on the southeastern quarter of the 13th District," Emileve answer. "That area borders the northern edge of the 12th District, near a rail yard where Preferred Logistics' private cargo rail starts."

"What are we going to do if we do find the facility?" Rognar asked, now rummaging through the remnants of our lunch. "I'll bet you anything this Blackhelm Security is actually a HAAMR division in disguise. We'll need a small army to break into a place like that."

I stood, brushing out my new frock coat as I drew a deep breath. "Don't worry, Rognar. I know some people who can get us in. Assuming they're not too busy tearing down deserted avenues or blasting their way out of a just-raided industrial compound, they should be easy enough to find." With that, I turned to Keldon and gave my apprentice a wide smile. "After all, the Nyasha Twins are not known for keeping low-key."

AN OILY RAIN BATTERED DOWN as we made our way through a low-town market in the western quarter of the 14th District. Leaning platforms, riveted-together catwalks, and dilapidated shanties wedged incongruously between a towering tenement cliff and the fabricrete wall of a long-abandoned foundry. Although Atracus would not rise until just before dawn, the hanging lanterns adorning the windows of makeshift food stalls and illicit rummage shops gave ample light to see by. A constant babble of half-whispered conversations rose from the milling masses of anonymous bystanders trudging along beside us, while the polyrhythmic drumbeats and strumming strings of nameless alley bands thrummed from one crowded watering hole or another.

Rognar had brought us here, having received word of an illegal locomobile rally terrorizing Mainspring Causeway. The racers had disbursed to evade the pursuing HAAMR units, but if Rognar's street contacts were correct, the majority had reconvened here to drink away the sum of their winnings or drown the pain of their losses. But having no inkling as to where the Nyasha Twins might be in this hurly-burly mess, I made for the loudest, most raucous of the ramshackle joints. It seemed the most logical place to start.

We ascended a precarious set of stairs, made all the more treacherous by the oily rain and the occasional puddle of some bodily malfunction I chose not to ponder. I motioned Keldon to follow closer, and he hustled to keep pace as we followed Rognar to the top of the busy, elevated structure. Although my apprentice would have been far safer in Armez's hideout helping Leta and Arleia in their research, he had to learn to navigate the seedier corners of the city if he was to ever become a detective magus.

Yet, as dangerous as this outlaw hotbed of debauchery might be, it was Emileve and her crew who were in real danger. Indeed, the only thing more perilous than scouting the 13th District for the Special Directorate's hidden facility would be the raid on the facility itself. And for that job, we were going to need a very special brand of crazy.

The Shifty Drifter was not the sort of place anyone should visit in the 4th hour of the morning while dressed in a bright blue frock coat and dapper top hat, unless one was looking to get mugged, rolled, and tossed over the side. The rough-built structure was less a single building and more a collection of rickety lean-tos and cobbled-together shacks. Built on an elevated platform, the dodgy dive was held aloft on four scaffold-like legs, complete with a makeshift boiler house, salvaged lifting cranes, and the control gondola of an old-style dirigible that now served as a lookout tower.

We pressed through the milling throng of bludgers, dregs, and dollymollies to find shelter beneath the Shifty Drifter's corrugated awning. Glad though I was to be out of the pattering rain, the clamor of rowdy cheers, smashing glassware, and ceaseless drums thundering from within drowned out whatever Rognar was saying to me.

"Everyone's staring at you!" Rognar yelled, finally loud enough for me to hear.

Though I made no overt show of glancing around, I had noticed the unsettling degree of attention we had attracted—a simmering animosity that only grew as we neared the establishment's entrance. But most of those looks were tempered by an edge of concern or confusion, as though even the most hardened ruffian was thrown by the poise and confidence with which I carried myself—a confidence that I hoped would signal that we meant business. After all, anyone who came tromping through here looking like Keldon and myself was either stark-raving mad or spelled seriously bad news. A few probably even recognized me, or perhaps guessed I was with Vandor Tower, and I could not help but notice a wave of whispers spreading across the crowd.

Although the city-wide curfew was still in effect, HAAMR had focused most of their efforts on securing the core districts. Even so, the threat of a full lockdown hung like a storm cloud above even the outer districts, and the patrons of the Shifty Drifter would not be pleased to see a well-known associate of Vandor Tower strolling about. Then again, there was another, even more worrisome explanation for the hushed whispers and side-long glances. HAAMR might have placed a bounty on my head.

"Where do you think they are?" Keldon yelled in my ear.

I looked over the side and spotted a cluster of ichor-fueled speedsters and pneumatic clockwork racers parked out of the rain, beneath the cantina's elevated platform. Among them I recognized two familiar motowheels, their rotary engines mounted below and behind the seats inside each wheel. Near them was another conspicuous vehicle, more like a locomotive engine in design, but with massive tires instead of train wheels. Bruntilga. The twins were here, and so was Gunther.

"They're here somewhere," I confirmed, then nodded to the door. "I don't know where, but—" A bloodied ruffian crashed through the shutters of a window on the far side of the structure. He staggered to his feet, shook his head, and scampered off as a chorus of cheers howled from within the riotous cantina. "Ah, yes. This is just the place to find them."

The nogknockers at the door looked us up and down, then saw Rognar and let us pass without question. Rognar waved and yelled at several people who called to him, receiving a few arm-clasps from a fellow Dworgh or two. Then he continued on, leading us past the shoulder-to-shoulder packed bar and deeper into the smoky recesses of the Shifty Drifter.

From the corner of my eye, I spotted a trio of rough-looking characters pushing their way through the crowd after us, hard-faced and with harder eyes, and hands moving to the weapons at their sides. I reached into my pocket, my fingers closing around my talismanic pen, and I felt the reassuring currents of aethergy pulsing like a heartbeat from its empowered vizstones. If any trouble did come our way, between Keldon's thaumaturgical training, Rognar's Varla, and my own reawakened abilities, we likely had nothing to fear. Even so, I preferred to avoid making a scene—a sentiment I realized was absurd once we reached the raucous brouhaha at the back of the unruly joint.

Boisterous cheers rang up from the tightly packed mob

as a hulking, bear-of-a-man staggered away from the table, clutching his bloodied nose. Throwing himself back at his smaller opponent, he received a cracking upper cut that sent him sprawling into the cheering crowd. Nera, or so I guess from her somewhat longer dreadlocks, spun away triumphantly and threw back a glass of some perilously clear liquid that was most certainly not water.

Just past Nera I spotted her sister, Vera, hurling a knife into one of the new regime's propaganda posters. The two men she had been competing with just shook their heads, admiring the spacing of her knives that had struck between each letter of the word 'Peace' headlining the poster's rather ironic motto 'Peace Under Law.' A few coins passed between the spectators, though there was not as much betting going on as I would have expected. Clearly, those who were willing to bet against the Nyasha Twins were few and far between. And for good reason.

Nera threw back another drink and motioned for someone else in the crowd to come at her. Then she froze, her eyes catching mine. A moment passed, and she lowered her glass to the table, her expression darkening as she realized I would only come here on a matter of utmost urgency.

"Vera!" she yelled over the din. "Get over here. Everybody else, get lost!"

The crowd moaned and grumbled, but one by one the gaggle of spectators grudgingly turned away. As the mob melted into the greater throng of the Shifty Drifter, I saw the three men who had taken an unhealthy interest in us. They stood for a moment, hands poised to draw knives, truncheons, or pistols, but Nera and Vera just glared back, sly smiles curling on their lips as they reached for their own clockwork pistols holstered in low-slung gun belts. The men glanced hesitantly at one another, then turned to leave, slamming headlong into the towering, barrel-chested, broad-shouldered form of Gunther Viggs. The would-be bounty hunters staggered back in a start, then scampered away to lose themselves in the anonymity of the ever-shifting crowd.

"Aw... That could'a been fun," Gunther griped. He cracked his knuckles as he made his way over to our table, then stroked his horseshoe mustache as he considered myself, the twins, Rognar, and Keldon. "Mind if I join you?"

"By all means," I replied, taking a seat as I did. "We could certainly use all the help we can get."

"What do you be doing here, Vescard?" Nera asked in her inflected Arkanan accent, barely audible over the cantina's deafening noise. She pushed her racing goggles further back, using it like a hairband for her dreadlocks. Then she leaned in closer so I could hear her better. "You be a wanted man, you know?"

"If we no be rolling in our winnings, we might be tempted to turn you in," Vera agreed with a smirk. Nera just rolled her eyes.

I glanced around. Although people crowded nearby tables or milled about the periphery of the throng, the pounding drumbeats and howling horns of the band made it unlikely anyone could eavesdrop without evoking an espial empowerment. Thanks to my restored abilities, I would know instantly if they were, as would Keldon.

"I need to stop the Shadow Man," I started off saying. Both sisters arched eyebrows, clearly unfamiliar with my own name for the villain. "The self-proclaimed Lord Protector of Corradon and former Commissioner General of Vandor Tower. As the Disciple of the Servants of Vosh, he has been secretly orchestrating events over the past year to bring us to where we are now."

"That do explain a few things," Nera admitted. "Not that we be buying the old 'martial law for the good of peace and order' line he and HAAMR be spouting."

"That be the sentiment of every soul here," Vera added, nodding to the roiling masses of the Shifty Drifter.

"Ain't that the truth!" Gunther agreed. He grabbed someone else's ale from a nearby table, momentarily evoking the injured party's ire until they saw who had taken the drink. "If HAAMR weren't so focused on the core districts, they might see us all as outlaws, dissidents, and rabble-rousers." Then he paused, considering his own words. "Well, I guess we are. But that's not my point."

"It's only a matter of time until they turn their attention this way," Rognar said. "You can bet good money they will. And when they do, it won't be pretty."

Vera nodded. "What you be needing, bossman?"

I took a moment to ponder how much I should reveal to Gunther and the twins, but to hold back from those I wished to enlist as allies would only work to harm my cause. After all, secrecy was the province of evil.

"I have strong evidence that the Shadow Man intends to open a portal to Atracus using the Aetherspire." Dark-skinned though they were, I could see the blood drain from the sisters' faces. "But first, we need to get into a secret research facility, hidden somewhere in the 13th District. The facility may have information on the over-science technology used in the Aetherspire's design."

Nera shook her head, eyeing me skeptically. "The 13th be one brutty war-zone. Only banging mercs and raving loons be going there." She glanced at her sister, then sighed. "Ah... Right. That be why you came to us, yes?"

"Why should we do this?" Vera asked, her tone growing suddenly serious. She folded her arms over her low-cut, leather racing suit and narrowed her eyes. "What be in it for us?"

"You should do it for the good of Corradon," Keldon pleaded. He glanced around, then spread his arms wide. "Maybe even for the good of the world! You can't just sit there and let HAAMR and the Shadow Man get away with this, can you?"

The twins glanced at one another doubtfully.

"It's a classified research facility for Consolidated Omniworks," I clarified.

Vera's face brightened with a wide grin. "Now you be speaking our language, bossman!"

"Why didn't you just say you wanting to poke a brutty bad sootstack in the grimy heinie?" Nera added, nodding emphatically. "You can count us in, so long as we keep a fair share of the booty."

I glanced at Gunther. "We could also use that monster locomobile of yours."

Gunther threw back the last of his illicitly acquired ale and slammed the mug on the table. "My Bruntilga's at your disposal!"

"Guns and gears we got aplenty, but we be needing a tooler, a ticker, and a trickster," Nera voiced. She gave Keldon a nod. "Illusions be good, but we be needing some brutty bad hokery-pokery, too."

"A thief and gearmeister we have," I assured, translating the street lingo. I pulled up one of my sleeves, revealing the absence of my severite wristbands. "And along with Keldon, we have another mage as well."

The twin's eyes widened. "You be cured!" Vera exclaimed.

Rognar laughed. "As cured as a brine-soaked haunch of ham." Then he glanced around and sighed. "Ah, now I'm hungry..."

Rognar's exclamation sounded louder than it should have, but only because the incessant clamor of the Shifty Drifter had dropped to an abrupt and inexplicable silence. There was only the angry rumble of the cantina's boiler house, the creak and groan of its support pilings, and the whine of a siren calling from the high up lookout gondola. Distantly, I could just discern the rising thrum of approaching ornithopters, and I realized the cause for the sudden alarm.

"Blast it!" Nera swore. I leaned aside as she jumped from her seat and threw herself across the table, her sister following just behind her. "Time to make scarce!"

As though following their lead, the entire population of

the Shifty Grifter scrambled for the exits, clambering down stairs, sliding down escape poles, or catching a ride on one of the cranes lowering cargo platforms to the ground. Nera and Vera both took an escape pole, but Gunther ushered Keldon, Rognar, and myself to the stairs. We followed the hurried footfalls of the quickly evacuating patrons. Nearly half the dissident mob had already vanished by the time we hit ground, and we dodged between dusty sprays of departing speedsters and steam-powered racers as we dashed for the iron behemoth called Bruntilga.

"Where to, bossman?" Nera yelled over the whine of her motowheel's ichor-pumped engine.

"We're rendezvousing with the Unseen Brotherhood below the freight car depot near the border of the 13th District," I yelled back.

The twins nodded, revving their engines before speeding away with the screech of their all-encompassing wheels.

We took our seats on the bench at the rear of Bruntilga's cab, and the ex-con-turned-racer threw a few shovelfuls of ebonite into the roaring furnace. Then he spun a few valves, released the pneumatic brakes, and shoved the throttle to full power. Before long we were thundering away from the low-town market, gaining speed with the ever-quickening *chug-chug-chug* of Bruntilga's supercritical steam engine. The vehicle lurched with a sudden bang as we crashed through a barrier wall, falling a good ten feet before slamming back to the ground and barreling into a trash-strewn sublevel plaza, trailing just behind the twins speeding for the safety of a storm tunnel.

I poked my head out the window beside me, holding onto my top hat as I looked back to the low-town market. The HAAMR thopters closed in on the Shifty Drifter, slowing and circling with arc-lights panning for any dissidents lingering near that hive of crime and rebellion. Two of the thopters continued on to follow us, but by then we had made it to the storm tunnel. The thrum of battering wings and the whine of sirens faded in the distance, replaced by the rumbling roar of Bruntilga's engine reverberating from the water-stained walls closing around us.

I sat back and settled in beside Keldon and Rognar. The tunnel was pitch-black, and Keldon summoned an orb of light just ahead of Bruntilga to supplement the paltry light of her forward lanterns. I drew my talismanic pen from my pocket, considering whether or not I should evoke an orb of essential light to flex my muscles, so to speak. Apart from a few simple exercises I had practiced this morning, it had been years since I last composed a proper aetheric empowerment.

"Don't go blowing us to pieces," Rognar muttered. "You're sorely out of practice, I'd wager."

Keldon glanced at me, then he turned back to Rognar and smiled. "There's an old saying among mages: once you've heard the music of the spheres, you'll never forget the tune."

Rognar shrugged inside his oversized duffle coat and gave a doubtful harrumph.

I twirled my talismanic pen between my fingers, then tightened my grip as I looped a quick circle in front of me. From everywhere and all around, I heard as much as saw the vast, aetheric sea of energy and vibrations humming through the fabric of reality. Like the keys, notes, and octaves of the musical scale, an infinite number of configurations existed within those resonating chords, but only a few carried any intelligible harmony. Almost reflexively, my mind picked out the familiar pattern I sought, and the chords of fire, force, and light collapsed into a coherent waveform of harmonic resonance. The empowerment surged through my talisman's orichalium coils, down the amplifying pathways etched within its vizstones, and struck from the spellworked focal lens at the tip of the pen's cap in a fizzling pop of sparkling blue embers and curling ribbons of prismatic light.

Keldon quirked an eyebrow, but I schooled my face and gave Rognar a wide 'I meant to do that' grin. The Dworgh, not knowing that I had actually been attempting to conjure the illusion of a roaring, fire-breathing dragon's head, blinked in a moment of dazzled astonishment.

"Knock it off or I'm let'n ya out right here!" Gunther threatened. He pushed the control tiller to his right, and my stomached lurched as Bruntilga thundered down a steep ramp leading from the storm tunnel to a vast, undercity cavern. "And by let'n ya off, I mean tossing ya out the door!"

I sighed and tucked the pen away. Either the patterns etched in my talisman's vizstones had decayed considerably from long-term disuse, or I was more out of practice than I had feared.

Bruntilga made a few more twists and turns, and Gunther eased back on the throttle. The hiss of pneumatic breaks and the squeal of metal grinding on metal preceded the lurch of rapid deceleration. I glanced out the window to see the dim gray haze of what little pre-dawn light seeped through the tangle of trestles, viaducts, and bridges rising high above. The inordinate number of broken-down railcars and discarded axleboxes scattered among the rusting junk heaps told me we had arrived at our destination.

I jumped from Bruntilga's slowing bulk, shoes splashing through fetid puddles as I made for the cloistered overhang where Nera and Vera had parked their motowheels. Armez and Quiniece had also arrived in their ensorcelled carriage, and I was relieved to see Emileve standing by as well, hopefully bearing news of her success.

"Took you long enough," Emileve chided. She gave a quick nod to Gunther as he, Keldon, and Rognar followed behind me. "Who's the bruiser?"

"Gunther Viggs," Gunther said, stabbing a sizable thumb at himself. "You've probably heard of me and my Bruntilga! I've raced in the Golden Gear four years in a row."

"And you no be placing even once," Nera snickered as she and her sister strolled up to join us. "But nobody place this year, all on account of that skulking dollymolly, Meretta, and that clodnog scheme of hers."

Gunther frowned, but his frown only deepened when Emileve answered.

"Sorry—never heard of you." She then turned back to me and cracked a wide smile, pinching the scar on her cheek. "We found them."

"You found the facility?" I asked, more in disbelief than as a question. Of course, I shouldn't have underestimated the resourcefulness of the Unseen Brotherhood.

If Emileve took offence at my incredulity, her expression didn't show it. "Once we knew what to look for, we followed Preferred Logistics' transfer stops through a tangled mess of smaller convoy routes, taking us straight to the facility in the 13th District. It's disguised as an abandoned steelworks, occupied by a deranged sorcerer and his lunatic cult. That at least keeps the local gangs away, but I wouldn't be surprised if there really is a mage there to keep up the illusion. Still, I figure with a couple of our own mages, a gearmeister, and some gratuitous firepower, we might actually have a chance."

"Glad to be of service," Quiniece chimed. She held up her clockwork gauntlet, arcs of sparking galvanic current jumping between its copper-coiled knuckles.

Nera and Vera both nodded. "And if we no be here for the gratuitous violence, why we be here at all?" Vera asked, patting her guns.

"Where are Leta and Arleia?" I asked Armez.

"Doing some additional research at my mansion," Armez replied. "Leta is convinced she can trace the Darkweaver's movement if it feeds again. I'm not sure how, but she mentioned something about the psychic dissonance of negative aetheric vibrations." He shrugged and rolled his eyes. "That's mystics for you."

I arched an eyebrow. "What do you mean, *feeds*?"

Armez clasped his hands behind his back, grinning at the prospect of lecturing me on some bookish detail for a change.

"From what Leta has pieced together, the creature is a bit like a vampire. But instead of gaining sustenance from the vitalic essence of blood, it drains the life energy directly from its victim's body, and at range no less. Not just vitalic energy, but very likely any form of energy: heat, light, aethergy, vitalic, or even necrolic."

"That's why the air turned so cold in its presence," Keldon said.

I nodded. "And perhaps that's how it took the alchemorph from me." I thought for a moment longer, then shook my head. "Keldon, I want you to return to Harrowdeep with Armez and see what you can do to help Leta and Arleia track down this Darkweaver."

Keldon frowned. "But—"

"Dangerous does not even begin to describe this operation," I said, cutting off his objection. "Not that tracking down a demonic servitor is any less dangerous, but at least it's a proper investigation, which is what an apprentice should be learning. Besides, you'll be teaming up with Arleia."

Even in the dim light I could see Keldon's blush, and he shifted uneasily before clearing this throat to reply. But Quiniece pounced like a cat upon a mouse, slapping his bottom and sending him jumping in the air with a yelp.

"Give your girlfriend my regards, lover boy!" she teased with a quick wink.

Armez quickly ushered a hopelessly flustered Keldon away, guiding him to the coach before glancing back to give his parting words. "Do try to behave, Quiniece," he admonished, but the wry smile he wore suggested otherwise. He then turned to me and tipped his top hat. "And you, my dear Vescard, had better make it back in one piece. I fear this city just wouldn't be the same without you."

With that, Armez jumped to the driver's box at the front of the coach, took the brass chains that served as reins, and urged the ensorcelled clockwork steeds to a thundering gallop. The midnight coach lifted away from the scrap-strewn ground, aetheric fire licking from pounding hooves as it rose to the tangled urban canopy above. Within moments I had lost sight of them, and I released a silent sigh of relief. What strange times these were that the safest place my apprentice could be was deep within a master vampire's secret lair.

"Time be wasting, bossman," Nera said, as she and her sister headed for their motowheels.

I motioned to Emileve, then turned and followed Gunther and Rognar back to Bruntilga. The whine of the twin's motowheels came to life as we piled into Gunther's vehicle, and the smaller engines were quickly eclipsed by the thundering boom of the iron beast's furnace firing at full steam. Soon we were rolling, Nera and Vera leading the way as we raced down long-abandoned storm tunnels and derelict access corridors, heading straight into the 13th District.

I did not know what we would find in the Special Directorate's secret facility, or even if we could breach its nigh-impenetrable defenses, but everything was riding on the fruits of our raid. Brute force alone could never defeat the Shadow Man. To have any hope of victory, we would need knowledge: knowledge of the Aetherspire, knowledge of its secret modifications, and knowledge of what role the Darkweaver had in his diabolical designs.

Knowledge... And a considerable degree of luck.

A BULLET PINGED OFF BRUNTILGA'S iron chassis as we sped down the wreckage-littered avenues of the 13th District's southwestern quarter. Whether fired intentionally or simply a wild shot from some nearby gunfight, I did not know, but the random attack brought home the grim reminder of just how dangerous this lawless district had become. The boom of some distant explosion echoed from the scorched façades of fire-gutted foundries while still more gunfire crackled between the windows and alleys of burned-out tenements.

Emileve directed Gunther down a hollowed-out trench to a graffiti-filled utility corridor, plowing through piles of refuse and debris, with the twins pulling in behind us. Minutes later, we emerged into an expansive cavern, which may once have been part of a sublevel industrial complex. Toppled pilings and scaffolding littered the ground, and a good two thirds of the cavern had caved in like one vast sinkhole, spilling the rubble of collapsed buildings from the war-torn streets above. Tendrils of rust scored the far western end of the cavern, heralding the slowly creeping blight of the Iron Barrens, which threatened not only to consume this district, but the 24th and 26th as well.

Following Emileve's directions, Gunther steered Bruntilga around a derelict viaduct and applied the pneumatic breaks, bringing us to a gradual stop. Four figures in rust-patterned cloaks emerged from the debris, the glint of their red-lensed goggles distinguishing them as members of the Unseen Brotherhood. Emileve climbed down from the cabin and I followed her, trailed by Quiniece and Rognar. Gunther joined us once he had disengaged the main drive gear of Bruntilga's fearsome engine. We were well concealed behind the collapsed viaduct, but if my guess was correct, the facility in question was the seemingly dilapidated steelworks on the other side of the cavern. Any closer than this and we would have been spotted for certain.

"Nebb, Tavin, what have you got?" Emileve asked as she approached her men. "Do any of the entrances look receptive?"

"Sure," said the first of the men—Nebb, I inferred, as Emileve had glanced at him when she spoke his name. "But avoiding those mercs guarding the place..." He hesitated, then shrugged. "Not happening."

"Mercenaries?" I asked.

The man named Tavin nodded. "We think it's the same outfit guarding the construction site beneath the Aetherspire. They've got this place buttoned up tighter than a dandy-fop's peacock suit." He looked me up and down and smirked. "No offence."

"You no be worrying about trigger boys," Nera said, her eyes gleaming with the prospect of a fight. She and her sister had parked their motowheels to either side of Gunther's locomotive racer, and both now wore protective armored corsets over their leather racing suits.

"They need be the ones worrying about us," Vera finished, sauntering up beside her sister, hands resting on her gun belt.

"I would prefer to infiltrate the facility as quietly as possible," I countered.

I glanced at the sisters who were now checking over their clockwork pistols, then looked to Rognar who had drawn Varla from his duffle coat, along with a sausage and cabbage sarnie. Gunther stood just behind the Dworgh, a large pipe wrench in one hand and some kind of hefty, pneumatic gun in the other. Quiniece fiddled with her gearmeister gauntlet, and although she was here to handle any technical obstacles we encountered, she was just as formidable a fighter as Rognar, Gunther, and the twins.

I sighed. "I suspect the word 'quiet' is not within this crew's vocabulary."

The twins rolled their eyes and Gunther gave a grunt of a laugh.

"There is one other way inside," Nebb went on to say. "But I'll let our little brother explain. He's the one who found it."

Hearing the prompt, a diminutive blue figure jumped out from behind some piece of scrap and landed on a broken slab of fabricrete. Almost immediately, the homunculus began chittering, hands flashing through signs.

"He says there's a sealed service tunnel beneath the loading docks," Emileve translated. "He was able to squeeze inside, and he thinks there's an access hatch farther down. But he didn't explore deeper. He sensed..." She hesitated, then signed back to the homunculus. He gave some reply and she nodded. "He sensed a threatening presence and left the area."

I nodded. Sentinel egregores, most likely. "That's our way in," I said, and turned to Gunther. "Gunther, I need you to stay with the vehicles." He frowned with disappointment, so I threw in an incentive. "Or would you prefer to leave Bruntilga here, in the middle of the 13th District, completely unattended?"

Gunther's eyes widened and he stood a bit straighter, looming over us all. "Ain't nobody stealing my Bruntilga." Then he gave a sharp nod toward Nera and Vera. "Or the twin's wheels, neither."

"These two will keep guard with you," Emileve offered, indicating the other two scouts standing behind Nebb and Tavin. "Tiamon knows we'll need these vehicles for our getaway."

With that settled, we followed Nebb and Tavin into a trench below the fallen viaduct, the little homunculus scurrying ahead while Rognar and the twins took up guard at the rear. Nebb led us up a small junk heap, giving a good vantage of the facility while keeping our own profiles concealed. Just as Emileve had said, the steelworks façade was made up to look like a cultish stronghold, complete with totems depicting monstrous faces, painted skulls on rusting poles, and ghastly scarecrows assembled from bones, gears, and twisted scraps of metal. Coiled razor wire surrounded the premises, and numerous makeshift signs, scrawled in gang graffiti, threatened doom upon anyone who trespassed.

"What do you think?" Emileve asked, adjusting the focusing dial on the side of her red-lensed goggles.

I glanced back at Nebb and Tavin, both of whom had donned the same eyewear as Emileve, then to Rognar and Quiniece who wore ocular headgear of their own, and finally to the twins with their racing goggles lowered over their eyes. Tavin offered me a set of the Brotherhood's eyewear, but I shook my head, drawing my talismanic pen from my frock coat's inner pocket.

After a moment's concentration, I recalled one of the simpler empowerments infused within my talisman, conducting a thin current of aetheric energy to bind the chords of its harmonic pattern. The world seemed to blur for an instant, then snapped back, clearer and crisper than before, but shaded in hues of vivid blue, viridian green, and iridescent violet. *Aetheric sight.* I drew a deep breath and smiled, feeling like a blind man able to see once more.

Surveying the scrapyard with my empowered vision, I was relieved to see the totems, skulls, and scarecrows were just as cold and inert as the rest of the rusting junk that littered the premises. Beyond them, ranks of floating, ghostly forms circled both inside and outside the facility—forms with jagged-edged appendages and jutting spikes, others like jellyfish with wispy tendrils, while still others were like undulating centipedes covered in eyes where their legs would have been. My breath caught. They had a veritable army of egregores...

"The totems and scarecrows are just for show, but the facility is teeming with egregores. But I can deal with them." Or at least, I hoped I could. Being out of practice would certainly not help matters. "Give me a moment to bring up an aetheric cloak."

Concentrating, I pulled in a second stream of aetheric current, spinning the energy through the patterns within my talisman to bind a composition of disruptive aetheric dissonance. Though invisible to the others, the shield expanded like a dome to envelop us, rendering us invisible to even the most masterfully composed egregore. But no sooner had it formed than cracks emerged, and I felt the aetheric cloak teetering on the verge of collapse. I clenched my teeth, straining as I pressed more aethergy into the empowerment in a desperate bid to strengthen its coherency. To my relief, the defects smoothed out, and I relaxed as I pushed the burden of sustaining the empowerment to the back of my mind. Rusty though I was, my reflex memory was fast returning.

"The aetheric cloak is up," I told everyone. "Stay within four paces of me and we probably won't be detected."

"Probably?" Rognar asked, eyebrow raised.

I sighed, self-consciously brushing some bit of dirt from my frock coat. "There's always a chance, so don't get careless."

Nera and Vera both nodded.

We continued along the trench with the homunculus leading the way to the service tunnel beneath the loading dock. The small creature scurried along ahead of us, well outside of my aetheric cloak, but since he had been here before and had not been detected or killed, I could only assume that he was too small for the egregores to recognize. They were likely tasked with detecting creatures larger than goblins, since otherwise the sheer number of vermin infesting the area would set off their alarms constantly.

The trench brought us close enough to the service tunnel that we were able to sneak the rest of the way without being spotted. But our progress was soon halted by the sealed service entrance the homunculus had discovered. A small gap at the top of the welded-on slab of steel was just large enough for the homunculus to squeeze through, but the rest of us were not so diminutive.

Quiniece sparked an intense electric arc between her gauntlet's fingers, but the light and noise were too much, and I motioned for her to shut it off. Instead, I took a vial of vitriolic chlorinate from my coat pocket and carefully applied a trickle of the corrosive liquid along the panel's welded seams. Minutes passed as the caustic reagent hissed and sizzled, slowly eating away at the welds. Everyone waited in silence as the alchemicals did their work.

Several more minutes passed before enough of the welds had dissolved for us to push open the panel and crawl into the old service tunnel. Rognar, Quiniece, Emileve, and her two men had no difficulty seeing in the near total darkness, thanks to the amplifying crystals of their goggles. My own aetheric vision gave a passable, if not oddly shaded, view of my surroundings, and I immediately caught sight of several faint embers of aetheric residue. I inspected one more closely, noticing then that the residue lingered on what could only be the charred remains of a corpse.

"Is that a body?" Emileve asked, seeing what had drawn my attention.

"It's hard to tell, but he was probably a scavenger looking to steal something," I replied grimly. I forced myself not to ponder the harrowing empowerments that had made such a grisly barbecue of flesh and double-checked my aetheric cloak. "The poor fool never even had a chance against the egregores. He was probably the reason they sealed this entrance better."

We continued down the service tunnel, finally stopping when we arrived at the hatch where our plucky homunculus chittered and pointed excitedly. Quiniece stepped up to the hatch, then selected a tool to pry off the access panel.

"You know what you be doing?" Nera asked in a whisper. "That could sound an alarm."

"Of course there's an alarm," Quiniece hissed as she popped off the panel. "It's the first thing I'll bypass."

She returned her attention to her work, taking the autorotor from her belt and positioning its adaptive melding bit to the clockwork gears now exposed within the hatch. But even as she did, I spotted a ghostly glimmer with my aetheric sight.

"Wait," I said, my hand snapping up to stop her.

She froze and looked at me, eyes narrowing. "What?"

"It's a nested tripspell," I explained. Although not as complex as an egregore, tripspells were just as dangerous—perhaps more so, as they were hard to spot. I grimaced, following the faint tendrils wrapped around the gears and rods of the hatch's locking mechanism. Judging from its design, the tripspell would melt the gears to slag the moment anyone began tampering with them, and it would likely do the same if someone tried to disarm it. “I can’t disarm it without it melting the gears, but I can probably restrain it long enough for you to unlock the hatch.” I brought my talisman up and gave a sharp nod. “Now!”

Quiniece jammed her autorotor home and I seized the tripspell in a tangle of aetheric threads, tightening my grip on my talismanic pen as the slippery empowerment thrashed in a flurry of writhing vibrations. I winced, caught off guard by its intensity, and nearly lost it as it slipped one way and another like a thrashing snake. A white-hot pulse of aethergy surged through the tripspell’s diaphanous tendrils, and I clenched my pen in a death-grip, straining to confine the empowerment for just a few seconds more.

Clockworks spun as the autorotor’s adaptive gears overrode the hatch’s locking mechanism, but the heat of its innermost components spiked despite my efforts. A quick succession of thunks signaled the release of the locking bolts and Quiniece yanked her autorotor free just as I lost my hold on the tripspell. A burst of scorching heat erupted from the open panel, reducing the interior of the hatch to molten metal.

“That could have slagged my autorotor,” Quiniece hissed, waving the custom-built device in my face. “Do you have any idea how long it takes to build these?”

“Probably as long as it takes a mage to construct a talisman,” I replied.

The door was too hot to touch, but as it was designed to swing inward, my foot was all I needed to push it open.

We were in.

I MOVED INSIDE FIRST, followed by Quiniece, Emileve, her two men, and the little homunculus. Rognar and the twins crowded in behind us all. The room was pitch-black, but I could still perceive the faint outlines of pipes, pumping equipment, and ventilation ducts as gentle currents of ambient aethergy rolled and coiled around the tightly packed equipment of the cluttered machine room. I glimpsed Emileve as she took the lead in front of me, while her men fanned out to either side. With my aetheric cloak still holding strong, I took a moment to extend my aetheric vision beyond the room, but someone bumped into me from behind.

Nera cursed. "It be darker than a Dworgh's heinie in here."

"Hey!" Rognar barked.

"Won't those egregore things detect that this hatch was opened?" Emileve asked.

"It was under my cloak at the time, and still is," I answered. "But it won't take long for the watchdogs to notice the breech."

The others grumbled irritably, but I wasn't going to lie about our predicament. I drew a breath and closed my eyes, focusing my aetheric senses beyond the room. I was not able to see far, twenty paces perhaps, but it was enough to detect several other people moving about, as well as the shark-like simulacrum of a prowler egregore swimming straight toward us. Whether it had sensed some anomaly in the aether caused by a defect in my cloak, or if this room was simply the next stop on its rote patrol, made little difference. As soon as it passed through my cloak it would either flee to alert its master or unleash a disruptive empowerment to bring down my camouflaging ward. I clenched my jaw, hands balling to fists.

Then I had an idea. A very bad idea.

"A prowler egregore is headed this way," I whispered to the others. "I'm going to bag it."

"Are you completely insane?" Quiniece hissed.

I didn't have time to answer—the egregore was already skimming the edge of the cloak. My breathing stilled in mindful awareness, and I turned the whole of my consciousness upon the artificed specter. Aethergy flowed from my talisman, spreading outward like a web of tendrils as I spun together a tightly bound net, poised to snap tight. I had one chance to snag the egregore, and even if I succeeded, the enemy mage would detect the incursion if he was actively monitoring his aetheric brood. As much as I might hope that he only checked the egregores periodically, all I needed was a pinch of bad luck and our covert raid would fast devolve into a running firefight. But this was our single best chance for success.

The egregore passed through the edge of my aetheric cloak, quivering as it detected the anomaly, and like a lurking trapdoor spider, I sprang the net in a split-second attack. The egregore thrashed violently about, but I pulled my catch in tight and rammed home a spike bound with threads of my own consciousness. *Contact!* In a sudden flash, I perceived the egregore's innerworkings like so many ghostly wheels, patterns, and geometric forms. I quickly nullified its payload of defensive and offensive spells, then froze the egregore entirely with a burst of entropic interference.

Although no more intelligent than an insect, the thought-form's artificed mind was a convolution of reflex actions, innate directives, and conditional contingencies—most of them common to all egregores, but a few were of stunning complexity. Knowing I had just seconds until a watchdog noticed its missing colleague, I dispelled the custom directives and replaced its autonomous instructions with a simple binding tethered to my conscious will. Outwardly, the egregore still resembled its original form, and the other egregores would still recognize it as such. But inwardly, the egregore was mine.

"I have a new pet," I said to the others. "I circumvented the egregore's directives and can now exercise full control over its actions."

"Just like an autorotor," Quiniece observed.

I blinked. I hadn't considered the parallel before, but she

was right. “Exactly. But we can’t doddle. The other egregores may see it as one of their own, but it won’t take long for the enemy mage to notice this one has been subverted.”

The egregore contained a mental map of the entire facility, and I quickly located the main research wing which was just one floor above us and several corridors down. Not wishing to chance any of the main hallways, I directed the egregore to lead us on a discreet route through the basement corridors. This was not the say the basement was devoid of occupants, but Emileve’s men were quite effective when it came to waylaying those few unfortunates that we came across. The workmen were merely clobbered, gagged, and bound, while the Blackhelm Security guards were less kindly treated.

“The research wing is up those stairs,” I said, indicating the stairs my captured egregore had led us to. I gazed upward, my aetheric vision giving me a hazy view of the floor above. At least two dozen people occupied the various offices, workshops, and laboratories, but I had no way of knowing how many were guards and how many were unarmed workers or scientists. “Get ready. As soon as we make our presence known, every guard in the facility will come down on us. Just remember, we have surprise on our—”

The air filled with the sudden undulating screech of a watchdog egregore, soon joined by a chorus of others. Whether they had detected the breached hatchway, some flaw in my aetheric cloak, or the men Nebb and Tavin had knocked out, I did not know. But the result was the same.

“We be made!” Vera yelled. She drew her pistols and nodded to her sister. “Go!”

The twins, Rognar, and Quiniece charged in a mad sprint for the stairs, trailed by Emileve, Nebb, Tavin, and the chittering homunculus. Thinking fast, I infused my captive egregore with a dazzle-flare empowerment and sent it shooting straight up through the floor directly above me. I dashed to catch up with my friends, who, in a matter of heartbeats, had reached the top of the stairs leading to the main hall of the research wing. Startled screams announced the arrival of my egregore and its blinding payload. We burst through the doors like a half-crazed bandit brigade just as the empowerment's dazzling pinwheel of strobing lights fizzled away.

Nera and Vera pressed ahead into the hub-like hall, clockwork pistols firing in a fury of chambering rounds and ratcheting gears. The startled guards were still trying to recover from the blinding light of my bedazzling spell, and five of them fell to the twin's attack. One of the guards managed to get off a lucky shot with his rifle, hitting Tavin square in the head, and the man crumpled to the floor like a puppet with his strings cut. Emileve screamed an oath, then dropped the killer with a thrown dagger.

The twins whipped around, pistols blazing as more guards stormed into the hub. Quiniece discharged a bolt of sparking electric arcs from her gauntlet while a scorching fireball belched from Rognar's empowered blunderbuss, blasting another guard into the wall. Panicked screams filled the air as clerks and engineers rushed from their offices and laboratories. Two went down in the crossfire, both hit by the guards who were meant to protect them.

"Get the civilians out of here!" I yelled to Emileve.

She acknowledged with a nod, then signaled to Nebb in mutespeak.

A squad of black uniformed mercenaries rushed in behind the fallen guards, guns training on us even as they spread out to flank our position. The execution of the maneuver was perfectly coordinated, like a well-trained military drill. If these weren't HAAMR commandos incognito, then they were a professional mercenary outfit of the highest caliber. But I had little time to ponder the implications, and threw myself behind a pallet of metal boxes as a deafening fusillade of breechblock rifles and pneumatic repeaters filled the air. Drawing upon the full power of my talismanic pen, I spun together harmonic chords of force, form, and vibration, and slammed the soldiers with a thunderclap shock wave.

The twins advanced on the stunned mercenaries with pistols blazing, and another fireball from Varla exploded through one of the more heavily armored mercs. Quiniece had already disabled the clockwork locks securing a vault-like door just off the main hub. I could only watch in wonder as she stepped through the door and into a symphony of clattering gears, clicking switches, and humming punch reels. I blinked in genuine surprise. I hadn't expected to find an analytical engine here—a few enumerators or tabulators perhaps, but not a room-sized, multi-function, automatronic analytical engine.

"Can you pull anything from those punch reels?" I yelled. Quiniece didn't answer, and I wasn't even sure she heard me over the clamor of the clattering machine and crackling gunfire. She was already prying off one of the machine's lower panels to access its internals. "I'll just leave you to it then."

Whether her efforts met with success or not, we still had to gather as much information as we could. A grenade blast shook the floor, filling the hub with smoke and debris. I used the diversion to dash from my covered position to what looked like a drafting room. With one glance I noted the shelves of engineering references, wall-spanning blueprints, and drafting desks stacked with reams of papers, books, and architectural schematics. Everywhere I saw the towering, needle-like profile of the Aetherspire and the detailed cutaways of the intricate machines and over-science devices comprising the tower's unfathomable design.

"Jonko!" I exclaimed in triumph.

My elation quickly faded, my blood turning cold when I saw the horrified faces of the engineers and draftsmen peering out from behind desks and tables, their eyes fixed on me, pleading in silent terror. But I had no time to explain, or even reassure them.

With a deafening blast, a figure crashed down from the ceiling, landing amidst a rapidly expanding fireball. The room filled with a chorus of screams as the howling firestorm billowed outward, consuming everything and everyone in its path. It was all I could do to throw up a hastily composed defensive ward before the explosion struck home, shattering my barrier and hurling me back out the door. I scrambled to my feet, smoke curling from my frock coat, and I stared in helpless horror as a raging inferno incinerated the drafting room—records, blueprints, men, and all.

The flames parted as their wielder strode from the heart of the murderous conflagration, his face scowling with bitter disdain. Although he lacked his empowered armor, I immediately recognized the corrupt battle-mage as HAAMR's second in command, just below Colonel Dolgrim himself.

"Major Caldrus!" I exclaimed.

"Interloper," the major snarled, a mantle of smoke and burning embers still swirling around him.

Saying nothing more, he leveled his brass and crystal staff to unleash a storm of crackling red lightning. The surprise attack left me half a heartbeat to react. Throwing out a burst of discordant resonance, the lightning arced away from me, ripping through the floor with ferocious intensity. I brought up my talisman to compose an offensive strike of my own, but Caldrus laid on a barrage of metaplasmic bolts forcing me to erect an aetheric ward. Seconds passed, and the battle-mage poured on his attack, grinning in triumph as my ward began to crack and flicker. I wheeled away the instant my barrier shattered, the searing edge of a bolt catching me on the shoulder as I dropped behind a bullet-chewed support pillar.

I winced, more in frustration than in pain, my heart racing and hopes fading fast. With the drafting room obliterated, our only chance at recovering some vital clue now stood with Quiniece. I glanced her way and saw she was still busy with the analytical engine, hands flying across cranks, dials, and switches as her autorotor did its work to override the machine's primary function. Even the homunculus now helped her, fetching rolls of punch tape streaming from the engine's clattering output registers.

With most of the mercenaries down, Nera and Vera stood guard for Quiniece, while Rognar helped Emileve and Nebb escort the civilians to the exit. They had almost made it when a third coterie of mercs and combat automatons appeared from the corridor in front of them, opening fire not on my friends, but on the scientists and engineers. Nebb went down in the hail of bullets as he tried, in vain, to protect the innocents, and though both Emileve and Rognar struck back hard, they were too late to save them.

"No!" I screamed, paling before the utter brutality of the massacre. "You've killed them all!"

"*You* killed them, Vescard," Major Caldrus balked. "We cannot allow you to have them. But had you not come here, they would have lived. Lived, to serve our glorious regime."

He whipped his staff around and conjured a seething orb of aethergy, primed to unleash upon the room where Quiniece was working. The twins opened fire, but their bullets were no match for the mage's defenses, and he hurled the roiling bolide toward its unsuspecting target. I threw myself out from behind the pillar, flinging up a barrier of entropic noise. The orb disintegrated into a rainbow of fizzling sparks, and Caldrus jerked his head around to face me, eyes narrowing with hate.

"You made one critical mistake," I admonished. "You failed to kill *me* first."

Caldrus snarled. "Easily corrected!"

A rapid burst of searing-hot bolts streamed from his staff, but I drew still more aethergy into my talisman, intensifying the entropic barrier and supplementing its effect with a backlash of shrieking dissonance that only a mage could hear. Caldrus winced in pain, then struck with a blazing silver lance to cut through my disruptive empowerments.

Seconds passed—seconds that seemed to us as minutes. We stretched our living quintessence to the breaking point, will against will and mind against mind, in a whirling tumult of jabs, feints, strikes, and counterstrikes—visible to no one but ourselves. Caldrus screamed, eyes bulging and face steaming red as he strained against the colossal forces building between us. I felt the strain as well, but my old training took hold.

An ocean of calm surrounded my mind, guarded by a crystal tower of harmony and focus, untouched by the crashing tides raging all around us. I had him, and he knew it.

Caldrus screamed again, drawing in far more aethergy than he could safely conduct as he prepared for a final, desperate attack. I struck at that very instant, compressing all my disruptive empowerments into a single burst of entropic dissonance. The backlash slammed him like a locomotive, electric fire tearing through every nerve and fiber of his brain and gripping him in the throes of a whole-body seizure. His staff shattered in his hand and he went limp, collapsing to the spell-scorched floor—dead or unconscious, I did not know. But if by some cruel twist of fate he did survive, he would likely awaken to find himself a blind epileptic, burned out of every mote of aetheric talent that he had.

"Quiniece!" I yelled as the drumming of combat boots sounded from more than one intersecting corridor.

She bolted from the analytical engine room, a broad grin showing her teeth as she held up a pair of punch tape spindles. The homunculus followed her, trailing more punch tape as it ran. "We've got it all!" she proudly proclaimed.

Though I had no idea what she had found, with more mercs about to burst into the hub and the thrum of ornithopters rising in the distance, I was inclined to accept her judgement on the matter. I motioned for the twins to take point as we hurried for the lobby, grimly noting that they were down to their last magazine cylinders. Gunfire cracked through the air just behind us, and Rognar returned with a parting gift from Varla, while I threw back a dazzling burst of strobing lights and ear-splitting booms to cover our tail. Three mercs held the lobby, but a few pointed remarks from the twin's pistols, followed by Varla's resounding objection, cleared the way for our escape.

Gunther was already coming around to pick us up, but Bruntilga showed no sign of slowing down. We broke into a mad dash to catch the locomotive as it continued building speed, jumping to grab hold of the cabin's handrails, and managed, however ungracefully, to clamber inside. Bullet's plinked against the locomotive's wrought iron chassis as we raced away, and the thrum of pursuing ornithopters faded fast behind.

Nera and Vera jumped from the cab as we rumbled past their parked motowheels, and the whirring hum of their racers' engines caught up with us just a few moments later.

"Where to, bossman?" Vera yelled over the whipping wind.

I leaned out the cabin door, yelling at the top of my lungs to be heard over the roar of Bruntilga's supercritical furnace. "The 5th District Underworks! We have our very own secret lair there."

The twins replied with impish grins and mock salutes, then revved their ichor-pumped engines and formed up to ride escort beside us. Gunther made a sharp turn, plowing through dunes of rust-blighted junk before dropping into a maze of derelict storm tunnels, speeding ever faster into the shadow-veiled heart of the Clockwork City.

CASE FILE 15:

THE DARK ABOVE, THE DARK BELOW

WE STOOD IN HARROWDEEP'S CAVERNOUS GREAT HALL, the tick-tock symphony of clattering cogs and interlocking rods echoing from the stone walls as the gearmill ground through its computations. Quiniece had brought the machine up from her workshop, both to collaborate with us while she worked and also for the additional space. Spools of meaningless numbers poured from the machine's output registers, a heap of ticker tape pooling on the floor around her. Meaningless to me, anyway—Quiniece apparently had no difficulty understanding the mathematically encoded notations. Nera and Vera helped her as well, going over the technical notes Quiniece had already deciphered. All three chattered excitedly about aetheric compression coils, harmonic inverters, and elemental reaction catalyzers.

"Mainspring Avenue will be too heavily guarded," Armez was saying to me. "Even if we take one of the sublevel streets below the thoroughfare, you can bet HAAMR will have patrols watching every plaza, tunnel, and corridor."

Although the map spread out across the banquet table was already heavily marked up, I drew another line from the gilded terraces of the 6th District to the cluttered foothills of the 1st. I continued the line to the high plateau of the Central Core, where rose Vandor Tower, the Governor's Tower, and the lofty Aetherspire. I then drew another line coming into the Central Core from the north, followed by two more from opposite directions along the East and West Axis.

"Even they cannot monitor every entrance into the Central Core," I asserted. "And with a large enough force, we could come at them from several different directions—street level, sublevels, and perhaps even from the air. Instigate, provocate, disperse, and regroup. There are a few more steps, of course, but that's the basic strategy."

"Us and what army?" Gunther boomed from across the Great Hall. The burly locomotive engineer lounged on one of the chairs near the roaring fireplace, and he gestured vaguely around the room with a half-eaten ham shank. "Now, I ain't as good with numbers as our toothy gear-girl over there, but last I counted there was eleven of us—and four ain't even here right now."

The diminutive, blue-skinned creature sitting next to Emileve chittered reproachfully.

"Uh, right... I meant there's twelve of us." Gunther tossed the homunculus a piece of his roast. "Sorry 'bout that, little fella'."

"Not to come off sounding overly pretentious," Armez began, his broadening grin betraying any illusion of feigned modesty, "but I would count Quiniece and myself as equivalent to two tactical assault squads. Each. The Nyasha Twins are nothing short of a light cavalry unit, Rognar is a one-man siege cannon, Leta is our mobile shield-wall, Keldon can summon decoy units at will, Arleia brings a host of elemental allies, Aldicus equates to a few more assault squads, and you, Gunther, are our battering ram. If that doesn't constitute an army, then I don't know what does. And I'm fairly certain the Queen of Thieves *does* have a small army of her very own."

"We're thieves, not soldiers," Emileve contended, her tone as dour as her expression. "And we've suffered more than our share of casualties these past few weeks. In addition to Nebb and Tavin, I've lost over a dozen brothers scouting the Central Core and the 13th District."

The hall fell silent, save for the clink and clatter of Quiniece's custom-built gearmill.

"Don't worry... We're with you, Aldicus," Emileve went on to assure. She glanced down, her eyes closing in mournful resignation. "If what you say is true, we'll all be dead anyway if that maniac opens a portal to Atracus. Better to try and die than to die cowering in fear."

I gave an appreciative nod, but had no idea what else to say. A mere 'thank you' seemed grotesquely inadequate, if not outright belittling of the sacrifices the Unseen Brotherhood had made and would continue to make as these final days unfolded. "I cannot promise that we will succeed in stopping the Shadow Man," I said in all honesty, "but I do know that we could not have made it this far without the Brotherhood's sacrifice."

Emileve nodded, but said nothing more.

I deliberated with Armez for another hour, listening to both Emileve and Gunther when they added their suggestions. We just didn't know enough about the enemy's plans to make any real progress.

When Leta, Arleia, and Keldon returned a short time later, they were not only exhausted by their latest reconnoitering excursion, but discouragingly empty handed as well. Part of me was grimly glad for their lack of success. If they had tracked down either the Darkweaver or Mistress Agona, it was a fair bet that they would never have returned at all.

"It's no use," Leta said, collapsing in a chair at the banquet table opposite Armez and myself. She fanned her shrug coat, then drew a deep breath before continuing. "I think the negative aetheric resonance I was detecting is coming from the Aetherspire, not the Darkweaver."

I quirked an eyebrow at her admission. "What do you mean? Didn't you begin sensing this negative resonance when the creature showed up?"

"Perhaps the Darkweaver is inside the Aetherspire," Armez suggested. He nodded to me. "You did deduce that they awoke the creature to serve as an engineering consultant, for lack of a better term."

Leta fidgeted nervously, then sighed. "The Darkweaver has a powerful aura, as black as the Void itself. But what I'm sensing is something else. Its resonance is far too regular." She glanced at Quiniece's gearmill. "Regular... Like a machine. And it's growing more powerful by the day."

A chill ran through me. "The Aetherspire is already starting up."

Keldon nodded, apparently already having come to the same conclusion. "It's the only thing that makes sense. The eclipse is a day away, but Atracus is already in alignment, for all practical purposes. If the machine uses convergent aetheric currents as part of its operation, they could be making a preliminary attempt to power it on."

"Fangle-fop," I swore. We were out of time, and no closer to forming a workable plan.

"I've got it!" Quiniece announced, throwing a mess of papers, ticker tape, and handwritten notes across the banquet table. "Oh, hi, Keldon," she teased, just then noticing him.

Arleia glared through her glasses, but said nothing. Keldon shifted anxiously in his chair, glancing between them.

"What's all this?" I asked, picking up a page that consisted of a coordinate grid scrawled with seemingly random numbers and letters.

"Technical schematics," Quiniece answered. I was about to point out that nothing I saw looked anything like a schematic when she went on to explain. "It's not a schematic like an engineer would draw—it's just the numbers describing its specifications, mathematically. I could spend months studying everything that's here and still wouldn't be able to understand it all, but I have deciphered enough to construct a rudimentary map."

She brought out several blank broadsheets and began sketching a crude outline of the sky-reaching spire with the massive power station at its base, consisting of six steam turbines, various control rooms, and an expansive complex of engineering shops and machine rooms. She even noted two rail stations, one for passengers and normal freight, and the other for daily shipments of ebonite coal to feed the monstrous furnaces.

Ostensibly, the Aetherspire had been built to provide Corradon with a limitless supply of aetheric energy, converting the raw power of its roaring turbines into aethergy through a series of orichalium dynamos, aetheric amplifiers, and empowered vizstones. Costing countless millions, the soaring structure would have paved the way for a new Golden Age of over-science marvels not seen since the days of Marada: levitating rails, gossamer flyers, projected marquees, and telaetheric missives.

But that dream had proven to be a lie, contrived by the Shadow Man—the Disciple of the Servants of Vosh—to conceal his sinister agenda. Now we had to destroy that great wonder of our age before it could unleash the very same nightmare that had brought Marada to its knees fifteen hundred years ago.

"From what I can tell," Quiniece continued, "the Aetherspire is a giant focusing tube for directing and magnifying aethergy, and the turbines, control rooms, and machine shops are all just for show. Forget about them." She then proceeded to X-out most of what she had drawn. "The important stuff, the *real* engine that drives the Aetherspire, is below the lower foundation levels."

Emileve nodded. "The covert construction work my men have been scouting."

"Exactly," Quiniece agreed. She drew a large, circular chamber beneath the spire's foundation. "Judging from the technical specifications, they've built a solaonic reactor core."

"What?" Keldon asked, his eyes widening.

"That's impossible!" I heard myself exclaim.

But it made sense. Solaonic reactors burned radiant aurium to sustain a perpetual elemental annihilation reaction, generating an unfathomable profusion of light, heat, and aethergy. All knowledge of constructing such reactors had been lost with the fall of Marada, but the Shadow Man had spent the past year accumulating relics of that forgotten age, including the Chaos Hexillion, a sizable quantity of radiant aurium, and a stasis box containing a fiendish Darkweaver. Not only did they have the radian aurium, but with the help of that Darkweaver, they would overcome whatever technical obstacles still remained.

"That all be good to know, but how do we get in to shut it down?" Nera asked. Her sister nodded in emphatic agreement.

"There's no easy way in," Emileve answered, folding her arms over her leather brigandine. She looked at Quiniece. "We would have found it by now if there was, but that place makes the Special Directorate's secret facility look like a picket fence by comparison."

"I'm still studying the specifications," Quiniece admitted, though her glum expression told far more than her words. "But I'm fairly sure I know where the Shadow Man and the Darkweaver are most likely to be."

She pulled out another broadsheet and began to sketch the sphere-shaped chamber beneath the Aetherspire. Then she drew the distinctive convex column in the center of the solaonic reactor, encircled by coil-like rings and what might have been enormous focal lenses, finally adding a single shaft leading directly up to the Aetherspire itself.

"Here," she said, circling an area just above the reactor and next to the shaft. "This is the only other control center mentioned in the records I recovered, and it's referred to as 'the nexus chamber.' I'm betting that's where you'll find the magine used to open the astral bridge to Atracus."

"A Maradian mage-engine?" Leta asked, raising an eyebrow.

Quiniece glanced at Armez, then to me. Armez nodded. They both already knew. After all, they had been there when the Shadow Man made off with it after the heist aboard the *Gambler's Boon.*

"No, not a Maradian magine," I corrected. "A Gollan magine. The Chaos Hexillion."

All eyes turned to me expectantly, but I had nothing more to add. What little I knew of the Chaos Hexillion came from the vaguest speculation by thaumaturgical researchers. Theories ranged from it being a component of an aetheric vortex weapon to the drive engine of an ancient Gollan warship to a sorcerous device capable of contacting the Demon Lords of Atracus. The latter guess was disturbingly close to the mark.

"So, we know where to go," Keldon said, breaking the silence, "but what good does this do us if we can't even get inside?" He looked to me, apparently hoping that I had some brilliant plan to unveil.

I still had nothing to say, but assuming Rognar returned soon, that would change.

"We'll smash our way in!" Gunther exclaimed, slamming his fist into his palm. He had come over to stand next to the table, apparently eager to voice his own distinctive brand of tactical advice. "They ain't expecting us to make an outright attack. Vescard's always just talk'n and think'n his way through. But this calls for a heap'n help'n of mayhem. My kind of mayhem!"

"You never be no good with the thinking," Nera agreed. She chuckled lightly, then smiled as she looked him up and down. "But you do be one brutty bruiser boy."

Emileve sighed. "Have you already forgotten about our attack on their research facility? I'm sure they haven't, and they've probably doubled their security at the Aetherspire by now."

"That might also explain why they're already trying to start up the machine," Arleia offered. "They suspect you've pieced together their plans, so they've accelerated their timetable. That means we've already forced their hand. If we act quickly, we might throw them off-balance."

Leta smiled, clearly impressed by her apprentice's grasp of the situation.

"There is one other thing," Quiniece said. Judging from her expression, she was uncertain whether or not it was even worth mentioning. "It might be nothing, but..."

"Go on," I encouraged. "Even the smallest detail could be critical."

She glanced over several lengths of ticker tape, then rifled through her own notes before continuing. "The Chaos Hexillion was mentioned as the key component of the nexus chamber powering the Aetherspire, but I also came across a reference to a negative energy catalyzer, which they had been unable to get working. The specifications warn that without this catalyzer, the reaction would be extremely unstable and subject to a catastrophic cascade implosion."

"Maybe that's why they needed the Darkweaver," Keldon ventured. "The science behind the astral bridge is too far beyond their ability to comprehend, even for the Shadow Man."

I laced my fingers together and I leaned forward in thought. "A negative energy catalyzer," I mulled. "From the sound of it, the catalyzer might have something to do with countering whatever aetheric turbulence or instabilities are inherent to the Chaos Hexillion. But without more information, there is no way to be certain."

I was about to suggest that we take a break from our deliberations when Rognar finally strolled into Harrowdeep's Great Hall, casually juggling a small silver orb between his hands.

"Well don't everybody cheer at once," he grumbled when

silence greeted his return. "I'm lucky to have made it back alive. Do you know how many HAAMR units they have blockading the 6th District?"

The Dworgh hobbled up to our gathering and set an egg-shaped orb on the banquet table. Four legs sprouted from the sides, and a vizstone extended vertically, glowing iridescent blue.

"Excellent," I said, smiling. "You were able to make contact with Barthemius?"

"The Grand Magister of the Magestrian Order?" Keldon asked, startled.

"Actually, this whatchamajigger was delivered by a street contact for one of the Order's deep cover agents," Rognar clarified. He reached into another coat pocket and pulled out a sizable fried dumpling—filled with who knew what—and began eating. "He runs a food stall, so that was nice."

I sighed. "Hopefully the others got theirs as well." Everyone continued to stare at me in confusion. "Grand Magister Barthemius put together six empowered telaetheric projectors to facilitate the conference," I explained, doing my best to contain the temptation to chuckle.

Leta narrowed her eyes, no doubt annoyed by the giddy amusement she sensed in me. "A conference with whom?"

I widened my smile. "With everyone else who's going to be helping us." I feigned surprise, glancing around. "Oh, did I forget to mention that?"

"I'm sure it just slipped your mind," Armez sighed.

In truth, I didn't know if Barthemius was going to complete his work in time, or if he would even be able to distribute the projectors under the grip of martial law. But if all went as planned, our chances for success were about to grow by several orders of magnitude.

The egg-shaped device hummed quietly, and I sensed the currents of the luminiferous aether stirring as rays of charged aethergy coiled outward from the crystal at its top. The coiling rays converged, and an illusory form took shape not four paces from the table. Everyone else either jumped with a start or gasped in surprise at the sudden appearance of the ghostly apparition. I only smiled, recognizing the voluminous robes, neatly cropped beard, and orichalium skullcap of my old master.

"Grand Magister," I greeted, taking off my top hat to give a respectful bow. "This is a welcome turn of events to be sure."

Keldon, still stunned, swept off his newsboy cap and performed a hasty bow of his own.

"Ah, Aldicus, there you are," Barthemius said, apparently fiddling with something to his right. "Just a moment..."

Two more images materialized a few paces away. The first was an Eldren woman, elegantly dressed in august robes and a totem-covered headpiece. The second was quite the opposite, being a stout Dworgh with broad shoulders and an even broader belly. His great braided beard hung heavy with jeweled rings and rune-etched ornaments.

"Eligarch!" Arleia greeted, placing her hands together and bowing her head in respect.

"Burgomaster!" Rognar exclaimed with equal surprise.

"Allow me to introduce Chief Elder Naraeth, Eligarch of the Eldren Preserve of Corradon in the 3rd District," Barthemius announced, although the long-distinguished Eldren needed no introduction. "And Hreldgarj, Burgomaster of the Dworgh Enclave in the 5th District."

"Rognar, you good-for-nothing scoundrel!" Hreldgarj barked, shaking his ceremonial mace. "What have you gotten me into this time?" Then he and Rognar both burst out with laughter, reveling in whatever joke the rest of us were not privy too.

The air shimmered as another figure came into focus, resolving into the crisp naval uniform of the Vandorian Air Corp, complete with golden epaulettes and an old-style captain's cap.

"Captain Cheyron, of the *true* Vandorian Guard,"

Barthemius indicated, though I recognized him at once.

"Aldicus Vescard," Captain Cheyron greeted, removing the emberless pipe from his mouth. "All is well, I hope."

"With any luck, Commissioner," I greeted in return, garnering an arched eyebrow from the captain. As the highest ranking member of the Vandorian Guard—the *true* Vandorian Guard, now holed up in the 10th and 11th Districts—he was the de facto commissioner of Corradon's rightfully and lawfully elected civil guardians, whether or not the title was official.

The last figure shimmered into view, revealing a dapper dressed man in a striped suit with a pork pie hat. "...told you those stuffy dandy-wands don't got no idea what..." he was saying to someone just out of view. Then he froze, looking around. "Well, I'll be a bulgore's uncle. This crazy hokery-pokery actually works!"

Barthemius gestured to the mobster. "Giono Gallinaro, newly installed boss for the Corradon branch of the Travenni crime..." he cleared his throat, then continued. "For the Travenni business interests."

"Vescard!" Giono exclaimed, doubtlessly recognizing me from our encounter on the *S.S. Gambler's Boon.* He then saw Captain Cheyron. "And what's this? Another hoity-toity bluejack? We ain't working with a bunch of jacks and badgers, you hear?"

"And I would rather not fraternize with the criminal underworld," Captain Cheyron grumbled in return. "Unfortunately, extremely desperate times require extremely desperate measures."

"I was not able to empower these projectors as well as I would have liked," Barthemius explained. His ghostly image, and that of the others, faded out briefly before snapping back again. "We may only have a few minutes before the connection destabilizes entirely."

"Mages," Giono Gallinaro mumbled. "Bah!"

I cleared my throat. "Then I will get straight to the point.

The man you know as the Commissioner General of Vandor Tower, now the self-proclaimed Lord Protector of Corradon, is the grand orchestrator of the fabricated revolution by the Brethren of Justice. He is also a sworn servitor of the Demon Lords of Atracus, the Disciple of the Servants of Vosh."

My announcement was met by stunned expressions, save for Captain Cheyron who had witnessed the Commissioner General's betrayal, and Barthemius who had already been informed.

"We call him the Shadow Man, for his true identity we will likely never know," I continued. "For years he has been quietly moving all the pieces into position, building up to our present state of martial law under the iron heel of HAAMR's paramilitary occupation." I held up my hand, staving off the deluge of questions I was about to receive. "There's more, and it's worse. The Aetherspire is not what it seems, and has, in fact, been constructed according to the Shadow Man's specifications for the sole purpose of opening a portal to Atracus. I believe this portal will open sometime tomorrow."

"What's all this now?" Giono demanded.

"Impossible!" Hreldgarj exclaimed.

"The eclipse," Chief Elder Naraeth said, shaking herself from the initial shock of my revelation. "They plan to utilize the aetheric attenuation of the astral conjunction to create a transpositional confluence, as was done when Marada opened their ill-starred portal fifteen centuries ago."

I arched an eyebrow, but I should not have been surprised. She was an Eldren eligarch after all—her great-great-grandmother had probably fought in the War of Golla and Marada. "Just so."

"Why not call in the Armillian army?" Hreldgarj rebuked. "City-state or not, Corradon's an Armillian protectorate under the provisions of the Medrean Concord."

"Armillia is currently fighting both the Karghen Warhold as well as the clans of the Erylion Frontier," Captain Cheyron explained. "And then there is the war in Tarrona that has prompted the entire Armillian navy to stand at high alert in the Sea of Isles. Presently, Parliament believes the situation here is stable under the Lord Protector's emergency powers, and it might take weeks to convince them otherwise."

"We have less than a day," I reiterated. "The eclipse will reach totality tomorrow afternoon, and that will be when the Shadow Man activates the astral bridge to Atracus—assuming they are not able to activate it sooner."

"Well, this certainly explains things," Barthemius said rubbing his short beard. "We detected an aetheric disturbance earlier today, though even our best astral delvers were unable to divine the true aspect of its nature or pinpoint its precise location."

"We sensed it as well," Chief Elder Naraeth said thoughtfully, her ancient eyes looking to some distant place beyond the material world. "A discordant resonance in the higher astral strata... It is beginning. The penumbra of the demon-moon fast approaches."

"Quit with the mystical mumbo-jumbo!" Giono exclaimed. "You said you were going to get to the point, Vescard, so get to the point. Why do you need the Travennis in this scheme?"

"Yes, why bring these criminals into this?" the Eligarch demanded, her eyes flashing as she turned to confront me. "You of all people, Vescard, should—"

I slammed my hands on the table. "We need muscle as much as magery to stand any chance of victory. We need courage, we need guile, and we need steel. We need the whole of Corradon to rally behind this great offensive. We need them *all*—hero and villain alike. This is *our* city, and we either stand together to defend it, or we fall before the fire and darkness that is to come!"

The Eligarch kept her eyes locked on mine. Then, ever so subtly, she tipped her head in deference to my words. "You have the support of the Eldren Preserve. We will answer the call when the call is given."

"The Vandorian Guard stands with you," Captain

Cheyron announced, touching the brim of his captain's cap. "At least, what remains of the Vandorian Guard still under my command. Consider *Justiciar* at your disposal, along with six patrol dirigibles, two full ornithopter squadrons, and five companies of loyal Guardsmen."

"If what you say is true, this madman must be stopped at all cost," Hreldgarj declared. "Every able-bodied Dworgh in our enclave who knows how to fight will throw in their lot with you—and that would be all of them." After a short pause, he amended, "Except you, Rognar. You're still on your own." Both of them broke out laughing again.

"Needless to say, you can count on the Grand Lodge of the Magestrian Order," Barthemius assured. "Most of our mages are dedicated to thaumaturgical research, scientific studies, or clerical duties, but those of us who are trained in defensive and offensive magery will lend our full support."

Giono threw his arms in the air, falling back into the chair behind him. "I guess I'm 'sposed to be grateful you called us and not those Seladono moochers." He shook his head, then shrugged. "I can't wait to see the look on old Evardo Seladono's face when he sees us fighting side by side with the bluejacks."

Emileve rolled her eyes, then moved to join me in the projector's field of view. "The Unseen Brotherhood has always stood up for the helpless and oppressed of the Clockwork City, but this time we stand for all."

The twins stepped up to either side of me, drawing a surprised look from Giono. "The Nyasha Twins be inviting ourselves to this little party, too," Nera put in.

"And not only us," Vera continued, "but all the raff and rabble of the Shifty Drifter, too."

"And I'll call in a couple of my old buddies from back in the day," Gunther added, now looming behind me. He stabbed his thumb at himself, a great big grin stretching below his horseshoe mustache. "Let the call go out—the Iron Thunder Gang rides again!"

Chief Elder Naraeth drew a deep breath, looking notably indignant, and Barthemius let out a long sigh as he rubbed his eyes.

"This is going to devolve into utter chaos," Barthemius groaned.

"That be the plan," Vera chimed. She looked my way and winked. "Ain't that right, bossman?"

I nodded. "That be the plan."

The ghostly images of my fellow conspirators faded, then flickered, and began fading again.

"The telaetheric coupling is losing coherency," Barthemius said, his image growing transparent before flickering back. He tended to something just out of sight, then shook his head. "There's nothing I can do. The resonate feedback has surpassed the empowerment's entropic limit."

"Captain Cheyron, I'll see you soon. The rest of you, we'll make our move tomorrow," I said as the image of the others dissolved into a jumble of smearing colors and collapsing bubbles. "Watch for the signal. You'll know it when you see it."

I saw nods before they faded entirely from view. The silver egg sparked and sputtered, and the vizstone at its top flashed one last time before growing dark.

"An army," Keldon muttered, leaning back in bewilderment. "We actually have an army."

"Sure, but if it's just havoc you were after, I'm pretty sure these two had you covered," Quiniece said, nodding to Nera and Vera. I had never seen the twins look more proud of themselves.

But Emileve only shook her head. "Mayhem alone won't get us inside the Aetherspire. Brute force can never win against an even more brutal force."

"And they be a mighty brutty force to reckon with," Nera agreed.

Armez let out a long, exasperated sigh, sinking deeper into the chair where he sat. "Oh, my dear Vescard. Please tell me you have something that amounts to a *real* plan."

Leta cocked her head, eyebrow arching as she sensed the gears turning in my mind. "Oh, he has a plan. Damn you, Vescard. You've had a plan all this time."

I nodded. "Initiation, conflagration, separation, circulation, congelation, transmutation, rectification."

Everyone gawked as though I had completely lost my mind. Everyone, save for Keldon, who grinned as he recognized the seven stages of alchemical transformation given by *The Precepts of the Great Work*. I closed my eyes and drew a deep breath, centering my mind and stilling all perturbment as I listened to the shifting silver harmonies of the higher astral light. The ebb and flow of the aether coursed around me—the energy of all energies and the force of all forces, ever-changing and eternal.

"Through these stages does the sage transform both the subtle and the gross," I quoted from *The Precepts*, "ascending from earth to heaven and back to earth again, unifying in exalted splendor that which is above with that which is below. In this way were all things created and in this way shall all things be uncreated, through the force of all forces, the power of all power, and the unity of all unity." I opened my eyes to the silent, expectant faces of my friends and gave them a single, encouraging nod. "So let it be done."

THE ROLLING DRONE OF THE SHIP'S IMPELLER engines vibrated the floor beneath my feet, while the howling alarms blared from every deck and corridor of the Vandorian Guard's indelible flagship. Officers and crewmen dashed about the bridge, yelling orders and hollering back replies. Brassy voices echoed through call tubes from every station aboard *Justiciar*. Beside me, in his chair in the center rear of the bridge, Captain Cheyron solemnly looked on. The spotters, manning the forward observation scopes, yelled the warning that all had dreaded, yet expected to hear.

"HAAMR ships, dead ahead!" the crewman announced.

"This is it," the captain mulled. He took the emberless pipe from his mouth and raised his voice above the babbling din. "All hands, prepare for attack!"

I gazed out the panoramic windows at the front of the ship to the skyline of reaching towers foresting the city's core districts. At the center stood the great, needle-like mast of the Aetherspire. Although the ship's chronometer read just past noon, the bright of day dimmed to crimson twilight hues as the fiery visage of Atracus fell fast across the face of the sun. By the fading glow of that quickly waning light, I saw what the forward observers had seen: ten HAAMR dirigibles, escorted by squadrons of ornithopters and aeronefs, and led by a single heavily armed aircruiser. The distant rise and fall of air-raid sirens howled from below, followed just moments later by a storm of flak, flares, and tracer fire lighting up the dusky midday sky.

Keldon, looking more awed than terrified, gripped the railing beside him as the ship trembled with the concussive blasts of exploding flak shells. I knew *Justiciar's* armored hull could sustain the bombardment for a time, but the unceasing barrage only intensified as we closed with the heavy artillery of the approaching HAAMR fleet.

"Main batteries, give me alternating forward salvos," Captain Cheyron ordered through the call tubes to his left. "Secondary batteries, remove those HAAMR thopters from my sky. All fire control and damage control teams, standby."

Six Vandorian dirigibles held formation around *Justiciar*, three to either side. Our own squadrons of ornithopters raced ahead to intercept the approaching flight of enemy aircraft and *Justiciar* shook again as more flak burst around us. I watched in dismay as one of our six dirigibles erupted in a swelling ball of flame, its armor-plated hull torn open by the direct impact of three enemy shells.

The captain turned to me and nodded. "We could really use a defensive barrier right about now."

The ship shook with another blast, and I hurried to the

front of the bridge, motioning Keldon to follow. My specialties had always been in delving, disruptive magery, and egregore automata, crucial fields for any detective magus. As a result, I was not as well versed in the art of defensive warding. Even so, with Keldon's help I was sure I could generate a kinetic barrier capable of shielding *Justiciar*. There was little chance that I could defend the other ships of our modest flotilla, but with *Justiciar* in the lead position, she would take the brunt of what the HAAMR ships dished out.

"This will be a basic convergent empowerment," I said to Keldon. He nodded, drawing his talismanic key from his belt. "Conduct as much aethergy as you can, then join on my mark."

I flipped my own talismanic pen from my frock coat to my hand as we made our way to the very front of the bridge. We stopped at the great arc of windows, and I looked down upon a turbulent sea of anarchy, riots, and protests surrounding the central plateau, where loomed the Aetherspire. Countless firefights and burning buildings brightened the streets even as the last rays of the sun dwindled behind the volcanic visage of the demon-moon.

To the north, a pair of motowheels sped down Mainspring Causeway, followed by a roaring menagerie of makeshift racers and tricked-out steam-coaches. These could only be the Shifty Drifter's Outlaw Riders. From the West Axis thundered a ten-ton monstrosity of iron and steam, enveloped by a shimmering field of mystical protection conjured by her passengers. A coterie of coal-fired locomobiles formed up beside Bruntilga, engines howling and horns sounding as the Iron Thunder Gang crashed through HAAMR checkpoints and barricades with heedless abandon. To the south, columns of Vandorian Guardsmen, their numbers bolstered by four companies of Dworghen warriors, marched along the boulevards of the 4th District. At their head rumbled over a dozen patrol wagons and street buggies. The flash of gunfire and explosions far to the east signaled the Travenni's own trouble-making efforts, and somewhere beneath the district sublevels prowled Emileve and the Unseen Brotherhood, out of sight and out of mind.

"Initiation," I whispered. *And so it began.*

Bullets pelted the tektite glass like rain, leaving little more than a dusting of lead, but jarring me from my musings all the same. In the sky ahead, HAAMR ornithopters and aeronefs broke this way and that to intercept our own thopters, while the fleet of HAAMR dirigibles, spearheaded by the menacing aircruiser, turned to bring their bristling broadsides to bear.

I held out my talisman and focused my thoughts on the aetheric currents converging around me. Chords of force and vibration converged into a harmonic pattern which, once suffused with aethergy, would solidify into a barrier equivalent to three feet of solid fabricrete. That instant, the flash of the enemy gunports lit up along their armored hulls.

"Now!" I yelled to Keldon.

Keldon stabbed his key forward, releasing the sum total of aetheric energy he had conjured. Drawing upon both the ambient aethergy and the sudden burst of power Keldon had released, I focused every bit I could safely conduct into the empowerment, projecting the coalescing barrier forward of our ship. The sky before us exploded in a roiling fireball as two dozen flak shells slammed home. I strained to maintain control as the ward flickered and cracked. Even as I did, another brilliant explosion lit up the darkening sky—the death flare of a second Vandorian dirigible pounded into burning scrap by the opposing fleet. I redoubled my efforts, forcing my overheating talisman to the breaking point as I channeled a torrent of force and energy into the defensive ward. Beside me, my apprentice strained to conduct more aethergy than he had ever managed before. Another salvo pounded into the ward, engulfing the ship's forward quarter in a halo of flame, yet still our tenuous barrier held.

"Signal the remaining ships to turn broadside and fire!"

Captain Cheyron yelled to the semaphore officer. Then he piped to the engine room, "Chief Beldwick, give me emergency speed and then some."

"The elemental turbines already be run'n hot, skipper," came the chief engineer's reply. "The hous'n won't hold for long, and when she blows, we'll have us a scream'n tempest hot enough to boil skin from bones."

"Then evacuate the engine room and open every coolant valve," the captain ordered. "I want to hear those turbines howling from the bridge!"

"Aye!"

The bombardment only intensified as *Justiciar* surged ahead, guns booming, turbines howling, impellers screaming, and over it all thundered the deafening punishment of the HAAMR aircruiser and her fleet. The cracks in my barrier grew with every successive impact, and there was only so much I could do to keep those cracks patched over. Cracks grew to holes, explosions tore through, and what remained of my shredded ward tittered on the verge of complete collapse. I was no master of defensive magery, and it was only brute force and raw power that had carried it this far. This far, and no farther.

"My barrier's failing!" I warned, although the impact of artillery shells ripping into our hull did more to explain our circumstances than my words ever could.

The ship lurched and heaved, fire exploding both port and starboard. Looking ahead, through the raging firestorm around *Justiciar*'s forward hull, I saw the enormous black shadow of HAAMR's indomitable aircruiser against the black, ecliptic sky—a veritable flying fortress of murderous artillery guns and devastating alchemical-air bombs.

"We have to bring down that monster at all costs!" Cheyron exclaimed, gripping both arms of the captain's chair.

He was right, of course. Unless we took down that airborne battleship, our ground forces would be pounded into bloody pulp from above. Yet, what remained of our little fleet didn't stand a chance against them.

"Captain, we could—" I started to say.

But the captain already had a plan in mind. He hit the one alarm no crewman wanted to hear, then yelled into the call tubes over its clamoring death knell. "All hands abandon ship. I say again, all hands abandon ship." He motioned for the bridge crew to resign their stations and make for the nearest escape dinghy. Then he stood, straightened out his uniform coat, and came forward to join me at the panorama of windows. "That goes for you, too, Vescard. Get yourself and your apprentice out of here."

"No, Commissioner," I said, my voice raised over the thunder of gunfire and explosions. Cheyron wheeled around and frowned, rightly unaccustomed to having his orders questioned in the heat of battle. Technically speaking, I could refuse or ignore any order he gave. I was a civilian, after all, operating strictly as a deputized freelance detective for Vandor Tower. "You're the one who's getting out of here."

"I'm the captain of this—"

"You're the Commissioner General now!" I interrupted. "The *real* Commissioner General. No one else is left in the senior levels of command who wasn't killed, corrupted, or subverted by the Shadow Man." I stepped closer, conjuring a quick glamour to amplify my voice and magnify my countenance, driving my point home. "Your duty is to the *true* Vandorian Guard, not just to a single vessel. Now, carry out your duty and I will carry out mine!"

Cheyron glared at me for a moment, drawing in a sharp breath. He looked to the aircruiser and to the darkening eclipse above, then turned back to me, his face a deepening scowl. "Damn you, Vescard." The ship shook as a massive explosion ripped into the forward hull. "Damn you for being so blasted right all the time! But this is a suicide run, and you know it."

"It's not suicide for an archmage," I replied in an even

tone. I placed a hand on Keldon's shoulder. "Go with him. As soon as you land, try to rendezvous with either the Unseen Brotherhood or Gunther's gang. Barring that, find what shelter you can in the 4th District." I tapped the brooch he wore pinned to his vest. As much as I wanted to borrow it, I wasn't about to leave my apprentice defenseless in a war zone. "And don't forget you have this."

Keldon said something, but the ear-splitting clap of cannon fire drowned his words. Captain Cheyron beckoned for my apprentice to follow, and he hesitated for just an instant, looking back at me with eyes more fearful for me than for his own circumstances. Then he turned and raced after the captain, disappearing down a ladder to the escape dinghies in the deck below.

"Now it's just you and me," I said to the enemy aircruiser, so close that it filled the bridge's entire view.

Between its bristling arsenal, near-impregnable armor, and roaring impeller turbines, the airborne fortress was beyond anything that could be justifiably commissioned for police or garrison duty. It was the very same warship that had attacked the *S.S. Gambler's Boon*, so the Shadow Man had the vessel in his pocket well before HAAMR's military takeover. I had no idea where he had obtained such impressive military hardware, but the war-hungry imperium of Kendes would be my first guess, to say nothing of the fact that Agona herself hailed from those demon-sworn lands.

Was the Shadow Man actually an agent of Kendes? Was this all a prelude to an invasion of Armillia, or perhaps all of Celaphania? The entire continent of Tarrona was embroiled in a war with Kendes and their dark allies, but whatever wider conspiracy there might have been, I did not presently care. For now, stopping the monstrous vessel was my sole concern.

Another salvo of artillery fire smashed through the hull, the explosions knocking the ship sharply off course. *Justiciar*'s own guns had fallen silent, the gunners having evacuated along with the rest of the crew. The impellers dropped in pitch as the overheating machinery finally began to fail. The only thing holding the ship aloft was her own momentum and the innate buoyancy of her novarite hull.

With no time to spare, I threw myself into the captain's chair and jammed my talismanic pen against the armrest, sending ribbons of aethergy spiraling into the deck and surging back along the fuselage. I focused every thought upon the noble vessel's buckling structure—her tattered skin of molten armor, her fire-gutted entrails of venting conduits and shattered gears, and her screaming turbines flying apart under their own incalculable strain. The ship was dead, but the elemental flames within her burning engine room lived still—a whirling maelstrom of fire, steam, and thunder.

"One last mission," I whispered to that blazing elemental fury, though surely those mindless aetheric flotsam could not truly understand me. *Or could they?* "One last battle. One last victory. And then, freedom. Freedom for you. Freedom for us. Freedom for all."

My mind touched the living fire within the turbines, infusing both will and intention, and with a blinding flash and thundering report, the twin vortices of elemental energy ripped free of the engines, unleashing the sum total of their power. The sheer force of the ignition shoved me back into the captain's chair, and every beam, bolt, and deck plate trembled as the dying ship rose back into the eclipse-blackened sky, a specter wreathed in flames and howling like some nightmarish barghest.

The HAAMR aircruiser renewed its barrage, pummeling *Justiciar* with explosive shells and close-in defense guns even as she began to turn and lift away. Fire rolled into the bridge, the tektite windows shattered inward, and burning support joists crashed to the deck behind me. I held fast to the bucking chair, weaving chords of aethergy around the blazing inferno at the heart of the dying vessel, shaping, guiding, and directing the tumultuous forces to propel us onward and upward toward the opposing aircruiser, now less than a thousand feet away. And yet, scarcely anything of *Justiciar* remained. She was now little more than a gutted, flaming tube, hollowed out like a barrel... Not unlike the barrel of a ship's gun, only a hundred orders of magnitude greater.

Focusing on my empowerment, I willed the twin vortices ripping through *Justiciar*'s heart to compress and release, driving the full force of their explosive energy through the ship's barrel-like hull while sheer momentum carried the vessel on a direct collision course for the enemy ship.

"Conflagration!" I screamed.

Blinding light and scorching fire exploded all around me, and I grabbed hold of my top hat, diving headfirst out the window. Wind whipped past as I plummeted downward, and I looked back to watch the compressed vortex of elemental energy rip through one end of the enemy aircruiser and out the other. Seconds later, the burning wreckage of *Justiciar* slammed into her target, crumpling on impact. Both ships vanished in a brilliant fireball as fuel and munitions detonated in a catastrophic chain reaction.

Acting quickly, I thrusted my talisman forward, projecting a defensive ward just in time to dampen the impact of the shock wave thundering away from the swelling firestorm. As soon as the thunderclap passed, I dropped the ward to divert its energy into a downward beam of repulsive force. My fall slowed and leveled out as the repulsive beam pushed back with its equal and opposite counterforce, propelling me above the Clockwork City, frock coat flapping in the wind as burning embers and flaming debris rained around me.

Flares, spotlights, and exploding flak filled the darkened sky as far as I could see. Tracer fire ripped deadly arcs before me while air-raid sirens wailed their warning cry. Ornithopters buzzed and gyred like angry wasps, and the last Vandorian airships, both aflame, pounded it out with the five remaining HAAMR dirigibles. An aeronef careened past me, airfoils burning and impeller sputtering, and I veered aside to avoid a streaking volley of anti-airship rounds.

Corradon was a warzone!

THROUGH THE HAZE OF SMOKE AND FIRE, I saw the battle raging on the streets and causeways encircling the Central Core's municipal plateau. Companies of Dworghen warriors and Vandorian Guardsmen pushed their way through the HAAMR troopers blockading the 1st District, while Travenni trigger boys chewed away at the enemy's flanks, drawing more HAAMR troopers away. Eldren archers loosed flights of brilliant white arrows from their empowered bows, backed by a dozen of their most accomplished elementors casting bolts of crackling lightning and blasts of concussive air.

A sudden flash of light drew my eye, and I watched as a blinding ray of energy lanced through one of the HAAMR dirigibles, obliterating it utterly. The beam had struck from one of six floating castle turrets, which I recognized as the turrets that normally orbited the Grand Lodge's central tower, and with them flew a dozen mage-empowered chariots with Barthemius at the head.

Small though I was compared to the great ships and armored companies battling it out, I was nevertheless a target, and I soon found myself dodging this way and that as rockets and flak bursts filled the air around me. Lacking sufficient aethergy to both maintain my altitude and invoke another defensive barrier, my predicament grew suddenly more dire when a HAAMR ornithopter picked me as the victim of its twin drum guns. The rain of bullets strafed my way, but from out of nowhere a bola-like chain tore through the thopter's thrumming wings, sending it tumbling to the burning streets below.

I searched the flak-filled sky for my savior and spotted a familiar midnight coach, its clockwork steeds thundering on blazing hooves of spectral fire. Armez waved to me as his ensorcelled coach swept into the heart of the aerial battle.

Salvos of spinning bolas, snaking spark-rockets, and spinning flechette canisters flew in every direction as Quiniece introduced the enemy to the fearsome repertoire of a gearmeister's arsenal.

Yet, even as our combined forces closed in on the Central Core, I realized we were already too late. I could only watch with mounting dread as the black orb of Atracus consumed the last sliver of the sun, and the volcanic halo of the demon-moon erupted into a burning red corona, bathing the city in all its terrible light. A reverberating rumble rose above the wail of the air-raid sirens, growing in strength and pitch as thrashing electric arcs and bubbles of aetheric energy swirled about the tip of the Aetherspire's needle-like pinnacle, converging into a tempest of crackling metaplasm.

I gasped, my eyes widening in horror. *The Aetherspire was activating!*

Even as I thought the words, an incalculable pulse of energy surged through the aether. I clutched my head in agony, reeling against the resonating screech of a thousand discordant notes like nails raking across slate. With a blinding flash and a deafening boom, an orb of complete and utter blackness materialized above the Aetherspire's pinnacle, rapidly expanding as though to engulf the Central Core. What it was, I did not know, but I could only assume the astral bridge to Atracus was opening.

I let up on my talisman, falling into a dive straight for the foot of the Central Core's plateau where our teams fought to secure the junction of Mainspring Causeway and the West Axis. With a final surge of repulsive force, I slowed to a feather-fall and touched down on the road, my coat whipping around me as the hot wind of an explosion howled past. Reaching up, I found I had lost my top hat somewhere along the way, but one lost hat was the least of my worries.

Gunfire rang and lightning cracked, and the whistle of mortar bombs culminated in a crescendo of explosions echoing from the rising heights of the tangled urban plateau.

Bullets peppered the ground around me while Dworghen blunderbusses boomed and Eldren arrows flew. A HAAMR ornithopter crashed nearby. Bruntilga barreled through the burning wreckage before pulling to a halt, pneumatic brakes screaming. The rest of the Iron Thunder Gang continued on down the West Axis—a roaring cavalry of coal-fired locomobiles, joining up with the Outlaw Riders of the Shifty Drifter to harry the HAAMR squads in pursuit. Nera and Vera sped past on their motowheels, pistols firing as they circled the perimeter of our muster point to fend off the encroaching troopers.

I made a dash for the considerable cover that Bruntilga's massive iron bulk provided. Leta, Arleia, and Rognar piled out of the locomotive racer as I drew near, followed by Gunther himself, covered in soot and grease and lugging a drum-chamber blunderbuss over his shoulder. Keldon was not with them.

"Where is Keldon?" I demanded, glancing about for my apprentice. "Did he not join up with you?"

"Wasn't he with you?" Arleia asked. Her eyes widened behind her glasses and she looked to the crimson sky—to the expanding cloud of smoke and fire left by *Justiciar*'s collision with the HAAMR aircruiser.

"A few dinghies came down not far from here," Vera said, jogging up to us with her sister not far behind. She clicked off a few casual shots at some distant target, then turned back to us. "Most be riddled with holes from all the flak."

Arleia looked even more horrified, but all eyes turned when Armez's ensorcelled coach came thundering down from the sky. Quiniece jumped from the top as they pulled around, slinging a bulky concussion gun over one shoulder as she sauntered over to us. But one look at Arleia, and a quick glance at me, and her sardonic grin faded to an expression of genuine worry.

"Keldon?" Quiniece asked, her voice a whisper barely audible over the clamor and gunfire of battle. Arleia was too worried to even be troubled by her rival's earnest concern.

I was about to voice my own concern when a coterie of cloaked figures and diminutive homunculi scrambled out from a nearby storm tunnel, then hurried over to meet up with us. Among them I spotted Emileve pushing back her hood, and beside her, to my relief, walked Keldon—a sheepish grin crooked on his face.

"Looking for your errant apprentice?" Emileve asked. "We found him covering Captain Cheyron from a HAAMR fire squad near their crashed dinghy. He was tossing out illusions and dazzlers faster than I could have believed possible." She glanced to her men and nodded. "The rest of my team is escorting the good captain back to the Vandorian command post, but I figured you'd want to know the kid was all right."

"Kid?" Keldon asked.

Arleia gasped, her eyes wide with both joy and surprise, and her tapered ears perked up in delight. She rushed forward as though to give him a hug, but Quiniece was already at Keldon's side. She threw an arm over his shoulder and leaned in to plant a quick kiss on his cheek. Arleia tensed, her face scrunching in a scowl as hands clenched into fists. Keldon, the poor lad, just looked bewildered.

"Oh, cool your ears, sweets," Quiniece chimed. Her amber eyes tracked up to the ever-expanding sphere of darkness engulfing the Aetherspire. "We've got bigger problems than you and me, in case you hadn't noticed."

"To say it's a problem puts it mildly," Leta grumbled. She stepped up beside Arleia, probably to make sure her fuming apprentice didn't blast Quiniece with a bolt of elemental light. "I can barely hear myself think, let alone sense anything over the screaming discords resonating from that..." she paused, unsure what to name the expanding anomaly. "...that portal."

Armez shook his head. "It's more than a portal, dear. Didn't the Eligarch suggest this was some kind of transpositional confluence between our world and Atracus? Looking at it now, I'll be damned if she wasn't right."

"But you *are* damned," Leta reminded.

Armez pushed up his red-tinted spectacles, then folded his hands on his dragon-headed cane and sighed. "Some perspective, please."

Rognar came forward, drawing Varla from inside his duffle coat. "Whatever it is, we need to shut it down."

Nera, Vera, and Gunther nodded their emphatic agreement. "If there be one thing I know for sure, it be this," Nera said, speaking for them all. She drew a clockwork pistol from her holster, spun it around, and checked the ammo drum. "No matter how big the brutty bad may be, it no be big enough or bad enough to beat the likes of we."

Explosions shook the ground, and the squad of Vandorian Guardsmen took position to return fire at whoever was throwing potshots our way. They were soon joined by the Dworghen blunderbussiers and Eldren archers with their empowered compound bows.

"So, what's the plan, boss?" Keldon asked.

Everyone looked to me expectantly. I studied the cluttered walls of the Central Core's plateau looming above us, and to the ever-expanding astral confluence which had grown to encompass the Aetherspire, Vandor Tower, and the Governor's tower. At this rate, the confluence would soon encompass the Central Core and the 1st District, and not long after that, the core districts as well. It was now or never, and we had not a moment to lose.

I turned to Quiniece. "Give us a rundown of the layout."

"We have three angles of attack." She looked to a large opening at the base of the Central Core's plateau, less than three blocks away. "This storm tunnel leads straight into the 1st District's waterworks, which opens into the Central Core's underframe support structure, buttressing not only Vandor Tower and the Governor's Tower, but the Aetherspire as well." She pointed farther up the Central Core's plateau, to a tangled mass of rail lines, trestle bridges, and overbuilt structures. "Second, the city's steamrail lines converge at Grand Wheel Terminal. The Wheel is probably heavily guarded, but the older cargo lines that run beneath have service tunnels connecting with the Aetherspire's loading docks." She then pointed down, indicating the sublevels below. "And finally, there's the sublevel maze of utility corridors and access shafts which, thanks to Emileve and her men, we know leads directly to the nexus chamber beneath the Aetherspire."

"Which way will it be?" Emileve asked.

"All of them," I answered. "Never bet all your chips on a single hand. We stand a better chance of at least some of us making it through if we take every possible avenue of attack."

"How?" Leta asked. She glanced at the others and shook her head. "It will take all of us together to have any chance of getting through even one of those routes, to say nothing of all three."

I looked to the handful of Vandorian Guardsmen, Dworghen warriors, and Eldren archers who had taken up defensive positions around our muster point.

"Separation and circulation," I explained, using the alchemical terms upon which my strategy was based. "Emileve, you're the dagger. You and your men will take the sublevel tunnels beneath the Central Core, then slip through the foundation substructure to the nexus chamber." I looked over the Eldren as they made their way over to join us, and surmised they were scouts from their mottled gray cloaks and compound bows. "You'll be accompanied by the Eldren scouts, who should be able to keep up and move just as silently as your men."

I received more than a few surprised looks, so I quickly turned my attention to Gunther and the twins before anyone could mount a protest.

"Gunther, you're the sledgehammer. I want you to drive Bruntilga through the cargo lines beneath Grand Wheel

Terminal, with Nera and Vera taking outrider points. Make your way down from there to the nexus chamber. Rognar, you'll go with them, along with these Dworghen warriors." I gestured to the four Dworghs who had joined our company, each one a 'Bruntilga' in their own right, donned in heavy plate with crenellated helms, and armed with iron maces and blunderbusses.

All nodded in agreement. I turned my attention to Leta and Armez.

"We're the spearhead, together with this squad of Vandorian Guardsmen." I nodded to the six men in their distinctive brass and blue armor, with shock-batons at the ready. "We'll take the 1st District waterworks tunnels to the underframe support structure, allowing us to hit the nexus chamber from above while Emileve comes at it from below."

"Why do I have the feeling we're the ones who will be striking deepest and most directly?" Leta grumbled.

"Perhaps because he said we're the spearhead," Armez ventured, his lips quirking in a grin. "Or perhaps you just read his mind."

I nodded to Gunther and the Nyasha Twins. "Don't worry. I'm fairly certain we won't be the ones making the most noise."

"Count on us, bossman," Vera assured, giving an enthusiastic thumbs up. "We do make a mighty roar!"

With that, the Nyasha Twins dropped their goggles over their eyes and jumped to their motowheels. Gunther hurried to fire up his own locomobile as Rognar and the Dworghen warriors piled into the cab behind him. Emileve rounded up her men and exchanged a few words with the Eldren scouts, then made for the nearest utility corridor leading to the sublevels below. I passed a few orders to the Vandorian lieutenant leading the small squad, then watched as they clambered into their patrol wagon. With no further orders to give, I followed Armez and Quiniece to their empowered coach, with Keldon, Leta, and Arleia joining up beside me.

"You keep leaving this behind," Armez said as he climbed up to the top of his coach. He threw my black bag down to me, and I caught it with some surprise, the familiar jangle of glassware and alchemical bottles greeting me.

"A fine sentiment, but I hardly think it's important," I said. "My curse is lifted, and I'm a mage once more with my powers and talisman restored."

"And do you see me filing down my teeth just because I have the Chalice of the Blood King?" Armez asked, taking hold of the brass chains that served as reins. "We are who we are, my dear Vescard. No tricks of sorcery or ancient relics, no matter how powerful, will ever change that. True change comes only from within. As an alchemist, you should know this."

Keldon, Leta, and Arleia had already seated themselves inside the coach, and Quiniece arranged herself on top at the rear, armed to the fangs. I climbed up to the driver's box and took the seat beside Armez. After all, as the de facto marshal of our great offensive, it just didn't feel right to bury myself inside the coach.

I adjusted my frock coat and secured my bag beside me, then chanced one last look at the hideous visage of Atracus, silhouetted by a seething red corona. Just below the ecliptic conjunction loomed the murky black dome of the expanding astral confluence, like a shadowy mirror of the demon-moon itself. The Aetherspire, the Governor's Tower, and even Vandor Tower were now completely enveloped, along with over half of the Central Core. I could not guess what we would find behind the outer fringes of the expanding anomaly, but whatever nightmares awaited us, we would meet them with unyielding determination.

"No matter what happens, we must make it through," I called over the rolling rumble of explosions, gunfire, and revving engines. "The fate of this city, and perhaps the world, rests solely upon our success."

"Ah, no pressure then," Armez immediately cut in. "Just

another merry jaunt to save the world from utter doom."

Lightning flashed and explosions boomed, the sky above afire with arcing tracer rounds, exploding dirigibles, thrumming ornithopters, and mage-empowered chariots. Nera and Vera looked up from their motowheels, Emileve paused before dropping into the sublevel tunnels, and even Gunther and Rognar poked their heads out from Bruntilga's cab. Armez arched an eyebrow, Quiniece turned to listen, and those inside the coach looked up at me from the windows. Perhaps they expected me to give some stirring words of encouragement, but I had nothing more to add. Nothing—save for a single heartfelt sentiment that I knew we all could share.

"Let's make some mayhem!" I yelled above the din.

The twins gave a hoot, their motowheels tearing ahead of Bruntilga as they made for the cargo lines leading into Grand Wheel Terminal. Our own coach gave a lurch when Armez whipped the chains. Ghostly energy fumed from the nostrils of the ensorcelled steeds, their hooves clopping and the coach wheels clattering as we gained speed. The Vandorian patrol wagon puttered along just behind us, following as we raced into a yawning storm tunnel beneath the Central Core's plateau. The darkness of the tunnel gave way to blue-hued silhouettes as I evoked my aetheric vision, but in the distance I saw only the impenetrable blackness of the expanding anomaly drawing ever closer.

I tensed as we sped recklessly onward, and in one fleeting yet seemingly eternal heartbeat, we passed through that inky black horizon and into the maelstrom of a screaming, demon-bound abyss.

A DIZZYING COLLAGE OF SIGHTS and sounds rushed past—harrowing visions of nightmare things glimpsed only fleetingly, lunging, grasping, and slashing, then vanishing amidst a turbulent sea of writhing shadows. One moment we were clattering down a dank waterworks tunnel, and in the next, we were bounding across a scorched terrain of smoldering chasms and jagged stone. The stench of ash and sulfur thickened the air as volcanic pumice fell from a fire-wreathed sky.

Yet, even as we flitted back to the familiar trappings of the pipe-lined waterworks tunnel, I still perceived the faint reflection of Atracus's charred landscape through my aetheric vision. It took all the fortitude I could muster not to shrink away from those nameless horrors awaiting us beyond the weakening veil of space and dimension.

Glancing back to the patrol wagon following behind us, I saw a look of utter dismay painted on the lieutenant's face. The driver and Guardsmen inside the wagon were likely just as mortified by the otherworldly happenings. None of their training could have prepared them for this, and I was more than a little impressed they had not already sped away in sheer terror.

"Stay close!" I yelled to them. "All of Corradon is counting on us!"

"Aldicus!" Armez called.

I whirled around as the world flickered again, the vast sublevel reservoir we had entered giving way to a treacherous embankment of crumbling shale skirting the outer ramparts of a colossal obsidian citadel, its reaching black walls topped by talon-crowned towers and bone-like spires. From the guardhouses and portcullises of that dread fortress stormed companies of hulking, armored brutes—each one bulging with gear-augmented muscles, riveted iron plates, and gruesome arms like serrated war-scythes. Armez never veered from our course, and in an instant we flickered back to our own world, speeding along the waterworks causeway. Yet, to my utter astonishment, a cohort of those fellspawn fiends had followed us back, their savage weapons slamming into the patrol wagon and sending it careening into a wall.

I threw myself from my seat, aetheric fire blazing from my talismanic pen as I landed amidst the brutish horde. Armez pulled the coach around, iron hooves clopping and steel wheels clattering, while Quiniece unleashed blast after blast from her oversized concussion gun. A scythe-like blade sliced through the air above me, then another swung in from my left as I dodged to the side. I fired another aetheric bolt through one of the attacking ironclad brutes, and two more fell to the crushing impact of Quiniece's conk gun. A flash of mystic light streaked from Leta's hand as she exited the coach, with Arleia and Keldon climbing out behind her.

Knowing we could not afford to get hung up fighting these invaders, I waved the others back to the coach and dashed for the overturned patrol wagon. Three Guardsmen had survived the crash and exited the wagon, including the lieutenant. All were busy pulling a fourth survivor from the wreck. The other two were unmistakably dead, one crushed beneath the wagon and the other scalded to death when the boiler exploded.

"Get us out of here!" I yelled to Armez as he steered his coach around to pick us up.

The lieutenant joined me in the driver's box beside Armez, along with one of the Guardsmen, while the other two crammed themselves in with Keldon, Leta, and Arleia. For a moment, I feared Armez would object to the added weight, but he only grinned before giving the chains a solid crack. The coach lurched forward before the clamoring horde reached us, then shook again as hooves and wheels lifted off from the ground. Ghostly flames flared from the hooves and nostrils of the clockwork horses as we soared on through the madness.

"This carriage can *fly*!" the lieutenant gasped, eyes wide with both terror and dismay as he gripped the small railing that rounded the roof.

"Why yes, lieutenant," Armez said matter-of-factly. "Four ensorcelled clockwork steeds to pull the midnight coach of one master vampire and his gearmeister sireling, Quiniece," he introduced, pointing first to himself and then to Quiniece, still manning her weapons at the rear. The lieutenant swallowed nervously, and I almost felt sorry for him. "But fear not, good mortal, for you are also in the company of the veilhunter, Leta Meridian, and her dutiful half-Eldren assistant, Arleia, together with Aldicus Vescard and Keldon Veldanor, whom I'm sure you already know. As for myself, you may call me Armez."

"L-lieutenant P-Pemberwick," the lieutenant stammered.

Armez tipped his top hat and gave a broad, toothy grin. "A pleasure to meet you, L-lieutenant P-Pemberwick," he mockingly stammered back. "Now, sit back and hang on to your helmet. This ride's about to get rough!"

We soared higher still, weaving in and out between the support pilings, buttressing columns, and trestles that forested the Central Core's underframe support structure. The scene around us faded in and out as we flew, flitting between a scorched volcanic wasteland and the vast underframe cavern beneath the Central Core.

"There!" Quiniece called from the rear. I looked to where she was pointing, focusing my aetheric vision to penetrate the darkness, and saw the contour of a massive, dome-shaped structure of fabricrete and steel. "That's the perimeter bulwark surrounding the solaonic reactor," she explained, voice raised over the rushing air. She pointed higher up. "But that maintenance access corridor should lead straight to the nexus chamber's control center. Watch out for the guard post."

"Guard post?" I asked, but Armez was already steering the coach for the corridor.

The crack of gunfire resounded above the blaring alarms as we closed with the secret control facility. The glittering blue haze of Leta's mystic barrier materialized around us and two identical flying coaches appeared beside us as Keldon invoked a mirror-mirage, drawing enemy fire away. Quiniece opened up with a succession of thundering blasts from her conk gun, taking down both sniper towers flanking the entrance. I loosed a wide plume of sparking aetheric energy, scattering the HAAMR guards who remained at their posts, and my attack was joined by the roaring fury of the single-minded air elementals Arleia unleashed. A shower of bomblets corkscrewed from Quiniece's pneumatic launcher, covering our tail in a flaring spread of explosions as we raced past the guard post and into the access corridor.

I immediately sensed a panoply of watchdog egregores, each one waking its neighbor and alerting them to our intrusion. I had no time to erect an aetheric cloak, and saw no reason to, either. Even if we did evade the egregores, they would simply attack the other teams as they charged into the facility. Like a swarm of hornets defending their nest, the egregores spiraled after us, invisible to unaided eyes, but all too clear to my aetheric vision. I brought up my talisman, binding chords of force and entropy to compose a massive disruption empowerment. Unfortunately, releasing such an empowerment would not only dispel the pursuing egregores, but would also interrupt the empowerment fueling the coach's clockwork steeds.

"How far are we from the nexus chamber?" I yelled to Quiniece.

"We're nearly there," she replied.

We shifted between worlds again, hurling through the ash-choked sky of Atracus in one instant, then snapping back to the access corridor a few moments later. I could still see a murky shadow of that other world overlaid with our own, a fact I found only marginally less disconcerting than the storm of sentinel egregores converging on our location. Each one bristled with murderous spells ready to unleash the instant they came into range.

"Never mind," Quiniece amended. "We're there!"

Our ensorcelled steeds smashed through an entry gate and we thundered into an immense vaulted chamber between the base of the Aetherspire above and the radiant furnace of the solaonic reactor below. The swarm of sentinel egregores closed to twenty paces, quivering as they prepared to unleash grisly death upon us, and I released the disruption burst I had been building within my talisman. My own aetheric vision winked out, the coach plunged to the platform just below, and Leta cursed as her mystical ward instantly dispelled.

We hit the platform with a clatter and bounced, the steeds tumbling like marionettes with their strings cut, and we skidded to a stop mere feet from the overhanging ledge. But my empowerment had worked, and every attacking egregore fizzled into the turbid aether from which they had come.

"You could have warned me!" Armez yelled. Not waiting for my apology, he grabbed his sword cane and threw himself from the driver box, drawing the blade as he charged the squads of HAAMR troopers and combat automatons pouring out to meet us.

"I hope you didn't permanently disrupt the empowerment on those horses," Quiniece complained. She checked over her clockwork gauntlet, grabbed her conk gun, and followed her master's reckless charge into battle. "We're going to need them to get out."

"Thanks, boss," Keldon griped, clambering out from the coach. "I had almost finished conjuring the biggest mirage you had ever seen. So much for that idea."

Both Leta and Arleia threw me rather unfavorable looks as they climbed out, followed by the two Vandorian Guardsmen. They seemed relieved until discovering our landing platform was suspended a hundred feet above a blazing elemental annihilation reactor. I nodded to Lieutenant Pemberwick and the bluejacks. They drew their bolt-batons before jumping down to join the others.

The expansive chamber we had entered was a clutter of catwalks and platforms fixed between pulsing aethergy conduits, humming crystal amplifiers, and towering coils alive with climbing electric arcs. And there, in the center of it all, rose the primary nexus conduit—blazing bright with a stupendous torrent of aethergy flowing from the solaonic reactor below to the peak of the Aetherspire high above. The effect of the astral confluence was strongest here, and even without aetheric sight I could see the ghostly shadow of Atracus bleeding through the weakening walls of reality. Yet, beyond even that horrifying spectacle, my eyes were inexorably drawn to the black orb spinning in the center of it all, ablaze in a maelstrom of elemental light and living fire—the Chaos Hexillion!

A nimble form in leather robes and a black tabard flipped through the air, crackling energy lancing out as she landed on a platform one tier up. I recognized Mistress Agona at once, and a host of Dungh'gar acolytes hastened out to join her, their sinister banners and ensorcelled staffs held high. From a wide set of doors at the other end of the chamber stormed a squad of armored HAAMR troopers, led by a half-ton moto-armor whose operator was unmistakable. Behind the tektite visor glowered the scarred face of Colonel Dolgrim with his distinctive optographic receptor. And there above, on the central platform supporting the Chaos Hexillion, I saw the black-shrouded silhouette of the Shadow Man, together with the hunched form of the Darkweaver—cloaked and terrible—standing by his side.

"Kill them all!" the Shadow Man boomed, his words echoing from the chamber's buttressed walls.

A frenetic exchange of bullets, lightning, aetheric bolts, and explosions erupted across the catwalks and platforms of the nexus chamber. Dolgrim and the HAAMR troopers clashed against the hopelessly outnumbered bluejacks, while Agona threw the full fury of her savage powers against Keldon, Leta, and Arleia. A thundering blast from Quiniece's concussion gun blew a pair of HAAMR soldiers off a nearby catwalk, and Armez lent his blade to defend the others from the gray-skinned sorceress and her cultic cronies.

No sooner had I readied my talisman to join the fray than a rolling thunder rose above the clamor of battle. A ten-ton locomotive exploded from the wall two levels up, sailing through the air before crashing back down and barreling into a squad of HAAMR soldiers and automatons. Dworghen warriors charged out from the cab, blunderbusses booming over their bellowing battle-cry. Just behind them followed Rognar, with Varla belching one fireball after another. Gunther emerged from Bruntilga next, heaving his blunderbuss and pipe wrench, and bulled his way into the fight.

The Nyasha Twins' motowheels roared past Gunther and the others, pistols firing and hand grenades flying as Nera and Vera peeled across the chamber's maze of catwalks and platforms. Five more vehicles raced in after them, the first three packed with Travenni trigger boys yelling and firing with nearly as much gusto as the twins, while the last two were Vandorian patrol wagons, sirens wailing.

"Congelation," I whispered, watching our forces converge with the brutish enemy cohorts.

Though it would take them longer, Emileve, her team, and the Eldren scouts would soon be here as well—and, with any luck, whatever other teams managed to make it through the urban battle ground of the Central Core. But in the end, this conflict had only two possible outcomes: the fall of Corradon or the fall of the Shadow Man. I fixed my eyes on my diabolical adversary and dashed forward, leveling my talisman behind me and boosting myself upward with a sudden kick of repulsive force.

"This ends, now!" I declared, my frock coat flapping as I flew upward toward the platform at the center of the chamber.

The Shadow Man dispelled his murky veil, revealing the face of the Commissioner General, twisted in a loathsome mix of hatred and contempt. He sneered, lifting a heavy scepter of spiraled black metal and onyx crystals. A beam of utter blackness poured from the scepter's onyx finial—a blackness that seemed to swallow the very light around it. I managed to spin aside mid-flight just in time, and the black beam raked across the catwalk behind me, cleaving it in half.

But I had no time to wonder at the artifact, for at that same instant the air around me grew suddenly cold as the very energy of the aether ripped away. The Darkweaver pressed his massive, taloned hands together, drawing in those stolen energies before hurling them out again in a deafening shock wave of resonating aetheric dissonance. I flung up my arms in a defensive reflex while propelling myself backwards in a desperate bid to roll with the impact.

My vision exploded in a white flash speckled with swimming black stars. The nauseating vertigo of free fall came over me as I plunged downward like a limp ragdoll, half expecting my final moments to end with the sickening crunch of my own shattering bones when my body met the platform below me. Instead, I passed through what seemed like layer upon layer of gossamer threads, and my momentum dropped considerably before I hit the platform, sprawling flat on my back.

"Honestly, Aldicus, have you completely lost your mind or are you actually trying to kill yourself?" I heard Leta ask. I blinked as my vision cleared and looked up at her, noting the eyebrow arched in mock concern. "We're not immortal, you know."

"Speak for yourself, veilhunter," Armez yelled from some distance away. A salvo of bullets tore his coat to tatters, but the vampire surged ahead in a superhuman blur, his rapier-like sword cane scoring precision strikes through the joints and seams of the armor covering three HAAMR soldiers, dropping each one in turn. "My only regret is not retaining my tailor before this riotous foolery began."

Leta rolled her eyes, then helped me stagger ungracefully to my feet. Another bout of vertigo swam over me, but I clutched my talismanic pen and steeled my nerves.

The nexus chamber had become a raucous battleground of rattling bullets, screaming men, and dazzling bolts of aethergy. Rognar and Gunther had found cover behind a conduit, Gunther popping off shots from his drum-chamber blunderbuss while Rognar blasted away with Varla. The heavily armed coterie of Dworghen warriors split off to flank the troopers pinning them down.

Lieutenant Pemberwick and his men joined up with the newly arrived Vandorian Guardsmen and Travenni mobsters, and together the unlikely allies went head-to-head against Colonel Dolgrim and his HAAMR troopers—shock bolts crackling and gunfire thundering. Colonel Dolgrim stomped forward in his moto-armor, barking orders to his troops, but the soldiers were forced to duck for cover as Nera and Vera raced past, zigging and zagging as they clicked off potshots and tossed grenades.

Farther along the main platform, Keldon, Arleia, and Quiniece battled it out with Mistress Agona and her black-robed cronies. A flood of crackling galvanic bolts struck from Quiniece's gauntlet, followed by the reverberating blast of her concussion gun aimed squarely at Agona. The shock wave dissipated against the Scaithi's defensive wards, and the infuriated sorceress unleashed a deluge of spectral flames as she poured her wrath against Keldon and Arleia. Both vanished in a cloud of glittering light before reappearing a short distance away—the fruits of a well-crafted illusion.

"We have to help them," Leta said. "They can't take her on alone!"

I turned, talisman ready, but our apprentices had only just begun to fight. A condensed blade of elemental air whipped from Arleia's runic totem, followed by a sparkling aetheric bolt from Keldon's key. Agona's acolytes countered both attacks, conjuring a disruption pulse from their empowered staffs, while Agona herself replied with a crackling red beam of metaplasm. The beam struck Keldon in the chest, knocking him down, but his protective brooch flashed brilliant blue as it reflected the sorceress's attack into one of her own acolytes.

Enraged, Agona unleashed a wide deluge of crackling red lightning straight at Keldon, Arleia, and Quiniece. The trio was too far for Leta to create a ward to protect them, and I had no time to compose a disruption blast to dispel the attack. But there was no need for either of us to act. Quiniece darted out with superhuman speed, tossing an aetheric countermeasure and tumbling away as the lightning surged into the device's polarized orichalium mesh. The three joined up back-to-back and side-by-side, Quiniece with her gauntlet and conk gun ready, Keldon conjuring a dazzling prismatic wall, and Arleia summoning a whirling orb of elemental fire and light.

"Perhaps we give them too little credit," I said to Leta.

Leta released a breathy laugh. "They do make quite a team."

I looked to the central platform again, watching as the Shadow Man turned to face the pulsing nexus conduit with his black scepter in hand. That scepter was most likely the Void Scepter of the Embersoul, stolen months ago along with the Reliquary of the Infernal Desolator. Beside him stood the Darkweaver—the so-call Desolator himself—its apish arms raised high as it uttered a series of undulating croaks and growls in some grotesque mockery of speech. Together they conducted the gestures and incantations of their sorcerous ritual, and the veil between our world and Atracus grew fainter still.

A chill ran through me as I watched the twisted, volcanic landscape of the demon-moon grow more distinct. Two dozen ironclad brutes phased in from the strengthening astral confluence—summoned by the Shadow Man's culminating ritual. Armez plunged headlong into that charging fellspawn horde, his sword cane becoming a whirlwind of steel. A flight of blazing white arrows covered the vampire's flank, cutting down nearly a third of that demonic brood. Those empowered arrows signaled the arrival of the Eldren scouts, and following them came Emileve and the Unseen Brotherhood, scrambling out from a service tunnel two platforms below.

Leta braced herself to join the fight—she was a veilhunter after all, and was more than qualified for the task. But I touched her arm to draw her attention back around.

"Our battle is there," I said, nodding to the Shadow Man and his dark servitor. "We must end this before the confluence reaches its culmination."

Leta nodded, gleaning the gist of my intentions from my surface thoughts.

I stepped closer to her, garnering an almost imperceptible gasp when I wrapped my arm around her waist. Then, aiming my talismanic pen behind me, I propelled us upward and forward in a bubble of kinetic force to meet our fearsome foes head on. The Darkweaver struck first, unleashing a freezing flood of necrolic energy, but Leta flung out her hand, gnashing her talismanic rings to invoke her mystical barrier. The wave of antilife slammed into the ward, inverted shadows spraying in all directions, and the air became bone-chillingly cold. Her ward weakened, then shattered, but we continued rising onward and upward until reaching the central platform. I stumbled forward as we touched down and Leta dropped into a ready stance beside me.

No sooner had we landed than a blast of concussive force slammed into us, hurling us backwards and nearly over the edge before I threw out a kinetic ward. That barrier lasted scarcely a second before it began to crack and fracture against the Darkweaver's relentless attack, and I winced from the sudden stab of pain as I redoubled the flow of aethergy to my talisman. Sweat beaded on my brow, and every muscle in my body seemed to strain as I held at bay the crushing wave of force thundering from the demonic foe's taloned hands. Leta projected another ward to help bolster my own, and the mystical barrier materialized not a split-second before a roiling tide of shrieking black flames poured against us.

"You are too late, Vescard!" the Shadow Man boomed, his

amplified words echoing through the chamber.

He now stood directly within the vortex of fire and light whirling about the Chaos Hexillion—the Void Scepter held high before him. Bathed in those surging energies, the flesh of his upraised arms peeled away like paper in a blast furnace, while sooty smoke boiled from his empty eye sockets. What had once been the face of the Commissioner General was now a mass of blacked cinder, a demonic emblem blazing like a red-hot brand upon his forehead.

"I am the chosen vessel of Voshthok-gol-ung'koth, blessed by the deathless ember of His Supreme Majesty. Behold, my master comes! He comes, and he shall cleanse this world in the black radiance of his divine splendor. As above, so below; the dark above, the dark below. So let it be done!"

Insane laughter barked from the Shadow Man's gaping mouth, twisting into a gurgling scream as his body tore open from within, unable to contain the primordial entity he had summoned from its eternal prison. Writhing protrusions and crystalline spines erupted from every side, while his back and chest ruptured with luminous orbs like so many compound eyes. I could only watch in dumbfounded awe as the whole of his transmogrifying body grew in both size and mass—the last of his flesh sloughing away like the wilting fibers of a dead cocoon.

"I am he! I am he!" shrieked the agonized cry of the man he once had been. His voice broke, booming in a deep, inhuman thunder that shook every beam, buttress, and platform in the chamber. "I am he! *And I am free!*"

Leta clutched her face and screamed, falling to her knees. I staggered back, my mind wrenched to near breaking by the unfathomable horror of what I was seeing. It took every whit of my courage not to turn and flee in freakish terror from the prodigious monstrosity metamorphosing before my eyes.

"Transmutation..." was all I managed to mutter, the word inaudible over the howling hot winds and thundering dissonance of turbulent aetheric chords.

The platform shook as the enormous mass of the Shadow Man's transmogrified form basked within the surging beam of energy powering the Chaos Hexillion and, through it, the Aetherspire. I pulled Leta to her feet, pushing her along as crackling black lightening and bubbling metaplasmic fragments surged around us. She staggered, but kept moving, and if the blood trickling from the edges of her eyes was any indication, she had sustained a severe backlash of psychic trauma.

Soon we were running for the other side of the platform, looking for something, *anything*, to defeat the demonic monstrosity. I loosed a pulsing stream of aetheric bolts from my talismanic pen to no avail, and Leta began to invoke another defensive ward to grant us some small measure of protection. But before she finished, the transmogrified Shadow Man—the living incarnation of Voshthok itself—projected another cyclonic blast of rippling concussive force.

"Get down!" I yelled, but it was too late.

The impact struck like the swat of a giant's hand, hurling us both through the air. The chamber spun, and my vision exploded with stars as I crashed back to the platform—the dark of unconsciousness drawing over me.

DAZED AND NUMB, I BLINKED MY EYES OPEN. The ringing silence in my ears was a sharp contrast to the streaking bullets, sparkling rockets, and sizzling aethergy bolts crisscrossing the chamber above me. With blurry double-vision, I watched the escalating battle unfold. Travenni and Guardsman fought HAAMR troopers side-by-side, while Keldon, Arleia, and Quiniece exchanged fire with Mistress Agona and her remaining acolytes. Emileve, the Unseen Brotherhood, and the Eldren scouts lent their support to the battle, yet more fellspawn brutes materialized from the astral confluence.

Blast after blast belched from Gunther's blunderbuss as he and the Nyasha Twins cut a path through the mounting chaos. But their efforts only drew the ire of Colonel Dolgrim, who turned his moto-armor's considerable firepower upon Gunther and the twins.

Gunther staggered back and slumped against a support buttress, dead or dying I did not know. Rognar's empowered blunderbuss belched in reply, and the blazing fireball slammed into Colonel Dolgrim's breastplate. The colonel raised his arms to fire again, but a secondary explosion tore through the left side of his suit, followed by a half-dozen smaller explosions as his ammunition belt detonated, blasting him apart.

"Gunther..." I moaned, my own voice a distant whisper to my still ringing ears. I looked to my fallen compatriot, and to Nera who stood above him, her eyes ablaze with rage and her mouth open in a scream as she unloaded her dual clockwork pistols on the attacking troopers.

A shadow fell over me and I looked up to see Leta, her mouth open in a silent scream—a mirror to Nera screaming above Gunther's unmoving form. As the ringing in my ears began to fade, I could just discern her urgent call. "Get up! We have to keep moving!"

She hoisted me to my feet, and I staggered forward, still dazed. Every bone and muscle in my body ached, as though I had been thrown through a fabricrete wall, or hit by one. I looked to my hands—my empty hands—and felt a sudden chill of sinking fear. *Where was my talismanic pen?* Frantic, I looked about, but amidst the clutter of bodies and debris, my talisman was nowhere to be seen.

"Aldicus!" Leta screamed.

Black fire spilled from the Darkweaver's taloned hands, washing over Leta's tentative ward. She cried out, dropping to one knee, her trembling arm outstretched as she strained to maintain the barrier. I tensed, fists clenched, wishing there was something I could do. But without my talisman I was both weaponless and defenseless.

"I can't... hold it..." Leta managed to say, her face contorted with pain and strain. "...much longer."

Her barrier cracked, then shattered in a spray of fizzling sparks, and the Darkweaver reached out as though to seize Leta's very soul. I clenched my fists and stepped forward—but there was nothing I could do. Deprived of my alchemorph and my talisman, I was as helpless as a newborn babe.

From the corner of my eye, I glimpsed a blur of black and red streaking across the platform to our position. Leta nearly fell into me as Armez shoved her aside, and in a flash his sword plunged straight into the Darkweaver's chest, through the place where its heart should have been. The Darkweaver bellowed what must have been a laugh, then rammed its massive hand through the vampire's chest, exploding blood and broken bits of bone as its wicked talons burst from his back.

But Armez just grinned. In his other hand he held a black leather bag—my black bag, which I had left atop his coach. A signal flare burned hot and bright within the open bag, and Armez upended my entire collection of potent alchemical reagents overtop the Darkweaver's snarling, reptilian face. The deafening, multicolored blast obliterated the Darkweaver's head, along with most of its upper torso, hurling Armez across the platform like a limp rag doll. Leta scrambled to his side, shaking what remained of his charred, gutted form. But it was no use. Not even a master vampire could survive those kinds of wounds.

On the platform below, Quiniece screamed as she watched her master fall.

"Armez..." I croaked, a trembling hand reaching out despite the numbness gripping every nerve and fiber in my body.

The last of Agona's acolytes lay dead, but the sorceress herself became a whirlwind of streaking aetheric bolts and crackling arcs of searing red lightning. I did not know what manner of empowerment she used, but the triangulated attack slammed Keldon from three different directions, overloading his defensive brooch in a flurry of electric arcs that sent him spasming to the ground. Her face a grotesque contortion of sadistic glee, Agona unleashed a torrent of metaplasmic flames to finish my apprentice off.

"Keldon!" I yelled, helpless to do anything but watch.

A wall of elemental energy slammed against the metaplasmic deluge, and Arleia stepped forward, placing herself between Keldon and Mistress Agona. Quiniece joined the young Eldren, her own anguish and fury now turned entirely against the sorceress. A canister flew from her pneumatic launcher, bursting in mid-air and scattering a cloud of severite chaff. Agona's metaplasmic firestorm and Arleia's elemental barrier vanished instantly—extinguished by the dampening metal.

Agona tumbled away, aethergy sparking across her talismanic jewelry as she struggled to restore her empowerments. An elemental lance struck from Arleia's totem, with Keldon joining in as he struggled to his feet, aetheric bolts streaking from his key. Neither of their attacks hit, disrupted as they were by the severite chaff, but a concussive blast from Quiniece's conk gun slammed into the sorceress like a sledgehammer, hurling her over the platform's edge. Still covered in severite dust, Mistress Agona found herself as helpless as I, and she plunged screaming into the solaonic reactor blazing far below.

Relieved though I was, the greatest threat still remained. The Shadow Man's transmogrified form loomed above me like a mountain of incandescent bone and bubbling flesh. I stumbled left as a blast of aethergy exploded through the platform where I had been. A rain of fire and shrapnel fell around me, and I staggered to the right, grunting at the pain of what was probably a few cracked or broken ribs.

Then I froze, my eyes drawn to the whirling disk of fire and light driving the Chaos Hexillion, writhing and shifting like some living thing even as I gazed upon it.

Gazed upon it... As it gazed back upon me.

"The alchemorph," I whispered, my voice trembling in

sudden recognition. “Fangle-fop!”

I should have realized the truth when Quiniece mentioned the Shadow Man’s need for a negative energy catalyzer to counter the Chaos Hexillion’s instability. *What had she said precisely?* That without the catalyzer, the reaction would result in a catastrophic cascade implosion. The researchers at the Special Directorate’s secret facility had been unable to develop the catalyzer, but the Darkweaver had given the Shadow Man the next best thing: a living elemental reactor, capable of that singular property unique to life itself—the conversion of random chaos into natural order. The insane Doctor Zaveroi had called the alchemorph a living alchemical reactor, and even acknowledged its ability to channel an elemental annihilation reaction, identical to that of the solaonic reactor now powering the astral bridge.

I raced for the stairs leading up to the elevated dais where the Chaos Hexillion spun within the raging tempest of my alchemorph. Fire and thunder crashed down from the transmogrified Shadow Man, blasting apart the platform below me and shaking the stairs as I sprinted up three steps with every bound. Whatever control the Darkweaver might have held over my alchemorph had released when Armez killed the monstrous foe, and my best hope—perhaps our only hope—lay in restoring my sympathetic bond with that infernal shadow of my soul.

We are who we are, my dear Vescard, I recalled, thinking back to what Armez had said to me. *No tricks of sorcery or ancient relics, no matter how powerful, will ever change that. True change comes only from within.*

Fire, hotter than the hottest blast furnace, surged and howled around me, my clothes burning to cinders as my skin blistered in the immolating fires of my alchemorph. Yet, despite the searing pain, I pressed deeper into that raging furor, focusing my thoughts on the alchemorph and opening that place within me left hollow by its absence. I touched its mind as it touched mine—a tumultuous storm of fire and madness, enraged by its confinement and reveling at the chance to at last break free.

Initiation, conflagration, separation, circulation, congelation, and transmutation. All were complete, save for one.

"Rectification!" I yelled, pronouncing the final stage of alchemical transformation.

Rage, euphoria, tranquility, and mania surged through me as I embraced my own diametric antithesis—the alchemical marriage of equal and opposite, of chaos and order, of discord and harmony, of darkness and light. My body dissolved within the alchemorph's living flames, then instantly coalesced and reformed—blood pulsing with liquid cinnabar, eyes blazing like brimstone embers, innards churning with digestive alkahest, and lungs heaving with burning phlogiston.

Above, the undulating mass of the demonic incarnation bellowed with all its implacable wrath. Below, surged the pure, elemental chaos of the solaonic reactor—a roiling cyclone of annihilating matter and howling energies, brighter than the sun itself. And in-between stood I, a living amalgamate of my conscious self and the brutish alchemorph, its flame-wreathed form still drawing upon the column of pure elemental energy driving the Chaos Hexillion.

A storm of freezing black fire and blinding violet rays erupted from Voshthok's incarnation, its deafening roar like the thunder of an avalanche. Suffused in the surging column of energy streaming up from below, my alchemorph struck back, pouring that fearsome deluge not upon my calamitous adversary, but twisting the in-rushing tide back upon the Chaos Hexillion. Inundated by the circulating flow, the timeless relic spun faster and faster, until reaching some unimaginable speed—the very fabric of reality seeming to warp and twist about it.

Shearing tidal forces began to rip apart the energized nexus conduit, shredding the central platform and shattering the nearby support pylons. Then, as the Chaos Hexillion reached such speed and brilliance that it could no longer be seen, the demon-forged artifact exploded in a terrific blast of diamond-shattering force and all-consuming light.

The explosion blew me back like a leaf in a hurricane, my alchemorph howling with pain and rage as we crashed onto the platform below, scorching fire and molten metal splashing in every direction. A deafening roar resounded through the chamber, and all who yet lived clutched their heads against the ear-piercing scream. My alchemorph looked up, and I watched through burning brimstone eyes as the walls and buttresses of the chamber twisted and bent inward, sheets of metal ripping away to tumble into the churning maelstrom of pure white energy vomiting up from the destabilized solaonic reactor roiling below.

With claws grasping and limbs thrashing, the incarnation of Voshthok-gol-ung'koth sank inexorably into the rapidly imploding portal, screaming as its cindery flesh and burning bones tore away to be pulverized in the white-hot heart of the shrinking vortex.

"We have to get out of here!" I heard Arleia yell as she helped Keldon off the floor. "The astral bridge is collapsing in on itself!"

The platforms and catwalks of the chamber became a flurry of commotion with every living soul scrambling to escape. Engines roared as the Vandorian patrol wagons and Travenni steamers wheeled around, men piling aboard even as they started to speed away. Surviving HAAMR troopers dropped their weapons and fled to the tunnels or threw themselves to the mercy of the evacuating Vandorian Guardsmen. Nera and Vera carried Gunther into Bruntilga, whose engine roared to life with Rognar at the controls, and a menagerie of Dworghs, bluejacks, and Travenni mobsters crowded into the cab behind them. Emileve and her men, along with the Eldren scouts, made their escape through the tunnels below, and Quiniece dashed to Leta's side to help drag Armez's corpse to his waiting coach, its spectral empowerment having regenerated.

My alchemorph rose, a flaming juggernaut of destruction and rage, and I charged straight for my friends gathering at the coach. Quiniece spun around, her alabaster face a picture of anguish, and without a word she leveled her gauntlet's pneumatic launcher and fired. The canister exploded directly in front of me, spraying my incandescent form with freezing particles of severite chaff, and I crashed to my knees as the inferno around me evaporated in a cloud of steam and ash. My body screamed with pain, both from the injuries of battle and the burns left by my transformation, but within moments I felt a sweltering surge as the alchemorph began to reassert itself.

Hands seized my arms, severite cuffs locked around my wrists, and Keldon threw a blanket over me as he and Lieutenant Pemberwick pulled me to my feet. Within seconds, they had me inside the coach—Keldon, Leta, Arleia and Pemberwick crowding in beside me, with Armez's charred corpse on the seat opposite from us.

The shriek of rending metal filled the air, followed by a deafening crash as the chamber's main support structure gave way. Quiniece leaped into the driver's box and we were off at a gallop. Nera and Vera raced past us on their motowheels and we thundered down the wildly shaking platform just behind Bruntilga, the Vandorian patrol wagons, and Travenni steamers. I chanced one look back through the coach's rear window, and my blood froze as a thundering avalanche of fabricrete and steel poured down like a waterfall.

The full height of the Aetherspire collapsed into the roiling furnace of the nexus chamber, ripping apart in a churning tornado of debris funneled into the receding astral portal. Ahead, Bruntilga smashed through the remains of a fallen bulkhead, spearheading our escape through the sublevel tunnels, with the twins, the bluejacks, and the mobsters racing close behind.

"Can't this thing drive any faster?" Keldon yelled up to Quiniece.

"Drive? No!" Quiniece answered from the driver's box. "Fly? Yes!"

The floor beneath us lurched, and I pinched my eyes shut against the blinding flash as the now unfettered solaonic reaction erupted in an uncontrolled elemental annihilation cascade. An ear-splitting blast wave slammed us like some colossal war-maul. Scorching hot winds howled past, and I held my breath, awaiting that final terrifying instant when we would be obliterated in the all-consuming firestorm. We surely would have been, along with the entire 1st District and all surrounding districts were it not for the inward pull of the imploding astral portal.

As quickly as it had erupted, the blinding detonation froze and contracted, rushing backwards like an explosion in reverse to become an ever-shrinking, ever-brightening ball of pure white light. The cave-in of the topside streets and buildings of the Central Core obscured the final pinpoint of infinitesimal light as it vanished completely from our reality, taking with it the nexus chamber, the Aetherspire, and whatever remained of the solaonic reactor.

"That's for Tibblemond!" I yelled behind us, my voice barely carrying over the thundering report.

We flew from the tunnel just moments later, our coach lifting into the air as Quiniece brought the clockwork steeds to full power. Bruntilga and the twins raced on ahead, skidding across the war-ravaged streets, followed closely by the Vandorian patrol wagons and Travenni steamers.

I pulled my blanket tighter and looked out the window as we rose higher into the sky, my breath catching when I saw the enormous crater hollowed out from the city's central plateau. At least twelve full blocks had been obliterated. Gone was the Aetherspire, the Governor's Tower, and even

Vandor Tower, along with countless buildings, plazas, and offices—all swallowed up in the crushing implosion of the collapsing portal. Smoke and ash billowed up from the place where the Aetherspire once had been, the red glow of molten metal fading in the shadow of the blood red eclipse.

I breathed out with a sigh, grimly thankful that HAAMR had forced all citizens out of the Central Core amidst their coup.

The coach veered suddenly as a crescent of brilliant white spilled from the far side of the demon-moon. I squinted against the golden brilliance of a second dawn, and in the light of the newly wakened sun I saw jubilant crowds filling the debris-littered streets. I saw Vandorian Guardsman and Dworghen warriors escorting away the HAAMR troopers that had surrendered en masse. I saw Travenni bruisers and trigger boys pressing back against those few opportunists trying to loot and steal. I saw Barthemius and his mages, together with the Eligarch and her Eldren, bringing aid to the wounded. I saw Emileve and her men emerge from a sublevel tunnel, with scores of undercity refugees rushing to greet them. I saw the Outlaw Riders of the Shifty Drifter and the Iron Thunder Gang wheeling through the celebrating crowds, shouting and hollering as they egged the revelries on. And I saw so many countless others, from every district and all walks of life, hooting, cheering, and embracing one another as word of our victory reverberated through every block and street of the Clockwork City.

The coach banked, empowered steeds galloping as we descended toward that magnificent helter-skelter we called home. I leaned back in my seat and closed my eyes, and, for the first time in as long as I could remember, I found myself at peace.

THE SUN SANK INTO THE WEST, the faded visage of Atracus scarcely visible in the golden sea of dusk, spilling like liquid flame across the expanse of towers, smokestacks, and great industrial enclaves. I pushed my hands into the pockets of my lurid fuchsia frock coat, thankful for the spare set of clothes Armez had stashed in the trunk of his coach. The clothes fit perfectly, and I could not help but wonder if the garish selection was not part of some final, perverse joke of his. I closed my eyes and swallowed, then looked back to the hollow beneath the elevated trestle span where my friends had gathered.

We had landed here only a few hours ago, the post-eclipse sunlight being too much for Quiniece who was the only one of us able to drive Armez's coach. Here we had remained, watching in solemn silence as celebrations played out across the city below. Rognar, Nera, and Vera had pulled up not long after we set down, and the three wasted no time carrying Gunther to the refuge of our urban encampment. Despite suffering four bullet wounds, two of them to his abdomen, the burly ex-con was somehow alive. Leta and Arleia both knew a modest amount of first aid, and the two did their best to staunch the bleeding and keep him alive.

But it was not until a pair of Vandorian ornithopters arrived that I felt confident Gunther would pull through. Commissioner Cheyron had dispatched the thopters to pick up Lieutenant Pemberwick and the other Vandorian Guardsmen who had joined us, but they also brought two field medics and an Eldren healer, anticipating that we might have casualties of our own. They could do nothing for Armez, but Gunther was now stable enough to be evacuated aboard one of the thopters.

"Good work, Inspector," I said to Lieutenant Pemberwick as he started for the ornithopters, their ichor engines thrumming in preparation for takeoff. "Few today can claim they went toe to toe against the dark legions of Atracus, and fewer still who can say they faced a demonic incarnation and lived."

"I'm just a lieutenant, sir," Pemberwick corrected, tapping the insignia on the side of his helmet. Despite his humble admission, his voice carried an air of confidence that had been notably lacking before. "Just another bluejack."

"Oh, I don't know," I maintained. "Inspector Pemberwick has a rather nice ring to it. Besides, I'm fairly certain Commissioner Cheyron is about to issue promotions to just about everyone. I expect the Vandorian Guard is going to be flooded with hundreds of new recruits after their heroic actions today."

Pemberwick gave a quick smile and a short nod. Then he hurried to the ornithopters, first helping to secure Gunther on the evacuation gurney before climbing into one of the passenger seats across from the medics.

"You no be worrying over Gunther, do you now?" Nera asked, stepping up beside me. She gave a sniff and watched the thopters lift off. Her hand came up to wipe a tear from her eye—a hand, I noted, that was still stained with his blood. "He be fine, you know. He be one brutty bruiser boy."

My frock coat whipped about me as the departing ornithopters' thundered overhead, speeding away on a course for the 2nd District precinct station. "He do be that," I replied.

Vera stepped up beside her sister and patted her on the shoulder. "And you no be worrying neither," she said with a grin and a wink.

Nera jumped at the remark, then crossed her arms and glanced down. Dark though her skin was, I could have sworn she was blushing.

"I'm not sure the Vandorian Guard will survive this," Keldon said as he made his way over to join me. He nodded to the now distant ornithopters. "By now, half the city knows the Commissioner General orchestrated the coup. He proclaimed himself Lord Protector and charged HAAMR with enforcing his will under martial law. Do you think anyone's ever going to trust the Vandorian Guard after this?"

I was about to point out that most people should know the difference between HAAMR and the standard Vandorian

Guard, but then I hesitated. Was I the one being naïve this time? After all, HAAMR was a division of Vandor Tower. They may have worn empowered armor and flaunted military firepower, but their standard uniforms were almost identical to those of the bluejacks, and so was their authority.

"He has a point, Aldicus," Emileve said. I looked up, surprised to see the Queen of Thieves jump down from the trestle span's framework. A diminutive blue form a wearing vest and goggles scurried along a support beam just above her, chittering as it signed a greeting. "The Unseen Brotherhood's got no love for anyone in uniform, but we'll make sure our people know who the real villains were. Still, for most of the underfolk, a jack's a jack." Then she shrugged and looked to some indistinct point in the city. "As much as I'll miss the hijinks you get me tangled in, I'm afraid we're back to being on opposite sides of the law. But that's the least of your concerns. The Travenni will be back to their usual mischief tomorrow, and by this time next week, they'll have solidified their hold over the East Wharf and the outer slums."

"And that goes for every crime lord, racketeer, and gang in this city," Leta put in. "With Vandor Tower fallen, *Justiciar* destroyed, and the Vandorian Guard at quarter force, it's going to be one great big outlaw holiday."

I sighed, realizing they were right. I began to reply, but another voice spoke up from nearby.

"I think we have an even bigger problem than that," Arleia said. She shrank away as all eyes turned to her, but with an encouraging smile from Keldon, she gave a sigh and forced herself to continue. "If there's anything the press loves more than wars and revolutions, its scandal. And I'm afraid the fall of Vandor Tower is the biggest scandal this city has seen in quite some time."

"Arleia's right," Keldon said. "The broadsheets are going to tear the Vandorian Guard to shreds over this. At the very least they'll blame Commissioner Cheyron, and maybe everyone in Vandor Tower, for failing to uncover the plot in time."

I nodded. They had a good point. The reporters of the *Corradon Daily Post* will be falling over themselves digging for the scoop, to say nothing of the far less discerning tabloids. That, more than anything else, filled my mouth with the astringent taste of bile.

"Faugh!" Rognar laughed as he meandered over. He drew a crumbling meat pie from his duffle coat pocket, sniffed it, and took a sizable bite. "They won't give a bulgore's hide about Vandor Tower. Not after someone leaks a few tantalizing tidbits about Consolidated Omniworks' involvement." He glanced in Quiniece's direction. "If only we knew someone who had copies of deeply damning records obtained from an analytical engine in one of their illegal research facilities." He shrugged again and sighed. "If only we knew someone with such records, I could make sure it fell into the right hands."

Everyone turned to look at Quiniece, but the young vampire was too focused on her own task to pay Rognar any mind. "It's time," she muttered as though to herself. She knelt beside Armez's desiccated husk, cupping the Chalice of the Blood King in her hands. "Close enough, anyway," she amended after a quick glance at the sun, its last rays melting into the jagged urban peaks of the western skyline.

"Quiniece," Leta said softly. She knelt on the other side of the body, trying to garner the orphaned sireling's attention. "We both know that a vampire's final death cannot be reversed."

Quiniece looked up suddenly, and the fury of her feral gaze stilled Leta's words. But the flash of anger passed as quickly as it had come, and Quiniece turned her head down, her tearless eyes dimming with sorrow. Arleia stepped up behind her, placing a consolatory hand on her shoulder, as did Keldon, who offered her his best commiserative expression. I followed them over as well, but kept back with

Rognar, Emileve, and the twins, standing as silent and solemn as the others.

This was her time to grieve—her time to come to terms with the reality that, no matter how much they professed the contrary, vampires were as mortal as any creature subject to death's inexorable embrace.

"No," Quiniece said finally. She looked at the Chalice, then turned her eyes back to her friends now gathered around. "No," she repeated louder. "There *is* a way."

Arleia adjusted her glasses. "What do you mean?"

Quiniece stared into the Chalice again, her eyes narrowing as she worried her lip. "This relic turns water into blood. But that is not its *true* power. Have none of you wondered what it does when filled with living, mortal blood?"

Leta's brow twitched, then her eyes widened in sudden realization. "You're talking about the *dhampyris quintessentia*... But that's a myth!"

"And until recently, so was this," Quiniece said, holding up the Chalice of the Blood King.

Leta drew a sharp breath, a trembling hand closing over her mouth. "No wonder Armez wanted it so badly. This is the wellspring of the entire vampire race!"

"Well, bowl me over and slap me dizzy!" Rognar laughed. "I think that relic's just as old as you, Varla." Then he snorted at something and patted the bulge in his coat. "Aw, don't get all petulant, Varla. I still love you."

"He saved my life," Leta whispered, her eyes fixed on the desiccated corpse. She snorted in a kind of ironic laugh, then nodded as she came to whatever decision she had been mulling. "How much blood do you need?"

Quiniece blinked. "I'm not sure. I don't even know if this will work at all. I just know that I have to try."

Leta held out her hand to Emileve, and Emileve drew a blade from her boot and passed it over, answering the unspoken request. With one quick slice, Leta cut open her left forearm, drawing gasps from both Keldon and Arleia. I felt my own stomach knot as I watched a profusion of blood run down her arm and splash into the Chalice's golden bowl. Half a minute passed, and Leta looked to Quiniece with a quaver of worry furrowing her brow. But the vampire's gaze never broke from the slowly filling Chalice, her feral eyes flitting between anguish and bloodlust as she struggled to rein in her own instinctive hunger.

Another minute passed, and Leta began to wobble, her eyelids drooping and her color growing notably pale. Then, just went I felt certain she could not possibly give any more, Quiniece pulled the Chalice away and Arleia and Vera both jumped into action, helping Leta sit down and winding a strip of cloth around the wound.

"Is it... Is it working?" Leta struggled to say, her voice weak and shaky.

Quiniece did not respond, but held the brimming Chalice above her master's corpse, her expression unchanged from its pensive glower. The last rays of the sun settled behind the western skyline, splashing brilliant ochre hues across the city's low-hanging smog, and I perceived the slightest shimmer within the sanguine libation. At first, I thought it had been a trick of the diminishing evening light, but the golden shimmer only grew as twilight dimmed. Quiniece's eyes widened, and I heard both Keldon and Arleia gasp as the contents of the Chalice shown with golden-red radiance.

"The power," Keldon said in a breathless whisper. "It's like a thousand dissonant chords, converging into a single thundering drum... like..."

"Like a heartbeat..." Arleia completed.

I glanced at my severite cuffs. I could no longer hear the symphony of the spheres, and could only imagine the form and beauty of the ancient relic's empowerment whirling into existence.

Quiniece drew a sharp breath, then poured half of the shimmering liquid into the burnt cavity of Armez's chest. She drizzled what remained across his desiccated face and into his mouth, then sat back in an anxious crouch with arms crossed over her abdomen. We all stood in wordless silence, watching the golden-red potion slowly soak into the grisly corpse.

Minutes passed, and at first nothing seemed to happen. Then, impossibly, the shriveled remains began to fill out and regenerate. Lifeless organs revivified before our eyes, his unbeating heart reformed in the cavity where it once had been, and ancient bones knitted together as necrolic flesh stretched over the quickly closing wounds.

The remortified vampire sat up with a start, wild eyes shooting open to reveal topaz irises blazing against his midnight black sclera.

"That *hurt*!" Armez choked, his voice hoarse and cracking. He gave himself a quick once over and gasped in horror. "Archons help me! That shirt was imported from Kaimbuka. And just look at my coat..."

Quiniece threw her arms around him, hugging him in a tight, daughterly embrace. Could vampires cry, her tears would surely have transmuted from sorrow to joy. Everyone else took a hesitant step back as she helped Armez off the ground, and he pulled what remained of his tattered coat around his half-clothed body.

"I suppose this means we won," he breathed. His skin was a ghastly shade of cadaverous blue, stretched thin and hungry over his jutting bones. It would probably take weeks for him to fully recover, if not months. The Chalice of the Blood King might have been a relic of some long-forgotten age of wonders, but even miracles had their limitations. "I do apologize for being dead during the climax of the battle. But how did you defeat that demonic incarnation and destroy the astral bridge to Atracus?"

"We have your sireling to thank for that," I replied. Armez cocked his head inquisitively, and I held up my arms, showing the severite handcuffs. "She was the one who found the information about the negative energy catalyzer and its importance in stabilizing the Chaos Hexillion. As it so happened, my alchemorph was the catalyzer, captured and controlled by the Darkweaver. Once I reunited with its essence, the astral vortex spun out of control, imploding even as the solaonic reactor detonated, bringing an end to Voshthok's invasion of our world and saving the city from total destruction."

Armez smiled, but his grin turned suddenly down as his eyes settled on Leta, still massaging her freshly bandaged arm. "Did you...?" he began to ask. He looked at the Chalice, then to Quiniece, and finally back to Leta again. "It was your blood that brought me back. Your blood, transmuted into the Gift of Amonakh by his very chalice." He stood a bit straighter and bowed his head. "I owe you my life."

Leta scoffed. "You gave your life to save mine. I wish I could say this makes us even, but the balance is still soundly in your favor."

"Oh, quite the contrary," Armez said. "In fact..."

"And I owe both of you," I put in, cutting off what was sure to be a hopeless argument. I looked from Armez and Leta to the faces of all my friends gathered around—Keldon, Arleia, Quiniece, Emileve, Nera, Vera, and Rognar. I also thought of Gunther, hoping him a speedy recovery, and Tibblemond who had given his life to set us on our course to victory. "I owe all of you a debt that can never be repaid. Without your courage, this city would now be in ashes, the Demon Lords would be free, and their fellspawn legions would have a foothold on our world."

"Bah!" Rognar rebuked. "Either everyone owes everyone everything or nobody owes anyone anything. Without each of us fighting for all of us, none of us would be left to owe any of us anything."

"Wiser words have never been spoken!" Armez laughed.

Keldon sighed and scratched his head. "More like confusing words."

"Well, I say you owe me for saving your butt from that

sorceress," Quiniece teased, throwing an arm around Keldon. She glanced at Arleia, who glared back in growing consternation. "What say the two of us kill a little time on Vaugaire Boulevard?" She pressed her face close to Keldon's neck, licking her lips. "Maybe drop by a nice confectionary, then head back to my place and—"

Arleia's face darkened with indignation, her ears flattening back and her eyes narrowing to a scathing glare. She pushed her glasses up, stomped forward, and shoved Quiniece aside. Before my apprentice could even articulate a gasp, Arleia seized him in her arms and planted her lips squarely on his. Keldon's eyes had never bulged so wide, but they soon flitted closed as Arleia's kiss lingered, and he wrapped his arms about her, oblivious to everything but that singular moment lost in the embrace of another.

"It's about time, sweets!" Quiniece laughed. "I was worried I might have to resort to extreme measures, and we *won't* get into what *that* would have entailed."

Arleia broke away from her kiss and blinked. She looked at Keldon, who smiled sheepishly, then turned her bewildered expression to Quiniece. "You mean... You mean you were just *goading* me all this time?"

Quiniece threw her head back laughing. "Between his thickheaded cluelessness and your coy reticence, someone had to intervene." She folded her arms over her tight-laced bodice and looked Keldon up and down. "Don't get me wrong. He *is* really cute. Especially with his scruffy mess of hair and that adorable blushes he gets when—"

"Enough!" Arleia blurted. She drew a deep breath and sighed, visibly calming herself before looking back to Keldon with a smile.

Keldon's blush deepened, his hands going to the newsboy cap covering his hopelessly tousled hair even as he grinned back in return. He began to say something, then stopped, apparently too smitten to enunciate with any discernable coherency.

Rognar gave a cynical harrumph. "For a couple of burgeoning investigators, you two sure know how to ignore the glaringly obvious. Why, if Quiniece hadn't done something, I'd have slapped both of you upside the head!"

"You're one to talk," Emileve snorted. "You and that gun of yours... Folks are going to start to wonder."

"Cool your chamber," Rognar muttered into his coat. Then he sniffed. "She didn't mean nothing by it."

Leta stepped up beside me, shaking her head as she quirked a smile at Keldon and Arleia. "Kids these days never seem to see what's right in front of them."

"Kids these days, indeed," Armez agreed. His eyes darted from me, to Leta, and back again, and his mouth formed a dangerous grin. "Perhaps another swift kick to someone's coyish self-denial is called for."

I glanced at Leta, then quickly turned away, avoiding her uncertain gaze. I cleared my throat, adjusted my fuchsia frock coat, and walked to the edge of our urban encampment overlooking the vast expanse of the city. Nera and Vera sauntered up on my left with hands resting on their gun belts, accompanied by Rognar as he finished off the last bite of his meat pie. Armez and Quiniece joined me on my right, both grinning with some freshly brewing mischief. Emileve followed close behind them, a chittering homunculus scurrying along the girders of the trestle bridge just above. Leta squeezed her way in between Armez and myself, pausing only to throw the vampire a reproachful glare, and Keldon and Arleia joined us a moment later.

"Will anything ever be the same again?" Keldon asked, his hand squeezing Arleia's as they stood together, their young eyes gazing out across the destruction spread far and wide.

I looked to my severite cuffs, balling my hands into fists as I felt the living fire of the alchemorph roiling inside. *Nothing was the same anymore, and yet, had anything really changed?*

Releasing a sigh, I returned my gaze to the city's

sprawling vista. Arc-lights from half a dozen dirigibles swept across what remained of the Central Core, while fire brigades worked tirelessly to extinguish the countless blazes raging through the 1st District. The wind picked up and I pulled my gaudy frock coat tighter, wrinkling my nose against the caustic stench of burning ash and the bitter tang of electric residue still lingering in the air.

I stood in silence, not knowing what, if anything, I should say. Then I looked beyond the smoking crater where the Aetherspire once had stood, to the glittering forest of brass and glass towers farther on, to the vast mesas of clockwork manufactories and churning alchemical refineries, and the ever-turning complication of busy airship ports, thundering steamrail lines, and knotted avenues which, even now, bustled with activity.

"Corradon will never be the same again," I said, turning to meet the eyes of all those gathered around. "And that, I think, is as it should be. We have lost many and sacrificed much, but only through the selfless efforts of those who paid the ultimate price were we able to win the day. The Shadow Man and his forces have been vanquished, the incarnation of Voshthok has been destroyed, and the Demon Lords of Atracus remain sealed within the fiery tombs of their infernal prison. This day will forever be remembered, and those who gave their lives shall never be forgotten. The scars our city bears will remain a monument to their sacrifice and a reminder of the tyranny that came and fell before the courage of those who would never surrender the eternal light of freedom."

My friends nodded as I spoke, and each one stood a bit taller, heads held higher, eyes looking out across the far-reaching cityscape.

I drew a deep breath, pausing before I continued. "But crime ever turns in the Clockwork City. When next the darkness comes, when next tyranny arises or evil makes our city its home, we shall stand together once more—united, unyielding, and unafraid—the champions of the Clockwork City."

A hand touched my hand, fingers curling to lace with my own. I glanced to my right to see Leta, smiling fondly, her eyes lightly closed. I breathed out, letting my shoulders relax as the tension drained from me. Her smile broadened, her empathic powers as keen as ever.

Returning her warming smile, I allowed my mental wall to finally come down.

END

THANK YOU

I hope you enjoyed reading *THE CASE FILES OF ALDICUS VESCARD* as much as I enjoyed writing it. Please consider leaving a quick review or star rating on Amazon or Goodreads.

https://www.amazon.com/dp/product-reviews/B093KK1XVR

https://www.goodreads.com/book/show/57954051-the-case-files-of-aldicus-vescard

ALSO AVAILABLE

SIEGE CHRONICLES: THE COMPLETE SERIES — Sell-spell sorcerers, vampire operatives, killer automatons, and a heist to nab a legendary dragon stone. It's all in a day's work for Davrick Caliburn.
US: https://www.amazon.com/dp/B08SSPXLF4

UK: https://www.amazon.co.uk/dp/B08SSPXLF4

AND COMING SOON

THE WAR OF WARS SAGA — An epic 5-book series, also set in the World of Mythania during the momentous War of Wars, the same conflict highlighted in *The Siege Chronicles*.

STEAM, STEEL, AND SORCERY — An anthology of short stories set in the World of Mythania.

Keep in Touch

If you enjoyed *The Case Files of Aldicus Vescard* and are eager to hear about upcoming books and other announcements, simply visit my website and sign up for my newsletter:

https://mwchase.com/newsletter

And just so you know, I hate spam just as much as you do. I won't bombard your inbox with trivial junk or tacky ads. I will try to send out a newsletter once a month, or when I release a book, but sometimes things get hectic and there may be months when I don't send out anything at all.

You can always visit me on the web at mwchase.com or mythania.com, and I also have a Facebook page and Twitter account where you can follow me as well.

Website: mwchase.com or mythania.com

Newsletter: mwchase.com/newsletter

Facebook: facebook.com/markwilliamchase

Twitter: twitter.com/markwchase

The World of Mythania

The Case Files of Aldicus Vescard is part of the World of Mythania—a fantastical realm of steam, steel, and sorcery, where juggernaut war machines ravage the landscape, where stupendous air fleets dominate the skies, and where the march of progress is moved as much by gears of iron as by weave of spell.

The Clockwork City of Corradon is the primary setting for *The Case Files of Aldicus Vescard.* If you want to know more about Corradon and see a full map and description of the city's districts, please visit https://mythania.com/corradon.

If you want to know more about the wider world of Mythania, please visit https://mythania.com/world. There you will find artwork, maps, history, world book information, and the latest news on upcoming books.

About the Author

Mark William Chase lives near Indianapolis with his wife and the occasional foster kid, and spends most of his free time reading science fiction and fantasy, keeping up with the latest news in science and technology, and writing the kinds of stories he most enjoys reading.

At his day job, he works as a software architect developing cloud-based financial and banking applications. He is an avid connoisseur of the steampunk aesthetic and has adorned his home office with curious devices and clockwork contrivances collected both from afar and crafted by his own hands.

He can occasionally be found attending science fiction conventions in his ever-accumulating steampunk attire.

Made in United States
North Haven, CT
01 March 2022